PLANET
OF
ADVENTURE

Tor books by Jack Vance

Araminta Station
Big Planet
Ecce and Old Earth
The Dragon Masters
Green Magic
The Languages of Pao
The Last Castle
Showboat World
Throy

PLANET
OF
ADVENTURE

CITY OF THE CHASCH

SERVANTS OF THE WANKH

THE DIRDIR

THE PNUME

JACK VANCE

TOR

A TOM DOHERTY ASSOCIATES BOOK
NEW YORK

PLANET OF ADVENTURE

This book is an omnibus edition, consisting of the novels *City of the Chasch*, copyright © 1968 by Jack Vance; *Servants of the Wankh*, copyright © 1969 by Jack Vance; *The Dirdir*, copyright © 1969 by Jack Vance; *The Pnume*, copyright © 1970 by Jack Vance.

A Tor Book
Published by Tom Doherty Associates, Inc.
175 Fifth Avenue
New York, N.Y. 10010

Tor® is a registered trademark of Tom Doherty Associates, Inc.

Map by Ellisa Mitchell

Design by Lynn Newmark

Library of Congress Cataloging-in-Publication Data

Vance, Jack
    Planet of adventure / Jack Vance.
        p.   cm.
    "A Tom Doherty Associates Book."
    ISBN 0-312-85487-0
    1. Life on other planets—Fiction.   I. Title.
    PS3572.A424P57   1993
    813'.54—dc20   dc—20   93-25919
                                                              CIP

First edition: October 1993

Printed in the United States of America

0 9 8 7 6 5 4 3 2 1

TABLE OF CONTENTS

Sea of Achenkin

Waste

Nerv

CHARCHAN

Spang
Varvodel
Settra

ISLES of CLOUD

Ballisidre
Jinga
Kabasas
CATH

Zara
Ish
KACHAN
RAKH
Smargash

Lake Falas

Ao Hidis
Ao Khaha

HOLANGAR

VORD

Cape Dread

TSCHAI

EHM '93

CITY
OF
THE
CHASCH

CITY OF THE CHASCH

To ONE SIDE of the *Explorator IV* flared a dim and aging star, Carina 4269; to the other hung a single planet, gray-brown under a heavy blanket of atmosphere. The star was distinguished only by a curious amber cast to its light. The planet was somewhat larger than Earth, attended by a pair of small moons with rapid periods of orbit. An almost typical K2 star, an unremarkable planet, but for the men aboard the *Explorator IV* the system was a source of wonder and fascination.

In the forward control pod stood Commander Marin, Chief Officer Deale, Second Officer Walgrave: three men similarly trim, erect, brisk of movement, wearing the same neat white uniforms, and so much in each other's company that the wry, offhand intonations in which they spoke, the half-sarcastic, half-facetious manner in which they phrased their thoughts, were almost identical. With scanscopes—hand-held binocular photomultipliers, capable of enormous magnification and amplification—they looked across to the planet.

Walgrave commented, "At casual observation, a habitable planet. Those clouds are surely water-vapor."

"If signals emanate from a world," said Chief Officer Deale, "we almost automatically assume it to be inhabited. Habitability follows as a natural consequence of habitation."

Commander Marin gave a dry chuckle. "Your logic, usually irrefutable, is at fault. We are presently two hundred and twelve light-years from Earth. We received the signals twelve light-years out; hence they were broadcast two hundred years ago. If you recall, they halted abruptly. This world may be habitable; it may be inhabited; it may be both. But not necessarily either."

Deale gave his head a doleful shake. "On this basis, we can't even be sure that Earth is inhabited. The tenuous evidence available to us—"

Beep beep went the communicator. "Speak!" called Commander Marin.

The voice of Dant, the communications engineer, came into the pod: "I'm picking up a fluctuating field; I think it's artificial but I can't tune it in. It just might be some sort of radar."

Marin frowned, rubbed his nose with his knuckle. "I'll send down the scouts, then we'll back away, out of range."

Marin spoke a code-word, gave orders to the scouts Adam Reith and Paul Waunder. "Fast as possible; we're being detected. Rendezvous at System axis, up, Point D as in Deneb."

"Right, sir. System axis, up, Point D as in Deneb. Give us three minutes."

Commander Marin went to the macroscope and began an anxious search of the planet's surface, clicking through a dozen wavelengths. "There's a window at about 3000 angstroms, nothing good. The scouts will have to do all of it."

"I'm glad I never trained as a scout," remarked Second Officer Walgrave. "Otherwise I also might be sent down upon strange and quite possibly horrid planets."

"A scout isn't trained," Deale told him. "He exists: half acrobat, half mad scientist, half cat burglar, half—"

"That's several halves too many."

"Just barely adequate. A scout is a man who likes a change."

The scouts aboard the *Explorator IV* were Adam Reith and Paul Waunder. Both were men of resource and stamina; each was master of many skills; there the resemblance ended. Reith was an inch or two over average height, dark-haired, with a broad forehead, prominent cheekbones, rather gaunt cheeks where showed an occasional twitch of muscle. Waunder was compact, balding, blond, with features too ordinary for description. Waunder was older by a year or two; Reith however, held senior rank, and was in nominal command of the scout-boat: a miniature spaceship thirty feet long, carried in a clamp under the *Explorator*'s stern.

In something over two minutes they were aboard the scout-boat. Waunder went to the controls; Reith sealed the hatch, pushed the detach-button. The scout-boat eased away from the great black hull. Reith took his seat, and as he did so a flicker of movement registered at the corner of his vision. He glimpsed a gray projectile darting up from the direction of the planet, then his eyes were battered by a tremendous purple-white dazzle.

There was rending and wrenching, violent acceleration as Waunder clutched convulsively upon the throttle, and the scout-boat went careening down toward the planet.

Where the *Explorator IV* had ridden space now drifted a curious object: the nose and stern of a spaceship, joined by a few shreds of metal, with a great void between, through which burnt the old yellow sun Carina 4269. Along with crew and technicians, Commander Marin, Chief Officer Deale, Second Officer Walgrave had become fleeting atoms of carbon, oxygen and hydrogen, their personalities, brisk mannerisms, and jocularity now only memories.

1

THE SCOUT-BOAT, STRUCK rather than propelled by the shockwave, tumbled bow over stern down toward the gray and brown planet, with Adam Reith and Paul Waunder bumping from bulkhead to bulkhead in the control cabin.

Reith, only half-conscious, managed to seize a stanchion. Pulling himself to the panel, he struck down the stabilization switch. Instead of a smooth hum there was hissing and thumping; nevertheless the wild windmilling motion gradually was damped.

Reith and Waunder dragged themselves to their seats, made themselves fast. Reith asked, "Did you see what I saw?"

"A torpedo."

Reith nodded. "The planet is inhabited."

"The inhabitants are far from cordial. That was a rough reception."

"We're a long way from home." Reith looked along the line of non-signifying dials and dead indicator lights. "Nothing seems to be functioning. We're going to crash, unless I can make some swift repairs." He limped aft to the engine room, to discover that a spare energy-cell, improperly stowed, had crushed a connection box, creating a chaotic tangle of melted leads, broken crystals, fused composites.

"I can fix it," Reith told Waunder, who had come aft to inspect the mess. "In about two months with luck. Providing the spares are intact."

"Two months is somewhat too long," said Waunder. "I'd say we have two hours before we hit atmosphere."

"Let's get to work."

An hour and a half later they stood back, eyeing the jury-rig with doubt and dissatisfaction. "With luck we can land in one piece," said Reith gloomily. "You go forward, put some power into the lifts; I'll see what happens."

A minute passed. The propulsors hummed; Reith felt the

pressure of deceleration. Hoping that the improvisations were at least temporarily sound, he went forward and resumed his seat.

"What's it look like?"

"Short range, not too bad. We'll hit atmosphere in about half an hour, somewhat under critical velocity. We can come down to a soft landing—I hope. The long-range prognosis—not so good. Whoever hit the ship with a torpedo can follow us down with radar. Then what?"

"Nothing good," said Reith.

The planet below broadened under their view: a world dimmer and darker than Earth, bathed in tawny golden light. They now could see continents and oceans, clouds, storms: the landscape of a mature world.

The atmosphere whined around the car; the temperature gauge rose sharply toward the red mark. Reith cautiously fed more power through the makeshift circuits. The boat slowed, the needle quivered, sank back toward a comfortable level. There came a soft report from the engine room and the boat began to fall free once more.

"Here we go again," said Reith. "Well, it's up to the airfoils now. Better get into ejection harness." He swung out the side-flaps, extended the elevators and rudder and the boat hissed down at a slant. He asked, "How does the atmosphere check out?"

Waunder read the various indices of the analyzer. "Breathable. Close to Earth normal."

"That's one small favor."

Looking through scanscopes, they could now observe detail. Below spread a wide plain or a steppe, marked here and there with low relief and vegetation. "No sign of civilization," said Waunder. "Not below, at any rate. Maybe up there, by the horizon—those gray spots . . ."

"If we can land the boat, if no one disturbs us while we rebuild the control system, we'll be in good shape . . . But these airfoils aren't intended for a fast landing in the rough. We'd better try to stall her down and eject at the last instant."

"Right," said Waunder. He pointed. "That looks like a forest—vegetation of some sort. The ideal spot for a crash."

"Down we go."

The boat slanted down; the landscape expanded. The fronds of a dank black forest reached into the air ahead of them.

"On the count of three: eject," said Reith. He pulled the boat up into a stall, braking its motion. "One—two—three. Eject!"

The ejection ports opened; the seats thrust; out into the air snapped Reith. But where was Waunder? His harness had fouled, or the seat had failed to eject properly; and he dangled helplessly outside the boat. Reith's parachute opened, swung him up pendulum-wise. On the way down he struck a glossy black limb of a tree. The blow dazed him; he swung at the end of his parachute shrouds. The boat careened through the trees, plowed into a bog, Paul Waunder hung motionless in his harness.

There was silence except for the creaking of hot metal, a faint hiss from somewhere under the boat.

Reith stirred, kicked feebly. The motion sent pain tearing through his shoulders and chest; he desisted and hung limp.

The ground was fifty feet below. The sunlight, as he had noted before, seemed rather more dim and yellow than the sunlight of Earth, and the shadows held an amber overtone. The air was aromatic with the scent of unfamiliar resins and oils; he was caught in a tree with glossy black limbs and brittle black foliage which made a rattling sound when he moved. He could look along the broken swath to the bog, where the boat sat almost on an even keel, Waunder hanging head-down from the ejection hatch, his face only inches from the muck. If the boat should settle, he would smother—if he was still alive even now. Reith struggled frantically to untangle himself from his harness. The pain made him dizzy and sick; there was no strength in his hands, and when he raised his arms there were clicking sounds in his shoulders. He was helpless to free himself, let alone assist Waunder. Was he dead? Reith could not be sure. Waunder, he thought, had twitched feebly.

Reith watched intently. Waunder was slipping slowly into the mire. In the ejection seat was a survival kit with weapons and tools. With his broken bones he could not raise his arms to reach the clasp. If he detached himself from the shrouds he would fall and kill himself . . . No help for it. Broken shoulder, broken collarbone or not, he must open the ejection seat, bring forth the knife and the coil of rope.

There was a sound, not too far distant, of wood striking wood. Reith desisted in his efforts, hung quietly. A troop of men armed with fancifully long rapiers and heavy hand-catapults marched quietly, almost furtively, below.

Reith stared dumbfounded, suspecting hallucination. The cosmos seemed partial to biped races, more or less anthropoid; but these were true men: people with harsh, strong features, honey-colored skin, blond, blond-brown, blond-gray hair and bushy drooping mustaches. They wore complicated garments: loose trousers of striped brown and black cloth, dark blue or dark red shirts, vests of woven metal strips, short black capes. Their hats were black leather, folded and creased with out-turned ear-flaps, each with a silver emblem four inches across at the front of a tall crown. Reith watched in amazement. Barbarian warriors, a wandering band of cutthroats: but true men, nonetheless, here on this unknown world over two hundred light-years from Earth!

The warriors passed quietly below, stealthy and furtive. They paused in the shadows to survey the boat, then the leader, a warrior younger than the rest, no more than a youth and lacking a mustache, stepped out into the open and examined the sky. He was joined by three older men, wearing globes of pink and blue glass on their helmets, who also searched the sky with great care. Then the youth signaled to the others, and all approached the boat.

Paul Waunder raised his hand in the feeblest of salutes. One of the men with the glass globes snatched up his catapult, but the youth yelled an angry order and the man sullenly turned away. One of the warriors cut the parachute shrouds, let Waunder fall to the ground.

The youth gave other orders; Waunder was picked up and carried to a dry area.

The youth now turned to investigate the space-boat. Boldly he clambered up on the hull and looked in through the ejection ports.

The older men with the pink and blue globes stood back in the shadows, muttering dourly through their drooping whiskers and glowering toward Waunder. One of them clapped his hand to the emblem on his hat as if the object had jerked or made a sound. Then, at once, as if stimulated by the contact, he stalked upon Waunder, drew his rapier, brought it flickering down. To Reith's horror Paul Waunder's head rolled free of his torso, and his blood gushed forth to soak into the black soil.

The youth seemed to sense the act and swung about. He cried

out in fury, leaped to the ground, marched over to the murderer. The youth snatched forth his own rapier, flicked it and the flexible end slashed in to cut away the emblem from the man's hat. The youth picked it up, and pulling a knife from his boot hacked savagely at the soft silver, then cast it down at the murderer's feet with a spate of bitter words. The murderer, cowed, picked up the emblem and moved sullenly off to the side.

From a great distance came a throb of sound. The warriors set up a soft hooting, either as a ceremonial response or in fear and mutual admonition, and quickly retreated into the forest.

Low in the sky appeared an aircraft, which first hovered, then settled: a sky-raft fifty feet long, twenty feet wide, controlled from an ornate belvedere at the stern. Forward and aft great lanterns dangled from convolute standards; the bulwarks were guarded by a squat balustrade. Leaning over the balustrade, pushing and jostling, were two dozen passengers, in imminent danger, so it seemed, of falling to the ground.

Reith watched in numb fascination as the craft landed beside the scout-boat. The passengers jumped quickly off: individuals of two sorts, non-human and human, though this distinction was not instantly obvious. The non-human creatures—Blue Chasch, as Reith was to learn—walked on short heavy legs, moving with a stiff-legged strut. The typical individual was massive and powerful, scaled like a pangolin with blue pointed tablets. The torso was wedge-shaped, with exoskeletal epaulettes of chitin curving over into a dorsal carapace. The skull rose to a bony point; a heavy brow jutted over the ocular holes, glittering metallic eyes and the complicated nasal orifice. The men were as similar to the Blue Chasch as breeding, artifice and mannerism allowed. They were short, stocky, with bandy-legs; their faces were blunt and almost chinless, with the features compressed. They wore what appeared to be false craniums which rose to a point and beetled over their foreheads; and their jerkins and trousers were worked with scales.

Chasch and Chaschmen ran to the scout-boat, communicating in fluting glottal cries. Some clambered up the hull, peered into the interior, others investigated the head and torso of Paul Waunder, which they picked up and carried aboard the raft.

From the control belvedere came a bawled alarm. Blue Chasch and Chaschmen looked up into the sky, then hurriedly pushed the raft under the trees and out of sight. Once again the little clearing was deserted.

Minutes passed. Reith closed his eyes and considered the evil nightmare from which he hoped to wake, secure aboard the *Explorator*.

A thudding of engines aroused him from torpor. Down from the sky sank still another vehicle: an airship which, like the raft, had been built with small regard for aerodynamic efficiency. There were three decks, a central rotunda, balconies of black wood and copper, a scrolled prow, observation cupolas, weapon ports, a vertical fin displaying a gold and black insignia. The ship hovered while those on the decks gave the space-boat a fastidious inspection. Some of these were not human, but tall attenuated creatures, hairless, pale as parchment, with austere countenances, languid and elegant attitudes. Others, apparently subordinates, were men, though they displayed the same attenuated arms, legs and torso, the sheep-like mannerisms. Both races wore elaborate costumes of ribbons, flounces, sashes. Later Reith would know the non-human folk as Dirdir and their human subordinates as Dirdirmen. At the moment, dazed by the immensity of his disaster, he noted the splendid Dirdir airship only with disinterested wonder. The thought, however, seeped into his mind that either these tall pale folk or their predecessors at the scene had destroyed the *Explorator IV*, and both had evidently tracked the arrival of the scout-boat.

Dirdir and Dirdirmen scrutinized the space-boat with keen interest. One of them called attention to the print left by the Chasch raft, and the discovery created an instant atmosphere of emergency. Instantly from the forest came stabs of purple-white energy; Dirdir and Dirdirmen fell writhing. Chasch and Chaschmen charged forth, Chasch firing hand-weapons, Chaschmen running to throw grapples at the ship.

The Dirdir discharged their own hand-weapons, which exuded a violet flare and whorls of orange plasma; Chasch and Chaschmen were consumed in a purple and orange blaze. The Dirdir ship lifted, to be constrained by grapples. The Dirdirmen hacked with knives, burnt with energy pistols; the ship broke free, to fluting cries of disappointment from the Chasch.

A hundred feet above the bog the Dirdir turned heavy plasma-beams upon the forest and burnt a series of reeking avenues, but failed to destroy the raft, from which the Chasch were now aiming their own great mortars. The first Chasch projectile missed. The second struck the ship under the hull; it slewed around under the impact, then gave a great dart off into the sky, flitting, lurching, jerking like a wounded insect, upside-down, then right-side up, with Dirdir and Dirdirmen falling off, black specks drifting down the slate-colored sky. The ship veered south, then east and presently was lost to sight.

Chasch and Chaschmen came forth to gaze after the Dirdir ship. The raft slid forth from the forest, hovered over the scout-boat. Grapples were dropped; the boat was lifted from the mire. Chasch and Chaschmen climbed aboard the raft; it slanted up into the air and moved off to the northeast, with the space-boat slung below.

Time passed. Reith hung in his harness, barely conscious. The sun settled behind the trees; dimness began to drift over the land-scape.

The barbarians reappeared. They went to the clearing, made a desultory inspection, looked up into the sky, then turned away.

Reith gave a hoarse call. The warriors snatched out their cata-pults, but the youth made a furious gesture to restrain them. He gave orders; two men climbed the tree, cut the parachute shrouds to leave the ejection seat and Reith's survival gear swinging in the branches.

Reith was lowered to the ground, none too gently, and his senses went dim at the grating of bones in his shoulder. Forms loomed above him, speaking in harsh consonants and broad vowels. he was lifted, placed in a litter; he felt the thud and swing of footsteps; then he either fainted or fell asleep.

2

REITH AWOKE TO the flicker of firelight, the murmur of voices. Above was a dark canopy, to either side a sky full of strange stars. The nightmare was real. Aspect by aspect, sensation by sensa-tion, Reith took stock of himself and his condition. He lay on a pallet of woven reeds which exuded a sourish odor, half-vegetable, half-human. His shirt had been removed; a harness of withe constricted his shoulders and provided support for his bro-ken bones. Painfully he raised his head and looked around. He lay in an open-sided shelter of metal poles covered with fabric. Another paradox, thought Reith. The metal poles indicated a high level of technology; the weapons and manners of the people were purely barbaric. Reith tried to look toward the fire, but the effort pained him and he lay back.

The camp was in the open country; the forest had been left behind; so much was evident from the stars. He wondered about his ejection seat and the attached survival pack. Seat and pack had been left dangling, so he recalled to his regret. He had only himself and his innate resources to depend upon—a quality somewhat augmented by the training forced upon a scout, some of which Reith had considered pedantic over-elaboration. He had assimilated vast quantities of basic science, linguistic and communication theory, astronautics, space and energy technology, biometrics, meteorology, geology, toxicology. So much was theory; additionally he had trained in practical survival techniques of every description: weaponry, attack and defense, emergency nutrition, rigging and hoisting, space-drive mechanics, electronic repair and improvisation. If he was not killed out of hand, as had been Paul Waunder, he would live—but to what purpose? His chances of returning to Earth must be considered infinitesimal—which made the intrinsic interest of the planet less stimulating.

A shadow fell across his face; Reith saw the youth who had saved his life. After peering through the dark the youth kneeled down, proffered a bowl of coarse gruel.

"Thanks very much," said Reith. "But I don't think I can eat; I'm constricted by the splints."

The youth leaned forward, speaking in a rather curt voice. Reith thought his face strangely stern and intense for a boy who could not be more than sixteen years old.

With great exertion Reith pulled himself up on his elbow and took the gruel. The youth rose, moved a few paces back, stood watching as Reith tried to feed himself. Then he turned and called a gruff summons. A small girl came running forward. She bowed, took the bowl and began to feed Reith with earnest care.

The boy watched a moment, evidently mystified by Reith, and Reith was perplexed no less. Men and women, on a world two hundred and twelve light-years from Earth! Parallel evolution? Incredible! Spoonful by spoonful the gruel was placed in his mouth. The girl, about eight years old, wore a ragged pajama-like garment, not too clean. A half-dozen men of the tribe came to watch; there was a growl of conversation which the youth ignored.

The bowl was empty; the girl held a mug of sour beer to Reith's mouth. Reith drank because it was expected of him, though the brew puckered his lips. "Thank you," he told the girl, who returned a diffident smile and quickly departed.

Reith lay back on the pallet. The youth spoke to him in a brusque voice: evidently a question.

"Sorry," said Reith. "I don't understand. But don't be irritated; I need every friend I can get."

The youth spoke no more and presently departed. Reith leaned back on his pallet and tried to sleep. The firelight flickered low; activity in the camp dwindled.

From far off came a faint call, half howl, half quavering hoot, which was presently answered by another, and another, to become an almost identical chanting of hundreds of voices. Raising up on his elbow once more, Reith saw that the two moons, of equal apparent diameter, one pink, the other pale blue, had appeared in the east.

A moment later a new voice, nearer at hand, joined the far ululation. Reith listened in wonder; surely this was the voice of a woman? Other voices joined the first, wailing a wordless dirge, which, joined to the far hooting, produced a colloquy of vast woe.

The chant at last halted; the camp became quiet. Reith became drowsy and fell asleep.

In the morning Reith saw more of the camp. It lay in a swale between a pair of broad low hills, among multitudes rolling off to the east. Here for reasons not immediately apparent to Reith the tribesmen elected to sojourn. Each morning four young warriors wearing long brown cloaks mounted small electric motorcycles and set off in different directions across the steppe. Each evening they returned, to make detailed reports to Traz Onmale the boy-ruler. Every morning a great kite was paid out, hoisting aloft a boy of eight or nine, whose function was evidently that of a lookout. Late in the afternoon the wind tended to die, dropping the kite more or less easily. The boy usually escaped with no more than a bump, though the men handling the lines seemed to worry more for the safety of the kite; a four-winged contraption of black membrane stretched over wooden splints.

Each morning, from beyond the hill to the east, sounded a

fearful squealing, which persisted for almost half an hour. The tumult, Reith presently learned, arose from the herd of multi-legged animals from which the tribe derived meat. Each morning the tribe butcher, a woman six feet tall and brawny to match, went through the herd with a knife and a cleaver, to excise three or four legs for the needs of the day. Occasionally she cut flesh from a beast's back, or reached through a wound to carve chunks from an internal organ. The beasts made little protest at the excision of their legs, which soon renewed themselves, but performed prodigies of complaint when their bodies were entered.

While Reith's bones mended his only contacts were with women, a spiritless group, and with Traz Onmale, who spent the greater part of each morning with Reith, talking, inspecting Reith's habiliments, teaching the Kruthe language. This was syntactically regular but rendered difficult by scores of tenses, moods and aspects. Long after Reith was able to express himself, Traz Onmale, in the stern manner so much at odds with his years, would correct him and indicate still another intricacy of usage.

The world was Tschai, so Reith learned; the moons were Az and Braz. The tribesmen were Kruthe or "Emblem Men," after the devices of silver, copper, stone and wood which they wore on their hats. A man's status was established by his emblem, which was reckoned a semi-divine entity in itself, with a name, detailed history, idiosyncrasies and rank. It was not too much to say that rather than the man carrying the emblem, the emblem controlled the man, as it gave him his name and reputation, and defined his tribal role. The most exalted emblem was Onmale, carried by Traz, who prior to assuming the emblem had been an ordinary lad of the tribe. Onmale was the embodiment of wisdom, craft, resolution and the indefinable Kruthe *virtu*. A man might inherit an emblem, take possession after killing its owner, or fabricate a new emblem for himself. In the latter case, the new emblem held no personality or *virtu* until it had participated in noteworthy feats and so acquired status. When an emblem changed hands the new owner willy-nilly assumed the personality of the emblem. Certain emblems were mutually antagonistic, and a man coming into possession of one of these at once became the enemy of the holder of the other. Certain emblems were thousands of years old, with complex histories; some were fey and carried a weight of doom; others impelled the wearer to hardihood or some specific sort of berserker élan. Reith was sure that his perception of the symbolic personalities was pale and gray compared to the intensity of the Kruthe's own comprehensions. Without his emblem the tribesman was a man without a face, without prestige or function. He was in fact what Reith presently learned himself to be; a helot, or a woman, the words in the Kruthe language being the same.

Curiously, or so it seemed to Reith, the Emblem Men believed him to be a man from a remote region of Tschai. Far from respecting him for his presence aboard the space-boat, they thought him a subordinate to some non-human race unknown to them, as the Chaschmen were subordinate to the Blue Chasch, or the Dirdirmen to the Dirdir.

When Reith first heard Traz Onmale express this point of view, he refuted the idea indignantly. "I am from Earth, a far planet; we are not ruled by anyone."

"Who built the space-boat then?" Traz Onmale asked in a skeptical voice.

"Men, naturally. Men of Earth."

Traz Onmale gave his head a dubious shake. "How could there be men so far from Tschai?"

Reith gave a laugh of bitter amusement. "I've been asking myself the same question: How did men come to Tschai?"

"The origin of men is well-known," said Traz Onmale in a frigid voice. "We are taught this as soon as we can speak. Did you not receive the same instruction?"

"On Earth we believe that men evolved from a protohominid, which in turn derived from an ancient mammal; and so on back to the first cells."

Traz Onmale looked askance at the women who worked nearby. He gave them a brusque signal. "Be off, we are discussing men's matters."

The women departed with clacking tongues, and Traz Onmale looked after them in disgust. "The foolishness will be all over camp. The magicians will be annoyed. I must explain to you the true source of men. You have seen the moons. The pink moon is Az, abode of the blessed. The blue moon is Braz, a place of torment, where evil folk and *kruthsh'geir** are sent after death. Long ago the moons collided; thousands of folk were dislodged and

---

*An untranslatable word; roughly: a man who has defied and defiled his emblem, and hence perverted his destiny.

fell to Tschai. All now seek to return to Az, good and evil alike. But the Judgers, who derive wisdom from the globes they wear, separate good men from the bad and send them to appropriate destinations.

"Interesting," said Reith. "What of the Chasch and the Dirdir?"

"They are not men. They came to Tschai from beyond the stars, as did the Wankh; Chaschmen and Dirdirmen are unclean hybrids. Pnume and Phung are spew of the northern caves. We kill all with zeal." He regarded Reith sidelong, brows knit severely. "If you derive from a world other than Tschai, you cannot be a man, and I should order you killed."

"That seems overly harsh," said Reith. "After all, I have done you no harm."

Traz Onmale made a gesture to indicate that the argument had no relevance. "I will defer judgment."

Reith exercised his stiff limbs, and diligently studied the language. The Kruthe, he learned, held to no fixed range, but wandered the vast Aman Steppe, which spread across the south of the continent known as Kotan. They had no great knowledge of conditions elsewhere on Tschai. There were other continents—Kislovan to the south; Charchan, Kachan, Rakh on the other side of the world. Other nomad tribes roamed the steppe; in the marshes and forests to the south lived ogres and cannibals, with a variety of supernatural powers. The Blue Chasch were established to the far west of Kotan; the Dirdir, who preferred a cold climate, lived on Haulk, a peninsula reached south and west of Kislovan, and on the northeast coast of Charchan.

Another alien race, the Wankh, were also established on Tschai, but the Emblem Men knew little of these folk. Native to Tschai was an eerie race known as the Pnume, also their mad relatives, the Phung, regarding whom the Kruthe were reluctant to speak, lowering their voices and looking over their shoulders when they did so.

Time passed: days of bizarre events, nights of despair and longing for Earth. Reith's bones began to knit and he unobtrusively explored the camp.

About fifty sheds had been erected in the lee of the hill, the roofs butted end to end to form what from the air would seem a fold or declivity on the hillside. Beyond the sheds was a cluster of enormous six-wheeled motor drays, camouflaged under tarpaulins. Reith was awed by the bulk of the vehicles and would have examined them more closely were it not for the band of sallow urchins which followed him about, attentive to his every move. Intuitively they sensed his strangeness and were fascinated. The warriors, however, ignored him; a man without an emblem was little more than a ghost.

At the far end of camp Reith found an enormous machine mounted on a truck: a giant catapult with a thrust-arm fifty feet long. A siege engine? On one side was painted a pink disc, on the other a blue disc: reference, so Reith assumed, to the moons Az and Braz.

Days passed, weeks, a month. Reith could not understand the inactivity of the tribe. They were nomads; why did they keep so long to this particular camp? Every day the four scouts rode forth, while overhead swung the black kite, veering and dipping while the rider's legs swung doll-like back and forth. The warriors were clearly restive, and occupied themselves practicing the use of their weapons. These were of three sorts: a long flexible rapier with a cutting and stabbing tip, like the tail of a ray: a catapult, which used the energy of elastic cables to shoot short feathered bolts; a triangular shield, a foot in length, nine inches across the base, with sharp elongated corners and razor-sharp side-edges serving additionally as a thrusting and hacking weapon.

Reith was tended first by the eight-year-old urchin, then by a small hunched crone with a face like a raisin, then by a girl who, were it not for her joylessness, might have been attractive. She was perhaps eighteen years old, with regular features, fine blonde hair typically tangled with twigs and bits of fodder. She went barefoot, wearing only a smock of coarse gray homespun.

One day, as Reith sat on a bench, the girl came past. Reith caught her around the waist, pulled her down upon his knee. She smelled of furze and bracken, and the moss of the steppes, and a faintly sour scent of wool. She asked in a husky alarmed voice, "What do you want of me?" And she tried half-heartedly to rise.

Reith found her warm weight comforting. "First, I'll comb the twigs from your hair . . . Sit still now." She relaxed, eyes turned sidelong at Reith; puzzled, submissive, uneasy. Reith combed her hair, first with his fingers, then with a chip of broken wood. The girl sat quietly.

"There," said Reith presently. "You look nice."

The girl sat as in a dream. Presently she stirred, rose to her feet. "I must go," she said in a hurried voice. "Someone might see." But she lingered. Reith started to pull her back, then thought better of the impulse and let her hurry away.

The next day she chanced past again, and this time her hair was combed and clean. She paused to look over her shoulder, and Reith could remember the same glance, the same attitude from a hundred occasions on Earth; and the thought made him sick with melancholy. At home the girl would be reckoned beautiful; here on Aman Steppe, she had no more than a dim awareness of such matters . . . He held out his hand to her; she approached, as if drawn against her will, which was undoubtedly the case, for she knew the ways of her tribe. Reith put his hands on her shoulders, then around her waist, kissed her. She seemed puzzled. Reith asked, smiling, "Hasn't anyone done that before?"

"No. But it's nice. Do it again."

Reith heaved a deep sigh. Well, why not? . . . A step behind him: a buffet sent him sprawling to the ground, accompanied by a spate of words too fast for his understanding. A booted foot struck into his ribs, sending shivers of pain through his mending shoulder.

The man advanced on the cringing girl, who stood with fists pressed to her mouth. He struck her, kicked her, pushed her out into the compound, cursing and bawling insults: "—disgusting intimacy with an outland slave; is this your regard for the purity of the race?"

"Slave?" Reith picked himself up from the floor of the shed. The word rang in his mind. Slave?

The girl ran off to huddle under one of the towering wagons. Traz Onmale came to look into the uproar. The warrior, a stalwart buck of about Reith's own age, pointed a quivering finger toward Reith. "He is a curse, a dark omen! Was not all this foretold? Intolerable that he should spawn among our women! He must be killed, or gelded!"

Traz Onmale looked dubiously toward Reith. "It seems that he did small damage."

"Small damage indeed! But only because I happened past! With so much energy for ardor, why is he not put out to work? Must we pamper his belly while he sits on pillows? Geld him and set him to toil with the women!"

Traz Onmale gave a reluctant assent, and Reith, with a sinking heart, thought of his survival kit dangling from the tree, with its drugs, transcom, spanscope, energy pack, and, most especially, weapons. For all their present benefit to him they might as well be with the *Explorator IV*.

Traz Onmale had summoned the butcher-woman. "Bring a sharp knife. The slave must be made placid."

"Wait!" gasped Reith. "Is this any way to treat a stranger? Have you no tradition of hospitality?"

"No," said Traz Onmale. "We do not. We are the Kruthe, driven by the force of our Emblems."

"This man struck me," protested Reith. "Is he a coward? Will he fight? What if I took his emblem from him? Would I not then be entitled to his place in the tribe?"

"The emblem itself is the place," Traz Onmale admitted. "This man Osom is the vehicle for the emblem Vaduz. Without Vaduz he would be no better than you. But if Vaduz is content with Osom, as must be so, you could never take Vaduz."

"I can try."

"Conceivably. But you are too late; here is the butcher-woman. Be good enough to disrobe."

Reith turned a horrified glance upon the woman, whose shoulders were broader than his own and inches thicker, and who advanced upon him wearing a face-splitting grin.

"There is still time," muttered Reith. "Ample time." He turned upon Osom Vaduz, who snatched forth his rapier with a shrill whine of steel against hard leather. But Reith had stepped in close, within the six-foot reach of the blade. Osom Vaduz tried to leap back; Reith caught his arm, which was hard as steel; in his present condition Osom Vaduz was by far the stronger man. Osom Vaduz gave his arm a mighty jerk to fling Reith to the ground. Reith pulled in the same direction, swung around to drag Osom Vaduz reeling off-balance. Reith thrust up his shoulder, Osom Vaduz rolled across his hip and crashed to the ground. Reith kicked him in the head, grounding his heel into Osom Vaduz's throat, to crush the windpipe. As Osom Vaduz lay twitching and croaking his hat rolled off; Reith reached for it but the Chief Magician snatched it away.

"No, by no means!" cried the magician in a passion. "This is not our law. You are a slave; a slave you remain!"

"Must I kill you too?" asked Reith, edging ominously forward.

"Enough!" cried Traz Onmale peremptorily. "There has been enough killing. No more!"

"What of the emblem?" asked Reith. "Do you not agree it is mine?"

"I must consider," declared the youth. "In the meanwhile, no more. Butcher-woman, take the body to the pyre. Where are the Judgers? Let them come forth and judge this Osom who carried Vaduz. Emblems, bring forth the engine!"

Reith moved off to the side. A few minutes later he approached Traz Onmale. "If you wish, I will leave the tribe and go off by myself."

"You will know my wishes when they are formulated," declared the lad, with the absolute decisiveness conferred upon him by the Onmale. "Remember, you are my slave; I ordered back the blades which would have killed you. If you try to escape, you will be tracked, taken, flogged. Meanwhile you must gather fodder."

It seemed to Reith as if Traz Onmale were straining for severity, perhaps to divert attention—his own as well as everyone else's—from the unpleasant order he had given to the butcher-woman and which, by implication, he had rescinded.

For a day the dismembered body of Osom, who once had carried the emblem Vaduz, smoldered within a special metal kiln, and the wind blew a vile stench through the camp. The warriors uncovered the monstrous catapult, started the engine and brought it into the center of the compound.

The sun sank behind a bank of graphite-purple clouds; sunset was an angry welter of crimson and brown. Osom's corpse had been consumed; the fire was ashes. With all the tribe crouching in murmurous ranks, the Chief Magician kneaded the ashes with beast-blood to form a cake, which was then packed into a box and lashed to the head of a great shaft.

The magicians looked into the east, where now rose Az the pink moon, almost at the full. The Chief Magician called in a great belling voice: "Az! The Judgers have judged a man and found him good! He is Osom; he carried Vaduz. Make ready, Az! We send you Osom!"

The warriors on the catapult engaged a gear. The great arm swung across the sky; the elastic cables ground with tension. The shaft with Osom's ashes was laid in the channel; the arm was aimed toward Az. The tribe set up a moan, rising to a throaty wail. The magician cried: "Away to Az!"

The catapult gave a heavy *twunggg-thwack!* The shaft sped away too swiftly to be seen. A moment later, high in the sky, appeared a burst of white fire; and the watchers gave a sigh of exaltation.

For another half-hour the folk of the tribe stood looking up toward Az. Did they envy Osom, Reith wondered, presumably now rejoicing in the Vaduz palace on Az? He sought among the dark shapes, lingering before going to his pallet, until, with a smile of grim amusement for his own weakness, he realized that he was hoping to locate the girl who had occasioned the entire affair.

On the following day Reith was sent forth to gather fodder, a coarse leaf terminating in a drop of dark-red wax. Far from resenting the work, Reith was happy to escape the monotony of the camp.

The rolling hills extended as far as the eye could reach, alternate cusps of amber and black under the windy sky of Tschai. Reith looked south, to the black line of forest, where his ejection seat still hung in a tree, or so he hoped. In the near-future he would ask Traz Onmale to conduct him to the spot . . . Someone was watching him. Reith swung around, but saw nothing.

Wary, watching from the corner of his eyes he went about his task, plucking leaves, filling the two baskets he carried on a shoulder-pole. He started down into a swale, where grew a copse of low bushes, with leaves like red and blue flame. He saw the flutter of a gray smock. It was the girl, pretending not to see him. Reith descended to meet her and they stood face to face, she half-smiling, half-cringing, awkwardly twisting her fingers together.

Reith reached forth, took her hands. "If we meet, if we are friends, we'll get in trouble."

The girl nodded. "I know . . . Is it true that you are from another world?"

"Yes."

"What is it like?"

"It's hard to describe."

"The magicians are foolish, aren't they? Dead people don't go to Az."

"I hardly think so."

She came closer. "Do that again."

Reith kissed her. Then he took her by the shoulders and held her back. "We can't be lovers. You'd be made unhappy, and get more beatings . . ."

She shrugged. "I don't care. I wish I could go with you back to Earth."

"I wish you could too," said Reith.

"Do that again," said the girl. Just once more . . ." She gave a sudden gasp, looking over Reith's shoulder. He jerked around, to see a flicker of movement. There was a hiss, a thud, a heartrending sob of pain. The girl sagged to her knees, fell over on her side, clutching at the feathered bolt buried in her chest. Reith gave a hoarse call, looked wildly here and there.

The skyline was clear; no one could be seen. Reith bent over the girl. Her lips moved, but he could not hear the words. She sighed and relaxed.

Reith stood looking down at the body, rage crowding all rational thought from his mind. He bent, lifted her—she weighed less than he expected—and carried her back to camp, reeling and straining. He took her to the shed of Traz Onmale.

The boy sat on a stool, holding a rapier which he glumly twitched back and forth. Reith lay down the body of the girl as gently as he was able. Traz Onmale looked from the body to Reith with a flinty stare. Reith said, "I met the girl picking fodder. We were talking—and the bolt hit her. It was murder. The bolt might have been meant for me."

Traz Onmale glanced down at the bolt, touched the feathers. Already warriors were sauntering close. Traz Onmale looked from face to face. "Where is Jad Piluna?"

There were mutters, a hoarse voice, a summons. Jad Piluna approached: one whom Reith had noticed on previous occasions: a man of dash and flair, with a keen high-colored face, a curious V-shaped mouth, conveying, perhaps unintentionally, a continual insolent mirth. Reith stared at him in a fascination of loathing. Here was the murderer.

Traz Onmale held out his hand. "Show me your catapult."

Jad Piluna tossed it, an act of casual disrespect, and Traz Onmale turned up a glittering glance. He looked at the catapult, checked the claw release and the film of grease customarily applied by the warriors after using their weapons. He said: "The grease is disturbed; you have fired this catapult today. The bolt"—he pointed down at the corpse—"has the three black bands of Piluna. You killed the girl."

Jad Piluna's mouth twitched, the V broadened and narrowed. "I meant to kill the man. He is a slave and a heretic. She was no better."

"Who are you to decide? Do you carry Onmale?"

"No. But I maintain that the act was accidental. It is no crime to kill a heretic."

The Chief Magician stepped forward. "The matter of intentional heresy is crucial. This person"—he pointed toward Reith—"is clearly a hybrid; I would suppose Dirdirman and Pnumekin. For reasons unknown he has joined the Emblem Men and now circulates heresy. Does he think we are too stupid to notice? How wrong he is! He suborned the young woman; he led her astray; she became worthless. Hence when—"

Traz Onmale, again displaying the decisiveness so astonishing in a lad so young, cut him short. "Enough. You talk nonsense. The Piluna is notoriously an emblem of dark deeds. Jad, the carrier, must be brought to account, and Piluna curbed."

"I claim innocence," said Jad Piluna indifferently. "I give myself to the justice of the moons."

Traz Onmale squinted in anger. "Never mind the justice of the moons. I will give you justice."

Jad Piluna gazed at him without concern. "The Onmale is not permitted to fight."

Traz Onmale looked around the group. "Is there no noble emblem to subdue the murderous Piluna?"

None of the warriors responded. Jad Piluna nodded in satisfaction. "The emblems stand aloof. Your call has no effect. But you have laid a slur on Piluna; you have used the word 'murderer.' I demand vindication from the moons."

In a controlled voice Traz Onmale said, "Bring forth the disc."

The Chief Magician departed, to return with a box carved from a single huge bone. He turned to Jad Piluna. "To which moon do you call for justice?"

"I demand vindication from Az, moon of virtue and peace; I ask Az to demonstrate my right."

"Very well," said Traz Onmale. "I beseech Braz, the Hellmoon, to claim you for her own."

The Chief Magician reached into the box, brought forth a disc, on one side pink, on the other blue. "Stand clear, all!" He spun the disc into the air. It tilted, wobbled, seemed to float and glide, and landed with the pink side on top. "Az, moon of virtue, has decided innocence!" called the magician. "Braz has seen no cause to act."

Reith gave a snort of sour amusement. He turned to Traz Onmale. "I call upon the moons for judgment."

"Judgment in regard to what?" demanded the Chief Magician. "Certainly not your heresy! That is demonstrable!"

"I ask that the moon Az concede me the emblem Vaduz, so that I may punish the murderer Jad."

Traz Onmale gave Reith a startled glance.

The Chief Magician cried out in indignation. "Impossible; how can a slave carry an emblem?"

Traz Onmale looked down at the pathetic corpse and gave a curt sign to the magician. "I release him from bondage. Throw the disc to the moons."

The Chief Magician stood curiously stiff and reluctant. "Is this wise? The emblem Vaduz—"

"—is hardly the most noble of emblems. Throw."

The magician glanced askance at Jad Piluna. "Throw," said Jad Piluna. "Should the moons give him to the emblem I will cut him into small strips. I have always despised the Vaduz trait."

The magician hesitated, considering first the tall hard-muscled figure of Jad Piluna, then Reith, equally tall but thinner and looser, and still lacking his full vigor.

The Chief Magician, a cautious man, thought to temporize. "The disc is drained of its force; we can have no more judgments."

"Nonsense," said Reith. "The disc is controlled, so you claim, by the power of the moons. How can the disc be drained? Throw the disc!"

"Throw the disc!" ordered Traz Onmale.

"Then you must take Braz, for you are evil and a heretic."

"I have called on Az, which can reject me if it chooses."

The magician shrugged. "As you wish. I will use a fresh disc."

"No!" exclaimed Reith. "The same disc."

Traz Onmale sat erect and leaned forward, his attention once again engaged. "Use the same disc. Throw!"

With an angry gesture the Chief Magician snatched up the disc, spun it high and twinkling into the air. As before, it wobbled, seemed to float, drifted down with the pink face up.

"Az favors the stranger!" declared Traz Onmale. "Fetch the emblem Vaduz!"

The Chief Magician stalked to his shed and brought it forth. Traz Onmale handed it to Reith. "You now carry Vaduz: you are an Emblem Man. Do you then challenge Jad Piluna?"

"I do."

Traz Onmale turned to Jad Piluna. "Are you prepared to defend your emblem?"

"At once." Jad Piluna whipped forth his rapier, flourished it whistling around his head.

"A sword and hand-foil for the new Vaduz," said Traz Onmale.

Reith took the rapier which presently was tendered him. He hefted it, whipped the blade back and forth. Never had he handled so supple a sword, and he had handled many, for swordsmanship was an element of his training. An awkward weapon, in some respects, useless for close-range fighting. The warriors at practice held their distance from each other, swinging, slashing, lunging, swerving the blade down and up, in and out, but using relatively little footwork. The triangular knife-foil for the left hand was also strange. He swung the blade back and forth, watching Jad Piluna from the corner of his eyes, who stood contemptuously at ease.

To attempt to fight the man in his own style was equivalent to suicide, thought Reith.

"Attention!" called Traz Onmale. "Vaduz challenges Piluna. Forty-one such encounters have occurred previously. Piluna has humiliated Vaduz on thirty-four occasions. Emblems, address yourselves."

Jad Piluna instantly lunged; Reith parried without difficulty, hacked down with his own blade: a blow which Jad Piluna glissed off with his knife-shield. As he did so Reith jumped forward, struck with the point of the knife-shield, to puncture Jad Piluna's chest: a trifling wound, but sufficient to destroy Piluna's complacence. Eyes bulging in wrath, the red in his face almost feverish, he leaped back, then launched a furious attack, overwhelming Reith by sheer strength and technical brilliance. Reith was extended to the utmost even to fend away the whistling blade, without thought for counterattack. His shoulder gave a sudden ominous twinge and began to burn; he panted for breath. The blade slashed into his thigh, then his left bicep; confident, gloating, Jad Piluna pressed the attack, expecting Reith to fall back, to be carved into tatters. But Reith lurched forward, knocked aside the blade with his knife-shield, slashed at Jad Piluna's head and struck the black hat askew. Jad Piluna stepped back to set his hat straight but Reith jumped forward again, inside comfortable fighting distance with the rapier. He struck with the knife-shield, batted again at Jad Piluna's hat, knocked it off, and with it the emblem Piluna. Reith dropped the knife-shield, seized the hat. Jad, bereft of Piluna, stood back aghast, his face ringed by brown curls. He lunged; Reith swung the hat, caught the rapier in the ear-flaps. He stabbed with his own rapier, piercing Jad's shoulder.

Jad frantically disengaged his rapier, gave ground, anxious to gain more room, but Reith, panting and sweating, pressed him.

Reith spoke: "I hold the emblem Piluna, which has rejected you in disgust. You, the murderer, are about to die."

Jad gave an inarticulate call, lunged to the attack. Again Reith swung the hat, to catch the rapier in the flaps. He thrust and ran Jad, one-time carrier of Piluna, through the abdomen. Jad struck down with his foil, knocked the rapier from Reith's grip. A grotesque moment he stood looking at Reith in horror and accusation, the blade protruding from his body. He tore it out, flung it aside, advanced on Reith who groped for his dropped knife-shield. As Jad lunged Reith picked up the foil, hurled it point first into Jad's face. The point struck into Jad's open mouth and became fixed, like a fantastic metal tongue. Jad's knees buckled; he collapsed to the ground, and lay with fingers twitching.

Reith, breath rasping in his throat, dropped the hat with proud Piluna into the dirt and went to lean on the pole of a shed.

There was no sound throughout the camp.

Finally Traz Onmale said, "Vaduz has overcome Piluna. The emblem takes on luster. Where are the Judgers? Let them come to judge Jad Piluna."

The three magicians came forward, glowering first at the new corpse, at Traz Onmale and sidelong at Reith.

"Judge," ordered Traz Onmale in his harsh, old-man's voice. "Be sure to judge correctly!"

The magicians consulted in a mutter; then the Chief Magician spoke. "Judgment is difficult. Jad lived a hero's life. He served Piluna with distinction."

"He murdered a girl."

"For good cause: the taint of heresy, traffic with an unclean hybrid! What other religious man might not do the same?"

"He acted beyond his competence. I instruct you to judge him evil. Put him on the pyre. When Braz appears, shoot the evil ashes to hell."

"So be it," muttered the Chief Magician.

Traz Onmale went off into his shed.

Reith stood alone at the center of the compound. In uneasy groups the warriors spoke together, glancing toward Reith with distaste. The time was late afternoon; a bank of heavy clouds obscured the sun. There were flickers and twitches of purple lightning, a hoarse mutter of thunder. Women scurried here and there, covering bundles of fodder and jars of food-pod. The warriors bestirred themselves to tighten the lines holding the tarpaulins down over the great wagons.

Reith looked down at the girl's corpse, which no one seemed interested in carrying away. To allow the body to lie out all night in the rain and wind was unthinkable. Already the pyre was alight, ready to receive the hulk of Jad. Reith lifted the girl's body, carried it to the pyre and, ignoring the complaints of the old women who tended the flames, laid the body into the kiln with as much composure and grace as he could manage.

With the first spatters of rain, Reith went to that storage shed which had been given over to his use.

Outside the rain pelted down. Sodden women built a rude shelter over the pyre and continued to feed the flames with brush.

Someone came into the shed. Reith backed into the shadows, then the firelight shone on the face of Traz Onmale. He seemed somber, dejected. "Reith Vaduz, where are you?"

Reith came forth. Traz Onmale looked at him, gave his head a glum shake. "Since you have been with the tribe, everything has gone wrong! Dissension, anger, death. The scouts return with news only of empty steppe. Piluna has been tainted. The magicians are at odds with the Onmale. Who are you, why do you bring us such woe?"

"I am what I told you I am," said Reith: "a man from Earth."

"Heresy," said Traz Onmale, without heat. "Emblem Men are the spill of Az. So say the magicians, at least."

Reith pondered a moment, then said, "When ideas are in contradiction, as here, the more powerful ideas usually win. Sometimes this is bad, sometimes good. The society of the Emblems seems bad to me. A change would be for the better. You are ruled by priests who—"

"No," said the boy decisively. "Onmale rules the tribe. I carry that emblem; it speaks through my mouth."

"To some extent. The priests are clever enough to have their own way."

"What do you intend? Do you wish to destroy us?"

"Of course not. I want to destroy no one—unless it becomes necessary to my own survival."

The boy heaved a heavy sigh. "I am confused. You are wrong—or the magicians are wrong."

"The magicians are wrong. Human history on Earth goes back ten thousand years."

Traz Onmale laughed. "Once, before I carried Onmale, the tribe entered the ruins of old Carcegus and there captured a Pnumekin. The magicians tortured him to gain knowledge, but he spoke only to curse each minute of the fifty-two thousand years that men had lived on Tschai . . . Fifty-two thousand years against your ten thousand years. It is all very strange."

"Very strange indeed."

Traz Onmale rose to his feet, looked up into the sky, where wind-driven wrack flew across the night sky. "I have been watching the moons," he said in a thin voice. "The magicians are watching likewise. The portents are poor; I believe that there is about to be a conjunction. If Az covers Braz, all is well. If Braz covers Az, then someone new will carry Onmale."

"And you?"

"I must carry aloft the wisdom of Onmale, and set matters right." And Traz Onmale departed the shed.

The tempest roared across the steppe: a night, a day, a second night. On the morning of the second day the sun rose into a clear windy sky. The scouts rode forth as usual, to return pellmell at noon. There was an instant explosion of activity. Tarpaulins were folded, sheds were struck, packed into bundles. Women loaded the drays; warriors rubbed their leap-horses with oil, threw on saddles, attached reins to the sensitive frontal palps. Reith approached Traz Onmale. "What goes on?"

"A caravan from the east has been sighted at long last. We

shall attack along the Ioba River. As Vaduz you may ride with us and take a share of plunder."

He ordered a leap-horse; Reith mounted the ill-smelling beast with trepidation. It jerked to the unfamiliar weight, thrashing up its knob of a tail. Reith yanked at the reins; the leap-horse crouched and sprang off across the steppe while Reith held on for dear life. From behind came a roar of laughter: the hooting and jeering of experts for the tribulations of a tenderfoot.

Reith finally brought the leap-horse under control and came plunging back. A few moments later the group swept off to the northeast, the black long-necked brutes lunging and foaming, the warriors leaning forward on the saddleplats, knees drawn up, black leather hats flapping; Reith could not help but feel an archaic thrill at riding in the savage cavalcade.

For an hour the Emblem Men pounded across the steppe, bending low when they crossed over skylines. The rolling hills flattened; ahead lay a vast expanse streaked with shadows and dull colors. The troop halted on a hill while the warriors pointed here and there. Traz Onmale now gave orders. Reith pulled his mount up close and strained to listen. "—the south track to the ford. We wait in Bellbird Covert. The Ilanths will make the ford first; they will scout Zad Woods and White Hill. Then we sweep upon the center and make off with the treasure vans. Is all clear? So onward, to Bellbird Covert!"

Down the long slope rushed the Emblems, toward a far line of tall trees and a group of isolated bluffs overlooking Ioba River. In the shelter of a deep forest the Emblem warriors concealed themselves.

Time passed. From afar sounded a faint rumble, and the caravan appeared. Several hundred yards in advance rode three splendid yellow-skinned warriors, wearing black caps surmounted by jawless human skulls. Their beasts were similar to, but larger and rather more bland than the leap-horses; they carried sidearms and short swords, with short rifles laid across their laps.

Now, from the standpoint of the Emblems, everything went awry. The Ilanths failed to plunge across the river but waited watchfully for the caravan. To the river-bank lumbered motordrays with six-foot wheels, piled to astonishing heights with bales, parcels and in certain cases, cages in which huddled men and women.

The caravan commander was a cautious man. Before the drays attempted the ford, he stationed gun-carts to command all the approaches, then sent Ilanths to scout the opposite bank.

In Bellbird Covert the Emblem warriors cursed and fumed. "Wealth, wealth! Goods galore! Sixty prime wagons! But suicide to attempt an attack."

"True. The sand-blasts would strike us down like birds!"

"Is it this for which we waited three tedious months in the Walgram Rolls? Is our luck then so vile?"

"The omens were wrong; last night I looked up at blessed Az; I saw it jib and career through the clouds: a definite admonition."

"Nothing goes right, all our ventures are thwarted! We are under the influence of Braz."

"Braz—or the work of the black-haired sorcerer who slew Jad Piluna."

"True! And he has come to scathe the raid, where we have always enjoyed success!"

And sour looks began to be turned toward Reith, who made himself inconspicuous.

The war leaders conferred. "We can achieve nothing; we would strew the field with dead warriors and drown our Emblems in Ioba River."

"Well, then—shall we follow and attack at night?"

"No. They are too well-guarded. The commander is Baojian; he takes no risks! His soul to Braz!"

"So, then—three months dawdling for naught!"

"Better for naught than for disaster! Back to camp. The women will have all packed, and so east to Meraghan."

"East, more destitute than when we came west! What abominable luck."

"The omens, the omens! All are at odds!"

"Back to camp, then; nothing for us here."

The warriors swung about and without a backward look sent the leap-horses plunging south across the steppe.

During the early evening, surly and glum, the troop arrived back at the campsite. The women, who had all packed, were cursed for neglect; why were not cauldrons bubbling? pots of beer ready to hand?

The women bawled and cursed in return, only to be drubbed. All hands finally pulled gear and food helter-skelter from the drays.

Traz Onmale stood brooding apart, while Reith was pointedly ignored. The warriors ate hugely, grumbling all the while, then, seated and exhausted, lay back beside the fire.

Az had already risen, but now up into the sky sailed the blue moon Braz, angling athwart the course of Az. The magicians were first to notice and stood with arms pointing in awe and premonition.

The moons converged; it seemed as if they would collide. The warriors gave guttural sounds of dread. But Braz moved before the pink disc, eclipsing it utterly. The Chief Magician gave a wild bellow to the sky: "So be it! So be it!"

Traz Onmale turned and went slowly off to the shadows where by chance stood Reith. "What is all the tumult?" Reith asked.

"Did you not see? Braz overpowered Az. Tomorrow night I must go to Az to expiate our wrongs. No doubt you will go as well to Braz."

"You mean, by way of fire and catapult?"

"Yes. I am lucky to have carried Onmale as long as I have. The bearer before me was not much more than half my age when he was sent to Az."

"Do you think this ritual has any practical value?"

Traz Onmale hesitated. Then: "It is what they expect; they will demand that I cut my throat into the fire. So I must obey."

"Better that we leave now," said Reith. "They will sleep like logs. When they awake we will be far from here."

"What? The two of us? Where would we fare?"

"I don't know. Is there no land where folk live without murder?"

"Perhaps such places exist. But not on Aman Steppe."

"If we could take possession of the scout-boat, and if I were given time to repair it, we could leave Tschai and return to Earth."

"Impossible. The Chasch took the ship. It is lost to you forever."

"So I fear. In any case, we'd do better to depart now than wait to be killed tomorrow."

Traz Onmale stood staring up at the moons. "Onmale orders me to stay. I cannot pervert the Onmale. It has never fled; it has always pursued duty to the death."

"Duty doesn't include futile suicide," said Reith. He made a sudden motion, seized Traz Onmale's hat, wrenched loose the emblem. Traz gave a croak of almost physical pain, then stood staring at Reith. "What do you do? It is death to touch the Onmale!"

"You are no longer Traz Onmale; you are Traz."

The boy seemed to shrink, to lessen in stature. "Very well," he said in a subdued voice. "I do not care to die." He looked around the camp. "We must go afoot. If we try to harness leap-horses they will scream and gnash their horns. You wait here. I will fetch cloaks and a parcel of food." He departed, leaving Reith with the emblem of Onmale.

In the light of the moons he looked at it and it seemed to stare back at him, issuing orders of baleful import. Reith dug a hole in the ground, dropped in Onmale. It seemed to shiver, give a soundless shriek of anguish; he covered the gleaming emblem, feeling haunted and guilty, and when he rose to his feet his hands were shaking and clammy, and sweat trickled down his back.

Time passed: an hour? Two hours? Reith was unable to estimate. Since arriving on Tschai his time sense had gone awry.

The moons slid down the sky; midnight approached, passed; night sounds came in off the steppe; a faint high-pitched yelping of night-hounds, a great muffled belch. In the camp the fires dwindled to embers; the mutter of voices ceased.

The boy came silently up behind him. "I'm ready. Here is your cloak and a pack of food."

Reith was aware that he spoke in a new voice, less certain, less brusque. His black hat seemed strangely plain. He looked at Reith's hands and briefly around the shed, but made no inquiry concerning the Onmale.

They slipped off to the north, climbed the hillside so as to walk along the ridge. "We'll be easier for the night-hounds to see," muttered Traz, "but the attanders keep to the shadows of the swales."

"If we can reach the forest, and the tree where I hope my harness still hangs, we'll be considerably safer. Then . . ." He paused. The future was a blank expanse.

They gained the crest of the hill and halted a moment to rest. The high moons cast a wan light across the steppes, filling the hollows with darkness. From not too far to the north came a series of low wails. "Down," hissed Traz. "Lie flat. The hounds are running."

They lay without moving for fifteen minutes. The eerie cries sounded again, toward the east. "Come," said Traz. "They're circling the camp, hoping for a staked child."

They struck off to the south, up and down, avoiding the dark swales as much as possible. "The night is old," said Traz. "When light comes the Emblems will trail us. If we reach the river we can lose them. If the marshmen take us, we'll fare as badly, or worse."

For two hours they walked. The eastern sky began to show a watery yellow light, barred by streaks of black cloud, and ahead rose the loom of the forest. Traz looked back the way they had come. "The camp will be astir. The women will be fire-building. Presently the magicians will come to seek out the Onmale. That would have been me. Since I am gone the camp will be in turmoil. There will be curses and shouts: high anger. The Emblems will run to their leap-horses, and be off pellmell!" Once more Traz searched the horizons. "They'll be along soon."

The two walked, and reached the edge of the forest, still dark and dank and pooled with night shadows. Traz hesitated, looking into the forest, then back across the steppes.

"How far to the bog?" asked Reith.

"Not far. A mile or two. But I smell a berl."

Reith tested the air and detected an acrid fetor.

"It might be only the spoor," said Traz in a husky voice. "The Emblems will be here in a very few minutes. We'd best try to reach the river."

"First the ejection harness!"

Traz gave a fatalistic shrug, plunged into the forest. Reith turned a last look over his shoulder. At the far dim edge of vision a set of hurrying black specks had appeared. He hurried after Traz, who moved with great care, stopping to listen and smell the air. In a fever of impatience Reith pressed at his back. Traz speeded his pace, and presently they were almost running over the sodden leaf-mold. From far behind Reith thought to hear a set of savage boots.

Traz stopped short. "Here is the tree." He pointed up. "Is that what you want?"

"Yes," said Reith with heartfelt relief. "I was afraid it might be gone."

Traz climbed the tree, lowered the seat. Reith snapped open

the flap, with drew his hand-gun, kissed it in rapture, thrust it in his belt.

"Hurry," said Traz anxiously. "I hear the Emblems; they're not far behind."

Reith pulled forth the survival pack, buckled it on his back. "Let's go. Now they follow at their own risk."

Traz led the way around the bog, taking pains to conceal the signs of their passage, doubling back, swinging across a twenty-foot finger of black muck on a hanging branch, climbing another tree, letting it bend beneath his weight to carry him sixty feet away to the opposite side of a dense clump of reeds. Reith followed each of his ploys. The voices of the Emblem warriors were now clearly audible.

Traz and Reith reached the edge of the river, a slow-flowing flood of black-brown water. Traz found a raft of driftwood, dead lianas, humus, held together by living reeds. He pushed it off into the stream. Then he and Reith hid in a nearby clump of reeds. Five minutes passed; four of the Emblem Men came crashing through the bog along their trail, followed by a dozen more, with catapults at the ready. They ran to the river's edge, pointed to the marks where Traz had dislodged the raft, searched the face of the river. The mass of floating vegetation had drifted almost two hundred yards downstream and was being carried by a swirl in the current to the other bank. The Emblems gave cries of fury, turned and raced at top speed through the murk and tangle, along the bank toward the drifting raft.

"Quick," whispered Traz. "They won't be fooled long. We'll go back along their tracks."

Back away from the river, across the bog and once more into the forest, Traz and Reith ran, the calls and shouts at first receding to the side, then becoming silent, then once again raised in a sound of furious exultation. "They've picked up our trail once again," gasped Traz. "They'll be coming on leap-horses; we'll never—" He stopped short, held up his hand, and Reith became aware of the acrid half-sweet fetor once again. "The berl," whispered Traz. "Through here . . . Up this tree."

With the survival pack dangling at his back Reith followed the boy up the oily green branches of a tree. "Higher," said Traz. "The beast can lunge high."

The berl appeared: a lithe brown monster with a wicked boar's-head split by a vast mouth. From its neck protruded a pair of long arms terminating in great horny hands which it held above its head. It seemed to be intent on the calls of the warriors and paid no heed to Traz and Reith other than a single swift glance up toward them. Reith thought he had never seen such evil in a face before. "Ridiculous. It's only a beast . . ."

The creature disappeared through the forest; a moment later the sound of pursuit halted abruptly. "They smell the berl," said Traz. "Let's be off."

They climbed down from the tree, fled to the north. From behind them came yells of horror, a guttural gnashing roar.

"We're safe from the Emblems," said Traz in a hollow voice. "Those who live will depart." He turned Reith a troubled glance. "When they go back to the camp there will be no Onmale. What will happen? Will the tribe die?"

"I don't think so," said Reith. "The magicians will see to that."

Presently they emerged from the forest. The steppe spread flat and empty, drenched in an aromatic honey-colored light. Reith asked, "What is to the west of us?"

"The West Aman and the country of the Old Chasch. Then the Jang Pinnacles. Beyond are the Blue Chasch and the Aesedra Bight."

"To the south?"

"The marshes. The marsh men live there, on rafts. They are different from us: little yellow people with white eyes. Cruel and cunning as Blue Chasch."

"They have no cities?"

"No. There are cities there"—Traz made a gesture generally toward the north—"all ruined. There are old cities everywhere along the steppes. They are haunted, and there are Phung, as well, who live among the ruins."

Reith asked further questions regarding the geography and life of Tschai, to find Traz's knowledge spotty. The Dirdir and Dirdirmen lived beyond the sea; where, he was uncertain. There were three types of Chasch: the Old Chasch, a decadent remnant of a once-powerful race, now concentrated around the Jang Pinnacles; the Green Chasch, nomads of the Dead Steppe; and the Blue Chasch. Traz detested all the Chasch indiscriminately, though he had never seen Old Chasch. "The Green are terrible: demons! They keep to the Dead Steppe. The Emblems stay to the south, except for raids and caravan pillage. The caravan we failed to loot skirted far south to avoid the Greens."

"Where was it bound?"

"Probably Pera, or maybe to Jalkh on the Lesmatic Sea. Most likely Pera. North-South caravans trade between Jalkh and Mazuún. East-West caravans move between Pera and Coad."

"These are cities where men live?"

Traz shrugged. "Hardly cities. Settled places. But I know little, only what I have heard the magicians say. Are you hungry? I am. Let us eat."

On a fallen log they sat and ate chunks of caked porridge and drank from leather flasks of beer. Traz pointed to a low weed on which grew small white globules. "We'll never starve so long as pilgrim plant grows . . . And see yonder black clumps? That is watak. The roots store a gallon of sap. If you drink nothing but watak you become deaf, but for short periods there is no harm."

Reith opened his survival pack: "I can draw water from the ground with this sheet of film, or convert sea-water with this purifier . . . These are food pills, enough for a month. . . . This is an energy cell . . . A medical kit . . . Knife, compass, scanscope. . . . Transcom . . ." Reith examined the transcom with a sudden thrill of interest.

"What is that device?" asked Traz.

"Half of a communication system. There was another in Paul Waunder's pack, which went with the space-boat. I can broadcast a signal which will bring an automatic response from the other set and give the other set's location." Reith pushed the *Find* button. A compass arrow swung to the northwest; a counter flashed a white 6.2 and a red 2. "The other set—and presumably the space-boat—is 6.2 times 10 to the second, or 620 miles northwest."

"That would be in the country of the Blue Chasch. We knew that already."

Reith looked off to the northwest, ruminating. "We don't want to go south into the marshes, or back into the forest. What lies to the east, beyond the steppes?"

"I don't know. I think the Draschade Ocean. It is far away."

"Is that where the caravans come from?"

"Coad is on a gulf which connects to the Draschade. Between is all of Aman Steppe, the Emblem Men and other tribes as well:

the Kite-fighters, the Mad Axes, the Berl Totems, the Yellow-Blacks and others beyond my knowledge."

Reith considered. His space-boat had been taken by the Blue Chasch into the northwest. Northwest therefore seemed the most reasonable direction in which to fare.

Traz sat dozing, chin on his chest. Wearing Onmale he had demonstrated a bleak unrelenting nature; now, with the soul of the emblem lifted from his own, he had become forlorn and wistful, though still far more reserved than Reith thought natural.

Reith's own eyelids were drooping with fatigue: the sunlight was warm; the spot seemed secure . . . What if the berl should return? Reith forced himself to wakefulness. While Traz slept he repacked his gear.

3

TRAZ AWOKE. HE turned Reith a sheepish look and rose quickly to his feet.

Reith arose; they set forth: by some unspoken understanding into the northwest. The time was middle morning, the sun a tarnished brass disc in the slate sky. The air was pleasantly cool, and for the first time since his arrival on Tschai Reith felt a lifting of the spirits. His body was mended, he had recovered his equipment, he knew the general location of the scout-boat: immeasurable improvement over his previous situation.

They trudged steadily across the steppe. The forest became a dark blur behind them: elsewhere the horizons were empty. After their midday meal they slept for a period; then, awakening in the late afternoon, they went on into the northwest.

The sun dropped into a bank of low clouds, casting an embroidery of dull copper over the top. There was no shelter on the open steppe; with nothing better to do they walked on.

The night was quiet and still; far to the east they heard the wailing of night-hounds but were not molested.

The following day they finished the food and water from the packs which Traz had supplied and began to subsist on the pods of pilgrim plant and sap from watak roots: the first bland, the second acrid.

On the morning of the third day they saw a fleck of white

drifting across the western sky. Traz flung himself flat behind a low shrub and motioned Reith to do likewise. "Dirdir! They hunt!"

Reith brought forth his scanscope, sighted on the object. With elbows on the ground he zoomed the magnification to fifty diameters, when air vibration began to confuse the image. He saw a long flat boat-like hull, riding the air on rakish cusps and odd half-crescents: an aesthetic style, apparently, rather than utilitarian design. Crouched on the hull were four pale shapes, unidentifiable as Dirdir or Dirdirmen. The flyer traveled a course roughly parallel to their own, passing several miles to the west. Reith wondered at Traz's tension. He asked, "What do they hunt?"

"Men."

"For sport?"

"For sport. For food, as well. They eat man-meat."

"I'd like to have that flyer," mused Reith. He rose to his feet, ignoring Traz's frantic protests. But the Dirdir flyer disappeared into the north. Traz relaxed, but searched the sky. "Sometimes they fly high and look down until they spot a lone warrior. Then they drop like perriaults, to noose the man, or engage him with electric swords."

They walked on, always north and west. Toward sunset Traz once again became uneasy, for reasons Reith could not discern, though there was a particularly eerie quality to the landscape. The sun, obscured by a mist, was small and dim and cast a light as wan as lymph over the vastness of the steppe. There was nothing to be seen save their own long shadows behind them, but as Traz walked he looked this way and that, pausing at times to search the way they had come. Reith finally asked, "What are you looking for?"

"Something is following us."

"Oh?" Reith turned to look back across the steppe. "How do you know?"

"It is a feeling I have."

"What would it be?"

"Pnumekin, who travel unseen. Or it might be nighthounds."

"Pnumekin: they are men, are they not?"

"Men in a sense. They are the spies, the couriers of the Pnume. Some say that tunnels run beneath the steppe, with secret entrance traps—perhaps under that very bush!"

Reith examined the bush toward which Traz had directed his attention, but it seemed ordinary enough. "Would they harm us?"

"Not unless the Pnume wanted us dead. Who knows what the Pnume want? . . . More likely the night-hounds are out early."

Reith brought forth his scanscope. He searched the steppe, but discovered nothing.

"Tonight," said Traz, "we had best build a fire."

The sun sank in a sad display of purple and mauve and brown. Traz and Reith collected a pile of brush and set a fire.

Traz's instinct had been accurate. As dusk deepened to dark a soft wailing sounded to the east, to be answered by a cry to the north and another to the south. Traz cocked his catapult. "They're not afraid of fire," he told Reith. "But they avoid the light, from cleverness . . . Some say they are a kind of animal Pnume."

The night-hounds surrounded them, moving just beyond range of the firelight, showing as dark shapes, with an occasional flash of lambent white eye-discs.

Traz kept his catapult ready. Reith brought forth his gun and his energy cell. The first fired tiny explosive needles, and was accurate to a distance of fifty yards. The cell was a multiple-purpose device. At one end a crystal emitted either a beam or a flood of light at the touch of a switch. A socket allowed the recharging of the scanscope and the transcom. At the other end a trigger released a gush of raw energy, but seriously depleted the energy available for future use, and Reith regarded the energy cell as an emergency weapon only.

With night-hounds circling the fire he kept both weapons ready, determined not to waste a charge unless it was absolutely necessary. A shape came close; Traz fired his catapult. The bolt struck home; the black shape bounded high, giving a contralto call of woe.

Traz re-cocked the catapult, and put more brush on the fire. The shapes moved uneasily, then began to run in circles.

Traz said gloomily, "Soon they will lunge. We are as good as dead. A troop of six men can hold off night-hounds; five men are almost always killed."

Reith reluctantly took up his energy-cell. He waited. Closer, in from the shadows danced and spun the night-hounds. Reith aimed, pulled the trigger, turned the beam halfway around the circle. The surviving night-hounds screamed in horror. Reith stepped around the fire to complete the job, but the night-hounds were gone and presently could be heard grieving in the distance.

Traz and Reith took turns sleeping. Each thought he kept sharp lookout, but in the morning, when they went to look for corpses, all had been dragged away. "Crafty creatures!" said Traz in a marveling voice. "Some say they talk to the Pnume, and report all the events of the steppe."

"What then? Do the Pnume act on the information?"

Traz shrugged doubtfully. "When something terrible happens it is safe to assume that the Pnume have been at work."

Reith looked all around, wondering where Pnume or Pnumekin, or even night-hounds, could hide. In all directions lay the open steppe, dim in the sepia dawn gloom.

For breakfast they ate pilgrim pod and drank watak sap. Then once more they began their march northwest.

Late in the afternoon they saw ahead an extensive tumble of gray rubble which Traz identified as a ruined city, where safety from the night-hounds could be had at the risk of encountering bandits, Green Chasch or Phung. At Reith's question, Traz described these latter: a weird solitary species similar to the Pnume, only larger and characterized by an insane craft which made them terrible even to the Green Chasch.

As they approached the ruins Traz told gloomy tales of the Phung and their macabre habits. "Still, the ruins may be empty. We must approach with caution."

"Who built these old cities?" asked Reith.

Traz shrugged. "No one knows. Perhaps the Old Chasch; perhaps the Blue Chasch. Perhaps the Gray Men, though no one really believes this."

Reith sorted over what he knew of the Tschai races and their human associates. There were Dirdir and Dirdirmen; Old Chasch, Green Chasch, Blue Chasch and Chaschmen; Pnume and the human-derived Pnumekin; the yellow marsh-men, the various tribes of nomads, the fabulous "Golds," and now the "Gray Men."

"There are Wankh and Wankhmen as well," said Traz. "On the other side of Tschai."

"What brought all these races to Tschai?" Reith asked—a rhetorical question, for he knew that Traz would have no answer; and Traz gave only a shrug in reply.

They came to mounds of silted-over rubble, slabs of tip-tilted concrete, shards of glass: the outskirts of the city.

Traz stopped short, listened, craned his neck uneasily, brought his catapult to the ready. Reith, looking about, could see nothing threatening; slowly they moved on, into the heart of the ruins. The old structures, once lofty halls and grand palaces, were toppled, decayed, with only a few white pillars, posts, pedestals lifting into the dark Tschai sky. Between were platforms and piazzas of wind-scoured stone and concrete.

In the central plaza a fountain bubbled up from an underground spring or aquifer. Traz approached with great circumspection. "How can there fail to be Phung?" he muttered. "Even now—" and he scrutinized the tumbled masonry around the plaza with great care. Reith tasted the water, then drank. Traz, however, hung back. "A Phung has been here."

Reith could see no evidence of the fact. "How do you know?"

Traz gave a half-diffident shrug, reluctant to expatiate upon a matter so obvious. His attention was diverted to another more urgent matter; he looked apprehensively around the sky, sensing something below the threshold of Reith's perceptions. Suddenly he pointed. "The Dirdir boat!" They took shelter under an overhanging slab of concrete; a moment later the flyer skimmed so close above that they could hear the swish of air from the repulsors.

The flyer swung in a great circle, returned to hover over the plaza at a height of two hundred yards.

"Strange," whispered Traz. "It's almost as if they know we're here."

"They may be searching the ground with an infrared screen," whispered Reith. "On Earth we can track a man by the warmth of his footprints."

The flyer floated off to the west, then gathered speed and disappeared. Traz and Reith went back out upon the plaza. Reith drank more water, relishing the cold clarity after three days of watak sap. Traz preferred to hunt the large roach-like insects which lived among the rubble. These he skinned with a quick jerk of the fingers and ate with relish. Reith was not sufficiently hungry to join him.

The sun sank behind broken columns and shattered arches; a peach-colored haze hung over the steppe which Traz thought to be a portent of changing weather. For fear of rain, Reith wished to take shelter under a slab, but Traz would not hear of it. "The Phung! They would sniff us out!" He selected a pedestal rising thirty feet above a crumbled staircase as a secure place to pass the night. Reith looked glumly at a bank of clouds coming up from the south but made no further protest. The two carried up armloads of twigs and fronds for a bed.

The sun sank; the ancient city became dim. Into the plaza wandered a man, reeling with fatigue. He rushed to the fountain and drank greedily.

Reith brought out his scanscope. The man was tall, slender, with long legs and arms, a long sallow head quite bald, round eyes, a small button nose, minute ears. He wore the tatters of a once-elegant garment of pink and blue and black; on his head was an extravagant confection of pink puffs and black ribbons. "Dirdirman," whispered Traz, and bringing forth his catapult, took aim.

"Wait!" protested Reith. "What do you do?"

"Kill him, of course."

"He is not harming us! Why not give the poor devil his life?"

"He only lacks the opportunity," grumbled Traz, but he put aside the catapult. The Dirdirman, turning away from the fountain, looked carefully around the plaza.

"He seems to be lost," muttered Reith. "I wonder if the Dirdir boat was seeking him. Could he be a fugitive?"

Traz shrugged. "Perhaps; who knows?"

The Dirdirman came wearily across the plaza and took shelter only a few yards from the foot of the pedestal, where he wrapped himself in his tattered garments and bedded himself down. Traz grumbled under his breath and lay back into the twigs and seemed to go instantly to sleep. Reith looked out across the old city and mused upon his extraordinary destiny . . . Az appeared in the east, glowing pale pink through the haze to send a strange light along the ancient avenues. The vista was one of eerie fascination: a scene unreal, the stuff of strange dreams. Now Braz lifted into the sky; the broken columns and toppled structures cast double shadows. One particular shape at the end of an avenue resembled a brooding statue. Reith wondered why he had not noticed it previously. It was a gaunt-man-shaped figure seven or eight feet tall, legs somewhat apart, head bowed as if in intense concentration, one hand under the chin, the other behind the back. The head was covered by a soft hat with a drooping brim; a cloak hung from the shoulders; the legs seemed encased in boots. Reith looked more intently. A statue? Why did it not move?

Reith brought forth his scanscope. The creature's visage was in dark shadow; but, adjusting focus, zoom and gain, Reith was able to glimpse a long, gaunt countenance. The gnarled half-human, half-insect features were set in a frozen grimace; as Reith watched, the mouth-parts worked slowly, moving in and out ... The creature moved, taking a single long stealthy step forward, again freezing into position. It held a long arm aloft in a minatory gesture, for no purpose comprehensible to Reith. Traz had awakened; he followed Reith's gaze. "Phung!"

The creature whirled about as if it had heard the sound and danced two great strides to the side.

"They are insane," whispered Traz. "Mad demons."

The Dirdirman was not yet aware of the Phung. He fretfully moved his cloak, trying to make himself comfortable. The Phung made a gesture of gleeful surprise, and gave three bounds which took him to a spot only six feet from the Dirdirman, who still fidgeted with his cloak. The Phung stood looking down, again nonmoving. It stooped, picked up several small bits of gravel. Holding its long arm over the Dirdirman, it dropped one of the pebbles.

The Dirdirman gave a fretful jerk, but, still not seeing the Phung, settled himself again. Reith winced and called out: "Hey!"

Traz hissed in consternation. The effect upon the Phung was comical. It gave a great leap back, turned to stare toward the pedestal, arms outspread in extravagant surprise. The Dirdirman, on his knees, discovered the Phung, and could not move for horror.

"Why did you do that?" cried Traz. "It would have been content with the Dirdirman."

"Shoot it with your catapult," Reith told him.

"Bolts won't touch it, swords won't cut it."

"Shoot at its head."

Traz gave a despairing sound, but bringing forth his catapult, he aimed and snapped the release. The bolt sped toward the pallid face. At the last second, the head jerked aside, the bolt clashed against a stone buttress.

The Phung picked up a chunk of rock, swung back its long arm, hurled the rock with tremendous force. Traz and Reith fell flat; the stone splintered behind them. Reith wasted no further time and aimed his gun at the creature. He touched the button; there was a click, a hiss; the needle struck into the Phung's thorax, exploded. The Phung leapt into the air, uttered a croak of dismay and came down in a heap.

Traz clutched Reith's shoulder. "Kill the Dirdirman, quick! Before he flees."

Reith descended from the pedestal. The Dirdirman snatched forth his sword; apparently the only weapon he carried. Reith put his gun in his belt, held up his hand. "Put up your sword; we have no reason to fight."

The Dirdirman, puzzled, moved back a step. "Why did you kill the Phung?"

"It was about to kill you; why else?"

"But we are strangers! And you"—the Dirdirman peered through the gloom—"are sub-men. Do you think to kill me yourself? If so—"

"No," said Reith. "I only want information; then, so far as I am concerned, you may go on your way."

The Dirdirman grimaced. "You are as mad as the Phung. Still, why should I persuade you differently?" He came a step or two forward, to inspect Reith and Traz at closer range. "Do you inhabit this place?"

"No; we are travelers."

"Then you would not know of a place suitable for me to spend the night?"

Reith pointed to a pedestal. "Climb to the top, as we have done."

The Dirdirman gave his fingers a petulant flicker. "That is not to my taste, not at all. And there may well be rain." He looked back to the slab of concrete under which he had taken shelter, then to the corpse of the Phung. "You are an obliging pair: docile and intelligent. As you see, I am tired and must be allowed to rest. You are at hand; I would like you to stand guard while I sleep."

"Kill the nauseous brute!" muttered Traz in a passion.

The Dirdirman laughed: a queer gasping chuckle. "That's more the way of a sub-man!" He spoke to Reith. "Now you are a queer one. I can't place your type. Some strange hybrid? Where, then, is your home region?"

Reith had decided that the less attention drawn to himself the better; he would say no more of his terrestrial origin. But Traz, stung by the Dirdirman's condescension, cried out: "Not a region! He is from Earth, a far world! The home of true men like myself! You are a freak!"

The Dirdirman wagged his head reproachfully. "Of madfolk, a pair. Well, then, what can one expect?"

Reith, uncomfortable at Traz's disclosures, quickly changed the subject. "What do you do here? Was the Dirdir flyer searching for you?"

"Yes, I fear so. They did not find me, I took good care to ensure."

"You are a fugitive?"

"Precisely."

"What is your crime?"

"No matter; you would hardly understand; it is beyond your capabilities."

Reith, more amused than annoyed, turned back to the pedestal. "I plan to sleep. If you intend to live till morning, I suggest that you climb high, out of reach of the Phung."

"I am puzzled by your solicitude," was the Dirdirman's wry remark.

Reith made no reply. He and Traz returned to their pedestal and the Dirdirman gingerly climbed another nearby.

The night passed. The clouds pressed heavily upon them, but produced no rain. Dawn came imperceptibly; and presently brought light the color of dirty water. The Dirdirman's pedestal was bare. Reith assumed that he had gone his way. He and Traz descended to the plaza, built a small fire to dispel the chill. Across the plaza the Dirdirman appeared.

Observing no signs of hostility, he approached step by step, at last to stand a wistful fifty feet away, a long loose-limbed harlequin with garments much the worse for wear. Traz scowled and prodded the fire, but Reith gave him a civil greeting: "Join us, if you're of a mind."

Traz muttered, "A mistake! The creature will do us harm! Such as he are smooth-tongued and supercilious; and maneaters to boot."

Reith had forgotten this latter characteristic and gave the Dirdirman a frowning inspection.

For a period there was silence. Then the Dirdirman said tentatively, "The longer I consider your conduct, your garments, your gear, the more puzzled I become. Whence did you claim to originate?"

"I made no claims," said Reith. "What of yourself?"

"No secret there. I am Ankhe at afram Anacho; I was born a man at Zumberwal in the Fourteenth Province. Now, having been declared a criminal and a fugitive, I am of no greater consequence than yourselves, and I will make no pretensions otherwise. So here we are, three unkempt wanderers huddled around a fire."

Traz growled under his breath. Reith, however, found the Dirdirman's frivolity, if such it was, refreshing. He asked, "What was your crime?"

"You would find it difficult to understand. Essentially, I disregarded the perquisites of a certain Enze Edo Ezdowirram, who brought me to the attention of the First Race. I trusted to ingenuity and refused to be chastened. I compounded my original offense; I exacerbated the situation a dozen times over. At last in a spasm of irritation, I dislodged Enze Edo from his seat a mile above the steppe." Ankhe at afram Anacho made a gesture of whimsical fatalism. "By one means or another I evaded the Derogators; so now I am here, without plans and no resources other than my—" Here he used an untranslatable word, comprising the ideas of intrinsic superiority, intellectual élan, the inevitability of good fortune deriving from these qualities.

Traz gave a snort and went off to hunt his breakfast. Anacho watched with covert interest and presently sauntered after him. The two ran here and there through the rubble, catching and eating insects with relish. Reith contented himself with a handful of pilgrim pods.

The Dirdirman, hunger appeased, returned to examine Reith's clothes and equipment. "I believe the boy said 'Earth, a far planet.' " He tapped his button-nose with a long white finger. "I could almost believe it, were you not shaped precisely like a sub-man, which renders the idea absurd."

Traz said in a somewhat lordly tone, "Earth is the original home of men. We are true men. You are a freak."

Anacho gave Traz a quizzical glance. "What is this, the creed of a new sub-man cult? Well then, it is all the same to me."

"Enlighten us," requested Reith in a silky voice. "How did men come to Tschai?"

Anacho made an airy gesture. "The history is well-known

and perfectly straightforward. On Sibot the home-world the Great Fish produced an egg. It floated to the shore of Remura and up the beach. One half rolled into the sunlight and became the Dirdir. The other rolled into the shade and became Dirdirmen."

"Interesting," said Reith. "But what of the Chaschmen? What of Traz? What of myself?"

"The explanation is hardly mysterious; I am surprised that you ask. Fifty thousand years ago the Dirdir drove from Sibol to Tschai. During the ensuing wars Old Chasch captured Dirdirmen. Others were taken by the Pnume; and later by the Wankh. These became Chaschmen, Pnumekin, Wankhmen. Fugitives, criminals, recalcitrants and biological sports hiding in the marshes interbred to produce the sub-men. And there you have it."

Traz looked to Reith. "Tell the fool of Earth; explain his ignorance to him."

Reith only laughed.

Anacho gave him a puzzled appraisal. "Beyond question you are a unique sort. Where are you bound?"

Reith pointed to the northwest. "Pera."

"The City of Lost Souls, beyond the Dead Steppe . . . You will never arrive. Green Chasch range the Dead Steppe."

"There is no way to avoid them?"

Anacho shrugged. "Caravans cross to Pera."

"Where is the caravan route?"

"To the north, at no great distance."

"We will travel with a caravan, then."

"You might be taken and sold for a slave. Caravan-masters are notoriously without scruple. Why are you so anxious to reach Pera?"

"Reasons sufficient. What are your own plans?"

"I have none. I am a vagabond no less than yourself. If you do not object, I will travel in your company."

"As you wish," said Reith, ignoring Traz's hiss of disgust.

They set forth into the north, the Dirdirmen maintaining an inconsequential chatter which Reith found amusing and occasionally edifying, and which Traz pretended to ignore. At noon they came to a range of low hills. Traz shot a skate-shaped ruminant with his catapult. They built a fire, broiled the animal on a spit and made a good meal. Reith asked the Dirdirman, "Is it true that you eat human flesh?"

"Certainly. It can be the most tender of meats. But you need not fear, unlike the Chasch, Dirdir and Dirdirmen are not compulsive gourmands."

They climbed up through the hills, under low trees with soft blue and gray foliage, trees laden with plump red fruits which Traz declared poisonous. Finally they breasted the ridge, to look out over the Dead Steppe: a flat, gray waste, lifeless except for tufts of gorse and pilgrim plant. Below, almost at their feet, ran a track of two wide ruts. It came up from the southeast, skirted the base of the hills, passed below, then three miles northwest turned among a cluster of rock towers, or outcrops, which rose near the base of the hills like dolmens. The track continued to the northwest, dwindled away across the steppe. Another track led south through a pass in the hills, another swung away to the north-east.

Traz squinted down at the outcrops, then pointed. "Look yonder through your instrument."

Reith brought forth his scanscope, scrutinized the outcrops.

"What do you see?" asked Traz.

"Buildings. Not many—not even a village. On the rocks, gun emplacements."

"This must be Kazabir Depot," mused Traz, "where caravans transfer cargo. The guns protect against Green Chasch."

The Dirdirman made an excited gesture. "There may even be an inn of sorts. Come! I am anxious to bathe. Never in my life have I known such filth!"

"How will we pay?" asked Reith. "We have no coin, no trade-goods."

"No fear," declared the Dirdirman. "I carry sequins sufficient for us all. We of the Second Race are not ingrates and you have served me well. Even the boy shall eat a civilized supper, probably for the first time."

Traz scowled and prepared a prideful retort; then, noticing Reith's amusement, managed a sour grin of his own. "We had best depart; this is a dangerous place, a vantage for the Green Chasch. See the spoor? They come up here to watch for caravans." He pointed to the south, where the horizon was marked by an irregular gray line. "Even now a caravan approaches."

"In that case," said Anacho, "we had best hurry to the inn, to take accommodation before the caravan arrives. I have no wish for another night on the gorse."

The clear Tschai air, the extent of the horizons, made distances hard to judge; by the time the three had descended the hills the caravan was already passing along the track: a line of sixty or seventy great vehicles, so tall as to seem top-heavy, swaying and heaving on six ten-foot wheels. Some were propelled by engines, others by hulking gray beasts with small heads which seemed all eyes and snout.

The three stood to the side and watched the caravan trundle past. In the van three Ilanth scouts, proud as kings, rode on leaphorses: tall men, wide-shouldered, narrow of hip, with keen sharp features. Their skins were radiant yellow; their raven-black hair, tied into stiff plumes, glistened with varnish. They wore long-billed black caps crowned by jawless human skulls, and the plume of hair rose jauntily just behind the skull. They carried a long supple sword like that of the Emblems, a pair of hand-guns at their belts, two daggers in their right boot. Riding past on their massive leap-horses they turned uninterested glances down at the three wayfarers, but deigned no more.

Great drays rumbled past. Some were top-heavy with bales and parcels; others carried tiers of cages, in which blank-faced children, young men, young women, were mixed indiscriminately. Every sixth vehicle was a gun-cart, manned by grayskinned men in black jerkins and black leather helmets. The guns were short wide-mouthed tubes for the discharge, apparently by propulsor-field, of projectiles. Others, longer, narrow of muzzle, were hung with tanks, and Reith presumed them flame-ejectors.

Reith said to Traz, "This is the caravan we met at Iobu Ford."

Traz gave a gloomy nod. "Had we taken it I might yet have carried Onmale . . . But I am not sorry. There was never such a weight as Onmale. At night it would whisper to me."

A dozen of the drays carried three-story lodges of blackstained timber, with cupolas, decks and shaded verandahs. Reith looked at them with envy. Here was the comfortable way to travel the steppes of Tschai! A particularly massive dray carried a house with barred windows and iron-bound doors. The front deck was enclosed by heavy wire mesh: in effect, a cage. Looking forth was a young woman, with a beauty so extraordinary that it seemed to have a vitality of its own, like the Onmale emblem. She was rather slight, with skin the color of dune sand. Dark hair brushed her shoulders; her eyes were the clear brown-gold of topaz. She wore a small rose-red skull-cap, a dull red tunic, trousers of white linen, rumpled and somewhat soiled. As the dray lurched past she looked down at the three wayfarers. For an instant Reith met her eyes, and was shocked by the melancholy of her expression. The dray rolled past. In an open doorway at the rear stood a tall woman, bleak-featured, with glittering eyes, an inch-long bristle of brown-gray hair. In vast curiosity Reith applied to Anacho for information, but to no avail. The Dirdirman had neither knowledge nor opinion.

The three followed the caravan past the fortified rock-juts, into a wide sandy compound. The caravan master, a small intensely active old man, ranged the vehicles in three ranks: the cargo wagons next to the depot warehouse, then the slave-carriers' houses and barracks, and finally the gun-carts with the weapons directed toward the steppe.

Across the compound stood the caravansary, a slope-sided two-storied structure of compacted earth. The tavern, kitchen and common-room occupied the lower floor; on the second was a row of small chambers opening upon a porch. The three wayfarers found the innkeeper in the common-room: a burly man in black boots and a brown apron, with skin as gray as wood-ash. With raised eyebrows he looked from Traz in nomad costume to Anacho and his once-elegant Dirdir garments to Reith, in Earth-style whipcord breeches and jacket, but made no difficulty about providing accommodation and agreed to provide new garments as well.

The chambers were eight feet wide, ten feet long. There was a bed of leathern thongs across a wooden frame, with a thin pallet of straw, a table with basin and ewer of water. After the journey across the steppe, the accommodations seemed almost luxurious. Reith bathed, shaved with the razor from his survival kit, donned his new garments in which he hoped to be less conspicuous: loose trousers of brown-gray canvas, a shirt of rough white homespun, a black short-sleeved vest. Stepping out on the porch, he looked down into the compound. His old life on Earth: how remote it seemed! Compared to the bizarre multiplicity of Tschai, the old existence was drab and colorless—though not the less desirable for all that. Reith was forced to admit that his initial desolation had become somewhat less poignant. His new life, for all its precariousness, held zest and adventure. Reith looked across the compound toward the dray with the iron-bound house. The girl was a prisoner: so much was evident. What was her destiny that she should display such anguish?

Reith tried to identify the dray, but among so many humped, peaked and angular shapes it could not be found. Just as well, he told himself. He had troubles enough without investigating the woe of a slave girl, glimpsed for five seconds in all. Reith went back into his room.

Certain items from his survival kit he thrust into his pockets; the rest he concealed under the ewer. Descending to the common-room, he found Traz sitting stiffly on a bench to the side. In response to Reith's question, he admitted that he had never before been in such a place and did not wish to make a fool of himself. Reith laughed and clapped him on the shoulder, and Traz managed a painful grin.

Anacho appeared, less obviously a Dirdirman in his steppe-dweller's garments. The three went to the refectory, where they were served a meal of bread and thick dark soup, the ingredients of which Reith did not inquire.

After the meal Anacho regarded Reith through eyes heavy-lidded with speculation. "From here you fare to Pera?"

"Yes."

"This is known as the City of Lost Souls."

"So I understand."

"Hyperbole, of course," Anacho remarked airily. " 'Soul' is a concept susceptible to challenge. The Dirdir theologies are subtle; I will not discuss them, except to remark that—no, best not to confuse you. But back to Pera, the 'City of Lost Souls,' as it were, and the destination of the caravan. Rather than walk, I prefer to ride; I suggest then that we engage the best and most comfortable transport the caravan-master can provide."

"An excellent idea," said Reith. "However, I—"

Anacho fluttered his finger in the air. "Do not concern yourself; I am, for the moment at least, disposed kindly toward you and the boy; you are mild and respectful; you do not overstep your status; hence—"

Traz, breathing hard, rose to his feet. "I carried Onmale! Can you understand that? When I left camp do you think that I neglected to take sequins?" He thumped a long bag down upon the table. "We do not depend on your indulgence, Dirdirman!"

"As you wish," said Anacho with a quizzical glance toward Reith.

Reith said, "Since I have no sequins, I gladly accept whatever is offered to me, from either of you."

The common-room had gradually filled with folk from the caravan: drivers and weaponeers, the three swaggering Ilanths, the caravan-master, others. All called for food and drink. As soon as the caravan-master had eaten, Anacho, Traz and Reith approached him and solicited transportation to Pera. "So long as you are in no hurry," said the caravan-master. "We wait here until the Aig-Hedajha caravan comes down from the North, then we travel by way of Golsse; if you are in haste you must make other arrangements."

Reith would have preferred to travel rapidly: what would be happening to his space-boat? But with no swifter form of transport available, he curbed his impatience.

Others also were impatient. Up to the table marched two women in long black gowns with red shoes. One of these Reith had seen previously, looking from the back of the dray. The other was thinner, but taller, with a skin even more leaden, almost cadaverous. The tall woman spoke in a voice crackling with restrained anger, or perhaps chronic antagonism: "Sir Baojian, how long do we wait here? The driver says it may be five days."

"Five days is a fair estimate."

"But this is impossible! We will be overdue at the seminary!"

Baojian the caravan-master spoke in a professionally toneless voice: "We wait for the southbound caravan, to exchange articles for trans-shipment. We proceed immediately thereafter."

"We cannot wait so long! We must be at Fasm for business of great importance."

"I assure you, old mother, that I will deliver you to your seminary with all the expedition possible."

"Not fast enough! You must take us on at once!" This was the hoarse expostulation of the other, the burly slab-cheeked woman Reith had seen previously.

"Impossible, I fear," said Baojian briskly. "Was there anything else you wished to discuss?"

The women swung away without response and went to a table beside the wall.

Reith could not restrain his curiosity. "Who are they?"

"Priestesses of the Female Mystery. Do you not know the cult? They are ubiquitous. What part of Tschai is your home?"

"A place far away," said Reith. "Who is the young woman they keep in a cage? Likewise a priestess?"

Baojian rose to his feet. "She is a slave, from Charchan, or so I suppose. They take her to Fasm for their triennial rites. It is nothing to me. I am a caravaneer; I ply between Coad on the Dwan to Tosthanag on the Schanizade Ocean. Whom I convoy, where, to what purpose—" He gave a shrug, a purse of the lips. "Priestess or slave, Dirdirman, nomad or unclassified hybrid: it's all the same to me." He gave them a cool grin and departed.

The three returned to their table.

Anacho inspected Reith with a thoughtful frown. "Curious, curious indeed."

"What is curious?"

"Your strange equipment, as fine as Dirdir stuff. Your garments, of a cut unknown on Tschai. Your peculiar ignorance and your equally peculiar competence. It almost might seem that you are what you claim to be: a man from a far world. Absurd, of course."

"I made no such claim," said Reith.

"The boy did."

"The question, then, is between you and him." Reith turned to watch the priestesses, who brooded over bowls of soup. Now they were joined by two more priestesses, with the captive girl between them. The first two reported their conversation with the caravan-master with many grunts, jerks of the arms, sour glances over the shoulder. The girl sat dispiritedly, hands in her lap, until one of the priestesses prodded her and pointed to a bowl of soup, whereupon she listlessly began to eat. Reith could not take his eyes from her. She was a slave, he thought in sudden excitement; would the priestess sell? Almost certainly not. The girl of extraordinary beauty was destined for some extraordinary purpose. Reith sighed, turned his gaze elsewhere, and noticed that others—namely the Ilanths—were no less fascinated than himself. He saw them staring, tugging at their mustaches, muttering and laughing, with such lascivious jocularity that Reith became annoyed. Were they not aware that the girl faced a tragic destiny?

The priestesses rose to their feet. They stared truculently in all directions and led the girl from the room. For a time they marched back and forth across the compound, the girl walking to the side, occasionally being jerked into a trot when her steps lagged. The Ilanth scouts, coming out of the common-room, squatted on their heels by the wall of the caravansary. They had exchanged their war-hats with the human skulls for square berets of soft brown velvet, and each had pasted a vermilion beauty-disc on his lemon-yellow cheek. They chewed on nuts, spitting the shells into the dirt and never taking their eyes from the girl. There was badinage between them, a sly challenge, and one rose to his feet. He sauntered across the compound and, accelerating his steps, came up behind the marching priestesses. He spoke to the girl, who looked at him blankly. The priestesses halted, swung about. The tall one raised her arm, forefinger pointed at the sky, and called out an angry reprimand. The Ilanth, grinning insolently, held his ground. He failed to notice the burly priestess who came up from the side and dealt him a vicious blow on the side of the head. The Ilanth tumbled to the compound, but leapt to his feet instantly, spitting curses. The priestess, grinning, moved forward; the Ilanth tried to strike her with his fist. She caught him in a bear hug, banged his head with her own, lifted him, bumped out her belly, propelled him away. Advancing, she kicked him, and the others joined her. The Ilanth, surrounded by priestesses, finally managed to crawl away and regain his feet. He shouted invective, spat in the first priestess's face, then, retreating swiftly, rejoined his hooting comrades.

The priestesses, with occasional glances toward the Ilanths, continued their pacing. The sun sank low, sending long shadows across the compound. Down from the hills came a group of ragged folk, somewhat undersized, with white skins, yellow-brown hair, clear sharp profiles, small slanting eyes. The men began to play on gongs, while the women performed a curious hopping dance, darting back and forth with the rapidity of insects. Wizened children, wearing only shawls, moved among the travelers with bowls, soliciting coins. Across the compound the travelers were airing blankets and shawls, hanging the squares of orange, yellow, rust and brown out to flap in the airs drifting down from the hills. The priestesses and the slave girl retired to their ironbound dray-house.

The sun set behind the hills. Dusk settled over the caravansary; the compound became quiet. Pale lights flickered from the dray-houses of the caravan. The steppes beyond the outcrops were dim, rimmed by plum-colored afterglow.

Reith ate a bowl of pungent goulash, a slab of coarse bread and a dish of preserves for his supper. Traz went to watch a gambling game; Anacho was nowhere to be seen. Reith went out into the compound, looked up at the stars. Somewhere among the unfamiliar constellations would be a faint and minuscule Cepheus, across the Sun from his present outlook. Cepheus, an undistinguished constellation, could never be identified by the naked eye. The Sun at 212 light-years would be invisible: a star of perhaps the tenth or twelfth magnitude. Somewhat depressed, Reith brought his gaze down from the sky.

The priestesses sat outside their dray, muttering together. Within the cage stood the slave girl. Drawn almost beyond his will, Reith circled the compound, came up behind the dray, looked into the cage. "Girl," he said. "Girl."

She turned and looked at him, but said nothing.

"Come over here," said Reith, "so that I can speak to you."

Slowly she crossed the cage to peer down at him.

"What do they do with you?" Reith asked.

"I don't know." Her voice was husky and soft. "They stole me from my home in Cath; they took me to the ship and put me in a cage."

"Why?"

"Because I am beautiful. Or so they say . . . Hush. They hear us talking. Hide."

Reith, feeling craven, dropped to his knees. The girl stood holding to the bars, looking from the cage. One of the priestesses came to look in the cage and, seeing nothing amiss, returned to her sisters.

The girl called softly down to Reith. "She is gone."

Reith rose to his feet, feeling somewhat foolish. "Do you want to be free of this cage?"

"Of course!" Her voice was almost indignant. "I don't want to be part of their rite! They hate me! Because they are so ugly!" She peered down at Reith, studied him in the flicker from a nearby window, "I saw you today," she said, "standing beside the track."

"Yes. I noticed you too."

She turned her head. "They come again. You had better go."

Reith moved away. From across the compound he watched the priestesses thrust the girl into the dray-house. Then he went into the common-room. For a period he watched the games. There was chess, played on a board of forty-nine squares with seven pieces to a side; a game played with a disc and small numbered chips, of great complication; several card games. A flask of beer stood by every hand; women of the hill tribes wandered through the room soliciting; there were several brawls of no great consequence. A man from the caravan brought forth a flute, another a lute, another drew sonorous bass tones from a long glass tube; the three played music which Reith found fascinating if only for the strangeness of its melodic structure. Traz and the Dirdirman had long gone to their chambers; Reith presently followed.

4

REITH AWOKE WITH a sense of imminence which for a space he could not comprehend. Then he understood its source: it derived from the girl and the Priestesses of the Female Mystery. He lay scowling at the plaster ceiling. Utter folly to concern himself with matters beyond his comprehension! What, after all, could he achieve?

Descending to the common-room, he ate a dish of porridge served by one of the innkeeper's slatternly daughters, then went out to sit on a bench, aching for a glimpse of the captive girl.

The priestesses appeared, proceeded to the caravansary with the girl in their midst, looking neither right nor left.

Half an hour later they returned to the compound, and went to talk to one of the small men from the hills, who grinned and nodded obsequiously, eyes glittering in a fascination of awe.

The Ilanths trooped from the common-room. With sidelong glances toward the priestesses and leers at the girl, they crossed the compound, brought forth their leap-horses and began to pare the horny growths which gathered on the gray-green hides.

The priestesses ended their discussion with the mountain-man and went to walk out on the steppe, back and forth in front of the outcrops, the girl lagging a few steps behind, to the exasperation of the priestesses. The Ilanths looked after, muttering to themselves.

Traz came out to sit by Reith. He pointed across the steppe. "Green Chasch are near: a large party."

Reith could see nothing. "How do you know?"

"I smell the smoke of their fires."

"I smell nothing," said Reith.

Traz shrugged. "It is a party of three or four hundred."

"Mmmf. How do you know that?"

"By the strength of the wind, the smell of the smoke. A small group makes less smoke than a large group. This is the smoke of about three hundred Green Chasch."

Reith threw up his hands in defeat.

The Ilanths, mounting their leap-horses, bounded off into the outcrops, where they halted. Anacho, standing by, gave a dry laugh. "They go to plague the priestesses."

Reith jumped to his feet, went out to watch. The Ilanths waited till the priestesses strode by, then bounded forth. The priestesses sprang back in alarm; the Ilanths, cawing and hooting, snatched up the girl, threw her over a saddle and carried her off toward the hills. The priestesses stared aghast; then, screaming hoarsely, they all ran back to the compound. Seizing upon Baojian the caravan-master, they pointed trembling fingers. "The yellow beasts have stolen the maid of Cath!"

"Just for a bit of sport," said Baojian soothingly. "They'll bring her back when they're through with her."

"Useless for our purposes! When we have journeyed so far and borne so much! It is utter tragedy! I am a Grand Mother of the Fasm Seminary! And you will not even help!"

The caravan-master spat into the dirt. "I help no one. I maintain order in the caravan. I steer my wagons, I have time for nothing else."

"Vile man! Are these not your underlings? Control them!"

"I control only my caravan. The event occurred upon the steppe."

"Oh, what shall we do? We are bereft! There will be no Rite of Clarification!"

Reith found himself in the saddle of a leap-horse, bounding across the steppe. He had been activated by an impulse far below the level of his conscious mind; even while the leap-horse took him on prodigious bounds across the steppe he marveled at the reflexes which had sent him springing away from the caravan-master and up onto the leap-horse. "What's done is done," he consoled himself, with somewhat bitter satisfaction; it seemed that the plight of a beautiful slave-girl had taken precedence over his own woes.

The Ilanths had not ridden far; up a little valley to a small flat sandy area under a beetling boulder. The girl stood bewildered and cowering against the stone; the Ilanths had only just finished tying their leap-horses when Reith arrived. "What do you want?" asked one without friendliness. "Away with you; we are about to test the quality of this Cath girl."

Another one gave a coarse laugh. "She will need instruction for the Female Mysteries!"

Reith displayed his gun. "I'll kill any or all of you, with pleasure." He motioned to the girl. "Come."

She looked wildly around the landscape, as if not knowing in which direction to run.

The Ilanths stood silently, black mustaches adroop. The girl slowly clambered up on the horse in front of Reith; he turned it about and rode off down the valley. She looked at him with an unreadable expression, started to speak, then became silent. Behind, the Ilanths mounted their own horses and bounded off past, yipping, hooting, cursing.

The priestesses stood by the entry to the compound, gazing across the steppe. Reith halted the horse and considered the four black-clad shapes, who at once began to make peremptory signals.

The girl spoke frantically: "How much did they pay you?"

"Nothing," said Reith. "I came of my own accord."

"Take me home," begged the girl. "Take me to Cath! My father will pay you far more—whatever you ask of him!"

Reith pointed to a moving black line at the horizon. "I suspect those are Green Chasch. We'd best go back to the inn."

"The women will take me! They will put me in the cage!" The girl's voice quavered; her composure—or perhaps it was apathy—began to disintegrate. "They hate me, they want to do their worst!" She pointed. "They come now! Let me go!"

"Alone? Out on the steppe?"

"I prefer it!"

"I won't let them take you," said Reith. He rode slowly toward the caravansary. The priestesses stood waiting at the passage between the rock juts. "Oh noble man!" called the Grand Mother. "You have done a fine deed! She has not been defiled?"

"It is no concern of yours," said Reith.

"What's this? Not our concern? How can you say so?"

"She is my property. I took her from the three warriors. Go to them for restitution, not to me. What I have taken, I keep."

The priestesses laughed hugely. "You ridiculous cockbird of a man! Give us our property, or it will go poorly with you! We are Priestesses of the Female Mystery."

"You will be dead priestesses if you interfere with me or my property," said Reith. He rode past, into the compound, leaving the priestesses staring after. Reith dismounted, helped the girl to the ground, and now he understood why his instinct had sent him in pursuit of the Ilanths, all the urging of good judgment to the contrary.

"What is your name?" he asked.

She reflected, as if Reith had asked the most perplexing of riddles, and answered with diffidence. "My father is lord of Blue Jade Palace." Then she said, "We are of the Aegis caste. Sometimes I am announced as Blue Jade Flower, at lesser functions Beauty Flower, or Flower of Cath . . . My flower-name is Ylin-Ylan."

"That is all somewhat complicated," stated Reith, to which the girl nodded, as if she too found the matter overly profound. "What do your friends call you?"

"That depends on their caste. Are you high-born?"

"Yes, indeed," said Reith, seeing no reason to claim otherwise.

"Do you intend me to be your slave? If so, it would not be proper to use my friend-name."

"I've never owned a slave," said Reith. "The temptation is great—but I think I'd rather use your friend-name."

"You may call me the Flower of Cath, which is a formal friend-name, or, if you wish, my flower-name, Ylin-Ylan."

"That should do, temporarily at least." He surveyed the compound, then, taking the girl's arm, led her into the common-room of the caravansary, and to a table at the back wall. Here he studied the girl, Ylin-Ylan, the Beauty Flower, the Flower of Cath. "I don't quite know what to do with you."

Out in the compound the priestesses were expostulating with the caravan-master, who listened with gravity and politeness.

Reith said, "The problem may be taken out of my hands. I'm not sure of my legal footing."

"There are no laws here on the steppe," the girl said. "Fear alone rules."

Traz came to join them. He appraised the girl with disapproval. "What do you intend with her?"

"I'd see her home, if I could."

"You would want nothing, if you did so," the girl told him

earnestly. "I am the daughter of a notable house. My father would build you a palace."

At this Traz showed less disapprobation, and looked off to the east as if envisioning the journey. "It is not impossible."

"For me it is," said Reith. "I must go to find my space-boat. If you want to conduct her to Cath, by all means do so, and make a new life for yourself."

Traz looked dubiously out at the priestesses. "Without warriors or weapons, how could I convey one like her across the steppes? We'd be enslaved or killed out of hand."

Baojian the caravan-master entered the room, approached. He spoke in an even voice: "The priestesses demand that I enforce their claims, which I will not do, since the transfer of property occurred away from my caravan. However, I agreed to put the question: what are your intentions in regard to the girl?"

"It is no concern of theirs," said Reith. "The girl has become my property. If they want compensation, they must approach the Ilanths. I have no business with them."

"This is a reasonable statement," remarked Baojian. "The priestesses understand as much, although they protest their misfortunes. I am inclined to agree that they have been victimized."

Reith looked to see if the caravan-master was keeping a straight face. "Are you serious?"

"I think only in terms of property rights and security of transfer," declared Baojian. "The priestesses have suffered a great loss. A certain sort of girl is necessary for their rite; they strove inordinately to procure a suitable participant, only to lose her at the last minute. What if they paid a salvage fee—let us say, half the price of a comparable female?"

Reith shook his head. "They suffered loss, but I feel no concern whatever. After all, they have not come to rejoice with the girl for having regained her freedom."

"I suspect that they are in no mood for merrymaking, even at so happy an occasion," remarked Baojian. "Well, I will communicate your remarks. Doubtless they will make other arrangements."

"I hope the situation will not affect the convenience of our travel?"

"Naturally not," declared the caravan-master emphatically. "I enforce total ban upon thieving and violence. Security is my stock in trade." He bowed and departed.

Reith turned to Traz and Anacho, who had come to join the group. "Well, what now?"

"You are as good as dead," said Traz gloomily. "The priestesses are witch-women. We had several such among the Emblems. We killed them and events went for the better."

Anacho inspected the Flower of Cath with the cool detachment he might have used for an animal. "She's a Golden Yao, an extremely old stock: hybrids of the First Tans and the First Whites. A hundred and fifty years ago they became arrogant and contrived to build certain advanced mechanisms. The Dirdir taught them a sharp lesson."

"A hundred and fifty years ago? How long is the Tschai year?"

"Four hundred and eighty-eight days, though I see no relevance to the discussion."

Reith calculated. A hundred and fifty Tschai years was equivalent to about two hundred and twelve Earth years. Coincidence? Or had the Flower's ancestors dispatched that radio beam which had brought him to Tschai?

The Flower of Cath was regarding Anacho with detestation. She said in a husky voice, "You are a Dirdirman!"

"Of the Sixth Estate: by no means an Immaculate."

The girl turned to Reith. "They torpedoed Settra and Balisidre; they wanted to destroy us, from envy!"

" 'Envy' is not the proper word," said Anacho. "Your people were playing with forbidden forces, matters beyond your comprehension."

"What happened after?" asked Reith.

"Nothing," said Ylin-Ylan. "Our cities were destroyed, and the receptories and the Palace of Arts, and the Golden Webs—the treasures of thousands of years. Is it any wonder we hate the Dirdir? More than the Pnume, more than the Chasch, more than the Wankh!"

Anacho shrugged. "Expunging the Yao was not my doing."

"But you defend the deed! This is the same!"

"Let us talk of something else," suggested Reith. "After all, the happening is two hundred and twelve years gone."

"Only a hundred and fifty!" the Flower of Cath corrected him.

"True. Well, then, what of you? Would you like a change of clothes?"

"Yes. I have worn these since the unspeakable women took me from my garden. I would like to bathe. They allowed me water only enough to drink . . ."

Reith stood guard while the girl scrubbed herself, then handed in steppe-travelers' garments which made no distinction between male and female. Presently she emerged, still half-damp, wearing the gray breeches and tan tunic, and they once more went down to the common-room, and out upon the compound, to discover an atmosphere of urgency, occasioned by the Green Chasch, who had approached to within a mile of the caravansary. The gun emplacements on the rock juts had been manned; Baojian was driving his gun-carts up into the openings where they commanded all avenues of approach.

The Green Chasch showed no immediate disposition to attack. They brought up their own wagons, ranged them in a long line, erected a hundred tall black tents.

Baojian pulled at his chin in vexation. "The North-South train will never join us with nomads so near. When their scouts see the camp they'll back away and wait. I foresee delay."

The Grand Mother set up an indignant outcry. "The Rite will proceed without us! Must we be thwarted in every particular?"

Baojian held out his hands to implore reason. "Can't you see the impossibility of leaving the compound? We would be forced to fight! We may have to do so in any event!"

Someone called, "Send the priestesses forth to dance their 'Rite' with the Chasch!"

"Spare the unfortunate Chasch," spoke another impudent voice. The priestesses retreated in a fury.

Dusk settled over the steppe. The Green Chasch started up a line of fires, across which their tall shapes could be seen to pass. From time to time they seemed to halt and stare toward the caravansary.

Traz told Reith, "They are a telepathic race; they know each other's minds. Sometimes they seem to read the thoughts of men . . . I myself doubt that they do. Still—who knows?"

A scratch meal of soup and lentils was served in the common-room, with dim lights to prevent the Chasch from silhouetting those on guard. A few quiet games were played to the side. The Ilanths drank distillation, and presently became loud and harsh, until the innkeeper warned them that he maintained as stringent a policy as did the caravan-master, and that if they wished to brawl they must go forth on the steppe. The three hunched forward over their table, hats pulled thwartwise across their yellow faces.

The common-room began to empty. Reith took Ylin-Ylan the Beauty Flower to a cubicle beside his own. "Bolt your door," he told her. "Do not come out until morning. If anyone tries the door, pound on the wall to wake me."

She looked at him through the doorway with an unreadable expression and Reith thought never had he seen more appealing a sight. She asked, "Then you really do not intend me to be a slave?"

"No."

The door closed, the bolt struck home. Reith went to his own cubicle.

The night passed. On the following day, with the Green Chasch still camped before the caravansary, there was nothing to do but wait.

Reith, with the Flower of Cath close by his side, inspected the caravan guns—the so-called "sand blasts"—with interest. He learned that the weapons indeed fired sand, charging each grain electrostatically, accelerating it violently almost to light speed, augmenting the mass of each grain a thousandfold. Such driven sand-grains, striking a solid object, penetrated, then gave up their energy in an explosion. The weapons, Reith learned, were obsolete Wankh equipment, and were engraved with Wankh writing: rows of rectangles of different sizes and shapes.

Returning to the caravansary, he found Traz and Anacho arguing as to the nature of the Phung. Traz declared them to be creatures generated by Pnumekin upon the corpses of Pnume. "Have you ever seen a pair of Phung? Or an infant Phung? No. They go singly. They are too mad, too desperate, to breed."

Anacho waved his fingers indulgently. "Pnume go singly as well, and reproduce in a peculiar manner. Peculiar to men and sub-men, I should say, for the system seems to suit the Pnume admirably. They are a persistent race. Do you know that they have records across a million years?"

"So I have heard," said Traz sourly.

"Before the Chasch came," said Anacho, "the Pnume ruled everywhere. They lived in villages of little domes, but all trace of these are gone. Now they keep to caves and passages under the old cities, and their lives are a mystery. Even the Dirdir consider it bad luck to molest a Pnume."

"The Chasch then came to Tschai before the Dirdir?" Reith inquired.

"This is well-known," said Anacho. "Only a man from an isolated province—or a far world—could be ignorant to the fact." He gave Reith a quizzical glance. "But the first invaders indeed were the Old Chasch, a hundred thousand years ago. Ten thousand years later the Blue Chasch arrived, from a planet colonized an era previously by Chasch spacefarers. The two Chasch races fought for Tschai, and brought in Green Chasch for shock-troops.

"Sixty thousand years ago the Dirdir arrived. The Chasch suffered great losses until the Dirdir arrived in large numbers and so became vulnerable, whereupon a stalemate went into effect. The races are still enemies, with little traffic between them.

"Comparatively recently, ten thousand years ago, space-war broke out between the Dirdir and the Wankh, and extended to Tschai when the Wankh built forts on Rakh and South Kachan. But now there is little fighting, other than skirmishes and ambushes. Each race fears the other two and bides its time until it can expunge all but itself. The Pnume are neutral and take no part in the wars, though they watch with interest and take notes for their history."

"What of men?" asked Reith guardedly. "When did they arrive on Tschai?"

Anacho's side-glance was sardonic. "Since you claim to know the world where men originated, this information should be in your possession."

Reith refused to be provoked and made no comment.

"Men originated," said the Dirdirman in his most didactic manner, "on Sibol and came to Tschai with the Dirdir. Men are as plastic as wax, and some metamorphosed, first into marsh-men, then, twenty thousand years ago, into this sort." He pointed toward Traz. "Others, enslaved, became Chaschmen, Pnumekin, even Wankhmen. There are dozens of hybrids and freakish races. Variety exists even among the Dirdirmen. The Immaculates are almost pure Dirdir. Others exhibit less refinement. This is the background for my own disaffection: I demanded prerogatives which were denied me, but which I adopted in any event . . ."

Anacho spoke on, describing his difficulties, but Reith's attention wandered. It was clear, to Reith at least, how men had come to Tschai. The Dirdir had known space-travel for more than seventy thousand years. During this time they evidently had visited Earth, twice at the very least. On the first occasion they had captured a tribe of photo-Mongoloids; on the second occasion—twenty thousand years ago, according to Anacho—they had collected a cargo of proto-Caucasoids. These two groups, under the special conditions of Tschai, had mutated, specialized, remutated, respecialized to produce the bewildering diversity of human types to be found on the planet.

So then: the Dirdir undoubtedly knew of Earth and its human population, but perhaps reckoned it still a savage planet. Nothing could be gained by advertising the fact that Earth was now a space-faring world; indeed Reith could envision calamity arising from the knowledge. There were no clues aboard the space-boat to point to Earth, except possibly the corpse of Paul Waunder. In any event the Dirdir had lost possession of the space-boat to the Blue Chasch.

Still unanswered was the question: who had fired the torpedo that destroyed the *Explorator IV*?

Two hours before sundown the Green Chasch broke camp. The high-wheeled wagons milled in a circle; the warriors mounted on monstrous leap-horses, lunged and bounded; then at some imperceptible signal—perhaps telepathic, reflected Reith—the band formed a long line and moved off toward the east. The Ilanth scouts set forth and followed at a discreet distance. In the morning they returned to report that the band seemed to be veering to the north.

Late in the afternoon the Aig-Hedajha caravan arrived, laden with leather, aromatic logs and mosses, tubs of pickles and condiments.

Baojian the caravan-master took his wagons and drays out upon the steppe, to effect exchanges and transshipments. Derricks rolled between the two caravans, swinging goods back and forth; porters and drivers toiled and strained, sweat rolling down their naked backs and into their loose brown breeches.

An hour before sunset the transfer of goods had been effected and a call came into the common-room for all passengers. Reith, Traz, Anacho and the Flower of Cath started across the compound. The priestesses were nowhere to be seen; Reith assumed that they were aboard their house.

They walked out under the rock juts toward the caravan. There was a sudden jostle; arms gripped Reith in a bear-hug and he was pressed against a soft wheezing body. He struggled; the two toppled to the ground. The Grand Mother gripped him in her massive legs. Another priestess seized the Flower of Cath and dragged her at an awkward lope out to the caravan. Reith lay enfolded in masses of flesh and muscle. A hand squeezed his throat; blood surged through his arteries and his eyes began to start. He managed to free an arm, drove stiff fingers up into the Grand Mother's face, into something moist. She gasped and wheezed; Reith found her nostrils, clenched, twisted; she cried out and kicked; Reith rolled free.

An Ilanth was rummaging through his pack; Traz lay limp on the ground; Anacho was coolly defending himself against the swordplay of the remaining two Ilanths. The Grand Mother grabbed for Reith's legs; Reith kicked furiously, won free, lurched aside as the Ilanth investigating his pack looked up and flicked a knife at him. Reith struck up at the lemon-yellow chin with his fist; the man went down. Reith leapt on the back of one of the Ilanths who were attacking the Dirdirman, bore him down, and Anacho deftly stabbed him. Reith side-stepped a thrust from the third Ilanth, seized the outstretched arm, threw the man cartwheeling over his shoulder. The Dirdirman, standing by, struck down with his sword, nearly cutting through the yellow neck. The remaining Ilanth took to his heels.

Traz, tottering to his feet, stood holding his head. The Grand Mother was at this moment mounting the steps into the drayhouse.

Reith in all his existence had never been so angry. He picked up his pack, marched to where Baojian the caravan-master stood directing the passengers to their compartments.

"I was attacked!" stormed Reith. "You must have noticed! The priestesses have dragged the Cath girl into their house and hold her prisoner!"

"Yes," said Baojian. "I saw something of the sort."

"Well, then, assert your authority! Enforce your ban on violence!"

Baojian gave his head a prim shake. "The affair occurred on that strip of the steppe between the compound and the caravan, where I make no effort to maintain order. It appears that the priestesses have recovered their property in the same manner by which they lost it. You have no cause for complaint."

"What?" roared Reith. "You'll let them inflict an innocent person with their Female Mystery?"

Baojian held out his hands. "I have no choice. I cannot police the steppe; I do not care to try."

Reith burnt him with a stare of fury and contempt, then turned to examine the priestesses' dray-house.

Baojian said, "I must caution you against disorderly conduct while you are a passenger. I meticulously enforce caravan discipline."

Reith for a space could find no words. At last he stuttered, "Have you no concern for evil deeds?"

" 'Evil'?" Baojian laughed sadly. "On Tschai the word has no meaning. Events exist—or they do not exist. If a person adheres to some other system of conduct he himself will swiftly cease to exist—or else becomes mad as a Phung. So now, permit me to show you your compartment, as we set forth at once. I want to put leagues behind us this night, before the Green Chasch return. It seems that now I have only a single scout."

5

REITH, TRAZ AND Anacho were assigned compartments on one of the barrack drays, each containing a hammock and a small locker. Four wagons ahead was the dray-house of the priestesses. All night it rolled on its great wheels, showing no lights.

Unable to contrive any feasible rescue scheme, Reith went to his hammock, and was sent into a sleep almost hypnotic by the motion of the wagon.

Shortly after the wan sun rose from the murk, the caravan halted. The folk of the caravan filed past a commissary wagon and each was handed a pancake heaped with hot meat, a mug of hot beer. Low mist hung in wisps and drifts; the small noises of the caravan only seemed to accentuate the vast silence of the steppe. Color was forgotten; there was only the slate of the sky, drab gray-brown of steppe, watered milk of the mist. From the dray-house came no sign of life; the priestesses did not appear, nor was the Flower of Cath permitted on the caged foredeck.

Reith sought out the caravan master. "How far is the way to the seminary? When will we arrive?"

The caravan-master munched his pancake while he considered. "We camp tonight by Slugah Knoll. Another day to Zadno's Depot, then the next morning to Fasm Junction. None too soon for the priestesses; they fear that they will be late for their Rite."

"What is this 'Rite'? What goes on?"

Baojian shrugged. "I can only report rumor. They are a select group, the priestesses, and they hate men, so I am told, with abnormal fervor. The feeling extends to every aspect of the ordinary male-female relationship, and includes such women who stimulate erotic conduct. The Rite seems to purge these intense emotions; and I am told the priestesses become afflicted with a frenzy during the solemnities."

"Two and a half days, then."

"Two and a half days to Fasm Junction."

The caravan moved across the steppe, on a course parallel to the hills which heaved up, now high, now low, to the south. Occasionally clefts or chasms led away into the hills; occasionally there were copses and groves of spindly vegetation. Reith, sweeping the landscape with his spanscope, glimpsed creatures watching from the shadows; he guessed them to be Phung, or possibly Pnume.

For the most part his attention was fixed on the dray-house. It evinced no life or motion by day, and the dimmest of flickering lamplight by night. Occasionally Reith jumped down from the great wagon on which he rode to walk beside the caravan. Whenever he approached the dray-house a weaponeer in a nearby gun-cart quickly swiveled around his weapon. Baojian clearly had given orders that the priestesses were not to be molested.

Anacho tried to divert him. "Why concern yourself for this isolated female? You have spared not a glance for the three slave troupes forward. Everywhere people live and die: you are oblivious. What of the victims of the Old Chasch and their games? What of the cannibal nomads who herd men and women through the Kislovan mid-region as other tribes herd fat-humps? What of the Dirdir and Dirdirmen in Blue Chasch dungeons? All these you ignore; you are bemused by moth-dust: a fascination with this one female and her grotesque tribulations!"

Reith managed a grin. "One man can't do everything. I'll make a start, saving the girl from the Rite . . . if I can."

An hour later Traz made a similar protest. "What of your space-boat? Are you abandoning your plans? If you interfere with the priestesses, they will have you killed or maimed."

To which Reith gave a series of patient nods, admitting the justice of Traz's remarks, but not allowing himself to be persuaded by them.

Towards the end of the second day the hills became stony and abrupt, and at times cliffs loomed over the steppe.

At sunset the caravan came to Zadno's Depot, a small caravansary dug into the face of one of the cliffs, where it halted to discharge parcels of goods and to take on rock crystals and slabs of malachite. Baojian marshaled his wagons close up under the cliff, with the gun-carts facing the steppe. Reith, passing the priestesses' dray-house, was galvanized by a low wail, the poignant call a person might give while dreaming. Traz, almost in a panic, seized his arm. "Don't you see that you are watched every instant? The master expects you to make a disturbance!"

Reith turned a wolfish grin around the caravan. "I'll make a disturbance, no fear as to that! Mind you, I want you to stay clear! Whatever happens to me, go on your way!"

Traz gave him a glance of reproach and indignation. "Do you think I would stand aside? Are we not comrades?"

"Yes. Still—"

"There is no more to be said," stated Traz, with more than a trace of the Onmale crispness.

Reith threw up his hands, walked away from the dray-house, out upon the steppe. Time was growing short. He must act—but when? During the night? During the trip to Fasm Junction? After the priestesses left the caravan?

To act now was to bring instant disaster upon himself.

Likewise during the night, or on the morrow, when the priestesses, realizing his desperation, would be at their most vigilant.

At Fasm Junction, after they had left the protection of the caravan-master, what then? This was the unknown quantity. Presumably they would take steps to guard themselves well.

Twilight gave way to night; menacing sounds came from the steppe. Reith went to his compartment, lay in his hammock. He could not sleep; he did not wish to sleep. He jumped to the ground.

The moons were in the sky. Az hung halfway down the west and presently disappeared behind a cliff. Braz, low in the east, threw a melancholy glimmer across the landscape. The depot was almost completely dark, except for a few guard-lights: no roisterous common-room here. Within the dray-house lights still flickered, as the occupants moved here and there, more active than usual, or so it seemed. Suddenly the lights were extinguished; the house went dark.

Reith, restless and uneasy, circled back around the dray. A sound? He stopped short, peering into the dark. Something was afoot. The sound came again: the scrape of a moving vehicle. Abandoning caution, Reith ran forward. He stopped short. Near at hand came the sound of low voices. Someone stood even nearer, a black bulk in the shadows. There was sudden vicious motion, something struck Reith's head. Lights danced in his brain, the world turned over—

He recovered consciousness to the same scraping sound that he had heard before: creak-scrape, creak-scrape. From a subconscious reservoir of memory came the knowledge that he had been handled, lifted, dealt with . . . He felt constricted; he could not move his arms and legs. Under him was a hard surface which thudded and jarred: the cargo deck of a small wagon. Above was the night sky, with crags and ridges bulking up at either hand. The wagon evidently proceeded by a rough track up through the hills. Reith strained to move his arms. They were tied with coarse twine; the effort caused him agonizing cramps. He relaxed, clenching his teeth. From the front came gruff conversation; someone looked back at him. Reith lay still, feigning insensibility; the dark shape turned away. Priestesses, almost certainly. Why was he bound, why had they not killed him out of hand?

Reith thought that he knew.

He strained at his bonds but again succeeded only in causing himself pain. Whoever had bound him had been in great haste. Only his sword had been taken from him; at his belt was still his pouch.

The wagon gave a great thump; Reith bounced, which gave him an idea. He squirmed, inched himself toward the rear of the wagon, sweating for fear that someone would turn to look at him. He reached the edge of the deck; again the wagon lurched and Reith dropped off. The wagon rumbled on, into the dark. Ignoring his bruises, Reith twisted, turned, rolled himself off the track, down a rocky slope into deep shade. He lay still, fearful that his fall from the wagon had been noticed. The squeak-scrape of the wagon had receded; the night was quiet except for a hoarse whisper of wind.

Reith heaved, lurched, raised to his knees. Groping through the dark, he found a rough edge of rock and began to grind at his bonds. The process was interminable. His wrists became raw and bloody; his head throbbed; a curious feeling of unreality overcame him, a nightmarish identification with the dark and the rocks, as if all shared the same elemental consciousness. He cleared his mind, sawed at his bonds. The cords finally parted; his arms came free.

For a moment he sat back, flexing his fingers, easing his muscles. Then he bent to free his legs, an operation maddeningly tedious in the dark.

At last rose to his feet, to stand swaying, holding to a rock for support. Over the highest ridge of mountainside came Braz to fill the valley with the palest of illuminations. Reith painfully climbed up the slope and at last gained the road. He looked up and down the track. Behind lay Zadno's Depot; ahead at some unknown distance rolled the wagon, going creak-scrape, creak-scrape, perhaps more rapidly now that the priestesses had discovered his absence. Aboard the wagon, almost certainly, was Ylin-Ylan. Reith set out in pursuit, limping, hobbling, at as rapid a pace as he could manage. According to Baojian, Fasm Junction was another half a day by caravan, the Seminary at an unknown distance from the junction. This mountain track was evidently a shorter and more direct route.

The way began to climb, angling up to a gap through the hills. Reith stumbled doggedly forward, gasping for breath. He had no hope of overtaking the wagon, which moved at that unvarying pace established by the pad pad pad of the pull-beast's eight soft feet. He reached the gap and paused to rest, then set off once more, descending toward a forested upland, indistinct in the ink-blue light of Braz. The trees were wonderful and strange, with trunks of glimmering white rising as spirals, winding round and round, sometimes engaging the spirals of near trees. The foliage was tattered black floss, and each tree terminated in a rough pitted ball, vaguely luminescent.

From the forest came sounds: croaks, groans laden with such

human woe that Reith paused often in his stride, hand in his pouch on the comforting shape of his energy cell.

Braz sank into the forest; wisps of foliage glinted, zones of shimmer moved through the trees to keep pace as Reith passed.

He walked, trotted, loped, slowed to a walk once more. A large pallid creature glided quietly through the air above him. It seemed as frail as a moth, with huge soft wings and a round baby's head. Another time Reith thought to hear grave voices speaking, at not too far a distance. When he stopped to listen, there was nothing to hear. He continued, fighting the conviction that he moved in a dream, through an endless mental landscape, his legs carrying him back rather than forward.

The road rose sharply, angled through a narrow gorge. At one time a high stone wall had barred the gap; now it lay in ruins. A tall arched portal remained standing, under which passed the road. Reith stopped short, disturbed by a prickling beneath the surface of his mind. The situation was too blandly innocent, or so it seemed.

Reith tossed a rock through the gap. No response, no reaction. He left the road and with great care picked his way across the ruined wall, pressing close against the side of the gorge. After a hundred feet he returned to the road. He looked back, but if danger actually existed at the portal it could not be detected in the dark.

Reith pushed forward. Every few minutes he stopped to listen. The walls of the gorge fell apart and dwindled in height, the sky came closer, the Tschai constellations lit the gray rock of the hillsides.

Ahead: a glow in the sky? A murmur, a sound half-strident, half-harsh. Reith went forward at a stumbling run. The road raised, twisted over a knoll, Reith stopped, looking down on a scene as weird and wild as Tschai itself.

The Seminary of the Female Mystery occupied an irregular flat area surrounded by crags and cliffs. A massive four-story edifice of stone was built in a ravine, to straddle a pair of crags. Elsewhere were sheds of timber and wattle, animal pens and hutches, outbuildings, cribs and racks. Directly below Reith a platform projected from the hill, with a two-story building to the sides and the rear.

Gala events were in progress. Flames from dozens of flambeaux cast red, vermilion and orange light upon two hundred women who moved back and forth, half-dancing, half-lurching, in a state of entranced frenzy. They wore black pantaloons, black boots and were elsewhere naked, with even the hair shaved from their heads. Many were without breasts, displaying a pair of angry red scars: these women, the most active, marched and trooped, bodies glistening with sweat and oil. Others sat on benches slack and dull, resting, or exalted beyond mere frenzy. Below the platform, in a row of low cages, a dozen naked men stood crouched. These men produced the harsh chant Reith had heard from the hills. When one faltered, jets of flame spurted up from the floor beneath him, and he once more screamed his loudest. The flames were controlled from a keyboard in the front; here sat a woman dressed completely in black, and it was she who orchestrated the demoniac uproar. *There,* thought Reith, *but for the bump of a wagon—there sing I.*

A singer collapsed. Jets of flame only caused him to twitch. He was dragged forth; a bag of transparent membrane was pulled over his head and tied at the neck; he was tossed into a rack at the side. Into the cage was thrust another singer: a strong young man, glaring in hatred. He refused to sing, and suffered the jets in furious silence. A priestess came forward, blew a waft of smoke into his face; presently he sang with the rest.

How they hated men! thought Reith. A troupe of entertainers appeared on the stage—tall emaciated clown-men with skins bleached white, eyebrows painted high and black. In horrified fascination Reith watched them cavort and caper and with earnest zest defile themselves, while the priestesses called out in delight.

When the clown-men retired a mime appeared: he wore a wig of long blonde hair, a mask with wide eyes and a smiling red mouth, to simulate a beautiful woman. Reith thought, *They hate not only men, but love and youth and beauty!*

As the mime expatiated his shocking message, a curtain to the back of the platform drew back revealing a huge naked cretin, hairy of body and limb, in a state of intense erotic excitement. He worked to gain entry into a cage of thin glass rods, but could not puzzle out the working of the latch. In the cage cowered a girl wearing a gown of thin gauze: the Flower of Cath.

The androgynous mime finished his curious performance. The singers were instructed to a new chant, a soft hoarse baying, and the priestesses crowded close around the platform, intent on the efforts of the fumbling brute.

Reith already had departed from his vantage. Keeping to the shadows, he circled down around toward the rear of the platform. He passed a shed where the clown-men rested. Nearby, a set of pens held two dozen young men, apparently destined to sing. They were guarded by a wizened old woman with a gun almost as large as herself.

From the front came a sudden avid murmur. The brute apparently had fumbled open the latch to the cage. Giving no thought to gallantry, Reith dropped down behind the old woman, felled her with a blow, ran along the line of pens, throwing open the doors. The men thrust pell-mell out into the corridor, while the troupe of clown-men watched in consternation.

"Take the gun," Reith told the freed men. "Free the singers."

He jumped up into the wings of the platform. The brute had entered the cage and was ripping the girl's gauze gown. Reith aimed his gun, sent an explosive needle into the bulging back. A *thwump!*—the brute jerked, seemed to puff. He raised on tiptoes, twisted about and fell dead. Ylin-Ylan the Flower of Cath, looking around with dazed eyes, saw Reith. He motioned; she stumbled from the cage, across the platform.

The priestesses cried out first in fury, then in fear, for certain of the free men, bringing the gun out on the stage, fired again and again into the audience. Others released the singers. The young man most recently caged charged for the priestess at the console. He seized her, dragged her to the vacated box, locked her within; then returning to the console, pressed home the firevalve, and the priestess sang an ululating contralto. Another of the erstwhile captives seized a torch, fired one of the sheds; others took clubs and began to bludgeon the wailing celebrants.

Reith led the sobbing girl down around the outskirts of the tumult, and was able to snatch up a cape which he drew about the shoulders of the girl.

Priestesses were trying to flee the area—up the hillside, down the east road. Some tried to wriggle their half-naked bodies under sheds, only to be dragged back by the heels and clubbed.

Reith led the girl down the main road toward the east. From the stable came rushing a wagon frantically urged by four priestesses. Tall and dominant bulked the Grand Mother. As Reith watched, a man vaulted up on the bed of the wagon, seized the

Grand Mother and sought to strangle her with his bare hands. She reached up with her massive arms, drew him down, cast him on the deck and started to stamp on his head. Reith leapt up behind her, gave her a push; she fell off the wagon. Reith turned to the other priestesses: the three who had traveled with the caravan. "Off! To the ground!"

"We'll be killed! The men are mad things! They are killing the Grand Mother!"

Reith turned to look; four men had surrounded the Grand Mother, who stood at bay, roaring like a bear. One of the priestesses, taking advantage of Reith's distraction, tried to knife him. Reith threw her to the ground, and the other two as well. He pulled the girl up beside him and drove down the east road toward Fasm Junction.

Ylin-Ylan the Flower of Cath huddled against him, exhausted, apathetic. Reith battered, bruised, dry of emotion, hunched in the seat. The sky behind them reddened; flames licked up into the black sky.

6

AN HOUR AFTER dawn they reached Fasm Junction: three bleak structures of earthen brick on the edge of the steppe, the tall walls punctuated by the smallest and narrowest of black windows, a stockade of timber surrounding. The gate was closed; Reith halted the wagon, pounded and called, to no effect. The two, comatose from fatigue and the dullness following extreme emotion, settled themselves to wait until the folk in the junction saw fit to open the gates.

Investigating the back of the wagon Reith found, among other effects, two small satchels containing sequins, to a number Reith could not even estimate.

"So now we have the priestesses' wealth," he told the Flower of Cath. "Enough, I should think, to buy you safe passage home."

The girl spoke in a puzzled voice: "You would give me the sequins and send me home and you demand nothing in return?"

"Nothing," said Reith with a sigh.

"The Dirdirman's joke seems real," said the girl sternly. "You act as if you were indeed from a distant world." And she turned half away from him.

Reith looked off across the steppe, smiling somewhat sadly. Assuming the unlikely, that he were able to return to Earth, would he then be content to remain, to live his life out and never return to Tschai? No, probably not, mused Reith. Impossible to predict official Earth policy, but he himself could never be content while the Dirdir, the Chasch and the Wankh exploited men and used them as despised subordinates. The situation was a personal affront. Somewhat absently he asked Ylin-Ylan, "What do your people think of the Dirdirmen, the Chaschmen, the others?"

She frowned in perplexity, and seemed, for some reason obscure to Reith, annoyed. "What is there to think? They exist. When they do not disturb us, we ignore them. Why do you speak of Dirdirmen? We were speaking of you and me!"

Reith looked at her. She watched him with passive expectancy. Reith drew a deep breath, started to move closer to her, when the gate into the depot raised and a man looked forth. He was squat, with thick legs, long arms; his face was big-nosed and askew, with skin and hair the color of lead: evidently a Gray.

"Who are you? That's a Seminary wagon. Last night flames burnt the sky. Was that the Rite? The priestesses are as eerie as potlinks during the Rite."

Reith gave him an evasive answer and drove the wagon into the enclosure.

They breakfasted on tea, stewed herbs, hard bread and went back out to the wagon to await the arrival of the caravan. The early morning mood had passed; both felt heavy and uncommunicative. Reith relinquished the seat to Ylin-Ylan and stretched out in the bed of the wagon. In the warm sunlight both became drowsy and slept.

At noon the caravan was sighted: a heaving line of gray and black. The surviving Ilanth scout—and a scowling round-faced youth promoted to the position from gunner arrived at the junction first, then, wheeling their leap-horses, bounded back to the caravan. The tall wagons drawn by soft-footed beasts arrived, the drivers hunched in voluminous cloaks, faces thin under long-billed hats. Then came barrack-wagons with passengers sitting in the openings to their cubicles. Traz greeted Reith with obvious pleasure; Anacho the Dirdirman gave an airy flutter of the fingers which might have meant anything. "We were sure that you had been killed or kidnapped," Traz told Reith. "We searched the hills, we went out on the steppe, but found nothing. Today we were going to seek you at the Seminary."

"We?" asked Reith.

"The Dirdirman and myself. He's not such a bad sort as one might think."

"The Seminary no longer exists," said Reith.

Baojian appeared, stopped short at the sight of Reith and Ylin-Ylan but asked no questions. Reith, who half-suspected Baojian of facilitating the priestesses' departure from Zadno's Depot, volunteered no information. Baojian assigned them to compartments, and accepted the priestesses' wagon as passage payment to Pera.

Bundles were discharged at the Junction, others were loaded aboard the wagons, and the caravan proceeded to the northeast.

Days passed: easy idle days of trundling across the steppe. For a period they skirted a wide shallow lake of brackish water, then with great caution crossed a marsh overgrown with jointed white reeds. The scout discovered an ambush laid by a dwarfish tribe of marsh-men, who at once fled into the reeds before the caravan guns could be brought to bear.

On three occasions Dirdir aircraft swooped low to inspect the caravan, on which occasions Anacho concealed himself in his compartment. Another time a Blue Chasch platform slid overhead.

Reith would have enjoyed the journey had he not been anxious in regard to his space-boat. There was also the problem of Ylin-Ylan, the Flower of Cath. Upon reaching Pera, the caravan would return to Coad on the Dwan Zher, where the girl could take passage aboard a ship for Cath. Reith assumed this to be her plan, though she said nothing of the matter and in fact had become somewhat cool, to Reith's puzzlement.

So went the days, and the caravan crept northward, under the slate-dark skies of Tschai. Twice thunderstorms shattered the afternoon, but for the most part the weather was even. They passed through a dark forest, and the next day followed an ancient causeway across a vast black quagmire covered with bubble-plants and bubble-insects simulating the bubble-plants. The quagmire was the habitat of many fascinating creatures: wingless frog-sized things which propelled themselves through the air by a vibration of fan-like tails; larger creatures, half-spider, half-bat, which, anchoring by means of an exuded thread, rode the breeze on extended wings like a kite.

At Wind Mountain Depot they met a caravan bound for Malagash, south behind the hills on the Hedajha Gulf. Twice small bands of Green Chasch were sighted, but on neither occasion did they attack. The caravan-master declared them to be mating groups en route to a procreation area north of the Dead Steppe. On another occasion a troop of nomads halted to watch them pass: tall men and tall women with faces painted blue. Traz identified them as cannibals and stated that the women fought in battle on an even footing with the men. Twice the caravan passed close to ruined cities; once it swung south to deliver aromatics, essences and amphire wood to an Old Chasch city which Reith found peculiarly fascinating. There were myriads of low white domes half-hidden under foliage, with gardens everywhere. The air held a peculiar freshness, exuded by tall yellow-green trees, not unlike poplars, known as adarak. These, so Reith learned, were cultivated by Old Chasch and Blue Chasch alike for the clarity which they gave the air.

The caravan halted on an oval area covered with thick short grass, and Baojian immediately called all the personnel of the caravan about him. "This is Golsse, an Old Chasch city. Do not leave the immediate area, or you may be subject to Old Chasch tricks. These can be mere mischiefs, such as trapping you in a maze or dosing you with an essence that will cause you to exude a frightful odor for weeks. But if they become excited, or feel particularly humorous, the tricks may be cruel or fatal. On one occasion they stupefied one of my drivers with essence, grafted new features on his face and a great gray beard as well. Remember, then: do not under any circumstances stray from this oval, even though the Chasch may tease or tempt you. They are an old and decayed race; they are without pity and think only of their odors and essences, and their fanciful jokes. So be warned: keep to the oval, do not wander off in the gardens, no matter what the beguilement, and if you value your life and sanity, do not enter the Old Chasch domes."

He said no more.

Goods were loaded upon the low Chasch motor-drays, operated by a few dispirited Chaschmen: smaller and perhaps not so evolved as the Blue Chaschmen Reith had seen before. They were slight and stooped, with gray wrinkled faces, bulging foreheads, mouths puckered into little buds above nonexistent chins. Like the Blue Chaschmen they wore a false scalp which butted over their eyes and rose to a point. Their demeanor was furtive and hurried, they spoke to none of the caravan personnel, and had eyes only for their work. Four Old Chasch presently appeared. They walked directly below the barrack car; Reith saw them close at hand and was reminded of large silverfish grotesquely endowed with semi-human legs and arms. Their skin was like ivory satin, almost imperceptibly scaled; they seemed fragile, almost desiccated; they had eyes like small silver pellets, independently swiveling and in constant motion. Reith watched them with great interest; they felt his gaze and paused to look up to where he sat. They nodded and gave him affable gestures, to which Reith replied in kind. For a moment longer they inspected him with their bright silver eyes, and then passed on.

Baojian wasted no time at Golsse. As soon as he had reloaded his drays with cases of drugs and tinctures, bales of lacy cloth, dried fruit in cakes and packs, he marshaled the wagons and set off once more to the north, preferring to pass the night on the open steppe rather than risk the caprices of the Old Chasch.

The steppe was empty grassland, flat as a table. Standing on the barrack-wagon Reith could see twenty miles through his scope, and so spied a large band of Green Chasch even before the scouts. He notified Baojian, who immediately ordered the caravan into a defensive ring with the guns commanding the entire surrounding area. The Green Chasch loped up on their massive beasts, holding yellow and black flags afloat on their lances, signifying truculence and bellicosity. "They have just come down from the north," Traz told Reith. "This is the meaning of the flags. They gorge on fluke-fish and angbut; their blood becomes rich and thick, which makes them irritable. When they fly yellow and black even the Emblems retire rather than face them in battle."

Yellow and black flags regardless, the Green warriors did not molest the caravan but halted a mile distant. Reith studied them through his scope, to see creatures vastly different from the Old Chasch. These were seven and eight feet tall, massive and thick-limbed, their scales clearly defined and of a glistening metallic green. Their faces were small, brooding, wickedly ugly under the massive jut of their scalps. They wore rude leather aprons and shoulder harness, in which hung swords, battle-picks and catapults similar to those of the Emblems. Troublesome creatures to encounter in close combat, thought Reith. They sat on their beasts studying the caravan for a full five minutes, then swung away and bounded off to the east.

The caravan re-formed itself and continued along the track. Traz was puzzled by the diffidence of the Green Chasch. "When they carry yellow and black, they are insensate. Perhaps they prepare an ambush from behind a forest."

Baojian suspected a similar stratagem and kept his scouts far forward for the next few days. At night there were no special precautions taken, inasmuch as the Green Chasch became torpid in the dark and huddled in groaning grunting masses until daybreak.

Pera lay ahead: the caravan terminus. Reith's transcom specified a vector of sixty miles west to the mate transcom. He made inquiry of the caravan-master, who informed him that the Blue Chasch city Dadiche was situated at this location. "Avoid them; a wicked lot they are, subtle as the Old Chasch, savage as the Greens."

"They have no commerce with men?"

"There is considerable trade; in fact, Pera is a depot for trade with the Blue Chasch, which is carried on by a caste of draymen operating out of Pera; only these draymen gain access to Dadiche. Of all the Chasch I find the Blues most detestable. The Old Chasch are not a friendly folk, but they are malicious, rather than harsh. Sometimes of course, the effect is the same, just as the storm"—he pointed toward the west where great masses of black cloud filled the sky—"will wet us no less than submersion in the ocean."

"You will turn directly about at Pera and return to Coad on the Dwan Zher?"

"Within three days."

"In all likelihood the Princess Ylin-Ylan will return with you and take ship for Cath."

"All very well; can she pay?"

"Certainly."

"Then there is no difficulty. What of you? Do you wish to go to Cath likewise?"

"No. I'll probably remain at Pera."

Baojian, with a darting glint of a glance for Reith, gave his head a wry shake. "The Golden Yao of Cath are estimable folk. But then, nothing of Tschai is predictable except trouble. The Green Chasch are dogging us. A miracle that they have not attacked. I begin to hope that we may reach Pera without incident."

Baojian was to be denied. With Pera already in view—a city of ruined halls and toppled monuments surrounding a central citadel, much like those others they had passed—the Green Chasch bounded in from the east. Coincidentally the storm broke. Lightning crashed down upon the steppe; to the south black brooms of rain swept down upon the land.

Baojian decided that Pera offered no refuge and ordered the caravan into its defensive circle. Barely soon enough: this time the Green Chasch showed neither indecision nor diffidence. Bent low on their great beasts, they came charging forward, intent only on penetrating the ring of wagons.

The caravan guns gave their curious gurgling belch, barely heard through the thunder, and the rain made efficient weapon handling difficult. The Green Chasch, coordinated perhaps telepathically, bounded forward; some were struck by the sand blast and killed; some were crushed under their toppling beasts. For a space there was sheer confusion, then new ranks sprang over the thrashing bodies. Again the gunners fired frantically through the rain, with the lightning and thunder providing a mind-jarring accompaniment to the battle.

The Green Chasch fell faster than they could advance, and changed their tactics. Those who had been dismounted, crouched behind leap-horse hulks, brought their catapults to bear; the first shower of bolts killed three gunners. The mounted warriors charged again, hoping to gain the circle by sheer momentum. Again, they were thrown back, the vacated guns having been manned by drivers, and again there was a shower of bolts and more gunners dropped from the gun platforms.

The Green Chasch lunged forward a third time, their mounts bounding and capering. Behind them, lightning fractured the black sky, with the thunder an incessant background to the cries and screams of the battle. The Green Chasch were taking terrible losses, the ground heaved with groaning shapes, but others leapt forward and at last the guns were in range of Green Chasch swords.

The result of the battle was no longer in doubt. Reith took the Flower of Cath's hand, beckoned to Traz. The three struck out for the city, joining a line of panic-stricken fugitives from the barrack-wagons, which now was joined by the drivers and surviving gunners. The caravan was abandoned.

Screaming in triumph, the Green Chasch bounded among the fugitives, hacking off heads, chopping down through necks and shoulders. A flaming-eyed warrior lunged at Reith, Ylin-Ylan and Traz. Reith had his gun ready, but hesitated to waste the precious pellets and dodged under the hissing sword-stroke. The leap-horse, swerving, skidded on the wet turf; the warrior was flung bellowing sidewise. Reith ran forward, raised his Emblem cutlass high, hacked at the thick neck, cut through cords, filaments and tubes. The warrior kicked and thrashed in appalling reluctance to die; the three did not wait. Reith took up the sword, which was somewhat crudely forged from a single bar of steel as tall as himself and wide as his arm. It was too heavy and long to be wieldy; he cast it down. The three proceeded through the rain, now falling in such heavy sheets as to obscure vision. The Green Chasch occasionally were glimpsed as bounding phantoms; occasionally the wraith-like shapes of fugitives could be seen, bending forward, crouched to the rain, hurrying with all speed for the ruins of Pera.

In sodden clothes, with the ground streaming beneath their feet, the three finally reached a tumble of concrete slabs marking the outskirts of Pera, and considered themselves somewhat safer from the Green Chasch. They took shelter under an overhanging jut of concrete, to stand shivering and miserable while the rain thrashed down in front of their faces. Traz said philosophically, "At least we are at Pera, where we intended to come."

"Ingloriously," said Reith, "but alive."

"Now what do you think to do?"

Reith reached into his pouch, brought forth the transcom, checked the vector indicator. "It points to Dadiche, twenty miles west. I suppose I'll go there."

Traz gave a disapproving sniff. "The Blue Chasch will deal severely with you."

The girl of Cath suddenly leaned against the wall, put her face in her hands and began to weep: the first time Reith had seen her give way to emotion. Somewhat tentatively he patted her shoulder. "What's the trouble? Other than being cold, wet, hungry and scared?"

"I'll never be home to Cath. Never! I know this."

"Of course you will! There will be other caravans!"

The girl, clearly unconvinced, wiped her eyes and stood looking out across the dismal landscape. The rain now began to slacken. The lightning flickered off to the east; the thunder became a sullen rumble. A few minutes later the clouds broke and sunlight slanted through the rain to glisten on wet stone and puddles. The three, still somewhat damp, emerged from their refuge, almost to collide with a small man in an ancient leather cloak, carrying a bundle of faggots. He jumped back in alarm, dropped his bundle, darted back to snatch it up and was about to race away when Reith caught hold of his cloak. "Wait! Not so fast! Tell us where we can find food and shelter!"

The man's face slowly relaxed. Warily, under bushy eyebrows, he looked from one to the other, then with great dignity jerked his cloak from Reith's grasp. "Food and shelter: these be hard to come by; only by toil. Can you pay?"

"Yes, we can pay."

The man considered. "Now, I have a comfortable dwelling, of three apertures . . ." Reluctantly he shook his head. "But best that you go to the Dead Steppe Inn. If I took you in, the Gnashters would gain my profit, and I would have naught."

"The Dead Steppe Inn is the best of Pera?"

"Yes, a fine hostelry indeed. The Gnashters will tax your wealth, but this is what we must pay for our security. In Pera no one may rob or rape but Naga Goho and the Gnashters; and this is a boon. What if everyone enjoyed this license?"

"Naga Goho is the ruler of Pera, then?"

"Yes, one might say so." He pointed to a massive structure of blocks and slabs on the central eminence of the city. "There is his palace, on the citadel, and there he lives with his Gnashters. But I will say no more; after all, they have worried the Phung out to North Pera; there is trade with Dadiche; bandits avoid the city; affairs could be the worse."

"I see," said Reith. "Well then, where do we find the inn?"

"Yonder, at the foot of the hill: at the caravan's end."

7

THE DEAD STEPPE INN was the most grandiose structure Reith had yet seen in a ruined city: a long building with a complicated set of roofs and gables built against the central hill of Pera. As in all the inns of Tschai, there was a large common-room with trestle-tables, but rather than rude benches, the Dead Steppe Inn boasted fine high-backed chairs of carved black wood. Three chandeliers of colored glass and black iron illuminated the room; on the walls hung a number of very old terra-cotta masks: visages of some fanciful half-human folk.

The tables were crowded with fugitives from the caravan; a savory odor of food hung in the air. Reith began to feel somewhat more cheerful. Here, at least, were a small few concessions to comfort and style.

The innkeeper was a small plump man with a neat red beard, protuberant red-brown eyes. His hands were in ceaseless motion and his feet shifted back and forth as if haste dominated his life. At Reith's request for accommodation he waved his hands in despair. "Have you not heard? The green demons destroyed Baojian's train. Here are the survivors, and I must find room. Some cannot pay; what of that? I am ordered by Naga Goho to extend shelter."

"We were also with the caravan," said Reith. "However, we can pay."

The innkeeper became more optimistic. "I'll find you a single room; you must make the best of this. A word of advice." Here he looked swiftly over his shoulder. "Be discreet. There have been changes at Pera."

The three were shown to a cubicle of adequate cleanliness; three pallets were brought in. The inn could provide no dry clothing; with garments still damp the three descended to the common-room, where now they discovered Anacho the Dirdirman, who had arrived an hour before. Off to the side, staring thoughtfully into the fire, was Baojian.

For supper they were served ample bowls of stew, wafers of hard bread. While they were eating seven men entered the room to stand looking truculently this way and that. All were strong big-boned men, a trifle fleshy with ease, florid with good living. Six wore dull red gowns, stylish black leather slippers, rakish caps hung with baubles. Gnashters, thought Reith. The seventh, wearing an embroidered surcoat, was evidently Naga Goho: a man tall and thin, with a peculiarly large vulpine head. He spoke to a room which had become hushed: "Welcome all, welcome all to Pera! We have a happy orderly city, as you will notice. Laws are sternly enforced. A sojourn tax is collected as well. If anyone lacks funds he must contribute his labor for the common benefit. So, then—are there questions or complaints?" He looked about the room, but no one spoke. The Gnashters circulated through the room, collecting coins. Reith grudgingly paid a tax of nine sequins for himself, Traz and the Flower of Cath. None of the folk present seemed to find the exaction unreasonable. So pervasive was the lack of social discipline, Reith decided, that exploitation of advantage was taken for granted.

Naga Goho noticed the Flower of Cath and stood erect, preening his mustache. He signaled to the innkeeper, who hastened to present himself. The two held a muttered colloquy, Naga Goho never taking his eyes from Ylin-Ylan.

The innkeeper crossed the room, muttered in Reith's ear. "Naga Goho has taken note of the woman." He indicated the Flower. "He wants to know her status: is she slave? daughter? wife?"

Reith glanced sidewise at Ylin-Ylan, at a loss for immediate response; already he saw the girl stiffening. If he declared her to be alone and independent he put her at the mercy of Naga Goho. If he claimed her as his own he would no doubt provoke her indignant disclaimer. He said, "I am her escort, she is under my protection."

The innkeeper pursed his lips, shrugged and went to report to Naga Goho, who made a small curt gesture and turned his attention elsewhere. Not long after he departed.

In the small room Reith found himself in a state of disturbing propinquity with the Flower of Cath. She sat on her pallet, clasping her knees disconsolately. "Cheer up," said Reith. "Things aren't all that bad."

She gave her head a mournful shake. "I am lost among barbarians: a pebble dropped in Tembara Deep, gone from mind."

"Nonsense," scoffed Reith. "You'll be traveling home with the next caravan to leave Pera."

Ylin-Ylan was unconvinced. "At home they will name another the Flower of Cath; she will take my flower at the Banquet of the Season. The princess will beseech the girls to name their names, and I will not be there. No one will ask me and no one will know my names."

"Tell me your names then," said Reith. "I'd like to hear."

The Flower turned to look at him. "Do you mean this? Do you mean what you ask?"

Reith was puzzled by her intensity. "Certainly."

The girl turned a swift glance toward Traz, who was occupied in arranging his pallet. "Come outside," she whispered in Reith's ear and jumped to her feet.

Reith followed her to the balcony. For a period they leaned together, elbows touching, looking out over the ruined city. Ax rode high among broken clouds; below were a few dismal lights; from somewhere came a reedy chant, the twang of a plectrum. The Flower spoke in a quick hushed voice: "My flower is the Ylin-Ylan, and this you know; my Flower name. But that is a name used only at demonstrations and pageants." She looked toward him breathlessly, leaning so close that Reith could smell the clean tart-sweet scent of her person.

Reith asked in a husky voice, "You have other names too?"

"Yes." Sighing, she edged closer to Reith, who began to feel out of his depth. "Why have you not asked before? You must have known I would tell."

"Well, then," asked Reith, "what are your names?"

Demurely, she said, "My court name is Shar Zarin." She hesitated then, leaning her head on his shoulder (for Reith's arm was around her waist), she said, "My child name was Zozi, but only my father calls me that."

"Flower name, court name, child name . . . What other names do you have?"

"My friend-name, my secret name, and—one other. My friend-name—would you hear it? If I tell you, then we are friends, and you must tell me your friend-name."

"Certainly," croaked Reith. "Of course."

"Derl."

Reith kissed her upturned face. "My first name is Adam."

"Is that your friend-name?"

"Yes . . . I suppose you'd call it that."

"Do you have a secret name?"

"No. Not that I know of."

She gave a small nervous laugh. "Perhaps it is just as well. For if I asked you, and you told me, then I would know your secret soul, and then—" Breathlessly she looked up at Reith. "You must have a secret name; one that only you know. I have."

Intoxicated, Reith tossed caution to the winds. "What is yours?"

She raised her mouth to his ear. "L'lae. She is a nymph who lives in clouds over Mount Daramthissa, and loves the star-god Ktan." She looked toward him, melting, expectant, and Reith kissed her fervently. She sighed. "When we are alone, you shall call me L'lae and I will call you Ktan and that shall be your secret name."

Reith laughed. "If you like."

"We shall wait here, and soon there will be a caravan east: back across the steppe to Coad, then by cog across the Draschade, to Vervode in Cath."

Reith put his hand on her mouth. "I must go to Dadiche."

"Dadiche? The city of the Blue Chasch? Are you still so obsessed? But why?"

Reith raised his eyes, looked off into the night-sky, as if to draw strength from the stars, though none of those visible could possibly be the Sun . . . What could he say? If he told the truth she would think him insane, even though her ancestors had beamed signals to Earth.

So he hesitated, disgusted by his own softness of spirit. The Flower of Cath—Ylin-Ylan, Shar Zarin, Zozi, Derl, L'lae, according to the social circumstances—put her hands on his shoulders and peered up into his face. "Since I know you for Ktan and you know me for L'lae, your mind is my mind; your pleasure is my pleasure. So—what prompts you for Dadiche?"

Reith drew a deep breath. "I came to Kotan in a space-boat. The Blue Chasch almost killed me, and conveyed the space-boat to Dadiche, or so I suppose. I must recover it."

The Flower was bewildered. "But where did you learn to fly a space-boat? You are no Dirdirman or Wankhman . . . Or are you?"

"No, of course not. No more than you. I was instructed."

"It is all such a mystery." Her arms twitched on his shoulders. "And—were you able to recover the space-boat, what would you do?"

"First, take you to Cath."

The fingers now gripped his shoulders, the eyes searched his through the darkness. "Then what? You would return to your own land?"

"Yes."

"You have a woman—a wife?"

"Oh no. No indeed."

"Someone who knows your secret name?"

"I had no secret name until you gave me one."

The girl took her hands from his shoulders, and, leaning on the rail, stared moodily out across old Pera. "If you go to Dadiche, they will smell you and kill you."

" 'Smell' me? How do you mean?"

She turned him a quick look. "You are a puzzle! So much you know, and so little! One would think you from the farthest island of Tschai! The Blue Chasch smell as accurately as we can see!"

"I still must make the trial."

"I don't understand," she said in a dull voice. "I have told you my name; I have given what is most precious to me; and you are unmoved. You do not alter your way."

Reith took her in his arms. She was stiff, then gradually yielded. "I am not unmoved," said Reith. "Far from it. But I must go to Dadiche—for your sake as well as mine."

"How my sake? To be carried back to Cath?"

"That, and more. Are you happy to be dominated by Dirdir and Chasch and Wankh, not to mention the Pnume?"

"I don't know . . . I had never thought of it. Men are freaks, afterthoughts, so they tell us. Though Mad King Hopsin insisted that men came from a far planet. He called to them for help, which of course never came. That was a hundred and fifty years ago."

"It's a long time to wait," said Reith. He kissed her once more; she submitted listlessly. The fervor was gone.

"I feel—strange," she mumbled. "I don't know how I feel."

They stood by the rail, listening to the sounds of the inn: soft hoots of laughter from the pot-room; complaints of children, the scolding of their mothers. The Flower of Cath said, "I think I will go to bed now."

Reith held her back. "Derl."

"Yes?"

"When I come back from Dadiche—"

"You will never come back from Dadiche. The Blue Chasch

will take you for their games . . . Now I will try to sleep, and forget that I am alive."

She went back into the cubicle. Reith remained out on the balcony, first cursing himself, then wondering how he could have acted differently—unless he were composed of something other than flesh and blood.

Tomorrow, then: Dadiche, to learn once and for all the shape of his future.

8

THE NIGHT PASSED; morning came: first a wash of sepia light, then a wan yellow glare, then the appearance of Carina 4269. From the kitchens rose the smoke of fires, the rattle of pans. Reith descended to the common-room, where he found Anacho the Dirdirman before him, sitting over a bowl of tea. Reith joined him and was likewise brought tea by a kitchen-wench. He asked, "What do you know of Dadiche?"

Anacho warmed his long pale fingers around the bowl. "The city is relatively old: twenty thousand years or so. It is the main Chasch spaceport, though they have little communication with their home-world Godag. South of Dadiche are factories and technical plants, and there is even some small trade between Dirdir and Chasch, though both parties pretend to the contrary. What do you seek at Dadiche?" And he fixed Reith with his owlish water-gray eyes.

Reith reflected. He gained nothing by confiding in Anacho, whom he still regarded as something of an unknown quantity. Finally he said, "The Chasch took something of value from me. I want to get it back, if possible."

"Interesting," said Anacho with a sardonic overtone to his voice. "I am piqued. What could the Chasch take from a sub-man that he would travel a thousand leagues to recover? And how could he expect to recover it, or even find it?"

"I can find it. What happens next is the problem."

"You intrigue me," said the Dirdirman. "What do you propose to do first?"

"I need information. I want to learn if persons such as you and I can enter Dadiche and depart without hindrance."

"Not I," said Anacho. "They would smell me for a Dirdirman. They have noses of astonishing particularity. The food you eat delivers essences to your skin; the Chasch can identify these, and separate Dirdir from Wankh, marsh-dwellers from steppe-men, rich from the poor; not to mention the variations caused by disease, uncleanliness, unguents, waters, a dozen other conditions. They can smell salt air in a man's lungs if he has been near the ocean; they can detect ozone on a man coming down from the heights. They sense if you are hungry, or angry, or afraid; they can define your age, your sex, the color of your skin. Their noses provide them an entire dimension of perception."

Reith sat reflecting.

Anacho arose, went to a nearby table where sat three men in rough garments: men with waxy white-gray skins, light-brown hair, mild large eyes. To Anacho's questions they gave deferent responses; Anacho ambled back to Reith.

"Those three are drovers; they visit Dadiche regularly. The country is safe to the west of Pera; the Green Chasch avoid the city guns. No one will molest us along the road—"

"'Us'? You are coming?"

"Why not? I have never seen Dadiche or its outlying gardens. We can hire a pair of leap-horses and approach Dadiche within a mile or so. The Chasch seldom leave the city, so the drovers tell me."

"Good," said Reith. "I'll have a word with Traz; he can keep the girl company."

At a corral to the rear of the inn Reith and the Dirdirman hired leap-horses of a tall rubber-legged breed strange to Reith. The ostler threw on the saddles, shoved guide-bars through holes in the creatures' brains, at which they screamed and whipped the air with their palps. The reins were attached, Reith and Anacho vaulted up into the saddles; the beasts made angry sidling leaps, then sprang off down the road.

They passed through the center of Pera, where, over a considerable area, folk had built all manner of dwellings from the rubble and slabs of concrete. There was a greater population than Reith had expected, numbering perhaps four or five thousand. And up on top of the old citadel, brooding over all, was the crude mansion in which lived Naga Goho and his retinue of Ghashters.

Coming into the central plaza Reith and Anacho stopped

short before a display of horrid objects. Beside a massive gibbet were flaying-stocks stained with blood. Poles held aloft a pair of impaled men. From a derrick swung a small cage; inside crouched a naked sun-blackened creature, barely recognizable as a man. A Gnashter lounged nearby, a heavy-jowled young man wearing a maroon vest and a knee-length black kilt: the Gnashter uniform. Reith reined up the leap-horse and, indicating the cage, addressed the Gnashter. "What was his crime?"

"Recalcitrance, when Naga Goho called his daughter to service."

"What then? How long does he swing thus?"

The Gnashter glanced up indifferently. "Another three days he'll last. The rain freshened him up; he's full of water."

"What of those?" Reith pointed to the impaled corpses.

"Defaulters. Certain graceless folk begrudge a tithe of their wealth to Naga Goho."

Anacho touched Reith's arm. "Come."

Reith slowly turned away; impossible to right all the wrongs of this dreadful planet. But looking back toward the wretch in the cage, he felt a flush of shame. Still—what options were open to him? To embroil himself with Naga Goho could easily mean the loss of his life, with no benefit to anyone. If he were able to regain his space-boat and return to Earth, the lot of all men on Tschai must be improved. So Reith told himself, and tried to put the dismal scene out of his mind.

Beyond Pera were large numbers of irregular plots, where women and girls cultivated all manner of crops. Drays loaded with food and farm produce moved westward along the road toward Dadiche: a commerce surprising to Reith, who had expected no such formalized trade.

The two rode ten miles, toward a low range of gray hills. Where the road rose into a steep-walled ravine a gate barred the way and they were forced to wait while a pair of Gnashters inspected a dray piled with crates of cabbage-like pulps, then levied a toll upon the drayman. Reith and Anacho, passing the gate, paid a sequin each.

"Naga Goho misses few chances to profit," Reith grumbled. "What does he do with his wealth?"

The Dirdirman shrugged. "What does anyone do with wealth?"

The road wound up, passed through a notch. Beyond lay the

land of the Blue Chasch: a wooded countryside meshed by dozens of little rivers, easing in and out of innumerable ponds. There were a hundred sorts of trees: red feather-palm, green conifer-like growths, black trunks and branches hung with white globes; and many groves of adarak. The entire landscape was a single garden, tended with meticulous care.

Below was Dadiche: low flat domes and curving white surfaces, half-submerged in foliage. The size and population of the city was impossible to estimate; there was no differentiation between city and park. Reith was forced to admit that the Blue Chasch lived in pleasant circumstances.

The Dirdirman, conditioned to other aesthetic precepts, spoke with condescension. "Typical of the Chasch mentality: formless, chaotic, devious. You have seen a Dirdir city? Truly noble! a sight to stop the heart! This half-bucolic botchery"—Anacho made a scornful gesture—"reflects the caprice of the Blue Chasch. Not as flaccid and decadent as the Old Chasch of course—remember Golsse?—but then the Old Church have been moribund for twenty thousand years . . . What do you do? What is that instrument?"

For Reith, unable to contrive a method to read his transcom dials discreetly, had brought it forth. "This," said Reith, "is a device which indicates the direction and distance of three and a half miles." He sighted along the needle. "The line passes through that large structure with the high dome." He pointed. "The distance is about right."

Anacho was looking at the transcom with gloomy fascination. "Where did you get this instrument? It is of a workmanship I have never seen before. And those markings: neither Dirdir nor Chasch nor Wankh! Is there some far corner of Tschai where sub-men make goods of this quality? I am astounded! I have believed the sub-men incapable of any activity more complicated than agriculture!"

"Anacho, my friend," said Reith, "you have a great deal to learn. The process will come as an appalling shock to you."

Anacho massaged his undershot jaw, pulled the soft black cap down over his forehead. "You are as mysterious as a Pnume."

Reith brought the scanscope from his pouch, inspected the landscape. He traced the course of the road, down the hill, through a grove of flame-shaped trees with enormous green and purple leaves, thence to a wall which he had not previously noticed and which evidently guarded Dadiche from the Green Chasch. The road passed through a portal in this wall and into the city. At intervals along the road were drays entering Dadiche loaded with comestibles, leaving with crates of manufactured goods.

Anacho, inspecting the scanscope, made a clicking sound of irritated puzzlement, but restrained his comments.

Reith said, "No point in going further down the road; however, if we rode along the ridge a mile or two, I could take another sight on that big building."

Anacho made no objection; they rode south almost two miles, then Reith took a new reading of the transcom. The line of sight passed through the same large domed structure. Reith gave a nod of certainty. "In that building are articles which at one time were mine, and which I want to recover."

The Dirdirman's lips twitched in a grin. "All very well—but how? You can't ride into Dadiche, pound on the door and cry 'Bring out my object!' You will be disappointed. I doubt if you are a thief sufficiently deft to fool the Chasch. What will you do?"

Reith looked longingly down at the great white dome. "First, closer reconnaissance. I need to look inside that building. Because what I want most might not be there at all."

Anacho shook his head in mild reproach. "You talk in riddles. First you declare that your articles are there, then that they may not be there after all."

Reith merely laughed, far more confidently then he felt. Now that he was close to Dadiche, and presumably to the space-boat, the task of regaining possession seemed overwhelming. "Enough for today, at any rate. Let's be back to Pera."

They rode, swaying and lurching on the leap-horses, and returned to the road, where they halted for a space watching the drays rumble past. Some were propelled by engines, others by slow-going pull-beasts. Those to Dadiche carried foodstuffs: melons, stacks of dead reed-walkers, bales of dingy white floss spun by swamp insects, nets bulging with purple bladders. "These drays go into Dadiche," said Reith. "I'll go with them. Why should there be difficulty?"

The Dirdirman gave his head a lugubrious shake. "The Blue Chasch are unpredictable. You might find yourself performing tricks for their amusement. Such as walking rods over pits full of filth or white-eyed scorpions. As you gain equilibrium, the

Chasch heat the rods, or send electricity through, so that you bound back and forth and perform desperate antics. Or perhaps you will find yourself in a glass maze with a tormented Phung. Or you might be blindfolded and set in an amphitheater with a cyclodon, also blindfolded. Or—were you Dirdir or Dirdirman— you might be set to solving logical problems to avoid unpleasant penalties. Their ingenuity is endless."

Reith scowled down at the city. "The draymen risk all this?"

"They are licensed and go and come unmolested, unless they violate an ordinance."

"Then I will go as a drayman."

Anacho nodded. "The obvious stratagem. I suggest that to- night you strip off your clothes, rub yourself with damp soil, stand in the smoke of burning bones, walk in pull-beast dung, eat panibals, ramp and smudgers, all of which permeate the body with odor, and wipe the grease into your skin. Then dress from skin outward in drayman's garments. As a last precaution, never pass upwind of a Blue Chasch and never exhale where one might detect the odor of your teeth or your breath."

Reith managed a wry grin. "The scheme sounds less feasible every minute. But I don't care to die. I have too many responsibil- ities. Such as returning the girl to Cath."

"Bah!" snorted Anacho. "You are a victim of sentimentality. She is a troublemaker, vain and self-willed. Leave her to her des- tiny."

"If she were not vain I'd suspect her of stupidity," declared Reith with feeling.

Anacho kissed his fingertips: a gesture of Mediterranean fer- vor. "When you say 'beauty,' you must mean the women of my race! Ah! Elegant creatures, pale as snow, with pates naked and glossy as mirrors! So near to Dirdir that the Dirdir themselves are beguiled . . . Each to his own taste. The Cath girl can never be other than a source of tribulation. Such women trail disaster as a cloud trails rain; think of the times she has led you into conten- tion!"

Reith shrugged, and kicked the leap-horse into motion; they bounded east along the road, back down upon the steppe, off to- ward the mound of gray-white rubble which was Pera.

Late in the afternoon they entered the ruined city. They re- turned the leap-horses to the stables, crossed the plaza to the long half-subterranean inn, with the low sun shining on their backs.

The common-room was half-full of folk consuming an early supper. Neither Traz nor the Flower of Cath was here, nor were they in the sleeping cubicles on the second floor. Reith returned downstairs and found the innkeeper. "Where are my friends: the boy and the Cath girl? They are nowhere on the premises."

The innkeeper drew a sour face, looked everywhere but into Reith's eyes. "You must know where she is; how could she be elsewhere? As for the lad, he went into an unreasonable fury when they came to take her. The Gnashters broke his head and dragged him off to be hanged."

In a voice precise and controlled Reith asked, "How long ago did this occur?"

"Not long. He'll still be kicking. The lad was a fool. A girl like that is flagrant enticement; he had no right to defend her."

"They took the girl to the tower?"

"So I suppose. What's it to me? Naga Goho does as he pleases; he wields power in Pera."

Reith turned to Anacho, handed over his pouch, retaining only his weapons. "Take care of my belongings. If I don't return, keep them."

"You plan to risk yourself again?" asked Anacho in wonder and disapproval. "What about your 'object'?"

"It can wait." Reith ran off toward the citadel.

9

THE LIGHT OF the setting sun shone full on the stone platforms and mounting blocks surrounding the gibbet. Colors held the curious fullness of all the Tschai colors: even the browns and grays, mustards, dull ochers, earthen colors in the garments of those who had come to watch the hanging imparted a sense of rich essence. The dull-red jackets of the Gnashters glowed rich and ripe; there were six of these. Two stood by the gibbet rope; two supported Traz, who stood on limp legs, head bowed, a trickle of blood down his forehead. One leaned negligently by a post, hand by his slung catapult; the last spoke to the apathetic herd before the gibbet.

"By order of Naga Goho, this furious criminal who dared use violence upon the Gnashters must be hanged!"

The noose was ceremoniously dropped around Traz's neck. He raised his head, turned a glassy look around the crowd. If he noticed Reith he gave no sign. "May the incident and its consequences teach obedience to all!"

Reith walked around to the side of the gibbet. No time now for delicacy or squeamishness—if, in fact, such occasions ever occurred on Tschai. The Gnashters at the hoist-rope saw him approach, but his demeanor was so casual that they gave him no heed and turned to watch for their signal. Reith slid his knife into the heart of the first, who croaked in surprise. The second looked about; Reith cut his throat with a back-hand stroke, then threw the knife to split the forehead of the Gnashter who stood by the gibbet-pole. In an instant the six had become three. Reith stepped forward with his sword and cut down the man who had uttered the proclamation, but now the two holding Traz, drawing blades, rushed at Reith, jostling each other in outrage. Reith jumped back, aimed his Emblem catapult, shot the foremost; the second, now the sole survivor of the six, stopped short, Reith attacked him, struck the sword from his hand, felled him with a blow to the side of the head. He freed the noose, yanked it tight around the neck of the fallen Gnashter, pointed to two men at the front of the fascinated onlookers. "Heave now; heave on the rope. We'll hang the Gnashter, not the boy." When the men hesitated, Reith cried: "Heave on the rope; do my bidding! We'll show Naga Goho who rules Pera! Up with the Gnashter!"

The men sprang to the rope: high into the air swung the Gnashter, kicking and flailing. Reith ran over to the derrick. He loosed the rope which held the cage aloft, lowered it to the ground, threw open the top. The wretch within, crouched and cramped, looked up in fearful expectation, then an impossible hope. He tried to raise himself, but he was too weak. Reith reached down, helped him forth. He signaled to the men who had hoisted on the rope. "Take this man and the lad to the inn; see that they are cared for. You need fear the Gnashters no more. Take weapons from the dead men; if Gnashters appear, kill them! Do you understand? There are to be no more Gnashters in Pera, no more taxes, no more hangings, no more Naga Goho!"

Diffidently men took the weapons, then turned to look up toward the citadel.

Reith waited only long enough to see Traz and the man from

the cage helped toward the inn, then he turned and ran up the hill toward Naga Goho's makeshift palace.

A wall of piled rubble lay across the path, enclosing a courtyard. A dozen Gnashters lounged at long tables, drinking beer and munching strips of pickled reed-walker. Reith looked right and left, slid along the wall.

The hill fell away below to become a precipice; Reith pressed closer to the wall, clung to the corners and crevices of the blocks. He came to an aperture: a window crisscrossed by iron bars. Cautiously Reith looked within, to see only darkness. Ahead was a larger window, but the way was perilous, sheer over a seventy-foot drop. Reith hesitated, then proceeded, moving with painful slowness, hanging to the rough edges and crevices by his fingertips. In the gathering dusk he was inconspicuous, a blot on the wall. Below spread old Pera, with yellow lights beginning to flicker among the ruins. Reith reached the window, which was screened by a grille of woven reeds. He looked through, into a bed-chamber. On a couch was the outline of someone sleeping—a woman. Sleeping? Reith peered through the gloom. The hands were raised in supplication, the legs were gracelessly sprawled. The body lay very still. The woman was dead.

Reith tore open the grille, climbed into the room. The woman had been beaten about the head and strangled; her mouth was open, her tongue protruded foolishly. Alive she had been not uncomely, or so Reith conjectured. Dead, she was a sad sight.

Reith took three long strides to the door, looked out into a garden courtyard. From an archway opposite came a murmur of voices.

Reith slipped across the courtyard, looked through the archway, into a dining hall hung with rugs patterned in yellow, black, red. Other rugs muffled the floor; the furnishings were heavy chairs, a table of age-blackened wood. Under a great candelabra flaring with yellow lights sat Naga Goho at his evening meal, a splendid fur cloak thrown back from his shoulders. Across the room sat the Flower of Cath, head downcast, hair hanging past her face. Her hands were clasped in her lap; Reith saw that her wrists were bound with thongs. Naga Goho ate with exaggerated delicacy, conveying morsels to his mouth with mincing twitches of finger and thumb. As he ate he spoke, and as he spoke he flourished a short-handled whip in a mood of sinister playfulness.

The Flower sat with a still countenance, never raising her eyes from her lap. Reith watched and listened for a moment, one part of him as singleminded as a shark, another disgusted and horrified, still another sardonically amused for the grotesque surprise awaiting Naga Goho.

He stepped quietly into the room. Ylin-Ylan looked up, face blank. Reith signaled her to silence, but Naga Goho perceived the focus of her eyes and swung around in his chair. He jumped to his feet, the fur cloak falling to the floor. "Ha ho!" he cried out, startled. "A rat in the palace!" He ran to seize his sword from the scabbard over the back of the chair; Reith was there first, and, not deigning to draw his own blade, struck Naga Goho with his fist and sent him sprawling across the table. Naga Goho, a strong active man, turned an agile somersault, came up on his feet. Reith leapt after him, and now it developed that Naga Goho was as skilled in Tschai hand-fighting as Reith in the intricate techniques of Earth. To confuse Naga Goho, Reith began to throw left jabs into his face. When Naga Goho grasped for Reith's left arm, to attempt a throw or a bone-break, Reith stepped in and hacked at Naga Goho's neck and face. Naga Goho, desperate, attempted a terrible sweeping kick, but Reith was ready; seizing the foot, he yanked, twisted, heaved, to break Naga Goho's ankle. Naga Goho fell on his back. Reith kicked his head and a moment later Naga Goho fell on his back. Reith kicked his head and a moment later Naga Goho lay with arms triced up behind him, a gag in his mouth.

Reith liberated Ylin-Ylan, who closed her eyes. So pale was she, so drawn, that Reith thought that she would faint. But she stood up, to stand weeping against Reith's chest. For a moment or two he held her, stroking her head; then he said, "Let's be out of here. So far we've had good luck; it may not last. There are a dozen or more of his men below."

Reith tied a length of thong around Naga Goho's neck, yanked. "To your feet, quick now."

Naga Goho lay back, glaring, making angry sounds through his gag. Reith picked up the whip, flicked the side of Naga Goho's face. "Up." He hauled on the thong; the erstwhile chieftain rose to his feet.

With Naga Goho hobbling in great pain, they passed along a hall lit with a reeking cresset, entered the courtyard where the Gnashters sat over tankards of beer.

Reith gave the thong to the Flower. "Walk on through; don't

hurry. Pay no heed to the men. Lead the Goho on down the road."

Ylin-Ylan, taking the thong, walked through the courtyard leading Naga Goho. The Gnashters swung around on their benches, staring in wonder. Naga Goho made hoarse urgent noises; the Gnashters rose irresolutely to their feet. One of them came slowly forward. Reith stepped into the courtyard holding the catapult. "Back; into your seats."

While they stood, he slipped across the courtyard. Ylin-Ylan and Naga Goho were starting down the hill. Reith told the Gnashters, "Naga Goho is finished. So are you. When you come down the hill, you had better leave your weapons behind." He backed out into the dark. "Don't any come after us." He waited. From within came a furious babble of talk. Two of the Gnashters strode toward the opening. Reith appeared in the gap, shot the foremost with his catapult, stepped back into the dark once more. Within the courtyard, while Reith dropped a new bolt into the slot, was utter silence. Reith looked back in. All stood at the far side of the courtyard, staring at the corpse. Reith turned, ran down the path, where the Flower struggled to control Naga Goho, who jerked at the neck thong, trying to pull her close so that he might fall upon her, perhaps knock her down. Reith took the thong, dragged Naga Goho stumbling and hopping at a smart pace to the foot of the hill.

Az and Braz both rode the eastern sky; the white blocks of old Pera seemed to glow with a wan intrinsic light.

In the plaza stood a crowd of people, brought forth by rumors and wild reports, ready to slink off among the ruins should the Gnashters come marching down from the palace. Seeing only Reith, the girl and the stumbling Naga Goho, they called out in soft surprise and came step by step closer.

Reith halted, looked around the circle of faces, pallid in the moonlight. He gave a yank on the thong, grinned at the crowd. "Well, here is Naga Goho. He is chieftain no more. He committed one crime too many. What shall we do with him?"

The crowd moved uneasily, eyes shifting up to the palace, then back to Reith and Naga Goho, who stood glaring from face to face, promising dire vengeance. A woman's voice low, husky, throbbing with hate, said: "Flay him, flay the beast!" "Impalement," muttered an old man. "He impaled my son; let him feel the pole!" "The flame!" shrilled another voice. "Burn him with slow fire!"

"No one counsels mercy," Reith observed. He turned to Naga Goho. "Your time has come." He pulled off the gag. "Do you have anything to say?"

Naga Goho could find no words, but made only strange noises at the back of his mouth.

Reith said to the crowd. "Let's make a quick end to him— though he probably deserves worse. You—you—you." He pointed. "Lower the Gnashter. It's the rope for Naga Goho."

Five minutes later, with the dark form kicking in the moonlight, Reith spoke to the crowd. "I am a newcomer to Pera. But it's clear to me, as it must be to you, that the city needs a responsible government. Look how Naga Goho and a few thugs brutalized the entire city! You are men! Why act like animals? Tomorrow you must meet together, to select five experienced men for your Council of Elders. Let them pick a chieftain to rule for, say, a year, subject to the approval of the Council, who should also judge criminals and impose penalties. Then you should organize a militia, a troop of armed warriors to fight off Green Chasch, perhaps hunt them down and destroy them. We are men! Never forget this!" He looked back up toward the citadel. "Ten or eleven Gnashters still hold the palace. Tomorrow your Council can decide what to do about them. They may try to escape. I suggest that a guard be posted: twenty men up along the path should be ample." Reith pointed to a tall man with a black beard. "You look to be a stalwart man. Take the job in hand. You are captain. Pick two dozen men, or more, and mount guard. Now I must go to see my friend."

Reith and the Flower started back to the Dead Steppe Inn. As they moved away they heard the black-bearded man say, "Very well, then; for many months we have performed as poltroons. We'll do better now. Twenty men with weapons; who'll step forward? Naga Goho escaped with simple hanging; let's give the Gnashters something better . . ."

Ylin-Ylan took Reith's hand, kissed it. "I thank you, Adam Reith."

Reith put his arm around her waist; she stopped, leaned against him and once again fell to sobbing, from sheer fatigue and nervous exhaustion. Reith kissed her forehead; then, as she turned up her face, her mouth, in spite of all his good intentions.

Presently they returned to the inn. Traz lay asleep in a chamber off the common-room. Beside him sat Anacho the Dirdirman. Reith asked, "How is he?"

Anacho said in a gruff voice, "Well enough, I bathed his head. A bruise, no fracture. He'll be on his feet tomorrow."

Reith went back to the common-room. The Flower of Cath was nowhere to be seen. Reith thoughtfully ate a bowl of stew and went up to the room on the second floor, where he found her waiting for him.

She said, "I have still my last name, my most secret name, to tell my lover alone. If you come close—"

Reith bent forward and she whispered the name in his ear.

10

ON THE FOLLOWING morning Reith visited the drayage depot at the extreme south of town: a place of platforms and bins piled with the produce of the region. The drays rumbled up to the loading areas, the teamsters cursing and sweating, jockeying for position, oblivious to dust, smell, protest of beast, complaints of the hunters and growers, whose merchandise was constantly threatened by the jostling wagons.

Some of the wagons carried a pair of teamsters, or a draymaster and a helper; others were managed by a single man. Reith approached one of these latter. "You haul to Dadiche today?"

The draymaster, a small thin man with black eyes in a face which seemed all nose and narrow forehead, gave a suspicious jerk of the head. "Aye."

"When you arrive in Dadiche, what is the procedure?"

"I'll never arrive to begin with, if I waste my time talking."

"Don't worry; I'll make it worth your while. What do you do?"

"I drive to the unloading dock; the porters sweep me clean; the clerk gives me my receipt; I pass the wicket and take either sequins or vouchers, depending on whether I have an order for return cargo. If I have return cargo I take my voucher to the proper factory or warehouse, load and then start back for Pera."

"So, then—there are no restrictions to where you drive in Dadiche?"

"Certainly there are restrictions. They don't like drays along the river-side among their gardens. They don't want folk to the south of the city near the race-course, where teams of Dirdir pull the chariots, or so it is said."

"Elsewhere, no regulations?"

The draymaster squinted at Reith across the impressive beak of his nose. "Why do you ask such questions?"

"I want to ride with you, to Dadiche and back."

"Impossible. You have no license."

"You will provide the license."

"I see. No doubt you are prepared to pay?"

"A reasonable sum. How much will you demand?"

"Ten sequins. Another five sequins for the license."

"Too much! Ten sequins for everything, or twelve if you drive where I bid you."

"Bah! Do you take me for a fool? You might bid me drive you out Fargon Peninsula."

"No risk of that. A short distance into Dadiche, to look at something which interests me."

"Done for fifteen sequins, no iota less."

"Oh, very well," said Reith. "But I'll expect you to provide me drayer's clothes."

"Very well, and I'll give you further instructions: carry none of your old metal; this retains a scent to alarm them. Throw off all your clothes, rub yourself in mire, and dry yourself with annel leaves, and chew annel to disguise your breath. And you must do this at once, for I load and leave in half an hour."

Reith did as he was bid, though his skin crawled at the clammy feel of the drayer's old garments, and the loose-brimmed old hat of wicker and felt. Emmink, as the drayer called himself, checked to make sure Reith carried no weapons, which were forbidden within the city. He pinned a plaque of white glass on Reith's shoulder. "This is the license. When you pass the gate, call out your number, like this: 'Eighty-six!' Then say no more and do not get down from the dray. If they smell you out for a stranger, I can do nothing to help, so do not look to me."

Reith, already uneasy, was not encouraged by the remarks.

The dray rumbled west toward the crumble of gray hills, carrying a cargo of reed-walker corpses, the yellow bills and staring dead eyes alternating with rows of yellow feet to form a macabre pattern.

Emmink was surly and uncommunicative, he showed no interest in the motive for Reith's visit and Reith, after several attempts at conversation, fell silent.

The dray ground up the road, the torque generators at each wheel spinning and groaning. They entered the pass which Emmink named Belbal Gap, and before them spread Dadiche: a scene of bizarre and somewhat menacing beauty. Reith's uneasiness became keener. Despite his soiled garments, he did not feel that he resembled the other drayers and could only hope that he smelled like a drayer. What of Emmink? Would he prove dependable? Reith considered him surreptitiously: a dry wisp of a man, with skin the color of boiled leather, all nose and narrow forehead, his little mouth pinched together. A man like Anacho, like Traz, like himself, ultimately derived from the soil of Earth, mused Reith. How dilute now, how tenuous, was the terrestrial essence! Emmink had become a man of Tschai, his soul conditioned by the Tschai landscape, the amber sunlight, the gunmetal sky, the quiet rich colors. Reith cared to trust the loyalty of Emmink no farther than the length of his arm, if as far. Looking out over the extent of Dadiche, he asked, "Where do you discharge your cargo?"

Emmink delayed before answering, as if searching for a plausible reason to decline response. Grudgingly he said, "Wherever I get the best price. It might be North Market or River Market. It might be Bonte Bazaar."

"I see," said Reith. He pointed to the great white structure he had located the day before. "That building there: what is that?"

Emmink gave his narrow shoulders a twitch of disinterest. "It is none of my affair. I buy, transport, and sell; beyond that, I care nothing."

"I see . . . Well, I want to drive past that building."

Emmink grunted. "It is to the side of my usual route."

"I don't care if it is. That's what I'm paying you for."

Emmink grunted again, and for a moment was silent. Then he said: "First to the North Market, to secure a quote on my corpses, then to the Bonte Bazaar. On the way I will pass the building."

They rolled down the hill, across a strip of barrens strewn with junk and refuse, then into a garden of feathery green shrubs and mottled black and green cycads. Ahead rose the wall surrounding Dadiche, a structure thirty feet high built of a brown glossy synthetic material. Through a gate passed drays from Pera submitting to scrutiny from a group of Chaschmen in purple pantaloons, gray shirts and tall conical hats of black felt. They carried sidearms and long thin rods, with which they prodded the loads of incoming drays. "What's the reason for that?" Reith asked, as the Chaschmen somewhat lackadaisically stabbed through the heaped cargo of the dray ahead.

"They prevent Green Chasch from stealing into the city. Forty years ago a hundred Green Chasch entered Dadiche hidden in cargo; there was a great slaughter before all the Green Chasch were killed. Oh, Blue Chasch and Green Chasch are bitter enemies! They love to see the other's blood!"

Reith asked, "What do I say if they ask me questions?"

Emmink shrugged. "That's your affair. If they ask me, I'll tell them you paid for transportation into Dadiche. Is it not the truth? Then you must tell your truth, if you dare . . . Shout your number when I shout mine."

Reith gave a sour grin but said nothing.

The way was clear; Emmink drove up through the portal and stopped upon a red rectangle. "Forty-five," he bawled. "Eighty-six," yelled Reith. The Chaschmen stepped forward, thrust rods into the stack of reed-walker corpses while another walked around the dray: a stocky man with bandy legs, features crowded together at the bottom of his face, as chinless as Emmink but with a small snub nose, a lowering forehead rendered grotesque by the false scalp which rose into a cone six inches or more above his normal skull. His skin was leaden, tinged with blue which might have been cosmetic. His fingers were short and stubby, his feet broad. In Reith's opinion he deviated from the human form, as Reith knew it, considerably further than did Anacho the Dirdirman. The man glanced indifferently at Emmink and Reith, stepped back with a wave of his arm. Emmink pushed forward the power-arm and the dray lurched ahead into a wide avenue.

Emmink turned to Reith with a sour grin. "You're lucky none of the Blue Chasch captains were on hand. They'd have smelled you sweating. I could almost smell you. When a man is afraid he sweats. If you want to pass as a drayman, you'll need a cold-blooded disposition."

"That's asking a lot," said Reith. "I'll do my best."

Into Dadiche rolled the dray. Blue Chasch could be seen in their gardens, tending arbors, stirring stone troughs, moving quietly in the shadows surrounding their round-roofed villas. Occasionally Reith sensed odors from a garden or a trough: wafts tart, pungent, spicy, reeks of burnt amber, candied musk, anomalous ferments, disturbing by their uncertainty: were they repulsive or exquisitely delightful?

The road continued among the villas for a mile or two. The Blue Chasch put no store by what Reith considered a normal regard for privacy; and their villas seemed spaced without any concern for the road. Occasionally Chaschmen and Chaschwomen could be seen at menial or laborious tasks; seldom did Reith notice Chaschmen in the company of the Blue Chasch; always they worked separately, and when they were by chance in physical contiguity, each ignored the other as if he did not exist.

Emmink made no comments or observations. Reith expressed wonder at the apparent obliviousness of the Blue Chasch to the drays. Emmink gave a snort of bitter amusement. "Don't be fooled! If you think them vague, only try to slip off the dray and walk into one of the villas! You'd be pinned down in a trice, and conveyed to the gymnasium to demonstrate at their games. Ah, cunning, cunning, cunning! As cruel as they are ludicrous! Pitiless and sly! Have you heard of their trick with poor Phosfer Ajan the drayer? He stepped down from his dray to answer a call of nature: mad folly, of course. What could he expect but resentment? So Phosfer Ajan, with feet tied, was placed in a vat, with putrid foulness up to his chin. At the bottom was a valve. When the slime became too hot, Phosfer Ajan must dive to the bottom, turn the valve, whereupon the stink would become bitter cold, and Phosfer must dive and grope again, while slime singed and froze him by turns. Still, he persevered; he dived and groped stoically, and on the fourth day they allowed him to his dray, so that he might bear his tale back to Pera. As may be adduced, they fit the game to the occasion, and a more resourceful set of humorists has never been known." Emmink turned to Reith his calculating glance. "What offense do you plan against them? I can predict to some degree of accuracy how they will respond."

"No offense," said Reith. "I am curious, no more, and wish to see how the Blue Chasch live."

"They live like facetious maniacs, from the standpoint of all who annoy them. I have heard that they especially enjoy pranks with a bull Green Chasch and a fledged Phung, together of course. Next, should they be lucky enough to capture a Dirdir and Pnume, these are urged through laughable antics. All in a spirit of fun, of course; the Blue Chasch above all dislike boredom."

"I wonder why there is not a great war to the finish," pondered Reith. "Are not the Dirdir more powerful than the Blue Chasch?"

"They are indeed; and their cities are grand, or so I have heard. But the Chasch have torpedoes and mines ready to destroy all the Dirdir cities in case of attack. It is a common situation: each is sufficiently strong to obliterate the other; hence neither dares more than minor unpleasantness . . . Ah well, so long as they ignore me, I shall do the same for them . . . There ahead is North Market. Notice, the Blue Chasch are everywhere at hand. They love to bargain, though they prefer to cheat. You must be silent. Make no sign, give no nod or shake! Otherwise they will claim that I have sold at some ruinous price."

Emmink turned his dray into an open area protected by an enormous parasol. Now began the most frantic bargaining Reith had ever seen. A Blue Chasch, approaching, examining the reed-walker corpses, would croak a proffer which Emmink would decline in a scream of outrage. For minutes the two would heap abuse on each other, sparing no aspect of the other, until suddenly the Blue Chasch would make a furious gesture of disgust and go to seek his reed-walkers at another dray.

Emmink gave Reith a malicious wink. "Once in a while I hold the price up, just to excite the Blues. Also I find out what the selling prices are about to be. Now we'll try Bonte Bazaar."

Reith started to remind Emmink of the wide oval building, then thought better of it. Crafty Emmink had forgotten nothing. He swung around the dray, drove it out along a road running south a quarter-mile inland from the river, with gardens and villas intervening. On the left were small domes and sheds among sparse-foliaged trees, areas of dirt where naked children played: the homes of the Chaschmen. Emmink said with a leer: "There's the start of the Blue Chasch themselves; so it was explained to me by one of the Chaschmen in loving detail."

"How so?"

"The Chaschmen believe that in each grows a homunculus which develops throughout life and is liberated after death, to become a full Chasch. So the Blue Chasch teach; is it not ludicrous?"

"So I would say," replied Reith. "Haven't the Chaschmen ever seen human corpses? Or Blue Chasch infants?"

"No doubt. But they supply explanations for every discord and discrepancy. This is what they want to believe: how else can they justify their servitude to the Chasch?"

Emmink was perhaps a more profound individual than his appearance suggested, thought Reith. "Do they think the Dirdir originate in the Dirdirmen? Or Wankh in the Wankhmen?"

"As to that," Emmink shrugged, "perhaps they do . . . Look now; yonder is your building."

The cluster of Chaschmen huts was behind, concealed by a bank of pale green trees with huge brown flowers. The dray skirted the central node of the city. Beside an avenue were public or administrative buildings, supported on shallow arches, with roof-lines of variously-curved surfaces. Opposite rose the great structure which contained the space-boat, or so Reith believed. It was as long as a football field and as wide, with low walls and a vast half-ellipsoidal roof: an architectural *tour de force* by any standards.

The function of the building was not apparent. There were few entrances, and no large openings nor facilities for heavy transport. Reith finally decided that they were traveling along the building's back elevation.

At Bonte Bazaar Emmink sold his corpses to the tune of furious haggling, while Reith kept to the side and downwind from Blue Chasch buyers.

Emmink was not totally pleased with the transaction. Returning to the dray after unloading, he grumbled, "I should have had another twenty sequins; the corpses were prime. . . . How could I make this clear to the Blue? He was watching you and trying to catch your air; the way you dodged and ducked would have aroused suspicion in an old Chaschwoman. By all standards of justice you should reimburse me for my loss."

"I hardly think he got the better of you," said Reith. "Come; let's drive back."

"What of my lost twenty sequins?"

"Forget them; they are imaginary. Look; the Blues are watching us."

Emmink hastily jumped into the driver's seat and started up the dray. Apparently from sheer perversity, he began to return by the same road he had come. Reith spoke sternly: "Drive by the east road, to the front of the big building; let's have no more tricks!"

"I always drive to the west," whined Emmink. "Why should I change now?"

"If you know what's best for you—"

"Ha, threats? In the middle of Dadiche? When all I need do is signal a Blue—"

"It would be the last signal of your life."

"What of my twenty sequins?"

"You've already had fifteen from me, plus your profit. No more of your complaints! Drive as I tell you or I'll wring your neck."

Wheezing, protesting, casting spiteful glances from the side of his face, Emmink obeyed.

The white building loomed ahead. The road ran parallel to the front at a distance of seventy-five yards, with a strip of garden intervening. An access road turned off from the main avenue, to run in front of the building. To drive along the access road would have rendered them highly conspicuous, and they continued along the main avenue in the company of other drays and wagons, and a few small cars driven by Blue Chasch. Reith gazed anxiously at the facade. Three large portals broke the front wall. Those to the left and center were shut; the far right portal was open. As they passed Reith looked in, to see the loom of machinery, the glow of hot metal, the hull of a platform similar to that which had lifted the space-boat away from the swamp.

Reith turned to Emmink. "This building is a factory where airships and spacecraft are built!"

"Yes, of course," grunted Emmink.

"I asked you as much; why did you not tell me?"

"You weren't paying for information. I give nothing away."

"Drive around the building again."

"I must charge you an additional five sequins."

"Two. And no complaints, or I'll rattle your teeth."

Cursing under his breath, Emmink swung the dray around the factory. Reith asked, "Have you ever looked into the center or the left of the building?"

"Oh yes; several times."

"What is there?"

"How much is the information worth?"

"Not very much. I'd have to see for myself."

"A sequin?"

Reith nodded shortly.

"Sometimes the other portals are ajar. In the center they construct sections of spaceships, which are then rolled out and carried away for assembly elsewhere. In the left they build smaller spaceships, when such are needed. Recently there has been little work; the Blue Chasch do not like to travel space."

"Have you seen them bring spaceships or space-boats here for repair? Several months ago?"

"No. Why do you ask?"

"The information will cost you money," said Reith. Emmink showed great yellow teeth in a grin of sardonic appreciation and said no more.

They started along the front a second time. "Slow," Reith ordered, for Emmink had pushed the power-arm hard over and the old dray rattled at full speed along the avenue.

Emmink grudgingly obliged. "If we go too slow they'll think us curious, and ask us why we peer and crane our necks."

Reith looked along the road adjacent to the building, along which walked a few Blue Chasch, a somewhat larger number of Chaschmen.

Reith said to Emmink, "Pull off the road; stop the dray for a minute or two."

Emmink began his usual protest, but Reith pulled back the power-lever and the dray wheezed to a halt. Emmink stared at Reith, speechless with fury.

"Get out; fix your wheels, or look at your energy cell," said Reith. "Do something to keep occupied." He jumped to the ground, stood looking at the great factory, for such seemed to be the nature of the building. The portal on the right was tantalizingly open. So near yet so far . . . If only he dared cross the seventy-five yards to the portal, and look inside!

What then? Suppose he saw the space-boat. It certainly would not be in operative condition; chances were good that Blue Chasch technicians had at least partially disassembled the mechanism. They would be a puzzled group, thought Reith. The technology, the engineering, the entire rationale of design would seem strange and unfamiliar. The presence of a human body would only puzzle them the more. The situation was by no means encouraging. The boat was possibly within, in a dismantled and non-usable condition. Or it was not. If it should be there he had not the remotest idea of how to gain possession of it. If it was not in the building, if only Paul Waunder's transcom was there, then he must revise his thinking and make new plans . . . But at the moment the first step was to look inside the factory. It seemed easy. He needed only to walk seventy-five yards and look . . . but he did not dare. If only he were in some disguise to deceive the Blue Chasch—which could only mean the guise of a Chaschman. Far-fetched, thought Reith. With his well-marked features, he resembled a Chaschman not at all.

The reflections had occupied him a very short time: hardly a minute, but Emmink clearly was becoming restive. Reith decided to seek his counsel.

"Emmink," said Reith, "suppose you wanted to learn if a certain object—for instance, a small spaceship—was inside that building, how would you go about it?"

Emmink snorted. "I would consider no such folly. I would resume my place on the dray and depart while I still had health and sanity."

"You can think of no errand to take us into the building?"

"None whatever. A fantasy!"

"Or close past that open portal?"

"No, no! Of course not!"

Reith longingly considered the building and the open portal. So near and yet so far . . . He became furious with himself, at the intolerable circumstances, at the Blue Chasch, Emmink, the planet Tschai. Seventy-five yards: the work of half a minute. He said curtly to Emmink: "Wait here." And he started walking with long strides across the planted area.

Emmink gave a hoarse call. "Come here, come back! Are you insane?"

But Reith only hastened his steps. On the walk beside the building were a few Chaschmen, apparently laborers, who paid him no heed. Reith gained the walk. The open portal was ten steps ahead. Three Blue Chasch stepped forth. Reith's heart pounded; his palms were damp. The Blue Chasch must smell his sweat; would they know it for the odor of fear? It seemed as if, engrossed in their own affairs, they might not notice him. Head bowed, loose-brimmed hat in front of his face, Reith hurried past. Then, with only twenty feet to the portal, the three swung around as if activated by the same stimulus. One of the Blue Chasch spoke in a gobbling mincing voice, the words formed by organs other than vocal chords. "Man! Where go you?"

Reith halted and responded with the explanation he had formed as he had crossed from the main avenue. "I came for scrap metal."

"What scrap metal?"

"By the portal, in a box; so they told me."

"Ah!—" a blowing gasping sound, which Reith was unable to interpret. "No scrap metal!"

One of the others muttered something quietly, and all three emitted a hiss, the Blue Chasch analogue of human laughter.

"Scrap metal, so? Not at the factory. There: notice that building yonder? Scrap metal yonder!"

"Thank you!" called Reith. "I'll but look." He went the last few steps to the open portal, looked into a great space murmurous with machinery, smelling of oil and metal and ozone. Nearby were platform components in the process of fabrication. Blue Chasch and Chaschmen alike worked, without obvious caste distinction. Around the walls, as in any Earthly factory or machine shop, were benches, racks and bins. In the center were a cylindrical section of what apparently would be a medium-sized spaceship. Beyond, barely visible, was a familiar shape: the space-boat on which Reith had come down to Tschai.

He could detect no damage to the hull. If the machinery had been dismantled, no evidence was apparent. But a good deal of distance intervened between himself and the boat, and he had time only for a single glimpse. Behind him the three Blue Chasch stood staring at him, massive blue-scaled heads half-inclined as if listening. They were, so Reith realized, smelling him. They seemed suddenly intent, suddenly interested and began to walk slowly back toward him.

One spoke, in his thick queer voice: "Man! Attention! Return here. There is no scrap metal."

"You smell of man-fear," said another. "You smell of odd substances."

"A disease," replied Reith.

Another spoke. "You smell like a strangely dressed man we found in a strange spaceship; there is about you a factitious quality."

"Why are you here?" demanded the third of the group. "For whom do you spy?"

"No one; I am a drayer, and I must return to Pera."

"Pera is a hive of spies; time perhaps that we sifted the population."

"Where is your dray? You did not arrive on foot?"

Reith started to move away. "My dray is out on the avenue." He pointed, then stared in consternation. Emmink and the dray were no longer to be seen. He called back to the three Blue Chasch, "My dray! Stolen! Who has taken it!" And with a gesture of hasty farewell for the puzzled Chasch, he darted off into the planted area separating the two roads. Behind a hedge of white wool and gray-green plumes he paused to look back and was by no means reassured. One of the Blue Chasch had run a few steps after him and was pointing some sort of instrument here and there through the planting. A second was speaking with great urgency into a hand microphone. The third had gone to the portal and was peering toward the space-boat, as if to verify its presence.

"I've done it for sure," Reith muttered to himself. "I've pulled the whole business down around my ears." He started to turn away, but paused an instant longer to watch as a squad of Chaschmen, wearing uniforms of purple and gray, drove up the factory road on long low-slung motorcycles. The Blue Chasch gave terse instructions, pointing toward the planted area. Reith waited no longer. He ran to the avenue, and as a dray loaded with empty baskets rolled smartly by, he sprang out, caught hold of the tailgate, pulled himself up on the bed and crawled behind a stack of baskets, without arousing the attention of the draymaster.

Behind came half a dozen motorcycles at great speed. They passed the dray with an angry whir of electric propulsion. To set up a roadblock? Or to reinforce the guards at the main gates?

Possibly both, thought Reith. The venture, as Emmink had predicted, was about to end in fiasco. Reith doubted that the Blue Chasch would involve him in their infamous games; they would prefer to extract information from him. And then? At best, Reith's freedom of action would be curtailed. At worst—but this bore little thinking about. The dray was rattling along at a good pace, but Reith knew he had no chance of passing through the gate. Close to the North Market Reith dropped to the ground and at once took cover behind a long low structure of porous white concrete: a warehouse or a storage shed. Finding his view constricted, he climbed upon a wall, thence to the roof of the shed. He could see down the main avenue to the gate, and his fears were amply justified: a number of purple and gray-uniformed security police stood beside the portal inspecting traffic with great care. If Reith was going to leave the city he must choose some other route. The river? Conceivably he could wait till night and float down the river unseen. But Dadiche extended a score or more miles along the riverbank, with other Blue Chasch villas and gardens beyond. Additionally, Reith had no knowledge of the creatures inhabiting the river. If they were as noxious as other forms of Tschai life, he wanted nothing to do with them.

A faint hum attracted Reith's attention. He looked up, startled to see an air-sled, not a hundred yards distant, sliding quietly by. The passengers were Blue Chasch, wearing peculiar headgear like enormous moth antennae. Reith was initially sure that he had been seen; then he was sure that the antennae were some sort of olfactory amplifiers: equipment being used to track him down.

The air-sled proceeded without change of course. Reith released his pent breath. His apprehension apparently had been unfounded. What were the tall antennae? Ceremonial vestments? Adornments? "I may never know," Reith told himself. He searched the sky for other sky-sleds, but none could be seen. Raising to his knees, he once again looked all around. Somewhat to the left, behind a screen of the ever-present adarak trees, was North Market: white concrete parasols, suspended discs, glass screens; moving figures wearing black, dull blue, dull red; scales glinting gunmetal blue. The breeze, blowing from the north, carried a complicated reek of spice; of sour vegetable matter; of meat cooked, fermented, pickled; of yeasts and mycelium cake.

To the right were the huts of Chaschmen, scattered through the gardens. Beyond, pressed up against the wall, was a large building screened by tall black trees. If Reith could climb to the top of this building he might possibly cross the wall. He looked at the sky. Dusk was the best time for such a venture, a matter of two or three hours.

Reith descended from the roof, and stood a moment thinking. The Blue Chasch, so sensitive to odors; would they not be able to track him by scent, like bloodhounds? It was not an unreasonable theory, and if so, he had no time to spare.

He found two short lengths of wood, tied them to his shoes,

and, taking long steps, stalked carefully away through the garden.

He had traveled only fifty yards when he heard sounds behind him, and instantly took cover. Peering back through the shrubbery, he saw that his hunch had not only been accurate, but timely. By the shed stood three Chaschmen security guards in purple and gray uniforms, with a pair of Blue Chasch, one of whom carried a detector-wand connected to a pack and thence to a mask across his nasal orifice. The Blue Chasch, waving the wand across the ground, sniffed out Reith's tracks without difficulty. At the back of the building the creature became confused, but presently discerned evidence of Reith's sojourn on the roof. All drew back warily, apparently believing Reith still on top.

From his vantage point fifty yards distant Reith chuckled, wondering what the Blue Chasch would think when they found no Reith on the roof and no perceptible trace of his departure. Then, still on his wooden clogs, he continued through the gardens toward the wall.

With a great caution he approached the large building and halted behind a tall tree to take stock of the situation. The building was dark and gloomy, apparently unoccupied. As Reith had supposed, the roof was very close to the top of the wall.

Reith looked back over the city. More sky-sleds were visible, at least a dozen. They flew low over the area he had just crossed, trailing black cylinders on wire: almost certainly olfactory pickups. If one passed overhead or downwind, whatever distinctive odor Reith exuded must be detected. It was obviously important that he take cover swiftly, and the somber building against the wall seemed the only practical covert: if it was unoccupied.

Reith watched another few minutes. He could discern no stir of movement within. He listened but heard no sounds; still he dared not approach. On the other hand, glancing over his shoulder at the air-sleds, he dared not remain. Discarding the clogs, he took a tentative step forward—then, hearing sounds behind him, sprang back into concealment.

There were measured tones of a gong. Up the road came a procession of Chaschmen muffled in gray and white. In the van four carried a white-draped corpse on a bier; behind marched Chaschmen and Chaschwomen sighing and keening. The building was a mausoleum or mortuary, thought Reith; the somber aspect was no deception.

The gong strokes slowed. The group halted below the portico of the building. The gong became still. In utter silence the bier was brought forward and placed upon the porch. The mourners drew back and waited. The gong struck a single tone.

A door slowly opened, a gap which seemed to extend into an infinite void. An intense golden ray slanted down upon the corpse. From right and left came a pair of Blue Chasch, wearing a ceremonial harness of straps, tabs, golden whorls and tassels. They approached the corpse, drew down the pall to expose the face and the beetling false skull, then stepped aside. A curtain descended to hide the corpse.

A moment passed. The ray of golden light became a glare; there was sudden plangent sound, as of a broken harpstring. The curtain lifted. The corpse lay as before, but the false skull was split and the cranium as well. In the cold brain sat a Blue Chasch imp, staring forth at the mourners.

The gong struck eleven jubilant strokes; the Blue Chasch cried out, "The elevation has occurred! A man has transcended his first life! Partake of beatitude! Inhale the jubilant odor! The man, Zugel Edgz, has given soul to this delightful imp! Could there be greater felicity? Through diligence, by application of approved principle, the same glory may come to all! In first life I was the man Sagaza Oso—" spoke one. "I was the woman Diseun Furwg," spoke the other. "—So with all the others. Depart then in joy! The imp Zugel Edgz must be anointed with healthful salve; the empty man-hulk will return to the soil. In two weeks you may visit your beloved Zugel Edgz!"

The mourners, no longer dejected, returned down the path to quick strokes of the gong, and were lost to sight. The bier with corpse and staring imp slid into the building. The Blue Chasch followed, and the door closed.

Reith gave a quiet laugh, which he quickly stifled as a sky-sled drifted alarmingly close. Creeping through the foliage, he approached the mortuary. No one, Chasch or Chaschman, was in sight; he slipped around to the rear of the building, which almost abutted the wall.

Low to the ground was an arched opening. Reith sidled close, listened, to hear a muffled grind of machinery, and he winced at the thought of the grisly work being done. He peered into the dimness to see what appeared to be a storeroom, a repository for discarded objects. On racks and shelves were pots, jars, heaps of old garments, a clutter of dusty mechanisms for purposes unimaginable. The room was untenanted, apparently little used. Reith took a final look at the sky and slipped into the building.

The room communicated with another, through a wide low arch. Another room lay beyond, and another, and another, all illuminated by a sickly glow from ceiling panels. Reith was content to crouch behind a rack and wait.

An hour passed, two hours. Reith became restless and made a cautious exploration. In a side chamber he found a bin containing false craniums, each with a label and a series of characters. He picked one up, tried it on. It seemed to fit; Reith detached and discarded the label. From a pile of garments he selected an old cloak and drew it up under his chin. From a distance, at a casual glance, he might conceivably be taken for a Chaschman.

There was a fading of light at the window; looking forth Reith saw that the sun had settled into a wrack of clouds. The adarak trees moved against a background of watery light. Reith climbed forth, scrutinized the sky; no sky-sleds were immediately evident. Reith went to a convenient tree and started to climb. The bark was a slippery pulp, which made the project more difficult than he had anticipated. At last, sticky with aromatic sap, sweating under his ill-smelling garments, he gained the roof of the mortuary.

He crouched, looked out over Dadiche. The sky-sleds had disappeared; the sky was brown-gray with oncoming dusk.

Reith went to the back edge of the roof, looked across at the wall. The top surface was about six feet distant, flat, with foot-high prongs at fifty-foot intervals. Warning devices? Reith could imagine no other purpose. On the other side was a drop of thirty feet—twenty-five feet, if he hung by his hands before he let himself fall. Reith appraised the chances of landing without broken bones or sprained joints: about two in three, depending upon the ground beneath. With a rope, the descent would be effortless. In the basement of the mortuary he had seen no ropes, but there were quantities of old garments to be knotted together. First: what would happen if he reached the top of the wall?

To learn, Reith doffed his cloak. Moving along the rooftop until he was opposite one of the prongs, he swung the cloak out and over the prong.

The result was instant and startling. From the prongs to either side lances of white fire darted forth, piercing the cloak, setting it aflame. Reith snatched it back, stamped out the blaze, looked hurriedly back and forth along the wall. Undoubtedly an alarm had been set off. Should he risk leaping the wall, fleeing across the waste? The chances, very bad in any case, would be nonexistent if he should become caught in the open. He ran to the tree, descended far more rapidly than he had mounted. Over the city sky-sleds were already appearing. Reith heard a far weird whistling which set his nerves on edge . . . He ran, cloak flapping, back under the trees. A gleam of water attracted his attention: a small pond, overgrown with pallid white water-plants. Throwing off his cloak and false cranium, Reith jumped into the water, submerged himself up to his nose, and waited.

Minutes passed. A squad of security guards on electric motorcycles dashed past. Two sky-sleds trailing scent-detectors drifted overhead, one to his right, the other to his left. They disappeared to the east; clearly the Blue Chasch thought he had crossed the wall, that he was at large outside the city. If this was the case, if they presently decided that he had escaped into the mountains, his chances would be thereby much improved . . . He became aware of something moving along the bottom of the pond. It felt muscular, purposeful. An eel? a water-snake? A tentacle? Reith jumped out of the pond. Ten feet away something broke the surface and made a sound like a snort of disgust.

Reith seized up the cloak and the false cranium and trudged dripping back down away from the mortuary.

He came upon a small lane winding among the Chaschmen bungalows. By night they seemed close, secretive, locked-in. The windows were small and none lower than eight feet from the ground. Some exuded a wavering yellow light, as if from a lamp, which puzzled Reith. Surely a race as technically capable as the Blue Chasch could provide their underlings electric or nucleonic illumination . . . Another paradox of Tschai.

The wet clothes not only chafed but smelled abominably—a situation which might camouflage his own scent, thought Reith. He pulled the false cranium over his skull, threw the cloak around his shoulders. Walking slow and stiff-legged, he continued toward the gate.

The sky was dark; neither Az nor Braz was in the sky, and the byways of Dadiche knew only the most casual illumination. Two Chaschmen came into view. Reith pulled down his chin, hunched his shoulders, walked stolidly forward. The two passed with no more than a glance.

Somewhat encouraged, Reith reached the central boulevard with the gate two hundred yards ahead. High lamps cast a yellow glare into the portal. Three guards in purple and gray were still in evidence, but they seemed slack and uninterested, and Reith was reinforced in his belief that the Blue Chasch thought him gone from the city.

Unfortunately, thought Reith, the Blue Chasch were wrong.

He considered the feasibility of sauntering up to the portal, dashing through and away into the darkness. The sky-sleds would instantly be after him, as well as platoons of guards on electric motorcycles. What with his reeking clothes, he would have no place to hide—unless he discarded all his garments and ran naked through the night.

Reith gave a soft grunt of disapproval . . . His attention was attracted by a tavern in the basement of a tall building. From the low windows came flickering red and yellow light, hoarse conversation, an occasional gust of bellowing laughter. Three Chaschmen came lurching forth; Reith turned his back and looked through the window down into a murky taproom, lit by firelight and the ubiquitous yellow lamps. A dozen Chaschmen, faces pinched and twisted under the grotesque false crania, sat hunched over stone pots of liquor, exchanging lewd banter with a small group of Chaschwomen. These wore gowns of black and green; bits of tinsel and ribbon bedizened their false scalps; their pug-noses were painted bright red. A dismal scene, thought Reith; still, it pointed up the essential humanity of the Chaschmen. Here were the universal ingredients of celebration: invigorating drink, gay women, camaraderie. The Chaschman version seemed somewhat leaden and dour . . . Another pair of Chaschmen passed close to Reith without remark. So far the disguise had been effective, though whether it would pass a more detailed examination Reith was uncertain. He walked slowly toward the gate, until he was barely fifty yards distant. He dared approach no further. He slid into a niche between two buildings and settled himself to watch the gate.

The night went on. The air became still and cold and Reith became aware of odors from the Dadiche gardens.

He dozed. When he awoke Az had appeared behind a line of

sentinel adarak. Reith shifted his position, groaned, massaged his neck, recoiling at the odor of the still damp garments.

At the gate two of the security guards had disappeared. The third stood torpidly, half-asleep. In the booths the attendants sat looking morosely out over the empty spaces. Reith settled back into his niche.

The east became bright with dawn; the city came alive. New personnel arrived at the portal. Reith watched the incoming and outgoing groups exchange information.

An hour later drays began to arrive from Pera. The first, drawn by a pair of great draft beasts, brought casks of pickles and fermented meat, and stank with a fervor that put Reith to shame. On the driver's bench sat two persons: Emmink, more sour, sulky and dire than ever, and Traz. "Forty-three," shouted Emmink. "A hundred and one," called Traz. The guards came out, counted barrels, inspected the wagon, then ordered Emmink to proceed.

As the wagon passed, Reith emerged from his niche, walked close beside. "Traz."

Traz looked down and made a small exclamation of satisfaction. "I knew you'd still be alive."

"Just barely. Do I look like a Chaschman?"

"Not too much. Keep the cloak over your chin and nose. . . . When we come back from market, up under the right foreleg of the right beast."

Reith turned aside into a secluded little nook behind a shed and watched the wagon move off toward the market.

An hour later it returned, moving slowly. Emmink guided it along the right side of the road. It passed Reith; he emerged from his hiding place. The wagon stopped; Traz jumped down as if to lash the barrels more securely, but blocking off the view from the rear.

Reith ran forward, ducked under the draft beast. Between the first and second right-hand legs hung a great leathery flap of skin. Between the belly and the skin five thongs had been tied to make a tight cramped hammock, into which Reith inserted himself. The wagon started forward; Reith could see nothing but the gray belly, the dangling flap, the first two legs.

The wagon paused at the gate. He heard voices, saw the pointed red sandals of the security guards. After a suspenseful wait, the wagon started forward, rumbled out toward the surrounding hills. Reith could see the gravel of the road, an occasional bit of vegetation, the ponderous legs, the dangling flap which at every step clamped in upon him.

At last the dray halted. Traz peered under the beast. "Out— no one is watching."

With almost insane relief Reith pulled himself from under the beast. He ripped off the false cranium, flung it in a ditch, threw off the cloak, the stinking jacket, the shirt, clambered up on the bed of the dray, where he slumped back against a barrel.

Traz resumed his seat beside Emmink, and the dray started forward. Traz looked back with concern. "Are you ill? Or wounded?"

"No. Tired. But alive—thanks to you. And Emmink, as well, or so it appears."

Traz gave Emmink a frowning glance. "Emmink has been no great help. It was necessary to make threats, to inflict a bruise or two."

"I see," said Reith. He turned a critical glance upon the draymaster's hunched shoulders. "I've had one or two harsh thoughts in connection with Emmink myself."

The shoulders quivered. Emmink swung around in his seat, thin face split in a yellow-toothed grin. "You'll recall, sir, that I conveyed you and instructed you, even before I knew your lordship's high rank."

" 'High rank'?" asked Reith. "What 'high rank'?"

"The council at Pera has appointed you chief executive," said Traz. And he added, in a disparaging tone: "High rank of a sort, I suppose."

11

REITH HAD NO inclination to rule Pera. The occupation would exhaust his energy, destroy his patience, restrict his scope of action and bring him no personal advantage. Perforce, he would tend to govern in terms of Earth social philosophy. He considered the population of Pera: a motley group. Fugitives, criminals, bandits, freaks, hybrids, nondescripts, nonesuchs: what would these poor wretches know of equity, juridical procedure, human dignity, the ideal of progress?

A challenge, to say the least.

What of the space-boat, what of his hopes of returning to Earth? His adventures in Dadiche had verified only the location of the space-boat. The Blue Chasch would doubtless be amused and interested should he demand the return of his property. Inducements? Reith could hardly promise Earth military assistance against the Dirdir or the Wankh—whichever were the current adversaries of the Blue Chasch. Compulsion? He had no leverage, no force to apply.

Another matter: the Blue Chasch were now aware of his existence. Undoubtedly they wondered as to his identity, his homeland. Tschai was vast, with remote regions where men might have produced almost anything. The Blue Chasch must even now be anxiously consulting their maps.

As Reith reflected, the dray ground up the hill, passed through Belbal Gap, rumbled down toward the steppe. Sunlight warmed Reith's skin; the steppe wind blew away the stench. He became drowsy and presently fell asleep.

He awoke to find the dray trundling over the ancient pavements of Pera. They entered the central plaza at the base of the citadel. As they passed the gibbets Reith saw swinging eight new bodies: Gnashters, the rakish swagger of their garments now a bedraggled and pathetic joke. Traz explained the circumstances, in the most casual of voices. "They decided to come down from the citadel, and so they did, waving their hands and laughing, as if the whole affair were a farce. How indignant they became when the militia seized them and hoisted them aloft! They were dead before they had ceased complaining!"

"So now the palace is empty," said Reith, looking up at the mass of slabs and stones.

"So far as I know. I suppose you will choose to live there?"

Traz's voice held a faint note of disapprobation. Reith grinned. The influence of Onmale persisted and occasionally manifested itself.

"No," said Reith. "Naga Goho lived there. If we moved in, people would think we were a new set of Gohos."

"It is a fine palace," said Traz, dubious now. "It contains many interesting objects . . ." He turned a quizzical glance toward Reith. "Apparently you have decided to rule Pera."

"Yes," said Reith. "Apparently I have."

* * *

At the Dead Steppe Inn Reith rubbed himself in oil, soft sand, sifted ashes. He rinsed himself in clean water and repeated the process, thinking that soap would be one of the first innovations he would bring to the people of Pera, and Tschai at large. Was it possible that a substance so relatively simple as soap was unknown on Tschai? He would ask Derl, Ylin-Ylan, whatever her name, if soap was known in Cath.

Scrubbed, shaved, in fresh linen and new sandals of soft leather, Reith ate a meal of porridge and stew in the commonroom. A change in the atmosphere was apparent. The personnel of the inn treated him with exaggerated respect; others in the room spoke in quiet voices, watching him from the side of their faces.

Reith noticed a group of men standing in the compound, muttering together and peering into the inn from time to time. When he had finished his meal they entered and came to stand in a line in front of him.

Reith looked them over, recognizing some who had been present at Naga Goho's execution. One was thin and yellow, with burning black eyes: a marsh-man, Reith guessed. Another appeared to be a mixture of Chaschman and Gray. Another was typical Gray, of medium height, bald with putty-colored skin, a fleshy lump of a nose, glossy protuberant eyes. The fourth was an old man from one of the nomad tribes, handsome in a haggard, wind-driven fashion; the fifth was short and barrel-shaped, with arms dangling almost to his knees, of derivation impossible to calculate. The old man of the steppes had been designated spokesman. He spoke in a husky voice. "We are the Committee of Five, formed according to your recommendation. We have held a long discussion. Inasmuch as you have been of assistance in destroying Naga Goho and the Gnashters, we wish to appoint you headman of Pera."

"Subject to our restraint and advice," appended the Chaschman-Gray.

Reith had still not come to a definite, irrevocable decision. Leaning back in his chair he surveyed the committee, and thought that seldom, if ever, had he seen a more heterogeneous group.

"It's not quite so easy," he said at last. "You might not be willing to cooperate with me. I wouldn't take on the job unless I was guaranteed that cooperation."

"Cooperation toward what?" the Gray asked.

"Toward changes. Extreme, far-reaching changes."

The committeemen examined him cautiously. "We are conservative folk," the Chaschman-Gray muttered. "Life is hard; we cannot afford risky experiments."

The old nomad gave a harsh crackling laugh. " 'Experiments'! We should welcome them! Any change can only be for the better! Let us hear what the man proposes!"

"Very well!" acceded the Chaschman-Gray. "It does no harm to listen; we are not committed."

Reith said, "I am of this man's opinion." He indicated the old nomad. "Pera is a tumble of ruins. The people here are little better than fugitives. They have no pride or self-respect; they live in holes, they are dirty and ignorant, they wear rags. What's worse, they don't seem to care."

The committee blinked in surprise. The old nomad gave a hoarse jeering laugh; the Chaschman-Gray scowled. The others looked doubtful. Retiring a few paces, they muttered among themselves, then turned back to Reith. "Can you explain in detail what you propose to do?"

Reith shook his head. "I haven't given the matter any thought. To be blunt, I am a civilized man; I was educated and trained in civilized circumstances. I know what men can achieve. It is a great deal—more perhaps than you can imagine. The folk of Pera are men; I would insist that they live like men."

"Yes, yes," cried the marsh-man, "but how? In what particular?"

"Well, in the first place, I would want a militia, disciplined, and well-trained, to maintain order, to protect the city and caravans from the Green Chasch. I would organize schools and a hospital; later a foundry, warehouses, a market. Meanwhile I would encourage people to build houses, in clean surroundings."

The committeemen fidgeted uneasily, looking askance at one another and at Reith. The old nomad grunted. "We are men, of course; who has denied it? And since we are men, we must live carefully. We do not desire to be Dirdir. Suffice that we survive."

The Gray said, "The Blue Chasch would never allow such pretensions. They tolerate us at Pera only because we are inconspicuous."

"But also because we supply certain of their wants," stated the short man. "They buy our produce cheap."

"It is never wise to irritate those in power," argued the Gray.

Reith held up his hand. "You've heard my program. If you won't cooperate wholeheartedly—select another chief."

The old nomad turned a searching glance at Reith, then drew the others apart. There was heated argument. Finally they returned. "We agree to your terms. You will be our chief."

Reith, who had been hoping that the committee would decide otherwise, heaved a small sigh. "Very well, so be it. I warn you, I'll demand a great deal from you. You'll work harder than ever before in your lives—for your own ultimate good. Or at least I hope so."

He spoke to the committee for an hour, explaining what he hoped to achieve, and succeeded in arousing interest, even guarded enthusiasm.

Late in the afternoon, Reith, with Anacho and three of the committee members, went to explore the erstwhile palace of Naga Goho.

Up the winding path they walked, with the grim pile of masonry looming overhead. They passed through the dank courtyard, into the main hall. Naga Goho's cherished possessions: the heavy benches and table, the rugs, wall-hangings, tripod lamps, the platters and urns were already filmed over with dust.

Adjoining the hall were sleeping chambers, smelling of soiled clothing and aromatic unguents. The corpse of Naga Goho's concubine lay as Reith had first discovered it. The group hastily drew back.

On the other side of the hall were storerooms stacked with great quantities of loot: bales of cloth, crates of leather, parcels of rare wood, tools, weapons, implements, ingots of raw metal, flasks of essence, books written in brown and gray dots upon black paper, which Anacho identified as Wankh production manuals. An alcove held a chest half-full of sequins. Two smaller coffers contained jewels, ornaments, trinkets, trifles: a magpie's hoard. The committeemen selected steel swords with filigree pommels and guards for themselves; Traz and Anacho did likewise. Traz, after a diffident glance at Reith, arrayed himself in a fine golden ocher cloak, boots of soft black leather, a beautifully wrought casque of thin steel, drooping and splaying to protect the nape of the neck.

Reith located several dozen energy pistols with spent powercells. These, according to Anacho, could be recharged from the power-cells which drove the drays: a fact evidently unknown to Naga Goho.

The sun was low in the west when they departed the gloomy palace. Crossing the courtyard Reith noticed a squat door set back in a niche. He heaved it open, to reveal a flight of steep stone stairs. Up wafted a dismal draft, reeking of mold, organic decay, filth—and something else: a musky dank stench which stiffened the hairs at the back of Reith's neck.

"Dungeons," said Anacho laconically. "Listen."

A feeble croaking murmur came up from below. Inside the door Reith found a lamp, but was unable to evoke light. Anacho tapped the top of the bulb, to produce a white radiance. "A Dirdir device."

The group descended the steps, ready for anything, and stepped forth into a high-vaulted chamber. Traz, seizing at Reith's arm, pointed; Reith saw a black shape gliding quietly off into the far shadows. "Pnume," muttered Anacho, hunching his shoulders. "They infest the ruined places of Tschai, like worms in old wood."

A high lamp cast a feeble light, revealing cages around the periphery of the room. In certain of these were bones, in others heaps of putrefying flesh, in others living creatures, from whom issued the sounds which the group had heard. "Water, water," moaned the shambling figures. "Give us water!"

Reith held the lamp close. "Chaschmen."

From a tank to the side of the room he filled pannikins of water and brought them to the cages.

The Chaschmen drank avidly and clamored for more, which Reith brought to them.

Heavy cages at the far end of the room held a pair of massive motionless figures with towering conical scalps.

"Green Chasch," whispered Traz. "What did Naga Goho do with these?"

Anacho said, "Notice: they peer in a single direction only, the direction of their horde. They are telepathic."

Reith dipped up two more pans of water, thrust them into the cages of the Green Chasch. The creatures reached ponderously, sucked the pans dry.

Reith returned to the Chaschmen. "How long have you been here?"

"A long, long time," croaked one of the captives. "I cannot say how long."

"Why were you caged?"

"Cruelty! Because we were Chaschmen!"

Reith returned to the committeemen. "Did you know they were here?"

"No! Naga Goho did as he pleased."

Reith moved the linch-pins, opened the doors. "Come forth; you are free. The men who captured you are dead."

The Chaschmen timorously crept forth. They went to the tank and drank more water. Reith turned back to examine the Green Chasch. "Very strange, strange indeed."

"Perhaps Goho used them as indicators," Anacho suggested. "He would know at all times the direction of their horde."

"No one can talk to them?"

"They do not talk; they transfer thoughts."

Reith turned to the committeemen. "Send up a dozen men, to carry the cages down to the plaza."

"Bah," muttered Bruntego the Gray. "Best kill the ugly beasts! Kill the Chaschmen as well!"

Reith turned him a quick glare. "We are not Gnashters! We kill from necessity only! As for the Chaschmen, let them go back to their servitude, or stay here as free men, whatever they wish."

Bruntego gave a sour grunt. "If we do not kill them, they will kill us."

Reith, making no answer, turned the lamp toward the remote parts of the dungeon, to find only dank stone walls. He could not learn how the Pnume had departed the chamber, nor could the Chaschmen give any coherent information. "They would come, silent as devils, to look at us, with never a word, nor would they bring us water!"

"Odd creatures," ruminated Reith.

"They are the weirds of Tschai!" cried the Chaschmen, trembling to the emotion of their new freedom. "They should be purged from the planet!"

"As well as the Dirdir, the Wankh and the Chasch," said Reith, grinning.

"No, not the Chasch. We are Chasch, did you not know?"

"You are men."

"No, we are Chasch in the larval stage; this is prime verity!"

"Bah!" said Reith, suddenly angry. "Take off those ridiculous false heads." He stepped forward, jerked away the conical head-pieces. "You are men, you are nothing else! Why do you allow the Chasch to victimize you?"

The Chaschmen fell silent, glancing fearfully at the cages as if they expected a new incarceration.

"Come," said Reith brusquely. "Let's get out of here."

A week passed. With nothing better to do, Reith flung himself into his job. He selected a group of the most obviously intelligent young men and women, whom he would teach and who would teach others. He formed a civic militia, delegating authority in this case to Baojian, the erstwhile caravan-master. With the help of Anacho and Tostig the old Nomad, he drew up a tentative legal code. Over and over he explained the benefits to be derived from his innovations, arousing a variety of responses: interest, apprehension, dubious sneers, enthusiasm, as often as not blank incomprehension. He learned that there was more to organizing a government than merely giving orders; he was required to be everywhere at once. And always at the back of his mind was apprehension: what were the Blue Chasch planning? He could not believe that they had so easily abandoned their efforts to capture him. Beyond doubt they employed spies. They would therefore be informed of events in Pera, and hence be in no great haste. But sooner or later they would come to take him. A man of ordinary prudence would flee Pera instantly. Reith, for a variety of reasons, was disinclined to flight.

The Chaschmen from the dungeons displayed no eagerness to return to Dadiche; Reith assumed that they were fugitives from Chasch justice. The Green Chasch warriors were a problem. Reith could not bring himself to kill them, but popular opinion would have been outraged had he released them outright. As a compromise the cages stood in the plaza, and the creatures served as a spectacle for the people of Pera. The Green Chasch ignored the attention, facing steadily to the north, telepathically linked—so stated Anacho—to the parent horde.

Reith's principal solace was the Flower of Cath, although the girl mystified him. He could not read her mood. During the long caravan journey she had been melancholy, distrait, somewhat haughty. She had become gentle and loving, if at times absent-minded. Reith found her more alluring than ever, full of a hundred sweet surprises. But her melancholy persisted.

Homesickness, decided Reith; almost certainly she longed for her home in Cath. With a dozen other preoccupations, Reith postponed the day when he must reckon with Derl's yearnings.

The three Chaschmen, so Reith presently learned, were not citizens of Dadiche, but hailed from Saaba, a city to the south. One evening in the common-room they took Reith to task for what they characterized as "extravagant ambitions." "You wish to ape the higher races; you will only come to grief! Sub-men are incapable of civilization."

"You don't know what you're talking about," said Reith, amused by their earnestness.

"Of course we do; are we not Chaschmen, the larval stage of the Blue Chasch? Who would know better?"

"Anyone with a smattering of biology."

The Chaschmen made fretful gestures. "A sub-man, you; and jealous of the advanced race."

Reith said, "In Dadiche I saw the mortuary or death-house—whatever you call it. I saw the Blue Chasch split a dead Chaschman's skull and put a Blue Chasch imp into the cold brains. They play games with you; they trick you to ensure your servitude. The Dirdir no doubt use a parallel technique upon the Dirdirmen, though I doubt if the Dirdirmen expect to become Dirdir." He looked down the table to Anacho. "What of that?"

Anacho's voice trembled slightly. "The Dirdirmen do not expect to become Dirdir; this is superstition. They are Sun, we are Shade; but both from the Primeval Egg. Dirdir are the highest form of cosmic life; Dirdirmen can only emulate, and this we do, with pride. What other race has produced such glory, achieved such magnificence?"

"The race of men," said Reith.

Anacho's face twitched in a sneer. "In Cath? Lotus-eaters. The Merribs? Vagrant artisans. The Dirdir stand alone on Tschai."

"No, no, no!" bawled the Chaschmen simultaneously. "Submen are the culls and dross of Chaschmen. Some become clients of the Dirdir. True men come from Zoör, the Chasch world."

Anacho turned away in disgust. Reith said, "This is not the case, though I don't expect you to believe me. You are both wrong."

Anacho the Dirdirman spoke in a voice carefully casual. "You are so definite; you puzzle me. Perhaps you can enlighten us further."

"Perhaps I can," said Reith. "At the moment I don't care to do so."

"Why not?" Anacho persisted. "Such enlightenment would be useful to all of us."

"The facts are as well-known to you as they are to me," said Reith. "Draw your own deductions."

"Which facts?" blurted the Chaschmen. "What deductions?"

"Aren't they plain? The Chaschmen are in servitude, precisely as are the Dirdirmen. Men are not biologically compatible with either of these races, nor with the Wankh nor the Pnume. Men certainly did not originate on Tschai. The deduction is that they were brought here as slaves, long ages ago, from the world of men."

The Chaschmen grunted; Anacho raised his eyes and studied the ceiling. The men of Pera sitting at the table sighed in wonder.

There was further talk, which became excited and vehement as the evening wore on. The Chaschmen went off to a corner and argued among themselves, two disputing with one.

On the following morning the three Chaschmen departed Pera for Dadiche, riding, so it happened, Emmink's dray. Reith watched them go with misgiving. They would undoubtedly report upon his activities and radical doctrines. The Blue Chasch would not approve. Existence, Reith reflected, had become extremely complex. The future seemed murky, even grim. Once again he considered hasty departure into the wilderness. But the prospect still had no appeal.

During the afternoon Reith watched the first draft of the militia at drill: six platoons of fifty men each, armed diversely with catapults, swords, short cutlasses, in striking variety of garments: pantaloons, smocks, burnouses, flared jackets with short skirts, rags and strips of fur. Some wore beards, others varnished topknots; the hair of others hung to their shoulders. Reith thought that never had he seen so sad a spectacle. He watched in mingled amusement and despair as they stumbled and slouched, with grumbling bad grace, through the exercises he had ordained. The six lieutenants, who showed no great enthusiasm, perspired and swore, gave orders more or less at random, while Baojian's aplomb was sorely taxed.

Reith finally demoted two lieutenants on the spot and appointed two new men from the ranks. He climbed up on a wagon, called the men in about him. "You are not performing well! Don't you understand what you are here for? To learn to protect yourselves!" He looked from one sullen face to another then pointed down to a man who had been muttering to his fellow. "You! What are you saying? Speak up!"

"I said that this prancing and marching is foolishness, a waste of energy; what benefit can arise from such antics?"

"The benefit is this. You learn to obey orders, quickly and decisively. You learn to function as a corps. Twenty men acting together are stronger than a hundred men at odds with each other. In a battle situation the leader makes plans; the disciplined warriors carry out these plans. Without discipline, plans are useless and battles are lost. Now do you understand?"

"Bah. How can men win battles? The Blue Chasch have energetics and battle-rafts. We have a few sand-blasts. The Green Chasch are indomitable; they would kill us like emmets. It is easier to hide among the ruins. This is how men have always lived in Pera."

"Conditions are different," said Reith. "If you don't want to do a man's work, you can do a woman's work and wear woman's clothes. Take your choice." He waited but the dissident only glowered and shuffled his feet.

Reith came down from the wagon and gave a series of orders. Certain men were sent up to the citadel to fetch bolts of cloth and leather. Others brought shears and razors; the men of the militia, despite protests, were shorn clean. Meanwhile the women of the city had gathered and were put to work cutting out and sewing uniforms: long sleeveless smocks of white cloth with black lightning-bolts appliquéd to the chest. Corporals and sergeants wore black shoulder tabs; the lieutenants had short red sleeves to their uniforms.

On the following day the militia, wearing the new garments, drilled again, and on this occasion were noticeably smarter—indeed, thought Reith, almost jaunty.

On the morning of the third day after the Chaschmen's departure Reith's doubts were resolved. A large raft, sixty feet long and thirty feet wide, came gliding over the steppe. It flew in a single slow circle over Pera, then settled into the plaza directly before the Dead Steppe Inn. A dozen burly Chaschmen—Security Guards in gray pantaloons and purple jackets—jumped out and stood with hands at their weapons. Six Blue Chasch stood on the deck of the raft staring around the plaza from under overhanging brows. These Blue Chasch appeared to be special personages; they wore tight suits of silver filigree, tall silver morions, silver caps at the joints of their arms and legs.

The Blue Chasch spoke briefly to the Chaschmen; two marched to the door of the inn, and spoke to the innkeeper. "A man calling himself Reith has established himself as your chief. Fetch him forth, to the attention of the Lord Chasch."

The innkeeper, half-awed, half-truculent, was prompted to a snarling obsequiousness. "He is somewhere at hand; you will have to wait till he arrives."

"Notify him! Be quick!"

Reith received the summons gloomily, but without surprise. He sat thinking a moment or two; then, heaving a deep sigh, he came to a decision, which, for better or worse, must alter the lives of all the men of Pera, and perhaps all the men of Tschai. He turned to Traz, gave a set of orders, then slowly went into the common-room of the inn. "Tell the Chasch that I'll speak to them in here."

The innkeeper relayed the message to the Chaschmen, who in turn spoke to the Blue Chasch.

The response was a set of glottal sounds. The Blue Chasch descended to the ground, approached the inn, to stand in a silver-glittering line. The Chaschmen entered the inn. One bawled, "Which is the man who is chief? Which is he? Let him hold up his hand!"

Reith thrust past them and stepped out into the compound. He faced the Blue Chasch, who stared back at him portentously. Reith examined the alien visages with fascination: the eyes like small metal balls glistening under the shadow of the cephalic overhang, the complex nasal processes, the silver morion and filigree armor. At the moment they seemed neither crafty, whimsical, capricious, nor given to cruel facetiousness; their mien rather was menacing.

Reith confronted them, arms folded across his chest. He waited, exchanging stare for stare.

One of the Blue Chasch wore a morion with a higher spine than the others. He spoke, in the strangled glottal voice typical of the race. "What do you do here in Pera?"

"I am the chosen chief."

"You are the man who made an unauthorized visit to Dadiche, who visited the District Technical Center."

Reith made no reply.

"Well then," called the Blue Chasch, "what do you say? Do not deny the charge; your scent is individual. In some fashion you entered and departed Dadiche; and made furtive investigations. Why?"

"Because I had never visited Dadiche before," said Reith. "You are now visiting Pera without express authorization; however, you are welcome, so long as you obey our laws. I would like to think that the men of Pera could visit Dadiche on the same basis."

The Chaschmen gave hoarse chuckles; the Blue Chasch stared in gloomy shock. The spokesman said, "You have been espousing a false doctrine, and persuading the men of Pera to folly. Where do you derive these ideas?"

"The ideas are neither 'false doctrine' nor 'folly.' They are self-evident."

"You must come with us to Dadiche," said the Blue Chasch, "and clarify a number of peculiar circumstances. Go aboard the sky-raft."

Reith smilingly shook his head. "If you have questions, ask them now. Then I will ask you my questions."

The Blue Chasch made a signal to the Chaschmen guards. They moved forward to seize Reith. He took a step back, looked up at the upper windows. Down came a fusillade of catapult bolts, piercing the Chaschmen's foreheads and necks. But those bolts aimed at the Blue Chasch swerved aside, diverted by a force-field, and the Blue Chasch stood unscathed. They seized their own weapons, but before they could aim and fire, Reith unfolded his arms. He held his energy cell. In a quick sweep of his arm he burnt off the heads and shoulders of the six Blue Chasch. The bodies sprang into the air by some peculiar reflex, then sprawled to the ground with a multiple thud, where they lay covered by globules of molten silver.

The silence was complete. The onlookers seemed to be holding their breaths. All turned to look from the corpses to Reith; then, as if by single presentiment, all turned to look toward Dadiche.

"What will we do now?" whispered Bruntego the Gray. "We are doomed. They will feed us to their red flowers."

"Precisely," said Reith, "unless we take steps to prevent them." He signaled to Traz; they collected weapons and other gear from the headless Blue Chasch and the Chaschmen; then Reith ordered the bodies carried away and buried.

He went to the sky-raft, climbed aboard. The controls—clusters of pedals, knobs and flexible arms—were beyond his comprehension. Anacho the Dirdirman came up to look casually into the raft. Reith asked, "Do you understand the working of this thing?"

Anacho gave a contemptuous grunt. "Of course. It is the old Daidne System."

Reith looked back along the length of the raft. "What are those tubes? Chasch energetics?"

"Yes. Obsolete, of course, compared to Dirdir weapons."

"What is the range?"

"No great distance. These are low-power tubes."

"Suppose we mounted four or five sand-blasts on the raft. We'd have considerable fire-power."

Anacho gave a curt nod. "Crude and makeshift, but feasible."

On the afternoon of the following day a pair of rafts drifted high above Pera and returned to Dadiche without landing. The next morning a column of wagons came down from Belbal Gap, conveying two hundred Chaschmen and a hundred Blue Chasch officers. Overhead slid four rafts, carrying Blue Chasch gun-crews.

The wagons halted a half-mile from Pera; the troops deployed into four companies, which separated and approached Pera from all four sides, while the rafts floated overhead.

Reith divided the militia into two squads, and sent them sidling through the ruins, to the outskirts of the city on the south and west sides, where the Chasch troops would make first contact.

The militia waited until the Chaschmen and the Blue Chasch, moving warily, had penetrated a hundred yards into the city. Suddenly appearing from concealment, all fired weapons: catapults, sand-blasts, hand-guns from the Goho arsenal, those taken from the Chasch corpses.

Fire was concentrated on the Blue Chasch, and of these two-thirds died in the first five minutes, as well as half the Chaschmen. The remainder faltered, then fled back out onto the open steppe.

The rafts overhead swooped low and began to sweep the

ruins with slay-beams. The militia now took shelter while the rafts descended even lower.

High above appeared another raft: that which Reith had armed with sand-blasts, then had taken five miles out on the steppe and hidden under brush. It dropped quietly upon the Chasch rafts, lower, lower, lower . . . The men at the sand-blasts and at the energetic beams opened fire. The four rafts dropped like stones. The raft then crossed the city and opened fire on the two companies which were entering the north and east sectors of the city, while the militia opened fire from the flanks. The Chasch troops drew back with heavy losses. Harassed by the bombardment from the air, they broke ranks and streamed off across the steppe in total disorder, pursued by the Peran militia.

12

REITH CONFERRED WITH his victory-flushed lieutenants. "We won today because they took us light. They still can bring overwhelming force against us. My guess is that tonight they will organize a strong war party: all their rafts, all their troops. Then tomorrow they will come forth to punish us. Does this sound reasonable?"

No one made dissent.

"Since we are committed to hostilities, best that we take the initiative, and try to arrange a few surprises for the Chasch. They have a poor opinion of men, and we might be able to do them some harm. This means taking our limited fire-power to where it can do the most damage."

Bruntego the Gray shuddered and clasped his hands to his face. "They have a thousand Chaschmen soldiers, and more. They have sky-rafts and energetic weapons—whereas we are only men, armed for the most part with catapults."

"Catapults kill a man just as dead as energy beams," Reith commented.

"But the rafts, the projectiles, the power and intelligence of the Blue Chasch! They will destroy us totally and reduce Pera to a crater."

Tostig the old nomad demurred. "We have served too well, too cheaply in the past. Why should they rob themselves for the sake of sheer drama?"

"Because that is the Blue Chasch way!"

Tostig shook his head. "Old Chasch perhaps. Blue Chasch no. They will prefer to besiege us, starve us, and take the leaders back to Dadiche for punishment."

"Reasonable," agreed Anacho, "but can we expect even Blue Chasch to behave reasonably? All Chasch are half-mad."

"For this reason," said Reith, "we must match them caprice for caprice!"

Bruntego the Gray said with a sniff, "Caprice is the only quality in which we can match the Blue Chasch."

The discussion continued; proposals were set forth and debated and at last agreement was grudgingly reached. Messengers were sent forth to arouse the population. Amid some small protest and wailing, women, children, the aged and the uncooperative were marshaled aboard drays and sent off through the night, to a dismal gorge twenty miles south, where they would establish a temporary camp.

The militia assembled with all its weapons, then marched off through the night toward Belbal Gap.

Reith, Traz and Anacho remained in Pera. The cage containing the Green Chasch warriors had been swathed in cloth and loaded aboard the raft. At sunrise Anacho took the raft aloft and sent it sliding in that direction toward which the Green Chasch sat staring: north by east. Twenty miles passed beneath, and another twenty; then Traz, who sat watching the Green Chasch through a peephole, cried out, "They are turning, twisting about—toward the west!"

Anacho swung the raft toward the west, and a few moments later a Green Chasch encampment was discovered in a grove of grass-trees beside a swamp. "Don't approach too closely," said Reith, examining the camp through his scanscope. "It's enough to know that they are here. Back to Belbal Gap."

The raft returned south, skimming the palisades which faced west toward the Schanizade Ocean. Passing over Belbal Gap, they settled upon a vantage point overlooking both Dadiche and Pera.

Two hours passed. Reith became increasingly fretful. His plans were based upon hypothesis and rational supposition; the Chasch were a notoriously capricious race. Then from Dadiche, to Reith's vast relief, came a long dark column. Looking through his scanscope Reith saw a hundred drays loaded with Blue

Chasch and Chaschmen, as many others carrying weapons and crates of equipment.

"This time," said Reith, they take us seriously." He scanned the sky. "No rafts visible. Undoubtedly they'll send something up for reconnaissance, at the very least . . . Time to be moving. They'll be coming through Belbal Gap in a half-hour."

They took the raft down to the steppe and landed several miles south of the road. They rolled the cage to the ground, pulled away the covering cloth. The monstrous green warriors sprang forward to peer out across the landscape.

Reith unlocked the door, slipped back the bolt and retreated to the raft, which Anacho at once took into the air. The Green Chasch sprang forth with ear-splitting yells of triumph, to stand like giants. They rolled their metallic eyes up at the raft, raised their arms in gestures of detestation. Turning swiftly north, they set off across the steppe, at the stiff-legged Green Chasch jog.

Over Belbal Gap came the drays from Dadiche. The Green Chasch stopped short, stared in wonder, then jogged forward to a clump of gart-furze and stood immobile, almost invisible.

Down the track came the great days, until the line of vehicles stretched a mile across the waste.

Anacho slid the raft up a dark gully, almost to the ridge, and landed. Reith searched the sky for rafts, then looked out across the panorama to the east. The Green Chasch, among the gart-furze copses, could not be seen. The war force from Dadiche was a menacing dark caterpillar crawling toward the ruins of old Pera.

Forty miles north the Green Chasch were camped.

Reith returned to the raft. "We've done what we can. Now—we wait."

The Blue Chasch expedition approached Pera, broke into four companies as before and surrounded the deserted ruins. Energetic beams were aimed at suspected strongpoints; scouts ran forward under cover of the weapons. They gained the first tumble of concrete blocks, then, drawing no fire, paused to regroup and to select new objectives.

Half an hour later the scouts emerged from the city, herding before them those folk who, from obstreperousness or simple inertia, had elected to remain in Pera.

Another fifteen minutes passed while these persons were interrogated. There was a period of indecision as the Blue Chasch leadership took counsel among themselves. Clearly the empty city was an unexpected development, and posed a perplexing dilemma.

The companies which had circled the city returned to the main force; presently all started back toward Dadiche, disconsolate and grim.

Reith searched the northern waste for movement. If there was validity in the theory of telepathic communication between the Green Chasch, if they hated the Blue Chasch as furiously as reported, they should now be appearing on the scene. But the steppe spread away into the northern murk empty and devoid of movement.

Back toward Belbal Gap moved the Blue Chasch war-force. From the dark green gart-furze, from copses of laggard bush, from salt-grass clumps, apparently from nowhere, erupted a horde of Green Chasch. Reith could not comprehend how so many warriors, riding gigantic leap-horses, had approached so inconspicuously. They hurled themselves upon the column, striking ten-foot arcs with their swords. The heavy weapons on the drays could not be brought to bear; the Green Chasch raged up and down the line doing carnage.

Reith turned away, half-sickened. He climbed aboard the raft. "Back across the mountains, to our own men."

The raft joined the militia at the agreed rendezvous, a gully half a mile south of Belbal Gap. The militia set off down the hill, keeping to the cover of trees and moss-hedge. Reith remained with the raft, searching the sky through the scanscope, apprehensive of Blue Chasch reconnaissance rafts. As he watched, a score of rafts rose from Dadiche to fly at full speed to the east: apparently reinforcement for the beleaguered war-party. Reith watched them disappear over Belbal Gap. Turning the scanscope back toward Dadiche, he glimpsed a sparkle of white uniforms up under the walls. "Now," he told Anacho. "As good a time as any."

The raft slid down toward the main portal into Dadiche: closer and closer. The guards, conceiving the raft to be one of their own, craned their necks in perplexity. Reith, steeling himself, pulled the trigger of the forward sand-blast. The way into Dadiche was open. The Pera militia surged into the city.

Jumping down from the raft, Reith sent two platoons to seize the raft depot. Another platoon remained at the portal with the greater part of the sand-blasts and energetics. Two platoons were sent to patrol the city and enforce the occupation.

These last two platoons, as fierce and unrelenting as any other inhabitants of Tschai, ranged through the half-deserted avenues, killing Blue Chasch and Chaschmen, and any Chaschwomen who offered resistance. The discipline of two days swiftly evaporated; a thousand generations of resentment exploded into blood-lust and massacre.

Reith, with Anacho, Traz and six others, rode the raft to the District Technical Center. The doors were closed; the building seemed vacant. The raft dropped beside the center portal; sand-blasts broke down the doors. Reith, unable to contain his anxiety, ran into the building.

There, as before: the familiar shape of the space-boat.

Reith approached with heart thumping in his throat. The hull was cut open; the drive-mechanisms, the accumulators, the converter: all had been removed. The boat was a hulk.

The prospect of finding the boat in near-operative condition had been an impossible dream. Reith had known as much. But irrational optimism had persisted.

Now, irrational optimism and all hope of return to Earth must be put aside. The boat had been gutted. The engines had been dismantled, the drive-tank opened, the exquisite balance of forces disrupted.

Reith became aware of Anacho standing at his shoulder. "This is not a Blue Chasch space-boat," said Anacho reflectively. "Nor is it Dirdir, nor Wankh."

Reith leaned back against a bench, his mind drained of vigor. "True."

"It is built with great skill; it shows refined design," mused Anacho. "Where was it built?"

"On Earth," said Reith.

" 'Earth'?"

"The planet of men."

Anacho turned away, his bald harlequin-face pinched and drawn, the axioms of his own existence shattered. "An interesting concept," he murmured over his shoulder.

Reith looked somberly through the space-boat but found little to interest him. Presently he returned outside, where he received a report from the platoon guarding the portal. Remnants of the Blue Chasch army had been sighted coming down the mountainside, in sufficient numbers to suggest that they had finally beaten off the Green Chasch.

Those platoons which had been sent to patrol the city were completely out of control and could not be recalled. Two platoons held the landing field, leaving only a single platoon at the portal—something over a hundred men.

An ambush was prepared. The portal was returned to the similitude of normalcy. Three men disguised as Chaschmen stood inside the wicket.

The remnants of the war-force approached the portal. They noticed nothing amiss and started to enter the city. Sand-blasts and energetics opened fire; the column withered, dissipated. The survivors were too stunned to resist. A few tottered wildly back into the parkland, pursued by yelling men in white uniforms; others stood in a stupid huddle to be passively slaughtered.

The battle-rafts were luckier. Observing the débâcle, they swooped back up into the sky. The militia-men, unfamiliar with the Blue Chasch ground guns, fired as best they could and, more by luck than by skill, destroyed four rafts. The others swung in high bewildered circles for five minutes, then bore south, toward Saaba, Dkekme, Audsch.

Spasms of fighting occurred throughout the rest of the afternoon, wherever the Peran militia encountered Blue Chasch who sought to defend themselves. The remainder—aged, females, imps alike—were slaughtered. Reith interceded with some success on behalf of the Chaschmen and Chaschwomen, saving all but the purple and gray-clad security guards, who shared the fate of their masters.

The remaining Chaschmen and Chaschwomen, throwing aside their false crania, gathered in a sullen crowd on the main avenue.

At sunset the militia, sated with killing, burdened with loot and unwilling to prowl the dead city after dark, assembled near the portal. Fires were built, food prepared and eaten.

Reith, taking pity on the miserable Chaschmen, whose world had suddenly collapsed, went to where they sat in a dispirited group, the women keening softly for those who were dead.

One burly individual spoke up truculently. "What do you propose to do with us?"

"Nothing," said Reith. "We destroyed the Blue Chasch because they attacked us. You are men; so long as you do us no harm, we shall do you none."

The Chaschman grunted. "Already you have harmed many of us."

"Because you chose to fight with the Chasch against men, which is unnatural."

The Chaschman scowled. "What is unnatural about that? We are Chaschmen, the first phase of the great cycle."

"Utter nonsense," said Reith. "You are no more Chasch than the Dirdirman yonder is Dirdir. Both of you are men. The Chasch and the Dirdir have enslaved you, plundered your lives. High time that you knew the truth!"

The Chaschwomen halted their keening, the Chaschmen turned blank faces toward Reith.

"So far as I am concerned," said Reith, "you can live as you like. The city of Dadiche is yours—so long as the Blue Chasch do not return."

"What do you mean by that?" quavered the Chaschmen.

"Precisely what I said. Tomorrow we return to Pera. Dadiche is yours."

"All very well—but what if the Blue Chasch come back, from Saaba, from Dkekme, from the Lizizaudre, as they surely will?"

"Kill them, chase them away! Dadiche is now a city of men! And if you don't believe that the Blue Chasch victimized you, go look into the death-house under the wall. You are told that you are larva, that the imp germinates in your brain. Go examine the brains of dead Chaschmen. You will find no imps—only the brains of men.

"So far as we are concerned, you can return to your homes. The only proscription I put upon you are the false heads. If you wear them we will consider you not men but Blue Chasch and deal with you accordingly."

Reith returned to his own camp; diffidently, as if they could not believe Reith's statement, the erstwhile Chaschmen slipped off through the dusk for their homes.

Anacho spoke to Reith. "I listened to what you said. You know nothing about the Dirdir and the Dirdirmen! Even were your theories valid, we would still remain Dirdirmen! We recognize excellence, superlativity; we aspire to emulate the ineffable—an impossible ideal, since Shade can never out-glow Sun, and men can never surpass Dirdir."

"For an intelligent man," snapped Reith, "you are extremely obstinate and unimaginative. Someday I am sure you will recognize your error; until then, believe whatever you care to believe."

13

BEFORE DAWN THE camp was astir. Drays laden with loot moved off westward, black against the ale-colored sky.

In Dadiche, the Chaschmen, peculiarly bald and gnomish without their false skulls, collected corpses, carried them to a great pit and buried them. A score of Blue Chasch had been flushed from hiding. The killing lust of the Perans having subsided, they were confined in a stockade, from which they stared in stone-eyed bewilderment at the coming and going of the men.

Reith was concerned over the possibility of counterattack from the Blue Chasch cities to the south. Anacho made light of the matter. "They have no stomach for fighting. They menace the Dirdir cities with torpedoes, but only to avoid war. They never challenge, they are content to live in their gardens. They might send Chaschmen to harass us, but I suspect they will do nothing whatever, unless we threaten them directly."

"Perhaps so." Reith released the captive Blue Chasch. "Go to the cities of the south," he told them. "Inform the Blue Chasch of Saaba and Dkekme that if they molest us we will destroy them."

"It is a long march," croaked the Blue Chasch. "Must we go on foot? Give us one of the rafts!"

"Walk! We owe you nothing!"

The Blue Chasch departed.

Still not wholly convinced that the Blue Chasch would refrain from seeking vengeance, Reith ordered weapons mounted on those nine rafts captured at the Dadiche depot and flew them to secluded areas on the hills.

On the following day, in the company of Traz, Anacho and Derl, he explored Dadiche in a more leisurely fashion. At the Technical Center he once more examined the hulk of his spaceboat, with an eye to its ultimate repair. "If I had the full use of this workshop," he said, "and if I had the help of twenty expert technicians, I might be able to build a new drive system. It might be more practical to try to adapt the Chasch drive to the boat—but then there would be control problems . . . Better to build a whole new boat."

Derl frowned at the quiet space-boat. "You are so intent, then, on departing Tschai? You have not yet visited Cath. You might wish never to depart."

"Possibly," said Reith. "But you have never visited Earth. You might not want to return to Tschai."

"It must be a very strange world," mused the Flower of Cath. "Are the women of Earth beautiful?"

"Some of them," Reith replied. He took her hand. "There are beautiful women on Tschai, as well. The name of one of them is—" And he whispered a name in her ear.

Blushing, she put her hand to his mouth. "The others might hear!"

SERVANTS
OF
THE
WANKH

1

TWO THOUSAND MILES east of Pera, over the heart of the Dead Steppe, the sky-raft faltered, flew smoothly for a moment, then jerked and bucked in a most ominous fashion. Adam Reith looked aft in dismay, then ran to the control belvedere. Lifting the voluted bronze housing, he peered here and there among the scrolls, floral hatchings, grinning imp faces which almost mischievously camouflaged the engine.* He was joined by the Dirdirman Ankhe at afram Anacho.

Reith asked, "Do you know what's wrong?"

Anacho pinched up his pale nostrils, muttered something about an "antiquated Chasch farrago" and "insane expedition to begin with." Reith, accustomed to the Dirdirman's foibles, realized that he was too vain to admit ignorance, too disdainful to avow knowledge so crass.

The raft shuddered again. Simultaneously from a four-pronged case of black wood to the side of the engine compartment came small rasping noises. Anacho gave it a lordly rap with his knuckles. The groaning and shuddering ceased. "Corrosion," said Anacho. "Electromorphic action across a hundred years or longer. I believe this to be a copy of the unsuccessful Heizakim Bursa, which the Dirdir abandoned two hundred years ago."

"Can we make repairs?"

"How should I know such things? I would hardly dare touch it."

They stood listening. The engine sighed on without further pause. At last Reith lowered the housing. The two returned forward.

Traz lay curled on a settee after standing a night watch. On

---

* Such elaborations were neither ornament nor functional disguise, but expressed, rather, the Chasch obsession for complication as an end in itself. Even the nomadic Green Chasch shared the trait. Examining their saddlery and weapons, Reith had been struck by a similarity to the metalwork of the ancient Scyths.

the green crush-cushioned seat under the ornate bow lantern sat the Flower of Cath, one leg tucked beneath the other, head on her forearms, staring eastward toward Cath. So had she huddled for hours, hair blowing in the wind, speaking no word to anyone. Reith found her conduct perplexing. At Pera she had yearned for Cath; she could talk of nothing else but the ease and grace of Blue Jade Palace, of her father's gratitude if Reith would only bring her home. She had described wonderful balls, extravaganzas, water-parties, masques according to the turn of the "round." ("Round? What did she mean by 'round'?" asked Reith. Ylin Ylan, the Flower of Cath, laughed excitedly. "It's just the way things are, and how they become! Everybody must know and the clever ones anticipate; that's why they're clever! It's all such fun!") Now that the journey to Cath was actually underway the Flower's mood had altered. She had become pensive, remote, and evaded all questions as to the source of her abstraction. Reith shrugged and turned away. Their intimacy was at an end: all for the best, or so he told himself. Still, the question nagged at him: why? His purpose in flying to Cath was twofold: first, to fulfill his promise to the girl; secondly, to find, or so he hoped, a technical basis to permit the construction of a spaceboat, no matter how small or crude. If he could rely upon the cooperation of the Blue Jade Lord, so much the better. Indeed, such sponsorship was a necessity.

The route to Cath lay across the Dead Steppe, south under the Ojzanalai Mountains, northeast along the Lok Lu Steppe, across the Zhaarken or the Wild Waste, over Achenkin Strait to the city Nerv, then south down the coast of Charchan to Cath. For the raft to fail at any stage of the journey short of Nerv meant disaster. As if to emphasize the point, the raft gave a single small jerk, then once more flew smoothly.

The day passed. Below rolled the Dead Steppe, dun and gray in the wan light of Carina 4269. At sunset they crossed the great Yatl River and all night flew under the pink moon Az and the blue moon Braz. In the morning low hills showed to the north, which ultimately would swell and thrust high to become the Ojzanalais.

At midmorning they landed at a small lake to refill water tanks. Traz was uneasy. "Green Chasch are near." He pointed to a forest a mile south. "They hide there, watching us."

Before the tanks were full, a band of forty Green Chasch on

leap-horses lunged from the forest. Ylin Ylan was perversely slow in boarding the raft. Reith hustled her aboard; Anacho thrust over the lift-arm—perhaps too hurriedly. The engine sputtered; the raft pitched and lurched.

Reith ran aft, flung up the housing, pounded the black case. The sputtering stopped; the raft lifted only yards ahead of the bounding warriors and their ten-foot swords. The leap-horses slid to a halt, the warriors aimed catapults and the air streamed with long iron bolts. But the raft was five hundred feet high; one or two of the bolts bumped into the hull at the height of their trajectory and fell away.

The raft, shuddering spasmodically, moved off to the east. The Green Chasch set off in pursuit; the raft, sputtering, pitching, yawing, and occasionally dropping its bow in a sickening fashion gradually left them behind.

The motion became intolerable. Reith jarred the black case again and again without significant effect. "We've got to make repairs," he told Anacho.

"We can try. First we must land."

"On the steppe? With the Green Chasch behind us?"

"We can't stay aloft."

Traz pointed north, to a spine of hills terminating in a set of isolated buttes. "Best that we land on one of those flat-topped peaks."

Anacho nudged the raft around to the north, provoking an even more alarming wobble; the bow began to gyrate like an eccentric toy.

"Hang on!" Reith cried out.

"I doubt if we can reach that first hill," muttered Anacho.

"Try for the next one!" yelled Traz. Reith saw that the second of the buttes, with sheer vertical walls, was clearly superior to the first—if the raft would stay in the air that long.

Anacho cut speed to a mere drift. The raft wallowed across the intervening space to the second butte, and grounded. The absence of motion was like silence after noise.

The travelers descended from the raft, muscles stiff from tension. Reith looked around the horizon in disgust: hard to imagine a more desolate spot than this, four hundred feet above the center of the Dead Steppe. So much for his hope of an easy passage to Cath.

Traz, going to the edge of the butte, peered over the cliff. "We may not even be able to get down."

The survival kit which Reith had salvaged from the wrecked scout boat included a pellet gun, an energy cell, an electronic telescope, a knife, antiseptics, a mirror, a thousand feet of strong cord. "We can get down," said Reith. "I'd prefer to fly." He turned to Anacho, who stood glumly considering the sky-raft. "Do you think we can make repairs?"

Anacho rubbed his long white hands together in distaste. "You must realize that I have no such training in these matters."

"Show me what's wrong," said Reith. "I can probably fix it."

Anacho's droll face grew even longer. Reith was the living refutation of his most cherished axioms. According to orthodox Dirdir doctrine, Dirdir and Dirdirmen had evolved together in a primeval egg on the Dirdir homeworld Sibol; the only true men were Dirdirmen; all others were freaks. Anacho found it hard to reconcile Reith's competence with his preconceptions, and his attitude was a curious composite of envious disapproval, grudging admiration, unwilling loyalty. Now, rather than allow Reith to excel him in yet another aspect, he hurried to the stern of the sky-raft and thrust his long pale clown's face under the housing.

The surface of the butte was scoured clean of vegetation, with here and there little channels half-full of coarse sand. Ylin Ylan wandered moodily across the butte. She wore the gray steppe-dwellers' trousers and blouse, with a black velvet vest; her black slippers were probably the first to walk the rough gray rock, thought Reith . . . Traz stood looking to the west. Reith joined him at the edge of the butte. He studied the dismal steppe, but saw nothing.

"The Green Chasch," said Traz. "They know we're here."

Reith once more scanned the steppe, from the low black hills in the north to the haze of the south. He could see no flicker of movement, no plume of dust. He brought out his scanscope, a binocular photo-multiplier, and probed the gray-brown murk. Presently he saw bounding black specks, like fleas. "They're out there, for a fact."

Traz nodded without great interest. Reith grinned, amused as always by the boy's somber wisdom. He went to the sky-raft. "How go the repairs?"

Anacho's response was an irritated motion of arms and shoulders. "Look for yourself."

Reith came forward, peered down at the black case, which Anacho had opened, to reveal an intricacy of small components. "Corrosion and sheer age are at fault," said Anacho. "I hope to introduce new metal here and here." He pointed. "It is a notable problem without tools and proper facilities."

"We won't leave tonight then?"

"Perhaps by tomorrow noon."

Reith walked around the periphery of the butte, a distance of three or four hundred yards, and was somewhat reassured. Everywhere the walls were vertical, with fins of rock at the base creating crevices, and grottos. There seemed no easy method to scale the walls, and he doubted if the Green Chasch would go to vast trouble for the trivial pleasure of slaughtering a few men.

The old brown sun hung low in the west; the shadows of Reith and Traz and Ylin Ylan stretched long across the top of the butte. The girl turned away from her contemplation of the east. She watched Traz and Reith for a moment, then slowly, almost reluctantly, crossed the sandstone surface and joined them. "What are you looking at?"

Reith pointed. The Green Chasch on their leap-horses were visible now to the naked eye: dark motes hopping and bounding in bone-jarring leaps.

Ylin Ylan drew her breath. "Are they coming for us?"

"I imagine so."

"Can we fight them off? What of our weapons?"

"We have sandblasts* on the raft. If they climbed the cliffs after dark they might do some damage. During daylight we don't need to worry."

Ylin Ylan's lips quivered. She spoke in an almost inaudible voice. "If I return to Cath, I will hide in the farthest grotto of the Blue Jade garden and never again appear. If ever I return."

Reith put his arm around her waist; she was stiff and unyielding. "Of course you'll return, and pick up your life where it left off."

"No. Someone else may be Flower of Cath; she is welcome . . . So long as she chooses other than Ylin Ylan for her bouquet."

---

* Sandblast: a weapon electrostatically charging and accelerating grains of sand to near-light speed, with consequent gain in mass and inertia. Upon penetrating a target, the energy is yielded in the form of an explosion.

The girl's pessimism puzzled Reith. Her previous trials she had borne with stoicism; now, with fair prospects of returning home, she had become morose. Reith heaved a deep sigh and turned away.

The Green Chasch were no more than a mile distant. Reith and Traz drew back to attract no notice in the event that the Chasch were unaware of their presence. The hope was soon dispelled. The Green Chasch bounded up to the base of the butte, then, dismounting from their horses, stood looking up the cliff face. Reith, peering over the side, counted forty of the creatures. They were seven and eight feet tall, massive and thick-limbed, with pangolin-scales of metallic green. Under the jut of their crania their faces were small, and, to Reith's eyes, like the magnified visage of a feral insect. They wore leather aprons and shoulder harness; their weapons were swords which, like all the swords of the Tschai, seemed long and unwieldy, and these, eight and ten feet long, even more so. Some of them armed their catapults; Reith ducked back to avoid the flight of bolts. He looked around the butte for boulders to drop over the side, but found none.

Certain of the Chasch rode around the butte, examining the walls. Traz ran around the periphery, keeping watch.

All returned to the main group, where they muttered and grumbled together. Reith thought that they showed no great zest for the business of scaling the wall. Setting up camp, they tethered their leap-horses, thrust chunks of a dark sticky substance into the pale maws. They built three fires, over which they boiled chunks of the same substance they had fed the leap-horses, and at last hulking down into toad-shaped mounds, joylessly devoured the contents of their cauldrons. The sun dimmed behind the western haze and disappeared. Umber twilight fell over the steppe. Anacho came away from the raft and peered down at the Green Chasch. "Lesser Zants," he pronounced. "Notice the protuberances to each side of the head? They are thus distinguished from the Great Zants and other hordes. These are of no great consequence."

"They look consequential enough to me," said Reith.

Traz made a sudden motion, pointed. In one of the crevices, between two vanes of rock, stood a tall dark shadow. "Phung!"

Reith looked through the scanscope and saw the shadow to be a Phung indeed. From where it had come he could not guess.

It was over eight feet in height, in its soft black hat and black cloak, like a giant grasshopper in magisterial vestments.

Reith studied the face, watching the slow working of chitinous plates around the blunt lower section of the face. It watched the Green Chasch with brooding detachment, though they crouched over their pots not ten yards away.

"A mad thing," whispered Traz, his eyes glittering. "Look, now it plays tricks!"

The Phung reached down its long thin arms, raised a small boulder which it heaved high into the air. The rock dropped among the Chasch, falling squarely upon a hulking back.

The Green Chasch sprang up, to glare toward the top of the butte. The Phung stood quietly, lost among the shadows. The Chasch which had been struck lay flat on its face, making convulsive swimming motions with arms and legs.

The Phung craftily lifted another great rock, once more heaved it high, but this time the Chasch saw the movement. Venting squeals of fury they seized their swords and flung themselves forward. The Phung took a stately step aside, then leaping in a great flutter of cloak snatched a sword, which it wielded as if it were a toothpick, hacking, dancing, whirling, cutting wildly, apparently without aim or direction. The Chasch scattered; some lay on the ground, and the Phung jumped here and there, slashing and slicing, without discrimination, the Green Chasch, the fire, the air, like a mechanical toy running out of control.

Crouching and shifting, the Green Chasch hulked forward. They chopped, cut; the Phung threw away the sword as if it were hot, and was hacked into pieces. The head spun off the torso, landed on the ground ten feet from one of the fires, with the soft black hat still in place. Reith watched it through the scanscope. The head seemed conscious, untroubled. The eyes watched the fire; the mouth parts worked slowly.

"It will live for days, until it dries out," said Traz huskily. "Gradually it will go stiff."

The Chasch paid the creature no further heed, but at once made ready their leap-horses. They loaded their gear and five minutes later had trooped off into the darkness. The head of the Phung mused upon the play of the flames.

For a period the men squatted by the edge of the precipice, looking across the steppe. Traz and Anacho fell into an argument regarding the nature of the Phung, Traz declaring them to be products of unnatural union between Pnumekin and the corpses of Pnume. "The seed waxes in the decay like a barkworm, and finally breaks out through the skin as a young Phung, not greatly different from a bald night-hound."

"Sheer idiocy, lad!" said Anacho with easy condescension. "They surely breed like Pnume: a startling process itself, if what I hear is correct."

Traz, no less proud than the Dirdirman, became taut. "How do you speak with such assurance? Have you observed the process? Have you seen a Phung with others, or guarding a cub?" He lowered his lip in a sneer. "No! They go singly, too mad to breed!"

Anacho made a finger-fluttering gesture of fastidious didacticism. "Rarely are Pnume seen in groups; rarely do we see a Pnume alone, for that matter. Yet they flourish in their peculiar fashion. Brash generalizations are suspect. The truth is that after many long years on Tschai we still know little of either Phung or Pnume."

Traz gave an inarticulate growl, too wise not to concede the conviction of Anacho's logic, too proud to abandon abjectly his point of view. And Anacho, in his turn, made no attempt to push a superficial advantage home. In time, thought Reith, the two might even learn to respect each other.

In the morning Anacho again tinkered with the engine, while the others shivered in the cold airs seeping down from the north. Traz gloomily predicted rain, and presently a high overcast began to form, and fog eased over the tops of the hills to the north.

Anacho finally threw down the tools in boredom and disgust. "I have done what I can. The raft will fly, but not far."

"How far, in your opinion?" asked Reith, aware that Ylin Ylan had turned to listen. "To Cath?"

Anacho flapped up his hands, fluttering his fingers in an unknowable Dirdir gesticulation. "To Cath, by your projected route: impossible. The engine is falling to dust."

Ylin Ylan looked away, studied her clenched hands.

"Flying south, we might reach Coad on the Dawn Zher," Anacho went on, "and there take passage across the Draschade. Such a route is longer and slower—but conceivably we will arrive in Cath."

"It seems that we have no choice," said Reith.

2

FOR A PERIOD they followed the southward course of the vast Nabiga River, traveling only a few feet above the surface, where the repulsion plates suffered the least strain. The Nabiga swept off to the west, demarcating the Dead Steppe from the Aman Steppe, and the raft continued south across an inhospitable region of dim forests, bogs, and morasses; and a day later returned to the steppe. On one occasion they saw a caravan in the distance: a line of high-wheeled carts and trundling house-wagons; another time they came upon a band of nomads wearing red feather fetishes on their shoulders, who bounded frantically across the steppe to intercept them, and were only gradually outdistanced.

Late in the afternoon they painfully climbed above a huddle of brown and black hills. The raft jerked and yawed; the black case emitted ominous rasping sounds. Reith flew low, sometimes brushing through the tops of black tree-ferns. Sliding across the ridge the raft blundered at head-height through an encampment of capering creatures in voluminous white robes, apparently men. They dodged and fell to the ground, then screaming in outrage fired muskets after the raft, the erratic course of which presented a shifting target.

All night they flew over dense forest, and morning revealed more of the same: a black, green, and brown carpet cloaking the Aman Steppe to the limit of vision, though Traz declared the steppe ended at the hills, that below them now was the Great Daduz Forest. Anacho condescendingly took issue, and displaying a chart tapped various topographic indications with his long white fingers to prove his point.

Traz's square face became stubborn and sullen. "This is Great Daduz Forest; twice when I carried Onmale among the Emblems,* I led the tribe here for herbs and dyes."

Anacho put away the chart. "It is all one," he remarked. "Steppe or forest, it must be traversed." At a sound from the engine he looked critically aft. "I believe that we will reach the outskirts of Coad, not a mile farther, and when we raise the housing we shall find only a heap of rust."

---

*The Emblems: nomads setting great store by small fetishes of metal, wood and stone, each with a name, history, and personality. The warrior wearing a particular emblem becomes imbued with its essence, and in effect becomes the emblem. Traz carried Onmale, the paramount emblem of the tribe, and so was the ritual chief.

"But we will reach Coad?" Ylin Ylan asked in a colorless voice.

"So I believe. Only two hundred miles remain."

Ylin Ylan seemed momentarily cheerful. "How different than before," she said. "When I came to Coad a captive of the priestesses!" The thought seemed to depress her and once more she became pensive.

Night approached. Coad still lay a hundred miles distant. The forest had thinned to a stand of immense black and gold trees, with intervening areas of turf, on which grazed squat six-legged beasts, bristling with bony tusks and horns. Landing for the night was hardly feasible and Reith did not care to arrive at Coad until morning, in which opinion Anacho concurred. They halted the motion of the raft, tied to the top of a tree and hovered on the repulsors through the night.

After the evening meal the Flower of Cath went to her cabin behind the saloon; Traz, after studying the sky and listening to the sounds of beasts below, wrapped himself in his robe and stretched out on one of the settees.

Reith leaned against the rail watching the pink moon Az reach the zenith just as the blue moon Braz rose behind the foliage of a far tall tree.

Anacho came to join him. "So then, what are your thoughts as to the morrow?"

"I know nothing of Coad. I suppose we inquire as to transportation across the Draschade."

"You still intend to accompany the woman to Cath?"

"Certainly," said Reith, mildly surprised.

Anacho hissed through his teeth. "You need only put the Cathwoman on a ship; you need not go yourself."

"True. But I don't care to remain in Coad."

"Why not? It is a city which even Dirdirmen visit from time to time. If you have money anything is for sale in Coad."

"A spaceship?"

"Hardly . . . It seems that you persist in your obsession."

Reith laughed. "Call it whatever you like."

"I admit to perplexity," Anacho went on. "The likeliest explanation, and one which I urge you to accept, is that you are amnesiac, and have subconsciously fabricated a fable to account for your own existence. Which of course you fervently believe to be true."

"Reasonable," Reith agreed.

"One or two odd circumstances remain," Anacho continued thoughtfully. "The remarkable devices you carry: your electronic telescope, your energy-weapon, other oddments. I cannot identify the workmanship, though it is equivalent to that of good Dirdir equipment. I suppose it to be home-planet Wankh; am I correct?"

"As an amnesiac, how would I know?"

Anacho gave a wry chuckle. "And you still intend to go to Cath?"

"Of course. What about you?"

Anacho shrugged. "One place is as good as another, from my point of view. But I doubt if you realize what awaits you in Cath."

"I know nothing of Cath," said Reith, "other than what I have heard. The people are apparently civilized."

Anacho gave a patronizing shrug. "They are Yao: a fervent race addicted to ritual and extravaganza, prone to excesses of temperament. You may find the intricacies of Cath society difficult to cope with."

Reith frowned. "I hope it won't be necessary. The girl has vouched for her father's gratitude, which should simplify matters."

"Formally the gratitude will exist. I am sure of this."

" 'Formally'? Not actually?"

"The fact that you and the girl have formed an erotic accommodation is of course a complication."

Reith smiled sourly. "The 'erotic accommodation' has long since run its course." He looked back toward the deck-house. "Frankly, I don't understand the girl. She actually seems disturbed by the prospect of returning home."

Anacho peered through the dark. "Are you so naïve? Clearly she dreads the moment when she must sponsor the three of us before the society of Cath. She would be overjoyed if you sent her home alone."

Reith gave a bitter laugh. "At Pera she sang a different tune. She begged that we return to Cath."

"Then the possibility was remote. Now she must deal with reality."

"But this is absurdity! Traz is as he is. You are a Dirdirman, for which you are not to blame—"

"No difficulties in either of these cases," stated the Dirdirman with an elegant flourish of the fingers. "Our roles are immutable. Your case is different; and it might be best for all if you sent the girl home on a cog."

Reith stood looking out over the sea of moonlit treetops. The opinion, assuming its validity, was far from lucid, and also presented a dilemma. To avoid Cath was to relinquish his best possibility of building a spaceboat. The only alternative then would be to steal a spaceship, from the Dirdir, or Wankh, or, least appealing of all, from the Blue Chasch: all in all, a nerve-tingling prospect. Reith asked, "Why should I be less acceptable than you or Traz? Because of the 'erotic accommodation'?"

"Naturally not. The Yao concern themselves with systematics rather than deeds. I am surprised to find you so undiscerning."

"Blame it on my amnesia," said Reith.

Anacho shrugged. "In the first place—possibly due to your 'amnesia'—you have no quality, no role, no place in the Cath 'round.' As a nondescript, you constitute a distraction, a zizyl-beast in a ballroom. Secondly, and more poignant, is your point of view, which is not fashionable in contemporary Cath."

"By this you mean my 'obsession'?"

"Unfortunately," said Anacho, "it is similar to an hysteria which distinguished a previous cycle of the 'round.' A hundred and fifty years* ago, a coterie of Dirdirmen were expelled from the academies at Eliasir and Anismna for the crime of promulgating fantasy. They brought their espousements to Cath, and stimulated a tendentious vogue: the Society of Yearning Refluxives, or the 'cult.' The articles of faith defied established fact. It was asserted that all men, Dirdirmen and sub-men alike, were immigrants from a far planet in the constellation Clari: a paradise where the hopes of humanity have been realized. Enthusiasm for the 'cult' galvanized Cath; a radio transmitter was constructed and signals were projected toward Clari. Somewhere, the activity was resented; someone launched torpedoes which devastated Settra and Ballisidre. The Dirdir are commonly held responsible, but this is absurd; why should they trouble themselves? I assure you that they are much too distant, too uninterested.

"Regardless of agency, the deed was done. Settra and Bal-

---

*The Tschai year: approximately seven-fifths the terrestrial year.

lisidre were laid low, the 'cult' was discredited; the Dirdirmen were expelled; the 'round' swung back to orthodoxy. Now even to mention the 'cult' is considered vulgarity, and so we arrive at your case. Clearly you have encountered and assimilated 'cult' dogma; it now manifests itself in your attitudes, your acts, your goals. You seem unable to distinguish fact from fancy. To speak bluntly, you are so disoriented in this regard as to suggest psychic disorder."

Reith closed his mouth on a wild laugh; it would only reinforce Anacho's doubts as to his sanity. A dozen remarks rose to his tongue; he restrained them all. At last he said, "All else aside, I appreciate your candor."

"Not at all," said the Dirdirman serenely. "I imagine that I have clarified the nature of the girl's apprehension."

The Dirdirman blinked up at the pink moon Az. "So long as she was outside the 'round' at Pera and elsewhere, she made sympathetic allowances. But now return to Cath is imminent . . ." He said no more, and presently went to his couch in the saloon.

Reith went to the forward pulpit under the great bow lantern. A cool draft of air fanned his face; the raft drifted idly about the treetop. From the ground came a furtive crackle of footsteps. Reith listened; they halted, then resumed and diminished off under the trees. Reith looked up into the sky where pink Az, blue Braz careened. He looked back at the deck-house where slept his comrades: a boy of the Emblem nomads, a clown-faced man evolved toward a race of gaunt aliens; a beautiful girl of the Yao, who thought him mad. Below sounded a new pad of footsteps. Perhaps he was mad indeed . . .

By morning Reith had recovered his equanimity, and was even able to find grotesque humor in the situation. No good reason to change his plans suggested itself, and the sky-raft limped south as before. The forest dwindled to scrub, and gave way to isolated plantings and cattle-runs, field huts, lookout towers against the approach of nomads, an occasional rutted road. The raft displayed an ever more aggravated instability, with an annoying tendency for the stern to sag. At mid-morning a range of low hills loomed ahead, and the raft refused to climb the few hundred feet necessary to clear the ridge. By the sheerest luck a cleft appeared through which the raft wobbled with ten feet to spare.

Ahead lay the Dwan Zher and Coad: a compact town with a

look of settled antiquity. The houses were built of weathered timber, with enormous high-peaked roofs and a multitude of skew gables, eccentric ridges, dormers, tall chimneys. A dozen ships rode to moorings; as many more were docked across from a row of factors' offices. At the north of town was the caravan terminus, beside a large compound surrounded by hostelries, taverns, warehouses. The compound seemed a convenient spot to set down the raft; Reith doubted if it could have held itself in the air another ten miles.

The raft dropped stern first; the repulsors gave a labored whine and went silent with a meaningful finality. "That's that," said Reith. "I'm glad we've arrived."

The group took up their meager luggage, alighted and left the raft where it had landed.

At the edge of the compound Anacho made inquiries of a dung-merchant and received directions to the Grand Continental, the best of the town's hostelries.

Coad was a busy town. Along the crooked streets, in and out of the ale-colored sunlight, moved men and women of many casts and colors: Yellow Islanders and Black Islanders, Horasin bark-merchants muffled in gray robes; Caucasoids such as Traz from the Aman Steppe; Dirdirmen and Dirdirmen hybrids; dwarfish Sieps from the eastern slopes of the Ojzanalai who played music in the streets; a few flat-faced white men from the far south of Kislovan. The natives, or Tans, were an affable fox-faced people, with wide polished cheekbones, pointed chins, russet or dark brown hair cut in a ledge across the ears and foreheads. Their usual garments were knee-length breeches, embroidered vest, a round black pie-plate hat. Palanquins were numerous, carried by short gnarled men with oddly long noses and stringy black hair: apparently a race to themselves; Reith saw them in no other occupation. Later he learned them to be natives of Grenie at the head of the Dwan Zher.

On a balcony Reith thought he glimpsed a Dirdir, but he could not be certain. Once Traz grabbed his elbow and pointed to a pair of thin men in loose black trousers, black capes with tall collars all but enveloping their faces, soft cylindrical black hats with wide brims: caricatures of mystery and intrigue. "Pnumekin!" hissed Traz in a something between shock and outrage. "Look at them! They walk among other men without a look aside, and their minds full of strange thinking!"

They arrived at the hostelry, a rambling edifice of three stories, with a café on the front veranda, a restaurant in a great tall covered arbor to the rear and balconies overlooking the street. A clerk at a wicket took their money, distributed fanciful keys of black iron as large as their hands and instructed them to their rooms.

"We have traveled a great dusty distance," said Anacho. "We require baths, with good quality unguents, fresh linen, and then we will dine."

"It shall be as you order."

An hour later, clean and refreshed, the four met in the downstairs lobby. Here they were accosted by a black-haired black-eyed man with a pinched melancholy face. He spoke in a gentle voice. "You are newly arrived at Coad?"

Anacho, instantly suspicious, drew himself back. "Not altogether. We are well-known and have no needs."

"I represent the Slave-taker's Guild, and this is my fair appraisal of your group. The girl is valuable, the boy less so. Dirdirmen are generally considered worthless except in clerical or administrative servitude, for which we have no demand. You would be rated a winkle-gatherer or a nut-huller, of no great value. This man, whatever he is, appears capable of toil, and would sell for the standard rate. Considering all, your insurance will be ten sequins a week."

"Insurance against what?" demanded Reith.

"Against being taken and sold," murmured the agent. "There is a heavy demand for competent workers. But for ten sequins a week," he declared triumphantly, "you may walk the streets of Coad night and day, secure as though the demon Harasthy rode your shoulders! Should you be sequestered by an unauthorized dealer the Guild will instantly order your free release."

Reith stood back, half-amused, half-disgusted. Anacho spoke in his most nasal voice: "Show me your credentials."

" 'Credentials'?" asked the man, his chin sagging.

"Show us a document, a blazon, a patent. What? You have none? Do you take us for fools? Be off with you!"

The man walked somberly away. Reith asked, "Was he in truth a fraud?"

"One never knows, but the line must be drawn somewhere. Let us eat; I have a good appetite after weeks of steamed pulses and pilgrim plant."

They took seats in the dining room: actually a vast airy arbor with a glass ceiling admitting a pale ivory light. Black vines climbed the walls; in the corners were purple and pale-blue ferns. The day was mild; the end of the room opened to a view of the Dwan Zher and a wind-curled bank of cumulus at the horizon.

The room was half-full; perhaps two dozen people dined from platters and bowls of black wood and red earthenware, talking in low voices, watching the folk at other tables with covert curiosity. Traz looked uneasily here and there, eyebrows raised in disapproval of so much luxury: undoubtedly his first encounter with what must seem a set of faddish and over-complicated niceties, reflected Reith.

He noticed Ylin Ylan staring across the room, as if astonished by what she saw. Almost immediately she averted her eyes, as if uncomfortable or embarrassed. Reith followed her gaze, but saw nothing out of the ordinary. He thought better of inquiring the cause of her perturbation, not wishing to risk a cool stare. And Reith grinned uncomfortably. What a situation: almost as if she were cultivating an active dislike for him! Perfectly comprehensible, of course, if Anacho's explanations were correct. His puzzlement regarding the girl's agitation was now resolved by the sardonic Dirdirman.

"Observe the fellow at the far table," murmured Anacho. "He in the green and purple coat."

Turning his head, Reith saw a handsome young bravo with carefully arranged hair and a rich mustache of a startling gold. He wore elegant garments, somewhat rumpled and well-used: a jacket of soft leather strips, dyed alternately green and purple, breeches of pleated yellow cloth, buckled at knee and ankle with brooches in the shape of fantastic insects. A square cap of soft fur, fringed with two-inch pendants of gold beads, slanted across his head; an extravagant garde-nez of gold filigree clung to the ridge of his nose. Anacho muttered, "Watch him now. He will notice us, he will see the girl."

"But who is he?"

Anacho gave his fingertips an irritated twitch. "His name? I do not know. His status: high, in his own opinion at least. He is a Yao cavalier."

Reith turned his attention to Ylin Ylan, who watched the young man from the corner of her eye. Miraculous how her mood had altered! She had become alive and aware, though obviously twitching with nervousness and uncertainty. She flicked a glance toward Reith, and flushed to find his eyes on her. Bending her head she busied herself with the appetizers: dishes of gray grapes, biscuits, smoked sea-insects, pickled fern-pod. Reith watched the cavalier, who was unenthusiastically dining upon a black seed-bun and a dish of pickles, his gaze off across the sea. He gave a sad shrug, as if discouraged by his thoughts, and shifted his position. He saw the Flower of Cath, who feigned the most artless absorption in her food. The cavalier leaned forward in astonishment. He jumped to his feet with such exuberance as nearly to overturn the table. In three long strides he was across the room and down on one knee with a sweeping salute which brushed his cap across Traz's face. "Blue Jade Princess! Your servant Dordolio. My goals are won."

The Flower bowed her head with an exact modicum of restraint and pleased surprise. Reith admired her aplomb. "Pleasant," she murmured, "in a far land to chance upon a cavalier of Cath."

" 'Chance' is not the word! I am one of a dozen who went forth to seek you, to win the boon proclaimed by your father and for the honor of both our palaces. By the wattles of the Pnume's First Devil, it has been given to me to find you!"

Anacho spoke in his blandest voice. "You have searched extensively, then?"

Dordolio stood erect, made a cursory inspection of Anacho, Reith, and Traz, and performed three precise nods. The Flower made a gay little motion, as if the three were casual companions at a picnic. "My loyal henchmen; all have been of incalculable help to me. But for them I doubt if I would be alive."

"In that case," declared the cavalier, "they may ever rely upon the patronage of Dordolio, Gold, and Carnelian. They shall use my field-name Alutrin Stargold." He performed a salute which included all three, then snapped his finger at the serving woman. "A chair, if you please. I will dine at this table."

The serving woman somewhat unceremoniously pushed a chair into place; Dordolio seated himself and gave his attention to the Flower. "But what of your adventures? I assume them to be harrowing. Still you appear as fresh as ever—decidedly unharrowed."

The Flower laughed. "In these steppe-dweller's garments? I

have not yet been able to change. I must buy dozens of sheer necessities before I dare let you look at me."

Dordolio, glancing at her gray garments, made a negligent gesture. "I had noticed nothing. You are as ever. But, if you wish, we will shop together; the bazaars of Coad are fascinating."

"Of course! Tell me of yourself. My father issued a behest, you say?"

"He did indeed, and swore a boon. The most gallant responded. We followed your trail to Spang where we learned who had taken you: Priestesses of the Female Mystery. Many gave you up for lost, but not I. My perseverance has been rewarded! In triumph we will return to Settra!"

Ylin Ylan turned a somewhat cryptic smile toward Reith. "I am of course anxious to return home. What luck to find you here in Coad!"

"Remarkable luck," said Reith dryly. "We arrived only an hour ago from Pera."

"Pera? I do not know the place."

"It lies at the far west of the Dead Steppe."

Dordolio gave an opaque stare, then once more he addressed himself to the Flower. "What hardships you must have suffered! But now you walk under the aegis of Dordolio! We return at once to Settra."

The meal proceeded, Dordolio and Ylin Ylan conversing with great vivacity. Traz, preoccupied with the unfamiliar table implements, turned them dour glances, as if he suspected their ridicule. Anacho paid them no heed; Reith ate in silence. Finally Dordolio sat back in his chair. "Now, as to the practicalities: the packet *Yazilissa* is at mooring, and shortly departs for Vervodei. A melancholy task to take leave of your comrades, good fellows all, I'm sure, but we must arrange our passage home."

Reith spoke in an even voice. "All of us, so it happens, are bound for Cath."

Dordolio presented his blank questioning stare, as if Reith spoke an incomprehensible language.

He rose, helped Ylin Ylan to her feet; the two went to saunter on the terrace beyond the arbour. The serving woman brought the score. "Five sequins, if you please, for five meals."

"Five?"

"The Yao ate at your table."

Reith paid over five sequins from his wallet. Anacho watched in amusement. "The Yao's presence is actually an advantage; you will avoid attention upon your arrival at Settra."

"Perhaps," said Reith. "On the other hand, I had hoped for the gratitude of the girl's father. I need all the friends I can find."

"Events sometimes display a vitality of their own," observed Anacho. "The Dirdir teleologists have interesting remarks to make on the subject. I recall an analysis of coincidences—this, incidentally, not by a Dirdir but by a Dirdirman Immaculate . . ." As Anacho spoke on, Traz went out on the terrace to survey the roofs of Coad; Dordolio and Ylin Ylan walked slowly past, ignoring his presence. Seething with indignation Traz returned to Reith and Anacho. "The Yao dandy urges her to dismiss us. She refers to us as nomads—rude but honest and dependable."

"No matter," said Reith. "Her destiny is not ours."

"But you have practically made it so! We might have remained in Pera, or taken ourselves to the Fortunate Isles; instead—" He threw up his arms in disgust.

"Events are not occurring as I expected," Reith admitted. "Still, who knows? It may be for the best. Anacho thinks so, at any rate. Would you please ask her to step over here?"

Traz went off on his errand, to return at once. "She and the Yao are off to buy what they call suitable garments! What a farce! I have worn steppe-dwellers' clothes all my life! The garments are suitable and useful."

"Of course," said Reith. "Well, let them do as they wish. Perhaps we also might make a change in our appearance."

Toward the dock area was the bazaar; here Reith, Anacho and Traz fitted themselves out in garments of somewhat less crude cut and material: shirts of soft light linen, short-sleeved vests, loose black breeches buckling at the ankle; shoes of supple gray leather.

The docks were but a few steps away; they continued on to inspect the shipping, and the *Yazilissa* immediately engaged their attention: a three-masted ship over a hundred feet long, with passenger accommodations in a tall many-windowed after-house, and in a row of 'tween-decks cabins along the waist. Cargo booms hung over the docks; bales of goods were hoisted aloft, swung up, over and into the holds.

Climbing the gangplank, they found the supercargo who verified that the *Yazilissa* sailed in three days, touching at ports in

Grenie and Horasin, then faring by way of Pag Choda, the Islands of Cloud, Tusa Tula at Cape Gaiz on the western thrust of Kachan, to Vervodei in Cath: a voyage of sixty or seventy days.

Inquiring as to accommodations, Reith learned that all first class staterooms were booked as far as Tusa Tula, and all but one of the 'tween-decks cabins. There was, however, unlimited deck-class accommodation, which according to the supercargo was not uncomfortable except during the equatorial rains. He admitted these to be frequent.

"Not satisfactory," said Reith. "At the minimum we would want four second-class cabins."

"Unfortunately I can't oblige you unless cancellations come in, which is always possible."

"Very well; I am Adam Reith. You may reach me at the Grand Continental Hotel."

The supercargo stared at him in surprise. " 'Adam Reith'? You and your group are already on the passenger list."

"I'm afraid not," said Reith. "We only arrived in Coad this morning."

"But only an hour ago, perhaps less, a pair of Yao came aboard, a cavalier and a noblewoman. They took accommodation in the name of 'Adam Reith'; the grand suite in the after-house—that is to say, two staterooms with a private saloon—and deck passage for three. I requested a deposit; they stated that Adam Reith would come aboard to pay the passage fee, which is two thousand three hundred sequins. Are you Adam Reith?"

"I am Adam Reith, but I plan to pay no two thousand three hundred sequins. So far as I am concerned, cancel the booking."

"What sort of tomfoolery is this?" demanded the supercargo. "I have no inclination for such frivolity."

"I have even less desire to cross the Draschade Ocean in the rain," said Reith. "If you want recourse, seek out the Yao."

"A pointless exercise," growled the supercargo. "Well then, so be it. If you will be happy with something less than luxury, try aboard the *Vargaz:* the cog yonder. She's departing in a day or so for Cath, and no doubt can find room for you."

"Thank you for your help." Reith and his companions walked down the dock to the *Vargaz:* a short high-pooped round-hulled ship with a long bowsprit, sharply aslant. The two masts supported a pair of lateen yards with sails hanging limp while crewmen sewed on patches of new canvas.

Reith inspected the cog dubiously, then shrugged and went aboard. In the shadow of the after-house two men sat at a table littered with papers, ink-sticks, seals, ribbons and a jug of wine. The most imposing of these was a burly man, naked from the waist up, save for a heavy growth of coarse black hair on his chest. His skin was brown, his features small and hard in a round immobile face. The other man was thin, almost frail, wearing a loose gown of white and a yellow vest the color of his skin. A long mustache drooped sadly beside his mouth; he wore a scimitar at his waist. Ostensibly a pair of sinister ruffians, thought Reith. "Yes, sir, what do you wish?" asked the burly man.

"Transportation to Cath in as much comfort as possible," said Reith.

"Little enough to ask." The man heaved himself to his feet. "I will show you what is available."

Reith eventually paid a deposit on two small cabins for Anacho and Ylin Ylan, a larger stateroom which he would share with Traz. The quarters were neither airy, spacious nor over-clean, but Reith thought that they might have been worse.

"When do you sail?" he asked the burly man.

"Tomorrow noon on the flood. By preference, be aboard by midmorning; I run a punctual ship."

The three returned through the crooked streets of Coad to the hotel. Neither the Flower nor Dordolio were on the premises. Late in the afternoon they returned in a palanquin, followed by three porters laden with bundles. Dordolio alighted, helped Ylin Ylan forth; they entered the hotel followed by the porters and the chief bearer of the palanquin.

Ylin Ylan wore a graceful gown of dark green silk, with a dark blue bodice. A charming little cap of crystal-frosted net constrained her hair. Seeing Reith she hesitated, turned to Dordolio and spoke a few words. Dordolio pulled at his extraordinary gold mustache, sauntered to where Reith sat with Anacho and Traz.

"All is well," said Dordolio. "I have taken passage for all aboard the *Yazilissa*, a ship of excellent reputation."

"I fear you have incurred an unnecessary expense," said Reith politely. "I have made other arrangements."

Dordolio stood back, nonplussed. "But you should have consulted me!"

"I can't imagine why," said Reith.

"On what ship do you sail?" demanded Dordolio.

"The cog *Vargaz*."

"The *Vargaz*? Bah! A floating pigpen. I would not wish to sail on the *Vargaz*."

"You do not need to do so, if you are sailing on the *Yazilissa*."

Dordolio tugged at his mustache. "The Blue Jade Princess likewise prefers to travel aboard the *Yazilissa*, the best accommodation available."

"You are a bountiful man," said Reith, "to take luxurious passage for so large a group."

"In point of fact, I did only what I could," admitted Dordolio. "Since you are in charge of the group's funds the supercargo will render an account to you."

"By no means," said Reith. "I remind you that I have already taken passage aboard the *Vargaz*."

Dordolio hissed petulantly through his teeth. "This is an insufferable situation."

The porters and the palanquin carrier drew near, and bowed before Reith. "Permit us to tender our accounts."

Reith raised his eyebrows. Was there no limit to Dordolio's insouciance? "Of course, why should you not? Naturally to those who commanded your services." He rose to his feet. He went to Ylin Ylan's room, knocked on the rattan door. There was the sound of movement within; she looked forth through a peep-lens. The upper panel of the door slid back a trifle.

Reith asked, "May I come in?"

"But I'm dressing."

"This has made no difference before."

The door opened; Ylin Ylan stood somewhat sullenly aside. Reith entered. Bundles were everywhere, some opened to reveal garments and leathers, gauze slippers, embroidered bodices, filigree headwear. Reith looked around in astonishment. "Your friend is extravagantly generous."

The Flower started to speak, then bit her lips. "These few things are necessities for the voyage home. I do not care to arrive at Vervodei like a scullery maid." She spoke with a haughtiness Reith had never before heard. "They are to be reckoned as traveling expenses. Please keep an account and my father will settle affairs to your satisfaction."

"You put me in a hard position," said Reith, "where inevitably I lose my dignity. If I pay, I'm a lout and a fool; if I don't, I'm a heartless pinchpenny. It seems that you might have handled the situation more tactfully."

"The question of tact did not arise," said the Flower. "I desired the articles. I ordered them to be brought here."

Reith grimaced. "I won't argue the subject. I came to tell you this: I have engaged passage to Cath aboard the cog *Vargaz*, which leaves tomorrow. It is a plain simple ship; you will need plain simple garments."

The Flower stared at him in puzzlement. "But the Noble Gold and Carnelian took passage aboard the *Yazilissa*!"

"If he chooses to travel aboard the *Yazilissa*, he of course may do so, if he can settle for his passage. I have just notified him that I will pay neither for his palanquin rides, nor his passage to Cath, nor"—Reith gestured toward the parcels—"for the finery which he evidently urged you to select."

Ylin Ylan flushed angrily. "I had never expected to find you niggardly."

"The alternative is worse. Dordolio—"

"That is his friend name," said Ylin Ylan in an undertone. "Best that you use his field name, or the formal address: Noble Gold and Carnelian."

"Whatever the situation, the cog *Vargaz* sails tomorrow. You may be aboard or remain in Coad as you choose."

Reith returned to the foyer. The porters and palanquin carrier had departed. Dordolio stood on the front veranda. The jeweled ornaments which had buckled his breeches at the knees were no longer to be seen.

3

THE COG *VARGAZ*, broad of beam, with high narrow prow, a cutaway midships, a lofty stern-castle, wallowed comfortably at its mooring against the dock. Like all else of Tschai, the cog's aspects were exaggerated, with every quality dramatized. The curve of the hull was florid, the bowsprit prodded at the sky, the sails were raffishly patched.

The Flower of Cath silently accompanied Reith, Traz and Anacho the Dirdirman aboard the *Vargaz*, with a porter bringing her luggage on a hand-truck.

Half an hour later Dordolio appeared on the dock. He appraised the *Vargaz* a moment or two, then strolled up the gangplank. He spoke briefly with the captain, tossed a purse upon the table. The captain frowned up sidewise from under bushy black eyebrows, thinking his own thoughts. He opened the purse, counted the sequins and found an insufficiency, which he pointed out. Dordolio wearily reached into his pouch, found the required sum, and the captain jerked his thumb toward the sterncastle.

Dordolio pulled at his mustache, raised his eyes toward the sky. He went to the gangplank, signaled a pair of porters who conveyed aboard his luggage. Then, with a formal bow toward the Flower of Cath, he went to stand at the far rail, looking moodily off across the Dwan Zher.

Five other passengers came aboard: a small fat merchant in a somber gray caftan and tall cylindrical hat; a man of the Isle of Cloud, with his spouse and two daughters: fresh fragile girls with pale skins and orange hair.

An hour before noon the *Vargaz* hoisted sails, cast off lines, and sheered away from the dock. The roofs of Coad became dark brown prisms laid along the hillside. The crew trimmed sails, coiled down lines, then unshipped a clumsy blast-cannon, which they dragged up to the foredeck.

Reith asked Anacho, "Who do they fear? Pirates?"

"A precaution. So long as a cannon is seen, pirates keep their distance. We have nothing to fear; they are seldom seen on the Draschade. A greater hazard is the victualing. The captain appears a man accustomed to good living, an optimistic sign."

The cog moved easily through the hazy afternoon. The Dawn Zher was calm and showed a pearly luster. The coastline faded away to the north; there were no ships to be seen. Sunset came: a wan display of dove-brown and umber, and with it a cool breeze which sent the water chuckling around the bluff bow.

The evening meal was simple but palatable: slices of dry spiced meat, a salad of raw vegetables, insect paste, pickles, soft white wine from a green glass demijohn. The passengers ate in wary silence; on Tschai strangers were objects of instinctive suspicion. The captain had no such inhibitions. He ate and drank with gusto and regaled the company with witticisms, reminiscences of previous voyages, jocular guesses regarding each passenger's purpose in making the voyage: a performance which gradually thawed the atmosphere. Ylin Ylan ate little. She appraised the two orange-haired girls and became gloomily aware of their appealing fragility. Dordolio sat somewhat apart, paying little heed to the captain's conversation, but from time to time looking sidewise toward the two girls and preening his mustache. After the meal he conducted Ylin Ylan forward to the bow where they watched phosphorescent sea-eels streaking away from the oncoming bow. The others sat on benches along the high quarterdeck, conducting guarded conversations while pink Az and blue Braz rose, one immediately behind the other, to send a pair of trails across the water.

One by one the passengers drifted off to their cabins, and presently the ship was left to the helmsman and the lookout.

Days drifted past: cool mornings with a pearly smoke clinging to the sea; noons with Carina 4269 burning at the zenith; ale-colored afternoons; quiet nights.

The *Vargaz* touched briefly at two small ports along the coast of Horasin: villages submerged in the foliage of giant gray-green trees. The *Vargaz* discharged hides and metal implements, took aboard bales of nuts, lumps of jellied fruit, butts of a beautiful rose and black timber.

Departing Horasin the *Vargaz* veered out into the Draschade Ocean, steering dead east along the equator both to take advantage of the counter-current and to avoid unfavorable weather patterns to north and south.

Winds were fickle; the *Vargaz* wallowed lazily across almost imperceptible swells.

The passengers amused themselves in their various ways. The orange-haired girls Heizari and Edwe played quoits, and teased Traz until he also joined the game.

Reith introduced the group to shuffleboard, which was taken up with enthusiasm. Palo Barba, the father of the girls, declared himself an instructor of swordsmanship; he and Dordolio fenced an hour or so each day, Dordolio stripped to the waist, a black ribbon confining his hair. Dordolio performed with foot-stamping bravura and staccato exclamations. Palo Barba fenced less flamboyantly, but with great emphasis upon traditional postures. Reith occasionally watched the two at their bouts, and on one occasion accepted Palo Barba's invitation to fence. Reith found the foils somewhat long and over-flexible, but conducted himself without discredit. He noticed Dordolio making critical observations to Ylin Ylan, and later Traz, who had overhead, informed him that Dordolio had pronounced his technique naïve and eccentric.

Reith shrugged and grinned. Dordolio was a man Reith found impossible to take seriously.

Twice other sails were spied in the distance; on one occasion a long black motor-galley changed course in a sinister fashion.

Reith inspected the vessel through his scanscope. A dozen tall yellow-skinned men wearing complicated black turbans stood looking toward the *Vargaz*. Reith reported as much to the captain, who made a casual glance. "Pirates. They won't bother us: too much risk."

The galley passed a mile to the south, then turned and disappeared into the southwest.

Two days later an island appeared ahead: a mountainous hump with foreshore cloaked under tall trees. "Gozed," said the captain, in response to Reith's inquiry. "We'll put in for a day or so. You've never touched at Gozed?"

"Never."

"You have a surprise in store. Or then, on the other hand"— here the captain gave Reith a careful inspection—"perhaps you don't. I can't say, since the customs of your own land are unknown to me. And unknown to yourself perhaps? I understand you to be an amnesiac."

Reith made a deprecatory gesture. "I never dispute other people's opinions of myself."

"In itself, a bizarre custom," declared the captain. "Try as I may, I cannot decide the land of your birth. You are a sort strange to me."

"I am a wanderer," said Reith. "A nomad, if you like."

"For a wanderer, you are at times strangely ignorant. Well then, ahead lies Gozed."

The island bulked large against the sky. Looking through the scanscope Reith could see an area along the foreshore where the trees had been defoliated and trimmed to the condition of crooked poles, each supporting one, two or three round huts. The ground below was barren gray sand, clear of refuse and raked smooth. Anacho the Dirdirman inspected the village through the scanscope. "About what I expected."

"You are acquainted with Gozed? The captain made quite a mystery of the place."

"No mystery. The folk of the island are highly religious; they worship the sea-scorpions native to the waters around the island. They are as large or larger than a man, or so I am told."

"Why then are the huts so high in the air?"

"At night the scorpions come up from the sea to spawn, which they accomplish by stinging eggs into a host animal, often a woman left down on the beach for that purpose. The eggs hatch, the 'Mother of the Gods' is devoured by the larvae. In the last stages, when pain and religious ecstasy produce a curious psychological state in the 'Mother,' she runs down the beach and flings herself into the sea."

"An unsettling religion."

The Dirdirman admitted as much. "Still it appears to suit the folk of Gozed. They could change anytime they chose. Sub-men are notoriously susceptible to aberrations of this sort."

Reith could not restrain a grin, and Anacho examined him with surprise. "May I inquire the source of your amusement?"

"It occurs to me that the relationship of Dirdirmen to Dirdir is not unlike that of the Gozed toward their scorpions."

"I fail to see the analogy," Anacho declared rather stiffly.

"Simplicity itself: both are victims to non-human beings who use men for their particular needs."

"Bah!" muttered Anacho. "In many ways you are the most wrong-headed man alive." He walked abruptly aft, to stand staring out over the sea. Pressures were working in Anacho's subconscious, thought Reith, causing him uneasiness.

The *Vargaz* nosed cautiously in toward the beach, swung behind a jut of barnacle-encrusted rock and dropped anchor. The captain went ashore in a pinnace; the passengers saw him talking to a group of stern-faced men, white-skinned, totally naked save for sandals and fillets holding down their long iron-colored hair.

Agreement was reached; the captain returned to the *Vargaz*. A half hour later a pair of lighters came out to the boat. A boom was rigged; bales of fiber and coils of rope were brought aboard, other bales and crates were lowered to the lighters. Two hours after arriving at Gozed the *Vargaz* backed sail, hoisted anchor and set off across the Draschade.

After the evening meal the passengers sat on the deck forward of the sterncastle with a lantern swinging overhead, and the talk veered to the people of Gozed and their religion. Val Dal Barba, wife of Palo Barba, mother of Heizari and Edwe, thought the ritual unjust.

"Why are there only 'Mothers of Gods'? Why shouldn't those flint-faced men go down on the beach and become 'Fathers of Gods'?"

The captain chuckled. "It seems as if the honors are reserved for the ladies."

"It would never be thus in Murgen," declared the merchant warmly. "We pay sizable tithes to the priests; they take all responsibility for appeasing Bisme; we have no further inconvenience."

"A system as sensible as any," agreed Pal Barba. "This year we subscribe to the Pansogmatic Gnosis, and the religion has much virtue to it."

"I like it much better than Tutelanics," said Edwe. "You merely recite the litany and then you are done for the day."

"Tutelanics was a dreadful bore," Heizari concurred. "All that memorizing! And remember that dreadful Convocation of Souls, where the priests were so familiar? I like Pansogmatic Gnosis much better."

Dordolio gave an indulgent laugh. "You prefer not to become intense. I myself incline in this direction. Yao doctrine, of course, is to some extent a syncresis; or, better to say, in the course of the 'round' all aspects of the Ineffable are given opportunity to manifest themselves, so that, as we move with the cycle, we experience all theopathy."

Anacho, still smarting from Reith's comparisons, looked across the deck. "Well then, what of Adam Reith, the erudite ethnologist? What theosophical insights can he contribute?"

"None," said Reith. "Very few, at any rate. It occurs to me that the man and his religion are one and the same thing. The unknown exists. Each man projects on the blankness the shape of his own particular world-view. He endows his creation with his personal volitions and attitudes. The religious man stating his case is in essence explaining himself. When a fanatic is contradicted he feels a threat to his own existence; he reacts violently."

"Interesting!" declared the fat merchant. "And the atheist?"

"He projects no image upon the blank whatever. The cosmic mysteries he accepts as things in themselves; he feels no need to hang a more or less human mask upon them. Otherwise, the correlation between a man and the shape into which he molds the unknown for greater ease of manipulation is exact."

The captain raised his goblet of wine against the light of the lantern, tossed it down his throat. "Perhaps you're right, but no one will ever change himself on this account. I have known a multitude of peoples. I have walked under Dirdir spires, through Blue Chasch gardens and Wankh castles. I know these folk and their changeling men. I have traveled to six continents of Tschai; I have befriended a thousand men, caressed a thousand women, killed a thousand enemies; I know the Yao, the Binth, the Walalukians, the Shemolei on one hand; on the other the steppe nomads, the marshmen, the islanders, the cannibals of Rakh and Kislovan; I see differences; I see identities. All try to extract a maximum advantage from existence, and finally all die. None seems the better for it. My own god? Good old *Vargaz*! Of course! As Adam Reith insists, it is myself. When *Vargaz* groans through the storm waves, I shudder and grind my teeth. When we glide the dark water under the pink and blue moons, I play the lute, I wear a red ribbon around my forehead, I drink wine. I and *Vargaz* serve each other and the day *Vargaz* sinks into the deep, I sink with her."

"Bravo!" cried Palo Barba, the swordsman, who had also drunk much wine. "Do you know, this is my creed as well?" He snatched up a sword, held it high so that lantern-light played up and down its spine. "What the *Vargaz* is to the captain, the sword is to me!"

"Father!" cried his orange-haired daughter Edwe. "And all the time we thought you a sensible Pansogmatist!"

"Please put down the steel," urged Val Dal Barba, "before you become excited and cut someone's ear off."

"What? Me? A veteran swordsman? How can you imagine such a thing? Well then, as you wish. I'll trade the steel for another goblet of wine."

The talk proceeded. Dordolio swaggered across the deck to stand near Reith. Presently he said, in a voice of facetious condescension, "A surprise to find a nomad so accomplished in disquisition, so apt in subtle distinctions."

Reith grinned at Traz. "Nomads are not necessarily buffoons."

"You perplex me," Dordolio declared. "Exactly which is your native steppe? What was your tribe?"

"My steppe is far away; my tribe is scattered in every direction."

Dordolio pulled thoughtfully at his mustache. "The Dirdirman believes you to be an amnesiac. According to the Blue Jade Princess you have implied yourself to be a man from another world. The nomad boy, who knows you best, says nothing. I admit to what may be an obtrusive curiosity."

"The quality signifies an active mind," said Reith.

"Yes, yes. Let me put what I freely acknowledge to be an absurd question." Dordolio examined Reith cautiously sidewise. "Do you consider yourself to be the native of another world?"

Reith laughed and groped for an answer. He said: "Four possible conditions exist. If I were indeed from another world I could answer either yes or no. If I were not from another world I could answer yes or no. The first case leads to inconvenience. The second diminishes my self-respect. The third case is insanity. The fourth represents the only situation you would not consider an abnormality. The question, hence, as you admit it, is absurd."

Dordolio tugged angrily at his mustache. "Are you, by any farfetched chance, a member of the 'cult'?"

"Probably not. Which 'cult' is this?"

"The Yearning Refluxives who rode up the cycle to destroy our two gorgeous cities."

"But I understood that an unknown agency torpedoed the cities."

"No matter; the 'cult' instigated the attack; they are the cause."

Reith shook his head. "Incomprehensible! An enemy destroys your cities; your bitterness is directed not against the cruel enemy but against a possibly sincere and thoughtful group of your own people. A displaced emotion, or so it seems."

Dordolio gave Reith a cold inspection. "Your analyses at times border upon the mordant."

Reith laughed. "Let it pass. I know nothing of your 'cult.' As for my place of origin, I prefer to be amnesiac."

"A curious lapse, when otherwise you seem so emphatic in your opinions."

"I wonder why you trouble to press the point," Reith mused. "For instance, what would you say if I claimed origin from a far world?"

Dordolio pursed his lips, blinked up at the lantern. "I had not taken my thoughts quite so far. Well, we will not pursue the subject. A frightening idea, to begin with: an ancient world of men!"

" 'Frightening'? How so?"

Dordolio gave an uneasy laugh. "There is a dark side to humanity, which is like a stone pressed into the mold. The upper side, exposed to sun and air, is clean; tilt it and look below, at the muck and scurrying insects . . . We of Yao know this well; nothing will put an end to *awaile*. But enough of such talk!" Dordolio gave his shoulders a jerk and a shake, and resumed his somewhat condescending tone of voice. "You are resolved to come to Cath; what will you do there?"

"I don't know. I must exist somewhere; why not in Cath?"

"Not too simple for a stranger," said Dordolio. "Affiliation with a palace is difficult."

"Odd that you should say that! The Flower of Cath declares that her father will welcome us to Blue Jade Palace."

"He would necessarily show formal courtesy, but you could no more take up residence at the Blue Jade Palace than you could on the bottom of the Draschade, merely because a fish invited you to swim."

"What would prevent me?"

Dordolio shrugged. "No man cares to make a fool of himself. Deportment is the definition of life. What does a nomad know of deportment?"

Reith had nothing to say to this. "A thousand details go into the conduct of a cavalier," stated Dordolio. "At the academy we learn degrees of address, signals, language configuration, in which I admit a deficiency. We take instruction in sword address and principles of dueling, genealogy, heraldry; we learn the niceties of costume and a hundred other details. Perhaps you consider these matters over-arbitrary?"

Anacho the Dirdirman, standing nearby, chose to reply. " 'Trivial' is a word more apt."

Reith expected an icy retort, at the least a glare, but Dordolio gave only an indifferent shrug. "Well, then, is your life more significant? Or that of the merchant, or the swordsman? Never forget the Yao are a pessimistic race! *Awaile* is always a threat; we are perhaps more somber than we seem. Recognizing the essential pointlessness of existence, we exalt the small flicker of vitality at our command; we extract the fullest and most distinctive flavor from every incident, by insisting upon an appropriate formality. Trivality? Decadence? Who can do better?"

"All very well," said Reith. "But why be satisfied with pessimism? Why not expand your horizons? Further, it seems that you accept the destruction of your cities with a surprising nonchalance. Vengeance is not the most noble activity, but submissiveness is worse."

"Bah," muttered Dordolio. "How could a barbarian understand the disaster and its aftermath? The Refluxives in vast numbers took refuge in *awaile;* the acts and the expiations kept our land in a ferment. There was no energy for anything else. Were you of good caste, I would cut your heart out for daring so gross an imputation."

Reith laughed. "Since my low caste protects me from retribution, let me ask another question: what is *awaile?*"

Dordolio threw his hands in the air. "An amnesiac as well as a barbarian! I have no conversation for such as you! Ask the Dirdirman; he is glib enough." And Dordolio strode off in a rage.

"An unreasonable display of emotion," mused Reith. "I wonder what my imputation was?"

"Shame," said Anacho. "The Yao are as sensitive to shame as an eyeball to grit. Mysterious enemies destroy their cities; they suspect the Dirdir but dare no recourse, and must cope with helpless rage and shame. It is their typical attribute and predisposes them to *awaile.*"

"And this is?"

"Murder. The afflicted person—one who feels shame—kills as many persons as he is able, of any sex, age or degree of relationship. Then, when he is able to kill no more, he submits and becomes apathetic. His punishment is dreadful and highly dramatic, and enlightens the entire population, who crowd the place of punishment. Each execution has its particular flavor and style and is essentially a dramatic pageant of pain, possibly enjoyed even by the victim. The institution permeates the life of Cath. The Dirdir on this basis consider all sub-men mad."

Reith grunted. "So then, if we visit Cath, we risk insensate murder."

"Small risk. After all, the acts are not ordinary events." Anacho looked around the deck. "But it seems that the hour is late." He bade Reith goodnight and stalked off to his bunk.

Reith remained by the rail, looking out over the water. After the bloodletting at Pera, Cath had seemed a haven, a civilized environment where just possibly he might contrive to patch together a spaceboat. The prospect seemed ever more remote.

Someone came to stand beside him: Heizari, the older of Palo Barbar's orange-haired daughters. "You seem so melancholy. What troubles you?"

Reith looked down into the pale oval of the girl's face: an arch impudent face, at this moment alive with innocent—or not so innocent?—coquetry. Reith restrained the first words that rose to his lips. The girl was unquestionably appealing. "How is it you are not in bed with your sister Edwe?"

"Oh, simple! She is not in bed either. She sits with your friend Traz on the quarterdeck, beguiling and provoking, teasing and tormenting. She is much more of a flirt than I."

Poor Traz, thought Reith. He asked, "What of your father and mother? Are they not concerned?"

"What's it to them? When they were young, they dallied as ardently as any; is that not their right?"

"I suppose so. Customs vary, as you know."

"What of you? What are the customs of your people?"

"Ambiguous and rather complicated," said Reith. "There's a great deal of variation."

"This is the case with Cloud Islanders," said Heizari, leaning somewhat closer. "We are by no means automatically amorous. But on occasions a certain mood comes over a person, which I believe to be the consequence of natural law."

"No argument there," Reith obeyed his impulse and kissed the piquant face. "Still, I don't care to antagonize your father, natural law or not. He is an expert swordsman."

"Have no fears on that score. If you require assurance, doubtless he is still awake."

"I don't know quite what I'd ask him," said Reith. "Well then, all things considered . . ." The two strolled forward and climbed the carved steps to the forepeak, and stood looking south across the sea. Az hung low in the west laying a line of amethyst prisms along the water. An orange-haired girl, a purple moon, a fairytale cog on a remote ocean: would he trade it all to be back on Earth? The answer had to be yes. And yet, why deny the attractions of the moment? Reith kissed the girl somewhat more fervently than before and now from the shadow of the anchor windlass, a person hitherto invisible jumped erect and departed in desperate haste. In the slanting moonlight Reith recognized Ylin Ylan, the Flower of Cath . . . His ardor was quenched; he looked miserably aft. And yet, why feel guilt? She had long since made it clear that the one-time relationship was at an end. Reith turned back to the orange-haired Heizari.

4

THE MORNING DAWNED without wind. The sun rose into a bird's-egg sky: beige and dove-gray around the horizon, pale gray-blue at the zenith.

The morning meal, as usual, was coarse bread, salt fish, preserved fruit, and acrid tea. The company sat in silence, each occupied with morning thoughts.

The Flower of Cath was late. She slipped quietly into the saloon and took her place with a polite smile to left and right, and ate in a kind of reverie. Dordolio watched her with perplexity.

The captain looked in from the deck. "A day of calm. Tonight clouds and thunder. Tomorrow? No way of knowing. Unusual weather!"

Reith irritably forced himself to his usual conduct. No cause for misgivings: he had not changed; Ylin Ylan had changed. Even at the most intense stage of their relationship she had at all times kept part of herself secret: a persona represented by another of her many names? Reith forced her from his mind.

Ylin Ylan wasted no time in the saloon, but went out on deck, where she was joined by Dordolio. They leaned on the rail, Ylin Ylan speaking with great urgency, Dordolio pulling his mustache and occasionally interposing a word or two.

A seaman on the quarterdeck gave a sudden call and pointed across the water. Jumping up on the hatch Reith saw a dark floating shape, with a head and narrow shoulders, disturbingly manlike; the creature surged, disappeared below the surface. Reith turned to Anacho. "What was that?"

"A Pnume."

"So far from land?"

"Why not? They are the same sort as the Phung. Who holds a Phung to account for his deeds?"

"But what does it do out here, in mid-ocean?"

"Perhaps it floats by night on the surface, watching the moons swing by."

The morning passed. Traz and the two girls played quoits. The merchant mused through a leather-bound book. Palo Barba and Dordolio fenced for a period. Dordolio was as usual flamboyant, whistling his steel through the air, stamping his feet, flourishing his arms.

Palo Barba presently tired of the sport. Dordolio stood twitching his blade. Ylin Ylan came to sit on the hatch. Dordolio turned to Reith. "Come, nomad, take up the foil; show me the skills of your native steppe."

Reith instantly became wary. "They are very few; additionally I am out of practice. Perhaps another day."

"Come, come," cried Dordolio, eyes glittering. "I have heard reports of your adroitness. You must not refuse to demonstrate your technique."

"You must excuse me; I am disinclined."

"Yes, Adam Reith!" called Ylin Ylan. "Fence! You will disappoint us all!"

Reith turned his head, examined the Flower for a long moment. Her face, pinched and wan and quivering with emotion, was not the face of the girl he had known in Pera. In some fashion, change had come; he looked into the face of a stranger.

Reith turned his attention to Dordolio, who evidently had been incited by the Flower of Cath. Whatever they planned was not to his advantage.

Palo Barba intervened. "Come," he told Dordolio. "Let the man rest, I will play another set of passes, and give you all the exercise you require."

"But I wish to engage this fellow," declared Dordolio. "His attitudes are exasperating; I feel that he needs to be chastened."

"If you intend to pick a quarrel," said Palo Barba coldly, "that of course is your affair."

"No quarrel," declared Dordolio in a brassy, somewhat nasal voice. "A demonstration, let us say. The fellow seems to equate the caste of Cath with common ruck. A significant difference exists, as I wish to make clear."

Reith wearily rose to his feet. "Very well. What do you have in mind for your demonstration?"

"Foils, swords, as you wish. Since you are ignorant of chivalrous address, there shall be none; a simple 'go' must suffice."

"And 'stop'?"

Dordolio grinned through his mustache. "As circumstances dictate."

"Very well." He turned to Palo Barba. "Allow me to look over your weapons, if you please."

Palo Barba opened his box. Reith selected a pair of short light blades.

Dordolio stared, eyebrows arched high in distaste. "Child's weapons, for the training of boys!"

Reith hefted one of the blades, twitched it through the air. "This suits me well enough. If you are dissatisfied, use whatever blade you like."

Dordolio grudgingly took up the light blade. "It has no life; it is without movement or backsnap—"

Reith lifted his sword, tilted Dordolio's hat down over his eyes. "But responsive and serviceable, as you see."

Dordolio removed the hat without comment, shot the cuffs of his white silk blouse. "Are you ready?"

"Whenever you are."

Dordolio raised his sword in a preposterous salute, bowed right and left to the spectators. Reith drew back. "I thought you planned to forgo the ceremonies."

Dordolio merely drew back the corners of his mouth, to show his teeth, and performed one of his foot-stamping assaults. Reith parried without difficulty, feinted Dordolio out of position and swung down at one of the clasps which supported Dordolio's breeches.

Dordolio jumped back, then attacked once more, the snarl replaced by a sinister grin. He stormed Reith's defense, picking here and there, resting, probing; Reith reacted sluggishly. Dordolio feinted, drew Reith's blade aside, lunged. Reith had already jumped away; Dordolio's blade met empty air. Reith hacked down hard at the clasp, breaking it loose.

Dordolio drew back with a frown. Reith stepped forward, struck down at the other clasp, and Dordolio's breeches grew loose about the waist.

Dordolio retreated, red in the face. He cast down the sword. "These ridiculous playthings! Take up a real sword!"

"Use any sword you prefer. I will remain with this one. But, first, I suggest that you take steps to support your trousers; you will embarrass both of us."

Dordolio bowed, with icy good grace. He went somewhat apart, tied his breeches to his belt with thongs. "I am ready. Since you insist, and since my purposes are punitive, I will use the weapon with which I am familiar."

"As you like."

Dordolio took up his long supple blade, flourished it around his head so that it sang in the air, then, nodding to Reith, came to the attack. The flexible tip swung in from right and left; Reith slid it away, and casually, almost as if by accident, tapped Dordolio's cheek with the flat of his blade.

Dordolio blinked, and launched a furious prancing attack. Reith gave ground; Dordolio followed, stamping, lunging, cutting, striking from all sides. Reith parried, and tapped Dordolio's other cheek. He then drew back. "I find myself winded; perhaps you have had enough exercise for the day?"

Dordolio stood glaring, nostrils distended, chest rising and falling. He turned away, gazed out to sea. He heaved a deep sigh, and turned back. "Yes," he said in a dull voice. "We have exercised enough." He looked down at his jeweled rapier, and for a moment appeared ready to cast it into the sea. Instead, he thrust it into his sheath, bowed to Reith. "Your swordplay is excellent. I am indebted for the demonstration."

Palo Barba came forward. "Well spoken, a true cavalier of Cath! Enough of blades and metal; let us take a goblet of morning wine."

Dordolio bowed. "Presently." He went off to his cabin. The Flower of Cath sat as if carved from stone.

Heizari brought Reith a goblet of wine. "I have a wonderful idea."

"Which is?"

"You must leave the ship at Wyness, come to Orchard Hill and assist my father's fencing academy. An easy life, without worries or fear."

"The prospect is pleasant," said Reith. "I wish I could ... but I have other responsibilities."

"Put them aside! Are responsibilities so important when one has a single life to live? But don't answer." She put her hand on Reith's mouth. "I know what you will say. You are a strange man, Adam Reith, so grim and so easy all at once."

"I don't seem strange to myself. Tschai is strange; I'm quite ordinary."

"Of course not!" laughed Heizari. "Tschai is—" She made a vague gesture. "Sometimes it is terrible . . . but strange? I know no other place." She rose to her feet. "Well then, I will pour you more wine and perhaps I will drink as well. On so quiet a day what else is there to do?"

The captain passing near, halted. "Enjoy the calm while you can; winds are coming. Look to the north."

On the horizon a bank of black clouds; the sea below glimmered like copper. Even as they watched a breath of air came across the sea, a curiously cool waft. The sails of the *Vargaz* flapped; the rigging creaked.

From the cabin came Dordolio. He had changed his garments; now he wore a suit of somber maroon, black velvet shoes, a billed hat of black velvet. He looked for Ylin Ylan; where was she? Far forward on the forepeak, she leaned on the rail, looking off to sea. Dordolio hesitated, then slowly turned away. Palo Barba handed him a goblet of wine; Dordolio silently took a seat under the great brass lantern.

The bank of clouds rolled south, giving off flashes of purple light, and presently the low grumble of thunder reached the *Vargaz.*

The lateen sails were furled; the cog moved sluggishly on a small square storm sail.

Sunset was an eerie scene, the dark brown sun shining under the black clouds. The Flower of Cath came from the stern-castle: stark naked she stood, looking up and down the decks, into the amazed faces of the passengers.

She held a dart pistol in one hand, a dagger in the other. Her face was set in a peculiar fixed smile; Reith, who had known the face under a host of circumstances, would never have recognized it. Dordolio, giving an inarticulate bellow, ran forward.

The Flower of Cath aimed the pistol at him; Dordolio dodged; the dart sang past his head. She searched the deck; she spied Heizari, and stepped forward, pistol at the ready; Heizari cried out in fear, ran behind the mainmast. Lightning sprang from cloud to cloud; in the purple glare Dordolio sprang upon the Flower; she slashed him with the dagger; Dordolio staggered back with blood squirting from his neck. The Flower aimed the dart-gun, Dordolio rolled over behind the hatch. Heizari ran forward to the forecastle; the Flower pursued. A crewman emerged from the forecastle—to stand petrified. The Flower stabbed up into his astounded face; the man tumbled backward, down the companionway.

Heizari stood behind the foremast. Lightning spattered across the sky; thunder came almost at once.

The Flower stabbed deftly around the mast; the orange-haired girl clutched her side, tottered forth with a wondering face. The Flower aimed the dart gun but Palo Barba was there to knock it clattering to the deck. The Flower cut at him, cut at Reith who was trying to seize her, ran up the ladder to the forepeak, climbed out on the sprit.

The cog rose to the waves; the sprit reared and plunged. The sun sank into the ocean; the Flower turned to watch it, hanging to the forestay with one arm.

Reith called to her, "Come back, come back!"

She turned, looked at him, her face remote. "Deal!" called Reith. "Ylin Ylan!" The girl gave no signal she had heard. Reith called her other names: "Blue Jade Flower!" Then her court name: "Shar Zarin!"

She only gave him a regretful smile.

Reith sought to coax her. He used her child name: "Zozi . . . Zozi . . . come back here."

The girl's face changed. She pulled herself closer to the stay, hugging it.

"Zozi! Won't you talk to me? Come here, there's a good girl."

But her mind was far away, off where the sun was setting.

Reith called her secret name: "L'lae! Come, come here! Ktan calls you, L'lae!"

Again she shook her head, never taking her eyes from the sea.

Reith called the final name though it felt strange to his lips: her love name. He called, but thunder drowned the sound of his voice, and the girl did not hear. The sun was a small segment, swimming with antique colors. The Flower stepped from the sprit, and dropped into a hissing surge of spume. For an instant Reith thought he saw the spiral of her dark hair, and then she was gone.

Later, in the evening, with the *Vargaz* pitching up the great slopes and wallowing in a rush down into the troughs, Reith put a question to Ankhe at afram Anacho, the Dirdirman. "Had she simply lost her reason? Or was that *awaile?*"

"It was *awaile*. The refuge from shame."

"But—" Reith started to speak, but could only make an inarticulate gesture.

"You gave attendance to the Cloud Isle girl. Her champion made a fool of himself. Humiliation lay across the future. She would have killed us all had she been able."

"I find it incomprehensible," muttered Reith.

"Naturally. You are not Yao. For the Blue Jade Princess, the pressure was too great. She is lucky. In Settra she would have been punished at a dramatic public torturing."

Reith groped his way out on deck. The brass lantern creaked as it swung. Reith looked out over the blowing sea. Somewhere far away and deep, a white body floated in the dark.

5

FREAKISH WINDS BLEW throughout the night: gusts, breaths, blasts, whispers. Dawn brought an abrupt calm, and the sun found the *Vargaz* wallowing in a confused sea.

At noon a terrible squall sent the ship scudding south like a toy, the bluff bow battering the sea to froth. The passengers kept to the saloon, or to the trunk deck. Heizari, bandaged and pale, kept to the cabin she shared with Edwe. Reith sat with her for an hour. She could speak of nothing but her terrible experience. "But why should she do so dreadful a deed?"

"Apparently the Yao are prone to such acts."

"I have heard as much; but even insanity has a reason."

"The Dirdirman says she was overwhelmed by shame."

"What folly! A person as beautiful as she? What could she have done to affect her so?"

"I wouldn't care to speculate," muttered Reith.

The squalls became gigantic hills lofting the *Vargaz* high, heaving the round hull bubbling and singing down the long slopes. Finally one morning the sun shone down from a dove-brown sky clean of clouds. The seas persisted a day longer, then gradually lessened, and the cog set all sail before a fair breeze from the west.

Three days later a dim black island loomed in the south,

which the captain declared to be the haunt of corsairs; he kept a sharp lookout from the masthead until the island had merged into the murk of evening.

The days passed without distinguishing characteristic: curiously antiseptic days overshadowed by the uncertainty of the future. Reith became edgy and nervous. How long ago had been the events at Pera: a time so innocent and uncomplicated! At that time, Cath had seemed a haven of civilized security, with Reith certain that the Blue Jade Lord through gratitude would facilitate his plans. What a callow hope!

The cog approached the coast of Kachan, where the captain hoped to ride north-flowing currents up into the Parapan.

One morning, coming on deck, Reith found a remarkable island standing off the starboard beam: a place of no great extent, less than a quarter-mile in diameter, surrounded at the water's edge by a wall of black glass a hundred feet high. Beyond rose a dozen massive buildings of various heights and graceless proportion.

Anacho the Dirdirman came to stand beside him, narrow shoulders hunched, long face dour. "There you see the stronghold of an evil race: the Wankh."

" 'Evil'? Because they are at war with the Dirdir?"

"Because they will not end the war. What benefit to either Dirdir or Wankh is such a confrontation? The Dirdir offer disengagement; the Wankh refuse. A harsh inscrutable people!"

"Naturally, I know nothing of the issues," said Reith. "Why the wall around the island?"

"To daunt the Pnume, who infest Tschai like rats. The Wankh are not a companionable folk. In fact—look down yonder below the surface."

Reith, peering into the water, saw gliding beside the ship at a depth of ten or fifteen feet a dark man-like shape, with a metal structure fixed across its mid-body, moving without motion of its own. The figure twisted, slanted away and vanished into the murk.

"An amphibious race, the Wankh, with electric jets for their underwater sport."

Reith once more raised the scanscope. The Wankh towers, like the walls, were black glass. Round windows were discs blacker than black; balconies of frail twisted crystal became walkways to far structures. Reith spied movement: a pair of Wankh? Looking more closely he saw the creatures to be men—Wankhmen, beyond all doubt—with flour-white skins and black pelts close to somewhat flat scalps. Their faces seemed smooth, with still, saturnine features; they wore what appeared to be one-piece black garments, with wide black leather belts, on which hung small implements, tools, instruments. As they moved into the building, they looked out at the *Vargaz* and for an instant Reith saw full into their faces. He jerked the scanscope from his eyes.

Anacho eyed him askance. "What is the trouble?"

"I saw two Wankhmen . . . Even you, weird mutated freak that you are, seem ordinary by comparison."

Anacho gave a sardonic chuckle. "They are in fact not dissimilar to the typical sub-man."

Reith made no argument; in the first place he could not define the exact quality he had seen behind the still white faces. He looked again, but the Wankhmen had disappeared. Dordolio had come out on deck and now stared in fascination at the scanscope. "What instrument is that?"

"An electronic optical device," said Reith without emphasis.

"I've never seen its like." He looked at Anacho. "Is it a Dirdir machine?"

Anacho made a quizzical dissent. "I think not."

Dordolio gave Reith a puzzled glance. "Is it Chasch or Wankh?" He veered at the engraved escutcheon. "What writing is this?"

Anacho shrugged. "Nothing I can read."

Dordolio asked Reith: "Can you read it?"

"Yes, I believe so." Impelled by a sudden mischievous urge, Reith read:

"Federal Space Agency
Tool and Instrument Division
Mark XI Photomultiplying Binocular Telescope
1x–1000x
Nonprojective, inoperable in total darkness.
BAF-1303-K-29023
Use Type D5 energy slug only. In poor light, engage color compensator switch. Do not look at sun or high-intensity illumination; if automatic light-gate fails, damage to the eyes may result."

Dordolio stared. "What language is that?"

"One of the many human dialects," said Reith.

"But from what region? Men everywhere on Tschai, to my understanding, speak the same language."

"Rather than embarrass you both," said Reith. "I prefer to say nothing. Continue to think of me as an amnesiac."

"Do you take us for fools?" growled Dordolio. "Are we children to have our questions answered with flippant evasions?"

"Sometimes," said Anacho, speaking into the air, "it is the part of wisdom to maintain a myth. Too much knowledge can become a burden."

Dordolio gnawed at his mustache. From the corner of his eye he glanced at the scanscope, then swung abruptly away.

Ahead three more islands had appeared, rising sharply from the sea, each with its wall and core of eccentric black buildings. A shadow lay on the horizon beyond: the mainland of Kachan.

During the afternoon the shadow took on density and detail, to become a hulk of mountains rising from the sea. The *Vargaz* coasted north, almost in the shadow of the mountains, with black dip-winged kites swooping around the masts, emitting mournful hoots and clashing their mandibles. Late in the afternoon the mountains fell away to reveal a landlocked bay. A nondescript town occupied the south shore; from a promontory to the north rose a Wankh fortress, like a growth of undisciplined black crystals. A spaceport occupied the flat land to the east, where a number of spaceships of various styles and sizes were visible.

Through the scanscope, Reith studied the landscape and the mountainside sloping down to the spacefield from the east. *Interesting*, mused Reith, *interesting indeed*.

The captain, coming past, identified the port as Ao Hidis, one of the important Wankh centers. "I had no intent of faring south so far, but since we're here, I'll try to sell my leathers and the Grenie woods; then I'll take on Wankh chemicals for Cath. A word of warning for those of you who intend to roister ashore. There are two towns here: Ao Hidis proper, which is Man-town, and an unpronounceable sound which is Wankh-town. In Man-town are several kinds of people, including Lokhars, but mainly Blacks and Purples. They do not mingle; they recognize their own kind only. In the streets you may walk without fear, you may buy at any shop or booth with an open front. Do not enter any closed shop or tavern, either Black or Purple; you'll likely not come out.

There are no public brothels. If you buy from a Black booth, do not stop at a Purple booth with your goods; you will be resented and perhaps insulted, or, in certain cases, attacked. The opposite holds true. As for Wankh-town, there is nothing to do except stare at the Wankh, to which you are welcome, for they do not seem to object. All considered, a dull port, with little amusement ashore."

The *Vargaz* eased alongside a wharf flying a small purple pennon. "I patronized Purple on my last visit," the captain told Reith who had come up to the quarterdeck. "They gave good service at a fair price; I see no reason to change."

The *Vargaz* was moored by Purple longshoremen: round-faced, round-headed men with a plum-colored cast to their complexion. From the neighboring Black dock Blacks looked on with aloof hostility. These were physiognomically similar to the Purples, but with gray skins oddly mottled with black.

"No one knows the cause," the Captain said, in regard to the color disparity. "The same mother may produce one Purple child and one Black. Some blame diet; others drugs; others hold that disease attacks a color-gland in the mother's egg. But Black and Purple they are born; and each calls the other pariah. When Black and Purple breed, the union is sterile, or so it is said. The notion horrifies each race; they would as soon couple with nighthounds."

"What of the Dirdirman?" asked Reith. "Is he likely to be molested?"

"Bah. The Wankh take no notice of such trivia. The Blue Chasch are known for sadistic malice. Dirdir stringencies are unpredictable. But in my experience the Wankh are the most indifferent and remote people of Tschai, and seldom trouble with men. Perhaps they do their evil in secret like Pnume; no one knows. The Wankhmen are a different sort, cold as ghouls, and it is not wise to cross them. Well then, we are docked. Are you going ashore? Remember my warnings; Ao Hidis is a harsh city. Ignore both Black and Purple; talk to no one; interfere with nothing. Last visit I lost a seaman who bought a shawl at a Black shop, then drank wine at a Purple booth. He staggered aboard the ship with foam coming from his nose."

Anacho chose to remain aboard the *Vargaz*. Reith went ashore with Traz. Crossing the dock they found themselves on a wide street paved with slabs of mica-schist. To either side were houses built crudely of stone and timber, surrounded by rubbish. A few motor vehicles of a type Reith had not previously seen moved along the street; Reith assumed them to be of Wankh manufacture.

Around the shore to the north rose the Wankh towers. In this direction also lay the spaceport.

There seemed to be no public conveyances; Reith and Traz set off on foot. The huts gave way to somewhat more pretentious dwellings, and then they came to a square surrounded on all sides by shops and booths. Half of the folk were Black, half Purple; neither took notice of the other. Blacks patronized Blacks; Purple shops and booths served Purples. Blacks and Purples jostled each other, without acknowledgment or apology. Detestation hung in the air like a reek.

Reith and Traz crossed the square, continued north along a road paved with concrete, and presently came to a fence of tall glass rods surrounding the spacefield. Reith halted, surveyed the lie of the land.

"I am not naturally a thief," he told Traz. "But notice the little spaceboat! I would gladly confiscate that from its present owner."

"It is a Wankh boat," Traz pointed out pessimistically. "You would not know how to control it."

Reith nodded. "True. But if I had time—a week or so—I could learn. Spacecraft are necessarily similar."

"Think of the practicalities!" Traz admonished him.

Reith concealed a grin. Traz occasionally reverted to the stern personality of Onmale, the near-vital emblem which Traz had worn at the time of their first meeting. Traz shook his head dubiously. "Are valuable vehicles left unattended, ready to fly off into the sky? Unlikely!"

"No one seems to be aboard the small ship," argued Reith. "Even the freighters seem to be empty. Why should there be vigilance? Who would wish to steal them, except a person like myself?"

"Well then, what if you managed to enter the ship?" Traz demanded. "Before you could understand how to operate the machinery, you would be found and killed."

"No question but that the project is risky," agreed Reith.

They returned to the port, and the *Vargaz*, when once more they were aboard, seemed a haven of normalcy.

Cargo was discharged and loaded all during the night. In the morning with all passengers and crew members aboard, the *Vargaz* threw off moorings, hoisted sail and glided back out into the Draschade Ocean.

The *Vargaz* sailed north under the bleak Kachan coast. On the first day a dozen Wankh keeps appeared ahead, passed abeam and were left in the haze astern. On the second day the *Vargaz* passed in front of three great fjords. From the last of these a motor galley plunged forth, wake churning up astern. The captain immediately sent two men to man the blast-cannon. The galley cut through the swells to pass behind the cog; the captain instantly put about and brought the cannon to bear once more. The galley swung away and off to sea, with the jeers and hoots from the men aboard coming faintly across the water.

A week later Dragan, first of the Isles of Cloud, appeared on the port beam. On the following day the cog put into Wyness; here Palo Barba, his spouse, and his orange-haired daughters disembarked. Traz looked wistfully after them. Edwe turned and waved; then the family was lost to sight among the yellow silks and white linen cloaks of the dockside crowd.

Two days the cog lay at Wyness, unloading cargo, taking on stores and fitting new sails; then the lines were thrown off and the cog put to sea.

With a brisk wind from the west the *Vargaz* drove through the chop of the Parapan. A day passed and a night and another day, and the atmosphere aboard the *Vargaz* became suspenseful, with all hands looking east, trying to locate the loom of Charchan. Evening came; the sun sank into a sad welter of brown and gray and murky orange. The evening meal was a platter of dried fruit and pickled fish, which no one ate, preferring to stand by the rail. The night drew on; the wind lessened; one by one the passengers retired to their cabins. Reith remained on deck, musing upon the circumstances of his life. Time passed. From the quarterdeck came a grumble of orders; the main yard creaked down the mast and the *Vargaz* lost way. Reith went back to the rail. Through the dark glimmered a shine of far lights: the coast of Cath.

6

DAWN REVEALED A low-lying shore, black against the sepia sky. The mainsail was hoisted to the morning breeze; the *Vargaz* moved into the harbor of Vervodei.

The sun rose to reveal the face of the sleeping city. To the north tall flat-faced buildings overlooked the harbor, to the south were wharves and warehouses.

The *Vargaz* dropped anchor; the sails rattled down the mast. A pinnace rowed out with lines and the *Vargaz* was heaved stern-first against a dock. Port officials came aboard, consulted with the captain, exchanged salutes with Dordolio and departed. The voyage was at an end.

Reith bade the captain goodbye and with Traz and Anacho went ashore. As they stood on the dock Dordolio approached. He spoke in an offhand voice. "I now take my leave of you, since I depart immediately for Settra."

Wary and wondering as to Dordolio's motives, Reith asked: "The Blue Jade Palace is at Settra?"

"Yes, of course." Dordolio pulled at his mustache. "You need not concern yourself in this regard; I will convey all necessary news to the Blue Jade Lord."

"Still, there is much that you do not know," said Reith. "In fact, nearly everything."

"Your information will be of no great consolation," said Dordolio stiffly.

"Perhaps not. But surely he will be interested."

Dordolio shook his head in sad exasperation. "Quixotic! You know nothing of the ceremonies! Do you expect simply to walk up to the Lord and blurt out your tale? Crassness. And your clothes: unsuitable! Not to mention the marmoreal Dirdirman and the nomad lad."

"We must trust to the courtesy and tolerance of the Blue Jade Lord," said Reith.

"Bah," muttered Dordolio. "You have no shame." But still he delayed, frowning off up the street. He said, "You definitely plan to visit Settra then?"

"Yes, of course."

"Accept my advice. Tonight stop at one of the local inns—the Dulvan yonder is adequate—then tomorrow or the next day visit a reputable haberdasher and put yourself into his hands. Then, suitably clothed, come to Settra. The Travelers' Inn on the Oval will furnish you suitable accommodation. Under these circumstances, perhaps you will do me a service. I seem to have misplaced my funds, and I would be obliged to you for the loan of a hundred sequins to take me to Settra."

"Certainly," said Reith. "But let us all go to Settra together."

Dordolio made a petulant gesture. "I am in haste. Your preparations will consume time."

"Not at all," said Reith. "We are ready at this moment. Lead the way."

Dordolio scanned Reith from head to toe, in vast distaste. "The least I can do, for our mutual comfort, is to see you into respectable clothes. Come along then." He set off along the esplanade toward the center of town. Reith, Traz and Anacho followed, Traz seething with indignation. "Why do we suffer his arrogance?"

"The Yao are mercurial folk," said Anacho. "Pointless to become disturbed."

Away from the docks the city took on its own character. Wide, somewhat stark, streets ran between flat-faced buildings of glazed brick under steep roofs of brown tile. Everywhere a state of genteel dilapidation was evident. The activity of Coad was absent; the few folk abroad carried themselves with self-effacing reserve. Some wore complicated suits, white linen shirts, cravats tied in complex knots and bows. Others, apparently of lesser status, wore loose breeches of green or tan, jackets and blouses of various subdued colors.

Dordolio led the way to a large open-fronted shop, in which several dozen men and women sat sewing garments. Signaling to the three following him, Dordolio entered the shop. Reith, Anacho, and Traz entered and waited while Dordolio spoke energetically to the bald old proprietor.

Dordolio came to confer with Reith. "I have described your needs; the clothier will fit you from his stock, at no large expense."

Three pale young men appeared, wheeling racks of finished garments. The proprietor made swift selection, laid them before Reith, Traz, and Anacho. "These I believe will suit the gentlemen. If they would care to change immediately, the dressing rooms are at hand."

Reith inspected the garments critically. The cloth seemed a trifle coarse; the colors were somewhat raw. Reith glanced at Anacho, whose reflective smile reinforced his own assumptions. Reith said to Dordolio: "Your own clothes are the worse for wear. Why not try on this suit?"

Dordolio stood back with eyebrows raised high. "I am satisfied with what I wear."

Reith put down the garments. "These are not suitable," he told the clothier. "Show me your catalog, or whatever you work from."

"As you wish, sir."

Reith, with Anacho watching gravely, looked through a hundred or so color sketches. He pointed to a conservatively cut suit of dark blue. "What of this?"

Dordolio made an impatient sound. "The garments a wealthy vegetable grower might wear to an intimate funeral."

Reith indicated another costume. "What of this?"

"Even less appropriate: the lounge clothes of an elderly philosopher at his country estate."

"Hm. Well then," Reith told the clothier, "show me the clothes a somewhat younger philosopher of impeccable good taste would wear on a casual visit to the city."

Dordolio gave a snort. He started to speak but thought better of it and turned away. The clothier gave order to his assistants. Reith looked at Anacho with an appraising frown. "For this gentleman, the traveling costume of a high-caste dignitary." And for Traz: "A young gentleman's casual dress."

New garments appeared, conspicuously different from those ordered out by Dordolio. The three changed; the clothier made small adjustments while Dordolio stood to the side, pulling at his mustache. At last he could no longer restrain a comment. "Handsome garments, of course. But are they appropriate? You will puzzle folk when your conduct belies your appearance."

Anacho spoke scornfully. "Would you have us visit Settra dressed like bumpkins? The clothes you selected hardly carried a flattering association."

"What does it matter?" cried Dordolio in a brassy voice. "A fugitive Dirdirman, a nomad boy, a mysterious nonesuch: is it not absurd to trick such folk out in noblemen's costume?"

Reith laughed; Anacho fluttered his fingers; Traz turned Dordolio a glance of infinite disgust. Reith paid the account.

"Now then," muttered Dordolio, "to the airport. Since you demand the best, we shall charter an air-car."

"Not so fast," said Reith. "As usual you miscalculate. There must be another, less ostentatious, means to reach Settra."

"Naturally," said Dordolio with a sneer. "But folk who dress like lords should act like lords."

"We are modest lords," said Reith. He spoke to the clothier. "How do you usually travel to Settra?"

"I am a man with no great regard or 'place';* I ride the public wheelway."

Reith turned back to Dordolio. "If you plan to travel by private air-car, this is where we part."

"Gladly; if you will advance me five hundred sequins."

Reith shook his head. "I think not."

"Then I also must travel by wheelway."

As they strode up the street Dordolio became somewhat more cordial. "You will find that the Yao set great store by consistency, and a harmony of attributes. You are dressed as persons of quality, no doubt you will conduct yourselves in consonance. Affairs will adjust themselves."

At the wheelway depot Dordolio bespoke first class accommodation from the clerk; a short while later a long car trundled up to the platform, riding a wedge-shaped concrete slot on two great wheels. The four entered a compartment, seated themselves on red plush chairs. With a lurch and a grind, the car left the station and trundled off into the Cath countryside.

Reith found the car intriguing and somewhat of a puzzle. The motors were small, powerful, of sophisticated design; why was the car itself so awkwardly built? The wheels—when the car reached top speed, perhaps seventy miles an hour—rode on cushions of trapped air, at times with silken smoothness, until the wheels came to breaks in the slot, whereupon the car jerked and vibrated abominably. The Yao, reflected Reith, seemed to be good theoreticians but poor engineers.

The car rumbled across an ancient cultivated countryside, more civilized than any Reith had yet seen on Tschai. A haze

---

*An untranslatable word: the quality a man acquires in greater or lesser extent by the grace of his evolutions upon aspects of the "round." A fragile, almost frivolous, equilibrium between a man and his peers, instantly disturbed by a hint of shame, humiliation, embarrassment.

hung in the air, tinting the sunlight antique yellow; shadows were blacker than black. In and out of forests rolled the car, beside orchards of gnarled black-leaved trees, past parks and manors, ruined stone walls, villages in which only half the houses seemed tenanted. After climbing to an upland moor, the car struck east over marshes and bogs, to outcrops of rotting limestone. No human being was in sight, though several times Reith thought to discern ruined castles in the distance.

"Ghost country," said Dordolio. "This is Audan Moor; have you heard of it?"

"Never," said Reith.

"A desolate region, as you can see. The haunt of outlaws, even an occasional Phung. After dark the night-hounds bell . . ."

Down from Audan Moor rolled the wheelway car, into a countryside of great charm. Everywhere were ponds and watercourses, overlooked by towering black, brown and rust-colored trees. On small islands stood tall houses with high-pitched gables and elaborate balconies. Dordolio pointed off to the east. "See yonder, the great manse in front of the forest? Gold and Carnelian: the palace of my connections. Behind—but you cannot see—is Halmeur, an outer district of Settra."

The car swung through a forest and came out into a region of scattered farmsteads with the domes and spires of Settra on the sky ahead. A few minutes later the car entered a depot and rolled to a halt. The passengers alighted, and walked to a terrace. Here Dordolio said: "Now I must leave you. Across the Oval you will find the Travelers' Inn, to which I recommend you and where I will send a messenger with the sum of my debt." He paused and cleared his throat. "If a freak of destiny brings us together in another setting—for instance, you have evinced a somewhat unrealistic ambition to make yourself acquainted with the Blue Jade Lord—it might serve our mutual purposes were we not to recognize each other."

"I can think of no reason for wanting to do so," said Reith politely.

Dordolio glanced at him sharply, then made a formal salute. "I wish you good fortune." He walked off across the square, his strides lengthening as he went.

Reith turned to Traz and Anacho. "You two go to the Travelers' Inn, arrange for accommodations. I'm off to the Blue Jade

Palace. With any luck I'll arrive before Dordolio, who seems in a peculiar state of haste."

He walked to a line of motorized tricycles, climbed aboard the first in line. "The Blue Jade Palace, with all speed," he told the driver.

The mechanism spun off to the south, past buildings of glazed brick and dim glass panes, then into a district of small timber cottages, then past a great outdoor market, a scene as brisk and variegated as any Reith had observed in Cath. Turning aside, the motor-buggy nosed across an ancient stone bridge, through a portal in a stone wall into a large circular plaza. Around the periphery were booths, for the most part unoccupied and barren of goods; at the center a short ramp led up to a circular platform, at the back of which rose a bank of seats. A rectangular frame occupied the front of the platform, of dimensions which Reith found morbidly suggestive.

"What is this place?" he asked the driver, who gave him a glance of mild wonder.

"The Circle, site of Pathetic Communion, as you can see. You are a stranger in Settra?"

"Yes."

The driver consulted a yellow cardboard schedule. "The next event is Ivensday, when a nineteen-score comes to clarify his horrible desperation. Nineteen! The most since the twenty-two of Agate Crystal's Lord Wis."

"You mean he killed nineteen?"

"Of course; what else? Four were children, but still a feat these days when folk are wary of *awaile*. All Settra will come to the expiation. If you're still in town you could hardly do more for your own soul's profit."

"Probably so. How far to Blue Jade Palace?"

"Through Dalmere and we're almost there."

"I'm in a hurry," said Reith. "As fast as possible."

"Indeed sir, but if I wreck or injure, I'll feel extraordinary shame, to my soul's sickness, and I would not care to risk despondency."

"Understandable."

The motor-buggy spun along a wide boulevard, dodging and veering to avoid potholes. Enormous trees, black-trunked with brown and purple-green foliage, overhung the way; to either side, shrouded in dark gardens, were mansions of the most extraordinary architecture. The driver pointed. "Yonder on the hill: Blue Jade Palace. Which entrance do you favor, sir?" He inspected Reith quizzically.

"Drive to the front," said Reith. "Where else?"

"As you say, your lordship. Although most of the fronters don't arrive in three-wheel motor-buggies."

Up the driveway rolled the vehicle, and under a *porte cochere* the buggy halted. Paying the fare, Reith alighted upon a silken cloth laid under his feet by a pair of bowing footmen. Reith walked briskly through an open arch into a room paneled with mirrors. A myriad prisms of crystal hung tinkling on silver chains. A majordomo wearing russet velvet livery bowed deeply. "Your lordship is at home. Will you rest or take a cordial, though my Lord Cizante impatiently awaits the privilege of greeting you."

"I will see him at once; I am Adam Reith."

"Lord of which realm?"

"Tell Lord Cizante that I bring important information."

The majordomo looked at Reith uncertainly, his face twisting through a dozen subtle emotions. Reith understood that already he had committed gaucheries. *No matter,* he thought, *the Blue Jade Lord will have to make allowance.*

The majordomo signaled, a trifle less obsequiously than before. "Be good enough to come this way."

Reith was taken into a small court murmuring to a waterfall of luminous green liquid.

Two minutes passed. A young man in green knickers and an elegant waistcoat appeared. His face was wax pale, as if he never saw sunlight; his eyes were somber and brooding; under a loose four-corner cap of soft green velvet his hair was jet black: a man richly handsome, by some extraordinary means contriving to seem both effete and competent. He examined Reith with critical interest, and spoke in a dry voice. "Sir, you claim to have information for the Blue Jade Lord?"

"Yes. Are you he?"

"I am his aide. You may impart your information to me with assurance."

"I have news relating to the fate of his daughter," said Reith. "I prefer to speak to the Blue Jade Lord directly."

The aide made a curious mincing motion and disappeared. Presently he returned. "Your name, sir?"

"Adam Reith."

"Follow me, if you will."

He took Reith into a wainscoted room enameled a brownish ivory, lit by a dozen luminous prisms. At the far end stood a frail frowning man in an extravagant eight-piece suit of black and purple silk. His face was round, dark hair grew down his forehead in an elflock; his eyes were dark, far apart, and his tendency was to glance sidelong. *The face*, thought Reith, *of a secretive suspicious man*. He examined Reith with a compression of the lips.

"Lord Cizante," said the aide, "I bring you the gentleman Adam Reith, heretofore unknown, who, chancing past, was pleased to learn that you were in the vicinity."

There was an expectant silence. Reith understood that the circumstances demanded a ritual response. He said, "I am pleased, naturally, to find Lord Cizante in residence. I have only this hour arrived from Kotan."

Cizante's mouth tightened, and Reith knew that once again he had made a graceless remark.

Cizante spoke in a crisp voice. "Indeed. You have news regarding the Lady Shar Zarin?"

This was the Flower's court name. Reith responded in a voice as cool as Cizante's own. "Yes. I can give you a detailed account of her experiences, and her unfortunate death."

The Blue Jade Lord looked toward the ceiling and spoke without lowering his eyes. "You evidently claim the boon?"

The majordomo entered the room, whispered to the aide, who discreetly murmured to Lord Cizante.

"Curious!" declared Cizante. "One of the Gold and Carnelian scions, a certain Dordolio, likewise comes to claim the boon."

"Send him away," said Reith. "His knowledge of the matter is superficial, as you will learn."

"My daughter is dead?"

"I am sorry to say that she drowned herself, after an attack of psychic malaise."

The Lord's eyebrows rose more sharply than before. "She gave way to *awaile*?"

"I would suppose so."

"When and where did this take place?"

"Three weeks ago, aboard the cog *Vargaz*, halfway across the Draschade."

Lord Cizante dropped into a chair. Reith waited for an invitation to do likewise, but thought better of seating himself. Lord Cizante spoke in a dry voice: "Evidently she had suffered deep humiliation."

"I couldn't say. I helped her escape from the Priestesses of the Female Mystery; thereafter she was secure and under my protection. She was anxious to return to Cath and urged me to accompany her, assuring me of your friendship and gratitude. But as soon as we started eastward she became gloomy, and, as I say, halfway across the Draschade she threw herself overboard."

While Reith spoke Cizante's face had shifted through phases and degrees of various emotions. "So now," he said in a clipped voice, "with my daughter dead, after circumstances I do not care to imagine, you come hurrying here to claim the boon."

Reith said coldly, "I knew then and know nothing now of this 'boon.' I came to Cath for several reasons, the least important of which was to make myself known to you. I find you indisposed to what I consider civilized standards of courtesy and I will now leave." Reith gave a curt nod and started for the door. He turned back. "If you wish to learn further details regarding your daughter, consult Dordolio, whom we found stranded at Coad."

Reith left the room. The Lord's sibilant murmur reached his ears: "You are an uncouth fellow."

In the hall waited the majordomo, who greeted Reith with the faintest of smiles. He indicated a rather dim passageway painted red and blue. "This way, sir."

Reith paid him no heed. Crossing into the grand foyer, he left the way he had come.

7

REITH WALKED BACK toward the Oval, pondering the city Settra and the curious temperament of its people. He was forced to admit that the scheme to build a small spaceboat, which in far-off Pera had appeared at least feasible, now seemed impractical. He had expected gratitude and friendship from the Blue Jade Lord; he had encountered hostility. As to the technical abilities of the Yao, he was inclined to pessimism, and he fell to appraising the vehicles which passed along the street. They appeared to function satisfactorily, though giving the impression that flair and elegance, rather than efficiency, had been first in the minds of the designers. Energy derived from the ubiquitious power cells produced by the Dirdir; the coupling was not altogether quiet: an indication, so Reith considered, of careless or incompetent engineering. No two were alike; each seemed an individual construction.

Almost certainly, reflected Reith, the Yao technology was inadequate to his purposes. Without access to standard components, maxima-minima sets, integrated circuit blocks, structural forms, computers, Fourier analyzers, macro-gauss generators, a thousand other instruments, tools, gauges, standards, not to mention clever and dedicated technical personnel, the construction of even the crudest spaceboat became a stupendous task—impossible in a single lifetime . . . He came to a small circular park, shadowed under tall psillas with shaggy black bark and leaves of russet paper. At the center rose a massive monument. A dozen male figures, each carrying an instrument or tool, danced in a dreadful ritual grace around a female form, who stood with arms raised high, upturned face twisted in some overpowering emotion. Reith could not identify her expression. Exultation? Agony? Grief? Beatification? Whatever the case, the monument was disturbing, and rasped at a dark corner of his mind like a mouse in the woodwork. The monument seemed very old—thousands of years? Reith could not be sure. A small girl and a somewhat younger boy came past. They paused first to study Reith; then gave fascinated attention to the gliding figures and their macabre instruments. Reith, in a somber mood, continued on his way and presently came to the Travelers' Inn. Neither Traz nor the Dirdirman were on the premises. They had, however, hired accommodations: a suite of four rooms overlooking the Oval.

Reith bathed, changed his linen. When he went down to the foyer, twilight had come to the Oval, which was now lit by a ring of great luminous globes in a variety of pastel colors. Traz and Anacho appeared on the other side of the Oval. Reith watched them with a wry grin. They were basically alien, like cat and dog; yet, when circumstances threw them together, they conducted themselves with cautious good-fellowship.

Anacho and Traz, so it developed, had chanced upon an area known as "the Mall," where cavaliers settled affairs of honor. In the course of the afternoon the two had watched three bouts:

near-bloodless affairs, Traz reported with a sniff of scorn. "The ceremonies exhaust their energy," said Anacho. "After the addresses and the punctilio there is little time for fighting."

"The Yao, if anything, are more peculiar than the Dirdirman," said Reith.

"Ha ha! I dispute that! You know a single Dirdirman. I can show you a thousand and confuse you totally. But come; the refectory is around the corner. If nothing else, the Yao cuisine is satisfactory."

The three dined in a wide room hung with tapestries. As usual Reith could not identify what he ate, and did not care to learn. There was yellow broth, faintly sweet, with floating flakes of pickled bark; slices of pale meat layered with flower petals; a celery-like vegetable crusted with crumbs of a fiery-hot spice; cakes flavored with musk and resin; black berries with a flavor of the swamp; clear white wine which tingled the mouth.

In an adjacent tavern the three took after-dinner liquors. The clientele included many non-Yao folk, who seemed to use the place as a rendezvous. One of these, a tall old man in a leather bonnet, somewhat the worse for drink, peered into Reith's face. "But I'm wrong, for a fact. I thought you a Vect of Holangar; then I asked myself, where are his tongs? And I said, no, it is just another of the anomes who creep into Travelers' Inn for a sight of their own kind."

"I'd like a sight of my own kind," said Reith. "Nothing would please me more."

"Yes, isn't this the case? What sort are you, then? I can't put a name to your face."

"A wanderer from far lands."

"No farther than mine, which is the far coast of Vord, where Cape Dread holds back the Schanizade. I have seen sights, I tell you! Raids on Arkady! Battles with sea-folk! I remember an occasion when we drove into the mountains and destroyed the bandits ... I was a young man then and a great soldier; now I toil for the ease of the Yao, and earn my own ease thereby, and it is not so hard a life."

"I should suppose not. You are a technician?"

"Nothing so grand. I inspect wheels at the car yard."

"Many foreign technicians are at work in Settra?"

"True. Cath is comfortable enough, if you can overlook the vagaries of the Yao."

"What about Wankhmen? Are there any such in Settra?"

"At work? Never. When I sojourned at Ao Zalil, to the east of Lake Falas, I saw how it went. The Wankhmen will not even work for the Wankh; they have sufficient exertion pronouncing the Wankh chimes. Though usually they play the chords on remarkable little instruments."

"Who works in the Wankh shops? Blacks and Purples?"

"Bah! One might be forced to handle an article the other had touched. Back-country Lokhars for the most part work in the shops. For ten or twenty years, or longer, they toil, then they return to their villages rich men. Wankhmen at work in the shops? What a joke! They are as proud as Dirdirman Immaculates! I see a Dirdirman beside you tonight."

"Yes, he is my comrade."

"Odd to find a Dirdirman so common!" marveled the old man. "I have seen only three previously and all treated me like dirt." He drained his goblet, set it down with a rap. "Now I must leave; I bid all good evening, Dirdirman as well."

The old man departed. With almost the same swing of the door a pale black-haired young man dressed unobtrusively in dark blue broadcloth entered the tavern. Somewhere, thought Reith, he had seen this young man, and recently . . . Where? The man walked slowly, almost absentmindedly, along the passage beside the wall. He went to the serving counter, was poured a goblet of sharp syrup. As he turned away his gaze met that of Reith's. He nodded politely and after a moment's hesitation approached. Reith now recognized him for Cizante's pallid young aide.

"Good evening," said the young man. "Perhaps you recognize me? I am Helsse of Isan, a Blue Jade connection. I believe that we met today."

"I had a few words with your master, true enough."

Helsse sipped from his goblet, made a fastidious grimace, placed the goblet on the bar. "Let's move to a more secluded place, where we can talk."

Reith spoke to Traz and Anacho, then turned back to Helsse. "Lead the way."

Helsse glanced casually toward the front entrance but chose to leave through the restaurant. As they departed Reith glimpsed a man thrusting into the tavern, to glare wildly around the room: Dordolio.

Helsse appeared not to notice. "Nearby is a little cabaret, not overly genteel, but as good as anywhere else for our talk."

The cabaret was a low-ceilinged room, lit by red and blue lamps with blue-painted booths around the periphery. A number of musicians sat on a platform, two of whom played small gongs and drum, while a male dancer strode sinuously this way and that. Helsse selected a booth near the door, as far as possible from the musicians; the two seated themselves on blue cushions. Helsse ordered two drams of "Wildwood Tincture" which were presently brought to the table.

The dancer departed, the musicians undertook a new selection, with instruments similar to oboe, flute, cello, and a kettledrum. Reith listened for a moment, puzzled by the plaintive scraping, the thumps of the kettledrum, the sudden excited trills of the flute.

Helsse leaned solicitously forward. "You are unfamiliar with Yao music? I thought as much. This is one of the traditional forms: a lament."

"It could never be mistaken for a cheerful composition."

"A question of degree." Helsse went on to list a series of musical forms, of decreasing optimism. "I do not mean to imply that the Yao are a dour folk; you need only attend one of the season balls to appreciate this."

"I doubt if I will be invited," said Reith.

The orchestra embarked upon another selection, a series of passionate phrases, taken up by each instrument at varying instants, to terminate in a wild sustained quaver. By some cross-sensoral stimulus, Reith thought of the monument in the circular park. "The music bears some connection with your ritual of expiation?"

Helsse smiled distantly. "I have heard it said that the spirit of Pathetic Communion permeates the Yao psyche."

"Interesting." Reith waited. Helsse had not brought him here to discuss music.

"I trust that the events of this afternoon caused you no inconvenience?" asked Helsse.

"None whatever, other than irritation."

"You did not expect the boon?"

"I knew nothing of it. I expected ordinary courtesy, certainly. My reception by Lord Cizante, in retrospect, seems remarkable."

Helsse nodded sagely. "He is a remarkable man. But now he

finds himself in an awkward position. Immediately upon your departure the cavalier Dordolio presented himself to denounce you as an interloper, and to demand the boon for himself. To be quite candid, such a proceeding, on Dordolio's terms, would embarrass Lord Cizante, when one takes all into consideration. You perhaps would not be aware that Blue Jade and Gold-Carnelian are rival houses. Lord Cizante suspects that Dordolio would use the boon to humiliate Blue Jade, with what consequences no one can foresee."

Reith asked: "Exactly what was the boon promised by Cizante?"

"Emotion overcame his reserve," said Helsse. "He declared: 'Whoever returns me my daughter or so much as brings me news, let him ask and I will fulfill as best I can.' Strong language, as you see, uttered only for the ears of Blue Jade, but the news circulated."

"It appears," said Reith, "that I do Cizante a favor by accepting his bounty."

"This is what we wish to ascertain," said Helsse carefully. "Dordolio has made a number of scurrilous statements in regard to you. He declares you a superstitious barbarian intent on reviving the 'cult.' If you demanded that Lord Cizante convert his palace into a temple and himself join the 'cult,' he might well prefer Dordolio's terms."

"Even though I appeared first on the scene?"

"Dordolio claims trickery, and is violently angry. But all this to the side, what might you demand of Lord Cizante, in light of the circumstances?"

Reith considered. Unfortunately, he could not afford the prideful luxury of refusal. "I'm not sure. I could use some unprejudiced advice, but I don't know where to find it."

"Try me," suggested Helsse.

"You are hardly unprejudiced."

"Much more than you might think."

Reith studied the pale handsome face, the still black eyes. A puzzling man was Helsse, the more so for his impersonality, neither cordial nor cold. He spoke with ostensible candor but permitted no inadvertent or unconscious signals to advertise the state of his inner self.

The orchestra had dispersed. To the platform came a somewhat obese man in a long maroon robe. Behind him sat a woman with long black hair plucking a lute. The man produced an ululating wail: half-words which Reith was unable to comprehend. "Another traditional melody?" he inquired.

Helsse shrugged. "A special mode of singing. It is not altogether without value. If everyone belabored themselves thusly, there would be far less *awaile*.'

Reith listened. "Judge me harshly, all," moaned the singer. "I have performed a terrible crime; it is because of my despair."

"Offhand," said Reith, "it seems absurd to discuss my best advantage over Lord Cizante with Cizante's aide."

"Ah, but your best advantage is not necessarily Lord Cizante's disadvantage," said Helsse. "With Dordolio the case is different."

"Lord Cizante showed me no great courtesy," mused Reith. "I am not anxious to do him a favor. On the other hand, I do not care to assist Dordolio, who calls me a superstitious barbarian."

"Lord Cizante was perhaps shocked by your news," suggested Helsse. "As for Dordolio's charge, it is obviously inaccurate and need no longer be considered."

Reith grinned. "Dordolio has known me a month; can you dispute him on the basis of such short acquaintance?"

If he had hoped to discomfit Helsse, he was unsuccessful. Helsse's smile was bland. "I am usually correct in my appraisals."

"Suppose that I were to make a set of apparently wild assertions: that Tschai was flat, that the tenets of the 'cult' were correct, that men could live underwater—what would become of your opinion?"

Helsse considered soberly. "Each case is different. If you told me Tschai was flat, I would certainly revise my judgment. If you argued the creed of the 'cult,' I would suspend a decision and listen to your remarks, for here is a matter of opinion and no evidence exists, at least to my knowledge. If you insisted that men could live underwater I might be inclined to accept the statement as a working premise. After all, the Pnume submerge, as do the Wankh; why not men, perhaps with special equipment?"

"Tschai is not flat," said Reith. "Men are able to live underwater for short periods using artificial gills. I know nothing of the 'cult' or its doctrines."

Helsse sipped from his goblet of essence. The singer had departed; a dance troupe now came forth: men in black leggings and sleeves, nude from upper thigh to rib cage. Reith stared in fascination for a moment or two, then looked away.

"Traditional dances," explained Helsse, "relating to Pathetic Communion. This is 'Precursory Movement of the Ministrants toward the Expiator.' "

"The 'ministrants' are torturers?"

"They are those who provide latitude for absolute expiation. Many become popular heroes because of their passionate techniques." Helsse rose to his feet. "Come. You have implied at least a mild interest in the 'cult.' As it happens, I know the location of their meeting place, which is not far from here. If you are interested, I will take you there."

"If the visit is not contrary to the laws of Cath."

"No fear of that. Cath has no laws, only customs, which seems to suit the Yao well enough."

"Peculiar," said Reith. "Killing is not proscribed?"

"It offends custom, at least under certain circumstances. However, the professional assassins of the Guild and the Service Company work without public reproach. In general the folk of Cath do what they see fit and suffer more or less opprobrium. So you may visit the 'cult' and incur, at the worse, invective."

Reith rose to his feet. "Very well; lead the way."

They walked across the Oval, through a winding alley into a dim avenue. The eccentric silhouettes of the houses opposite leaned across the sky, where Az and Braz both ranged. Helsse rapped at a door displaying a pale blue phosphor. The two men waited in silence. The door opened a crack; a long-nosed face peered forth.

"Visitors," said Helsse. "May we come in?"

"You are associates? I must inform you that here is the district center for the Society of Yearning Refluxives."

"We are not associates. This gentleman is an outlander who wishes to learn something of the 'cult.' "

"He is welcome and yourself as well, since you seem to have no concern for 'place.' "

"None whatever."

"Which marks you either the highest of the high or the lowest of the low. Enter then. We have little entertainment to offer—convictions, a few theories, fewer facts." The Refluxive swept aside a curtain. "Enter."

Helsse and Reith stepped into a large low room. To one side, forlorn in so much vacant space, two men and two women sat drinking tea from iron pots.

The Refluxive made a half-obsequious, half-sardonic gesture. "Here we are; stare yourself full at the dreadful 'cult.' Have you ever seen anything less obstreperous?"

"The 'cult,' " said Helsse, somewhat sententiously, "is despised not for the look of its meeting halls, but for its provocative assumptions."

" 'Assumptions' bah!" declared the Refluxive in a voice of peevish complaint. "The others persecute us but we are the chosen in knowledge."

Reith asked: "What, precisely, do you know?"

"We know that men are strangers to Tschai."

"How can you know this?" demanded Helsse. "Human history fades into murk."

"It is an intuitive Truth. We are equally certain that someday the Human Magi will call their seed back Home! And then what joy! Home is a world of bounty, with air that rejoices in the lungs, like the sweetest Iphthal wine! On Home are golden mountains crowned with opals and forests of dreams! Death is a strange accident, not a fate; all men wander with joy and peace for company, with delicious viands everywhere for the eating!"

"A delightful vision," said Helsse, "but do you not consider it somewhat conjectural? Or more properly, institutional dogma?"

"Possibly so," declared the stubborn Refluxive. "Still, dogma is not necessarily falsehood. These are revealed truths, and behold: the revealed image of Home!" He pointed to a world globe three feet in diameter hanging at eye-level.

Reith went to inspect the globe, tilting his head this way and that, trying to identify outline of sea and shore, finding here a haunting familiarity, there utter disparity. Helsse came to stand beside him. "What does it look like to you?" His voice was light and careless.

"Nothing in particular."

Helsse gave a soft grunt of mingled relief and perhaps disappointment, or so it seemed to Reith.

One of the women lifted her obese body from the bench and came forward. "Why not join the Society?" she wheedled. "We need new faces, new blood, to augment the vast new tide. Won't you help us make contact with Home?"

Reith laughed. "Is there a practical method?"

"To be sure! Telepathy! Indeed, we have no other recourse."

"Why not a spaceship?"

The woman seemed bewildered, and looked sharply to see if Reith was serious. "Where could we lay our hands on a spaceship?"

"They are nowhere to be bought? Even a small one?"

"I have never heard of such a case."

"Nor I," was Helsse's dry comment.

"Where would we fare?" demanded the woman, half-truculently. "Home is situated in the constellation Clari, but space is vast; we would drift forever."

"The problems are large," Reith agreed. "Still, assuming that your premise is correct—"

" 'Assume'? 'Premise'?" demanded the fat woman in a shocked voice. 'Revelation,' rather."

"Possibly so. But mysticism is not a practical approach to space travel. Let us suppose that by one means or another, you find yourself in command of a spaceship, then you might very easily verify the basis of your belief. Simply fly into the constellation Clari, halting at appropriate intervals to monitor the area for radio signals. Sooner or later, if the world Home exists, a suitable instrument will detect the signals."

"Interesting," said Helsse. "You assume that such a world, if it exists, is sufficiently advanced to propagate these signals?"

Reith shrugged. "Since we're assuming the world, why not assume the signals?"

Helsse had nothing to say. The Refluxive declared, "Ingenious but superficial! How, for instance, would we obtain a spaceship?"

"With sufficient funds and technical competence you could build a small vessel."

"To begin with," said the Refluxive, "we have no such funds."

"The least of the difficulties, or so I would think," murmured Helsse.

"The second possibility is to buy a small boat from one of the spacefaring peoples: the Dirdir, the Wankh, or perhaps even the Blue Chasch."

"Again a question of sequins," said the Refluxive. "How much would a spaceboat cost?"

Reith looked at Helsse, who pursed his lips. "Half a million sequins, should anyone be willing to sell, which I doubt."

"The third possibility is the most direct," said Reith. "Confiscation, pure and simple."

"Confiscation? From whom? Though members of the 'cult' we are not yet lunatics."

The fat woman gave a sniff of disapproval. "The man is a wild romantic."

The Refluxive said gently, "We would gladly accept you as an associate, but you must discover orthodox methodology. Classes in thought-control and projective telepathy are offered twice a week, on Ilsday and Azday. If you care to attend—"

"I'm afraid that this is impossible," said Reith. "But your program is interesting and I hope it brings fruitful returns."

Helsse made a courteous sign; the two departed.

They walked along the quiet avenue in silence. Then Helsse inquired: "What is your opinion now?"

"The situation speaks for itself," said Reith.

"You are convinced then that their doctrine is implausible?"

"I would not go quite so far. Scientists have undoubtedly found biological links between Pnume, Phung, night-hounds, and other indigenous creatures. Blue Chasch, Green Chasch, and Old Chasch are similarly related, as are all the races of man. But Pnume, Wankh, Chasch, Dirdir, and Man are biologically distinct. What does this suggest to you?"

"I agree that the circumstances are puzzling. Have you any explanation?"

"I feel that more facts are needed. Perhaps the Refluxives will become adept telepathists, and surprise us all."

Helsse walked along in silence. They turned a corner. Reith pulled Helsse to a halt. "Quiet!" He waited.

The shuffle of footsteps sounded; a dark shape rounded the corner. Reith seized the figure, spun it around, applied an arm and neck lock. Helsse made one or two tentative motions; Reith, trusting no one, kept him in his field of vision. "Make a light," said Reith. "Let's see whom we have. Or what."

Helsse brought forth a glow-bulb, held it up. The captive squirmed, kicked, lurched; Reith tightened his grip and felt the snap of a bone, but the figure, sagging, toppled Reith off balance. From the unseen face came a hiss of triumph; it snatched itself free. Then, to a flicker of metal, it gave a gasp of pain.

Helsse held up his glow-bulb, disengaged his dagger from the back of the twitching shape, while Reith stood by, mouth twisted in disapproval. "You are quick with your blade."

Helsse shrugged. "His kind carry stings." He turned the body over with his foot; a small tinkle sounded as a glass sliver fell against the stone.

The two peered curiously into the white face, half-shrouded under the brim of an extravagantly wide black hat.

"He hats himself like a Pnumekin," said Helsse, "and he is pale as a ghost."

"Or a Wankhman," said Reith.

"But I think he is something different from either; what, I could not say. Perhaps a hybrid, a mingling, which, so it is said, makes the best personnel for spy work."

Reith dislodged the hat, to reveal a stark bald pate. The face was fine-boned, somewhat loosely-muscled; the nose was thin and limber and terminated in a lump. The eyes, half-open, seemed to be black. Bending close, Reith thought that the scalp had been shaven.

Helsse looked uneasily up and down the street. "Come, we must hurry away, before the patrol finds us and issues an information."

"Not so fast," said Reith. "No one is near. Hold the light; stand yonder, where you can see along the street." Helsse reluctantly obeyed and Reith was able to watch him sidelong as he searched the corpse. The garments had a queer musky odor; Reith's stomach jerked as he felt here and there. From an inner pocket of the cloak he took a clip of paper. At the belt hung a soft leather pouch, which he detached.

"Come!" hissed Helsse. "We must not be discovered, we would lose all 'place.'"

They proceeded back to the Oval and across to the Travelers' Inn. In the arcade before the entrance they paused. "The evening was interesting," said Reith. "I learned a great deal."

"I wish I could say the same," said Helsse. "What did you take from the dead man?"

Reith displayed the pouch, which contained a handful of sequins. He brought forth the clip of paper, and the two examined it in the light streaming out of the inn, to find rows of a peculiar writing: a series of rectangles, variously shaded and marked.

Helsse looked at Reith. "Do you recognize this script?"

"No."

Helsse gave a short sharp bark of laughter. "It is Wankh."

"Hm. What would be the significance of this?"

"Simply more mystery. Settra is a hive of intrigue. Spies are everywhere."

"And spy devices? Microphones? Eye-cells?"

"It is safe to assume as much."

"Then it would be safe to assume that the Refluxive's hall is monitored . . . Perhaps I was too free with advice."

"If the dead man were the monitor, your words are now lost. But allow me to take custody of the notes. I will have them translated; there is a colony of Lokhars nearby and some of them have a smattering of Wankh."

"We will go together," said Reith. "Will tomorrow suit you?"

"Well enough," said Helsse glumly. He looked off across the Oval. "Finally then: what must I tell Lord Cizante as to the boon?"

"I don't know," said Reith. "I'll have an answer tomorrow."

"The situation may be clarified even sooner," said Helsse. "Here is Dordolio."

Reith swung around, to find Dordolio striding toward him, followed by two suave cavaliers. Dordolio was clearly in a fury. He halted a yard in front of Reith and, thrusting forth his head, blurted: "With your vicious tricks, you have ruined me! Have you no shame?" He took off his hat, hurled it into Reith's face. Reith stepped aside, the hat went wheeling off into the Oval.

Dordolio shook his finger in Reith's face; Reith backed away a step. "Your death is assured," bellowed Dordolio. "But not by the honor of my sword! Low-caste assassins will drown you in cattle excrement! Twenty pariahs will drub your corpse! A cur will drag your head along the street by the tongue!"

Reith managed a painful grin. "Cizante will arrange the same for you, at my request. It's as good a boon as any."

"Cizante, bah! A wicked parvenu, a moping invert. Blue Jade shall be nothing; the fall of that palace will culminate the 'round'!"

Helsse came slightly forward. "Before you enlarge upon your remarkable assertions, be advised that I represent the House of Blue Jade, and that I will be impelled to report to his Excellency Lord Cizante the substance of your comments."

"Do not bore me with triviality!" stormed Dordolio. He furiously motioned to Reith. "Fetch my hat, or tomorrow expect the first of the Twelve Touches!"

"A small concession," said Reith, "if it ensures your departure." He picked up Dordolio's hat, shook it once or twice, handed it to him. "Your hat, which you threw across the square." He stepped around Dordolio, entered the foyer of the inn. Dordolio gave a somewhat subdued caw of laughter, slapped his hat against his thigh, and, signaling his comrades, walked away.

In the foyer of the inn Reith asked Helsse, "What are the 'Twelve Touches'?"

"At intervals—perhaps a day, perhaps two days—an assassin will tap the victim with a twig. The twelfth touch is fatal; the man dies. By accumulated poison, by a single final dose, or by morbid suggestion, only the Assassins' Guild knows. And now I must return to Blue Jade. Lord Cizante will be interested in my report."

"What do you intend to tell him?"

Helsse only laughed. "You, the most secretive of men, asking me that! Still, Cizante will hear that you have agreed to accept a boon, that you probably will soon be departing Cath—"

"I said nothing of this!"

"It will still be an element of my report."

8

REITH AWOKE TO wan sunlight shining through the heavy amber panes of the windows. He lay on the unfamiliar couch, collecting the threads of his existence. It was difficult not to feel a profound gloom. Cath, where he had hoped to find flexibility, enlightenment, and perhaps cooperation, was hardly less harsh an environment than the Aman Steppe. It was obvious folly to dream of building a spaceboat in Settra.

Reith sat up on the couch. He had known horror, grief, disillusionment, but there had been corresponding moments of triumph and hope, even a few spasmodic instants of joy. If he were to die tomorrow—or in twelve days after twelve "touches"—he had already lived a miraculous life. Very well then, he would put his destiny to the test. Helsse had predicted his departure from Cath; Helsse had read the future, or Reith's own personality, more accurately than Reith himself.

Breakfasting with Traz and Anacho he described his adventures of the previous evening. Anacho found the circumstances perturbing. "This is an insane society, constrained by punctilio as a rotten egg is held by its shell. Whatever your aims—and sometimes I think that you are the most flamboyant lunatic of all—they will not be achieved here."

"I agree."

"Well then," said Traz, "what next?"

"What I plan is dangerous, perhaps rash folly. But I see no other alternative. I intend to ask Cizante for money; this we shall share. Then I think it best that we separate. You, Traz, might do worse than to return to Wyness, and there make a life for yourself. Perhaps Anacho will do the same. Neither of you can profit by coming with me; in fact, I guarantee the reverse."

Anacho looked off across the square. "Until now you have managed to survive, if precariously. I find myself curious as to what you hope to achieve. With your permission, I will join your expedition, which I suspect is by no means as desperate as you make it out to be."

"I intend to confiscate a Wankh spaceship from the Ao Hidis spaceport, or elsewhere, if it seems more convenient."

Anacho threw his hands in the air. "I feared no less." He proceeded to state a hundred objections which Reith did not trouble to contradict. "All very true; I will end my days in a Wankh dungeon or a night-hound's belly; still this is what I intend to attempt. I strongly urge that you and Traz make your way to the Isles of Cloud and live as best you may."

"Bah," snorted Anacho. "Why won't you attempt some reasonable exploit, like exterminating the Pnume, or teaching the Chasch to sing?"

"I have other ambitions."

"Yes, yes, your faraway planet, the home of man. I am tempted to help you, if only to demonstrate your lunacy."

"As for me," said Traz, "I would like to see this far world. I know it exists, because I saw the spaceboat in which Adam Reith arrived."

Anacho inspected the youth with eyebrows raised. "You have not mentioned this previously."

"You never asked."

"How might such an absurdity enter my mind?"

"A person who calls facts absurdities will often be surprised," said Traz.

"But at least he has organized the cosmic relationship into categories, which sets him apart from animals and sub-men."

Reith intervened. "Come now; let's put our energies to work, since you both seem bent on suicide. Today we seek information. And here is Helsse, bringing us important news, or so it appears from his aspect."

Helsse approached and gave a polite greeting. "Last night, as you may imagine, I had much to report to Lord Cizante. He urges that you make some reasonable request, which he will be glad to fulfill. He recommends that we destroy the papers taken from the spy and I am inclined to agree. If you acquiesce, Lord Cizante may grant further concessions."

"Of what nature?"

"He does not specify, but I suspect he has in mind a certain slackening of protocol in regard to your presence in Blue Jade Palace."

"I am more interested in the documents than in Lord Cizante. If he wants to see me he can come here to the inn."

Helsse gave a brittle chuckle. "Your response is no surprise. If you are ready I will conduct you to South Ebron where we will find a Lokhar."

"There are no Yao scholars who read the Wankh language?"

"Such facility would seem pointless expertise."

"Until someone wanted a document translated."

Helsse gave an indifferent twitch. "At this play of the 'round,' Utilitarianism is an alien philosophy. Lord Cizante, for instance, would find your arguments not only incomprehensible but disgusting."

"We shall never argue the matter," said Reith equably.

Helsse had come in an extremely elegant equipage: a blue carriage with six scarlet wheels and a profusion of golden festoons. The interior was like a luxurious drawing room, with gray-green wainscoting, a pale gray carpet, an arched ceiling covered with green silk. The chairs were deeply upholstered; to the side, under the windows of pale green glass, a buffet offered trays of sweetmeats. Helsse ushered his guests into the car with the utmost politeness; today he wore a suit of pale green and gray, as if to blend himself into the decor of the carriage.

When all were seated, he touched a button to close the door

and retract the steps. Reith observed, "Lord Cizante, while deriding utilitarianism as a doctrine, apparently does not flout its applications."

"You refer to the door-closing mechanism? He is not aware that it exists. Someone is always at hand to touch the button for him. Like others of his class he touches objects only in play or pleasure. You find this odd? No matter. You must accept the Yao gentry as you find them."

"Evidently you do not regard yourself as a member of the Yao gentry."

Helsse laughed. "More tactful might be the conjecture that I enjoy what I am doing." He spoke into a mesh. "To the South Ebron Mercade."

The carriage eased into motion. Helsse poured goblets of syrup and proffered sweetmeats. "You are about to visit our commercial district; the source of our wealth, in fact, though it is considered vulgar to discuss it."

"Strange," mused Anacho. "Dirdir, at the highest level, are never so hoity-toity."

"They are a different race," said Helsse. "Superior? I am not convinced. The Wankh would never agree, should they trouble to examine the concept."

Anacho gave a contemptuous shrug but said no more.

The carriage rolled through a market area: the Mercade, then into a district of small dwellings, in a wonderful diversity of style. At a cluster of squat brick towers the carriage halted. Helsse pointed to a nearby garden where sat a dozen men of spectacular appearance. They wore white shirts and trousers, their hair, long and abundant, was also white; in striking contrast to the lusterless black of their skins. "Lokhars," said Helsse. "Migrating mechanics from the highlands north of Lake Falas in Central Kislovan. That is not their natural coloration; they bleach their hair and dye their skin. Some say the Wankh enforced the custom upon them thousands of years ago to differentiate them from Wankhmen, who of course are white-skinned and black-haired. In any event, they come and go, working where they gain the highest return, for they are a remarkably avaricious folk. Some, after laboring in the Wankh shops, have migrated north to Cath; a few of these know a chime or two of Wankh-talk and occasionally can puzzle out the sense of Wankh documents. Notice the old man yonder playing with the child; he is reckoned as adept in

Wankh as any. He will demand a large sum for his efforts, and in order to forestall even more exorbitant demands in the future I must haggle with him. If you will be good enough to wait, I will go to make the arrangements."

"A moment," said Reith. "At a conscious level I am convinced of your integrity, but I can't control my instinctive suspicions. Let us make the arrangement together."

"As you wish," said Helsse graciously. "I will send the chauffeur for the man." He spoke into the mesh.

Anacho murmured, "If the arrangements were already made, the qualms of a trusting person might easily be drugged."

Helsse nodded judiciously. "I believe I can assuage your anxieties."

A moment later the old man sauntered up to the carriage.

"Inside, if you please," said Helsse.

The old man poked his white-maned face through the door. "My time is valuable; what do you want of me?"

"A matter for your profit."

"Profit, eh? I can at least listen." He entered the carriage, and seated himself with a comfortable grunt. The air took on the odor of a spicy, slightly rancid pomade. Helsse stood in front of him. With a side glance toward Reith he said, "Our arrangement is canceled. Do not heed my instructions."

" 'Arrangement'? 'Instructions'? What are you talking about? You must mistake me for another. I am Zarfo Detwiler."

Helsse made an easy gesture. "It's all one. We want you to translate a Wankh document for us, the guide to a treasure hoard. Translate correctly, you shall share the booty."

"No, no, none of that." Zarfo Detwiler waved a black finger. "I'll share the booty with pleasure; additionally I want a hundred sequins, and no recriminations if I fail to satisfy you."

"No recriminations, agreed. But a hundred sequins for possibly nothing? Ridiculous. Here: five sequins and eat your fill of the expensive sweetmeats."

"That last I'll do anyway; am I not your invited guest?" Zarfo Detwiler popped a handful of dainties into his mouth. "You must think me a moon-calf to offer but five sequins. Only three persons in Settra can so much as tell you which side of a Wankh ideogram is up. I alone can read meaning, by virtue of thirty toilsome years in the Ao Hidis machine shops."

The haggling proceeded; Zarfo Detwiler eventually agreed to

fifty sequins and a tenth share of the assumptive spoils. Helsse signaled Reith, who produced the documents.

Zarfo Detwiler took the papers, squinted, frowned, ran his fingers through his white mane. He looked up and spoke somewhat ponderously: "I will instruct you in Wankh communication at no charge. The Wankh are a peculiar folk, totally unique. Their brain works in pulses. They see in pulses and think in pulses. Their speech comes in a pulse, a chime of many vibrations which carries all the meaning of a sentence. Each ideogram is equivalent to a chime, which is to say, a whole unit of meaning. For this reason, to read Wankh is as much a matter of divination as logic; one must enunciate an entire meaning with each ideogram. Even the Wankhmen are not always accurate. Now this matter you have here—let me see. This first chime—hm. Notice this comb? It usually signifies an equivalence, an identity. A square of this texture shading off to the right sometimes means 'truth' or 'verified perception' or 'situation' or perhaps 'present condition of the cosmos.' These marks—I don't know. This bit of shading—I think it's a person talking. Since it's at the bottom, the base tone in the chord, it would seem that—yes, this trifle here indicates positive volition. These marks—hm. Yes, these are organizers, which specify the order and emphasis of the other elements. I can't understand them; I can only guess at the total sense. Something like 'I wish to report that conditions are identical or unchanged' or 'A person is anxious to specify that the cosmos is stable.' Something of the sort. Are you sure that this is information regarding treasure?"

"It was sold to us on this basis."

"Hm." Zarfo pulled at his long black nose. "Let me see. This second symbol: notice this shading and this bit of an angle? One is 'vision'; the other is 'negation.' I can't read the organizers, but it might mean 'blindness' or 'invisibility . . .' "

Zarfo continued his lucubrations, poring over each ideogram, occasionally tracing out a fragment of meaning, more often confessing failure, and becoming ever more restive. "You have been gulled," he said at last. "I'm certain there is no mention of money or treasure. I believe this is no more than a commercial report. It seems to say, as close as I can fathom: 'I wish to state that conditions are the same.' Something about peculiar wishes, or hopes, or volitions. 'I will presently see the dominant man, the leader of our group.' Something unknown. 'The leader is not helpful,' or perhaps 'stays aloof.' 'The leader slowly changes, or metamorphoses, to the enemy.' Or perhaps, 'The leader slowly changes to become like the enemy.' Change of some sort—I can't understand. 'I request more money.' Something about arrival of a newcomer or stranger 'of utmost importance.' That's about all."

Reith thought to sense an almost imperceptible relaxation in Helsse's manner.

"No great illumination," said Helsse briskly. "Well, you have done your best. Here is your twenty sequins."

" 'Twenty sequins'!" roared Zarfo Detwiler. "The price agreed was fifty! How can I buy my bit of meadowland if I am constantly cheated?"

"Oh very well, if you choose to be niggardly."

"Niggardly, indeed! Next time read the message yourself."

"I could do as well, for all the help you've given us."

"You were duped. That is no guide to treasure."

"Apparently not. Well then, good day to you."

Reith followed Zarfo from the carriage. He looked back in at Helsse. "I'll remain here, for a word or two with this gentleman."

Helsse was not pleased. "We must discuss another matter. It is necessary that the Blue Jade Lord receives information."

"This afternoon I will have a definite answer for you."

Helsse gave a curt nod. "As you wish."

The carriage departed, leaving Reith and the Lokhar standing in the street. Reith said, "Is there a tavern nearby? Perhaps we can chat over a bottle."

"I am a Lokhar," snorted the black-skinned old man. "I do not addle my brains and drain my pockets with drink; not before noon, at any rate. However you may buy me a fine Zam sausage, or a clut of head-cheese."

"With pleasure."

Zarfo led the way to a food shop; the two men took their purchases to a table on the street.

"I am amazed by your ability to read the ideograms," said Reith. "Where did you learn?"

"At Ao Hidis. I worked as a die cutter beside an old Lokhar who was a true genius. He taught me to recognize a few chimes, and showed me where the shadings matched intensity vibrations, where sonority equated with shape, where the various chord components matched texture and gradation. Both the chimes and the ideograms are regular and rational, once the eye and the ear are tuned. But the tuning is difficult." Zarfo took a great bite of sausage. "Needless to say, the Wankhmen discourage such learning; if they suspect a Lokhar of diligent study, he is discharged. Oh, they are a crafty lot! They jealously guard their role as intercessors between the Wankh and the world of men. A devious folk! The women are strangely beautiful, like black pearls, but cruel and cold, and not prone to dalliance."

"The Wankh pay well?"

"Like everyone else, as little as possible. But we are forced to concede. If labor costs rose, they would take slaves, or train Blacks and Purples, one or the other. We would then lose employment and perhaps our freedom as well. So we strive without too much complaint, and seek more profitable employment elsewhere once we are skilled."

"It is highly likely," said Reith, "that the Yao Helsse, in the gray and green suit, will ask what we discussed. He may even offer you money."

Zarfo bit off a chunk of sausage. "I shall naturally tell all, if I am paid enough."

"In that case," said Reith, "our conversation must deal in pleasantries, profitless to both of us."

Zarfo chewed thoughtfully. "How much profit had you in mind?"

"I don't care to specify, since you would only ask Helsse for more, or try to extract the same from both of us."

Zarfo sighed dismally. "You have a sorry opinion of the Lokhar. Our word is our bond; once we strike a bargain we do not deviate."

The haggling continued on a more or less cordial level until for the sum of twenty sequins Zarfo agreed to guard the privacy of the conversation as fiercely as he might the hiding place of his money, and the sum was paid over.

"Back to the Wankh message for a moment," said Reith. "There were references to a 'leader.' Were there hints or clues by which to identify him?"

Zarfo pursed his lips. "A wolf-tone indicating high-level gentry; another honorific brevet which might signify something like 'a person of the excellent sort' or 'in your own image,' 'of your sort.' It is very difficult. A Wankh reading the ideogram would understand a chime, which then would stimulate a visual image complete in essential details. The Wankh would be furnished a mental image of the person, but for someone like myself there are only crude outlines. I can tell no more."

"You work in Settra?"

"Alas. A man of my years and impoverished: isn't it a pity? But I near my goal, and then—back to Smargash, in Lokhara, for a bit of meadow, a young wife, a comfortable chair by the hearth."

"You worked in the space shops at Ao Hidis?"

"Yes, indeed; I transferred from the tool works to the space shops, where I repaired and installed air purifiers."

"Lokhar mechanics must be very skillful, then."

"Oh, indeed."

"Certain mechanics specialize upon the installation of, say, controls and instruments?"

"Naturally. Complex trades, both."

"Have such mechanics immigrated to Settra?"

Zarfo gave Reith a calculating glance. "How much is the information worth to you?"

"Control your avarice," said Reith. "No more money today. Another sausage, if you like."

"Later, perhaps. Now as to the mechanics: in Smargash are dozens, hundreds, retired after lifetimes of toil."

"Could they be tempted to join in a dangerous venture?"

"No doubt, if the danger were scant and the profit high. What do you propose?"

Reith threw caution to the winds. "Assume that someone wished to confiscate a Wankh spaceship and fly it to an unspecified destination: how many specialists would be required, and how much would it cost to hire them?"

Zarfo, to Reith's relief, did not stare in bewilderment or shock. He gnawed for a moment at the last of the sausage. Then, after a belch, he said, "I believe that you are asking if I consider the exploit feasible. It has often been discussed in a jocular manner, and for a fact the ships are not stringently guarded. The project is feasible. But why should you want a spaceship? I do not care to visit the Dirdir on Sibol or test the infinity of the universe."

"I can't discuss the destination."

"Well then, how much money do you offer?"

"My plans have not progressed to that stage. What do you consider a suitable fee?"

"To risk life and freedom? I would not stir for less than fifty thousand sequins."

Reith rose to his feet. "You have your fifty sequins; I have my information. I trust you to keep my secret."

Zarfo sat sprawled back in his chair. "Now then, not so fast. After all I am old and my life is not worth so much after all. Thirty thousand? Twenty? Ten?"

"The figure starts to become practical. How much of a crew will we need?"

"Four or five more, possibly six. You envision a long voyage?"

"As soon as we are in space, I will reveal our destination. Ten thousand sequins is only a preliminary payment. Those who go with me will return with wealth beyond their dreams."

Zarfo rose to his feet. "When do you propose to leave?"

"As soon as possible. Another matter: Settra is overrun with spies; it's important that we attract no attention."

Zarfo gave a hoarse laugh. "So this morning you approach me in a vast carriage, worth thousands of sequins. A man watches us even now."

"I've been noticing him. But he seems too obvious to be a spy. Well, then, where shall we meet, and when?"

"Upon the stroke of midmorning tomorrow, at the stall of Upas the spice merchant in the Cercade. Be certain you are not followed . . . That fellow yonder I believe to be an assassin, from the style of his garments."

The man at this moment approached their table. "You are Adam Reith?"

"Yes."

"I regret to say that the Security Assassination Company has accepted a contract made out in your name: the Death of the Twelve Touches. I will now administer the first inoculation. Will you be so good as to bare your arm? I will merely prick you with this splint."

Reith backed away. "I'll do nothing of the sort."

"Depart!" Zarfo Detwiler told the assassin. "This man is worth ten thousand sequins to me alive; dead, nothing."

The assassin ignored Zarfo. To Reith he said, "Please do not make an undignified display. The process then becomes protracted and painful for us all. So then—"

Zarfo roared: "Stand away; have I not warned you?" He

snatched up a chair and struck the assassin to the ground. Zarfo was not yet satisfied. He picked up the splint, jabbed it into the back of the man's thigh, through the rust-ocher corduroy of his trousers. "Halt!" wailed the assassin. "That is Inoculation Number One!"

Zarfo seized a handful of splints from the splayed-open wallet. "And here," he roared, "are numbers Two to Twelve!" And with a foot on the man's neck he thrust the handful into the twitching buttocks. "There you are, you knave! Do you want the next episode, Numbers Thirteen to Twenty-four?"

"No, no, let me be; I am a dead man now!"

"If not, you're a cheat as well as an assassin!"

Passersby had halted to watch. A portly woman in pink silk rushed forward. "You hairy black villain, what are you doing to that poor assassin? He is only a workman at his trade!"

Zarfo picked up the assassin's work sheet, looked down the list. "Hm. It appears that your husband is next on his list."

The woman looked with startled eyes after the assassin now tottering off down the street.

"Time we were leaving," said Reith.

They walked through back alleys to a small shed, screened from the street by a lattice of woven withe. "It is the neighborhood corpse-house," said Zarfo. "No one will bother us here."

Reith entered, looked gingerly around the black benches on one of which lay the hulk of a small animal.

"Now then," said Zarfo, "who is your enemy?"

"I suspect a certain Dordolio," said Reith. "I can't be sure."

Zarfo scrutinized the work sheet. "Well, we shall see. 'Adam Reith, the Travelers' Inn—Contract Number Two-three-o-five, Style Eighteen; prepaid.' Dated today, surcharged 'Rush.' Prepaid, eh? Well then, let us try a ruse. Back to my cottage."

He took Reith to one of the brick towers, entered by an arched doorway. On a table rested a telephone. Zarfo lifted the instrument with cautious fingers. "Connect me with the Security Assassination Company."

A grave voice spoke. "We are here to serve your needs."

"I refer to Contract Number Two-three-o-five," said Zarfo, "relating to a certain Adam Reith. I can't find the estimate and I wish to pay the charges."

"A moment, my lord."

The voice presently returned. "The contract was prepaid, my lord; and was scheduled for execution this morning."

"Prepaid? Impossible. I did not prepay. What is the name on the receipt?"

"The name is Helsse Izam. I'm sure there is no mistake, sir."

"Perhaps not. I'll discuss the matter with the person involved."

"Thank you, sir, for your custom."

9

REITH RETURNED TO the Travelers' Inn, and with a certain trepidation, entered the foyer where he found Traz. "What has occurred, if anything?"

Traz, the most lucid and decisive of individuals, was less deft when it came to communicating a mood. "The Yao—Helsse, is that his name?—became silent after you left the carriage. Perhaps he found us strange company. He told us that tonight we would dine with the Blue Jade Lord, that he would come early to instruct us in decorum. Then he drove off in the carriage."

A perplexing sequence of events, reflected Reith. An interesting point: the contract had specified Twelve Touches. If his death were urgently required, a knife, a bullet, an energy bolt would serve the purpose. But the first of twelve injections? A device to stimulate haste?

"Many things are happening," he told Traz. "Events I don't pretend to understand."

"The sooner we leave Settra the better," gloomed Traz.

"Agreed."

Anacho the Dirdirman appeared, freshly barbered and splendid in a new high-collared black jacket, pale blue trousers, scarlet ankle-high slippers with modish upturned toes. Reith took the two to a secluded alcove and described the events of the day. "So now we need only money, which I hope to extract from Cizante tonight."

The hours of the afternoon passed slowly. At last Helsse appeared, wearing a modish suit of canary yellow velvet. He gave polite greetings to the group. "You are enjoying your visit to Cath?"

"Indeed yes," said Reith. "I have never felt so relaxed."

Helsse maintained his aplomb. "Excellent. Now, in regard to this evening, Lord Cizante suspects that you and your friends might find a formal dinner somewhat tedious. He recommends rather a casual and unstructured tiffin, at a time to suit your convenience: now, if you so desire."

"We are ready," said Reith. "But, to anticipate any misunderstanding, please remember that we insist upon a dignified reception. We do not intend to slink into the palace by a back entrance."

Helsse made an easy gesture. "For a casual occasion, casual protocol. That's our rule."

"I will be specific," said Reith. "Our 'place' demands that we use the front entrance. If Lord Cizante objects, then he must meet us elsewhere: perhaps at the tavern around the Oval."

Helsse uttered an incredulous laugh. "He would as soon don a buffoon's cap and cut capers in Merrymaker's Round!" He shook his head dolefully. "To avoid difficulties we will use the front entrance; after all what difference does it make?"

Reith laughed. "Especially since Cizante has ordered us brought in by the scullery and will assume that this is how we entered . . . Well, it's a fair compromise. Let's go."

The trip to Blue Jade Palace was made in a sleek black landau. At Helsse's instructions it drove up to the formal portal. Helsse alighted, and with a thoughtful glance along the façade of the palace, conducted the three outlanders through the main portal and into the great foyer. He muttered a few words to a footman, then ushered the three up a flight of shallow stairs, into a small green and gold salon overlooking the courtyard.

Lord Cizante was nowhere to be seen.

"Please be seated," said Helsse affably. "Lord Cizante will be with you shortly." He gave a jerk of the head and departed the chamber.

Several minutes passed, then Lord Cizante appeared. He wore a long white gown, white slippers, a black skullcap. His face was petulant and brooding; he looked from face to face. "Which is the man to whom I spoke before?"

Helsse muttered in his ear; he turned to face Reith. "I see. Well then, make yourself easy. Helsse, you have ordered a suitable refreshment?"

"Indeed, your Excellency."

A footman rolled in a buffet and offered trays of sweet wafers, salt-barks, cubes of spiced meat, decanters of wine, flagons of essence. Reith accepted wine; Traz a goblet of syrup. Anacho took green essences; Lord Cizante selected a stick of incense and walked back and forth, jerking it through the air. "I have negative news for you," he said abruptly. "I have decided to withdraw all proffers and undertakings. In short, you may expect no boon."

Reith sipped the wine and gave himself time to think. "You are honoring Dordolio's claim?"

"I cannot elaborate upon the matter. The statement may be interpreted in its most general sense."

"I have no claim upon you," said Reith. "I came here yesterday only to convey the news of your daughter."

Lord Cizante held the incense stick under his nostrils. "The circumstances no longer interest me."

Anacho emitted a somewhat startling caw of laughter. "Understandable! To acknowledge them would force you to honor your pledge!"

"Not at all," said Lord Cizante. "I spoke only for the attention of Blue Jade personnel."

"Ha ha! Who will believe that, now that you have hired assassins against my friend?"

Lord Cizante held the incense still and poised. "Assassins? What of this?"

"Your aide"—Reith indicated Helsse—"took out a Type Eighteen contract against me. I intend to warn Dordolio; your penury carries a vicious sting."

Lord Cizante turned a frowning glance upon Helsse. "What of this?"

Helsse stood with black eyebrows fretfully raised. "I endeavored only to fulfill my function."

"Misplaced zeal! Would you make Blue Jade a laughing stock? If this sordid tale gains circulation . . ." His voice suddenly trailed off. Helsse gave a shrug, and poured himself a goblet of wine.

Reith rose to his feet. "Our business appears to be at an end."

"A moment," said Lord Cizante curtly. "Let me consider . . . You realize that this so-called assassination is a mare's-nest?"

Reith slowly shook his head. "You have blown hot and cold too often; I am totally skeptical."

Lord Cizante swung on his heel. The incense stick fell to the rug, where it began to smolder. Reith picked it up, placed it on the tray. "Why do you do that?" asked Helsse in sardonic wonder.

"You must supply your own answer."

Lord Cizante strode back into the room. He gestured to Helsse, took him into the corner, muttered a moment, and once again departed.

Helsse turned to Reith. "Lord Cizante has empowered me to pay over to you a sum of ten thousand sequins on condition that you depart Cath instantly, returning to Kotan by the first cog out of Vervodei."

"Lord Cizante's impertinence is amazing," said Reith.

Anacho asked casually, "How high will he go?"

"He specified no precise sum," Helsse admitted. "He is interested only in your departure, which he will facilitate in every detail."

"A million sequins, then," said Anacho. "If we must acquiesce to this undignified scheme, we might as well sell ourselves dear."

"Much too dear," said Helsse. "Twenty thousand sequins is more reasonable."

"Not reasonable enough," said Reith. "We need more, much more."

Helsse surveyed the three in silence. He said at last: "To avoid wasting time I will announce the maximum sum Lord Cizante cares to pay. It is fifty thousand sequins, which I personally consider generous, and transportation to Vervodei."

"We accept," said Reith. "Needless to say, you must cancel the contract with the Security Company."

Helsse smiled a small tremulous smile. "I have already received my instructions in this regard. And when will you depart Settra?"

"In a day or so."

With fifty strips of purple-celled sequins, the three left Blue Jade Palace, and climbed into the waiting black landau. Helsse did not accompany them.

The landau wheeled east through the cinnamon dusk, under

luminants which as yet cast no illumination. Off in the parks, palaces and town houses showed clusters of blurred lights, and in one great garden a fête was in progress.

The landau rumbled across a carved wooden bridge hung with lanterns, to enter a district of crowded timber buildings, with tearooms and cafés jutting over the street. They passed through an area of bleak half-deserted tenements, and at last came into the Oval.

Reith descended from the landau. Traz sprang past and threw himself on a dark silent figure. At the glint of metal Reith ducked to the ground, but failed to escape a violent purple-white flash. A hot blow pounded his head; he lay half-stunned, while Traz struggled with the assailant. Anacho stepped forward, pointed his sting. Out sprang the thin shaft, piercing the man's shoulder. The gun clattered to the cobbles.

Reith picked himself up, stood weaving. The side of his head smarted as if by a scald; the smell of ozone and burnt hair filled his nostrils. He tottered over to where Traz held the hooded figure in an armlock while Anacho removed his wallet and dagger. The man wore a half-hood; Reith raised it, revealing, to his astonishment, the face of the Yearning Refluxive to whom he had spoken the night before.

People here and there about the Oval, at first cautious of the struggle, now started to approach. There came the shrill hoot of the patrol whistle. The Refluxive struggled to free himself. "Release me; they'll make me a terrible example!"

"Why did you try to kill me?" demanded Reith.

"Need you ask? Let me go, I beg you!"

"Why should I? You just tried to murder me! Let them take you."

"No! The association will suffer!"

"Well then—why did you try to kill me?"

"Because you are dangerous! You would divide us! Already there is dissension! A few weak souls have no faith; they want to find a spaceship and go off on a journey! Folly! The only way is the orthodox way! You are a danger; I thought it best to expunge your dissidence."

Reith took a deep breath of exasperation. The patrol was almost upon them. He said: "Tomorrow we leave Settra; you've had your trouble for nothing." He gave the man a shove which sent him staggering and crying for the pain in his shoulder. "Be thankful we are merciful men!"

The Refluxive disappeared in the darkness. The patrol ran up: tall men in striped suits of red and black holding staffs terminating in incandescent tips. "What is the trouble?"

"A thief," said Reith. "He tried to rob us, then ran off behind the buildings."

The patrol departed; Reith, Anacho, and Traz went into the inn. As they supped Reith told of his arrangements with Zarfo Detwiler. "Tomorrow, if all goes well, we depart Settra."

"By no means too soon," remarked Anacho sourly.

"True. Already I've been spied on by the Wankh, persecuted by the gentry, shot at by the 'cult.' My nerves won't allow much more."

A boy wearing dark red livery came up to their table. "Adam Reith?"

"Who wants him?" Reith asked warily.

"I have a message."

"Give it here." Reith tore apart the folded paper, puzzled out the sense of the florid symbols:

> The Security Company sends greetings. Be it known that, since you, Adam Reith, have attacked an authorized employee in the innocent pursuit of his duties, spoiling his equipment and inflicting pain and inconvenience, we demand a retributive fee of eighteen thousand sequins. If the sum is not immediately paid at our main office, you will be killed by a combination of several processes. Your prompt cooperation will be appreciated. Please do not depart Settra or seek to deny us in any way, as in that case the penalties must be amplified.

Reith flung the letter down on the table. "Dordolio, the Wankh, Lord Cizante, and Helsse, the 'cult,' the Security Company: who is left?"

Traz commented: "Tomorrow may hardly be soon enough."

10

THE FOLLOWING MORNING Reith communicated with Blue Jade Palace by means of the queer Yao telephones, and was allowed to speak to Helsse. "You have naturally canceled the contract with the Security Company?"

"The contract has been canceled. I understand that they have decided to take independent action, which of course you must deal with as you see fit."

"Exactly," said Reith. "We are leaving Settra at once and we accept Lord Cizante's offer of assistance."

Helsse made a noncommittal sound. "What are your plans?"

"Essentially, to escape Settra with our lives."

"I will arrive shortly and take you to an outlying wheelway station. At Vervodei ships leave daily for all quarters and no doubt you will be able to make a convenient departure."

"We will be ready at noon, or before."

Reith set out on foot for the Cercade, taking all precautions, and arrived at the rendezvous with fair assurance that he had not been followed. Zarfo stood waiting, his white hair confined in a bonnet as black as his face. He immediately led the way to the cellar of an ale house. They sat at a stone table; Zarfo signaled the pot-boy and they were presently served heavy stone mugs of a bitter earthy ale.

Zarfo came quickly to business. "Before I disrupt my life by so much as a twitch, show me the color of your money."

Without words Reith threw down ten strips of winking purple sequins.

"Aha!" gloated Zarfo Detwiler. "This is true beauty! Is it to be mine? I will take custody of it at once, and guard it from all harm."

"Who will guard you?" asked Reith.

"Tish, tush, lad," scoffed Zarfo. "If comrades can't trust comrades in a cool ale-cellar, how will it go under adversity?"

Reith returned the money to his wallet. "Adversity is here now. The assassins are disturbed by the affair of yesterday. Instead of taking revenge upon you, they have threatened me."

"Yes, they are an unreasonable lot. If they demand money, defy them. A man can always fight for his life."

"I've been warned not to leave Settra until such a time as they choose to kill me. Nevertheless, I propose to depart, and as soon as possible."

"Shrewd." Zarfo quaffed ale and set the mug down with a thud. "But how will you evade the assassins? Naturally they ponder your every move."

Reith jerked around at a noise, only to find the pot-boy at hand to refill Zarfo's mug. Zarfo pulled at his long black nose to conceal a grin. "The assassins are pertinacious, but we shall outwit them, one way or another. Return to your hotel and make all ready. At noon I will join you and we shall see what we shall see."

"Noon? So late?"

"What difference an hour or two? I must wind up my affairs."

Reith returned to the inn, where Helsse had already arrived in the black landau. The atmosphere was strained and taut; at the sight of Reith, Helsse jumped to his feet. "Time is short; we have been waiting! Come; we have only enough time to catch the first afternoon car for Vervodei!"

Reith asked: "Won't the assassins be expecting just this? It seems an unimaginative plan."

Helsse gave an irritable shrug. "Do you have a better idea?"

"I'd like to work one out."

Anacho asked, "Does Lord Cizante keep an air-car?"

"It is not in operation."

"Are any others available?"

"For a purpose of this sort? I should think not."

Five minutes passed. Helsse said mildly, "The longer we wait, the less time remains to you." He pointed out of the window. "See the two men in the round hats? They wait for you to come forth. Now we cannot even use the car."

"Go out and tell them to go away," suggested Reith.

Helsse laughed. "Not I."

Another half an hour went by. Zarfo swaggered into the foyer. He saluted the group with a wave of the hand. "Are all ready?"

Reith pointed to the assassins standing to the side of the Oval. "They are waiting for us."

"Detestable creatures," said Zarfo. "Only in Cath would they be tolerated." He looked sidelong at Helsse. "Why is he here?"

Reith explained the circumstances; Zarfo looked out upon the Oval. "The black car with the silver and blue crest—is that the vehicle in question? If so, nothing is simpler. We shall ride off in the car."

"Not feasible," said Helsse.

"Why not?" asked Reith.

"Lord Cizante does not care to become involved in this matter, nor do I. At the very least, the Company would include me in the contract."

Reith laughed bitterly. "When you contracted with them in the first place? Out to the car, and drive us away from this city of madmen!"

After a moment of incredulous disdain, Helsse gave a curt nod. "As you wish."

The group left the inn and walked to the car. The assassins came forward. "I believe that you, sir, are Adam Reith?"

"What of it?"

"May we inquire your destination?"

"The Blue Jade Palace."

"Correct," said Helsse tonelessly.

"You understand our regulations and schedule of penalties?"

"Yes, of course."

The assassins muttered together, then one said: "In this case we think it advisable to accompany you."

"There is no room," said Helsse in a cool voice.

The assassins paid no heed. One started to enter the landau. Zarfo pulled him back. The assassin looked over his shoulder. "Have a care; I am a guildsman."

"And I am a Lokhar." Zarfo struck him a great clout, sending him sprawling. The second assassin stood astounded, then snatched forth a gun. Anacho's sting snapped forth, to penetrate his chest. The first assassin tried to crawl away; Zarfo gave him a tremendous kick under the chin; he fell flat and limp. "Into the car," said Zarfo. "It is time to leave."

"What a fiasco," whispered Helsse. "I am ruined."

"Away from Settra!" cried Zarfo. "By the least obvious route!"

The landau rolled along narrow streets, into a narrow lane, and presently out into the countryside.

"Where are you taking us?" demanded Reith.

"Vervodei."

"Ridiculous!" snorted Zarfo. "Drive east into the back country. We must make our way to the Jinga River and fare downstream to Kabasas on the Parapan."

Helsse tried a voice of calm reason. "To the east is wilderness. The car will stop. We have no spare energy cells."

"No difference!"

"Not to you. But how will I return to Settra?"

"Is this your plan, after what has happened?"

Helsse muttered something under his breath. "I am a marked man. They will demand fifty thousand sequins, which I cannot pay—all through your insane manipulations."

"Whatever you like. But continue east, until the car stops or the road gives out—whichever first."

Helsse made a gesture of fateful despair.

The road led through a weirdly beautiful flatland with slow streams and ponds to either side. Trees with drooping black limbs trailed tobacco-brown foliage into the water. Reith kept a lookout to the rear, but discovered no sign of pursuit. Settra became one with the murk of distance.

Helsse no longer seemed to be sulking, but watched the road ahead with an expression that almost seemed anticipation. Reith became suddenly suspicious. "Stop a moment."

Helsse looked around. "Stop? Why?"

"What lies ahead?"

"The mountains."

"Why is the road in such good repair? There seems to be no great traffic."

"Ho!" crowed Zarfo. "The mountain camp for insane folk! It must lie ahead!"

Helsse contrived a sickly grin. "You told me to drive you to the end of the road; you did not stipulate that I should avoid taking you to the asylum."

"I do so now," said Reith. "Please, no more innocent errors of this sort."

Helsse compressed his lips and once more began to brood. At a crossroad he swung south. The ground began to rise. Reith asked, "Where does the road lead?"

"To the old quicksilver mines, to mountain retreats, a few peasant holdings."

Into a forest hung with black moss rolled the car, and the road slanted up even more steeply. The sun passed behind a cloud, the forest became dark and dank, then gave way to a foggy meadow.

Helsse glanced at an indicator. "An hour more of energy."

Reith indicated the thrust of mountains ahead. "What lies beyond?"

"Wilderness. The Hoch Har tribes. Black Mountain Lake, source of the Jinga. The route is neither safe nor convenient. It is, however, an exit from Cath."

Across the meadow they drove. Thick-trunked trees rose at intervals with leaves like shelves of yellow fungus.

The road began to fail, and in places was blocked by fallen boughs. The ridge loomed above, a great rocky jut.

At an abandoned mine the road ended. Simultaneously the power index reached zero. The car halted with a thud and a bump; there was silence except for a sigh of wind.

The group alighted with their meager possessions. The fog had dissipated; the sun shone cool through a high overcast, washing the landscape in honey-colored light.

Reith surveyed the mountainside, tracing a path to the ridge. He turned to Helsse. "Well, which is it to be? Kabasas, or back to Settra?"

"Settra, naturally." He looked disconsolately at the car.

"Afoot?"

"Better than afoot to Kabasas."

"What of the assassins?"

"I must take my chances."

Reith brought out his scanscope and studied the way they had come. "There seems no sign of pursuit; you—" He halted, surprised by the expression on Helsse's face.

"What is that object?" demanded Helsse.

Reith explained.

"Dordolio spoke accurately," said Helsse in a wondering voice. "He was telling the truth!"

Half-amused, half-annoyed, Reith said, "I don't know what Dordolio told you, other than that we were barbarians. Goodbye, then, and my regards to Lord Cizante."

"Wait a moment," said Helsse, staring indecisively west toward Settra. "Kabasas may be safer, after all. The assassins would be sure to consider me an auxiliary to your offense." He turned, assessed the bulk of the mountain, heaved a gloomy sigh. "Total insanity, of course."

"Needless to say, we are not here by our own volition," returned Reith. "Well, we might as well start."

They climbed the tailings dump in front of the mine, peered into the tunnel, from which issued an ooze of reddish slime. A set of footprints led into the tunnel. They were about human size, the shape of a bowling pin or a gourd; two inches ahead of the narrow forward end were three indentations as of toes. Looking down at the marks Reith felt the hairs rise at the nape of his neck. He listened, but no sounds came from the tunnel. He asked Traz, "What sort of prints are these?"

"An unshod Phung, possibly—a small one. More likely a Pnume. The prints are fresh. It watched our approach."

"Come along; let's leave," muttered Reith.

An hour later they reached the ridge and halted to gaze out over the panorama. The land to the west lay drowned in late afternoon murk, with Settra showing as a discolored spot, like a bruise. Far to the east glimmered Black Mountain Lake.

The travelers spent an eerie night at the edge of the forest, starting up at far noises; a thin uncanny screaming, a rap-rap-rap, like blows against a block of hard wood, the crafty hooting of nighthounds.

Dawn came at last. The group made a glum breakfast on pods from a pilgrim plant, then proceeded down over a basalt palisade to the floor of a wooded valley. Ahead lay the Black Mountain Lake, calm and still. A fishing boat inched across the water and presently disappeared behind a jut of rock. "Hoch Har," said Helsse. "Ancient enemies of the Yao. Now they remain behind the mountains."

Traz pointed. "A path."

Reith looked. "I see no path."

"Nevertheless it is there, and I smell wood smoke, from a distance of three miles."

Five minutes later Traz made a sudden gesture. "Several men are approaching."

Reith listened; he could hear nothing. But presently three men appeared on the trail ahead: very tall men with thick waists, thin arms and legs, wearing skirts of a dirty white fiber and short capes of the same stuff. They stopped short at the sight of the travelers, then turned and retreated along the trail, looking anxiously back over their shoulders.

After a quarter-mile the trail left the jungle, and angled off across the swampy foreshore of the lake. The Hoch Har village stood on stilts over the water, terminating in a float to which a dozen plank boats were tied. On the shore a score of men stood in attitudes of nervous truculence, striding back and forth, bush-knives and long spring-bows at the ready.

The travelers approached.

The tallest and heaviest of Hoch Hars called out in a ridiculously shrill voice: "Who are you?"

"Travelers on the way to Kabasas."

The Hoch Hars stared incredulously, then peered back up the trail toward the mountains. "Where is the rest of your band?"

"There is no band; we are alone. Can you sell us a boat and some food?"

The Hoch Hars put aside their weapons. "Food is hard to come by," groaned the first man. "Boats are our dearest possessions. What can you offer us in exchange?"

"Only a few sequins."

"What good are sequins when we must visit Cath to spend them?"

Helsse muttered in Reith's ear. Reith said to the Hoch Hars, "Very well then, we shall continue. I understand that there are other villages around the lake."

"What? Would you deal with petty thieves and cheats? It is all those folks are. Well, to save you from your own folly, we will strain ourselves to work out some sort of arrangement."

In the end Reith paid two hundred sequins for a boat in fair condition and what the Hoch Har chief gruffly claimed to be sufficient provisions to take them all the way to Kabasas: crates of dried fish, sacks of tubers, rolls of pepper-bark, fresh and preserved fruit. Another thirty sequins secured the services, as a guide, of a certain Tsutso, a moon-faced young man somewhat portly, with an affable big-toothed smile. Tsutso declared the first stages of their journey to be the most precarious: "First, the rapids; then the Great Slant, after which the voyage becomes no more than drifting downstream to Kabasas."

At noon, with the small sail set, the boat departed the Hoch Har village, and through the long afternoon sailed the dark water south toward a pair of bluffs which marked the outlet of the lake and the head of the Jinga River. At sunset the boat passed between the bluffs, each crowned by a tumble of ruins, black on the brown-ash sky. Under the bluff to the right was a small cove with a beach; here Reith wanted to camp for the night but Tsutso would not hear of it. "The castles are haunted. At midnight the ghosts of old Tschai walk the pavings. Do you want us all put under a taint?"

"So long as the ghosts keep to the castle, what's to prevent us from using the cove?"

Tsutso gave Reith a wondering look, and held the boat to midstream between the opposing ruins. A mile downstream the Jinga split around a rocky islet, to which Tsutso took the boat. "Here nothing from the forest can molest us."

The travelers supped, laid themselves down around the campfire and were troubled by no more than soft whistles and trills from the forest, and once, far in the distance, the mournful call of the night-hounds.

On the next day they passed across ten miles of violent rapids, during which Tsutso ten times over earned his fee, in Reith's estimation. Meanwhile the forest dwindled to clumps of thorn; the banks became barren, and presently a strange sound made itself heard from ahead: a sibilant all-pervading roar. "The Slant," explained Tsutso. The river disappeared at a brink a hundred yards ahead. Before Reith or the others could protest, the boat had pitched over the verge.

Tsutso said, "Everyone alert; here is the Slant. Hold to the middle!"

The roar of water almost overwhelmed his voice. The boat was sliding into a dark gorge; with amazing velocity the rock walls passed astern. The river itself was a trembling black surface, lined with foam static in relation to the boat. The travelers crouched as low as possible, ignoring Tsutso's condescending grin. For minutes they dashed down the race, finally plunged into a field of foam and froth, then floated smoothly out into still water.

The walls rose sheer a thousand feet: brown sandstone pocked with balls of black starbush. Tsutso steered the boat to a fringe of shingle. "Here I leave you."

"Here? At the bottom of this canyon?" Reith asked in wonder.

Tsutso pointed to a trail winding up the slope. "Five miles away is the village."

"In that case," said Reith, "goodbye and many thanks."

Tsutso made an indulgent gesture. "It is nothing in particular. Hoch Hars are generous folk, except where the Yao are concerned. Had you been Yao, all might not have gone so well."

Reith looked toward Helsse, who said nothing. "The Yao are your enemies?"

"Our ancient persecutors, who destroyed the Hoch Har empire. Now they keep to their side of the mountain, which is well for them, as we can smell out a Yao like a bad fish." He jumped nimbly ashore. "The swamps lie ahead. Unless you lose yourselves or arouse the swamp-people you are as good as at Kabasas." With a final wave he started up the path.

The boat drifted through sepia gloom, the sky a watered silk ribbon high above. The afternoon passed, with the walls of the chasm gradually opening out. At sunset the travelers camped on a small beach, to pass a night in eerie silence.

The next day the river emerged into a wide valley overgrown with tall yellow grass. The hills retreated; the vegetation along the shore became thick and dense, and alive with small creatures, half-spider, half-monkey, which whined and yelped and spurted jets of noxious fluid toward the boat. Other streams made confluence; the Jinga became broad and placid. On the following day trees of remarkable stature appeared along the shore, raising a variety of silhouettes against the smoke-brown sky, and by noon the boat floated with jungle to either side. The sail hung limp; the air was dank with odors of wet wood and decay. The hopping tree-creatures kept to the high branches; through the dimness below drifted gauze-moths, insects hanging on pale bubbles, bird-like creatures which seemed to swim on four soft wings. Once the travelers heard heavy groaning and trampling sounds, another time a ferocious hissing and again a set of strident shrieks, from sources invisible.

By slow degrees the Jinga broadened to become a placid flood, flowing around dozens of small islands, each overgrown with fronds, plumes, fan-shaped dendrons. Once, from the corner of his eye, Reith glimpsed what seemed to be a canoe carrying three youths wearing peacock-tail headdresses, but when he turned to look he saw only an island, and was never sure what in fact he had seen. Later in the day a sinuous twenty-foot beast swam after them, but fifty feet from the boat it seemed to lose interest and submerged.

At sundown the travelers made camp on the beach of a small island. Half an hour later Traz became uneasy and, nudging Reith, pointed to the underbrush. They heard a stealthy rustling and presently sensed a clammy odor. An instant later the beast which had swum after them lunged forth screaming. Reith fired one of his explosive pellets into the very maw of the beast; with its head blown off it careened in a circle, using a peculiar prancing gait, finally floundering in the water to sink.

The group gingerly resumed their seats around the campfire. Helsse watched Reith return the handgun to his pouch, and could no longer restrain his curiosity. "Where, may I ask, did you obtain your weapon?"

"I have learned," said Reith, "that candor makes problems. Your friend Dordolio thinks me a lunatic; Anacho the Dirdirman prefers the term 'amnesiac.' So—think whatever you like."

Helsse murmured, as if for his own ears: "What strange tales we all could tell, if candor indeed were the rule."

Zarfo guffawed. "Candor? Who needs it? I'll tell strange tales as long as someone will listen."

"No doubt," said Helsse, "but persons with desperate goals must hold their secrets close."

Traz, who disliked Helsse, looked sideways with something like a sneer. "Who could this be? I have neither secrets nor desperate goals."

"It must be the Dirdirman," said Zarfo with a sly wink.

Anacho shook his head. "Secrets? No. Only reticences. Desperate goals? I travel with Adam Reith since I have nothing better to do. I am an outcast among the sub-men. I have no goals whatever, except survival."

Zarfo said, "I have a secret: the location of my poor hoard of sequins. My goals? Equally modest: an acre or two of river meadow south of Smargash, a cabin under the tayberry trees, a polite maiden to boil my tea. I recommend them to you."

Helsse, looking into the campfire, smiled faintly. "My every thought, willy-nilly, is a secret. As for my goals—if I return to Settra and somehow can appease the Security Company, I'll be well content."

Reith looked up to where clouds were clotting out the stars. "I'll be content to stay dry tonight."

The group carried the boat ashore, turned it over and, with the sail, made a shelter. Rain began to fall, extinguishing the campfire and sending puddles of water under the boat.

Dawn finally arrived: a blear of rain and umber gloom. At

noon, with the clouds breaking apart, the travelers once more floated the boat, loaded the provisions and set off to the south.

The Jinga widened until the shores were no more than dark marks. The afternoon passed; sunset was a vast chaos of black, gold, and brown. Drifting through the gloom, the travelers sought for a place to land. Mud flats lined the shore, but at last, as purple-brown dusk became night, a sandy bluff appeared under which the travelers landed for the night.

On the following day they entered the swamps. The Jinga, dividing into a dozen channels, moved sluggishly among islands of reeds, and the travelers passed a cramped night in the boat. Toward evening of the day following they came upon a canted dyke of gray schist which, rising and falling, created a chain of rocky islands across the swamp. At some immensely remote time, one or another people of old Tschai had used the islands to support a causeway, long toppled to a crumble of black concrete. On the largest of the islands the travelers camped, dining on the dried fish and musty lentils provided by the Hoch Hars.

Traz was restless. He made a circuit of the island, clambered to the highest jut, looked back and forth along the line of the ancient bridge. Reith, disturbed by Traz's apprehension, joined him. "What do you see?"

"Nothing."

Reith looked all around. The water reflected the dusky mauve of the sky, the hulks of the nearby islands. They returned to the campfire, and Reith set sentry watches. He awoke at dawn and instantly wondered why he had not been called. Then he noticed that the boat was gone. He shook Traz, who had stood the first watch. "Last night, whom did you call?"

"Helsse."

"He did not call me. And the boat is missing."

"And Helsse as well," said Traz.

Reith saw this to be the case.

Traz pointed to the next island, forty yards across the water. "There is the boat. Helsse went for a midnight row."

Going down to the water's edge Reith called: "Helsse! Helsse!"

No response. Helsse was not visible.

Reith considered the distance to the boat. The water was smooth and opaque as slate. Reith shook his head. The boat so near, so obvious: bait? From his pouch he took the hank of cord, originally a component of his survival kit, and tied a stone to one end. He heaved the stone at the boat. It fell short. Reith dragged it back through the water. For an instant the line went taut and quivered to the presence of something strong and vital.

Reith grimaced. He heaved the stone again, and now it wedged inside the boat. He pulled; the boat came back across the water.

With Traz, Reith returned to the neighboring island, to find no trace of Helsse. But under a jut of rock they found a hole slanting down into the island. Traz put his head close to the opening, listened, sniffed, and motioned Reith to do the same. Reith caught a faint clammy odor, like that of earthworms. In a subdued voice he called down into the hole: "Helsse!" and once again, louder: "Helsse!" To no effect.

They returned to their companions. "It seems that the Pnume play jokes," said Reith in a subdued voice.

They ate a silent breakfast, waited an indecisive fidgeting hour. Then slowly they loaded the boat and departed the island. Reith looked back through the scanscope until the island no longer could be seen.

11

THE CHANNELS OF the Jinga came together; the swamp became a jungle. Fronds and tendrils hung over the black water; giant moths floated like ghosts. The upper strata of the forest were a distinct environment: pink and pale yellow ribbons writhed through the air like eels; black-furred globes with six long white arms swung nimbly from branch to branch. Once, far off along an avenue of vision, Reith saw a cluster of large woven huts high in the branches and a little later the boat passed under a bridge of sticks and coarse ropes. Three naked people came to cross the bridge as the boat drifted close: frail thin-bodied folk with parchment-colored skin. Observing the boat, they halted in shock, then raced across the bridge and disappeared into the foliage.

For a week they sailed and paddled uneventfully, the Jinga growing ever wider. One day they passed a canoe from which an old man netted fish; the next day they saw a village on the banks; the day after a power-boat throbbed past. On the night following they halted at a town and spent the night in a riverside inn, standing on stilts over the water.

Two more days they sailed downstream, to a brisk wind from astern. The Jinga was now wide and deep and the wind raised sizable waves. Navigation began to be a problem. Coming to another town they saw a river packet headed downstream; abandoning the boat they took passage for Kabasas on the Parapan.

Three days they rode the packet, enjoying the comfort of hammocks and fresh food. At noon on the fourth day, with the Jinga so broad that the far shore could not be seen, the blue domes of Kabasas appeared on rising land to the west.

Kabasas, like Coad, served as a commercial depot for extensive hinterlands and like Coad seemed to seethe with intrigue. Warehouses and sheds faced the docks; behind, ranks of arched and colonnaded buildings, of beige, gray, white and dark blue plaster, mounted the hills. A wall of each building, for reasons never clear to Reith, leaned either inward or out, giving the city a curiously irregular appearance by no means dissonant with the conduct of the inhabitants. These were a slender alert people, with flowing brown hair, wide cheekbones, burning black eyes. The woman were notably handsome and Zarfo cautioned all: "If you value your lives, pay no heed to the women! Do not so much as look after them, even though they provoke and tease! They play a strange game here in Kabasas. At any hint of admiration they set up furious outcry and a hundred other women, screaming and cursing, rush up to knife the miscreant."

"Hmmf," said Reith. "And the men?"

"They'll save you if they can, and beat the women off, which suits all parties very well. Indeed this is the way of courtship. A man desiring a girl will set upon her and beat her black and blue. No one would think to interfere. If the girl approves, she comes the same way again. When he rushes forth to pummel her, she throws herself on his mercy. Such is the painful wooing of the Kabs."

"It seems somewhat awkward," said Reith.

"Exactly. Awkward and perverse. Such are affairs in Kabasas. During our stay you had best rely on my counsel. First, I nominate the Sea Dragon Inn as a base of operations."

"We'll hardly be here that long. Why not go directly to the dock and find a ship to take us across the Parapan?"

Zarfo pulled at his long black nose. "Things are never so easy! And why cheat ourselves of a sojourn at the Sea Dragon Inn? ... Perhaps a week or two."

"You naturally intend to pay for your own accommodations?"

Zarfo's white eyebrows dipped sharply. "I am as you know a poor man. My every sequin represents toil. On a joint venture of this sort openhanded generosity should certainly be the rule."

"Tonight," said Reith, "we stay at the Sea Dragon Inn. Tomorrow we leave Kabasas."

Zarfo gave a dismal grunt. "It is not my place to dispute your wishes. Hmmf. As I understand the matter, you plan to arrive at Smargash, recruit a team of technicians, then continue to Ao Hidis?"

"Correct."

"Discretion then! I suggest that we take ship to Zara across the Parapan and up the Ish River. You have not lost your money?"

"Definitely not."

"Take good care of it. The thieves of Kabasas are deft; they use thongs which reach out thirty feet." Zarfo pointed. "Observe that structure just above the beach? The Sea Dragon Inn!"

The Sea Dragon Inn was indeed a grand establishment, with wide public rooms and pleasant sleeping cubicles. The restaurant was decorated to suggest a submarine garden, even to the dark grottos where members of a local sect, who would not publicly perform the act of deglutition, were served.

Reith ordered fresh linen from the staff haberdashery and descended to the great bath on the low terrace. He scrubbed himself and was sprayed with tonic and massaged with handfuls of fragrant moss. Wrapping himself in a gown of white linen he returned to his chamber.

On the couch sat a man in a soiled dark blue suit. Reith stared. Helsse looked back at him with an unfathomable expression. He made no move and uttered no sound.

The silence was intense.

Reith slowly backed from the room, to stand uncertainly on the balcony, heart pounding as if he had seen a ghost. Zarfo appeared, swaggering back to his room with white hair billowing.

Reith signaled to him. "Come, I want to show you something." He took Zarfo to the door, thrust it ajar, half-expecting to find the room unoccupied. Helsse sat as before. Zarfo whispered: "Is he mad? He sits and stares and mocks us but does not speak."

"Helsse," said Reith. "What are you doing here? What happened to you?"

Helsse rose to his feet. Reith and Zarfo moved involuntarily back. Helsse looked at them with the faintest of smiles. He stepped out on the balcony, walked slowly to the stairs. He turned his head; Reith and Zarfo saw the pale oval of his face; then, like an apparition, he was gone.

"What is the meaning of all this?" Reith asked in a husky voice.

Zarfo shook his head, for once subdued. "The Pnume love their pranks."

"Should we have held him?"

"He could have stayed, had he wished."

"But—I doubt if he is sane."

Zarfo's only response was a hunch-shouldered shrug.

Reith went to the edge of the balcony, looked out over the town. "The Pnume know the very rooms in which we sleep!"

"A person floating down the Jinga ends up at Kabasas," said Zarfo testily. "If he is able, he patronizes the Sea Dragon Inn. This is not an intricate deduction. So much for Pnume omniscience."

On the following day Zarfo went off by himself and presently returned with a short man with skin the color of mahogany, walking with a sore-footed swagger as if his shoes were too tight. His face was seamed and crooked; small nervous eyes looked slantwise past the beak of his nose. "And here," declared Zarfo grandly, "I give you Sealord Dobagq Hrostilfe, a person of sagacity, who will arrange everything."

Reith thought that he had never seen a more obvious rascal.

"Hrostilfe commands the *Pibar*," explained Zarfo. "For a most reasonable sum he will deliver us to our destination, be it the far coast of Vord."

"How much across the Parapan?" Reith asked.

"Only five thousand sequins, would you believe it?" exclaimed Zarfo.

Reith laughed scornfully. He turned to Zarfo: "I need your help no longer. You and your friend Hrostilfe can try to swindle someone else."

"What?" cried Zarfo. "After I risked my life in that infernal chute and endured all manner of hardship?"

But Reith had walked away. Zarfo came after him, somewhat crestfallen. "Adam Reith, you have made a serious mistake."

Reith nodded grimly. "Instead of an honest man I hired you."

Zarfo swelled up indignantly. "Who dares name me other than honest?"

"I do. Hrostilfe would rent his boat for a hundred sequins. He gave you a price of five hundred. You told him: 'Why should we not both profit? Adam Reith is credulous. I'll name a price and anything over a thousand sequins is mine.' So, be off with you."

Zarfo pulled ruefully at his black nose. "You do me vast wrong. I have only just come from chiding Hrostilfe, who admitted knavery. He now offers his boat at"—Zarfo cleared his throat—"twelve hundred sequins."

"Not a bice more than three hundred."

Zarfo threw his hands into the air and stalked away. Not long after Hrostilfe himself appeared with the plea that Reith inspect his ship. Reith followed him to the *Pibar:* a jaunty craft forty feet long, powered by electrostatic jet. Hrostilfe kept up a half-hectoring, half-plaintive commentary. "A fast seaworthy vessel! Your price is absurd. What of my skills, my sea-lore? Do you appreciate the cost of energy? The voyage will exhaust a power cell: a hundred sequins which I cannot afford. You must pay for energy and additionally for provisions. I am a generous man but I cannot subsidize you."

Reith agreed to pay for energy and a reasonable amount for provisions, but not the installation of new water tanks, extra foul-weather gear, good-luck fetishes for the prow; furthermore he insisted on departure the following day, at which Hrostilfe gave a sour chuckle. "There's one in the eye for the old Lokhar. He had counted on swanking it a week or more at the Sea Dragon."

"He can stay as long as he likes," said Reith, "provided that he pays."

"Small chance of that," chuckled Hrostilfe. "Well then, what about provisions?"

"Buy them. Show me an itemized tally, which I will check in detail."

"I need an advance: a hundred sequins."

"Do you take me for a fool? Remember, tomorrow noon we sail."

"The *Pibar* will be ready," said Hrostilfe in a sullen voice.

Returning to the Sea Dragon Inn, Reith found Anacho on the terrace. Anacho pointed to a black-haired shape leaning against the seawall. "There he stands: Helsse. I called him by name. It was as if he never heard."

Helsse turned his head; his face seemed deathly white. For a moment or two he watched them, then turned and walked slowly away.

At noon the travelers embarked on the *Pibar*. Hrostilfe gave his passengers a brisk welcome. Reith looked skeptically here and there, wondering in what fashion Hrostilfe thought he had won advantage for himself. "Where are the provisions?"

"In the main saloon."

Reith examined boxes and crates, checked them against Hrostilfe's tally sheet, and was forced to admit that Hrostilfe had secured good merchandise at no great price. But why, he wondered, were they not stored forward in the lazaret? He tried the door, and found it locked.

Interesting, thought Reith. He called Hrostilfe: "Best to stow the stores forward in the lazaret, before we start pitching to the waves."

"All in good time!" declared Hrostilfe. "First things first! Now it's important that we make the most of the morning current!"

"But it will only require a moment. Here, open the door; I will do it myself."

Hrostilfe made a waggish gesture. "I am the most finicky of seamen. Everything must be done just so."

Zarfo, who had come into the saloon, gave the lazaret door a speculative frown. Reith said, "Very well then, just as you like." Zarfo started to speak but catching Reith's gaze, shrugged and held his tongue.

Hrostilfe nimbly hopped here and there, casting off lines, starting the jet, and finally jumping into the control pulpit. The boat surged out to sea.

Reith spoke to Traz, who went to stand behind Hrostilfe. Bringing forth his catapult Traz checked its action, dropped a bolt into the slot, cocked it and hung it loosely at his belt.

Hrostilfe grimaced. "Careful, boy! A foolhardy way to carry your catapult!"

Traz seemed not to hear.

Reith, after a word or two with Zarfo and Anacho, went to the foredeck. Setting fire to some old rags, he held them in the forward ventilator, so that smoke poured down into the lazaret.

Hrostilfe cried out in anger: "What nonsense is this? Are you trying to set us afire?"

Reith set more rags burning and dropped them into the ventilator. From below came a choked cough, then a mutter of voices and a stamping of feet. Hrostilfe jerked his hand toward his pouch, but noticed Traz's intent gaze and his ready catapult.

Reith sauntered aft. Traz said, "His weapon is in his pouch."

Hrostilfe stood rigid with dismay. He made a sudden move but stopped short as Traz jerked up the catapult. Reith detached the pouch, handed it to Traz, took two daggers and a poniard from various parts of Hrostilfe's person. "Go below," said Reith. "Open the door to the lazaret. Instruct your friends to come forth one at a time."

Hrostilfe, gray-faced with fury, hopped below and, after an exchange of threats with Reith, opened the door. Six ruffians came forth, to be disarmed by Anacho and Zarfo and sent up to the deck where Reith thrust them over the side.

The lazaret at last was empty of all but smoke. Hrostilfe was hustled up on deck, where he became unctuous and over-reasonable. "All can be explained! A ridiculous misunderstanding!" But Reith refused to listen and Hrostilfe joined his fellows over the side, where, after shaking his fist and bellowing obscenities at the grinning faces aboard the *Pibar*, he struck out for the shore.

"It appears," said Reith, "that we now lack a navigator. In what direction lies Zara?"

Zarfo's manner was very subdued. He pointed a gnarled black finger. "That should be our heading." He turned to look aft toward the seven bobbing heads. "Incomprehensible to me, the greed of men for money! See to what disasters it leads!" And Zarfo gave a sanctimonious cluck of the tongue. "Well then, an unfortunate incident, happily in the past. And now we command the *Pibar*! Ahead: Zara, the Ish River, and Smargash!"

12

ALL DURING THE first day the Parapan was serene. The second day was brisk with the *Pibar* pitching up and over a short chop. On the third day a black-brown cloud loomed out of the west, stabbing the sea with lightning. Wind came in massive gusts; for two hours the *Pibar* heaved and tossed; then the storm passed over, and the *Pibar* drove into clement weather.

On the fourth day Kachan loomed ahead. Reith steered the *Pibar* alongside a fishing craft and Zarfo asked the direction of Zara. The fisherman, a swarthy old man with steel rings in his ears, pointed wordlessly. The *Pibar* surged forward, entering the Ish estuary at sunset. The lights of Zara flickered along the western shore, but now, with no reason to put into port, the *Pibar* continued south up the Ish.

The pink moon Az shone on the water; all night the *Pibar* drove. Morning found them in a rich country with rows of stately keel trees along the banks. Then the land began to grow barren, and for a space the river wound through a cluster of obsidian spires. On the next day a band of tall men in black cloaks were seen on the riverbank. Zarfo identified them as Niss tribesmen. They stood motionless, watching the *Pibar* surge upstream. "Give them a wide berth! They live in holes like night-hounds and some say the night-hounds are kinder."

Late in the afternoon sand dunes closed in upon the river and Zarfo insisted that the *Pibar* be anchored in deep water for the night. "Ahead are sandbars and shallows. We would be certain to run aground and undoubtedly the Niss have followed. They would grapple the boat and swarm aboard."

"Won't they attack us if we lay at anchor?"

"No, they fear deep water and never use boats. At anchor we are as safe as if we were already at Smargash."

The night was clear with both Az and Braz wheeling through the sky of old Tschai. On the riverbank the Niss boldly lit their fires and boiled their pots, and later started up a wild music of fiddles and drums. For hours the travelers sat watching the agile shapes in black cloaks dancing around the fires, kicking, jumping, heads up, heads low; swinging, whirling, prancing with arms akimbo.

In the morning the Niss were nowhere to be seen. The *Pibar* passed through the shallows without incident. Late in the afternoon the travelers came to a village, guarded from the Niss by a line of posts to each of which was chained a skeleton in a rotting black cloak. Zarfo declared the village to be the feasible limit of navigation with Smargash yet three hundred miles south, across a land of deserts, mountain pinnacles and chasms. "Now we must travel by caravan, over the old Sarsazm Road, to Hamil Zut under the Lokhara Uplands. Tonight I'll make inquiry and learn what's to our advantage."

Zarfo stayed ashore overnight, returning in the morning with the news that by dint of the most furious bargaining he had exchanged the *Pibar* for first class passage by caravan to Hamil Zut.

Reith calculated. Three hundred miles? Two hundred sequins a person, at maximum: eight hundred for the four. The *Pibar* was worth ten thousand, even at a sacrifice price. He looked at Zarfo, who ingenuously returned the gaze. "You will recall," said Reith, "the ill feeling and dissension at Kabasas?"

"Of course," declared Zarfo. "To this day I become anguished by the injustice of your hints."

"Here is another hint. How much extra did you demand for the *Pibar*—and receive?"

Zarfo gave an uneasy grimace. "Naturally, I was saving the news to be a glad surprise."

"How much?"

"Three thousand sequins," muttered Zarfo. "No more, no less. I consider it a fair price up here, far from wealth."

Reith allowed the figure to pass without challenge. "Where is the money?"

"It will be paid when we go ashore."

"And when does the caravan leave?"

"Soon—a day or so. There is a passable inn; we can spend the night ashore."

"Very well; let us all go now and collect the money."

Somewhat to Reith's surprise the sack which Zarfo received from the innkeeper contained exactly three thousand sequins, and Zarfo gave a sour sneer and, going into the tavern, called for a pot of ale.

Three days later the caravan started south: a file of twelve power wagons, four mounted with sandblasts. Sarsazm Road led through awesome scenery: gorges and great precipices, the bed of an ancient sea, vistas of distant mountains, sighing forests of keel and blackfern. Occasionally Niss were sighted but they kept their distance and on the evening of the third day the caravan pulled into Hamil Zut, a squalid little town of a hundred mud huts and a dozen taverns.

In the morning Zarfo engaged pack-beasts, equipment and a pair of guides, and the travelers set forth up the trail into the Lokharan highlands.

"This is wild country," Zarfo warned them. "Dangerous beasts are occasionally seen, so be ready with your weapons."

The trail was steep, the terrain indeed wild. On several occasions they sighted Kar Yan, subtle gray beasts slinking through the rocks, sometimes erect on two legs, sometimes dropping to all six. Another time they encountered a tiger-headed reptile gorging upon a carcass, and were able to pass unmolested.

On the third day after leaving Hamil Zut, the travelers entered Lokhara, a great upland plain; and in the mid-afternoon Smargash appeared ahead. Zarfo now told Reith: "It occurs to me, as it must have to you, that yours is a very ticklish venture."

"Agreed."

"Folk here are not indifferent to the Wankh, and a stranger might easily talk to the wrong people."

"So?"

"It might be better for me to select the personnel."

"Certainly. But leave the question of payment to me."

"As you wish," growled Zarfo.

The countryside was now a prosperous well-watered land, populated by peasant farms. The men, like Zarfo, were tattooed or dyed black, with a mane of white hair. The skins of the women, in contradistinction, were chalky white, and their hair was black. Urchins showed white or black hair according to their sex, but their skins were uniformly the color of the dirt in which they played.

A road ran on a riverbank, under majestic old keels. To either side were small bungalows, each in its bower of vines and shrubs. Zarfo sighed with vast feeling. "Observe me, the transient worker returning to his home. But where is my fortune? How may I buy my cottage by the river? Poverty has forced me to strange ways; I am thrown in with a stone-hearted zealot, who takes his joy thwarting the hopes of a kind old man!"

Reith paid no heed, and presently they entered Smargash.

13

REITH SAT IN the parlor of the squat cylindrical cottage he had rented, overlooking the Smargash common, where the young folk spent much time dancing.

Across from him, in wicher chairs, sat five white-haired men of Smargash, a group screened from the twenty Zarfo originally had approached. The time was middle afternoon; out on the common dancers skipped and kicked to music of concertina, bells and drums.

Reith explained as much of his program as he dared: not a great deal. "You men are here because you can help me in a certain venture. Zarfo Detwiler has informed you that a large sum of money is involved; this is true, even if we fail. If we succeed, and I believe the chances are favorable, you will earn wealth sufficient to satisfy any of you. There is danger, as might be expected, but we shall hold it to a minimum. If anyone does not care to consider such a venture, now is the time to leave."

The oldest of the group, one Jag Jaganig, an expert in the overhaul and installation of control systems, said, "So far we can't say yes or no. None of us would refuse to drag home a sack of sequins, but neither would we care to challenge impossibility for a chancy bice."

"You want more information?" Reith looked from face to face. "This is natural enough. But I don't want to take the merely curious into my confidence. If any of you are definitely not disposed for a dangerous but by no means desperate venture, please identify yourself now."

There was a slight stir of uneasiness, but no one spoke out.

Reith waited a moment. "Very well; you must bind yourselves to secrecy."

The group bound themselves by awful Lokhar oaths. Zarfo, plucking a hair from each head, twisted a fiber which he set alight. Each inhaled the smoke. "So we are bound, one to all; if one proves false, the others as one will strike him down."

Reith, impressed by the ritual, had no more qualms about speaking to the point. "I know the exact location of a source of wealth, at a place not on the planet Tschai. We need a spaceship and a crew to operate it. I propose to commandeer a spaceship from the Ao Hidis field; you men shall be the crew. To demonstrate my sanity and good faith, I will pay to each man on the day of departure five thousand sequins. If we try but fail, each man receives another five thousand sequins."

"Each surviving man," grumbled Jag Jaganig.

Reith went on: "If we succeed, ten thousand sequins will seem like ten bice. Essentially, this is the scope of the venture."

The Lokhars shuffled dubiously in their chairs. Jag Jaganig spoke. "We obviously have the basis for an adequate crew here, at least for a Zeno, or a Kud, or even one of the small Kadants. But it is no small matter to so affront the Wankh."

"Or worse, the Wankhmen," muttered Zorofim.

"As I recall," mused Thadzei, "no great vigilance prevailed. The scheme, while startling, seems feasible—provided that the ship we board is in operative condition."

"Aha!" exclaimed Belje. "That 'provided that' is the key to the entire exploit!"

Zarfo jeered: "Naturally there is risk. Do you expect money for nothing?"

"I can hope."

Jag Jaganig inquired: "Assume that the ship is ours. Is further risk entailed?"

"None."

"Who will navigate?"

"I will."

"In what form is this 'wealth'?" demanded Zorofim. "Gems? Sequins? Precious metal? Antiques? Essences?"

"I don't care to go any further into detail, except to guarantee that you will not be disappointed."

The discussion proceeded, with every aspect of the venture subjected to attack and analysis. Alternative proposals were considered, argued, rejected. No one seemed to regard the risk as overwhelming, nor did anyone doubt the group's ability to handle the ship. But none evinced enthusiasm. Jag Jaganig put the situation into focus. "We are puzzled," he told Reith. "We do not understand your purposes. We are skeptical of boundless treasures."

Zarfo said, "Here I must speak. Adam Reith has his faults which I won't deny. He is stubborn and unwieldy; he is crafty as a zut; he is ruthless when opposed. But he is a man of his word. If he declares a treasure to exist for our taking, that aspect of the matter is closed."

After a moment Belje muttered: "Desperate, desperate! Who wants to learn the truth of the black boxes?"

"Desperate, no," countered Thadzei. "Risky, yes, and may demons run off with the black boxes!"

"I'll take the chance," said Zorofim.

"I as well," said Jag Jaganig. "Who lives forever?"

Belje finally capitulated and declared himself committed. "When shall we leave?"

"As soon as possible," said Reith. "The longer I wait, the more nervous I get."

"And more the chance of someone else running off with our treasure, hey?" exclaimed Zarfo. "That would be a sad case!"

"Give us three days to arrange our affairs," said Jag Jaganig.

"And what of the five thousand sequins?" demanded Thadzei. "Why not distribute the money now, so that we may have the use of it?"

Reith hesitated no longer than a tenth of a second. "Since you must trust me, I must trust you." He paid to each of the marveling Lokhars fifty purple sequins, worth a hundred white sequins each.

"Excellent!" declared Jag Jaganig. "Remember all! Utter discretion! Spies are everywhere. In particular I distrust that peculiar stranger at the inn who dresses like a Yao."

"What?" cried Reith. "A young man, black-haired, very elegant?"

"The person precisely. He stares out over the dancing field with never a word to say."

Reith, Zarfo, Anacho and Traz went to the inn. In the dim taproom sat Helsse, long legs in tight black twill breeches stretched under the heavy table. Brooding, he looked straight ahead and out the doorway to where black-skinned white-haired boys and white-skinned black-haired girls skipped and caracoled in the tawny sunlight.

Reith said: "Helsse!"

Helsse never shifted his gaze.

Reith came closer. "Helsse!"

Helsse slowly turned his head; Reith looked into eyes like lenses of black glass.

"Speak to me," urged Reith. "Helsse! Speak!"

Helsse opened his mouth, uttered a mournful croak. Reith

drew back. Helsse watched him incuriously, then returned to his inspection of the dancing field and the dim hills beyond.

Reith joined his comrades to the side where Zarfo poured him a pot of ale. "What of the Yao? Is he mad?"

"I don't know. He might be feigning. Or under hypnotic control. Or drugged."

Zarfo took a long draft from his pot, wiped the foam from his nose. "The Yao might think it a favor were we to cure him."

"No doubt," said Reith, "but how?"

"Why not call in a Dugbo practitioner?"

"What might that be?"

Zarfo jerked his thumb to the east. "The Dugbo have a camp back of town: shiftless folk in rags and tatters, given to thieving and vice, and musicians to boot. They worship demons, and their practitioners perform miracles."

"So you think the Dugbo can cure Helsse?"

Zarfo drained his pot. "If he is feigning, I assure you he won't feign long."

Reith shrugged. "We have no better occupation for a day or two."

"Exactly my way of thinking," said Zarfo.

The Dugbo practitioner was a spindly little man dressed in brown rags and boots of uncured leather. His eyes were a luminous hazel, his russet hair was confined in three greasy knobs. On his cheek pale cicatrices worked and jumped as he spoke. He did not appear to consider Reith's requirements surprising and with clinical curiosity studied Helsse, who sat sardonically indifferent in one of the wicker chairs.

The practitioner approached Helsse, looked into his eyes, inspected his ears, and nodded as if a suspicion had been verified. He signaled the fat youth who assisted him, then ducking behind Helsse touched him here and there while the youth held a bottle of black essence under Helsse's nose. Helsse presently became passive and relaxed into the chair. The practitioner set heaps of incense alight and fanned the fumes into Helsse's face. Then, while the youth played a nose flute the practitioner sang: secret words, close to Helsse's ears. He put a wad of clay into Helsse's hand; Helsse furiously began to mold the clay and presently set up a mutter.

The practitioner signaled to Reith. "A simple case of possession. Notice: the evil flows from the fingers into the clay. Talk to him if you like. Be gentle but command, and he will answer you."

"Helsse," said Reith, "describe your association with Adam Reith."

In a clear voice Helsse spoke. "Adam Reith came to Settra. There had been rumor and speculation, but when he arrived, all was different. By strange chance he came to Blue Jade, my personal vantage, and there I saw him first. Dordolio came after and in his rage maligned Reith as one of the 'cult': a man who fancied himself from the far world Home. I spoke with Adam Reith but learned only confusion. To clarify by acquiescence, third of the Ten Techniques, I took him to the headquarters of the 'cult' and received contradictions. A courier new to Settra followed us. I could not dramatically divert, sixth of the Techniques. Adam Reith killed the courier and took a message of unknown importance; he would not allow me inspection; I could not comfortably insist. I referred him to a Lokhar, again 'clarifying by acquiescence': as it eventuated, the wrong technique. The Lokhar read far into the message. I ordered Reith assassinated. The attempt was bungled. Reith and his band fled south. I received instructions to accompany him and penetrate his motivations. We journeyed east to the Jinga River and downstream by boat. On an island—" Helsse gave a gasping cry and sank back, rigid and trembling.

The practitioner waved smoke into Helsse's face and pinched his nose. "Return to the 'calm' state, and henceforth, when your nose is pinched, return; this shall be an absolute injunction. Now then, answer such questions as are put to you."

Reith asked, "Why do you spy on Adam Reith?"

"I am obligated to do so; furthermore I enjoy such work."

"Why are you obligated?"

"All Wankhmen must serve Destiny."

"Oho. You are a Wankhman?"

"Yes."

And Reith wondered how he could ever have thought otherwise. Tsutso and the Hoch Hars had not been deceived: "Had you been Yao, all would not have gone so well," so had said Tsutso.

Reith glanced ruefully at his comrades, then turned back to Helsse. "Why do the Wankhmen keep spies in Cath?"

"They watch the turn of the 'round'; they guard against a renascence of the 'cult.' "

"Why?"

"It is a matter of stasis. Conditions now are optimum. Any change can only be for the worse."

"You accompanied Adam Reith from Settra to an island in the swamps. What happened there?"

Helsse once more croaked and became catatonic. The practitioner tweaked his nose.

Reith asked, "How did you travel to Kabasas?"

Again Helsse became inert. Reith tweaked his nose. "Tell us why you cannot answer the questions?"

Helsse said nothing. He appeared to be conscious. The practitioner fanned smoke in his face; Reith tweaked his nose and, doing so, saw that Helsse's eyes looked in separate directions. The practitioner rose to his feet, and began to put away his equipment. "That's all. He's dead."

Reith stared from the practitioner to Helsse and back. "Because of the questioning?"

"The smoke permeates the head. Sometimes the subjects live: often, in fact. This one died swiftly; your questions ruptured his sensorium."

The following evening was clear and windy with puffs of dust racing over the vacant dancing field. Through the dusk men in gray cloaks came to the rented cottage. Within, lamps were low and windows shrouded; conversations were conducted in quiet voices. Zarfo spread an old map out on the table, and pointed with a thick black finger. "We can travel to the coast and down, but this is all Niss country. We can fare east around the Sharf to Lake Falas: a long route. Or we can move south, through the Lost Counties, over the Infnets and down to Ao Hidis: the direct and logical route."

Reith asked, "Sky-rafts aren't available?"

Belje, the least enthusiastic of the adventurers, shook his head. "Conditions are no longer as they were when I was a youth. Then you might have selected among half a dozen. Now there are none. Sequins and sky-rafts are both hard to come by. So now, in pursuit of the one, we lack the use of the other."

"How will we travel?"

"To Blalag we ride by power wagon, where perhaps we can hire some sort of conveyance as far as the Infnets. Thereafter, we must go afoot; the old roads south have been destroyed and forgotten."

14

FROM SMARGASH TO the old Lokhar capital, Blalag, was a three-day journey across a windy wasteland. At Blalag the adventurers took shelter at a dingy inn, where they were able to arrange transportation by motor-cart to the mountain-settlement Derduk, far into the Infnets. The journey occupied the better part of two days under uncomfortable conditions. At Derduk the only accommodation was a ramshackle cabin which provoked grumbling among the Lokhars. But the owner, a garrulous old man, stewed a great cauldron of game and wild berries, and the peevishness subsided.

At Derduk the road south became a disused track. At dawn the now somewhat cheerless group of adventurers set forth on foot. All day they traveled through a land of rock pinnacles, fields of rubble and scree. At sundown with a chill wind sighing through the rocks they came upon a small black tarn where they passed the night. The next day brought them to the brink of a vast chasm and another day was spent finding a route to the bottom. On the sandy floor beside the river Desidea, on its way east to Lake Falas, the group camped, to be disturbed for much of the night by uncanny hoots and near-human yells, echoing and re-echoing through the rocks.

In the morning, rather than attempt the south face of the precipice, they followed the Desidea and presently found a cleft which brought them out upon a high savannah rolling off into the murk.

Two days the adventurers marched south, reaching the extreme ramparts of the Infnets by twilight of the second day, with a tremendous vista across the lands to the south. When night came a sparkle of far lights appeared. "Ao Hidis!" cried the Lokhars in mingled relief and apprehension.

Over the minuscule campfire that night there was much talk of Wankh and Wankhmen. The Lokhars were unanimous in their detestation of the Wankhmen: "Even the Dirdirmen, for all their erudition and preening, are never so jealous of their prerogatives," declared Jag Jaganig.

Anacho gave an airy laugh. "From the Dirdirman point of view Wankhmen are scarcely superior to any of the other sub-races."

"Give the rascals credit," said Zarfo, "they understand the Wankh chimes. I myself am resourceful and perceptive; still, in twenty-five years, I learned only pidgin chords for 'yes,' 'no,' 'stop,' 'go,' 'right,' 'wrong,' 'good,' 'bad.' I must admit to their achievement."

"Bah," muttered Zorofim. "They are born to it; they hear chimes from the first instant of their lives; it is no great achievement."

"One that they make the most of, however," said Belje with something like envy in his voice. "Think; they work at nothing, they have no responsibilities, but to stand between the Wankh and the world of Tschai, and they live in refinement and ease."

Reith spoke in a puzzled voice. "A man like Helsse now: he was a Wankhman who lived as a spy. What did he hope to achieve? What Wankh interests did he safeguard in Cath?"

"Wankh interests—none. But remember, the Wankhmen are opposed to change, since any alteration of circumstances can only be to their disadvantage. When a Lokhar begins to understand chimes he is sent away. In Cath—who knows what they fear?" And Zarfo warmed his hands at the campfire.

The night passed slowly. At dawn Reith looked toward Ao Hidis through his scanscope, but could see little for the mist.

Surly with tension and lack of sleep the group once more set off to the south, keeping to such cover as offered itself.

The city slowly became distinct; Reith located the dock where the *Vargaz* had discharged—how long ago it seemed! He traced the road which led through the market and north past the spacefield. From the heights the city seemed placid, lifeless; the black towers of the Wankhmen brooded over the water. On the spacefield, plain to be seen, were five spaceships.

By noon the party reached the ridge above the city. With great care Reith studied the spacefield, now directly below, through his scanscope. To the left were the repair shops, and nearby a bulk-cargo vessel in a state of obvious disrepair, with scaffolds raised beside exposed machinery. Another ship, this the closest, at the back of the field, seemed to be an abandoned hulk. The condition of the other three vessels was not obvious, but the Lokhars declared them all operable. "It is a matter of routine," said Zorofim. "When a ship is down for overhaul, it is moved close to the shops. The ships in transit dock yonder, in the 'Load Zone.' "

"It would seem then that three ships are potentially suitable for our purposes?"

The Lokhars would not go quite so far.

"Sometimes minor repairs are done in the 'Load Zone,' " said Belje.

"Notice," said Thadzei, "the repair cart by the access ramp. It carries components, cases, and they must come from one of the three ships in the 'Load Zone.' "

These were two small cargo ships and a passenger vessel. The Lokhars favored the cargo ships, with which they felt familiar. In regard to the passenger vessel, which Reith considered the most suitable, the Lokhars were in disagreement, Zorofim and Thadzei declaring it to be a standard ship in a specialized hull; Jag Jaganig and Belje equally certain that this was either a new design or an elaborate modification, in either case certain to present difficulties.

All day the group studied the spacefield, watching the activity of the workshop and the traffic along the road. During the middle afternoon a black air-car drifted down to land beside the passenger vessel, which now obscured the view, but it appeared that there was a transfer between ship and air-car. Somewhat later Lokhar mechanics brought a case of energy tubes to the ship, which according to Zarfo was a sure signal that the ship was preparing for departure.

The sun sank toward the ocean. The men fell silent, studying the ships which, hardly more than a quarter-mile distant, seemed tantalizingly accessible. Still the question lingered: Which of the three ships in the "Load Zone" offered the maximum opportunity for a successful departure? The consensus favored one of the cargo ships, only Jag Jaganig preferring the passenger ship.

Reith's nerves began to crawl. The next few hours would shape his future, and far too many variables lay beyond his control. Strange that the ships should be guarded so lightly! On the other hand who was apt to attempt the theft of a spaceship? Probably not in the last thousand years had such an act occurred, if ever.

Dusk fell over the landscape; the group began to descend the mountainside. Floodlights illuminated the ground beside the warehouses, the repair shop, the depot in back of the loading zone. The remainder of the field remained in greater or less darkness, the ships casting long shadows away from the lights.

The men scrambled the last few feet down to the base of the hill, crossed a path of dank marshland, and came to the edge of the field, and here they waited five minutes, watching and listening. The warehouses showed no activity; in the shops a few men still worked.

Reith, Zarfo and Thadzei went forth to reconnoiter. Crouching they ran to the abandoned hulk, where they stood in the shadows.

From the machine shop came the whine of machinery; from the depot a voice called something unintelligible. The three waited ten minutes. In the town at the back of the spacefield long skeins of light had come into being; across the harbor the Wankh towers showed a few glimmers of yellow.

The machine shop became quiet; the workers appeared to be leaving. Reith, Zarfo and Thadzei moved across the field keeping to the long shadows. They reached the first of the small cargo ships, where again they halted to look and listen: there were no sounds, no alarms. Zarfo and Thadzei went to the entry hatch, heaved it open and entered, while Reith with beating heart stood guard outside.

Ten interminable minutes passed. From within came furtive sounds and once or twice a glimmer of light, which aroused in Reith an intense nervousness.

Finally the two Lokhars returned. "No good," grunted Zarfo. "No air, no energy. Let's try the other."

They stole quickly across the bands of light and shadow to the second cargo ship; as before Zarfo and Thadzei entered while Reith stood at the port. The Lokhars returned almost immediately. "Under repair," Zarfo reported glumly. "This is where the component cases come from."

They turned to look at the passenger vessel. "It's not a standard design," Zarfo grumbled. "Still, the instruments and layout may be familiar to us."

"Let's go aboard and look," said Reith. But now a light flared across the field. Reith's first thought was that they had been discovered. But the light played toward the passenger vessel. From the direction of the gate came a low easy-moving shape. The vehicle stopped beside the passenger vessel; a number of dark figures alighted—how many could not be ascertained in the glare. With a curiously abrupt and heavy motion, the figures entered the ship.

"Wankh," muttered Zarfo. "They're going aboard."

"It would mean that the ship is ready for departure," said Reith. "A chance we can't afford to miss!"

Zarfo demurred. "It's one thing to steal an empty ship, another coping with a half dozen Wankh, and Wankhmen as well."

"How do you know Wankhmen are aboard?"

"Because of the lights. Wankh project pulses of radiation and observe the reflections."

Behind them came a faint sound. Reith whirled to find Traz. "We became worried; you were gone so long."

"Go back; bring everyone here. If we have opportunity, we'll board the passenger ship. It's the only one available."

Traz vanished into the darkness. Five minutes later the entire group stood in the shadow of the cargo ship.

Half an hour went by. In the passenger ship shapes moved across the lights, performing activities beyond the comprehension of the nervous men. In husky whispers they debated possible courses of action. Should they try to storm the ship now? Almost certainly departure was in the offing. Such action was obviously reckless. The group decided to pursue a conservative course and return into the mountains to await a more propitious occasion. As they started back, a number of Wankh issued from the vessel and lurched to the vehicle, which almost immediately left the field. Within the ship lights still glowed. No further activity was evident.

"I'm going to give it a look," said Reith. He ran across the field, followed by the others. They mounted the ramp, passed through an embarkation port into the ship's main saloon, which was unoccupied. "Everybody to his station," said Reith. "Let's take it up!"

"If we can," grumbled Zorofim.

Traz cried out a warning: turning, Reith saw that a single Wankh had entered the saloon, watching in nonplussed disapproval. It was a black creature somewhat larger than a man, with a heavy torso, a squat head from which two black lenses flickered at half-second intervals. The legs were short; the feet were played webs; it carried no weapons or implements; in fact wore no garment or harness of any sort. From a sound organ at the base of the skull came four reverberating chimes, which, considering the circumstances, seemed measured and unexcited. Reith stepped forward, pointed to a settee, to indicate that it should sit down. The

Wankh stood motionless, looking after the Lokhars who had gone their various ways, checking engines, energy, supplies, oxygen. The Wankh at last seemed to understand the events which were taking place. It took a step toward the exit port, but Reith barred the way and once again pointed to the settee. The Wankh loomed in front of him, the glassy eyes flickering. Once again the chimes sounded, more peremptory than before.

Zarfo returned to the saloon. "The ship is in order. But it's an unfamiliar model, as I feared."

"Can we take it up?"

"We'll have to make sure we know what we are doing. It may be minutes or hours."

"Then we can't let the Wankh go."

"Awkward," said Zarfo.

The Wankh thrust forward; Reith pushed it back and displayed his handgun. The Wankh uttered a loud chime. Zarfo made a chirping sound. The Wankh drew back.

Reith asked: "What did you say?"

"I just gave the pidgin sound for 'danger.' It seems to understand well enough."

"I wish it would sit down; it makes me nervous standing there."

"Wankh almost never sit," said Zarfo and went to seal the entrance port.

Time passed. From various locations about the ship came calls and exclamations from the Lokhars. At Reith's direction, Traz stood in the observation dome, watching over the field. The Wankh stood stolidly, apparently at a loss for action.

The ship shuddered; the lights flickered, went dim, came on bright once more. Zarfo looked into the saloon. "We've got the engines pumping. Now if Thadzei can figure out the control configurations—"

Traz called down: "The car is coming back. The floodlight has just gone on, to light the field."

Thadzei ran through the saloon, jumped up to the control console. He peered this way and that, while Zarfo stood by his side urging him to haste. Reith set Anacho to guarding the Wankh, joined Traz in the observation dome. The car was slowing to a stop beside the ship.

Zarfo pointed here and there across the control panel; Thadzei nodded doubtfully, thrust at a set of pressure pads. The ship shuddered and heaved; Reith felt acceleration underfoot. He was departing Tschai! Thadzei made adjustments; the ship pitched. Reith reached for a stanchion; the Wankh stumbled and fell upon the settee, where it remained. From elsewhere about the ship came full-throated Lokhar curses.

Reith made his way to the bridge, to stand beside Thadzei, who desperately worked the controls, testing first one pad, then another. Reith asked: "Is there an automatic pilot?"

"Bound to be, somewhere. I can't locate the engagement. These are by no means standard controls."

"Do you know what you are doing?"

"No."

Reith looked down at the dark face of Tschai. "So long as we are going up and not down, we're in good shape."

"If I had an hour, a single hour," moaned Thadzei, "I could trace out the circuits."

Jag Jaganig came into the saloon to make a querulous protest. Thadzei called back: "I'm doing the best I can!"

"It's not good enough! We'll crash!"

"Not yet," said Thadzei grimly. "I see a lever I haven't tried." He pulled the lever; the ship skidded alarmingly and thrust off at great speed to the east. Once more the Lokhars gave a series of anguished cries. Thadzei moved the lever back to its original position. The ship came to a trembling stasis. Thadzei gave a great tremulous sigh, peering back and forth across the panel. "Like none I have ever seen!"

Reith looked out the port but saw nothing but darkness. Zarfo spoke in a calm voice: "Our altitude is not quite a thousand feet . . . Now it is nine hundred . . ."

Thadzei desperately worked the controls. Once again the ship lurched and fled eastward. "Up, up!" screamed Zarfo. "We're diving into the ground!"

Thadzei brought the ship back to a halt. "Well then, this toggle will surely activate the repulsors." He gave it a twitch. From aft came a sinister crackle, a muffled explosion. The Lokhars yelled mournfully. Zarfo read the altimeter. "Five hundred . . . Four hundred . . . Three . . . Two . . . One . . ."

Contact: a splash, a bobbing and pitching, then silence. The ship was afloat, apparently undamaged, in an unknown body of water. The Parapan? The Schanizade? Reith threw up his hands in fatalistic despair. Back once more in Tschai.

Reith jumped down to the saloon. The Wankh stood like a statue. Whatever its emotions, none were evident.

Reith went aft to the engine room, where Jag Jaganig and Belje looked disconsolately at a smoldering panel. "An overload," said Belje. "Circuits and nodes are certainly melted."

"Can we make repairs?"

Belje made a glum sound. "If tools and parts are aboard."

"If time is given to us," said Jag Jaganig.

Reith returned to the saloon. He threw himself down upon a settee and stared bleakly at the Wankh. The plan had succeeded . . . almost. He leaned back, sodden with fatigue. The others must be feeling the same. No useful purpose could be served by going longer without rest. He got to his feet, called the group together. Two-man watches were set; the others slumped upon settees to sleep as best they could.

The night passed. Az raced across the sky, followed by Braz. Dawn revealed a placid expanse which Zarfo identified as Lake Falas. "And never has it served a more useful purpose!"

Reith went out on the top surface of the hull, and searched the horizons through his scanscope. Hazy water stretched to south, east and west. To the north was a low shore toward which the ship was drifting, propelled by a gentle breeze from the south. Reith went back into the ship. The Lokhars had detached a panel and were unenthusiastically discussing the damage. Their attitudes gave Reith all the information he needed.

In the saloon he found Anacho and Traz gnawing on spheres of black paste encased in a hard white rind which they had taken from a locker. Reith offered one of the spheres to the Wankh, who paid no heed. Reith ate the sphere himself, finding it similar to cheese. Zarfo presently joined him and verified what Reith already had guessed. "Repairs are not feasible. A whole bank of crystals is destroyed. There are no spares aboard."

Reith gave a gloomy nod. "As I expected."

"What next?" demanded Zarfo.

"As soon as the wind blows us ashore we disembark and return to Ao Hidis for another try."

Zargo grunted. "What of the Wankh?"

"We'll have to let him go his own way. I certainly don't plan to murder him."

"A mistake," sniffed Anacho. "Best kill the repulsive beast."

"For your information," said Zarfo, "the main Wankh citadel Ao Khaha is situated on Lake Falas. It will not be far distant."

Reith went back out on the foredeck. The first tussocks of the shore were only half a mile distant; beyond lay quagmire. To ground at the edge of such a morass would be highly inconvenient, and Reith was glad to see that the wind, shifting to the east, seemed to be moving the ship slowly to the west, perhaps aided by a sluggish current. Turning the scanscope along the shore Reith was able to distinguish a set of irregular juts and promontories far to the west.

From within came the sound of expostulation, followed by the thud of heavy footsteps. Out on the foredeck came the Wankh, followed by Anacho and Traz. The Wankh fixed Reith for half a second with its flicking vision, long enough to register an image, then turned by slow degrees to look around the horizon. Before Reith could prevent it—even were he able to do so—the Wankh stepped forward, ran with its peculiar lurching gait down the side of the ship and plunged into the water. Reith caught a glimpse of wet black hide, then the creature was gone into the depths.

Reith searched the surface for a period but saw no more of the Wankh. An hour later, checking the progress of the vessel, he once more turned the scanscope on the western shore. To his cold dismay he saw that the shapes he had thought to be crags were the black glass towers of an extensive Wankh fortress city. Wordlessly Reith examined the swamp to the north with a new interest born of desperation.

Tussocks of white grass protruded like hairy wens from fields of black slime and stagnant ponds. Reith went below to seek material for a raft, but found nothing. The padding of the settee was welded to the structure and came away in shreds and chunks. There was no lifeboat aboard. Reith returned to the deck and wondered what his next move should be. The Lokhars joined him: disconsolate figures in wheat-colored smocks, wind blowing the white hair back from their craggy black faces.

Reith spoke to Zarfo: "Do you know the place yonder?"

"It must be Ao Khaha."

"If we are taken, what can we expect?"

"Death."

* * *

The morning passed; the sun climbing toward noon dissolved the haze which shrouded the horizons, and the towers of Ao Khaha stood distinct.

The ship was noted. On the water under the city appeared a barge, which surged across the water leaving a ribbon of white wake. Reith studied it through the scanscope. Wankhmen stood on the deck, perhaps a dozen, curiously alike; slender men with death-pale skins, saturnine or, in some instances, ascetic features. Reith considered resistance: perhaps a desperate attempt to seize the barge? He decided against such a trial, which almost certainly could not succeed.

The Wankhmen scrambled aboard the ship. Ignoring Reith, Traz and Anacho, they addressed the Lokhars. "All down to the barge. Do you carry weapons?"

"No," grunted Zarfo.

"Quick then." Now they noticed Anacho. "What is this? A Dirdirman?" And they gave chuckles of soft surprise. They inspected Reith. "And what sort is that one? A motley crew, to be sure! Now then, all down to the barge!"

The Lokhars went first, hulk-shouldered, knowing what lay ahead. Reith, Traz and Anacho followed.

"All! Stand on the deck, at the gunwales, in a neat line. Turn your backs." And the Wankhman brought out their handguns.

The Lokhars started to obey. Reith had not expected such casual and perfunctory slaughter. Furious that he had not resisted from the first he cried out: "Should we let them kill us so easily? Let's make a fight of it!"

The Wankhmen gave sharp orders: "Unless you wish worse, quick! To the gunwales!"

Near the barge the water roiled. A black shape floated lazily to the surface and produced four plangent chimes. The Wankhmen stiffened; their faces sagged into sneers of annoyance. They waved at their captives. "Back then, into the cockpit."

The barge returned to the great black fortress, the Wankhmen muttering among themselves. It passed behind a breakwater, magnetically clamped itself to a pier. The prisoners were marshaled ashore and through a portal, into Ao Khaha.

15

SURFACES OF BLACK glass, stark walls and areas of black concrete, angles, blocks, masses: a negation of organic shape. Reith wondered at the architecture; it seemed remarkably abstract and severe. Into a cul-de-sac, walled on three sides with dark concrete, the captives were taken. "Halt! Remain in place!" came the command.

The prisoners, with no choice, halted and stood in a surly line.

"Water yourselves at that spigot. Perform evacuation into that trough. Make no noise or disturbance." The Wankhmen departed, leaving the prisoners unguarded.

Reith said in a wondering voice, "We haven't even been searched! I still have my weapons."

"It's not far to the portal," said Traz. "Why should we wait here to be killed?"

"We'd never reach the portal," growled Zarfo.

"So we must stand here like docile animals?"

"That's what I plan to do," said Belje, with a bitter glance toward Reith. "I'll never see Smargash more, but I may escape with my life."

Zorofim gave a rude laugh. "In the mines?"

"I know only rumor of the mines."

"Once a man goes underground he never emerges. There are ambushes and terrible tricks by Pnume and Pnumekin. If we are not executed out of hand we will go to the mines."

"All for avarice and mad folly!" lamented Belje. "Adam Reith, you have much to answer for!"

"Quiet, poltroon," said Zarfo without heat. "No one forced you to come. The fault is your own. We should abase ourselves before Reith; he trusted our knowledge; we showed him ineptitude."

"All of us did our best," said Reith. "The operation was risky; we failed; it's as simple as that . . . As for trying to escape from here—I can't believe that they'd leave us alone, unguarded, free to walk away."

Jag Jaganig snorted sadly. "Don't be too sure; to the Wankhmen we are animals."

Reith turned to Traz, whose perceptions at times bewildered him. "Could you find your way to the portal?"

"I don't know. Not directly. There were many turns. The buildings confuse me."

"Then we had best remain here . . . There's a bare chance that we can talk our way out of the situation."

The afternoon passed, then the long night, with Az and Braz creating fantasies of shapes and shadows. In the chill morning, cantankerous with stiff joints and hunger, and increasingly restless because of their captors' inattention, even the most fearful of the Lokhars were peering out of the cul-de-sac and speculating as to the whereabouts of the portal through the black glass wall.

Reith still counseled patience. "We'd never make it. Our only hope as I see it is that the Wankh may decide to be lenient with us."

"Why should they be lenient?" sneered Thadzei. "Their justice is forthright: the same justice we use toward pests."

Jag Jaganig was no less pessimistic. "We will never see the Wankh. Why else do they maintain the Wankhmen, except to stand between themselves and Tschai?"

"We shall see," said Reith.

The morning passed. The Lokhars slumped torpidly against a wall. Traz, as usual, maintained his equanimity. Contemplating the boy, Reith could not help but wonder as to the source of his fortitude. Innate character? Fatalism? Did the personality of Onmale, the emblem he had worn so long, still shape his soul?

But other problems were more immediate. "This delay can't be accidental," Reith fretted to Anacho. "There must be a reason. Are they trying to demoralize us?"

Anacho, as peevish as any of the others, said, "There are better ways than this."

"Are they waiting for something to happen? What?"

Anacho could supply no answers.

Late in the afternoon three Wankhmen appeared. One of these, wearing thin silver greaves and a silver medallion on a chain around his neck, appeared to be a person of importance. He surveyed the group with eyebrows lofted in mingled disapproval and amusement, as if at naughty children. "Well then," he said briskly, "which among you is the leader of this group?"

Reith came forward with as much dignity as he could summon. "I am."

"You? Not one of the Lokhars? What did you hope to achieve?"

"May I ask who adjudicates our offense?" Reith asked.

The Wankhman was taken aback. " 'Adjudication'? What needs to be adjudicated? The only point at issue, and a minor one, is your motive."

"I can't agree with you," said Reith in a reasonable voice. "Our transgression was a simple theft; only by sheer accident did we take aloft a Wankh."

"A Wankh! Do you realize his identity? No, of course not. He is a savant of the highest level, an Original Master."

"And he wants to know why we took his spaceship?"

"What then? It is no concern of yours. You need only transmit the information on through me; that is my function."

"I'll be glad to do so, in his presence, and, I hope, in surroundings more appropriate than a back alley."

"Zff, but you are a cool one. Do you answer to the name of Adam Reith?"

"I am Adam Reith."

"And you recently visited Settra in Cath, where you associated with the so-called 'Yearning Refluxives'?"

"Your information is at fault."

"Be that as it may, we want your reason for stealing a spaceship."

"Be on hand when I communicate with the Original Master. The matter is complex and I am certain he will have questions which cannot be answered casually."

The Wankhman swung away in disgust.

Zarfo muttered, "You are a cool one indeed! But what do you gain by talking to the Wankh?"

"I don't know. It's worth trying. I suspect that the Wankhmen report only as much as suits their purposes."

"That's understood by everyone but the Wankh."

"How can it be? Are they innocent? Or remote?"

"Neither. They have no other sources of information. The Wankhmen make sure the situation remains that way. The Wankh have small interest in the affairs of Tschai; they're only here to counter the Dirdir threat."

"Bah," said Anacho. "The 'Dirdir threat' is a myth; the Expansionists are gone thousands of years."

"Then why are they still feared by the Wankh?" demanded Zarfo.

"Mutual distrust; what else?"

"Natural antipathy. The Dirdir are an insufferable race."

Anacho walked away in a huff. Zarfo laughed. Reith shook his head in mild disapproval.

Zarfo now said, "Take my advice, Adam Reith: don't antagonize the Wankhmen, because you can't win but through them. Ingratiate, truckle, fawn—and at least they'll bear you no malice."

"I'm not too proud to truckle," said Reith, "if it would do any good—which it won't. Our only hope is to push ahead. . . . And I've come up with an idea or two which may help our case, if we get a chance to talk with the Wankh."

"You won't defeat the Wankhmen that way," gloomed Zarfo. "They'll tell the Wankh only as much as they see fit, and you'll never know the difference."

"What I'd like to do," said Reith, "is work up to a situation where only the truth makes sense and where every other statement is an obvious falsity."

Zarfo shook his head in puzzlement and walked to the spigot to drink. Reith remembered that none of the group had eaten for almost two days; small wonder they were listless and irritable.

Three Wankhmen appeared. The official who previously had spoken to Reith was not among them. "Come along. Look sharp, now; form a neat line."

"Where are we going?" Reith asked, but received no reply.

The group walked five minutes, through odd-angled streets and irregular courts, by acute and obtuse angles, past unexpected juts and occasional clear vistas, through deep shadow and the wan shine of Carina 4269. They entered the ground floor of a tower, entered an elevator which took them up a hundred feet and opened upon a large octagonal hall.

The chamber was dim; a great lenticular bulge in the roof held water; windblown ripples modulated light from the sky and sent it dancing around the hall. Tremors of sound were barely audible, sighing chords, complex dissonances; sound both more and less than music. The walls were stained and discolored, a fact which Reith found peculiar, until looking closer he recognized Wankh ideograms, immense and intricately detailed, one to each wall. Each ideogram, thought Reith, represented a chime; each chime was the sonic equivalent of a visual image. Here, reflected Reith, were highly abstract pictures.

The chamber was empty. The group waited in silence while

the almost unheard chords drifted in and out of consciousness, and amber sunlight, refracted and broken into shimmers, swam through the room.

Reith heard Traz gasp in surprise: a rare event. He turned. Traz pointed. "Look yonder!"

Standing in an alcove was Helsse, head bent in an attitude of brooding reverie. His guise was new and strange. He wore black Wankhman garments; his hair was close-cropped; he looked a person worlds apart from the suave young man Reith had encountered in Blue Jade Palace. Reith looked at Zarfo. "You told me he was dead!"

"So he seemed to me! We put him out in the corpse shed, and in the morning he was gone. We thought the night-hounds had come for him."

Reith called: "Helsse! Over here! It's Adam Reith."

Helsse turned his head, looked at him and Reith wondered how he ever could have taken Helsse for anything but a Wankhman. Helsse came slowly across the chamber, a half-smile on his face. "So here: the sorry outcome to your exploits."

"The situation is discouraging," Reith agreed. "Can you help us?"

Helsse raised his eyebrows. "Why should I? I find you personally offensive, without humility or ease. You have subjected me to a hundred indignities; your pro-'cult' bias is repulsive; the theft of a space vessel with an Original aboard makes your request absurd."

Reith considered him a moment. "May I ask why you are here?"

"Certainly. To supply information in regard to you and your activities."

Reith mulled the matter over. "Are we so important?"

"So it would seem," said Helsse indifferently.

Four Wankh entered the chamber, and stood by the far wall: four massive black shadows. Helsse stood straighter; the other Wankhmen became silent. It was apparent, thought Reith, that whatever the total attitude of the Wankhmen toward the Wankh might be, that attitude included a great deal of respect.

The prisoners were urged forward, and ranged in a line before the Wankh. A minute passed, during which nothing happened. Then the Wankh exchanged chimes: soft muffled sounds at half-second intervals, apparently unintelligible to the Wankhmen. Another silence ensued, then the Wankh addressed the Wankhmen, producing triads of three quick notes, like xylophone trills, in what seemed to be a simplified or elemental usage.

The oldest Wankhman stepped forward, listened, turned to the prisoners. "Which of you is the pirate-master?"

"None of us," said Reith. "We are not pirates."

One of the Wankh uttered interrogatory chimes. Reith thought he recognized the Original Master. The Wankhman, somewhat grudgingly, brought forth a small keyed instrument which he manipulated with astonishing deftness.

"Tell him further," said Reith, "that we regret the inconvenience we caused him. Circumstances compelled us to take him aloft."

"You are not here to argue," said the Wankhman, "but to render information, after which the usual processes will occur."

Again the Master uttered chimes and was answered. Reith asked: "What is he saying, and what did you tell him?"

The senior Wankhman said, "Speak only when you are directly addressed."

Helsse came forward, and producing his own instrument, played chimes at length. Reith began to feel uneasy and frustrated. Events were ranging far beyond his control. "What is Helsse saying?"

"Silence."

"At least inform the Wankh that we have a case which we want to present."

"You will be notified if it becomes necessary for you to testify. The hearing is almost at an end."

"But we haven't had a chance to speak!"

"Silence! Your persistence is offensive!"

Reith turned to Zarfo. "Tell the Wankh something! Anything!"

Zarfo blew out his cheeks. Pointing at the Wankhmen he made chirping sounds. The senior Wankhman said sternly: "Quiet, you are interrupting."

"What did you tell him?" asked Reith.

"I said, 'Wrong, wrong, wrong.' That's all I know."

The Master spoke chimes, indicating Reith and Zarfo. The senior Wankhman, visibly exasperated, said: "The Wankh want to know where you planned to commit your piracies, or, rather, where you planned to take the spaceship."

"You are not translating correctly," protested Reith. "Did you tell him that we are not pirates?"

Zarfo again made sounds for "Wrong, wrong, wrong!"

The Wankhman said, "You are obviously pirates, or lunatics." Turning back to the Wankh, he played his instrument, misrepresenting, so Reith was sure, what had been said. Reith turned to Helsse. "What is he telling them? That we are not pirates?"

Helsse ignored him.

Zarfo guffawed, to everyone's astonishment. He muttered in Reith's ear: "Remember the Dugbo? Pinch Helsse's nose."

Reith said, "Helsse."

Helsse turned him an austere gaze. Reith stepped forward, tweaked his nose. Helsse seemed to become rigid. "Tell the Wankh that I am a man of Earth, the world of human origin," said Reith, "that I took the spaceship only in order to return home."

Helsse woodenly played a set of trills and runs. The other Wankhmen became instantly agitated—sufficient proof that Helsse had translated accurately. They began to protest, to press forward, to drown out Helsse's chimes, only to be brought up short by a great belling sound from the Master.

Helsse continued, and at last came to an end.

"Tell them further," said Reith, "that the Wankhmen falsified my remarks, that they consistently do so to further their private purposes."

Helsse played. The other Wankhmen again started a great protest, and again were rebuked.

Reith warmed to his task. He voiced one of his surmises, striking boldly into the unknown: "Tell them that the Wankhmen destroyed my spaceship, killing all aboard except myself. Tell them that our mission was innocent, that we came investigating radio signals broadcast a hundred and fifty Tschai-years ago. At this time the Wankhmen destroyed the cities Settra and Ballisidre from which the signals emanated, with great loss of life, and all for the same reason: to prevent a new situation which might disturb the Wankh-Dirdir stalemate."

The instant uproar among the Wankhmen convinced Reith that his accusations had struck home. Again they were silenced.

Helsse played the instrument with the air of a man astounded by his own actions.

"Tell them," said Reith, "that the Wankhmen have systematically distorted truth. They undoubtedly have prolonged the Dirdir war. Remember, if the war ended, the Wankh would return to their home world, and the Wankhmen would be thrown upon their own resources."

Helsse, gray-faced, struggled to drop the instrument, but his fingers refused to do his bidding. He played. The other Wankhmen stood in dead silence. This was the most telling accusation of all. The senior Wankhman shouted: "The interview is at an end! Prisoners, form your line! March!"

Reith told Helsse: "Request that the Wankh order all the other Wankhmen to depart, so that we may communicate without interruption."

Helsse's face twitched; sweat poured down his face.

"Translate my message," said Reith.

Helsse obeyed.

Silence held the chamber, with the Wankhmen gazing in apprehension toward the Wankh.

The Master uttered two chimes.

The Wankhmen muttered among themselves. They came to a terrible decision. Out came their weapons; they turned them, not upon the prisoners, but upon the four Wankh. Reith and Traz sprang forward, followed by the Lokhars. The weapons were wrested away.

The Master uttered two quiet chimes.

Helsse listened, then slowly turned to Reith. "He commands that you give me the weapon you hold."

Reith relinquished the gun. Helsse turned toward the other three Wankhmen, pushed the trigger-button. The three fell dead, their heads shattered.

The Wankh stood a moment in silence, assessing the situation. Then they departed the hall. The erstwhile prisoners remained with Helsse and the corpses. Reith took the gun from Helsse's cold fingers, before he thought to use it again.

The chamber began to grow murky with the coming of dusk. Reith studied Helsse, wondering how long the hypnotic state would persist. He said, "Take us outside the walls."

"Come."

Through the black and gray city Helsse took the group, finally to a small steel door. Helsse touched a latch; the door swung aside. Beyond, a spine of rock led through the dusk to the mainland.

The group filed through the gap into the open air. Reith turned to Helsse. "Ten minutes after I touch your shoulder, resume your normal condition. You will remember nothing of what has happened during the last hour. Do you understand?"

"Yes."

Reith touched Helsse's shoulder; the group hurried away through the twilight. Before a jut of rock hid them from sight Reith looked back. Helsse stood where they had left him, looking somewhat wistfully after them.

16

IN A PATCH of rough forestland the group slumped down in total fatigue, their stomachs crawling with hunger. By the light of the two moons Traz searched through the undergrowth and found a clump of pilgrim plant, and the group made their first meal in two days. Somewhat refreshed, they moved on through the night, up a long slope. At the top of the ridge, they turned to look back, toward the gloomy silhouette of Ao Khaha on the moonlit sky. For a few minutes they stood, each man thinking his own thoughts, then they continued north.

In the morning over a breakfast of toasted fungus, Reith opened his pouch. "The expedition has been a failure. As I promised, each man receives another five thousand sequins. Take them now, with my gratitude for your loyalty."

Zarfo took the purple-glowing pellets gingerly, weighed them in his fingers. "Above all I am an honest man, and since this was the structure of the contract, I will accept the money."

Jag Jaganig said: "Let me ask you a question, Adam Reith. You told the Wankh that you were a man from a far world, the home of man. Is this correct?"

"It is what I told the Wankh."

"You are such a man, from such a planet?"

"Yes. Even though Anacho the Dirdirman makes a wry face."

"Tell us something of this planet."

Reith spoke for an hour, while his comrades sat staring into the fire.

Anacho at last cleared his throat. "I do not doubt your sincerity. But, as you say, the history of Earth is short compared to the history of Tschai. It is obvious that far in the past the Dirdir visited Earth and left a colony from which all Earthmen are descended."

"I could prove otherwise," said Reith, "if our venture had been successful and we had all journeyed to Earth."

Anacho poked the fire with a stick. "Interesting . . . The Dirdir of course would not sell or transfer a spaceship. Such a theft as we perpetrated upon the Wankh would be impossible. Still—at the Great Sivishe Spaceyards almost any component can be acquired, by purchase or discreet arrangement. One only needs sequins—a considerable sum, true."

"How much?" asked Reith.

"A hundred thousand sequins would work wonders."

"No doubt. At the moment I have barely the hundredth part of that."

Zarfo threw over his five thousand sequins. "Here. It pains me like the loss of a leg. But let these be the first coins in the pot."

Reith returned the money. "At the moment they would only make a forlorn rattling sound."

Thirteen days later the group came down out of the Ifnets to Blalag, where they boarded a power wagon and so returned to Smargash.

For three days Reith, Anacho and Traz ate, slept and watched the young folk at their dancing.

On the evening of the third day Zarfo joined them in the taproom. "All look sleek and lazy. Have you heard the news?"

"What news?"

"First, I have acquired a delightful property on a bend of the Whisfer River, with five fine keels, three psillas and an asponistra, not to mention the tayberries. Here I shall end my days—unless you tempt me forth on another mad venture. Secondly, two technicians this morning returned to Smargash from Ao Hidis. Vast changes are in the wind! The Wankhmen are departing the fortresses; they have been driven out and now live in huts with the Blacks and Purples. It appears that the Wankh will no longer tolerate their presence."

Reith chuckled. "At Dadiche we found an alien race exploiting men. At Ao Hidis we found men exploiting an alien race. Both conditions are now changed. Anacho, would you care to be liberated from your enervating philosophy and become a sane man?"

"I want demonstration, not words. Take me to Earth."

"We can hardly walk there."

"At the Great Sivishe Spaceyards are a dozen spaceboats, needing only procurement and assembly."

"Yes, but where are the sequins?"

"I don't know," said Anacho.

"Nor I," said Traz.

THE
DIRDIR

1

THE SUN CARINA 4269 had passed into the constellation Tartusz, to mark the onset of Balul Zac Ag, the "unnatural dream time," when slaughter, slave-taking, pillage and arson came to a halt across the Lokhar Highlands. Balul Zac Ag was the occasion for the Great Fair at Smargash, or perhaps the Great Fair had come first, eventually to generate Balul Zac Ag after unknown hundreds of years. From across the Lokhar Highlands and the regions surrounding Xar, Zhurveg, Seraf, Niss and others came to Smargash to mingle and trade, to resolve stale feuds, to gather intelligence. Hatred hung in the air like a stench; covert glances and whispered curses, in-drawn hisses of detestation accented the color and confusion of the bazaar. Only the Lokhars (the men black-skinned and white-haired, the women white-skinned and black-haired) maintained faces of placid unconcern.

On the second day of Balul Zac Ag, as Adam Reith wandered through the bazaar, he became aware that he was being watched. The knowledge came as a dismal shock; on Tschai, surveillance always led to a grim conclusion.

Perhaps he was mistaken, Reith told himself. He had dozens of enemies; to many others he represented ideological disaster; but how could any of these have traced him to Smargash? Reith continued along the crowded lanes of the bazaar, pausing at the booths to look back the way he had come. But his follower, if in fact he existed, was lost in the confusion. There were Niss in black robes, seven feet tall, striding like rapacious birds: Xars; Serafs; Dugbo nomads squatting over their fires; Human Things expressionless behind pottery face-plates; Zhurvegs in coffee-brown caftans; the black and white Lokhars of Smargash themselves. There was odd staccato noise: the clank of iron, squeak of leather, harsh voices, shrill calls, the whine, rasp and jangle of Dugbo music. There were odors: fern-spice, gland-oil, submusk, dust rising and settling, the reek of pickled nuts, smoke from grilled meats, the perfume of the Serafs. There were colors: black, dull brown, orange, old scarlet, dark blue, dark gold. Leaving the bazaar Reith crossed the dancing field. He stopped short, and from the corner of his eye glimpsed a figure sliding behind a tent.

Thoughtfully Reith returned to the inn. Traz and the Dirdirman, Ankhe at afram Anacho, sat in the refectory making a meal of bread and meat. They ate in silence; disparate beings, each found the other incomprehensible. Anacho, tall, thin and pallid like all Dirdirmen, was completely hairless, a quality he now tended to minimize under a soft tasseled cap after the style of the Yao. His personality was unpredictable; he inclined toward garrulity, freakish jokes, sudden petulances. Traz, square, somber and sturdy, was in most respects Anacho's obverse. Traz considered Anacho vain, over-subtle, over-civilized; Anacho thought Traz tactless, severe and over-literal. How the two managed to travel in comparative amity was a mystery to Reith.

Reith seated himself at the table. "I think I'm being watched," he announced.

Anacho leaned back in dismay. "Then we must prepare for disaster—or flight."

"I prefer flight," said Reith. He poured himself ale from a stone jug.

"You still intend to travel space to this mythical planet of yours?" Anacho spoke in the voice of one who reasons with an obstinate child.

"I want to return to Earth, certainly."

"Bah," muttered Anacho. "You are the victim of a hoax, of an obsession. Can you not cure yourself? The project is easier to discuss than to effectuate. Spaceships are not wart-scissors, to be picked up at any bazaar booth."

Reith said sadly, "I know this only too well."

Anacho spoke in an offhand manner: "I suggest that you apply at the Grand Sivishe Spaceyards. Almost anything can be procured, if one has enough sequins."

"I suspect that I don't," said Reith.

"Go to the Carabas. Sequins can be had by the bucketful."

Traz gave a short snort of derision. "Do you take us for maniacs?"

"Where is the Carabas?" asked Reith.

"The Carabas is in the Dirdir Hunting Preserve, at the north of Kislovan. Men with luck and strong nerves sometimes prosper."

"Fools, gamblers and murderers, rather," muttered Traz.

Reith asked, "How do these men, whatever their nature, gain the sequins?"

Anacho's voice was flippant and airy. "By the usual method: they dig up nodes of chrysospine."

Reith rubbed his chin. "Is this the source of sequins? I thought that the Dirdir or some such folk minted them."

"Your ignorance is that of another planet indeed!" declared Anacho.

The muscles around Reith's mouth gave a rueful twitch. "It could hardly be otherwise."

"The chrysospine," said Anacho, "grows only in the Black Zone, which is to say, the Carabas, where uranium compounds occur in the soil. A full node yields two hundred and eighty-two sequins, of one or another color. A purple sequin is worth a hundred clears; a scarlet is fifty, and down through the emeralds, blues, sards and milks. Even Traz knows as much."

Traz looked at Anacho with a curled lip. " 'Even Traz'?"

Anacho paid him no heed. "All this to the side; we have no certain evidence of surveillance. Adam Reith may well be mistaken."

"Adam Reith is not mistaken," said Traz. " 'Even Traz,' as you put it, knows better than this."

Anacho raised his hairless eyebrows. "How so?"

"Notice the man who just entered the room."

"A Lokhar; what about him?"

"He is no Lokhar. He watches our every move."

Anacho's jaw fell a trifle slack.

Reith studied the man surreptitiously; he seemed less burly, less direct and abrupt than the typical Lokhar. Anacho spoke in a subdued voice: "The lad is right. Notice how he drinks his ale, head down instead of back . . . Disturbing."

Reith muttered, "Who would be interested in us?"

Anacho gave a bark of caustic laughter. "Do you think that our exploits have gone unnoticed? The events at Ao Hidis have aroused attention everywhere."

"So this man—whom would he serve?"

Anacho shrugged. "With his skin dyed black I can't even guess his breed."

"We'd better get some information," said Reith. He considered a moment. "I'll walk out through the bazaar, then around into the Old Town. If the man yonder follows, give him a start and come behind. If he stays, one of you stay, the other come after me."

Reith went out into the bazaar. At a Zhurveg pavilion he paused to examine a display of rugs, woven, according to rumor, by legless children, kidnapped and maimed by the Zhurvegs themselves. He glanced back the way he had come. No one appeared to be following. He went on a little way, and paused by the racks where hideous Niss women sold coils of braided leather rope, leap-horse harness, crudely beautiful silver goblets. Still no one behind. He crossed the passage to examine a Dugbo display of musical instruments. If he could take a cargo of Zhurveg rugs, Niss silver, Dugbo musical instruments back to Earth, thought Reith, his fortune would be made. He looked over his shoulder, and now he observed Anacho dawdling fifty yards behind. Anacho clearly had learned nothing.

Reith sauntered on. He paused to watch a Dugbo necromancer: a twisted old man squatting behind trays of misshapen bottles, jugs of salve, junction-stones to facilitate telepathy, love-sticks, sheafs of curses indited on red and green paper. Above flew a dozen fantastic kites, which the old Dugbo manipulated to produce a wan wailing music. He proffered Reith an amulet, which Reith refused to buy. The necromancer spat epithets and caused his kites to dart and shriek discords.

Reith moved on, into the Dugbo encampment proper. Girls wearing scarves and flounced skirts of black, old rose and ocher solicited Zhurvegs, Lokhars, Serafs, but taunted the prudish Niss who stalked silently past, heads out-thrust, noses like scythes of polished bone. Beyond the encampment lay the open plain and the far hills, black and gold in the light of Carina 4269.

A Dugbo girl approached Reith, jangling the silver ornaments at her waist, smiling a gap-toothed grin. "What do you seek out here, my friend? Are you weary? This is my tent; enter, refresh yourself."

Reith declined the invitation and stepped back before her fingers or those of her younger sister could flutter near his pouch.

"Why are you reluctant?" sang the girl. "Look at me! Am I not graceful? I have polished my limbs with Seraf wax; I am scented with haze-water; you could do far worse!"

"No doubt whatever," said Reith. "Still . . ."

"We will talk together, Adam Reith. We will tell each other of many strange matters."

"How do you know my name?" demanded Reith.

The girl waved her scarf at the younger girls, as if at insects. "Who at Smargash does not know Adam Reith, who strides abroad like an Ilanth prince, and his mind always full of thoughts?"

"I am notorious then?"

"Oh, indeed. Must you go?"

"Yes. I have an engagement." Reith continued on his way. The girl watched after him with an odd half-smile, which Reith, looking over his shoulder, found disconcerting.

A few hundred yards further along, Anacho approached from a side-lane. "The man dyed like a Lokhar remained at the inn. For a period you were followed by a young woman dressed as a Dugbo. In the encampment she accosted you, then followed no more."

"Strange," muttered Reith. He looked up and down the street. "No one follows us now?"

"No one is visible. We might well be under observation. Turn about, if you will."

Anacho ran his long white fingers over the fabric of Reith's jacket. "So I suspected." He displayed a small black button. "And now we know who tracks you. Do you recognize this?"

"No. But I can guess. A tell-tale."

"A Dirdir adjunct for hunting, used by the very young or the very old to guide them after their quarry."

"So the Dirdir are interested in me."

Anacho's face became long and pinched, as if he tasted something acrid. "The events at Ao Khaha have naturally attracted their attention."

"What should they want with me?"

"Dirdir motives are seldom subtle. They want to ask a few questions and then kill you."

"The time has come to move on."

Anacho glanced toward the sky. "That time has come and gone. I suspect that a Dirdir sky-car approaches at this very moment . . . Give me the button."

A Niss approached, black robes flapping to the stride of his legs. Anacho stepped forth, made a swift movement toward the black gown. The Niss sprang around with a grunt of menace, and for a moment seemed ready to abandon the unnatural restraints of Balul Zac Ag. Then he wheeled and continued along his way.

Anacho gave his thin fluting chuckle. "The Dirdir will be puzzled when Adam Reith proves to be a Niss."

"Before they learn differently, we had best be gone."

"Agreed, but how?"

"I suggest that we consult old Zarfo Detwiler."

"Luckily we know where to find him."

Skirting the bazaar, the two approached the ale-house, a ramshackle structure of stone and weather-beaten planks. Today Zarfo sat within, to escape the dust and confusion of the bazaar. A stone crock of ale almost hid his black-dyed face. He was dressed in unaccustomed elegance: polished black boots, a maroon cape, a black tricorn hat pulled down over his flowing white hair. He was somewhat drunk and even more garrulous than usual. With difficulty Reith made him aware of his problem. Zarfo at last became exercised. "So, the Dirdir now! Infamous, and during Balul Zac Ag! They had better control their arrogance, or know the wrath of the Lokhars!"

"All this to the side," said Reith, "how can we most quickly leave Smargash?"

Zarfo blinked and dipped another ladle of ale from the crock. "First I must learn where you wish to go."

"The Isles of Cloud, or perhaps the Carabas."

Zarfo let the ladle sag in shock. "The Lokhars are the most avaricious of people, yet how many attempt the Carabas? Few! And how many return with wealth? Have you noticed the great manor house to the east, with the chain of carved ivory around the bower?"

"I have seen the manor."

"There are no other such manors near Smargash," said Zarfo portentously. "Do you get my meaning?" He rapped on the bench. "Pot-boy! More ale."

"I mentioned the Isles of Cloud as well," said Reith.

"Tusa Tala on the Draschade is more convenient for the Isles. How to reach Tusa Tala? The motor-wagon fares only to Siadz at the edge of the highlands; I know of no route down the chasms to the Draschade. The caravan to Zara is two months gone. A sky-raft is the only sensible conveyance."

"Well, then, where can we obtain a sky-raft?"

"Not from the Lokhars; we have none. Look yonder: a sky-raft and a party of rich Xars! They are about to depart. Maybe their destination is Tusa Tala. Let us inquire."

"A moment. We must get word to Traz." Reith called the pot-boy, sent him running to the inn.

Zarfo strode out across the compound with Reith and Anacho behind. Five Xars stood by their old sky-raft: short bull-shouldered men with congested complexions. They wore rich robes of gray and green; their black hair rose in rigid varnished columns, flaring slightly outward and sheared off flat.

"Leaving Smargash so soon, friend Xars?" Zarfo called out in a cheerful voice.

The Xars muttered together and turned away.

Zarfo ignored the lack of affability. "Where then are you bound?"

"Lake Falas; where else?" declared the oldest Xar. "Our business is done; as usual we were cheated. We are anxious to return to the swamps."

"Excellent. This gentleman and his two friends need transportation to a point in your general direction. They asked me whether they should offer to pay; I said, 'Nonsense! The Xars are princes of generosity—' "

"Hold!" the Xar called sharply. "I have at least three remarks to make. First, our raft is crowded. Second, we are generous unless we lose sequins in the process. Third, these two nondescripts have a reckless and desperate air about them, not at all reassuring. Is this the third?" The reference was to Traz, who had arrived on the scene. "A mere lad but no less dubious for all that."

Another Xar spoke. "Two further questions: How much can they pay? Where do they wish to go?"

Reith, considering the uncomfortably scant supply of sequins in his pouch, said, "A hundred sequins is all we can offer; and we want to be taken to Tusa Tala."

The Xars threw up their hands in outrage. "Tusa Tala? A thousand miles northwest! We head southeast to Lake Falas! A hundred sequins? Is this a joke? Mountebanks! Off with all of you!"

Zarfo swaggered threateningly forward. "A mountebank,

you call me? Were it not Balul Zac Ag, the 'unnatural dream time,' I would tweak all of your ludicrously long noses!"

The Xars made spitting sounds between their teeth, climbed aboard the raft and departed.

Zarfo stared after the departing raft. He heaved a sigh. "In this case, failure . . . Well, all may not prove so churlish. In the sky comes another craft; we shall put the proposal to those aboard, or at an extremity, render them drunk and borrow the vehicle. A handsome craft, that. Surely—"

Anacho gave a startled outcry. "A Dirdir sky-car! Already they are here! Away to concealment, for our very lives!"

He started to dart away. Reith seized his arm. "Don't run; do you want them to identify us so quickly?" To Zarfo: "Where shall we hide?"

"In the ale-house storeroom—but never forget that this is Balul Zac Ag! The Dirdir would never dare violence!"

"Bah," sneered Anacho. "What do they know of your customs, or care?"

"I will explain to them," declared Zarfo. He led the three to a shed beside the ale-house, ushered them within. Through a crack in the plank Reith watched the Dirdir sky-car settle into the compound. On sudden thought he turned to Traz, felt over his garments, and in vast dismay discovered a black disc.

"Quick," said Anacho. "Give it here." He left the shed, went into the ale-house. A minute later he returned. "An old Lokhar departing for his cottage now carries the tell-tale." He went to a crack, peered out toward the field. "Dirdir, sure enough! As always when sport is to be had!"

The sky-car lay quiet: a craft different from any Reith had seen heretofore, the product of a sure and sophisticated technology. Five Dirdir stepped to the ground: impressive creatures, harsh, mercurial, decisive. They stood approximately at human height, and moved with sinister quickness, like lizards on a hot day. Their dermal surfaces suggested polished bone; their crania raised into sharp blade-like crests, with incandescent antennae streaming back at either side. The contours of the faces were oddly human, with deep eye-sockets, the scalp crests descending to suggest nasal ridges. They half-hopped, half-loped, like leopards walking erect; it was not hard to see in them the wild creatures which had hunted the hot plains of Sibol.

Three persons approached the Dirdir: the false Lokhar, the

Dugbo girl, a man in nondescript gray garments. The Dirdir spoke with the three for several minutes, then brought forth instruments, which they pointed in different directions. Anacho hissed: "They locate their tell-tales. And the old Lokhar in the ale-house still dawdles over his pot!"

"No matter," said Reith. "As well in the ale-house as anywhere else."

The Dirdir approached the ale-house, moving with their curious half-loping stride. Behind came the three spies.

The old Lokhar chose this moment to lurch from the ale-house. The Dirdir inspected him in puzzlement, and approached by great leaps. The Lokhar drew back in alarm. "What have we here? Dirdir? Don't interfere with me!"

The Dirdir spoke in sibilant lisping voices which suggested the absence of a larynx. "Do you know a man called Adam Reith?"

"Indeed not! Stand aside!"

Zarfo thrust himself forward. "Adam Reith, you say? What of him?"

"Where is he?"

"Why do you ask?"

The false Lokhar stepped forward, muttered to the Dirdir. The Dirdir said. "You know Adam Reith well?"

"Not well. If you have money for him, leave it with me; he would have wanted it so."

"Where is he?"

Zarfo looked out across the sky. "You saw the sky-raft which departed as you arrived?"

"Yes."

"It might be that he and his friends were aboard."

"Who claims this to be true?"

"Not I," said Zarfo. "I offer only the suggestion."

"Nor I," said the old Lokhar who had carried the telltale.

"What is the direction?"

"Pah! You are the great trackers," sneered Zarfo. "Why ask us poor innocents?"

The Dirdir retreated across the compound in long strides. The sky-car darted off into the air.

Zarfo confronted the three Dirdir agents, his big face twisted into a malevolent grin. "So here you are in Smargash, violating our laws. Do you not know this is Balul Zac Ag?"

"We committed no violence," stated the false Lokhar, "but merely did our work."

"Dirty work, conducive to violence! You shall all be flogged. Where are the constables? I give these three into custody!"

The three agents were hustled away, protesting and crying and making demands.

Zarfo came to the shed. "Best that you leave at once. The Dirdir will not delay long." He pointed across the compound. "The wagon to the west is ready to depart."

"Where does it take us?"

"Out to the highland rim. Beyond lie the chasms! A grim territory. But if you remain here, you will be taken by the Dirdir. Balul Zac Ag or no."

Reith looked around the compound, at the dusty stone and timber structures of Smargash, at the black and white Lokhars, at the shabby old inn. Here had been the single interim of peace and security he had known on Tschai; now events were forcing him once more into the unknown. In a hollow voice he said, "We need fifteen minutes to collect our gear."

Anacho said in a dismal voice, "The situation does not accord with my hopes ... But I must make the best of it. Tschai is a world of anguish."

2

ZARFO CAME TO the inn with white Seraf robes and spine helmets. "Wear these; conceivably you may win an additional hour or two. Hurry—the wagon is at the point of departure."

"One moment." Reith surveyed the compound. "There may be other spies, watching our every move."

"Well, then, by the back lane. After all, we cannot anticipate every contingency."

Reith made no further comments; Zarfo was becoming peevish and anxious to get them out of Smargash, no matter in what direction.

Silently, each man thinking his own thoughts, they went to the motor-wagon terminus. Zarfo told them: "Say nothing to anyone; pretend to meditate: that is the way of the Serafs. At sundown face the east and utter a loud cry: 'Ah-oo-cha!' No one knows what it means but that is the Seraf way. If pressed, state that you come to buy essences. So then: aboard the wagon! May you avoid the Dirdir and succeed in all your future undertakings. And if not, remember that death comes only once!"

"Thank you for the consolation," said Reith.

The motor-wagon trundled off on its eight tall wheels: away from Smargash, out over the plain toward the west. Reith, Anacho and Traz sat alone in the aft passenger cubicle.

Anacho was pessimistic in regard to their chances. "The Dirdir will not be confused for long. The difficulties will only make them keen. Do you know that the Dirdir young are like beasts? They must be tamed, then trained and educated. The Dirdir spirit remains feral; hunting is a lust."

"Self-preservation is no less a lust with me," Reith stated.

The sun sank behind the rim; gray-brown dust settled over the landscape. The wagon paused at a dismal little village; the passengers stretched their legs, drank brackish water raised from a well, haggled for buns with a withered old crone who asked outrageous prices and laughed wildly at counter-proposals.

The wagon proceeded, leaving the old woman muttering beside her tray of buns.

The dusk faded through umber into darkness. From across the wasteland came a weird hooting: the call of night-hounds. In the east rose the pink moon Az, followed presently by blue Braz. Ahead loomed a jut of rock: an ancient volcanic neck, so Reith surmised. From the summit glowed three wan yellow lights. Looking up through his scanscope* Reith saw the ruins of a castle . . . He dozed for an hour and awoke to find the wagon rolling through soft sand beside a river. On the opposite bank psillas stood outlined against the moonlit sky. Presently they passed a many-cupolaed manor-house, apparently uninhabited and in the process of decay.

Half an hour later, at midnight, the wagon rumbled into the compound of a large village, to halt for the night. The passengers composed themselves to sleep on their benches or on top of the wagon.

Carina 4269 finally rose: a cool amber disc only gradually dispelling the morning mist. Vendors brought trays of pickled

---

*A binocular photo-multiplying device, with a variable magnification ratio up to 1000 × 1: one of the articles Reith had salvaged from his survival kit.

meats, pastes, strips of boiled bark, toasted pilgrim pod, from which the passengers made a breakfast.

The wagon proceeded to the west toward the Rim Mountains, now jutting high into the sky. Reith occasionally swept the sky with his scanscope but discovered no signs of pursuit.

"Too early yet," said Anacho cheerlessly. "Never fear; it will come."

At noon the wagon reached Siadz, the terminus: a dozen stone huts surrounding a cistern.

To Reith's intense disgust, no transportation, neither motor-wagon nor leap-horse, could be hired for transportation onward across the rim.

"Do you know what lies beyond?" demanded the elder of the village. "The chasms."

"Is there no trail, no trade-route?"

"Who would enter the chasms, for trade or otherwise? What sort of folk are you?"

"Serafs," said Anacho. "We explore for asofa root."

"Ah, the Serafs and their perfumes. I have heard tales. Well, don't play your immortal antics on us; we are a simple people. In any event, there is no asofa among the chasms; only cripthorn, spumet and rack-belly."

"Nevertheless, we will go forth to search."

"Go then. There is said to be an ancient road somewhere to the north, but I know of none who have seen it."

"What people inhabit the chasms? Are they friendly?"

" 'People'? A joke. A few pysantillas, red cors under every rock, bode-birds. If you are extremely unlucky you might meet a fere."

"It seems a dire region."

"Aye, a thousand miles of cataclysm. Still, who knows? Where cowards never venture, heroes find splendor. So it may be with your perfume. Strike out to the north and seek the ancient road to the coast. It will be no more than a mark, a crumble. When darkness comes, make yourself secure: night-hounds range the wastes!"

Reith said, "You have dissuaded us; we will return east with the motor-wagon."

"Wise, wise! Why, after all, throw away your lives, Seraf or no?"

Reith and his companions rode the motor-wagon a mile back

down the road, then inconspicuously slid to the ground. The wagon lumbered east and presently disappeared into the amber murk.

There was silence about them. They stood on coarse gray soil, with here and there wisps of salmon-colored thorn and at even greater intervals a coarse tangle of pilgrim plant, which Reith saw with a certain glum satisfaction. "So long as we find pilgrim plant we won't starve."

Traz gave a dubious grunt. "We had best reach the mountains before dark. On the flat night-hounds have advantage over three men."

"I know an even better reason for haste," said Anacho. "The Dirdir won't be puzzled long."

Reith searched the empty sky, the bleak landscape. "They might conceivably become discouraged."

"Never! When thwarted they grow excited, furious with zeal."

"We're not far from the mountains. We can hide in the shadow of the boulders, or in one of the ravines."

An hour's travel brought them under the crumbling basalt palisade. Traz suddenly halted, sniffed the air. Reith could smell nothing, but long since had learned to defer to Traz's perceptions.

"Phung* droppings," said Traz. "About two days old."

Reith nervously checked the availability of his handgun. Eight explosive pellets remained. When these were gone the gun became useless. It might be, thought Reith, that his luck was running out. He asked Traz, "Is it likely to be close at hand?"

Traz shrugged. "The Phung are mad things. For all I know, one stands behind that boulder."

Reith and Anacho looked uneasily about. Anacho finally said, "Our first concern must be the Dirdir. The critical period has begun. They will have traced us aboard the motor-wagon; they can easily follow us to Siadz. Still, we are not completely without advantage, especially if they lack game-finding instruments."

"What instruments are these?" asked Reith.

"Detectors of human odor or heat radiation. Some trace footprints by residual warmth, others observe exhalations of carbon dioxide and locate a man from a distance of five miles."

*Phung: solitary nocturnal creature indigenous to Tschai.

"And when they catch their game?"

"The Dirdir are conservative. They do not recognize change," said Anacho. "They need not hunt but are driven by inner forces. They consider themselves beasts of prey, and impose no restraint upon themselves."

"In other words," said Traz, "they will eat us."

Reith was gloomily silent. At last he said, "Well, we must not be captured."

"As Zarfo the Lokhar said, 'Death comes but once.'"

Traz pointed. "Notice the break into the palisade. If ever a road existed, there it must go."

Across barren hummocks of compacted gray soil, around tangles of thorn and tumbled beds of rubble, the three hurried, perspiring and constantly watching the sky. At last they reached the shadow of the notch, but could find no trace of the road. If ever it existed, detritus and erosion had long ago expunged it from view.

Anacho suddenly gave a low sad call. "The sky-car. It comes. We are hunted."

Reith forced back a panicky urge to run. He looked up the notch. A small stream trickled down the center, to terminate in a stagnant tarn. To the right rose a steep slope; to the left, a massive buttress overhung an area of deep shade, at the back of which was an even deeper shadow: the mouth of a cave.

The three crouched behind the tumble which choked half the ravine. Out over the plain the Dirdir boat, with chilling deliberation, slid toward Siadz.

Reith said in a neutral voice, "They can't detect our radiation through the rocks. Our carbon dioxide blows up the notch." He turned to look up the valley.

"No point in running," said Anacho. "There's no sanctuary. If they follow us this far they will chase us forever."

Five minutes later the sky-car returned from Siadz, following the road east, at an altitude of two or three hundred yards. Suddenly it swerved and circled. Anacho said in a fateful voice, "They have found our tracks."

The sky-car came across the plain, directly toward the notch. Reith brought forth his handgun. "Eight pellets left. Enough to explode eight Dirdir."

"Not enough to explode one. They carry shields against such missiles."

In another half-minute the sky-car would be overhead. "Best that we take to the cave," said Traz.

"Obviously the haunt of Phung," muttered Anacho. "Or an adit of the Pnume. Let us die cleanly, in the open air."

"We can walk through the pond," said Traz, "and stand below the overhang. Our trail is then broken; they may follow the stream up the valley."

"If we stand here," said Reith, "we're finished for sure."

The three ran through the shallow fringes of the pond, Anacho gingerly bringing up the rear. They huddled under the loom of the cliff. The odor of Phung was strong and rich.

Over the shoulder of the mountain opposite came the sky-boat. "They'll see us!" said Anacho in a hollow voice. "We're in plain sight!"

"Into the cave," hissed Reith. "Back, further back!"

"The Phung—"

"There may be no Phung. The Dirdir are certain!" Reith groped back into the dark, followed by Traz and finally Anacho. The shadow of the sky-car passed over the pond, flitted on up the valley.

Reith flashed his light here and there. They stood in a large chamber of irregular shape, the far end obscured in murk. Light brown nodules and flakes covered the floor ankle-deep; the walls were crusted over with horny hemispheres, each the size of a man's fist.

"Night-hound larvae," muttered Traz.

Anacho stole to the cave-mouth, looked cautiously forth. He jerked back. "They've missed our trail; they're circling."

Reith extinguished the light and looked cautiously from the cave-mouth. A hundred yards away the sky-car descended to the ground, silent as a falling leaf. Five Dirdir alighted. For a moment they stood in consultation; then, each carrying a long transparent shield, they advanced into the notch. As if at a signal, two leaped forward like silver leopards, peering along the ground. Two others came behind at a slow lope, weapons ready; the fifth remained to the rear.

The pair in the lead stopped short, communicating in odd squeaks and grunts. "The hunting language," Anacho muttered, "from the time they were yet beasts."

"They look no different now."

The Dirdir halted at the far shore of the pond. They looked, listened, smelled the air, obviously aware their prey was close at hand.

Reith sighted along his handgun, but the Dirdir continually twitched their shields, frustrating his aim.

One of the leading Dirdir searched the valley through binoculars; the other held a black instrument before his eyes. At once he found something of interest. A great bound took him to the spot where Reith, Traz and Anacho had halted before crossing to the cave. Sighting through the black instrument, the Dirdir followed the tracks to the pond, then searched the space below the overhang. He gave a series of grunts and squeaks; the shields jerked about.

Anacho muttered, "They see the cave. They know we're here."

Reith peered into the back reaches of the cave.

Traz said in a matter-of-fact voice, "There is a Phung back there. Or it has not long departed."

"How do you know?"

"I smell it. I feel the pressure."

Reith turned to the Dirdir. Step by step they came, effulgences sparkling up from their heads. Reith spoke in a fateful croak: "Back, into the cave. Perhaps we can set up some kind of ambush."

Anacho gave a stifled groan; Traz said nothing. The three retreated through the dark, across the carpet of brittle granules. Traz touched Reith's arm. He whispered, "Notice the light behind us. The Phung is close at hand."

Reith halted, to strain his eyes into the dark. He saw no light. Silence pressed upon them.

Reith now thought to hear the faintest of scraping sounds. Cautiously he crept back through the dark, gun ready. And now he sensed yellow light: a wavering glimmer reflecting against the cave-wall. The *scrape-scrape-scrape* was somewhat louder. With the utmost caution Reith peered around a jut of rock, into a chamber. A Phung sat, back half-turned, burnishing its brachial plates with a file. An oil lamp emitted a yellow glow; to the side a broad-brimmed black hat and a cloak hung from a peg.

Four Dirdir stood in the mouth of the cave, shields in front, weapons ready; their effulgences, standing high, furnished their only light.

Traz plucked one of the horny hemispheres from the wall. He

threw it at the Phung, which gave a startled cluck. Traz pressed Anacho and Reith back behind the jut of rock.

The Phung came forth; they could see its shadow against the glimmer of lamp-light. It returned into its chamber, once more came forth, and now it wore its hat and cloak.

For a moment it stood silent, not four feet from Reith, who thought the creature must surely hear the thud-thud-thud of his heart.

The Dirdir came three bounds forward, effulgences casting a wan white glow around the chamber. The Phung stood like an eight-foot statue, shrouded in its cloak. It gave a cluck or two of chagrin, then a sudden series of whirling hops took it among the Dirdir. For a taut instant, Dirdir and Phung surveyed each other. The Phung swung out its arms, swept two Dirdir together, squeezing and crushing both. The remaining Dirdir, backing silently away, swung up their weapons. The Phung leaped on them, dashing the weapons aside. It tore the head from one; the other fled, with the Dirdir who had stood guard outside. They ran through the pond; the Phung danced a queer circular jig, sprang forth, leaped ahead of them, kicking water into a spray. It pushed one under the surface and stood on him, while the other ran up the valley. The Phung presently stalked in pursuit.

Reith, Traz and Anacho darted from the cave and made for the sky-car. The surviving Dirdir saw them and gave a despairing scream. The Phung was momentarily distracted; the Dirdir dodged behind a rock, then with desperate speed dashed past the Phung. He seized one of the weapons which had previously been knocked from his hand, and burned off one of the Phung's legs. The Phung fell in a sprawling heap.

Reith, Traz and Anacho were now scrambling into the sky-car; Anacho settled to the controls. The Dirdir screamed a wild admonition, and ran forward. The Phung made a prodigious hop, to alight on the Dirdir with a great flapping of the cloak. With the Dirdir at last a tangle of bones and skin, the Phung hopped to the center of the pond where it stood like a stork, ruefully considering its single leg.

3

BELOW LAY THE chasms, separated by knife-edged ridges of stone. Black gash paralleled black gash; looking down Reith wondered whether he and his party could possibly have survived to reach the Draschade. Almost certainly not. He speculated: Did the chasms tolerate life of any sort? The old man at Siadz had mentioned pysantillas and fere; who knows what other creatures inhabited the gulches far below? He now noticed, wedged in a crevice high between two peaks, a crumble of angular shapes like an efflorescence from the mother rock: a village, apparently of men, though none could be seen. Where did they find water? In the depths of the chasm? How did they provide themselves with food? Why did they choose so remote an aerie for their home? There were no answers to his questions; the aerie was left behind in the murk.

A voice broke into Reith's musings: a sighing, rasping, sibilant voice, which Reith could not understand.

Anacho touched a button; the voice cut off. Anacho showed no concern; Reith forbore to ask questions.

The afternoon waned; the chasms spread to become flat-bottomed gorges full of darkness, while the intervening ridges showed fringes of dark gold. A region as grim and hopeless as the grave, thought Reith. He recalled the village, now far behind, and became melancholy.

The peaks and ridges ended abruptly to form the front of a gigantic scarp; the floors of the gorges extended and joined. Ahead lay the Draschade. Carina 4269, sinking, laid a topaz trail across the leaden water.

A promontory jutted into the sea, sheltering a dozen fishing craft, high at bow and stern. A village struggled along the foreshore, lights already glimmering into the dusk.

Anacho circled slowly above the village. He pointed. "Notice the stone building with the two cupolas and the blue lamps? A tavern, or perhaps an inn. I suggest that we put down to refresh ourselves. We have had a most tiring day."

"True, but can the Dirdir trace us?"

"Small risk. They have no means to do so. I long since isolated the identity crystal. And in any event, that is not their way."

Traz peered suspiciously down at the village. Born to the inland steppes, he distrusted the sea and sea-people, considering both uncontrollable and enigmatic. "The villagers may well be hostile, and set upon us."

"I think not," said Anacho in the lofty voice which invariably irritated Traz. "First, we are at the edge of the Wankh realm; these folk will be accustomed to strangers. Secondly, so large an inn implies hospitality. Thirdly, sooner or later we must descend in order to eat and drink. Why not here? The risk can be no greater than at any other inn upon the face of Tschai. Fourthly, we have no plans, no destination. I consider it foolish to fly aimlessly through the night."

Reith laughed. "You have convinced me. Let's go down."

Traz gave his head a sour shake, but put forward no further objections.

Anacho landed the sky-car in a field beside the inn, close under a row of tall black chymax trees which tossed and sighed to a cold wind off the sea. The three alighted warily, but their arrival had attracted no great attention. Two men, hunching along the lane with capes gripped close against the wind, paused a moment to survey the sky-car, then continued with only an idle mutter of comment.

Reassured, the three proceeded to the front of the inn and pushed through a heavy timber door into a great hall. A half-dozen men with sparse sandy hair and pale bland faces stood by the fireplace nursing pewter mugs. They wore rough garments of gray and brown fustian, knee-high boots of well-oiled leather; Reith took them for fishermen. Conversation halted. All turned narrow gazes toward the newcomers. After a moment they reverted to the fire, their mugs, their terse conversations.

A strapping woman in a black gown appeared from a back chamber. "Who be you?"

"Travelers. Can you give us meals and lodging for the night?"

"What's your nature? Are you fjord men? Or Rab?"

"Neither."

"Travelers often be folk who do evil in their own lands and are sent away."

"This is often the case, I agree."

"Mmf. What will you eat?"

"What is to be had?"

"Bread and steamed eel with hilks."

"This then must be our fare."

The woman grunted once more and turned away, but served additionally a salad of sweet lichen and a tray of condiments. The inn, so she informed them, had originally been the residence of the Foglar pirate kings. Treasure was reputedly buried below the dungeons. "But digging only uncovers bones and more bones, some broken, some scorched. Stern men, the Foglars. Well, then, do you wish tea?"

The three went to sit by the fire. Outside the wind roared past the eaves. The landlady came to stoke the blaze. "The chambers are down the hall. If you need women, I must send out; I myself can't serve owing to my sore back, and there will be additional charge."

"Don't trouble in this regard," Reith told her. "So long as the couches are clean we will be content."

"Strange travelers that come in so grand a sky-car. You"—she pointed a finger toward Anacho—"might well be a Dirdirman. Is that a Dirdir sky-car?"

"I might be a Dirdirman and it might be a Dirdir sky-car. And we might be engaged upon important work where absolute discretion is necessary."

"Aha, indeed!" The woman's jaw slacked. "Something to do with the Wankh, no doubt! Do you know, there's been great changes to the south? The Wankhmen and the Wankh are all at odds!"

"We are so informed."

The woman leaned forward. "What of the Wankh? Are they in withdrawal? So it is rumored."

"I think not," said Anacho. "While the Dirdir inhabit Haulk, so long will the Wankh hold their Kislovan forts, and the Blue Chasch keep their torpedo pits ready."

The woman cried, "And we, poor miserable humans: pawns of the great folk, never knowing which way to jump! I say Bevol take 'em all, and welcome!"

She shook her fist to south, to southwest and northwest, the directions in which she located her principal antagonists; then she departed the chamber.

Anacho, Traz and Reith sat in the ancient stone hall, watching the fire flicker.

"Well, then," asked Anacho. "What of tomorrow?"

"My plans remain the same," said Reith. "I intend to return to

Earth. Somewhere, somehow, I must gain possession of a space-ship. This program is meaningless for you two; you should go where you feel secure: the Isles of Cloud, or perhaps back to Smargash. Wherever you decide, we will go; then perhaps you will allow me to continue in the sky-car."

Anacho's long harlequin face assumed an expression almost prim. "And where will you take yourself?"

"You mentioned the spaceyards at Sivishe; this will be my destination."

"What of money? You will need a great deal, as well as sub-tlety and, most of all, luck."

"For money there is always the Carabas."

Anacho nodded. "Every desperado of Tschai will tell you the same. But wealth does not come without extreme risk. The Cara-bas lies within the Dirdir Hunting Preserve; trespassers are fair game. If you evade the Dirdir, there is Buszli the Bandit, the Blue Band, the vampire women, the gamblers, the hook-men. For every man who gains a handful of sequins, another three leave their bones, or fill Dirdir guts."

Reith gave an uneasy grimace. "I'll have to take my chances."

The three sat looking into the fire. Traz stirred. "Once long ago I wore Onmale and never am I entirely free of the weight. Sometimes I feel it calling from under the soil. In the beginning it ordained life for Adam Reith; now, even if I wished, I would not desert Adam Reith for fear of Onmale."

"I am a fugitive," said Anacho. "I have no life of my own. We have destroyed the first Initiative,* but sooner or later there will be a second Initiative. The Dirdir are pertinacious. Do you know where we might find the most security? At Sivishe, close under the Dirdir city Hei. As for the Carabas . . ." Anacho gave a doleful sigh. "Adam Reith seems to have a knack for survival. I have nothing better to do. I will take my chances."

"I'll say no more," said Reith. "I'm grateful for your com-pany."

For a space the three looked into the flames. Outside the wind whistled and blustered. "Our destination, then, is the Carabas," said Reith. "Why should not the sky-car give us an advantage?"

---

*An inexact rendering of the word *tsau'gsh:* more accurately, a band of determined hunters who have claimed the right to prosecute a quest or a task, in order to win status and reputation.

Anacho fluttered his fingers. "Not in the Black Zone. The Dirdir would take note and instantly be upon us."

"There must be tactics of some sort to lessen the danger," said Reith.

Anacho gave a grim chuckle. "Everyone who visits the Zone has his private theories. Some enter by night; others wear camouflage and puff boots to muffle their tracks. Some organize brigades and march as a unit; others feel more secure alone. Some enter from Zimle; others come down from Maust. The eventualities are usually the same."

Reith rubbed his chin reflectively. "Do Dirdirmen join the hunt?"

Anacho smiled into the flames. "The Immaculates have been known to hunt. But your concept has no value. Neither you nor Traz nor I could successfully impersonate an Immaculate."

The fire became coals; the three went to their tall dim chambers and slept on hard couches under linens smelling of the sea. In the morning they ate a breakfast of salt biscuit and tea, then settled their tariff and departed the inn.

The day was dreary. Cold tendrils of fog sifted through the chymax trees. The three boarded the sky-car. Up they rose through the overcast, and finally broke out into the wan amber sunlight. Westward they flew, over the Draschade Ocean.

4

THE GRAY DRASCHADE rolled below: the ocean which Reith—it seemed an eon ago—had crossed aboard the cog *Vargaz*. Anacho flew close above the surface, to minimize the risk of detection by Dirdir search-screens. "We have important decisions to make," he announced. "The Dirdir are hunters; we have become prey. In principle, a hunt once initiated must be consummated, but the Dirdir are not a cohesive folk like the Wankh; their programs result from individual initiatives, the so-called *zhna-dih*. This means a great dashing leap, trailing lightning-like sparks. The zeal expended upon finding us depends upon whether the hunt-chief—he who performed the original *zhna-dih*—was aboard the sky-car and is now dead. If so, there is a considerable diminution of risk, unless another Dirdir wishes to assert *h'so*—a word meaning 'marvelous dominance'—and organizes another *tsau'gsh*, whereupon conditions are as before. If the hunt-chief is alive, he becomes our mortal enemy."

Reith asked in wonder, "What was he before?"

Anacho ignored the remark. "The hunt-chief has the force of the community at his disposal, though he asserts his *h'so* more emphatically by *zhna-dih*. However, if he suspects that we fly the sky-car, he might well order up search-screens." Anacho offhandedly indicated a disk of gray glass to the side of the instrument panel. "If we touch a search-screen you'll see a mesh of orange lines."

The hours went by. Anacho somewhat condescendingly explained the operation of the sky-car; both Traz and Reith familiarized themselves with the controls. Carina 4269 swung across the sky, overtaking the sky-car and dropping into the west. The Draschade rolled below, an enigmatic gray-brown waste, blurring and merging into the sky.

Anacho began to talk of the Carabas: "Most sequin-takers enter at Maust, fifty miles south of the First Sea. At Maust are the most complete outfitters' shops, the finest charts and handbooks, and other services. I consider it as good a destination as any."

"Where are the nodes usually found?"

"Anywhere within the Carabas. There is no rule, no system of discovery. Where many folk seek, nodes are naturally few."

"Then why not choose a less popular entry?"

"Maust is popular because it is most convenient."

Reith looked ahead toward the yet unseen coast of Kislovan and the unknown future. "What if we use none of these entries, but some point in between?"

"What is there to gain? The Zone is the same from any direction."

"There must be some way to minimize risks and maximize gains."

Anacho shook his head in disparagement. "You are a strange and obstinate man! Isn't this attitude a form of arrogance?"

"No," said Reith. "I don't think so."

"How," argued Anacho, "should you succeed with such facility where others have failed?"

Reith grinned. "It's not arrogant to wonder why they failed."

"One of the Dirdir virtues is *zs'hanh*," said Anacho. "It means 'contemptuous indifference to the activity of others.' There are twenty-eight castes of Dirdir, which I will not enumerate, and four castes of Dirdirmen: the Immaculates, the Intensives, the Estranes, the Cluts. *Zs'hanh* is reckoned an attribute of the fourth through the thirteenth Dirdir grades. The Immaculates also practice *zs'hanh*. It is a noble doctrine."

Reith shook his head in wonder. "How have the Dirdir managed to create and coordinate a technical civilization? In such a welter of conflicting wills—"

"You misunderstand," said Anacho in his most nasal voice. "The situation is more complex. To rise in caste a Dirdir must be accepted into the next highest group. He wins acceptance by his achievements, not by causing conflicts. *Zs'hanh* is not always appropriate to the lower castes, nor for the very highest, which use the doctrine of *pn'hanh*: 'corrosive or metal-bursting sagacity.' "

"I must belong in a high caste," said Reith. "I intend to use *pn'hanh* rather than *zs'hanh*. I want to exploit every possible advantage and avoid every risk."

Reith, looking sidewise at the long sour face, chuckled to himself. *He wants to point out that my caste is too low for such affectations*, thought Reith, *but he knows that I'll laugh at him.*

The sun sank with unnatural deliberation, its rate of decline slowed by the westward progress of the sky-car. Toward the end of the afternoon a gray-violet bulk rose above the horizon, to meet the disc of the pale brown sun. This was the island, Leume, close under the continent of Kislovan.

Anacho turned the sky-car somewhat to the north and landed at a dingy village on the sandy north cape. The three spent the night at the Glass Blower's Inn, a structure contrived of bottles and jugs discarded by the shops at the sand-pits behind the town. The inn was dank and permeated with a peculiar acrid odor; the evening meal of soup, served in heavy green glass tureens, evinced something of the same flavor. Reith remarked on the similarity to Anacho, who summoned the Gray* servant and put a haughty question. The servant indicated a large black insect darting across the floor. "The skarats do indeed be pungent creatures, and exhale a chife. Bevol made a plague on us, until we put

---

*Gray: Loose term for the various peoples hybridized of Dirdirmen, Marshmen, Chaschmen and others, generally stocky and large-headed, often with yellow-gray complexions, occasionally somewhat albinoid.

them to use and found them nutritious. Now we hardly capture enough."

Reith long had been careful never to make inquiry regarding foods set before him, but now he looked askance into the tureen. "You mean . . . the soup?"

"Indeed," declared the servant. "The soup, the bread, the pickles: all be skarat-flavored, and if we did not use them of purpose, they'd infest us to the same effect, so we make a virtue of convenience, and think to enjoy the taste."

Reith drew back from the soup. Traz ate stolidly. Anacho gave a petulant sniff and also ate. It occurred to Reith that never on Tschai had he noticed squeamishness. He heaved a deep sigh, and since no other food was forthcoming, swallowed the rancid soup.

In the dim brown morning breakfast was again soup, with a garnish of sea vegetables. The three departed immediately after, flying northwest across Leume Gulf and the stony wastes of Kislovan.

Anacho, usually nerveless, now became edgy, searching the sky, peering down at the ground, scrutinizing the knobs and bubbles, the patches of brown fur and vermilion velvet, the quivering mirrors which served as instruments. "We approach the Dirdir realm," he said. "We will veer north to the First Sea, then bear west to Khorai, where we must leave the sky-car and travel the Zoga'ar zum Fulkash am* to Maust. Then . . . the Carabas."

5

OVER THE GREAT Stone Desert flew the sky-car, parallel to the black and red peaks of the Zopal Range, over parched dust-flats, fields of broken rock, dunes of dark pink sand, a single oasis surrounded by plumes of white smoke-tree.

Late in the afternoon a windstorm drove lion-colored rolls of dust across the landscape, submerging Carina 4269 in murk. Anacho swung the sky-car north. Presently a black-blue line on the horizon indicated the First Sea.

Anacho immediately landed the sky-car upon the barrens, some ten miles short of the sea.

---

*Literally: the way of death's-heads with purple-gleaming eye-sockets.

"Khorai is yet hours ahead; best not to arrive after dark. The Khors are a suspicious folk, and flourish their knives at a harsh word. At night they strike without provocation."

"These are the folk who will guard our sky-car?"

"What thief would be mad enough to trouble the Khors?"

Reith looked around the waste. "I prefer supper at the Glass Blower's Inn to nothing whatever."

"Ha!" said Anacho. "In the Carabas you will recall the silence and peace of this night with longing."

The three bedded themselves down into the sand. The night was dark and brilliantly clear. Directly overhead burned the constellation Clari, within which, unseen to the eye, glimmered the Sun. Would he ever again see Earth? Reith wondered. How often then would he lie under the night sky looking up into Argo Navis for the invisible brown sun Carina 4269 and its dim planet Tschai?

A flicker inside the sky-car attracted his attention: he went to look and found a mesh of orange lines wavering across the radar screen.

Five minutes later it disappeared, leaving Reith with a sense of chill and desolation.

In the morning the sun rose at the edge of the flat plain in a sky uncharacteristically clear and transparent, so that each small irregularity, each pebble, left a long black shadow. Taking the sky-car into the air, Anacho flew low to the ground; he too had noticed the orange flicker of the night before. The waste became less forbidding: clumps of stunted smoke-tree appeared, and presently black dendron and bladder-bush.

They reached the First Sea and swung west, following the shoreline. They passed over villages: huddles of dull brown brick with conical roofs of black iron, beside copses of enormous dyan trees, which Anacho declared to be sacred groves. Rickety piers like dead centipedes sprawled out into the dark water; double-ended boats of black wood were drawn up the beach. Looking through the scanscope Reith noted men and women with mustard-yellow skins. They wore black gowns and tall black hats; as the sky-car passed over they looked up without friendliness.

"Khors," stated Anacho. "Strange folk with secret ways. They are different by day and by night—at least this is the report. Each individual owns two souls which come and go with dawn and sunset, so that each is two different persons. Peculiar tales are told." He pointed ahead. "Notice the shore, where it draws back into a funnel."

Reith, looking in the direction indicated, saw one of the now-familiar dyan copses and a huddle of dull brown huts with black iron roofs. From a small compound a road led south over the rolling hills toward the Carabas.

Anacho said, "Behold the sacred grove of the Khors, in which, so it is said, souls are exchanged. Yonder you see the caravan terminus and the road to Maust. I dare not take the sky-car further; hence we must land and make our way to Maust as ordinary sequin-takers, which is not necessarily a disadvantage."

"And when we return will the sky-car still be here?"

Anacho pointed down to the harbor. "Notice the boats at anchor."

Looking through his scanscope Reith observed three or four dozen boats of every description.

"Those boats," said Anacho, "brought sequin-takers to Khorai from Coad, Hedaijha, the Low Isles, from the Second Sea and the Third Sea. If the owners return within a year, they sail from Khorai and to their homes. If within the year they do not return, the boat becomes the property of the harbor-master. No doubt we can arrange the same contract."

Reith made no arguments against the scheme, and Anacho dropped the sky-car toward the beach.

"Remember," Anacho warned, "the Khors are a sensitive people. Do not speak to them; pay them no heed except from necessity, in which case you must use the fewest possible words. They consider garrulity a crime against nature. Do not stand upwind of a Khor, nor if possible downwind; such acts are symbolic of antagonism. Never acknowledge the presence of a woman; do not look toward their children—they will suspect you of laying a curse; and above all ignore the sacred grove. Their weapon is the iron dart which they throw with astonishing accuracy; they are a dangerous people."

"I hope I remember everything," said Reith.

The sky-car landed upon the dry shingle; seconds later a great gaunt brown-skinned man, with deep-sunk eyes, concave cheeks, a crag of a nose, came running forward, his coarse brown smock flapping. "Are you for the Carabas, the dreadful Carabas?"

Reith gave a cautious assent: "This is our design."

"Sell me your sky-car! Four times I have entered the Zone, creeping from rock to rock; now I have my sequins. Sell me your sky-car, so that I may return to Holangar."

"Unfortunately we will need the sky-car upon our return," said Reith.

"I offer you sequins, purple sequins!"

"They mean nothing to us; we go to find sequins of our own."

The gaunt man gave a gesture of emotion too wild to be expressed in words and lunged off down the beach. A pair of Khors now approached: men somewhat slender and delicate of physique, wearing black gowns and cylindrical black hats which gave the illusion of height. The mustard-yellow faces were grave and still, the noses thin and small, the ears fragile shells. Fine black hair grew up rather than down, to be contained within the tall hat. They seemed to Reith a stream of humanity as divergent as the Chaschmen—perhaps a distinct species.

The older of the two spoke in a thin soft voice: "Why are you here?"

"We go to take sequins," said Anacho. "We hope to leave the sky-car in your care."

"You must pay. The sky-car is a valuable device."

"So much the better for you should we fail to return. We can pay nothing."

"If you return, you must pay."

"No, no payment. Do not insist or we will fly directly to Maust."

The mustard-yellow faces showed no quiver of emotion. "Very well, but we allow you only to the month Temas."

"Only three months? Too short a period! Give us until the end of Meumas, or better Azaimas."

"Until Meumas. Your sky-car will be secure against all but those from whom you stole it."

"It will be totally secure; we are not thieves."

"So be it. Until the first day of Meumas, on the precise instant."

The three took their possessions and walked through Khorai, to the caravan terminus. Under an open shed a motor-wagon was being prepared for a journey, with a dozen men of as many races standing by. The three made arrangements for passage, and an hour later departed Khorai, along the road south to Maust.

* * *

Over barren hills and dry swales rolled the motor-wagon, halting for the night at a hostel operated by an order of white-faced women. They were either members of an orgiastic religious sect or simple prostitutes; long after Reith, Anacho and Traz had stretched out upon the benches which served as beds, drunken shouts and wild laughter came from the smoky common room.

In the morning the common room was dim and quiet, reeking with spilled wine and the smoke of dead lamps. Men huddled face-down over tables, or sprawled along benches, their faces the color of ash. The women of the place entered, now harsh-voiced and peremptory, with cauldrons of thin yellow goulash. The men stirred and groaned, somberly ate from earthenware bowls and staggered out to the motor-wagon, which presently set forth to the south.

By noon Maust appeared in the distance: a jumble of tall narrow buildings with high gables and crooked roof-lines, built of dark timber and age-blackened tile. Beyond, a barren plain extended to the dim Hills of Recall. Running boys came out to meet the motor-wagon. They shouted slogans and held up signs and banners: "Sequin-takers attention! Kobo Hux will sell one of his excellent sequin-detectors." "Formulate your plans at the Inn of Purple Lights." "Weapons, puff-pads, maps, digging implements from Sag the Mercantilist are eminently useful." "Do not grope at random; the Seer Garzu divines the location of large purple nodes." "Flee the Dirdir with all possible agility; use supple boots provided by Awalko." "Your last thoughts will be pleasant if, before death, you first consume the euphoric tablets formulated by Laus the Thaumaturge." "Enjoy a jolly respite, before entering the Zone, at the Platform of Merriment."

The motor-wagon halted in a compound at the edge of Maust. The passengers alighted into a crowd of bawling men, urgent boys, grimacing girls, each with a new proffer. Reith, Traz and Anacho pushed through the throng, avoiding as best they could the hands which reached to grasp them and their possessions.

They entered a narrow street running between tall, age-darkened structures, the beer-colored sunlight barely penetrating to the street. Certain of the houses sold gear and implements conceivably useful to the sequin-taker: grading kits, camouflage, spoor eliminators, tongs, forks, bars, monoculars, maps, guides, talismans and prayer powders. From other houses came the clash of cymbals, a raucous honking of oboes, accompanied by calls of drunken exaltation. Certain of the buildings catered to gamblers; others functioned as inns, with restaurants occupying the ground floor. Everywhere lay the weight of antiquity, even to the dry aromatic odor of the air. Stones had been polished by the casual touch of hands; interior timbers were dark and waxy; the old brown tiles showed a subtle luster to glancing light.

At the back of the central plaza stood a spacious hostelry, which appeared to offer comfortable accommodation and which Anacho favored, though Traz grumbled at what he considered excessive and unnecessary luxury. "Must we pay the price of a leap-horse merely to sleep the night?" he complained. "We have passed a dozen inns more to my taste."

"In due course you will learn to appreciate the civilized niceties," said Anacho indulgently. "Come, let us see what is offered within."

Through a portal of carved wood they entered the foyer. Chandeliers fashioned to represent sequin-clusters hung from the ceiling; a magnificent rug, black of field with a taupe border and five starbursts of scarlet and ocher, cushioned the tile floor.

A majordomo approached to inquire their needs. Anacho spoke for three chambers, clean linen, baths and unguents. "And what do you demand in the way of tariff?"

"For such accommodation each must pay a hundred sequins* per day," replied the majordomo.

Traz gave an exclamation of shock; even Anacho was moved to protest. "What?" he exclaimed. "For three modest chambers, you demand three hundred sequins? Have you no sense of proportion? The charges are outrageous."

The majordomo gave his head a curt inclination. "Sir, this is the famous Alawan Inn, at the threshold of the Carabas. Our patrons never begrudge themselves; they go forth either for wealth or the experience of a Dirdir intestine. What then a few sequins more or less? If you are unable to pay our fees I suggest the Den of Restful Repose or the Black Zone Inn. Notice, however, that the tariff includes access to a buffet of good-quality victuals as well as a library of charts, guides and technical advice, not to mention the services of an expert consultant."

"All very well," said Reith. "First we will look into the Black Zone Inn, and one or two other establishments."

---

*Sums expressed in sequins are in terms of the unit value sequin, the "clear."

The Black Zone Inn occupied the loft above a gambling establishment. The Den of Restful Repose was a cold barracks a hundred yards north of town, beside a refuse dump.

After inspecting several other hospices the three returned to the Alawan, where by dint of furious haggling they managed to secure a somewhat lower rate, which they were forced to pay in advance.

After a meal of stewed hackrod and mealcake, the three repaired to the library, at the back of the second floor. The side wall displayed a great map of the Zone; shelves held pamphlets, portfolios, compilations. The consultant, a small sad-eyed man, sat to the side and responded to questions in a confidential whisper. The three passed the afternoon studying the physiography of the Zone, the tracks of successful and unsuccessful ventures, the statistical distribution of Dirdir kills. Of those who entered the Zone, something under two-thirds returned, with an average gain of sequins to the value of about six hundred. "The figures here are somewhat misleading," Anacho stated. "They include the fringe-runners who never venture more than half a mile into the Zone. The takers who work the hills and the far slopes account for most of the deaths and most of the wealth."

There were a thousand aspects to the science of sequin-taking, with arrays of statistics to illuminate every possible inquiry. Upon sighting a Dirdir band a sequin-taker might run, hide or fight with chances of clean escape calculated in terms of physiography, the time of day, proximity to the Portal of Gleams. Takers organized into bands for self-protection attracted an overcompensating number of Dirdir and their chances of survival decreased. Nodes were found in all parts of the Zone, most being found in the Hills of Recall and upon the South Stage, the savanna at the far side of the hills. The Carabas was reckoned no-man's-land, takers occasionally ambushing each other; such acts were reckoned as eleven percent of the risk.

Dusk approached, and the library became filled with gloom. The three went down to the refectory, where under the light of three great chandeliers, servitors in black silk livery had already laid out the evening meal. Reith was moved to remark at so much elegance, to which Anacho gave a bark of sardonic amusement. "How else to justify such exorbitant tariffs?" He went off to the buffet and returned with three cups of spiced wine.

The three, leaning back in the ancient settees, observed the other sojourners, most of whom sat alone. A few were in pairs, and a single group of four huddled at a far table, in dark cloaks and hoods which revealed only long ivory noses.

Anacho spoke: "Eighteen men in the room, with ourselves. Nine will find sequins, nine will find none. Two may locate a node of high value, purple or scarlet. Ten, perhaps twelve, will pass through Dirdir guts. Six, or perhaps eight, will return to Maust. Those ranging the farthest to find the choicest nodes run the most risk; the six or eight will show no great profit."

Traz said dourly, "Every day in the Zone a man faces one chance in four of death. His average gain is about four hundred sequins: it would seem that these men, and ourselves as well, value life at only sixteen hundred sequins."

"Somehow we've got to change the odds," said Reith.

"Everyone who comes to the Zone makes similar plans," said Anacho dryly. "Not all succeed."

"Then we must try something no one else has considered."

Anacho made a skeptical sound.

The three went forth to explore the town. The music houses showed red and green lights; on the balconies frozen-faced girls twitched and postured and sang strange soft songs. The gambling houses showed brighter lights and more fervent activity. Each seemed to specialize in a particular game, as simple as the throw of fourteen-faced dice, as complex as chess played against the house professionals.

They stopped to watch a game call Locate the Prime Purple Node. A board thirty feet long by ten feet wide represented the Carabas. The Forelands, the Hills of Recall, the South Stage, the gorges and valleys, the savannas, the streams and forests were faithfully depicted. Blue, red and purple lights indicated the location of nodes, sparse along the Forelands, more plentiful in the Hills of Recall and on the South Stage. Khusz, the Dirdir hunting camp, was a white block, with purple prongs rising from each corner. A numbered grid was superimposed upon all. A dozen players overlooked the board, each controlling a manikin. Also on the board were the effigies of four lunging Dirdir hunters. The players in turn cast fourteen-sided dice to determine the movement of all the manikins across the grid, as each player elected. The Dirdir hunters, moving to the same numbers, endeavored to cross an intersection on which rested a manikin, whereupon the manikin was declared destroyed and removed from the game.

Each manikin sought to cross the lights representing sequin nodes, thus augmenting his score. Whenever he chose, he left the Zone by the Portal of Gleams and was paid his winnings. More often, prompted by greed, the player held his manikin on the board until a Dirdir struck it down, by which he lost the totality of his gain. Reith watched the game in fascination. The players sat clenching the rails of their booths. They stared and fidgeted, calling hoarse orders to the operators, yelling in exultation when they won a node, groaning at the approach of the Dirdir, leaning back with sick faces when their manikins were destroyed and their winnings lost.

The game ended. No further manikins roamed the Carabas.

No Dirdir hunted an empty Zone. The players stiffly descended from their booths; those who had won free of the Zone took their winnings. The Dirdir returned to Khusz beyond the South Stage. New players bought manikins, climbed into the booths and the game began once more.

Reith, Traz and Anacho continued along the street. Reith paused at a booth to scan packets of folded paper on display. Placards read:

> Meticulously annotated across seventeen years: the chart of Sabour Yan, for a mere 1000 sequins, guaranteed to be unexploited.

and

> The chart of Goragonso the Mysterious, who lived in the Zone like a shadow, nurturing his secret nodes like children, at a mere 3500 sequins. Never exploited.

Reith looked to Anacho for explanation.

"Simple enough. Such folk as Sabour Yan and Goragonso the Mysterious over the years explore the safer regions of the Carabas, seeking out low-grade nodes, the waters and milks, the pale blues which are known as sards, the pale greens. When they locate such nodes they carefully note their position and conceal them as best they may, under heaps of gravel or slabs of shale, thinking to return in later years after the nodes mature. If they find purple nodes so much the better, but in the near regions which for safety's sake they frequent, purple nodes are few—

save those which as 'waters' or 'milks' or 'sards,' were discovered and concealed a generation before. When such men are killed, their charts become valuable documents. Unfortunately, buying such a chart can be risky. The first person to come into possession of the chart might 'exploit' it, removing the choicest nodes, and then putting the chart up for sale as 'unexploited.' Who can prove otherwise?"

The three returned to the Alawan. In the foyer a single chandelier exuded the light of a hundred sullen jewels, which lost itself in the shadows, with only a colored gleam here and there on the dark wood. The refectory was also dim, occupied by a few murmuring groups. From an urn they drew bowls of pepper-tea and settled themselves in a booth.

Traz spoke in a disgruntled voice: "This place is insane: Maust and the Carabas together. We should leave and seek wealth in some normal manner."

Anacho gave an airy wave of white fingers and spoke in a didactic and fluting voice: "Maust is merely an aspect of the interplay between men and money, and must be viewed on this basis."

"Must you always talk gibberish?" demanded Traz. "To gain sequins either in Maust or in the Zone is a gamble, at poor odds. I do not care to gamble."

"As far as I am concerned," said Reith, "I plan to gain sequins, but I do not intend to gamble."

"Impossible!" Anacho declared. "In Maust you gamble with sequins; in the Zone you gamble with your life. How can you avoid doing so?"

"I can try to reduce the odds to a tolerable level."

"Everyone hopes to do the same. But Dirdir fires burn nightly across the Carabas, and at Maust the shopkeepers earn more than most sequin-takers."

"Taking sequins is uncertain and slow," said Reith. "I prefer sequins already gathered."

Anacho pursed his lips in quizzical calculation. "You plan to rob the sequin-gatherers? The process is risky."

Reith looked up at the ceiling. How could Anacho still misread the processes of his mind? "I plan to rob no sequin-takers."

"Then I am puzzled," said Anacho. "Whom do you intend to rob?"

Reith spoke with care. "While we watched the hunting game,

I began to wonder: when Dirdir kill a taker, what happens to his sequins?"

Anacho gave his fingers a bored flutter. "The sequins are booty; what else?"

"Consider a typical Dirdir hunt-party: long long will it remain in the Zone?"

"Three to six days. Grand hunts and commemoratives are longer; competition hunts are somewhat less extended."

"And, in a day, how many kills will a typical party make?"

Anacho considered. "Each hunter naturally hopes for a trophy each day out. The usual well-seasoned party kills two or three times each day, sometimes more. They waste much meat, necessarily."

"So that the typical hunting party returns to Khusz with sequins from as many as twenty takers."

Anacho said curtly, "So it might be."

"The average taker carries sequins to the value of, let us say, five hundred. Hence each hunting party returns with a value of ten thousand sequins."

"Don't allow the calculation to excite you," Anacho remarked in the driest of voices. "The Dirdir are not a generous folk."

"The game-board, I take it, is an accurate representation of the Zone?"

Anacho gave a dour nod. "Reasonably so. Why do you ask?"

"Tomorrow I want to trace the hunt routes out from Khusz and back again. If the Dirdir come to the Carabas to hunt men, they can hardly protest if men hunt Dirdir."

"Who can imagine men hunting the Effulgents?" croaked Anacho.

"It's never been done before?"

"Never! Do gekkos hunt smur?"

"In this case we gain the benefit of surprise."

"No doubt of that!" declared Anacho. "But you must proceed without me; I will have none of it."

Traz choked back a guffaw; Anacho swung about. "What amuses you?"

"Your fear."

Anacho leaned back in his seat. "If you knew the Dirdir as I do, you would fear too."

"They are alive. Kill, they die."

"They are hard to kill. When they hunt, they use a separate

region of their mind, what they call the 'Old State.' No man can stand against them. Reith's concept verges upon insanity."

"Tomorrow we'll study the hunt-board again," said Reith in a soothing voice. "Something may suggest itself."

6

THREE DAYS LATER, an hour before dawn, Reith, Traz and Anacho departed Maust. Passing through the Portal of Gleams, they set out across the Foreland toward the Hills of Recall, black on the mottled dark brown and violet sky, ten miles to the south. Ahead and behind, a dozen other shapes ran half-crouched through the cool gloom. Some had burdened themselves with equipment: digging implements, graders, weapons, deodorizing ointment, face-stains, camouflage; others had no more than a sack, a knife, a wad of alimentary paste.

Carina 4269 shouldered up through the murk, and some of the takers, crawling into patches of scrub, concealed themselves under camouflage cloth, to await the coming of dusk before proceeding further. Others plunged ahead, anxious to reach the Boulder Patch, accepting the risk of interception. Stimulated by evidence of this risk—ashes mingled with burned bones and scraps of leather—Reith, Traz and Anacho accelerated their pace. Half-trotting, half-running they gained the haven of the Boulder Path, where Dirdir did not care to hunt, without untoward incident.

They put down their packs and stretched out to rest. Almost at once a pair of hulking figures drew near: men of no race identifiable to Reith, brown of skin with long tangled black hair and curly beards. They wore rags; they stank abominably and inspected the three with truculent assurance. "We are in command of these premises," groaned one in a guttural voice. "Your cost for respite is five sequins each; if you refuse we will thrust you into the open, and notice! Dirdir stalk the northern ridge."

Anacho instantly leapt to his feet and with his shovel struck the speaker a great blow on the head. The second man swung his cudgel; Anacho cut up with his shovel blade, catching the man a maiming blow under the wrists. The cudgel flew aside; the man tottered back, looking in horror at his hands. They flapped under his wrists like a pair of empty gloves. Anacho said, "Go forth yourself to face the Dirdir." He jumped forward with shovel raised; the two shambled off into the rocks. Anacho watched them go. "We had better move."

The three took their packs and started away; almost as they did so a great chunk of rock flew down to smash into the ground. Traz jumped up on a boulder and fired his catapult, evoking a wail of distress.

The three took themselves a hundred yards south, somewhat up the slope from the Boulder Patch, where they commanded a view across the Forelands and yet could not easily be approached from the rear.

Settling back, Reith brought out his scanscope and studied the landscape. He discerned half a dozen furtive takers, and a band of Dirdir on a promontory to the east. For ten minutes the Dirdir stood immobile, then suddenly disappeared. A moment later he picked them out again, moving with long lunging strides down the slope and out upon the Forelands.

During the afternoon, with no Dirdir in view, takers began to venture from the Boulder Patch. Reith, Traz and Anacho climbed the slope, making for the ridge as directly as caution permitted. They were alone now. Not a sound could be heard.

What with the need for stealth, progress was slow; sunset found them toiling up a gulch just below the ridge, and they came forth just in time to see the last corroded sliver of Carina 4269 fade from sight. To the south the ground sloped in long rolls and swales down to the Stage: rich ground for sequins, but highly dangerous owing to the proximity of Khusz, about ten miles to the south.

With twilight a curious mood, mixed of melancholy and horror, settled over the Carabas. In all directions, winking fires appeared, each with its macabre implication. Amazing, thought Reith, that men, for any inducement whatever, would enter such a place. No more than a quarter-mile distant a fire sprang into existence, and the three quickly crouched into the shadows. The pale shapes of the Dirdir were clear to the naked eye.

Reith studied them through the scanscope. They stalked back and forth, their effulgences streaming like long phosphorescent antennae, and they seemed to be emitting sounds too soft to be heard.

Anacho whispered, "They use the 'Old State' of their brains;

they are truly wild beasts, just as on the Sibol plains a million years ago."

"Why do they walk back and forth?"

"It is their custom; they ready themselves for their feeding frenzy."

Reith scrutinized the ground around the fire. In the shadows lay two heaving shapes. "They're alive!" whispered Reith in dismay.

Anacho grunted. "The Dirdir don't care to carry burdens. The prey must run alongside, hopping and leaping like the Dirdir—all day if need be. If the prey flags, they sting him with nerve-fire and he runs with greater agility."

Reith put down the scanscope.

Anacho spoke in a voice carefully toneless: "You see them now in the 'Old State,' as wild beasts, which is their elemental nature. They are magnificent. In other cases they show magnificence of a different sort. Men cannot judge them, but merely stand back in awe."

"What of the elite Dirdirmen?"

"The Immaculates? What of them?"

"Do they imitate the Dirdir at hunting?"

Anacho looked off over the dark Zone. In the east a pink flush heralded the rising of the moon Az. "The Immaculates hunt. Naturally they cannot match Dirdir fervor and they are not privileged to hunt the Zone." He glanced toward the nearby fire. "In the morning the wind will blow from us to them. Best that we move on through the dark."

Az, low in the sky, cast a pink sheen over the landscape; Reith could think only of watered blood. They moved east and south, picking a painful way across the rocky bones of old Tschai. The Dirdir fire receded and passed from sight behind a bluff. For a period the three descended toward the Stage. They halted to sleep a fitful few hours, then once more continued down through the Hills of Recall. Az now hung low in the west, while Braz lifted into the east. The night was clear; every object showed a double pink and blue shadow.

Traz went into the lead, watching, listening, testing each step. Two hours before dawn he stopped short and motioned his comrades to stillness. "Dead smoke," he whispered. "A camp ahead . . . something is stirring."

The three listened. The landscape gave back only silence.

Moving with utmost stealth, Traz angled away on a new route, up over a ridge, down through a copse of feather-fronds. Once more halting to listen, Traz suddenly gestured the other two back into deep shade. From concealment they saw on the brow of the hill a pair of pale shapes, which stood silent and alert for ten minutes, then abruptly vanished.

Reith whispered, "Did they know we were near?"

"I don't think so," Traz muttered. "Still, they might have picked up our scent."

Half an hour later they went cautiously forward, keeping to the shadows. Dawn colored the east; Az was gone, followed by Braz. The three hurried through plum-colored gloom, and finally took shelter in a dense clump of torquil. At sunrise, among the litter of twigs and curled black leaves, Traz found a node the size of his two fists. When cracked loose from its brittle stem and split, hundreds of sequins spilled forth, each glowing with a point of scarlet fire.

"Beautiful!" whispered Anacho. "Enough to excite avidity! A few more finds like this and we could abandon Adam Reith's insane plan."

They searched further through the copse, but found nothing more.

Daylight revealed the South Stage savanna stretching east and west into the haze of distance. Reith studied his map, comparing the mountain behind with the depicted relief. "Here we are." He touched down his finger. "The Dirdir returning to Khusz pass yonder, west of the Boundary Woods, which is our destination."

"No doubt our destiny as well," remarked Anacho with a pessimistic sniff.

"I would as soon die killing Dirdir as any other way," said Traz.

"One does not die killing Dirdir," Anacho corrected him delicately. "They do not permit it. Should someone make the attempt they prickle him with nerve-fire."

"We'll do our best," said Reith. Lifting the scanscope he searched the landscape and along the ridge discovered three Dirdir hunting parties, scanning the slopes for game. A wonder, thought Reith, that any men whatever survived to return to Maust.

The day passed slowly. Traz and Anacho searched under the

scrub for nodes, without success. During the middle afternoon a hunt crossed the slope not half a mile distant. First came a man bounding like a deer, his legs extending mightily forward and back. Fifty yards behind ran three Dirdir without exertion. The fugitive, despairing, halted with his back to a rock and prepared to fight; he was swarmed upon and overwhelmed. The Dirdir crouched over the prostrate form, performed some sort of manipulation, then stood erect. The man lay twitching and thrashing. "Nerve-fire," said Anacho. "Somehow he annoyed them, perhaps by carrying an energy weapon." The Dirdir trooped away. The victim, by a series of grotesque efforts, gained his feet, and started a lurching flight toward the hills. The Dirdir paused, looked after him. The man halted and gave a great cry of anguish. He turned and followed the Dirdir. They began to run, bounding in feral exuberance. Behind, running with crazy abandon, came their captive. The group disappeared to the north.

Anacho said to Reith, "You intend to pursue your plans?"

Reith felt a sudden yearning to be out of the Carabas, as far away as possible. "I understand why the plan hasn't been tried before."

Afternoon faded into a sad and gentle evening. As soon as fires appeared along the hillsides, the three departed their covert and set off to the north.

At midnight they reached the Boundary Wood. Traz, fearing the sinuous half-reptilian beast known as the smur, was reluctant to enter. Reith made no argument and the three kept to the fringe of the forest until dawn.

With the coming of light they performed a cautious exploration, and found nothing more noxious than fluke lizards. From the western edge of the woods Khusz was clearly visible, only three miles south; entering and leaving the Zone the Dirdir skirted the forest.

In the afternoon, after careful assessment of all the potentialities of the woods, the three set to work. Traz dug, Anacho and Reith worked to fabricate a great rectangular net, using twigs, branches and the cord they had brought in their packs.

On the evening of the following day the apparatus was complete. Surveying the system Reith alternated between hope and despair. Would the Dirdir react as he hoped they might? Anacho seemed to think so, though he spoke much of nerve-fire and exhibited intense pessimism.

Middle morning and early afternoon, when the hunts returned to Khusz, were theoretically the productive periods. Earlier and later the Dirdir tended to go forth; the attention of these groups the three did not care to attract.

The night passed and the sun rose on a day which one way or another must prove to be fateful. For a time it seemed that rain would fall, but by midmorning the clouds had drifted south; in the suddenly clear air the light of Carina 4269 was like an antique tincture.

Reith waited at the edge of the woods, sweeping the landscape through his scanscope. To the north appeared a party of four Dirdir loping easily along the trail of Khusz. "Here they come," said Reith. "This is it."

The Dirdir came bounding down the trail, giving occasional whistles of exuberance. Hunting had been good; they had enjoyed themselves. But look! What was there? A man-beast at the edge of the forest! What did the fool do here so close to Khusz? The Dirdir sprang in happy pursuit.

The man-beast ran for his life, as did all such creatures. It faltered early and stood at bay, back to a tree. Venting their horrifying death-cry the Dirdir lunged forward. Under the feet of the foremost the ground gave way; he dropped out of sight. The remaining three halted in amazement. A sound: a crackle, a thrash; on top of them fell a mat of twigs, under which they were trapped. And here came men, unspeakably triumphant! A ruse, a ploy! With rage tearing their viscera, they struggled vainly against the mat, desperately intent to win free, to submerge the wicked men in hate and horror . . .

The Dirdir were killed, by stabbing, hewing and blows of the shovel.

The mat was raised, the bodies stripped of sequins and dragged away, the deadfall repaired.

A second group came down from the north: only three, but creatures resplendent in casques, with effulgences like incandescent wires. Anacho spoke in awe: "These are Hundred-Trophy Excellences!"

"So much the better," Reith signaled to Traz. "Bring them in; we'll teach them excellence."

Traz behaved as before, showing himself, then fleeing as if in panic. The Excellences pursued without vehemence; they had enjoyed a fruitful hunt. The way under the dendrons had been trodden before, perhaps by other hunters. The quarry, curiously enough, showed little of the frantic agility which added zest to the hunt; in fact, he had turned to face them, his back to an enormous gnarled torquil. Fantastic! He waved a blade. Did he challenge them, the Excellences? Launch forward, leap on him, rend him to the ground, with the trophy to the first to touch him! But—shock!—the ground collapsing, the forest falling; a delirium of confusion! And look: submen coming forth with blades, to hack, to stab! Mind-bursting rage, a frenzy of struggle, hissing and screaming—then the blade.

There were four slaughters that day, four on the next, five on the third day, by which time the process had become an efficient routine. During mornings and evenings the bodies were buried and the gear repaired. The business seemed as passionless as fishing—until Reith recalled the hunts he had witnessed and so restored his zeal.

The decision to halt the operation derived not from the diminution of profit—each party of hunters carried booty to a value of as much as twenty thousand sequins—or any lessening of fervor on the part of the three. But even after sorting out the clears, milks and sards the booty was an almost unmanageable bulk, and Anacho's pessimism had become apprehension. "Sooner or later the parties will be missed. There will be a search; how could we escape?"

"One more kill," said Traz. "Here now comes a group, rich from their hunting."

"But why? We have all the sequins we can carry!"

"We can discard our sards and some emeralds, and carry only reds and purples."

Anacho looked at Reith, who shrugged. "One more band."

Traz went to the edge of the forest and performed his now well-schooled simulation of panic. The Dirdir failed to react. Had they seen him? They advanced with no acceleration of pace. Traz hesitated a moment, then once again showed himself. The Dirdir saw him; apparently they had also seen him on the first occasion, for instead of leaping into immediate pursuit, they continued their easy jog. Watching from the shadows, Reith tried to decide whether they were suspicious or merely sated with hunting.

The Dirdir halted to examine the track into the forest. They came into the wood slowly, one in the lead, another behind, two holding up the rear. Reith faded back to his post.

"Trouble," he told Anacho. "We may have to fight our way out."

" 'Fight'?" cried Anacho. "Four Dirdir, three men?"

Traz, a hundred yards down the trail, decided to stimulate the Dirdir. Stepping into the open, he aimed his catapult at the foremost and fired a bolt into the creature's chest. It gave a whistle of outrage and sprang forward, effulgences stiff and furiously bright.

Traz dodged back, went to stand in his usual spot, a grin of irrational pleasure on his face. He brandished his blade. The wounded Dirdir charged, and crashed into the pitfall. Its yells became a weird keening of shock and pain. The remaining three stopped short, then came balefully forward, step by step. Reith pulled the net release; it dropped, capturing two; one danced back.

Reith came forth. He yelled to Anacho and Traz. "Kill those under the net!" He jumped through the tangle to confront the remaining Dirdir. Under no circumstances must it escape.

Escape was remote from its mind. It sprang upon Reith like a leopard, ripping with its talons. Traz ran forward brandishing his dagger and threw himself on the Dirdir's back. The Dirdir rolled over backward, and tearing Traz's legs loose, made play with his own dagger. Anacho leaped forward; with one mighty swordstroke he hacked apart the Dirdir's arm; with a second blow he clove the creature's head. Staggering and tottering, cursing and panting, the three finished off the remaining Dirdir, then stood in vast relief that they had fared so well. Blood pumped from Traz's leg. Reith applied a tourniquet, opened the first-aid kit he had brought with him to Tschai. He disinfected the wound, applied a toner, pressed the wound together, sprayed on a film of synthetic skin, and eased off the tourniquet. Traz grimaced, but made no complaint. Reith brought forth a pill. "Swallow this. Can you stand?"

Traz rose stiffly to his feet.

"Can you walk?"

"Not too well."

"Try to keep moving, to prevent the leg from going stiff."

Reith and Anacho searched the corpses for booty, to their enormous profit: a purple node, two scarlets, a deep blue, three pale greens and two pale blues. Reith shook his head in marvel and vexation. "Wealth! But useless unless we get it back to Maust."

He watched Traz limping back and forth with obvious effort. "We can't carry it all."

The corpses they rolled into the pitfall, and covered them over. The net they hauled off into the underbrush. Then they sorted out the sequins, making three packs, two heavy and one light. There still remained a fortune in clears, milks, sards, deep blues and greens. These they wrapped into a fourth parcel, which they secreted under the roots of the great torquil.

Two hours remained until dusk. They took up their packs, went to the eastern edge of the forest, accommodating their gait to Traz. Here they argued the feasibility of camping until Traz's leg had healed. Traz would hear none of it. "I can keep up, so long as we don't have to run."

"Running won't help us in any case," said Reith.

"If they catch us," said Anacho, "then we must run. With nerve-fire at our necks."

The afternoon light deepened through gold and dark gold; Carina 4269 disappeared and sepia murk fell over the landscape. The hills showed minuscule flickers of flame. The three set forth, and so the dismal journey began: across the Stage from one black clump of dendron to another. At last they came to the slopes, and doggedly began to climb.

Dawn found them under the ridge, with both hunters and hunted already astir. Shelter was nowhere in sight; the three descended into a gulch and contrived a covert of dry brush.

The day advanced. Anacho and Reith dozed while Traz lay staring at the sky; the enforced idleness had caused his leg to stiffen. At noon a hunt of four proud Dirdir, resplendent in glittering casques, crossed the ravine. For a moment they paused, apparently sensing the near-presence of quarry, but other affairs attracted their attention and they continued off to the north.

The sun declined, illuminating the eastern wall of the gulch. Anacho gave an uncharacteristic snort of laughter. "Look there." He pointed. Not twenty feet distant the ground had broken, revealing the wrinkled dome of a large mature node. "Scarlets at least. Maybe purples."

Reith made a gesture of sad resignation. "We can hardly carry the fortune we already have. It is sufficient."

"You underestimate the rapacity and greed of Sivishe," grumbled Anacho. "To do what you propose will require two fortunes, or more." He dug up the node. "A purple. We can't leave it behind."

"Very well," said Reith. "I'll carry it."

"No," said Traz. "I'll carry it. You two already have most of the load."

"We'll divide it into three parts," said Reith. "It won't be all that much more."

Night came at last; the three shouldered their packs and continued. Traz hopping, hobbling, grimacing in pain. Down the north slope they moved, and the closer they approached the Portal of Gleams, the more ghastly and detestable seemed the Zone.

Dawn found them at the base of the hills, with the Portal yet ten miles north. As they rested in a shadowed fissure, Reith swept the landscape through his scanscope. The Forelands seemed quiet and almost devoid of life. Far to the northwest a dozen shapes made for the Portal of Gleams, hoping to reach safety before full daylight. They ran with the peculiar scuttling gait that men instinctively used within the Zone, as if they thereby made themselves inconspicuous. A band of hunters stood on a relatively nearby crag, still and alert as eagles. They watched the fleeing men with regret. Reith put aside all hope of reaching the Portal before dark. The three passed another dreary day behind a boulder, with camouflage cloth overhead.

During the middle morning a sky-car drifted overhead. "They're looking for the missing hunts," said Anacho in a hushed voice. "Undoubtedly there will be a *tsau'gsh* . . . We are in great danger."

Reith looked after the sky-car, then gauged the miles to the Portal. "By midnight we should be safe."

"We may not last till midnight, if the Dirdir close off the Forelands, as well they may do."

"We can't set out now; they'd take us for sure."

Anacho gave a dour nod. "Agreed."

Towards middle afternoon another sky-car came to hover over the Forelands. Anacho hissed between his teeth. "We are trapped." But after half an hour the sky-car once more drifted south beyond the hills.

Reith made a careful scrutiny of the landscape. "I see no

hunts. Ten miles means at least two hours. Shall we make a run for it?"

Traz looked down at his leg with a wistful expression. "You two go on. I'll follow when the sun goes down."

"Too late by then," said Anacho. "Already it is too late."

Once more Reith searched the ridges. He helped Traz to his feet. "It's all of us or none."

They started out across the barrens, feeling naked and vulnerable. Any hunt which chanced to look down from the ridge into this particular sector could not fail to notice them.

They proceeded for half an hour, scuttling half-crouched like the others. From time to time Reith paused to sweep the landscape to the rear with his scanscope, dreading lest he see the dire shapes in pursuit. But the miles fell behind, and hope correspondingly began to rise. Traz's face was gray with pain and exhaustion; nevertheless he forced the pace, tottering at a half-run, until Reith suspected that he ran from sheer hysteria.

But suddenly Traz stopped. He looked back at the ridges. "They are watching us."

Reith scrutinized the ridges, slopes and dark gulches, but saw nothing. Traz had already set off at an erratic lope, with Anacho hunching along behind. Reith followed. A few hundred yards further north he paused again, and this time thought he saw a flicker of light reflecting from metal. Dirdir? Reith gauged the distance ahead. They had come roughly halfway across the barrens. Reith drew a deep breath and ran off after Traz and Anacho. Conceivably the Dirdir might not choose to pursue so far across the Forelands.

A second time he halted and looked back. All uncertainty was gone: four shapes bounded down the slopes. There could be no doubt as to their intent.

Reith caught up with Traz and Anacho. Traz ran with glaring eyes, mouth open so that his teeth showed. Reith took the heaviest bag from the lad's shoulder, threw it over his own. If anything, Traz slowed his pace a trifle. Anacho gauged the distance ahead, studied the pursuing Dirdir. "We have a chance."

The three ran, hearts pounding, lungs burning. Traz's face was like a skull. Anacho relieved him of the remaining parcel.

The Portal of Gleams was visible: a haven of wonderful security. Behind came the hunters, by prodigious leaps.

Traz was faltering, with the Portal yet a half-mile ahead. "Onmale!" called Reith.

The effect was startling. Traz seemed to expand, to grow tall. He stopped short and swung about to face the pursuers. His face was that of a stranger: a person sagacious, fierce and dominant—the personification in fact of the emblem Onmale.

Onmale was too proud to flee.

"Run!" cried Reith in a panic. "If we must fight, let's fight on our own terms!"

Traz, or Onmale—the two were confused—seized a pack from Reith and one from Anacho and sprang ahead toward the Portal.

Reith wasted a half-second gauging the distance to the first Dirdir, then continued his flight. Traz soared across the barrens. Anacho, his face pink and distorted, pounded behind.

Traz gained the Portal. He turned and waited, catapult in one hand, sword in the other. Anacho passed through, then Reith, not fifty feet in advance of the foremost Dirdir. Traz backed to stand just beyond the boundary, challenging the Dirdir to attack. The Dirdir gave a shrill scream of fury. It shook its head, and its effulgences, standing high, vibrated. Then, curvetting, it loped south, after its comrades, already on their way back to the hills.

Anacho leaned panting against the Portal of Gleams. Reith stood with the breath rasping in his throat. Traz's face was vacant and gray. His knees buckled; he fell to the ground and lay quiet, giving not so much as a twitch.

Reith staggered forward, turned him over. Traz seemed not to breathe. Reith straddled his body and applied artificial respiration. Traz gave a throat-wrenching gasp. Presently he began to breathe evenly.

The solicitors, touts and beggars who normally kept station by the Portal of Gleams had scattered, aghast at the approach of the Dirdir. First to return was a young man in a long maroon gown, who now stood making gracious movements of concern. "An outrage," he lamented. "The conduct of the Dirdir! Never should they chase so close to the gate! They have almost killed this poor young man!"

"Quiet," snapped Anacho. "You disturb us."

The young man stood aside. Reith and Anacho lifted Traz to his feet, where he stood in something of a stupor.

The young man once again came forward, his soft brown eyes

all-seeing, all-knowing. "Allow me to assist. I am Issam the Thang; I represent the Hopeful Venture Inn, which promises a restful atmosphere. Allow me to assist you with your parcels." Picking up Traz's pack he turned a startled gaze toward Reith and Anacho. "Sequins?"

Anacho seized his pack. "Be off with you! Our plans are established!"

"As you will," said Issam the Thang, "but the Hopeful Venture Inn is near at hand, and something apart from the tumult and gaming. While comfortable, the expense does not approach the exorbitant fees of the Alawan."

"Very well," said Reith. "Take us to the Hopeful Venture."

Anacho muttered under his breath; to which Issam the Thang made a delicate gesture of reproach. "This way, if you will."

They trudged toward Maust, Traz hobbling on his lame leg.

"My memory is a jumble," he muttered. "I recall crossing the Forelands; I remember that someone shouted into my ear—"

"It was I," said Reith.

"—then after, nothing real, and next I lay beside the Portal." And a moment later he mused: "I heard roaring voices. A thousand faces looked past me, warriors' faces, raging. I have seen such things in dreams." His voice dwindled; he said no more.

7

THE HOPEFUL VENTURE Inn stood at the back of a narrow alley, a brooding, age-blackened structure, doing no great business, to judge from the common room, which was dark and still. Issam, it now appeared, was the proprietor. He made an effusive show of hospitality, ordering water, lamps and linen up to the "grand suite," which orders were effected by a surly servant with enormous red hands and a shock of coarse red hair. The three mounted a twisting stairway to the suite, which comprised a sitting-room, a wash-room, several irregular alcoves furnished with sour-smelling couches. The servant arranged the lamps, brought flasks of wine and departed. Anacho examined the lead and wax stoppers, then put the flasks aside. "Too much risk of drugs or poison. When the man awakes—if he awakes—his sequins are gone and he is bereft. I am dissatisfied; we would have done better at the Alawan."

"Tomorrow is time enough," said Reith, sinking into a chair with a groan of fatigue.

"Tomorrow we must be gone from Maust," said Anacho. "If we are not marked men now, we soon will be." He went forth and presently returned with bread, meat and wine.

They ate and drank; then Anacho checked the bars and bolts. "Who knows what transpires in these old piles? A knife in the dark, a single sound, and who is the wiser save Issam the Thang?"

Again checking the locks, the three prepared themselves for sleep. Anacho, declaring himself to be easily aroused, put the sequins between himself and the wall. Except for a single wavering night light the lamps were extinguished. A few moments later Anacho slipped noiselessly across the room to Reith's couch. "I suspect peepholes and listening pipes," he whispered. "Here—the sequins. Put them beside you. Let us sit quietly and watch for a period."

Reith forced himself into a state of alertness. Fatigue defeated him; his eyelids drooped. He slept.

Time passed. Reith was aroused by a prod from Anacho's elbow; he sat up with a jerk of guilt. "Quiet," said Anacho in the ghost of a whisper. "Look yonder."

Reith peered through the darkness. A scrape, a movement in the shadows, a dark shape—a light suddenly flared up. Traz stood, crouched and glaring, arms concealed in the shadow of his body.

The two men by Anacho's couch turned to face the lamp, faces blank and startled. One was Issam the Thang; the second was the burly servant who had been groping with his enormous hands for the neck of Anacho, presumably asleep on the couch. The servant emitted a curious whisper of excitement and hopped across the room, hands clutching. Traz fired his catapult into the twisted face. The man fell silently, going to oblivion without apprehension or regret. Issam sprang for an opening in the wall. Reith bore him to the floor. Issam fought desperately; for all his slenderness and delicacy he was as strong and quick as a serpent. Reith seized him in an arm-lock and jerked him erect, squeaking in pain.

Anacho flipped a cord around Issam's neck and prepared to

tighten the noose. Reith grimaced but made no protest. This was the justice of Maust; it was only fitting that here, in the flaring lamplight, Issam should go to his doom.

Issam fervently cried out: "No! I am only a miserable Thang! Don't kill me! I'll help you, I swear! I'll help you escape!"

"Wait," said Reith. To Issam: "How do you mean, help us escape? Are we in danger?"

"Yes, of course. What should you expect?"

"Tell me of this danger."

Sensing reprieve, Issam drew himself up, indignantly shrugged away Anacho's hands. "The information is valuable. How much will you pay?"

Reith nodded to Anacho. "Proceed."

Issam gave a heart-rending wail. "No, no! Trade me my life for your three lives—is that not enough?"

"If such be the case."

"It is the case. Stand back, then; remove the noose."

"Not until we know the kind of bargain we are making."

Issam looked from face to face and saw nothing to encourage him. "Well, then, secret word has come to me. The Dirdir are in a state of frothing fury. Someone has destroyed an unlikely number of hunting parties, and stolen the booty—as much as two hundred thousands' worth of sequins. Special agents are on watch—here and elsewhere. Whoever submits any information will derive great benefit. If you are the person of the case, as I suspect, you will never leave Maust except in prickle-collars—unless I help you."

Reith asked cautiously, "Help us how?"

"I can and will save you—for a price."

Reith looked toward Anacho, who drew taut the cord. Issam clawed at the constriction, eyes bulging in the lamplight. The noose loosened. Issam croaked, "My life for yours, that is our bargain."

"Then talk no more of 'price.' Needless to say, don't try to trick us."

"Never, never!" croaked Issam. "I live or die with you! Your life is my life! We must leave now. Morning will be too late."

"Leave how? Afoot?"

"It may not be necessary. Make yourselves ready. Do those bags and parcels actually contain sequins?"

"Scarlets and purples," said Anacho with sadistic relish. "If you want the same, go into the Zone and kill Dirdir."

Issam shuddered. "Are you ready?" He waited impatiently while the three resumed their garments. On sudden thought he dropped down to rifle the corpse of the servant and clucked with satisfaction at the handful of clears and milks he found in the pouch.

The three were ready. In spite of Issam's protest Anacho maintained the noose around his neck. "So that you will not misunderstand our intentions."

"Must I always be cursed with suspicious associates?"

The main avenue of Maust vibrated with movement, the shift of faces, colored lights; from the taverns came wailing music, drunken belches of laughter, an occasional angry outcry. By furtive shortcuts and dark detours Issam took them to a stable at the north of town, where a scowling attendant finally responded to Issam's pounding. Five minutes of surly haggling resulted in the saddling of four leap-horses; ten minutes later, as the moons of Az and Braz simultaneously rolled up the eastern sky, Reith, Anacho, Traz and Issam bounded north on the gaunt white leap-horses of Kachan, and left Maust behind.

Through the night they rode and at dawn entered Khorai. Smoke trickling up from iron chimneys drifted north over the First Sea, which by some trick of light appeared as black as a sea of pitch, with the plum-colored northern sky for a backdrop.

Through Khorai they pounded and down to the harbor where they dismounted. Issam, wearing the most modest of smiles, bowed to Reith, hands folded behind his dark red gown. "I have achieved my goal; my friends have been delivered safe to Khorai."

"The friends you hoped to strangle a few hours ago."

Issam's smile became tremulous. "That was Maust! One's behavior in Maust must be tolerated."

"As far as I am concerned, you may return."

Issam bowed low once more. "May nine-headed Sagorio maim your enemies! So now, farewell!" Issam took the pale leap-horses back through Khorai and disappeared to the south.

The sky-car rested where they had left it. As they climbed aboard, the harbormaster looked on with a saturnine sneer, but made no comment. Mindful of Khor truculence the three took pains to ignore his presence.

The sky-car rose into the morning sky, curved along the shore of the First Sea. So began the first stage of the journey to Sivishe.

8

THE SKY-CAR FLEW west. To the south spread a vast dusty desert; to the north lay the First Sea. Below and ahead mudflats alternated with promontories of sandstone in a monotonous succession, one beyond the other, into the haze at the limit of vision.

Traz slept the sleep of sheer exhaustion. Anacho, to the contrary, sat unconcerned and careless, as if fear and emergency were foreign to his experience. Reith, though he ached with fatigue, could not wrench his gaze away from the radar-screen, except to search the sky. Anacho's carefree manner at last became exasperating. Reith glared at him through red-rimmed eyes and spoke in a dour voice: "For a fugitive you show surprisingly little apprehension. I admire your composure."

Anacho made an easy gesture. "What you call composure is childlike faith. I have become superstitious. Consider: we have entered the Carabas, killed dozens of First Folk and carried off their sequins. So now, how can I take seriously the prospect of casual interception?"

"Your faith is greater than mine," growled Reith. "I expect the whole force of the Dirdir system to be scouring the skies for us."

Anacho gave an indulgent laugh. "That is not the Dirdir way! You project your own concepts into the Dirdir mind. Remember, they do not look upon organization as an end in itself; this is a human attribute. The Dirdir exists only as himself, a creature responsible only to his pride. He cooperates with his fellows when the prospect suits him."

Reith shook his head skeptically, and went back to studying the radar-screen. "There must be more to it than that. How does the society hold together? How can the Dirdir sustain long-term projects?"

"Very simple. One Dirdir is much like another; there are racial forces which compel all alike. In great dilution, the submen know these forces as 'tradition,' 'caste authority,' 'zest to over-achieve'; in the Dirdir society they become compulsions. The individual is bound to customs of the race. Should a Dirdir need assistance he need only cry out *hs'ai hs'ai, hs'ai* and he is helped. If a Dirdir is wronged, he calls *dr'ssa dr'ssa, dr'ssa* and commands arbitration. If the arbitration fails to suit him he can challenge the arbitrator, who is usually an Excellence; if he defeats the arbitrator, he is vindicated. More often he himself is defeated; his effulgences are plucked out and he becomes a pariah ... There are few challenges of arbitration."

"Under such conditions, the society would seem to be highly conservative."

"This is the case, until there is need for change, and then the Dirdir applies himself to the problem with 'zest to over-achieve.' He is capable of creative thinking; his brain is supple and responsive; he wastes no energy upon mannerism. Multiple sexuality and the 'secrets' of course are a distraction, but like the hunt they are a source of violent passion beyond human comprehension."

"All this to the side, why should they give up the search for us so easily?"

"Is it not clear?" demanded Anacho testily. "How could even the Dirdir suspect that we fly toward Sivishe in a sky-car? Nothing identifies the men sought at Smargash with the men who destroy Dirdir in the Carabas. Perhaps in time a connection will be made, if, for example, Issam the Thang is questioned. Until then they are ignorant that we fly a sky-car. So why put up search-screens?"

"I hope you're right," said Reith.

"We shall see. Meanwhile—we are alive. We fly a sky-car in comfort. We carry better than two hundred thousand sequins. Notice ahead: Cape Braize! Beyond lies the Schanizade. We will now alter course and come down upon Haulk from above. Who will notice a single sky-car among a hundred? At Sivishe we will mingle with the multitude, while the Dirdir seek us across the Zhaarken, or at Jalkh, or out on the Hunghus tundra."

Ten miles passed below the sky-car with Reith pondering the soul of the Dirdir race. He asked. "Suppose you or I were in trouble and cried *dr'ssa dr'ssa, dr'ssa?*"

"That is the call for arbitration. *Hs'ai hs'ai, hs'ai* is the cry for help."

"Very well, *hs'ai hs'ai, hs'ai*—would a Dirdir be impelled to help?"

"Yes; by the force of tradition. This is automatic, a reflexive act: the connective tissue which binds an otherwise wild and mercurial race."

Two hours before sunset a storm blew in from the Schanizade. Carina 4269 became a brown wraith, then disappeared as black clouds tumbled up the sky. Surf like dirty beer-foam swept across the beach, close to the boles of the black dendrons which shrouded the foreshore. The upper fronds twisted to gusts of wind, turning up glossy gray undersides; roiling patterns moved across the black upper surfaces.

The sky-car fled south through the umber dusk, then, with the last glimmer of light, landed in the lee of a basalt jut. The three, huddling upon the settees and ignoring the odor of Dirdir bodies, slept while the storm hissed through the rocks.

Dawn brought a strange illumination, like light shining through brown bottle-glass. There was neither food nor drink in the sky-car, but pilgrim pod grew out on the barrens and a brackish river flowed nearby. Traz went quietly along the bank, craning his neck to peer through the reflections. He stopped short, crouched, plunged into the water to emerge with a yellow creature, all thrashing tentacles and jointed legs, which he and Anacho devoured raw. Reith stolidly ate pilgrim pod.

With the meal finished they leaned back against the sky-car, basking in the honey-colored sunlight and enjoying the morning calm. "Tomorrow," said Anacho, "we arrive in Sivishe. Our life once more changes. We are no longer thieves and desperadoes, but men of substance, or so we must let it appear."

"Very well," said Reith. "What next?"

"We must be subtle. We do not simply apply at the space-yards with our money."

"Hardly," said Reith. "On Tschai whatever seems reasonable is wrong."

"It is impossible," said Anacho, "to function without the support of an influential person. This will be our first concern."

"A Dirdir? Or a Dirdirman?"

"Sivishe is a city of sub-men; the Dirdir and Dirdirmen keep to Hei on the mainland. You will see."

9

HAULK HUNG LIKE a cramped and distorted appendix from the distended belly of Kislovan, with the Schanizade Ocean to the west and the Gulf of Ajzan to the east. At the head of the gulf was the island Sivishe, with an untidy industrial jumble at the northern end. A causeway led to the mainland and Hei, the Dirdir city. At the center of Hei and dominating the entire landscape stood a box of gray glass five miles long, three miles wide, a thousand feet high: a structure so large that the perspectives seemed distorted. A forest of spires surrounded the box, a tenth as high, scarlet and purple, then mauve, gray and white toward the periphery.

Anacho indicated the towers. "Each house a clan. Someday I will describe the life of Hei: the promenades, the secrets of multiple sex, the castes and class. But of more immediate interest, yonder lie the spaceyards."

Reith saw an area at the center of the island surrounded by shops, warehouses, depots and hangars. Six large spaceships and three smaller craft occupied bays to one side. Anacho's voice broke into his speculations.

"The spaceships are well secured. The Dirdir are far more stringent than the Wankh—by instinct rather than by reason, for no one in history has stolen a spaceship."

"No one in history has come with two hundred thousand sequins. Such money will grease a lot of palms."

"What good are sequins in the Glass Box?"

Reith said no more. Anacho took the sky-car down to a paved area beside the spaceyards.

"Now," said Anacho in a calm voice, "we shall learn our destiny."

Reith took instant alarm. "What do you mean by that?"

"If we have been traced, if we are expected, then we will be taken; and soon there will be an end to us. But the car yard seems as usual; I expect no disaster. Remember now, this is Sivishe, I am the Dirdirman, you are the sub-men; act accordingly."

Reith dubiously searched the yard. As Anacho had stated there seemed no untoward activity.

The sky-car landed. The three alighted. Anacho stood austerely aside while Reith and Traz removed the packs.

A power-wagon approached and fixed clamps to the sky-car. The operator, a hybrid of Dirdirman and another race unknown, inspected Anacho with impersonal curiosity, ignoring Reith and Traz. "What is to be the disposition?"

"Temporary deposit, on call," said Anacho.

"To what charge?"

"Special. I'll take the token."

"Number sixty-four." The clerk gave Anacho a brass disc. "I require twenty sequins."

"Twenty, and five for yourself."

The lift-wagon conveyed the sky-car to a numbered slot. Anacho led the way to a slide-way, with Reith and Traz trudging behind with the packs. They stepped aboard and were conveyed out to a wide avenue, along which ran a considerable traffic of power-wagons, passenger cars, drays.

Here Anacho paused to reflect. "I have been gone so long, I have traveled so far, that Sivishe is somewhat strange. First, of course, we need lodgings. Across the avenue, as I recall, is a suitable inn."

At the Ancient Realm Inn the three were led down a white-and black-tiled corridor to a suite overlooking the central court, where a dozen women sat on benches watching the windows for a signal.

Two seemed to be Dirdirwomen: thin sharp-faced creatures, pallid as snow, with a sparse fuzz of gray hair at the back of their scalps. Anacho surveyed them thoughtfully for a moment or so, then turned away. "We are fugitives, of course," he said, "and we must be wary. Nevertheless, here in Sivishe where many people come and go, we are as safe as we might be anywhere. The Dirdir do not concern themselves with Sivishe unless circumstances fail to suit them, in which case the Administrator goes to the Glass Box. Otherwise, the Administrator has a free hand; he taxes, polices, judges, punishes, appropriates as he sees fit and is therefore the least corruptible man in Sivishe. For influential assistance we must seek elsewhere; tomorrow I will make an inquiry. Next we will need a structure of suitable dimensions, close by the spaceyards, yet inconspicuous. Again, a matter requiring discreet inquiry. Then—most sensitive of all—we must hire technical personnel to assemble the components and perform the necessary tuning and phasing. If we pay high wages we can no doubt secure the right men. I will represent myself as a Dirdirman Superior—in fact, my former status—and hint of Dirdir reprisals against loose-mouthed men. There is no reason why the project should not go easily and smoothly, except for the innate perversity of circumstances."

"In other words," said Reith, "the chances are against us."

Anacho ignored the remark. "A warning: the city seethes with intrigue. Folk come to Sivishe for a single purpose: to win advantage. The city is a turmoil of illicit activity, robbery, extortion, vice, gambling, gluttony, extravagant display, swindling. These are endemic, and the victim has small hope of recourse. The Dirdir are unconcerned; the antics and maneuvers of the submen are nothing to them. The Administrator is interested only in maintaining order. So: caution! Trust no one; answer no questions! Identify yourselves as steppe-men seeking employment; profess stupidity. By such means we minimize risk."

10

IN THE MORNING Anacho went forth to make his inquiries. Reith and Traz descended to the street café and sat watching the passersby. Traz was displeased with everything he saw. "All cities are vile," he grumbled. "This is the worst: a detestable place. Do you notice the stink? Chemicals, smoke, disease, rotting stone. The smell has infected the folk; observe their faces."

Reith could not deny that the inhabitants of Sivishe were an unprepossessing lot. Their complexions ranged from muddy brown to Dirdirman white; their physiognomies reflected thousands of years of half-purposeful mutation. Never had Reith seen so wary and self-contained a people. Living in contiguity with an alien race had fostered no fellowship: in Sivishe each man was a stranger. As a positive consequence, Reith and Traz were inconspicuous: no one looked twice in their direction.

Reith sat musing over his bowl of pale wine, relaxed and almost at peace. As he pondered old Tschai, it occurred to him the single homogenizing force was the language, the same across the entire planet. Perhaps because communication often represented the difference between life and death, because those who failed to communicate died, the language had retained its universality. Presumably the language had its roots on ancient Earth. It resembled no language with which he was familiar. He considered key words. *Vam* was "mother"; *tatap* was "father"; *issir* was "sword." The cardinal numbers were *aine, sei, dros, enser, nif, hisz, yaga, managa, nuwai, tix.* No significant parallels, but somehow, a hunting echo of Earth sounds . . .

In general, reflected Reith, life on Tschai ranged a wider gamut than did life on Earth. Passions were more intense: grief more poignant, joy more exalted. Personalities were more decisive. By contrast the folk of Earth seemed pensive, conditional, sedate. Laughter on Earth was less boisterous; still, there were fewer gasps of horror.

As he often did, Reith wondered: *Suppose I return to Earth, what then? Can I adjust to an existence so placid and staid? Or all my life will I long for the steppes and seas of Tschai?* Reith gave a sad chuckle. A problem he would be glad to confront.

Anacho returned. After a quick glance to left and right he settled himself at the table. His manner was subdued. "I've been optimistic," he muttered. "I've trusted too much to my memories."

"How so?" Reith demanded.

"Nothing immediate. It seems, merely, that I have underestimated our impact on the times. Twice this morning I heard talk of the madmen who invaded the Carabas and slaughtered Dirdir as if they were lippets. Hei throbs with agitation and anger, or so it is said. Various *tsau'gsh* are in progress; all would regret to be the madmen once they are captured."

Traz was outraged. "The Dirdir go to the Carabas to kill men," he stormed. "Why should they resent the case when they themselves are killed?"

"Hist!" exclaimed Anacho. "Not so loud! Do you wish to attract attention? In Sivishe no one blurts forth his thoughts; it is unwholesome!"

"Another black mark against this squalid city!" declared Traz, but in a more restrained voice.

"Come now," said Anacho nervously. "It is not so disheartening after all. Think of it! While Dirdir range the continents, we three rest in Sivishe, at the Ancient Realm Inn."

"A precarious satisfaction," said Reith. "What else did you learn?"

"The Administrator is Clodo Erlius. He has just assumed office—not necessarily advantageous from our point of view since a new official is apt to stringency. I have made guarded inquiries, and since I am a Dirdirman Superior, I did not encounter total frankness. However a certain name has been mentioned twice. That name is Aila Woudiver. His ostensible occupation is the supply and transport of structural materials. He is a notable gourmand and voluptuary, with tastes at once so refined, so gross and so inordinate as to cost him vast sums. This information was given freely, in a tone of envious admiration. Woudiver's illicit capabilities were merely implied."

"Woudiver would appear to be an unsavory colleague," said Reith.

Anacho snorted in derision. "You demand that I find someone proficient at conniving, chicanery, theft; when I produce this man, you look down your nose at him."

Reith grinned. "No other names were mentioned?"

"Another source explained, in a carefully facetious manner, that any extraordinary activity must surely attract the attention of Woudiver. It would seem that he is the man with whom we must deal. In a certain sense, his reputation is reassuring; he is necessarily competent."

Traz entered the conversation. "What if this Woudiver refuses to help us? Are we not then at his mercy? Could he not extort our sequins from us?"

Anacho pursed his lips, shrugged: "No scheme of this sort is absolutely reliable. Aila Woudiver would seem to be a sound choice, from our point of view. He has access to the sources of supply, he controls transport vehicles, and possibly he can provide a suitable building in which to assemble a space-boat."

Reith said reluctantly, "We want the most competent man, and if we get him I suppose we can't cavil at his personal attributes. Still, on the other hand . . . Oh, well. What pretext should we use?"

"The tale you gave the Lokhars—that we need a spaceship to take possession of a treasure—is as good as any. Woudiver will discredit all he is told; he will expect duplicity, so one tale is as good as another."

Traz muttered: "Attention! Dirdir are approaching."

There were three, striding with a portentous gait. Cages of silver mesh clung to the back of their bone-white heads; the effulgences splayed down to either side of their shoulders. Flaps of soft pale leather hung from their arms, almost to the ground.

Other strips hung down front and back, indited with vertical rows of red and black circular symbols.

"Inspectors," muttered Anacho through down-drooping lips. "Not once a year do they come to Sivishe—unless complaints are made."

"Will they know you for a Dirdirman?"

"Of course. I hope they do not know me for Ankhe at afram Anacho, the fugitive."

The Dirdir passed; Reith glanced at them indifferently, though his flesh crept at their proximity. They ignored the three and continued along the avenue, pale leather flaps swinging to their stride.

Anacho's face relaxed from its glare of tension. In a subdued voice, Reith said, "The sooner we leave Sivishe the better."

Anacho drummed his fingers on the table and gave a final decisive rap. "Very well. I will telephone Aila Woudiver and arrange an exploratory meeting." He stepped into the inn and presently returned. "A car will arrive shortly to pick us up."

Reith had not been ready for so swift a response. "What did you tell him?" he asked uneasily.

"That we wanted to consult him in regard to a business matter."

"Hmf." Reith leaned back in his chair. "Too much haste is as bad as too little."

Anacho threw up his hands in vexation and defeat. "What reason to delay?"

"No real one. I feel strange to Sivishe and unsure of my responses—hence worried."

"No worry there. With familiarity Sivishe becomes even less reassuring."

Reith said no more. Fifteen minutes later an antique black vehicle, which at one time had been a grand saloon, halted in front of the hotel. A middle-aged man, harsh and grim, looked forth. He jerked his head toward Anacho. "You await a car?"

"To Woudiver?"

"Get in."

The three climbed into the vehicle, seated themselves on benches. The car rolled at no great speed down the avenue, then, turning off toward the south, entered a district of slatternly apartment houses: buildings erected with neither judgment nor precision. No two doorways were alike; windows of irregular shape and size opened at random in the thick walls. Wan-faced folk stood in alcoves or peered down into the streets; all turned to watch the passage of the car. "Laborers," said Anacho with a sniff of distaste. "Kherman, Thangs, Sad Islanders. They come from all Kislovan and lands beyond, as well."

The car continued across a littered plaza, into a street of small shops, all fitted with heavy metal shutters. Anacho asked the driver, "How far to Woudiver's?"

"Not far." The reply was uttered with hardly a motion of the lips.

"Where does he live? Out on the Heights?"

"On Zamia Rise."

Reith considered the hooked nose, the dour cords of muscle around the colorless mouth: the face of an executioner.

The way led up a low hill. The houses became abandoned gardens. The car halted at the end of a lane. The driver with a curt gesture signaled the three to alight, then silently led them along a shadowy passage smelling of dankness and mold, through an archway, across a courtyard, up a shallow flight of stairs into a room with walls of mustard-colored tile.

"Wait here." He passed through a door of black psilla bound with iron, and a moment later looked forth. He crooked his finger. "Come."

The three filed into a large white-walled chamber. A scarlet and maroon rug muffled the floor; for furniture there were settees padded with pink, red and yellow plush, a heavy table of carved wax-wood, a censer exuding wisps of heavy smoke. Behind the table stood an enormous yellow-skinned man in robes of red, black and ivory. His face was round as a melon; a few strands of sandy hair lay across his mottled pate. He was a man vast in every dimension and motivated, so it seemed to Reith, by a grandiose and cynical intelligence. He spoke: "I am Aila Woudiver." His voice was under exquisite control; now it was soft and fluting. "I see a Dirdirman of the First—"

"Superior!" Anacho corrected.

"—a youth of a rough unknown race, a man of even more doubtful extraction. Why does such an ill-matched trio seek me out?"

"To discuss a matter possibly of mutual interest," said Reith.

The lower third of Woudiver's face trembled in a grin. "Continue."

Reith looked around the room, then turned back to Woudiver. "I suggest that we move to another location, out of doors, by preference."

Woudiver's thin, almost-nonexistent eyebrows lofted high in surprise. "I fail to understand. Will you explain?"

"Certainly, if we can move to another area."

Woudiver frowned in sudden petulance, but marched forward. The three followed him through an archway, up a ramp and out on a deck which overlooked a vast hazy distance to the west. Woudiver spoke in a voice now carefully resonant: "Does this situation seem suitable?"

"Better," said Reith.

"You puzzle me," said Woudiver, settling into a massive chair. "What noxious influence do you so dread?"

Reith looked meaningfully across the panorama, toward the colored towers and cloud-gray Glass Box of far Hei. "You are an important man. Your activities conceivably interest certain folk to the extent that they monitor your conversations."

Woudiver made a jovial gesture. "Your business appears highly confidential, or even illicit."

"Does this alarm you?"

Woudiver pursed his lips into a fountain of gray-pink gristle. "Let us get down to affairs."

"Certainly. Are you interested in gaining wealth?"

"Poof," said Woudiver. "I have enough for all my small needs. But anyone can use more money."

"In essence, the situation is this: we know where and how to obtain a considerable treasure at no risk."

"You are the most fortunate of men!"

"Certain preparations are necessary. We believe that you, a man of known resource, will be able to provide assistance in return for a share of the gain. I do not, of course, refer to financial assistance."

"I cannot say yes or no until I am apprised of all details," said Woudiver in the most suave of voices. "Naturally, you may speak without reserve; my reputation for discretion is a byword."

"First we need a clear indication of your interest. Why waste time for nothing?"

Woudiver blinked. "I am as interested as is possible in a factual vacuum."

"Very well, then. Our problem is this: we must procure a small spaceship."

Woudiver sat motionless, his eyes boring into Reith's face. He glanced swiftly at Traz and Anacho, then gave a short brisk laugh. "You credit me with remarkable powers! Not to say reckless audacity! How can I possibly provide a spaceship, large or small? Either you are madmen or you take me for one!"

Reith smiled at Woudiver's vehemence, which he diagnosed as a tactical device. "We have considered the situation carefully," said Reith. "The project is not impossible with the help of a person such as yourself."

Woudiver gave his great lemon-colored head a peevish shake. "So I merely point my finger toward the Grand Spaceyards and produce a ship? Is this your belief? You would have me bounding through the Glass Cage before the day was out."

"Remember," said Reith, "a large vessel is not necessary. Conceivably we could acquire an obsolete craft and put it into workable condition. Or we might obtain components from persons who could be induced to sell, and assemble them in a makeshift hull."

Woudiver sat pulling at his chin. "The Dirdir certainly would oppose such a project."

"I mentioned the need for discretion," said Reith.

Woudiver puffed out his cheeks. "How much wealth is involved? What is the nature of this wealth? Where is it located?"

"These are details which at the moment can have no real interest for you," said Reith.

Woudiver tapped his chin with a yellow forefinger. "Let us discuss the matter as an abstraction. First, the practicalities. A large sum of money would be required: for inducements, technical help, a suitable place of assembly, and of course for the components you mention. Where would this money come from?" His voice took on a sardonic resonance. "You did not expect financing from Aila Woudiver?"

"Financing is no problem," said Reith. "We have ample funds."

"Indeed!" Woudiver was impressed. "How much, may I ask, are you prepared to spend?"

"Oh, fifty to a hundred thousand sequins."

Woudiver gave his head a shake of indulgent amusement. "A hundred thousand would be barely adequate." He turned a glance toward Hei. "I could never concern myself in any illicit or forbidden enterprise."

"Naturally not."

"I might be able to advise you, on a friendly and informal basis, for say, a fixed fee, or perhaps a percentage of outlay, and a small share in any eventual rewards."

"Something of the sort might suit our needs," said Reith. "How long, at an estimate, would such a project require?"

"Who knows? Who can prophesy such things? A month? Two months? Information is essential, which we now lack. A knowledgeable person from the Grand Spaceyards must be consulted."

"Knowledgeable, competent, and trustworthy," amended Reith.

"That goes without saying. I know the very man, a person for whom I have done several favors. In the course of a day or two I will see him and bring up the matter."

"Why not now?" asked Reith. "The sooner the better."

Woudiver raised a hand. "Haste leads to miscalculation. Come back in two days; I may have news for you. But first the matter of finance. I cannot invest my time without a retainer. I will need a small sum—say five thousand sequins—as earnest-money."

Reith shook his head. "I'll show you five thousand." He produced a card of purple sequins. "In fact here is twenty thousand. But we can't afford to spend a sequin except on actual costs."

Woudiver's face was one vast hurt. "What of my fee, then? Must I toil for joy alone?"

"Of course not. If all goes well, you will be rewarded to your satisfaction."

"This must serve for the moment," declared Woudiver in sudden heartiness. "In two days I will send Artilo for you. Discuss the matter with no one! Secrecy is absolutely essential!"

"This we well understand. In two days then."

11

SIVISHE WAS A dull city, gray and subdued, as if oppressed by the proximity of Hei. The great homes of Prospect Heights and

Zamia Rise were pretentious enough, but lacked style and finesse. The folk of Sivishe were no less dull: a somber, humorless race, gray-skinned and tending toward overweight. At their meals they consumed great bowls of clabber, platters of boiled tuber, meat and fish seasoned with a rancid black sauce that numbed Reith's palate, though Anacho declared that the sauce occurred in numerous variants and was in fact a cultivated taste. For organized entertainment there were daily races, run not by animals but by men. On the day after the meeting with Woudiver, the three watched one of the races. Eight men participated, wearing garments of different colors and carrying a pole topped with a fragile glass globe. The runners not only sought to outrun their opponents but also to trip them by agile side-kicks, so that they fell and broke their glass globes, and were hence disqualified. The spectators numbered twenty thousand and maintained a low guttural howl during the duration of each race. Reith noticed a number of Dirdirmen among the spectators. They bet with as much verve as anyone, but kept themselves fastidiously apart. Reith wondered that Anacho would risk recognition by some previous acquaintance, to which Anacho gave a bitter laugh.

"Wearing these clothes I am safe. They will never see me. If I wore Dirdirmen clothes I would be recognized at once and reported to the Castigators. Already I have seen half a dozen former acquaintances. None have so much as glanced at me."

The three visited the Grand Sivishe Spaceyards, where they strolled around the periphery observing the activity within. The spaceships were long, spindle-shaped, with intricate fins and sponsons—totally different from the bulky Wankh vessels and the flamboyant craft of the Blue Chasch, just as these differed from the starships of Earth.

The yards appeared to operate at less than top efficiency and far below capacity; even so, a respectable volume of work was in progress. Two cargo vessels were in the process of overhaul; a passenger ship seemed to be under construction. Elsewhere they noted three smaller ships, apparently uncommissioned warcraft, five or six space-boats in various stages of repair, a clutter of hulks on a junk heap to the rear of the shops. At the opposite end of the spaceyard three ships in commission rested on large black circles.

"They fare occasionally to Sibol," said Anacho. "There is no great traffic. Long ago when the Expansionists held sway Dirdir ships went out to many worlds. No longer. The Dirdir are quiescent. They would like to force the Wankh off of Tschai and slaughter the Blue Chasch, but they do not marshal their energies. It is somehow frightening. They are a terrible and active race and cannot lie quiet too long. One of these days they must explode, and go forth again."

"What of the Pnume?" Reith asked.

"There is no established pattern." Anacho pointed to the palisades behind Hei. "Through your electric telescope you might see Pnume warehouses, where they store metals for trade with the Dirdir. Pnumekin occasionally come out into Sivishe for one purpose or another. There are tunnels through all the hills and out into the country beyond. The Pnume observe every move the Dirdir make. They never come forth, however, for fear of the Dirdir, who kill them for vermin. On the other hand a Dirdir who goes hunting alone may never return. The Pnume have taken him down into their tunnels, so it is believed."

"It could only happen on Tschai," said Reith. "The folk trade in mutual detestation and kill each other on sight."

Anacho gave a sour snort. "I see nothing remarkable in the fact. The trading conduces to mutual profit; the killing gratifies the mutual detestation. The institutions have no common ground."

"What of the Pnumekin? Do the Dirdir or Dirdirmen molest them?"

"Not in Sivishe. A truce is observed. Elsewhere they too are destroyed, though rarely do they show themselves. There are, after all, relatively few Pnumekin, who must be the strangest and most remarkable folk of Tschai . . . We must depart before we attract the attention of the yard police."

"Too late," said Traz in a dreary voice. "We are being watched at this moment."

"By whom?"

"Behind us, along the way, stand two men. One wears a brown jacket and a loose black hat; the other a dark blue cloak and the head-shroud."

Anacho glanced along the avenue. "They are not police—at least not yard guards."

The three turned back to the dingy jumble of concrete which marked the center of Sivishe. Carina 4269, glowing through a high layer of haze, cast cool brown light over the landscape. Full in the light came the two men, and something in their noiseless gait sent a pang of panic through Reith. "Who can they be?" he muttered.

"I don't know." Anacho turned a quick glance over his shoulder, but the men were no more than silhouettes against the light. "I don't think they are Dirdirmen. We have been in contact with Aila Woudiver; it may be that he is watched. Woudiver's own men conceivably. Or a criminal gang? After all, we might have been noticed coming down in the sky-car, or taking sequins to the vaults—Worse! Our descriptions from Maust may have been circulated. We are not undistinctive."

Reith said grimly, "We'll have to find out, one way or another. Notice where the street passes closes to that broken building."

"Suitable."

The three strolled past a crumbling buttress of concrete, then, once out of sight, jumped to the side and waited. The two men came running past on long noiseless strides. As they passed the buttress, Reith tackled one, Anacho and Traz seized the other. With a sudden exclamation Anacho and Traz released their grip. For an instant Reith sensed a curious rancid odor, like camphor and sour milk. Then a bone-racking shudder of electricity sent him lurching back. He gave a croak of dismay. The two men fled.

"I saw them," said Anacho in a subdued voice. "They were Pnumekin, or perhaps Gzhindra. Did they wear boots? Pnumekin walk with bare feet."

Reith went to look after the pair, but in some miraculous fashion they had disappeared. "What are Gzhindra?"

"Pnumekin outcasts."

The three trudged back through the dank streets of Sivishe.

Anacho presently said, "It might have been worse."

"But why should Pnumekin follow us?"

Traz muttered, "They have been following us since we departed Settra. And maybe before."

"The Pnume think strange thoughts," said Anacho in a heavy voice. "Their actions seldom admit of sensible explanation; they are the stuff of Tschai itself."

12

THE THREE SAT at a table outside the Ancient Realm Inn, sipping soft wine and watching the passing folk of Sivishe. Music was the key to a people's genius, thought Reith. This morning, passing a tavern, he had listened to the music of Sivishe. The orchestra consisted of four instruments. The first was a bronze box studded with vellum-wrapped cones which when rubbed produced a sound like a cornet played at the lowest possible range. The second, a vertical wooden tube a foot in diameter, with twelve strings across twelve slots, emitted resonant twanging arpeggios. The third, a battery of forty-two drums, contributed a complex muffled rhythm. The fourth, a wooden slide-horn, bleated, honked and produced wonderful squealing glissandos as well.

The music performed by the ensemble seemed to Reith peculiarly simple and limited: a repetition of simple melody, played with only the smallest variation. A few folk danced: men and women, face to face, hands at sides, hopping carefully from one leg to the other. Dull! thought Reith. Yet, at the end of the tune the couples separated with expressions of triumph, and recommenced their exertions as soon as the music started again. As minutes passed, Reith began to sense complexities, almost imperceptible variations. Like the rancid black sauce which drowned the food, the music required an intensive effort even to ingest; appreciation and pleasure must remain forever beyond the reach of a stranger. Perhaps, thought Reith, these almost-unheard quavers and hesitations were the elements of virtuosity; perhaps the folk of Sivishe enjoyed hints and suggestions, fugitive lusters, almost unnoticeable inflections: their reaction to the Dirdir city so close at hand.

No less an index to the thought-processes of a people was their religion. The Dirdir, so Reith knew from conversations with Anacho, were irreligious. The Dirdirmen, to the contrary, had evolved an elaborate theology, based on a creation myth which derived Man and Dirdir from a single primordial egg. The submen of Sivishe patronized a dozen different temples. The observances, as far as Reith could see, followed the more or less universal pattern—abasement, followed by a request for favors, as often as not foreknowledge regarding the outcome of the daily races. Certain cults had refined and complicated their doctrines;

their doxology was a metaphysical jargon subtle and ambiguous enough to please even the folk of Sivishe. Other creeds serving different needs had simplified procedures so that the worshipers merely made a sacred sign, threw sequins into the priest's bowl, received a benediction and were off about their affairs.

The arrival of Woudiver's black car interrupted Reith's musing. Artilo, leaning forth with a leer, made a peremptory gesture, then sat crouched over the wheel staring off down the avenue.

The three entered the car, which lurched off across Sivishe. Artilo drove in a southeast direction, generally toward the spaceyards. At the edge of Sivishe, where a last few shacks dwindled out across the salt flats, a cluster of ramshackle warehouses surrounded piles of sand, gravel, bricks, sintered marl. The car rolled across the central compound and halted by a small office built of broken brick and black slag.

Woudiver stood in the doorway. Today he wore a vast brown jacket, blue pantaloons, and a blue hat. His expression was bland and unrevealing; his eyelids hung halfway across his eyes. He raised his arm in a gesture of measured welcome, then backed into the dimness of the hut. The three alighted and went within. Artilo, coming behind, drew himself a mug of tea from a great black urn, then, hissing irritably, went to sit in a corner.

Woudiver indicated a bench; the three seated themselves. Woudiver paced back and forth. He raised his face to the ceiling and spoke. "I have made a few casual inquiries. I fear that I find your project impractical. There is no difficulty as to work-space— the south warehouse yonder would suit admirably and you could have it at a reasonable rent. One of my trusted associates, the assistant superintendent of supply at the spaceyards, states that the necessary components are available . . . at a price. No doubt we could salvage a hull from the junkyard; you would hardly require luxury, and a crew of competent technicians would respond to a sufficiently attractive wage."

Reith began to suspect that Woudiver was leading up to something. "So, then, why is the project impractical?"

Woudiver smiled with innocent simplicity. "For me, the profit is inadequate to the risks involved."

Reith nodded somberly and rose to his feet. "I'm sorry then to have occupied so much of your time. Thank you very much for the information."

"Not at all," said Woudiver graciously. "I wish you the best of luck in your endeavor. Perhaps when you return with your treasure, you will want to build a fine palace; then I hope you will remember me."

"Quite possibly," said Reith. "So now . . ."

Woudiver seemed in no hurry to have them go. He settled into a chair with an unctuous grunt. "Another dear friend deals in gems. He will efficiently convert your treasure into sequins, if the treasure is gems, as I presume? No? Rare metal, then? No? Aha! Precious essences?"

"It might be any or none," said Reith. "I think it best, at this stage, to remain indefinite."

Woudiver twisted his face into a mask of whimsical vexation. "It is precisely this indefiniteness which gives me pause! If I knew better what I might expect—"

"Whoever helps me," said Reith, "or whoever accompanies me, can expect wealth."

Woudiver pursed his lips. "So now I must join this piratical expedition in order to share the booty?"

"I'll pay a reasonable percentage before we leave. If you come with us"—Reith rolled his eyes toward the ceiling at the thought—"or when we return, you'll get more."

"How much more, precisely?"

"I don't like to say. You'd suspect me of irresponsibility. But you wouldn't be disappointed."

From the corner Artilo gave a skeptical croak, which Woudiver ignored. He spoke in a voice of great dignity. "As a practical man I can't operate on speculation. I would require a retaining fee of ten thousand sequins." He blew out his cheeks and glanced toward Reith. "Upon receipt of this sum, I would immediately exert my influence to set your scheme into motion."

"All very well," said Reith. "But, as a ridiculous supposition, let us assume that, rather than a man of honor, you were a scoundrel, a knave, a cheat. You might take my money, then find the project impossible for one reason or another, and I would have no recourse. Hence I can pay only for actual work accomplished."

A spasm of annoyance crossed Woudiver's face, but his voice was blandness itself. "Then pay me rent for yonder warehouse. It is a superb location, unobtrusive, close to the spaceyards, with every convenience. Furthermore, I can obtain an old hull from the junkyards, purportedly for use as a storage bin. I will charge but a nominal rent, ten thousand sequins a year, payable in advance."

Reith nodded sagely. "An interesting proposition. But since we won't need the premises for more than a few months, why should we inconvenience you? We can rent more cheaply elsewhere, in even better circumstances."

Woudiver's eyes narrowed; the flaps of skin surrounding his mouth trembled. "Let us deal openly with each other. Our interests run together, as long as I gain sequins. I will not work on the cheap. Either pay earnest-money, or our business is at an end."

"Very well," said Reith. "We will use your warehouse, and I will pay a thousand sequins for three months' rent on the day a suitable hull arrives on the premises and a crew starts to work."

"Hmf. That could be tomorrow."

"Excellent!"

"I will need funds to secure the hull. It has worth as scrap metal. Drayage will be a charge."

"Very well. Here is a thousand sequins." Reith counted the sum upon the desk. Woudiver slapped down his great slab of a hand. "Insufficient! Inadequate! Paltry!"

Reith spoke sharply. "Evidently you do not trust me. This does not predispose me to trust you. But you risk nothing but an hour or two of your time whereas I risk thousands of sequins."

Woudiver turned to Artilo. "What would you do?"

"Walk away from the mess."

Woudiver turned back to Reith, spread wide his arms. "There you have it."

Reith briskly picked up the thousand sequins. "Good day, then. It is a pleasure to have known you."

Neither Woudiver nor Artilo stirred.

The three returned to the hotel by public passenger wagon.

A day later Artilo appeared at the Ancient Realm Inn. "Aila Woudiver wants to see you."

"What for?"

"He's got you a hull. It's in the old warehouse. A gang is stripping and cleaning it. He wants money. What else?"

13

THE HULL WAS satisfactory, and of adequate dimensions. The metal was sound; the observation ports were clouded and stained but well seated and sealed.

Woudiver stood to the side as Reith inspected the hull, an expression of lofty tolerance on his face. Every day, so it seemed, he wore a new and more extravagant garment, today a black and yellow suit, a black hat with a scarlet panache. The clasp securing his cape was a silver and black oval, bisected along the minor axis. From one end protruded the stylized head of a Dirdir, from the other the head of a man. Woudiver, noticing Reith's gaze, gave a profound nod. "You would never suspect as much from my physique, but my father was Immaculate."

"Indeed! And your mother?"

Woudiver's mouth twitched. "A noblewoman of the north."

Artilo spoke from the entry port: "A tavern wench of Thang, marsh-woman by blood."

Woudiver sighed. "In the presence of Artilo, romantic delusion is impossible. In any event, but for the accidental interposition of an incorrect womb, here would stand Aila Woudiver, Dirdirman Immaculate of the Violet Degree, rather than Aila Woudiver, dealer in sand and gravel, and gallant prosecutor of lost causes."

"Illogical," murmured Anacho. "In fact, improbable. Not one Immaculate in a thousand retains Primitive Paraphernalia."

Woudiver's face instantly became a peculiar magenta color. Whirling with astounding swiftness, he pointed a thick finger. "Who dares talk of logic and probability? The renegade Ankhe at afram Anacho! Who wore Blue and Pink without undergoing the Anguish? Who disappeared coincidentally with the Excellent Azarvim issit Dardo, who has never been seen again? A proud Dirdirman, this Ankhe at afram!"

"I no longer consider myself a Dirdirman," said Anacho in a level voice. "I definitely have no ambition for the Blue and Pink, nor even the trophies of my lineage."

"In this case kindly do not comment upon the plight of one who is unluckily barred from his rightful caste!"

Anacho turned away, fuming with anger, but obviously deeming it wise to hold his tongue. It appeared that Aila Woudiver had not been idle, and Reith wondered how far his researches had extended.

Woudiver gradually regained his composure. His mouth twitched, his cheeks puffed in and out. He made a scornful noise. "To more profitable matters. What is your opinion of this hulk?"

"Favorable," said Reith. "We could expect no better from the scrap-heap."

"This is my opinion as well," said Woudiver. "The next phase of course will be somewhat more difficult. My friend at the space-yards is by no means anxious to run the Glass Box, no more I. But an adequacy of sequins works wonders. Which brings us to the subject of money. My out-of-pocket expenses are eight hundred and ninety sequins for the hull, which I consider good value. Drayage charge: three hundred sequins. Shop rental for one month: one thousand sequins. Total: twenty-one hundred and ninety sequins. My commission or personal profit I reckon at ten percent, or two hundred and nineteen sequins, to a total of twenty-four hundred and nine sequins."

"Wait, wait, wait!" cried Reith. "Not a thousand sequins a month, a thousand for *three* months; that was my offer."

"It is too little."

"I'll pay five hundred, not a clear more. Now in the matter of your commission, let us be reasonable. You provide drayage at a profit; I pay a large rent on your warehouse; I see no reason to hand over an additional ten percent on these items."

"Why not?" inquired Woudiver in a reasonable voice. "It is a convenience to you that I can offer these services. I wear two hats, so to speak: that of the expediter and that of the supplier. Why, merely because the expediter finds a certain supplier convenient, inexpensive and efficient, should he be denied his fee? If the drayage were performed elsewhere, the charges would be no less, and I would receive my fee without complaint."

Reith could not deny the logic of the presentation, nor did he try. He said, "I don't intend to pay more than five hundred sequins for a ramshackle old shed you'd be happy renting for two hundred."

Woudiver held up a yellow finger. "Consider the risk! We are about to suborn the thievery of valuable property! I am rewarded, please understand, partly for services rendered and partly to allay my fear of the Glass Box."

"This is a reasonable statement, from your point of view,"

said Reith. "As far as I am concerned, I want to complete the spaceship before the money runs out. After the ship is complete, fueled and provisioned, you can take every sequin remaining, for all I care."

"Indeed!" Woudiver scratched his chin. "How many sequins do you have then, so that we can plan accordingly?"

"Something over a hundred thousand."

"Mmf. I wonder if the job can be done at all—let alone allow for surplus."

"My point exactly. I want to keep non-construction expenses to the minimum."

Woudiver turned his face toward Artilo. "See how I am reduced. All prosper but Woudiver. As usual, he suffers for his generosity."

Artilo gave a noncommittal grunt.

Reith counted out sequins. "Five hundred—exorbitant rent for this ramshackle shed. Drayage: three hundred. The hull: eight hundred and ninety. I'll pay ten percent on the hull. Another eighty-nine. A total of seventeen hundred and seventy-nine."

Woudiver's broad yellow face mirrored a succession of emotions. At last he said, "I must remind you that a policy of parsimony is often the most expensive in the end."

"If the work goes efficiently," said Reith, "you won't find me parsimonious. You'll see more sequins than you ever dreamed existed. But I intend to pay only for results. It is to your interest to expedite the space-boat as best you can. If the money runs out we're all the losers."

For once Woudiver had nothing to say. He stared dolefully at the glittering heap on the table, then, separating purples, scarlets, dark greens, he counted. "You drive a hard bargain."

"To our mutual benefit, ultimately."

Woudiver dropped the sequins into his pouch. "If I must I must." He drummed his fingers against his thigh. "Well, as to the components, what do you require first?"

"I know nothing about Dirdir machinery. We need the advice of an expert technician. Such a man should be here now."

Woudiver squinted sidelong. "Without knowledge, how do you expect to fly?"

"I am acquainted with Wankh space-boats."

"Hmmf. Artilo, go fetch Deine Zarre from the Technical Club."

* * *

Woudiver stalked off to his office, leaving Reith, Anacho and Traz alone in the shed.

Anacho surveyed the hull. "The old hulk has done well. This is the Ispra, a series now obsolete, in favor of the Concax Screamer. We must obtain Ispra components, to simplify the work."

"Are these available?"

"Undoubtedly. I believe you got the better of the yellow beast. His father an Immaculate—what a joke! His mother a marsh-woman—that I can believe! He's evidently gone to pains to learn our secrets."

"I hope he doesn't learn too much."

"As long as we can pay, we're safe. We have a sound hull at a fair price, and even the rental is not too exorbitant. But we must be careful: normal profits won't suit him."

"No doubt he'll swindle us," said Reith. "If we end up with a functioning space-boat, I don't really care." He walked around the hull, occasionally reaching out to touch it, in a kind of wonder. Here, solid and definite, the basis of a vessel to take him home! Reith felt a surge of affection for the cold metal, in spite of its alien Dirdir look.

Traz and Anacho went outside to sit in the wan afternoon sunlight, and Reith presently joined them. With images of Earth in his mind, the landscape became suddenly strange, as if he were viewing it for the first time. The crumbling gray city Sivishe, the spires of Hei, the Glass Box reflecting a dark bronze shine from Carina 4269, the loom of the palisades through the murk: this was Tschai. He looked at Traz and Anacho: these were men of Tschai.

Reith sat down on the bench. He asked, "What's inside the Glass Box?"

Anacho seemed surprised at his ignorance. "It is a park, a simulation of old Sibol. Young Dirdir learn to hunt; others take exercise and relaxation. There are galleries for onlookers. Criminals are the prey. There are rocks, Sibol vegetation, cliffs, caves; sometimes a man avoids the hunt for days."

Reith looked across to the Glass Box. "The Dirdir hunt in there now?"

"So I suppose."

"What of the Dirdirmen Immaculates?"

"They are sometimes allowed to hunt."

"They devour their prey?"

"Of course."

Along the rutted road came the black car. It splashed through a puddle of oily slime, halted before the office. Woudiver came to stand in the doorway, a grotesque lump in black and yellow finery. Artilo stepped down from the driver's bench; from the cab came an old man. His face was haggard and his body seemed distorted or twisted; he moved slowly, as if every effort cost him pain. Woudiver strutted forward, spoke a word or two, then conducted the old man to the shed.

Woudiver spoke: "This is Deine Zarre, who will supervise our project. Deine Zarre, I introduce to you this man of no distinguishable race. He calls himself Adam Reith. Behind you see a defalcated Dirdirman: a certain Anacho; and a youth who appears to derive from the Kotan steppes. These are the folk with whom you must deal. I am no more than an adjunct; make all your arrangements with Adam Reith."

Deine Zarre gave his attention to Reith. His eyes were clear gray, and in contrast to the black of the pupils seemed almost luminous. "What is the project?"

Another man to know the secret, thought Reith. Already with Aila Woudiver and Artilo, the list was overlong. But no help for it. "In the shed is the hull of a space-boat. We want to put it into operative condition."

Deine Zarre's expression changed little. He searched Reith's face a moment, then turned and limped into the shed. Presently he reappeared. "The project is possible. Anything is possible. But feasible? I don't know." His gaze once more searched Reith's face. "There are risks."

"Woudiver shows no great alarm. Of all of us he is the most sensitive to danger."

Deine Zarre gave Woudiver a dispassionate glance. "He is also the most supple and resourceful. For myself, I fear nothing. If the Dirdir come to take me, I shall kill as many as possible."

"Come, come," chided Woudiver. "The Dirdir are as they are: folk of fantastic skills and courage. Are we not all Brothers of the Egg?"

Deine Zarre gave a dismal grunt. "Who is to supply machinery, tools, components?"

"The spaceyards," said Woudiver dryly. "Who else?"

"We will need technicians: at least six men, of absolute discretion."

"A chancy matter," Woudiver admitted. "But the chance can be minimized by inducements. If Reith pays them well, the inducement of money. If Artilo counsels them, the inducement of reason. If I indicate the consequences of a loose tongue, the inducement of fear. Never forget, Sivishe is a city of secrets! As witness we who stand here."

"True," said Deine Zarre. Again he searched Reith with his remarkable eyes. "Where do you wish to go in your spaceship?"

Woudiver spoke with overtones either of mockery or malice: "He goes to claim a fabulous treasure, which we all will share."

Deine Zarre smiled. "I want no treasure. Pay me a hundred sequins a week; it is all I require."

"So little?" demanded Woudiver. "You reduce my commission."

Deine Zarre gave him no heed. "You intend to start work at once?" he asked Reith.

"The sooner the better."

"I will list immediate needs." To Woudiver: "When can you arrange delivery?"

"As soon as Adam Reith provides the wherewithal."

"Put through the order tonight," said Reith. "I'll bring money tomorrow."

"What of the honorarium for my friend?" demanded Woudiver testily. "Does he work for nothing? What of the fee for the warehouse guards? Do they look sideways for their health?"

"How much?" asked Reith.

Woudiver hesitated, then said in a dull voice, "Let us avoid a tiresome quarrel. I will present the minimum price first. Two thousand sequins."

"So much? Incredible. How many men must be bribed?"

"Three. The assistant supervisor, two guards."

Deine Zarre said, "Give it to him. I dislike haggling. If you must economize, pay me less."

Reith started to complain, then shrugged, managed a painful grin. "Very well. Two thousand sequins."

"Remember," said Woudiver, "you must bear the inventory cost of the merchandise; it is difficult to steal outright."

* * *

During the evening four power-wagons unloaded at the shed. Reith, Traz, Anacho and Artilo trundled the crates into the shed, as Deine Zarre checked them off his master list. Woudiver appeared on the scene at midnight. "All is well?"

Deine Zarre said, "As far as I can tell, the basic needs are here."

"Good." Woudiver turned to Reith, handed him a sheet of paper. "The invoice. Notice that it is itemized, and bluster will serve no purpose."

Reith read the total in a weak whisper "Eighty-two thousand sequins."

"Did you expect less?" Woudiver asked jauntily. "My fee is not included. Ninety thousand two hundred sequins in all."

Reith asked Deine Zarre, "Is there everything we need?"

"By no means."

"How much time will be required?"

"Two or three months. Longer if the components are seriously out of phase."

"What must I pay the technicians?"

"Two hundred sequins a week. Unlike myself, they are motivated by the need for money."

On the screen of Reith's imagination appeared a picture of the Carabas: the dun hills, the gray outcrops, the thickets of thorn, the horrid fires by night. He remembered the furtive passage across the Forelands, the Dirdir-trap in Boundary Forest, the race back to the Portal of Gleams. Ninety thousand sequins represented almost half of this . . . If the money dwindled too fast, if Woudiver became too brazenly corrupt, what then? Reith could not bear to think the thought. "Tomorrow I will bring the money."

Woudiver gave a fateful nod. "Good. Or tomorrow night the goods return to the warehouse."

14

WITHIN THE SHED the old Ispra began to come alive. The propulsors were raised into their sockets, bolted and welded. Up through the stern access panel the generator and converter were hoisted, then slid forward and secured. The Ispra was no longer a hulk. Reith, Anacho and Traz wire-brushed, ground, polished, removed rotten padding, sour-smelling old settees. They cleaned the observation ports, reamed air conduits, installed new seals around the entry hatch.

Deine Zarre did no work. He hobbled here and there, his gray eyes missing no details. Artilo occasionally looked into the shed, a sneering droop to his gray mouth. Woudiver was seldom to be seen. During his rare appearances he was cold and businesslike, all trace of his first jocundity gone.

For an entire month Woudiver did not show himself. Artilo, in a confiding mood, spat down at the ground and said, "Big Yellow's out at his country place."

"Oh? What's he do out there?"

Artilo twisted his head sidewise, showing Reith a lopsided grin. "Thinks he's a Dirdirman, that's what. That's where his money goes, on his fences and scenery and hunts, wicked old beast."

Reith stood stock-still staring at Artilo. "You mean he hunts men?"

"For sure. He and his cronies. Yellow has two thousand acres to his place, almost as big as the Glass Box. Walls aren't so good, but he's got them circled by electric wires and sting snaps. Don't go to sleep on Yellow's wine; you'll wake up to find yourself in the hunt."

Reith forbore to inquire the disposition of the victims; it was information he did not want.

Another of the ten-day Tschai weeks passed, and Woudiver appeared, in a surly mood. His upper lip was stiff as a shingle, totally concealing his mouth; his eyes darted truculently right and left. He strutted close to Reith; the great hulk of his torso blotted out half the landscape. He held out his hand. "Rent." His voice was flat and cold.

Reith brought forth five hundred sequins and placed them on a shelf. He did not care to touch the yellow hand.

Woudiver, in a spasm of petulance, struck out with the back of his hand, knocking Reith head over heels. Reith picked himself up in astonishment. His skin began to prickle, signaling the onset of fury. From the corner of his eye he noticed Artilo lounging against the wall. Artilo would shoot him as calmly as he might crush an insect, this he knew. Nearby stood Traz, watching Artilo intently. Artilo was neutralized.

Woudiver stood looking at him, eyes cold and expressionless. Reith heaved a deep sigh, choked back his wrath. To strike back at Woudiver would gain none of his respect, but only stimulate the whole of his rancor. Inevitably something dreadful would occur. Reith slowly turned away. "Bring me my rent!" barked Woudiver. "Do you take me for a mendicant? I have been sufficiently wounded by your arrogance. In the future extend me the respect due to my caste!"

Again Reith hesitated. How much easier to attack the monstrous Woudiver and accept the consequences! Which would be wreckage of the program. Again Reith sighed. If it were necessary to eat crow, a mouthful was no worse than a taste.

In cold and austere silence he handed the sequins to Woudiver, who only glared and made a waggling motion of the hips. "It is insufficient! Why should I subsidize your undertaking! Pay me my due! The rent is one thousand sequins a month!"

"Here is another five hundred sequins," said Reith. "Please do not demand more, because it will not be forthcoming."

Woudiver made a contemptuous sound, wheeled and stalked away. Artilo looked after him and spat in the dust. Then he gave Reith a speculative glance.

Reith went inside the shed. Deine Zarre, who had observed the episode, made no comment. Reith tried to soothe his humiliation in work.

Two days later Woudiver reappeared, wearing his gaudy black and yellow outfit. His truculence of the previous occasion had vanished; he was blandly polite. "Well, then, and what is the current state of your project?"

Reith responded in a flat voice. "There have been no major problems. The heavy components are in place and connected. The instruments have been installed, but are not operative. Deine Zarre is preparing another list: the magnetic justification system, navigation sensors, the environment conditioners. Perhaps we should also purchase fuel cells at this time."

Woudiver pursed his lips. "Just so. Again the sad occasion arises, of parting with your hard-gained sequins. How, may I ask, did you garner so large a sum? It is a fortune in itself. With so much in hand I wonder that you risk all on a wild-goose chase."

Reith managed a wintry smile. "Evidently I do not regard the expedition as a wild-goose chase."

"Extraordinary. When will Deine Zarre have his list in hand?"

"Perhaps it is finished now."

Deine Zarre had not finished his list but did so while Woudiver waited.

Scanning the list with head thrown back and eyes half-closed, Woudiver said, "I fear that the expense will be in excess of your reserves."

"I hope not," said Reith. "How much do you reckon?"

"I can't say for certain; I do not know. But with rent, labor costs, your original investments, you cannot have too much money left." He looked at Reith questioningly.

The last thing Reith planned to do was confide in Woudiver. "It is essential then that we keep costs to a minimum."

"Three basic costs must be met without fail," intoned Woudiver. "The rent, my fees, honorariums to my associates. What remains may be spent as you will. This is my point of view. And now be so good as to tender me two thousand sequins, for the honorariums. The materials, should you be unable to pay, can be returned without prejudice and at no cost other than drayage fees."

Gloomily Reith handed over two thousand sequins. He made a mental calculation: of something like two hundred and twenty thousand sequins brought from the Carabas, less than half remained.

Somewhat later a smaller wagon arrived, with eight canisters of fuel. Traz and Anacho started to unload these, but Reith stopped them. "One moment." He went into the shed where Deine Zarre checked items off his list. "Did you order fuel?"

"Yes."

Deine Zarre seemed pensive, thought Reith, as if his mind wandered afield.

"How long will a canister of fuel drive the ship?"

"Two are needed, one for each cell. These will give about two months' service."

"Eight canisters have been delivered."

"I ordered four, to ensure two spares."

Reith returned to the dray. "Take off four," he told Traz and Anacho. The driver sat in the shadow of the cab. Reith leaned in to address him, and to his surprise saw Artilo, apparently in no anxiety to identify himself. Reith said, "You brought eight cans of fuel; we ordered four."

"Yellow said to bring eight."

"We only need four. Take four back."

"Can't be done. Talk to Big Yellow."

"I need only four cans. That's all I'm taking. Do what you like with the others."

Artilo, whistling between his teeth, jumped from the cab, unloaded the four extra canisters, carried them over to the shed. Then he climbed back into the dray and drove off.

The three stood looking after him. Anacho said in a toneless voice, "Trouble is on its way."

"I expect so," said Reith.

"The fuel cells," said Anacho, "are no doubt Woudiver's own property. Perhaps he stole them, perhaps he bought them on the cheap. Here is an excellent chance to dispose of them at a profit."

Traz made a growling sound in his throat. "Woudiver should be made to carry away the cells on his back."

Reith gave an uneasy laugh. "If I only knew how to make him."

"He fears for his life, like anyone else."

"True. But we can't cut off our nose to spite our face."

In the morning Woudiver did not arrive to hear the statements which Reith had brooded upon a large part of the night. Reith drove himself to work, with the thought of Woudiver pressing on him like the weight of doom.

On this morning Deine Zarre was not on hand either, and the technicians muttered among themselves more freely than they dared in Deine Zarre's presence. Reith presently desisted from his work and made a survey of the project. There were, he thought, good grounds for optimism. The major components were installed; the delicate job of tuning proceeded at a satisfactory rate. At these jobs Reith, though acquainted with Earth space-drive systems, was helpless. He was not even certain that the drives functioned by the same principles.

About noon a line of black clouds broke over the palisades like a scud of surf. Carina 4269 went wan, faded through tones of brown, and disappeared; moments later rain swept the eerie landscape, blotting Hei from sight, and now plodding through the rain came Deine Zarre, followed by a pair of thin children: a boy of twelve, a girl three or four years older. The three trudged into the shed, where they stood shivering. Deine Zarre seemed drained of energy; the children were numb.

Reith broke up some crates, lit a fire in the middle of the shed. He found some coarse cloth and tore it into towels. "Dry yourselves. Take off your jackets and get warm."

Deine Zarre looked at him uncomprehendingly, then slowly obeyed. The children followed suit. They were evidently brother and sister, quite possibly Deine Zarre's grandchildren. The boy's eyes were blue; those of the girl were a beautiful slate gray.

Reith brought forth hot tea and at last Deine Zarre spoke. "Thank you. We are almost dry." And a moment later: "The children are in my care; they will be with me. If you find the prospect inconvenient, I must give up my employment."

"Of course not," said Reith. "They are welcome here, as long as they understand the need for silence."

"They will say nothing." Deine Zarre looked at the two. "Do you understand? Whatever you see must not be mentioned elsewhere."

The three were in no mood for conversation. Reith, sensing desolation and misery, lingered. The children watched him warily. "I can't offer you dry clothes," said Reith. "But are you hungry? We have food on hand."

The boy shook his head with dignity; the girl smiled and became suddenly charming. "We have had no breakfast."

Traz, who had been standing to the side, ran to the larder and presently returned with seed-bread and soup. Reith watched gravely. It appeared that Traz's emotions had been affected. The girl was appealing, if somewhat peaked and miserable.

Deine Zarre finally stirred himself. He pulled his steaming garments taut and went to inspect the work done in his absence.

Reith tried to make conversation with the children. "Are you becoming dry?"

"Yes, thank you."

"Deine Zarre is your grandfather?"

"Our uncle."

"I see. And now you are to live with him?"

"Yes."

Reith could find nothing more to say. Traz was more direct. "What happened to your father and mother?"

"They were killed, by Fairos," said the girl softly. The boy blinked.

Anacho said, "You must be from the Eastern Skyrise."

"Yes."

"How did you get from there to here?"

"We walked."

"It is a long way, and dangerous."

"We were lucky." The two stared into the fire. The girl winced, recalling the circumstances of their flight.

Reith went off to find Deine Zarre. "You have new responsibilities."

Deine Zarre darted Reith a sharp look. "That is correct."

"You work here for less than you deserve to be paid, and I want to increase your salary."

Deine Zarre gave a gruff nod. "I can put the money to use."

Reith returned to the floor of the shed, to find Woudiver standing in the doorway, a vast bulbous silhouette. His attitude was one of shocked disapproval. Today he wore another of his grand outfits: black plush breeches tight around his massive legs, a coat of purple and brown with a dull yellow sash. He marched forward to stare fixedly down at the boy and girl, one to the other. "Who built this fire? What do you do here?"

The girl quavered: "We were wet; the gentleman warmed us before the fire."

"Aha. And who is this gentleman?"

Reith came forward. "I am the gentleman. These are relations of Deine Zarre. I built the fire to dry them."

"What of my property? A single spark and all goes up in flames!"

"In the rain I conceived the danger to be slight."

Woudiver made an easy gesture. "I accept your reassurances. How does all proceed?"

"Well enough," said Reith.

Woudiver reached into his sleeve and brought forth a paper. "I have here an account for the deliveries of last night. The total, you will notice, is extremely low, because I was given an inclusive lot price."

Reith unfolded the paper. Black sprawling characters spelled out: *Merchandise, as supplied: Sequins 106,800.*

Woudiver was saying: "—appears we are proceeding in really wonderful luck. I hope it will last. Only yesterday the Dirdir trapped two thieves working out of the export warehouse and took them instantly to the Glass Box. So, you see, our present security is fragile."

"Woudiver," said Reith, "this bill is too high. Far too high. Further, I don't intend to pay for extra energy-cans."

"The price, as I noted," said Woudiver, "is an inclusive one. The extra cans come at no extra cost. In a sense, they are free."

"This is not the case, and I refuse to pay five times what is reasonable. In fact, I don't have enough money."

"Then you must get some more," said Woudiver softly.

Reith snorted. "You make the task sound so easy."

"It is for some," said Woudiver airily. "A most remarkable rumor circulates the city. It appears that three men, entering the Carabas, slaughtered an astonishing number of Dirdir, subsequently robbing the bodies. The men are described as a youth, fair, like a Kotan steppe-dweller; a renegade Dirdirman; and a dark quiet man of no distinguishable race. The Dirdir are anxious to hunt down these three. Another rumor purports to concern the same three men. The dark man reportedly states his origin to be a far-off world from which he insists all men derive: in my opinion a blasphemy. What do you think of all this?"

"Interesting," said Reith, trying to conceal his despair.

Woudiver permitted himself to smirk. "We are in a vulnerable position. There is danger to myself, grave danger. Should I expose myself for nothing? I assist you from motives of comradeship and altruism of course, but I must receive my recompense."

"I cannot pay so much," said Reith. "You knew approximately the extent of my capital; now you attempt to extort more."

"Why not?" Woudiver could no longer restrain a grin. "Assume that the rumors I cited are accurate; assume that by some wild accident you and your henchmen were the persons in question: then is it not true that you have shamefully deceived me?"

"Assuming as much—not at all."

"What of the wonderful treasure?"

"It is real. Assist me to the best of your abilities. In one month we can depart Tschai. In another month you will be repaid beyond your dreams."

"Where? How?" Woudiver hitched himself forward; he loomed over Reith and his voice came deep and rich from the far caverns of his chest. "Let me ask outright: did you promulgate a tale that the original home of man is a far world? Or even more to the point: do you believe this hideous fantasy?"

Reith, with spirits plunging even deeper, tried to sidestep the quagmire. "We are dealing with side issues. Our arrangement was clear; the rumors you mention have no relevance."

Woudiver slowly, deliberately, shook his head.

"When the spaceship leaves," said Reith, "you shall have every sequin in my possession. I can do no better than that. If you make unreasonable demands . . ." He searched for a convincing threat.

Woudiver tilted up the great expanse of his face, chuckled. "What can you do? You are helpless. One word from me and you are instantly taken to the Glass Box. What are your options? None. You must do as I demand."

Reith looked around the shed. In the doorway stood Artilo, applying ash-gray snuff to his nostrils. At his belt hung a handgun.

Deine Zarre approached. Ignoring Woudiver he spoke to Reith. "The energy-cans are not to my order. They are a nonstandard size and appear to have been used for an indeterminate period. They must be rejected."

Woudiver's eyes narrowed, his mouth jerked. "What? They are excellent canisters."

Deine Zarre said in a toneless but utterly definite voice, "For our purposes they are useless." He departed. The boy and the girl looked after him wistfully. Woudiver turned to examine them, with what appeared to Reith a peculiar intensity.

Reith waited. Woudiver swung about. For a moment he regarded Reith through narrow-lidded eyes. "Well, then," said Woudiver, "it seems that different energy-cans are needed. How do you propose to pay for them?"

"In the usual way. Take back those eight cans of junk; provide four fresh cans and submit an itemized bill. A fair account I am able to pay—just barely. Don't forget, I must meet labor costs."

Woudiver considered. Deine Zarre crossed the shed to speak to the boy and girl and Woudiver was distracted. He strutted over to join the group. Reith, limp with fatigue, went to the workbench and poured himself a mug of tea, which he drank with a shaking hand.

Woudiver had become extremely affable, and went so far as to pat the boy on the head. Deine Zarre stood stiff, his face the color of wax.

Woudiver at last turned away. He crossed the shed to Artilo, spoke a moment or two. Artilo went outside, where blasts of wind sent ripples scurrying across the puddles.

Woudiver signaled Reith with one hand, Deine Zarre with the other. The two approached. Woudiver sighed with vast melancholy. "You two are dedicated to my poverty. You insist on the most exquisite refinements but refuse to pay. So be it. Artilo is taking away the canisters you so condemn. Zarre, come with me now and select cells to suit your needs."

"At this moment? I must take care of the two children."

"Now. At once. Tonight I visit my little property. I will not return for a period. It is evident that my help is undervalued here."

Deine Zarre acquiesced with poor grace. He spoke to the boy and girl, then departed with Woudiver.

Two hours passed. The sun, breaking through the clouds, sent a single ray down upon Hei, so that the scarlet and purple towers glittered against the black sky. Down the road came Woudiver's black car. It rolled to a halt in front of the shed; Artilo alighted. He sauntered into the shed. Reith watched him, wondering as to his air of purposefulness. Artilo approached the boy and girl, stood looking down at them, and they in turn looked up, eyes wide in their pale faces. Artilo spoke a few terse words; Reith could see the corded muscles at the back of his jaw jerk as he spoke. The children looked dubiously across the room at Reith, then reluctantly started to move toward the door. Traz spoke to Reith in a low urgent voice: "Something is wrong. What does he want with them?"

Reith moved forward. He asked, "Where are you taking these two?"

"No affair of yours."

Reith turned to the children. "Don't go with this man. Wait until your uncle returns."

The girl said, "He says he is taking us to our uncle."

"He can't be believed. Something is wrong."

Artilo turned to face Reith, an act as sinister as the coiling of a snake. He spoke in a soft voice. "I have my orders. Stand away."

"Who gave you the orders? Woudiver?"

"It is no concern of yours." He motioned to the two children. "Come." His hand went under his old gray jacket and he watched Reith sidelong.

The girl said, "We are not going with you."

"You must. I'll carry you."

"Touch them and I'll kill you," said Reith in a flat voice.

Artilo gave him a cool stare. Reith braced himself, muscles creaking with tension. Artilo brought forth his hand; Reith saw the dark shape of a weapon. He lunged, chopped down at the cold hard arm. Artilo had been expecting this; from the sleeve of his other hand sprang a long blade, which he thrust at Reith's side, so swiftly that Reith, whirling away, felt the sting of the edge. Artilo sprang back, knife poised, though he had lost the handgun. Reith, intoxicated with fury and the sudden release of tension, edged forward, eyes fixed on the unblinking Artilo. Reith feinted. Artilo reacted by not so much as a quiver. Reith struck with his left hand; Artilo cut up; Reith seized his wrist, whirled, bent, heaved, threw him far across the room where he lay in a crumpled heap.

Reith dragged him to the door, threw him outside into a puddle of slime.

Artilo painfully hoisted himself to his feet and limped over to the black car. In a passionless matter-of-fact fashion, never looking toward the shed, he scraped the mud from his garments, entered the car and departed.

Anacho said in a disapproving voice, "You should have killed him. Matters will be worse than ever."

Reith had no reply to make. He became conscious of the blood oozing down his side. Pulling up his shirt he found a long thin slash. Traz and Anacho applied a dressing; the girl somewhat timidly approached and tried to help. She seemed deft and capable; Anacho moved aside. Traz and the girl completed the job.

"Thank you," said Reith.

The girl looked up at him, her face full of a hundred different meanings. But she could not bring herself to speak.

The afternoon waned. The girl and boy stood in the doorway looking up the road. The technicians departed; the shed was silent.

The black car returned. Deine Zarre stepped stiffly forth, followed by Woudiver. Artilo, going to the luggage compartment, brought forth four energy cells, which he carried at a painful hobble into the shed. His manner, as far as Reith could see, was no different from usual: dour, impersonal, silent.

Woudiver turned a single glance toward the girl and the boy, who shrank back into the shadows. Then he approached Reith. "The energy canisters are here. They are approved by Zarre. They cost a great deal of money. Here is my statement for next month's rent and Artilo's salary—"

"Artilo's salary?" demanded Reith. "You must be joking."

"—the total, as you see, is exactly one hundred thousand sequins. The sum is not subject to diminution. You must pay at once or I will evict you from the premises." And Woudiver pursed his lips in a cold smile.

Reith's eyes misted with hate. "I can't afford this amount of money."

"Then you must go. Further, since you are no longer my client, I will be obligated to make a report of your activities to the Dirdir."

Reith nodded. "One hundred thousand sequins. And after that, how much more?"

"Whatever sums you require me to lay out."

"No further blackmail?"

Woudiver drew himself up. "The word is capricious and vulgar. I warn you, Adam Reith, that I expect the same courtesy that I accord."

Reith managed a sad laugh. "You'll have your money in five or six days. I don't have it now."

Woudiver cocked his great head skeptically sidewise. "Where do you propose to secure this money?"

"I have money waiting for me in Coad."

Woudiver snorted, wheeled and marched to his car. Artilo hobbled after him. They departed.

Traz and Anacho came to watch after the car.

In a wondering voice Traz asked, "Where will you get a hundred thousand sequins?"

"We left as much buried in the Carabas," said Reith. "The only problem is bringing it back—and perhaps it won't be so much of a problem after all."

Anacho's lank white jaw dropped. "I've always suspected you of insane optimism . . ."

Reith held up his hand. "Listen. I will fly north by the same route the Dirdir themselves use. They will take no notice, even should a search-screen be operating, which is doubtful. I will land after dark, to the east of the forest. In the morning I will dig up the sequins and take them back to the sky-car and at dusk I will fly back to Sivishe like a party of Dirdir returning from the hunt."

Anacho gave a derogatory grunt. "You make it sound so simple."

"As probably it will be, if all goes well."

Reith looked wistfully back toward the shed and the half-complete spaceship. "I might as well start now."

"I'll go with you," said Traz. "You'll need help."

Anacho made a dreary sound. "I had better go as well."

Reith shook his head. "One can do the job as well as three. You two remain here and keep our affairs moving."

"And if you don't return?"

"There are sixty or seventy thousand sequins still in the pouch. Take the money and leave Sivishe . . . But I'll be back. I can't doubt this. It's not possible that we should toil and suffer so greatly only to fail."

"Hardly a rational assessment," Anacho said drily: "I expect never to see you again."

"Nonsense," said Reith. "Well, I'll get started. The sooner I leave, the sooner I return."

15

THE SKY-CAR SAILED quietly through the night of old Tschai, over landscape ghostly in the light of the blue moon. Reith felt like a man drifting through a strange dream. He mused over the events of his life—his childhood, his years of training, his missions among the stars and finally his assignment to the *Explorator IV*. Then Tschai: destruction and disaster, his time with the Emblem nomads, the journey across Aman Steppe and the Dead Steppe to Pera; the sack of Dadiche; the subsequent journey to Cath and his adventures at Ao Hidis. Then the journey to Carabas, the slaughter of the Dirdir, the construction of the spaceship in Sivishe. And Woudiver! On Tschai both virtue and vice were exaggerated; Reith had known many evil men, among whom Woudiver ranked high.

The night advanced; the forests of central Kislovan gave way to barren uplands and silent wasteland. In all the circle of vision, no light, no fire, no sign of human activity was visible. Reith consulted the course monitor, adjusted the automatic pilot. The Carabas lay only an hour ahead. The blue moon hung low; when it set the landscape would be dark until dawn.

The hour passed. Braz sank behind the horizon; in the east appeared a sepia glimmer announcing the nearness of dawn. Reith, dividing his attention between the course monitor and the ground below, finally thought to glimpse the shape of Khusz. At once, he dropped the car low to the ground and veered to the east, swinging behind the Boundary Forest. As Carina 4269 thrust a first cool brown sliver over the edge of the horizon Reith landed, close under the first great torquils of the forest.

For a period he sat watching and listening. Carina 4269 rose into the sky and the low light shone directly upon the sky-car. Reith gathered broken fronds and branches, which he laid against the car, camouflaging it to some extent.

The time had come when he must venture into the forest. He could delay no longer. Taking a sack and a shovel, tucking weapons into his belt, Reith set forth.

The trail was familiar. Reith recognized each bole, every dark sheaf of fungus, every hummock of lichen. As he passed through the forest he became aware of a sickening odor: the reek of carrion. This was to be expected. He halted. Voices? Reith jumped off the trail, listened.

Voices indeed. Reith hesitated, then stole forward through the heavy foliage.

Ahead lay the site of the trap. Reith approached with the most extreme caution, creeping on his hands and knees, finally crawling on his elbows . . . He looked forth upon an eerie sight. To one side, in front of a great torquil, stood five Dirdir in hunting regalia. A dozen gray-faced men stood in a great hole, digging with shovels and buckets: this was the hole, greatly enlarged, in which Reith, Traz and Anacho had buried the Dirdir corpses. From the splendid rotting carrion came an odious stench . . . Reith stared. One of these men was surely familiar—it was Issam the Thang. And next to him worked the hostler, and next, the porter at the Alawan. The others Reith could not positively identify, but all seemed somehow familiar, and he assumed them to be folk with whom he had dealings at Maust.

Reith turned to inspect the five Dirdir. They stood stiff and attentive, effulgences flaring out behind. If they felt emotion, or disgust, none was evident.

Reith did not allow himself to reason, to weigh, to calculate. He brought forth his hand-gun; he aimed, he fired. Once, twice, three times. Three Dirdir fell dead; the other two sprang around in questioning fury. Four times, five times: two glancing hits. Emerging from his cover Reith fired twice more down into the thrashing white bodies before they became still.

The men in the pit stood frozen in wonder. "Up!" cried Reith. "Out of there!"

Issam the Thang yelled hoarsely, "It is you, the murderer! Your crimes brought us here!"

"Never mind that," said Reith. "Get up out of that hole and fly for your life!"

"What good is that? The Dirdir will track us! They will kill us in some abominable fashion—"

The hostler was already out of the hole. He went to the Dirdir corpses, availed himself of a weapon, and turned back to Issam the Thang. "Don't bother to climb from the hole." He fired; the Thang's yell was cut short; his body rolled down among the decaying Dirdir.

The hostler said to Reith, "He betrayed us all, hoping for gain; he gained only what you saw; they took him with the rest of us."

"These five Dirdir—were there more?"

"Two Excellences who have gone back to Khusz."

"Take the weapons and go your way."

The men fled toward the Hills of Recall. Reith dug under the roots of the torquil. There, the sack of sequins. To the value of a hundred thousand? He could not be sure.

Shouldering the pouch, looking for a last time on the scene of carnage and the pitiful corpse of Issam the Thang, he departed the scene.

Back at the sky-car he loaded the sequins into the cabin and set himself to wait, anxiety gnawing at his stomach. He dared not depart. If he flew low he might be seen by hunt parties; if he flew high the screen across the Carabas would detect him.

The day passed. Carina 4269 dropped behind the far hills. Sad brown twilight fell over the Zone. Along the hills the hateful flickers sprang into existence. Reith could wait no longer. He took the sky-car into the air.

Low over the ground he skimmed until he was clear of the Zone, then rising high drove south for Sivishe.

16

THE DARK LAND passed astern. Reith sat staring ahead, visions flitting across his inner eye: faces, twisted in passion, horror, pain. The shapes of Blue Chasch, Wankh, Pnume, Phung, Green Chasch, Dirdir, all leaped upon the stage of his imagination, to stand, turn, perform a gesture and leap away.

The night passed. The sky-car slid south and when Carina 4269 rose into the east the spires of Hei glistened far ahead.

Without incident Reith landed the sky-car, though it seemed that a passing party of Dirdirmen scrutinized him with suspicious intensity as he departed the field with his sack of sequins.

Reith went first to his room at the Ancient Realm. Neither Traz nor Anacho were on the premises, but Reith thought nothing of this; they often passed the nights at the shed.

Reith stumbled to his couch, threw the bag of sequins against the wall, stretched out and almost immediately slept.

He awoke to a hand on his shoulder. He rolled over to find Traz standing above him.

Traz spoke in a husky voice: "I was afraid you'd come here. Hurry, we must leave. The apartment is now dangerous."

Reith, still torpid, swung himself to a sitting position. The time was early afternoon, or so he judged by the shadows outside the window.

"What's the trouble?"

"The Dirdir took Anacho into custody. I was out buying food, or they would have taken me as well."

Reith was now fully awake. "When did this happen?"

"Yesterday. It was Woudiver's doing. He came to the shed, and asked questions about you. He wanted to know if you claimed to come from another world; he persisted and would not accept evasion. I refused to speak, as did Anacho. Woudiver began to reproach Anacho as a renegade. 'You, a former Dirdirman, how can you live like a sub-man among sub-men?'" Anacho became provoked and said that Bifold Genesis was a myth. Woudiver went away. Yesterday morning the Dirdir came here to the rooms and took Anacho. If they force him to talk, we are not safe and the ship is not safe."

Reith's fingers were numb as he pulled on his boots. All at once the structure of his life, contrived at such cost, had collapsed. Woudiver, always Woudiver.

Traz touched his arm. "Come; best that we leave! The rooms may be watched."

Reith picked up the bundle of sequins. They departed the building. Through the alleys of Sivishe they walked, ignoring the pale faces looking forth from doorways and odd-shaped windows.

Reith became aware that he was ravenously hungry; at a small restaurant they ate boiled sea-thrush and spore-cake. Reith began to think more clearly. Anacho was in Dirdir custody; Woudiver would certainly be expecting some sort of reaction from him. Or would he be so assured of Reith's essential helplessness that he would expect matters to go on as before? Reith grinned a ghastly grin. If Woudiver reckoned as much, he would be right. Unthinkable to jeopardize the ship for any circumstance whatever! Reith's hate for Woudiver was like a tumor in his brain—and he must ignore it; he must make the best of an agonizing dilemma.

Reith asked Traz, "You have not seen Woudiver?"

"I saw him this morning. I went to the shed; I thought you might have gone there. Woudiver arrived and went into his office."

"Let's see if he's still there."

"What do you intend to do?"

Reith gave a strangled laugh, "I could kill him—but it would do no good. We need information. Woudiver is the only source."

Traz said nothing; as usual Reith was unable to read his thoughts.

They rode the creaking six-wheeled public carrier out to the construction yard, and every turn of the wheels wound the tension tighter. When Reith arrived at the yard and saw Woudiver's black car the blood surged through his brain and he felt lightheaded. He stood still, drew a deep breath and became quite calm.

He thrust the pouch of sequins upon Traz. "Take it into the shed and hide it."

Traz took the sack dubiously. "Don't go alone. Wait for me."

"I expect no trouble. We can't afford the luxury, as Woudiver well knows. Wait for me by the shed."

Reith went to Woudiver's eccentric stone office and entered. With his back to the charcoal brazier stood Artilo, legs splayed, arms behind his back. He examined Reith without change of expression.

"Tell Woudiver I want to see him," said Reith.

Artilo sauntered to the inner door, thrust his head in, spoke. He backed away. The door swung aside with a wrench that almost tore it from its hinges. Woudiver expanded into the room: a glaring-eyed Woudiver with great upper lip folded down over his mouth. He looked across the room with the unfocused all-seeing glare of a wrathful god, then seemed to catch sight of Reith, and his malevolence concentrated itself.

"Adam Reith," spoke Woudiver in a voice like a bell. "You have returned. Where are my sequins?"

"Never mind your sequins," said Reith. "Where is the Dirdir-man?"

Woudiver hunched his shoulders. For a moment Reith thought he was about to strike out. If so Reith knew that his self-control would dissolve, for better or worse.

Woudiver spoke in a throbbing voice: "Do you think to fatigue me with wrangling? Think again! Give me my money and depart."

"You shall have your money," said Reith, "as soon as I see Ankhe at afram Anacho."

"You wish to see the blasphemer, the renegade?" roared Woudiver. "Go to the Glass Box, you will see him clearly enough."

"He is in the Glass Box?"

"Where else?"

"You are certain?"

Woudiver leaned back against the wall. "Why do you wish to know?"

"Because he is my friend. You betrayed him to the Dirdir; you must answer to me."

Woudiver began to swell, but Reith said in a weary voice, "No more drama, no more shouting. You gave Anacho to the Dirdir; now I want you to save him."

"Impossible," said Woudiver. "Even if I wished I could do nothing. He is in the Glass Box, do you hear?"

"How can you be sure?"

"Where else should he be sent? He was taken for his old crimes; the Dirdir will learn nothing of your project, if that is your worry." And Woudiver showed his mouth in a gigantic sneer. "Unless, of course, he himself reveals your secrets."

"In which case," said Reith, "you would likewise find yourself in difficulties."

Woudiver had no comment to make.

Reith asked in a gentle voice, "Can money buy Anacho's escape?"

"No," intoned Woudiver. "He is in the Glass Box."

"So you say. How can I be sure?"

"As I informed you—go look."

"Anyone who wishes can watch?"

"Certainly. The Box holds no secrets."

"What is the procedure?"

"You cross to Hei, you walk to the Box, you climb to the upper gallery which overlooks the fields."

"Could a person lower a rope, or a ladder?"

"Certainly, but he could not hope for long life; he would be thrust at once down upon the field . . . If you plan anything of this nature I myself will come to watch."

"Suppose I were to offer you a million sequins," said Reith, "could you arrange that Anacho escape?"

Woudiver darted his great head forward. "A million sequins? And you have been crying poverty to me for three months? I have been deceived!"

"Could you arrange the escape for a million sequins?"

Woudiver showed a dainty pink tip of tongue. "No, I fear not . . . a million sequins . . . I fear not. There is nothing to be done. Nothing. So you have gained a million sequins?"

"No," said Reith. "I only wanted to learn if Anacho's escape was possible."

"It is not possible," said Woudiver crossly. "Where is my money?"

"In due course," said Reith. "You betrayed my friend; you can wait."

Again Woudiver seemed on the verge of swinging his great arm. But he said, "You misuse language. I did not 'betray': I exposed a criminal to his just deserts. What loyalty do I owe you or yours? You have given none to me, and would do worse if opportunity offered. Bear in mind, Adam Reith, that friendship must work in two directions. Do not expect what you are unwilling to give. If you find my attributes distasteful, remember that I feel the same about yours. Which of us is correct? By the standards of this time and this place, it is certainly I. You are the interloper; your protests are ludicrous and unrealistic. You blame me for inordinacy. Do not forget, Adam Reith, that you chose me as a man who would perform illegal acts for pay. This is your expectation of me; you care nothing for my security or prospects. You came here to exploit me, to urge me to dangerous acts for trifling sums; you must not complain if my conduct seems merely a mirror of your own."

Reith could find no answer. He turned and left the office.

In the shed work was proceeding at its usual pace: a haven of normalcy after the Carabas and the mind-twisting colloquy with Woudiver. Traz waited just inside the portal. "What did he say?"

"He said Anacho was a criminal, that I came here to exploit him. How can I argue?"

Traz curled his lip. "And Anacho?"

"In the Glass Box. Woudiver says it's easy to get in but impossible to get out." Reith walked back and forth across the shed. Halting in the doorway, he looked across the water toward the great gray shape. He spoke to Traz: "Will you ask Deine Zarre to step out here?"

Deine Zarre appeared. Reith asked, "Have you ever visited the Glass Box?"

"Long ago."

"Woudiver tells me that a man might lower a rope from the upper gallery."

"Should he care so little for his life."

"I want two quantities of high-potency battarache—enough, say, to destroy this shed ten times over. Where can I get it in a hurry?"

Deine Zarre reflected a moment, then gave a slow fateful nod. "Wait here."

He returned in something over an hour with two clay pots. "Here is battarache; here are fuses. It is contraband material; please do not reveal where you obtained it."

"The subject will never arise," said Reith. "Or so I hope."

17

SHROUDED IN GRAY cloaks Reith and Traz crossed the causeway to the mainland. By a fine wide avenue, surfaced with a rough white substance that rasped underfoot, they entered the Dirdir city Hei. To either hand rose spires, purple and scarlet; those of gray metal and silver stood far to the north behind the Glass Box. The avenue led close beside a hundred-foot shaft of scarlet. Surrounding this was an expanse of clean white sand upon which rested a dozen peculiar objects of polished stone. Art-things? Fetishes? Trophies? There was no way of knowing. In front of the spire, on a circular plat of white marble, stood three Dirdir. For the first time Reith saw a Dirdir female. The creature was shorter and seemed less resilient, less flexible, than the male; her head was wider at the scalp and pointed at the area corresponding to a chin; she was somewhat darker in color: a pallid gray subtly shaded with mauve. The two stood contemplating the third, a male Dirdir whelp, half the size of the adult. From time to time the effulgences of the three twitched to point to one or another of the polished rock-pieces, an activity which Reith made no effort to understand.

Reith watched them in a mingling of revulsion and reluctant admiration, and he could not avoid thinking of the "mysteries."

Some time previously Anacho had explained the Dirdir sexual processes. "Essentially, the facts are these: there are twelve styles of male sexual organs, fourteen of the female. Only certain pairings are possible. For instance, the Type One Male is compatible only with Types Five and Nine Female. Type Five Female adjusts only to Type One Male, but Type Nine Female has a more general organ and is compatible with Types One, Eleven and Twelve Male.

"The matter becomes fantastically complex. Each male and female style has its specific and theoretical attributes, which are very seldom realized—as long as an individual's type is secret! These are the Dirdir 'mysteries'! Should an individual's type become known, he is expected to conform to the theoretical attributes of the type, regardless of inclination; he rarely does so, and is constantly embarrassed on this account.

"As you can imagine, a matter so complicated absorbs a great deal of attention and energy and, perhaps, by keeping the Dirdir fragmented, obsessed and secretive, has prevented them from overrunning the world of space."

"Amazing," said Reith. "But if the types are secret and generally incompatible, how do they mate? How do they reproduce?"

"There are several systems: trial marriage, the so-called 'dark gatherings,' anonymous notices. The difficulties are transcended." Anacho paused a moment, then proceeded delicately. "I need hardly point out that low-caste Dirdirmen and Dirdirwomen, lacking the 'noble divinity' and without 'secrets,' are thus held to be deficient and somewhat clownish."

"Hmm," said Reith. "Why do you specify 'low-caste Dirdirmen'? What of the Immaculates?"

Anacho cleared his throat. "The Immaculates obviate shame by elaborate surgical methods. They are allowed to alter themselves in accordance with one of eight styles; thus they are conceded 'secrets' as well, and may wear Blue and Pink."

"What about mating?"

"It is more difficult, and in fact becomes an ingenious analogue of the Dirdir system. Each style will match at most two styles of the other sex."

Reith could no longer restrain his mirth. Anacho listened with an expression, half-grim, half-rueful. "What of yourself?" asked Reith. "How far did you involve yourself?"

"Not far enough," said Anacho. "For certain reasons I wore Blue and Pink without providing myself the requisite 'secret.' I was declared an outlaw and an atavism: this was my situation at our first meeting."

"A curious crime," said Reith.

Now Anacho darted for his life across the simulated landscape of Sibol.

The avenue leading to the Glass Box became even broader, as if in some attempt to keep it in scale with the vast bulk. Those who walked the rasping white surface—Dirdir, Dirdirmen, common laborers in gray cloaks—seemed artificial and unreal, like figures in classical perspective exercises. As they walked they looked neither right nor left, passing Reith and Traz as if they were invisible.

Scarlet and purple spires reared to all sides; ahead stood the Glass Box, dwarfing all else. Reith began to suffer oppression of the spirit; Dirdir artifacts and the human psyche were in discord. To tolerate such surroundings, a man eventually must deny his heritage and submit to the Dirdir world-view. In short, he must become a Dirdirman.

They came up beside two other men, like themselves muffled in hooded gray cloaks. Reith spoke: "Perhaps you will inform us. We want to visit the Glass Box but we do not understand the procedure."

The two men gave him an uncertain appraisal. They were father and son, both short, round-faced, with round little paunches, thin arms and legs. The older man said in a reedy voice, "One merely mounts by the gray ramps; there is no more to know."

"You yourselves go to the Glass Box?"

"Yes. There is a special hunt at noon, for a great Dirdirman villain, and there may well be a tossing."

"We had heard nothing of this. Who is this Dirdirman villain?"

The two again examined him dubiously, apparently from a condition of innate uncertainty. "A renegade, a blasphemer. We are scourers at the Number Four Fabrication Plant; we received information from the Dirdirmen themselves."

"You go often to the Glass Box?"

"Often enough." The father spoke rather tersely. The son amplified: "It is authorized and endorsed by the Dirdirmen; there is no expense."

"Come," said the father. "We must hurry."

"If you have no objection," said Reith, "we will follow you and take advantage of your familiarity with the procedures."

The father agreed with no great enthusiasm. "We do not care to be delayed." The two set off up the avenue, heads crouched upon their shoulders, a gait characteristic to the Sivishe laborers. Imitating the sag-necked slouch Reith and Traz followed. The glass walls reared overhead like vitreous cliffs, showing spots of a red-magenta glow where the illumination from within penetrated the glass. Angling along the sides were ramps and escalators coded by color; purple, scarlet, mauve, white and gray, each rising to different levels. The gray ramps led to a balcony only a hundred feet from the ground, evidently the lowest. Reith and Traz, joining a stream of men, women and children, climbed the ramp, passed through an ill-smelling passage which twisted forward and back and suddenly emerged upon a bright bleak expanse, illuminated by ten miniature suns. There were low crags and rolling hills, thickets of harsh vegetation: ocher, tan, yellow, bone-white, pale whitish brown. Below was a brackish pond, a thicket of hard white cactus-like growths; in the near distance stood a forest of bone-white spires identical in shape and size to the Dirdir residential towers. The similarity, thought Reith, could not be coincidental; on Sibol the Dirdir evidently inhabited hollow trees.

Somewhere among the hills and thickets wandered Anacho, in fear of his life, bitterly regretting the impulse which had brought him to Sivishe. But Anacho was not to be seen; in fact nowhere was there sign of either man or Dirdir. Reith turned to the two laborers for explanation.

"It is a quiet period," stated the father. "Notice the hill yonder? And its equal at the far north? These are base camps. During a quiet period the game takes refuge at one or the other of the camps. Let me see; where is my schedule?"

"I carry it," said the son. "Quiet continues yet an hour; the game is at this close hill."

"We are in good time. According to rules of this particular cycle, there will be darkness in one hour, for a period of fourteen minutes. Then South Hill becomes fair territory and the game must vacate to North Hill, which in its turn becomes refuge. I am surprised that with so notorious a criminal, they do not allow Competition rules."

"The schedule was established last week," replied the son. "The criminal was taken only a day or so ago."

"We still may see good techniques, and perhaps a tossing or two."

"In one hour, then, the field goes dark?"

"For fourteen minutes, during which the hunt begins."

Reith and Traz returned to the outside balcony and the suddenly dim landscape of Tschai. Pulling their hoods close, hunching their necks, they sidled down the ramp to the ground.

Reith looked in all directions. Cloaked laborers marched stolidly up the gray ramp. Dirdirmen used the white ramps; Dirdir rode mauve, scarlet and purple escalators to the high balconies.

Reith went to the gray glass wall. He sat down and pretended to adjust his shoe. Traz stood in front of him. From his pouch Reith brought forth a pot of battarache and an attached timer. He carefully adjusted a dial, pulled a lever, laid it beside a shrub, against the glass wall.

No one heeded. He adjusted the timer on the second pot of battarache, gave pouch, battarache and timer to Traz. "You know what to do."

Traz reluctantly took the pouch. "The plan may succeed, but you and Anacho will both certainly be killed."

Reith pretended that Traz was wrong for once, for the encouragement of them both. "Drop off the battarache—you'll have to hurry. Remember, just opposite to here. There isn't much time. And I'll see you at the construction shed."

Traz turned away, concealing his face in the folds of his hood. "Very well, Adam Reith."

"But just in case something goes wrong: take the money and leave as fast as you can."

"Goodbye."

"Hurry now."

Reith watched the gray shape diminish along the base of the Glass Box. He drew a deep breath. There was little time. He must commit himself at once; if darkness arrived before he had located Anacho, all the effort and risk were in vain.

He returned back up the gray ramp, passed through the portal into the Sibol glare.

He scanned the field, taking careful note of landmarks and directions, then moved south around the deck, toward South Hill. The spectators became less numerous, most tending toward the middle or the north.

Reith selected a spot near a stanchion. He looked right and left. No one stood within two hundred feet of him. The decks above were empty. He brought out a coil of light rope, parted it, passed it around the stanchion, threw the parts down. With a look to right and left he swung himself over the rail, lowered himself to the hunting ground.

He did not go unnoticed. Pallid faces peered down in wonder. Reith paid them no heed. He no longer shared their world; he was game. He pulled the rope down and ran off toward South Hill, coiling the rope as he ran through forests of bristle, over limestone juts and coffee-colored chert.

He neared the first slopes of South Hill, sighting neither hunters nor game. The hunters would now be taking such positions as tactics dictated; the game would be lurking at the base of South

Hill, wondering how best to reach the sanctuary of North Hill. Reith suddenly came upon a young Gray, crouched in the shadow of a white bamboo-like growth. He wore sandals and a breech-clout; he carried a club and a cactus-prong dagger. Reith asked him, "Where is the Dirdirman, the one just put out on the field?"

The Gray gave his head an indifferent jerk. "There might be one such around the hill. Leave me; you create a flurry of darkness with your cloak. Drop it off; your skin is the best camouflage. Don't you know the Dirdir observe your every move?"

Reith ran on. He saw two elderly men, stark naked, with stringy muscles and white hair, standing poised like specters. Reith called out, "Have you seen the Dirdirman anywhere near?"

"Up beyond, or so it may be. Take yourself off, with your dark cloak."

Reith scrambled up a jut of sandstone. He called out: "Anacho."

No response. Reith looked at his watch. In ten minutes the field would go dark. He searched the side of South Hill. A little distance away he glimpsed movement: persons running off through the thicket. His cloak seemed to arouse antagonism; he removed it, threw it over his arm.

In a hollow Reith found four men and a woman. They showed him the faces of hunted animals, and would not reply to his question. Reith labored up the hill, to gain a better view. "Anacho!" he called. A figure in a white smock swung around. Reith felt engulfed in relief; his knees felt weak; tears came to his eyes. "Anacho!"

"What do you do here!"

"Hurry. This way. We're about to escape."

Anacho looked at him in stupefaction. "No one escapes the Glass Box."

"Come along! You'll see!"

"Not that way," cried Anacho hoarsely. "Safety lies to the north, on North Hill! When the darkness comes the hunt starts!"

"I know, I know! We don't have much time. Come this way. We must take cover somewhere over yonder; we must be ready."

Anacho threw his hands in the air. "You must know something I don't know."

They ran back the way Reith had come, to the western face of South Hill. As they ran Reith gasped out the details of the plan.

Anacho asked in a hollow voice, "You did all this . . . for me? You came down here on the field?"

"No matter about that. Now—we want to be close to that tall clump of white bristles. Where shall we take cover?"

"Within the clump—as good as any. Notice the hunters! They take their positions. They must keep off half a mile until the darkness comes. We are just barely within the sanctuary. Those four are marking us!"

"Darkness will be coming in seconds. Our plan is this: we run due west, toward that mound. From there we work to that bank of brown cactus and around the southern edge. Most important: we must not become separated!"

Anacho made a plaintive gesture. "How can we avoid it? We can't call out; the hunters will hear us."

Reith gave him an end of the rope. "Hold to that. And if we are separated we meet on the west edge of that yellow clump."

They waited for darkness. Out on the field the young Dirdir took up their positions, with here and there more experienced hunters. Reith looked to the east. By some trick of light and atmosphere the fields seemed to be open and to extend to far horizons; only by dint of concentration could Reith make out the east wall.

Darkness came. The lights dulled to red, flickered out. Far to the north glowed a single purple light, to indicate direction. It cast no illumination. Darkness was complete. The hunt had begun. From the north came Dirdir hunting calls: chilling hoots and ululations.

Reith and Anacho moved west. From time to time they halted to listen through the dark. To their right came a sinister jingling. They stood stock-still. The jingling and a *pad-pad-pad* faded off to the rear.

They arrived at their landmark hummock, and continued toward the clump of cactus. Something was near. They halted to listen. It seemed to their straining ears, or nerves, that something else paused as well.

From high, high above came a many-voiced cry, ranging up and down the sonic range, then another and another. "The hunt-calls of all the septs," Anacho whispered. "A traditional ritual. Now from the field, all the sept-members present must give voice." The calls from above halted; from all parts of the hunting field, eerie out of the dark, came the responses. Anacho nudged Reith. "While the responses sound, we are free to move. Come."

They set out with long strides, their feet sensitive as eyes. The hunt-slogans dwindled away into the distance; again there was silence. Reith struck a loose rock with his feet, to cause a distressing rattle. They froze, teeth gritted.

There was no reaction. On they walked, on and on, feeling out with their feet for the cactus clump, but encountering only air and harsh soil. Reith began to fear that they had passed it by, that the lights would go on to expose them to all the hunters, all the spectators.

Seven minutes of darkness had elapsed, or so he estimated. In another minute, at the latest, they should find the outskirts of the clump . . . A sound! Running feet, apparently human, passed not thirty feet distant. A moment later a jogging thud, shrill whispers, a jingle of hunting gear. The sounds passed, dwindled. Silence returned.

Seconds later they came to the cactus. "Around to the southern side," Reith whispered. "Then on hands and knees into the center."

The two pushed through the coarse stalks, meeting sharp side-prongs.

"Light! Here it comes!"

The dark began to dissipate in the style of a Sibol sunrise: up through gray, pallid white, into the full glare of day.

Reith and Anacho looked about them. The cactus provided fair concealment; they seemed in no imminent peril, though not a hundred yards distant three Dirdir scions bounded across the field, heads high, searching in all directions for fleeing game. Reith consulted his watch. Fifteen minutes remained—if Traz had suffered no mishap, if he had been able to reach the opposite wall of the Glass Box.

The forest of white bristle lay a quarter of a mile ahead, across somewhat open ground. It might, thought Reith, be the longest quarter-mile he had ever traversed.

The two wormed through the cactus to the northern verge. "The hunters keep to middle ground for an hour or so," said Anacho. "They restrain quick penetration to the north, then they work to the south."

Reith handed Anacho a power-gun, tucked his own into his waistband. He raised to his knees. A mile distant he glimpsed movement, Dirdir or game he could not be sure. Anacho suddenly pulled him down into concealment. From behind the cactus bush trotted a group of Immaculates, hands sheathed in artificial talons, simulated effulgences trailing over their shining white pates. Reith's stomach twisted; he stifled the impulse to confront the creatures, to shoot them.

The Dirdirmen loped past, and it seemed that they missed seeing the fugitives only through the sheerest chance. They angled away to the east, and, sighting game, bounded off at full speed.

Reith checked his watch; time was growing short. Rising to his knees, he looked in all directions. "Let's go."

They jumped erect, ran off for the white forest.

They paused halfway, crouched behind a little thicket. By South Hill a hot hunt was in progress; two bands of hunters converged on game which had taken cover on South Hill itself. Reith checked his watch. Nine minutes. The white forest was only a minute or two away. The lone spire which he had established as a landmark could now be seen, a few hundred yards west of the forest. They set forth again. Four hunters stepped from the forest, where they had stationed themselves to spy out the game. Reith's heart sank into his boots. "Keep going," he said to Anacho. "We'll fight them."

Anacho looked dubiously at the power-gun. "If they take us with guns, they'll toss us for days . . . but I was to be tossed in any event."

The Dirdir watched in fascination as Reith and Anacho approached. "We must take them into the forest," muttered Anacho. "The judges will intervene if they see our guns."

"Around to the left then, and behind that clump of yellow grass."

The Dirdir did not advance to meet them, but moved to the side. With a final burst Reith and Anacho gained the edge of the forest. The Dirdir screamed their hunt slogans and sprang forward, while Reith and Anacho retreated.

"Now," said Reith. They brought forth their guns. The Dirdir gave a croak of dismay. Four quick shots: four dead Dirdir. Instantly from high above came a great howl: a mind-jarring ululation. Anacho shouted out in sheer frustration, "The judges saw. They'll watch us now, and direct the hunt. We are lost."

"We have a chance," Reith insisted. He wiped the sweat from his face, squinting against the glare. "In three minutes—if all goes well—the explosion. Let's go on to the long spire."

They ran through the forest, and as they emerged they saw hunt-teams loping in their direction. The howling overhead rose and fell, then stopped.

They reached the single spire, with the glass wall only a hundred yards distant. Above, obscured by glare and reflections, ran the observation decks; Reith was barely able to make out the gaping spectators.

He checked his watch.

Now.

An interval, to be expected: the Box was three miles across. Seconds passed, then came a great puff of shock and a thunderous reverberation. Lights flickered; far to the east they were extinguished. Reith peered but could not see the effect of the blast. From overhead, up and down the length of the field, came a frantic baying, expressing rage so savage and stupendous that Reith's knees became weak.

Anacho was more matter-of-fact. "They direct all hunts east to the rupture, to prevent the escape of game."

The hunts which had been converging upon Reith and Anacho turned and raced off to the east.

"Get ready," said Reith. He looked at his watch. "To the ground."

A second explosion: a tremendous shatter to gladden Reith's heart, to lift him into a state of near religious exaltation. Shards and chunks of gray glass whistled overhead; the lights dimmed, went dark. Before them appeared a gap, like an opening into a new dimension, a hundred feet wide, almost as high as the first observation deck.

Reith and Anacho jumped to their feet. Without difficulty they reached the wall and sprang through—away from the arid Sibol, out into the dim Tschai afternoon.

Down the broad white avenue they ran, then at Anacho's direction turned off to the north, toward the factories and the white Dirdirman spires, then to the waterfront, and across the causeway into Sivishe.

They halted to catch their breath. "Best that you go direct to the sky-car," said Reith. "Take it and leave. You won't be safe in Sivishe."

"Woudiver issued the information against me; he'll do the same for you," said Anacho.

"I can't leave Sivishe now, with the spaceship so near to completion. Woudiver and I must have an understanding."

"Never," said Anacho bleakly. "He is a great wad of malice."

"He can't betray the spaceship without endangering himself," argued Reith. "He is our accomplice; we work in his shed."

"He'd explain it away somehow."

"Perhaps, perhaps not. In any event, you must leave Sivishe. We'll share the money—then you must go. The sky-car is no more use to me."

Anacho's white face became mulish. "Not so fast, I am not the goal of a *tsau'gsh*, remember this. Who will take the initiative to seek me out?"

Reith looked back toward the Glass Cage. "You don't think they'll seek you in Sivishe?"

"They are unpredictable. But I'm as safe in Sivishe as anywhere else. I can't go back to the Ancient Realm. They won't seek me at the shed unless Woudiver betrays the project."

"Woudiver must be controlled," said Reith.

Anacho only grunted. They set off once more, through the mean alleys of Sivishe.

The sun passed behind the spires of Hei and dimness seeped into the already shadowed streets. Reith and Anacho rode by public power-wagon to the shed. Woudiver's office was dark; within the shed dim lights glimmered. The mechanics had gone home; there seemed to be no one on the premises . . . In the shadows a figure moved. "Traz!" cried Reith.

The lad came forward. "I knew that you would come here, if you won free."

Neither the nomads nor the Dirdirmen were given to demonstration; Anacho and Traz merely took note of each other.

"Best that we leave this place," said Traz. "And quickly."

"I said to Anacho, I say to you: take the sky-car and go. There is no reason for you to risk another day in Sivishe."

"And what about you?"

"I must take my chances here."

"The chances are very small, what with Woudiver and his vindictiveness."

"I will control Woudiver."

"An impossibility!" Anacho cried out. "Who can control such perversity, so much monstrous passion? He is beyond reason."

Reith nodded somberly. "There is only one certain way, and it may be difficult."

"How do you intend this miracle?" Anacho demanded.

"I intend simply to take him at gunpoint, and bring him here. If he will not come, I will kill him. If he comes, he will be my captive, under constant guard. I can think of nothing better."

Anacho grunted. "I would not object to guarding Big Yellow."

"The time to act is now," said Traz. "Before he knows of the escape."

"For you two, no!" Reith declared. "If I get killed . . . too bad but unavoidable. It is a risk I have to take. Not so for you. Take the sky-car and money, leave now while you are able!"

"I remain," said Traz.

"And I as well," said Anacho.

Reith made a gesture of defeat. "Let's go after Woudiver."

18

THE THREE STOOD in the dark court outside Woudiver's apartments, judging how best to open the postern. "We don't dare force the lock," muttered Anacho. "Woudiver undoubtedly guards himself with alarms and death-traps."

"We'll have to go over the top," said Reith. "It shouldn't be too hard to reach the roof." He studied the wall, the cracked tile, a twisted old psilla. "Nothing to it." He pointed. "Up there—across to there—then there and over."

Anacho shook his head gloomily. "I'm surprised to find you still so innocent. Why do you think the route appears so simple! Because Woudiver is convinced no one can climb? You'd find strings, traps and jangle-buttons every place you put your hand."

Reith chewed his lip in mortification. "Well, then, how do you propose we get in?"

"Not through here," said Anacho. "We must defeat Woudiver's craft with cleverness of our own."

Traz made a sudden motion, and drew the other two back into the deep shadows of an area-way.

Along the alley came a shuffle of footsteps. A tall thin shape limped past them and went to stand by the postern. Traz whispered: "Deine Zarre! He's in a bitter state."

Deine Zarre stood motionless; he brought forth a tool and worked on the lock. The postern swung open; he walked through, his pace inexorable as doom. Reith sprang forward and held the gate ajar. Deine Zarre limped on unseeing. Traz and Anacho passed through the postern; Reith let the gate rest against the lock. They now stood in a paved loggia, with a dimly lit passage leading to the main bulk of the house. "For the moment," said Reith, "you two wait here; let me confront Woudiver alone."

"You'll be in great danger," said Anacho. "It's obvious that you came for no good!"

"Not necessarily!" said Reith. "He will be suspicious, certainly. But he can't know that I've seen you. If he sees the three of us he'll be on his guard. Alone, I have a better chance of outwitting him."

"Very well," said Anacho. "We'll wait here, for a certain period, at any rate. Then we'll come in after you."

"Give me fifteen minutes." Reith set off down the passage, which opened into a courtyard. Across, in front of a brassbound door, stood Deine Zarre, plying his tool. Light suddenly flooded the courtyard. Deine Zarre had apparently tripped an alarm.

Into the courtyard stepped Artilo. "Zarre," he said.

Deine Zarre turned about.

"What do you do here?" Artilo asked in a gentle voice.

"It is no concern of yours," said Deine Zarre tonelessly. "Leave me be."

With an uncharacteristic flourish, Artilo brought forth a power-gun. "I have been so ordered. Prepare to die."

Reith stepped quickly forward, but the motion of Deine Zarre's eyes gave warning to Artilo; he started to look about. With two long strides, Reith was on him. He struck a terrible blow at the base of Artilo's skull, and Artilo collapsed dead. Reith took up the power-gun, rolled Artilo to the side. Deine Zarre was already turning away, as if the circumstances held no interest.

Reith said, "Wait!"

Deine Zarre turned around once more. Reith came forward. Deine Zarre's gray eyes were astonishingly clear. Reith asked, "Why are you here?"

"To kill Woudiver. He has savaged my children." Deine Zarre's voice was calm and expository. "They are dead, both dead, and gone from this sad world Tschai."

Reith's voice sounded muffled and distant to his own ears.

"Woudiver must be destroyed . . . but not until the ship is complete."

"He will never let you complete the ship."

"That is why I am here."

"What can you do?" Deine Zarre spoke contemptuously.

"I intend to take him captive, and keep him until the ship is finished. Then you may kill him."

"Very well," said Deine Zarre in a dull voice. "Why not? I will make him suffer."

"As you please. You go ahead, I will come close behind, as before. When we find Woudiver, upbraid him, but offer no violence. We don't want to drive him to desperate action."

Deine Zarre turned without a word. He worked open the door, to reveal a room furnished in scarlet and yellow. Deine Zarre entered, and after a quick look over his shoulder Reith followed. A dwarfish, dark-skinned servant in an enormous white turban stood startled.

"Where is Aila Woudiver?" asked Deine Zarre in his most gentle voice.

The servant became haughty. "He is importantly busy. He has great dealings. He cannot be disturbed."

Seizing the servant by the scruff of the neck Reith half raised him off the ground, dislodging the turban. The servant keened in pain and wounded dignity. "What are you doing? Take your hands away or I will summon my master!"

"Precisely what we want you to do," said Reith.

The servant stood back, rubbing his neck and glaring at Reith. "Leave the house at once!"

"Take us to Woudiver, if you want to avoid trouble!"

The servant began to whine. "I may not do so. He'll have me whipped!"

"Look yonder in the courtyard," said Deine Zarre. "You'll see Artilo's dead body. Do you wish to join him?"

The servant began to shake and fell on his knees. Reith hoisted him erect. "Quick now! To Woudiver!"

"You must tell him I was forced, on threat of my life!" cried the servant with chattering teeth. "Then you must swear—"

The portiere at the far end of the room parted. The great face of Aila Woudiver peered through. "What is this disturbance?"

Reith pushed the servant away. "Your man refused to summon you."

Woudiver examined him with the cleverest and most suspicious gaze imaginable. "For good reason, I am occupied with important affairs."

"None so important as mine," said Reith.

"A moment," said Woudiver. He turned, spoke a word or two to his visitors, swaggered back into the scarlet and yellow salon. "You have the money?"

"Yes, of course. Would I be here otherwise?"

For another long moment Woudiver surveyed Reith. "Where is the money?"

"In a safe place."

Woudiver chewed at his pendulous lower lip. "Do not use that tone with me. To be candid, I suspect you of contriving an infamy, that which today allowed the escape of numerous criminals from the Glass Box."

Reith chuckled. "Tell me, if you please, how I could be two places at once?"

"If you were in a single place, that is enough to damn you. A man corresponding to your description lowered himself to the field only an hour before the event. He would not have done so had he not been sure of escape. It is noteworthy that the renegade Dirdirman seemed to be among those missing."

Deine Zarre spoke: "The battarache came from your store; you will be held responsible if I should utter a word."

Woudiver seemed to notice Deine Zarre for the first time. In simulated surprise he spoke. "What do you do here, old man? Better be off about your business."

"I came to kill you," said Deine Zarre. "Reith asked that I wait."

"Come along, Woudiver," said Reith. "The game is over." He displayed his weapon. "Quickly, or I'll burn some of your hide."

Woudiver looked from one to the other without apparent concern. "Do the mice bare their teeth?"

Reith, from long experience, knew enough to expect wrangling, obstinacy, and generally perverse behavior. In a resigned voice he said, "Come along, Woudiver."

Woudiver smiled. "Two ridiculous little sub-men." He raised his voice a trifle. "Artilo!"

"Artilo is dead," said Deine Zarre. He looked right and left in something like puzzlement. Woudiver watched him blandly. "You seek something?"

Deine Zarre, ignoring Woudiver, muttered to Reith, "He is too easy, even for Woudiver. Take care."

Reith said in a sharp voice, "On the count of five, I'll burn you."

"First, a question," said Woudiver. "Where do we go?"

Reith ignored him. "One . . . two . . ."

Woudiver sighed hugely. "You fail to amuse me."

". . . three . . ."

"Somehow I must protect myself . . ."

". . . four . . ."

". . . so much is clear." Woudiver backed against the wall. The velvet canopy instantly slumped on Reith and Deine Zarre.

Reith fired the gun but the folds struck down his arm, and the ray scarred only the black and white tiles of the floor.

Woudiver's chuckle sounded muffled but rich and unctuous. The floor vibrated to his ominous tread. A vast weight suffocated Reith; Woudiver had flung himself down upon his body. Reith lay half-dazed. Woudiver's voice sounded close. "So the jackanapes thought to trouble Aila Woudiver? See how he is now!" The weight lifted. "And Deine Zarre, who courteously refrained from assassination. Well then, farewell, Deine Zarre. I am more decisive."

A sound, a sad sodden gurgle and then a scraping of fingernails upon the tiles.

"Adam Reith," said the voice. "You are a peculiar mad case. I am interested in your intentions. Drop the gun, put your arms to the front and do not move. Do you feel the weight on your neck? That is my foot. Quick then, arms forward, and no sudden motions. Hisziu, make ready."

The folds were pulled back, away from Reith's extended arms. Nimble dark fingers bound his wrists with silk ribbon.

The velvet was further drawn back. Reith, still somewhat dazed, looked up at the spraddle-legged bulk. Hisziu the servant skipped back and forth, around and under, like a puppy.

Woudiver hoisted Reith erect. "Walk, if you will." He sent Reith stumbling with a shove.

19

IN A DARK room, against a metal rack, stood Reith. His out-stretched arms were taped to a transverse bar; his ankles were likewise secured. No light entered the room save the glimmer of a few stars through a narrow window. Hisziu the servant crouched four feet in front of him, with a light whip of braided silk, little more than a length of supple cord attached to a short handle. He seemed able to see in the dark and amused himself by snapping the tip of the whip, at unpredictable intervals, upon Reith's wrists, knees and chin. He spoke only once. "Your two friends have been taken. They are no better than you: worse, indeed. Woudiver works with them."

Reith stood limp, his thoughts sluggish and dismal. Disaster was complete; he was conscious of nothing else. The malicious little snaps of Hisziu's whip barely brushed the edge of his awareness. His existence was coming to an end, to be no more remarked than the fall of a raindrop into one of Tschai's sullen oceans. Somewhere out of sight the blue moon rose, casting a sheen across the sky. The slow waxing and equally slow waning of moonlight told the passing of the night.

Hisziu fell into a drowse and snored softly. Reith was indifferent. He raised his head, looked out of the window. The shimmer of moonlight was gone; a muddy color towards the east signaled the coming of Carina 4269. Hisziu awoke with a start, and flicked the whip petulantly at Reith's cheeks, raising instant blood-blisters. He left the chamber and a moment later returned with a mug of hot tea, which he sipped by the window. Reith croaked: "I'll pay you ten thousand sequins to cut me loose."

Hisziu paid him no heed.

Reith said, "And another ten thousand if you help me free my friends."

The servant sipped the tea as if Reith had never spoken.

The sky glowed dark gold; Carina 4269 had appeared. Steps sounded; Woudiver's bulk filled the doorway. A moment he stood quietly, assessing the situation, then, seizing the whip, he gestured Hisziu from the room.

Woudiver seemed exalted, as if drugged or drunk. He slapped the whip against his thigh. "I can't find the money, Adam Reith. Where is it?"

Reith attempted to speak in a casual voice. "What are your plans?"

Woudiver raised his hairless eyebrows. "I have no plans. Events proceed; I exist as well as I may."

"Why do you keep me tied here?"

Aila Woudiver slapped the whip against his leg. "I have naturally notified my kinsmen of your apprehension."

"The Dirdir?"

"Of course." Woudiver gave his thigh a rap with the whip.

Reith spoke with great earnestness. "The Dirdir are no kinsmen of yours! Dirdir and men are not even remotely connected; they come from different stars."

Woudiver leaned indolently against the wall. "Where do you learn such idiocy?"

Reith licked his lips, wondering where lay his best hope of succor. Woudiver was not a rational man; he was motivated by instinct and intuition. Reith tried to project utter certainty as he spoke. "Men originated on the planet Earth. The Dirdir know this as well as I. They prefer that Dirdirmen deceive themselves."

Woudiver nodded thoughtfully. "You intend to seek out this 'Earth' with your spaceship?"

"I don't need to seek it out. It lies two hundred light-years distant, in the constellation Clari."

Woudiver pranced forward. With his yellow face a foot from Reith's he bellowed, "And what of the treasure you promised me? You misled, you deceived!"

"No," said Reith. "I did not. I am an Earthman. I was shipwrecked here on Tschai. Help me back to Earth; you will receive whatever treasure you care to name."

Woudiver backed slowly away. "You are one of the Yao redemptionist cult, whatever it calls itself."

"No. I am telling the truth. Your best interest lies in helping me."

Woudiver nodded sagely. "Perhaps this is the case. But first things first. You can easily demonstrate your good faith. Where is my money?"

"*Your* money? It is not your money. It is my money."

"A sterile distinction. Where is, shall we say, *our* money?"

"You'll never see it unless you perform your obligations."

"This is utter obstinacy!" stormed Woudiver. "You are captured, you are done, and your henchmen as well. The Dirdirman must return to the Glass Cage. The steppe-boy will be sold into slavery—unless you care to buy his life with the money."

Reith sagged and became listless. Woudiver strutted back and forth across the room, darting glances at Reith. He came close and prodded Reith in the stomach with the whip. "Where is the money?"

"I don't trust you," said Reith in a dreary voice. "You never keep your promises." With a great effort, he lifted himself erect and tried to speak in a calm voice. "If you want the money, let me go free. The spaceship is almost finished. You may come along to Earth."

Woudiver's face was inscrutable. "And then?"

"A space-yacht, a palace—whatever you want. You shall have it."

"And how shall I return to Sivishe?" demanded Woudiver scornfully. "What of my affairs? It is plain that you are mad; why do you waste my time? Where is the money? The Dirdirman and the steppe-lad have declared with conviction that they do not know."

"I don't know either. I gave it to Deine Zarre and told him to hide it. You killed him."

Woudiver stifled a groan of dismay. "My money?"

"Tell me," said Reith, "do you intend that I finish the spaceship?"

"It has never been my intention!"

"You defrauded me?"

"Why not? You tried the same. The man that beats Aila Woudiver is cunning indeed."

"No question as to that."

Hisziu entered the room and, standing on tiptoe, whispered into Woudiver's ear. Woudiver stamped with rage. "So soon? They are early! I have not even started." He turned to Reith, his face seething like water in a boiling pot. "Quick then, the money, or I sell the lad. Quick!"

"Let us go! Help us finish the spaceship. Then you shall have your money!"

"You unreasonable ingrate!" hissed Woudiver. Footsteps sounded. "I am thwarted!" he groaned. "What a sad life is mine. Vermin!" Woudiver spat into Reith's face and beat him furiously with the whip.

Into the room, proudly conducted by Hisziu, came a tall Dirdirman, the most splendid and strange Reith had yet seen: by all odds an Immaculate. Woudiver muttered to Hisziu from the side of his mouth; Reith's bonds were cut. The Dirdirman attached a chain to Reith's neck, clasped the other end to his belt. Without a word he walked away, shaking his fingers in fastidious disdain.

Reith stumbled after.

20

BEFORE WOUDIVER'S HOUSE stood a white-enameled car. The Immaculate snapped Reith's chain to a ring at the rear. Reith watched in dreary wonder. The Immaculate stood almost seven feet tall, with artificial effulgences attached to wens at either side of his peaked scalp. His skin gleamed white as the enamel of the car; his head was totally hairless; his nose was a ridged beak. For all his strange appearance and undoubtedly altered sexuality, he was a man, ruminated Reith, derived from the same soil as himself. From the house, at a quick stumble, as if shoved, came Anacho and Traz. Chains encircled their necks; behind, jerking the loose ends, ran Hisziu. Two Dirdirman Elites followed. They shackled the chains to the back of the car. The Immaculate spoke a few sibilant words to Anacho and indicated a shelf running across the rear of the car. Without looking back, he stepped into the car, where the two Elites already sat. Anacho muttered, "Climb aboard, otherwise we'll be dragged."

The three crawled up on the rear shelf, clutched the rings to which their neck chains were shackled. In such undignified fashion they departed Woudiver's residence. Woudiver's black saloon trundled fifty yards behind, with Woudiver's huge bulk crouched over the steering apparatus.

"He wants recognition," said Anacho. "He has assisted at an important hunt; he wants a share of the status."

"I made the mistake," said Reith in a thick voice, "of dealing with Woudiver as if he were a man. If I had treated him as an animal we might be better off."

"We could hardly be worse."

"Where are we going?"

"To the Glass Box; where else?"

"We are to have no hearing, no opportunity to speak for ourselves?"

"Naturally not," said Anacho curtly. "You are sub-men. I am a renegade."

The white car veered into a plaza and halted. The Dirdirmen alighted and stood stiffly apart, watching the sky. A plump, middle-aged man in a rich dark brown suit came forward: a person of status and evident vanity, with his hair elaborately curled and jeweled. He addressed the Dirdirmen in an easy manner; they replied after a moment's meaningful silence.

"That is Erlius, Administrator of Sivishe," grunted Anacho. "He wants to be in at the kill too. It seems that we are important game."

Attracted by the activity, the folk of Sivishe began to gather around the white car. They formed a wide respectful circle, eyeing the captives with macabre speculation, crouching back whenever the glance of a Dirdirman drifted in their direction.

Woudiver remained in his car, at a distance of fifty yards or so, apparently arranging his thoughts. At last he alighted and seemed to concern himself with the matter indited on a fold of paper. Erlius, noticing, quickly turned his back.

"Look at the two of them," growled Anacho. "Each hates the other: Woudiver ridicules Erlius for lacking Dirdirman blood; Erlius would like to see Woudiver in the Glass Box."

"So would I," said Reith. "Speaking of the Glass Box, why are we waiting?"

"For the leaders of the *tsau'gsh*. You will see the Glass Box soon enough."

Reith fretfully wrenched at the chain. The Dirdirmen turned him glances of admonition. "Ridiculous," muttered Reith. "There must be something we can do. What of the Dirdir traditions? What if I cried *h'sai h'sai, h'sai,* or whatever the call for arbitration?"

"The call is *dr'ssa dr'ssa, dr'ssa!*"

"What would happen if I called for arbitration?"

"You would be no better than before. The arbitrator would find you guilty and, as before: the Glass Box."

"And if I challenged the arbitration?"

"You'd be forced to fight, and killed all the sooner."

"And no one can be taken unless he is accused?"

"In theory," said Anacho curtly, "that is the custom. Who do you plan to challenge? Woudiver? It will do no good. He has not accused you, but only cooperated with the hunt."

"We will see."

Traz pointed into the sky. "Here come the Dirdir."

Anacho studied the descending sky-car. "The Thisz crest. If the Thisz are involved, we can expect brisk treatment indeed. They may even issue a proscription, that none but Thisz can hunt us."

Traz strained against the chain shackle without avail. He gave a hiss of frustration and turned to watch the descending sky-car. The gray-hooded crowd drew back from underneath; the sky-car landed not fifty feet from the white vehicle. Five Dirdir alighted: an Excellent and four of lower caste.

The Immaculate Dirdirman stepped grandly forward, but the Dirdir ignored him with the same indifference he had shown Erlius.

For a moment or two the Dirdir appraised Reith, Anacho and Traz. Then they made a signal to the Immaculate and uttered a few brief sounds.

Erlius stepped forward to pay his respects, knees bent, head bobbing. Before he could speak Woudiver marched forward and thrust his vast yellow bulk in front of Erlius, who was forced to stumble aside.

Woudiver spoke in a high-pitched voice: "Here, Thisz dignitaries, are the criminals sought by the hunt. I have participated to no small degree; let this be noted upon my scroll of honors!"

The Dirdir gave him only cursory attention. Woudiver, apparently expecting no more, bowed his head, swung his arms in an elaborate flourish.

The Immaculate approached the captives and unsnapped the chains. Reith snatched his chain free. The Immaculate looked up in slack-jawed surprise, the false effulgences drooping to the side of his white face. Reith walked forward, heart pounding in his throat. He felt the pressure of every eye; with great effort he held his gait to a steady, deliberate step. Six feet in front of the Dirdir he halted, so close that he could smell their body odor. They regarded him without display of any kind.

Reith raised his voice in order to speak clearly: *"Dr'ssa! Dr'ssa! Dr'ssa!"*

The Dirdir made small movements of surprise.

"Dr'ssa! Dr'ssa! Dr'ssa!" Reith called once more.

The Excellent spoke in a nasal, oboe-sounding voice. "Why

do you cry *dr'ssa?* You are a sub-man, incapable of discrimination."

"I am a man, your superior. Hence I cry *dr'ssa.*"

Woudiver pushed forward with a self-important huffing and heaving. "Bah! He is mad!"

The Dirdir seemed somewhat perplexed. Reith called out, "Who accuses me? Of what crime? Let him come forward and let the case be judged by an arbitrator."

The Excellent spoke: "You invoke a traditional force stronger than contempt or disgust. You may not be denied. Who accuses this sub-man?"

Woudiver spoke. "I accuse Adam Reith of blasphemy, of disputing the Doctrine of Double Genesis, of claiming status equal to the Dirdir. He has stated that Dirdirmen are not the pure line of the Second Yolk; he has called them a race of mutated freaks. He insists that men derive from a planet other than Sibol. This is not in accord with orthodox doctrine, and is repugnant. He is a mischief-maker, a liar, a provocator." Woudiver accented each of his accusations with a stab of his massive forefinger. "Such are my charges!" He favored the Dirdir with a companionable smirk, then turned and roared at the crowd. "Stand back! Do not press so close upon the dignitaries!"

The Dirdir fluted to Reith. "You claim this accusation to be false?"

Reith stood in perplexity. He faced a dilemma. To deny the charge was to endorse Dirdirman orthodoxy. He asked cautiously, "Essentially, I am accused of unorthodox views. Is this a crime?"

"Certainly, if the arbitrator declares it so."

"What if these views are accurate?"

"Then you must hold the arbitrator to account. Ridiculous as such an eventuality may be, it is tradition and wields its own force."

"Who is the arbitrator?"

The polished bone countenance of the Excellent showed no change, nor did his voice. "In this instance I appoint the Immaculate yonder."

The Immaculate stepped forward. In plangent mock-Dirdir tones he spoke: "I will be expeditious; the ordinary ceremonies are inappropriate." He spoke to Reith. "Do you deny the charges?"

"I neither confirm nor deny them; they are ridiculous."

"It is my opinion that your statement is evasive. It signifies guilt. Additionally your attitudes are disrespectful. You are guilty."

"I refuse to accept your verdict," said Reith, "unless you can enforce it. I hold you to account."

The Immaculate regarded Reith with scorn and revulsion. "You challenge me, an Immaculate?"

"It seems to be the only way I can prove my innocence."

The Immaculate looked at the Dirdir Excellent. "Am I so obligated?"

"You are so obligated."

The Immaculate measured Reith. "I will kill you with my hands and teeth as befits a Dirdirman."

"As you please. First, remove this chain from my neck."

"Remove the chain," said the Dirdir Excellent.

The Immaculate said fretfully, "Vulgarity! I lose dignity performing before a gaggle of sub-men."

"Do not complain," said the Excellent. "It is I, Captain of the Hunt, who loses a trophy. Continue; enforce your arbitration."

The chain was removed. Reith stretched, relaxed, stretched, relaxed, hoping to restore tone to his muscles. He had hung all night by his wrists, his body felt heavy with fatigue. The Dirdirman stepped forward. Reith became a trifle light-headed.

"What are the rules of combat?" asked Reith. "I do not wish to commit any fouls upon you."

"There are no fouls," said the Immaculate. "We use hunt rules: you are the game!" He uttered a wild screech and launched himself upon Reith, in what seemed an ineffectual sprawl, until Reith touched the creature's white body and found it all tense muscle and gristle. Reith fended aside the rush, but was ripped by artificial talons. He attempted an armlock, but could not secure a leverage. He struck the Immaculate a blow under the ear, tried to hack the larynx and missed. The Immaculate stood back in annoyance. The spectators gasped in excitement. The Immaculate again launched himself upon Reith, who caught the long forearm and sent the Dirdirman staggering. Woudiver could not contain himself; he rushed out and struck Reith a buffet across the side of his head. Traz yelled in protest and whipped his chain across Woudiver's face. Woudiver screamed in agony and sat squashily upon the ground. Anacho wrapped his chain around

Woudiver's neck and yanked it tight. The Elite Dirdirman leaped forward, snatched away the chain. Woudiver lay gasping, his face the color of mud.

The Immaculate had taken advantage of Woudiver's attack to seize Reith and bear him to the ground. The wire-tense arms clasped Reith's body; sharp long teeth tore at his neck. Reith freed his arms. With all his force he clapped his cupped hands upon the white ears. The Immaculate emitted a strangled squeal and rolled his head in agony. Momentarily he went limp. Reith straddled the thin body, as if he rode a white eel. He began to work at the bald head. He tore away the false effulgences, teased the head this way and that, then gave a great twist. The Immaculate's head hung askew; his body thrashed and floundered, then lay still.

Reith rose to his feet. He stood shaking and panting. "I am vindicated," he said.

"The charges of the fat sub-man are invalid," intoned the Excellent. "He may therefore be held to account."

Reith turned away. "Halt!" said the Excellent, its voice taking on a throaty vibrato. "Are there further charges?"

A Dirdir of the Elite caste, effulgences rigid and sparkling with crystal coruscations, spoke: "Does the beast still call *dr'ssa?*"

Reith swung around, half-intoxicated by fatigue and the aftermath of struggle. "I am a man, you are the beast."

"Do you demand arbitration?" the Excellent asked. "If not, let us be away."

Reith's heart sank. "What are the new charges?"

The Elite stepped forward. "I charge that you and your henchmen trespassed upon the Dirdir Hunting Preserve and there treacherously slaughtered members of the Thisz Sept."

"I deny the charge," said Reith in a hoarse voice.

The Elite turned to the Excellent. "I request that you arbitrate. I request that you give me this beast and his henchmen and mark him exclusive quarry of the Thisz."

"I accept the onus of arbitration," fluted the Excellent. To Reith, in a tone nasal and coarse: "You trespassed in the Carabas, this is true."

"I entered the Carabas. No one ordered me not to do so."

"The proscription is general knowledge. You furtively assaulted several Dirdir; this is true."

"I assaulted no one who did not attack me first. If the Dirdir

wish to act like wild beasts then they must suffer the consequences."

From the crowd came a murmur of wonder and what seemed
muted approval. The Excellent turned to glance around the
plaza. Instantly the sound was muted.

"It is Dirdir tradition to hunt. It is sub-man tradition and his
essential character to serve as quarry."

"I am no sub-man," said Reith. "I am a man and quarry to no
one. If a wild beast attacks me I will kill it."

The bone-white face of the Excellent showed no quiver of feeling. But the effulgences began to glow, and to become rigid. "The
verdict must adhere to tradition," the creature intoned. "I find
against the sub-man. This farrago is now at an end. You must be
taken to the Glass Cage."

"I challenge the arbitration!" cried Reith. Stepping forward,
he buffeted the Excellent on the side of the head. The skin was
cold and somewhat flexible, like tortoiseshell; Reith's hand stung
from the blow. The Excellent's effulgences stood like hot wires; it
vented a thin whistle. The crowd stood in unbelieving silence.

The Excellent reached its great arms to the front in a clutching,
ripping gesture. It vented a gurgling scream and poised to leap.

"A moment," said Reith, stepping back. "What are the rules
of combat?"

"There are no rules. I kill as I choose."

"And if I kill you, I am vindicated, and my friends as well?"

"That is the case."

"Let us fight with swords."

"We will fight as we stand."

"Very well," said Reith.

The fight was no contest. The Excellent came forward, swift and
massive as a tiger. Reith took two quick steps back; the Excellent
launched itself. Reith seized the horny wrist, planted a foot in the
torso; falling backwards he threw the creature in a sprawling
somersault. It landed on its neck, to lie in a daze. Instantly Reith
was upon it, locking the taloned arms. The Excellent writhed and
thrashed; Reith banged its head against the pavement until the
bone cracked and whitish-green ichor began to exude. He
panted: "What of the arbitration? Was it right or wrong?"

The Excellent keened—a weird wailing sound, expressing no
emotion known to human experience. Reith banged down the

harsh white head again and again. "What of the arbitration?" He slammed the head against the pavement. The Dirdir made a great effort to dislodge Reith and failed. "You are the victor. My arbitration is refuted."

"And I, with my friends, are now held guiltless? We may pursue our activities without persecution?"

"This is the case."

Reith called to Anacho, "Can I trust it?"

Anacho said, "Yes, it is tradition. If you want a trophy, pluck out his effulgences."

"I want no trophy." Reith rose to his feet and stood swaying.

The crowd regarded him with awe. Erlius turned on his heel and strode hastily away. Aila Woudiver backed slowly toward his black car.

Reith pointed a finger: "Woudiver—your charges were false and you now must answer to me."

Woudiver snatched out his power-gun: Traz leaped forward, hung on the vast wrist. The gun discharged, scorching Woudiver's leg. He bawled in agony and fell to the ground. Anacho took the gun; Reith tied one of the chains around Woudiver's neck and gave it a harsh tug. "Come, Woudiver." He led the way to the black car, through the hastily retreating onlookers.

Woudiver hulked himself within and lay groaning in a heap. Anacho started the vehicle and they departed the oval plaza.

21

THEY DROVE TO the shed. The technicians, in the absence of Deine Zarre, had not reported for work. The shed felt dead and abandoned; the space-boat, which had seemed on the verge of coming alive, lay desolate on its chocks.

The three marshaled Woudiver within, as they might lead a cantankerous bull, and tied him between two posts, Woudiver making a continual moaning complaint.

Reith watched him a moment. Woudiver was not yet expendable. Certainly he was still dangerous. For all his display and expostulation, he watched Reith with a clever and hard gaze.

"Woudiver," said Reith, "you have worked great harm upon me."

Woudiver's great body became racked with sobbing; he seemed a monstrous and ugly baby. "You plan to torment me, and kill me."

"The thought has presented itself," Reith admitted. "But I have more urgent desires. To finish the ship and return to Earth with news of this hellish planet I would even forgo the pleasure of your death."

"In that case," said Woudiver, suddenly businesslike, "all is as before. Pay over the money, and we will proceed."

Reith's jaw hung in disbelief. He laughed in admiration for Woudiver's wonderful insouciance.

Anacho and Traz were less amused. Anacho poked the great belly with a stick. "What of last night?" he demanded in a suave voice. "Do you recall your conduct? What of the electric probes, and the wicked harness?"

"What of Deine Zarre, the two children?" spoke Traz.

Woudiver looked appealingly toward Reith. "Whose words carry weight?"

Reith chose his words carefully. "All of us have cause for resentment. You would be a fool to expect ease and conviviality."

"Indeed, he shall suffer," said Traz through gritted teeth.

"You shall live," said Reith, "but only to serve our interests. I don't care a bice for your life unless you make yourself useful."

Again in Woudiver's eyes Reith discerned a cold and crafty glint. "So it shall be," said Woudiver.

"I want you to hire a competent replacement for Deine Zarre, at once."

"Expensive, expensive," said Woudiver. "We were lucky in Zarre."

"The responsibility for his absence is yours," said Reith.

"No one goes through life without making mistakes," Woudiver admitted. "This was one of mine. But I know just the man. He will come high, I warn you."

"Money is no object," said Reith. "We want the best. Secondly, I want you to summon the technicians back to work. All by telephone, of course."

"No difficulties whatever," declared Woudiver heartily. "The work will proceed with dispatch."

"You must arrange immediate delivery of the materials and supplies yet needed. And you must pay all costs and salaries incurred henceforth."

"What?" roared Woudiver.

"Further," said Reith, "you will remain tied between those posts. For your sustenance you must pay a thousand—or better, two thousand—sequins each day."

"*What!*" cried Woudiver. "Do you think to cheat and bewilder poor Woudiver?"

"Do you agree to the conditions?" Reith asked. "If not I will ask Anacho and Traz to kill you, and both of them bear you grudges."

Woudiver drew himself to his full height. "I agree," he said in a stately voice. "And now, since it seems that I must sponsor your hallucinations and suffer the backbreaking expense in the bargain, let us instantly get to work. The moment I see you vanish into space will be a happy one, I assure you! Now then, release these chains so that I may go to the telephone."

"Stay where you are," said Reith. "We will bring the telephone to you. And now, where is your money!"

"You can't be serious," Woudiver exclaimed.

THE PNUME

1

IN THE WAREHOUSE at the edge of the Sivishe salt flats Aila Woudiver sat perched on a stool. A chain connected the iron collar around his neck to a high cable; he could walk from his table to the closet against the wall where he slept, the chain sliding behind him.

Aila Woudiver was a prisoner on his own premises, insult added to injury, which by all accounts should have provoked him to spasms of tooth-chattering fury. But he sat placidly on the stool, great buttocks sagging to either side like saddlebags, waring an absurd smile of saintly forbearance.

Beside the spaceship which occupied the greater part of the warehouse Adam Reith stood watching. Woudiver's abnegation was more unsettling than rage. Reith hoped that whatever schemes Woudiver was hatching would not mature too quickly. The spaceship was nearly operative; in a week, more or less, Reith hoped to depart old Tschai.

Woudiver occupied himself with tat-work, now and then holding it up to admire the pattern—the very essence of patient affability. Traz, coming into the warehouse, scowled toward Woudiver and asserted the philosophy of the Emblem nomads, his forebears: "Kill him this moment; kill him and have an end!"

Reith gave an equivocal grunt. "He's chained by the neck; he does us no harm."

"He'll find a means. Have you forgotten his tricks?"

"I can't kill him in cold blood."

Traz gave a croak of disgust and stamped from the warehouse. Anacho the Dirdirman declared, "For once I agree with the young steppe-runner: kill the great beast!"

Woudiver, divining the substance of the conversation, displayed his gentle smile. He had lost weight, so Reith noticed. The once-bloated cheeks hung in wattles; the great upper lip drooped like a beak over the pointed little chin.

"See him smirk!" hissed Anacho. "If he could he'd boil us in nerve-fire! Kill him now!"

Reith made another sound of moderation. "In a week we'll be gone. What can he do, chained and helpless?"

"He is Woudiver!"

"Even so, we can't slaughter him like an animal."

Anacho threw up his hands and followed Traz outside the warehouse. Reith went into the ship and for a few minutes watched the technicians. They worked at the exquisitely delicate job of balancing the power pumps. Reith could offer no assistance. Dirdir technology, like the Dirdir psyche, was beyond his comprehension. Both derived from intuitive certainties, or so he suspected; there was little evidence of purposeful rationality in any aspect of Dirdir existence.

Long shafts of brown light slanted through the high windows; the time was almost sunset. Woudiver thoughtfully put aside his fancy-work. He gave Reith a companionable nod and went off to his little room against the wall, the chain dragging behind him in a rattling half-catenary.

The technicians emerged from the ship as did Fio Haro the master mechanic. All went off to their supper. Reith touched the unlovely hull, pressing his hands against the steel, as if he could not credit its reality. A week—then space and return to Earth! The prospect seemed a dream; Earth had become the world remote and bizarre.

Reith went to the larder for a chunk of black sausage, which he took to the doorway. Carina 4269, low in the sky, bathed the salt flats in ale-colored light, projecting long shadows behind every tussock.

The two black figures which of late had appeared at sunset were nowhere to be seen.

The view held a certain mournful beauty. To the north the city of Sivishe was a crumble of old masonry tinted tawny by the slanting sunlight. West across Ajzan Sound stood the spires of the Dirdir city Hei and, looming above all, the Glass Box.

Reith went to join Traz and Anacho. They sat on a bench tossing pebbles into a puddle: Traz, blunted-featured, taciturn, solid of bone and muscle, Anacho, thin as an eel, six inches taller than Reith, pallid of skin, long and keen of feature, as loquacious as Traz was terse. Traz disapproved of Anacho's airs; Anacho considered Traz crass and undiscriminating. Occasionally, however, they agreed—as now, on the need to destroy Aila Woudiver. Reith, for his own part, felt more concern for the Dirdir. From their spires they could almost look through the portals of the warehouse at the work within. The Dirdir inactivity seemed as unnatural as Aila Woudiver's smile, and to Reith implied a dreadful stealth.

"Why don't they do something?" Reith complained, gnawing at the black sausage. "They must know we're here."

"Impossible to predict Dirdir conduct," Anacho replied. "They have lost interest in you. What are men to them but vermin? They prefer to chivy the Pnume from their burrows. You are no longer the subject of *tsau'gsh**: this is my supposition."

Reith was not wholly reassured. "What of the Phung or Pnume,† whatever they are, that come to watch us? They aren't there for their health." He referred to the two black shapes which had been appearing of late on the salt flats. Always they came to stand against the sunset, gaunt figures wearing black cloaks and wide-brimmed black hats.

"Phung go alone; they are not Phung," said Traz. "Pnume never appear by daylight."

"And never so close to Hei, for fear of the Dirdir," Anacho said. "So, then—they are Pnumekin, or more likely Gzhindra.‡"

On the occasion of their first appearance the creatures stood gazing toward the warehouse until Carina 4269 fell behind the palisades; then they vanished into the gloom. Their interest seemed more than casual; Reith was disturbed by the surveillance but could conceive of no remedy for it.

The next day was blurred by mist and drizzle; the salt flats remained vacant. On the day following, the sun shone once more, and at sundown the dark shapes came to stare toward the shed, again afflicting Reith with disquietude. Surveillance portended unpleasant events: this on Tschai was an axiom of existence.

Carina 4269 hung low. "If they're coming," said Anacho, "now is the time."

---

tsau'gsh: prideful endeavor, unique enterprise, lunge toward glory. An essentially untranslatable concept.

†*Phung:* a man-like indigene of Tschai, given to erratic and reckless behavior.

Pnume: a diffident, tranquil and secretive folk, similar to the Phung but of lesser stature.

‡*Pnumekin:* men associated with the Pnume over a period of tens of thousands of years, with consequent assimilation of Pnume habits and mental processes.

Gzhindra: Pnumekin ejected from the underground world, usually for reason of "boisterous behavior"; wanderers of the surface, agents of the Pnume.

Reith searched the salt flats through his scanscope.* "There's nothing out there but tussocks and swamp-bush. Not even a lizard."

Traz pointed over his shoulder. "There they are."

"Hmmf," said Reith. "I just looked there!" He raised the magnification of the scanscope until the jump of his pulse caused the figures to jerk and bounce. The faces, back-lit, could not be distinguished. "They have hands," said Reith. "They are Pnumekin."

Anacho took the instrument. After a moment he said: "They are Gzhindra: Pnumekin expelled from the tunnels. To trade with the Pnume you must deal through the Gzhindra; the Pnume will never dicker for themselves."

"Why should they come here? We want no dealings with the Pnume."

"But they want dealings with us, or so it seems."

"Perhaps they're waiting for Woudiver to appear," Traz suggested.

"At sunset and sunset alone?"

To Traz came a sudden thought. He moved away from the warehouse and somewhat past Woudiver's old office, an eccentric little shack of broken brick and flints, and looked back toward the warehouse. He walked a hundred yards further, out upon the salt flats, and again looked back. He gestured to Reith and Anacho, who went out to join him. "Observe the warehouse," said Traz. "You'll now see who deals with the Gzhindra."

From the black timber wall a glint of golden light jumped and flickered.

"Behind that light," said Traz, "is Aila Woudiver's room."

"The fat yellow shulk is signaling!" declared Anacho in a fervent whisper.

Reith drew a deep breath and controlled his fury: foolish to expect anything else from Woudiver, who lived with intrigue as a fish lives with water. In a measured voice he spoke to Anacho: "Can you read the signals?"

"Yes; ordinary stop-and-go code. '... Suitable ... compensation ... for ... services ... time ... is ... now ... at ... hand ...'" The flickering light vanished. "That's all."

---

*Scanscope: photo-multiplying binoculars.

"He's seen us through the crack," Reith muttered.

"Or he has no more light," said Traz, for Carina 4269 had dropped behind the palisades. Looking across the salt flats, Reith found that the Gzhindra had gone as mysteriously as they had come.

"We had better go talk to Woudiver," said Reith.

"He'll tell anything but the truth," said Anacho.

"I expect as much," said Reith. "We may be informed by what he doesn't tell us."

They went into the shed. Woudiver, once again busy with his tat-work, showed the three his affable smile. "It must be close to suppertime."

"Not for you," said Reith.

"What?" exclaimed Woudiver. "No food? Come now; let us not carry our little joke too far."

"Why do you signal the Gzhindra?"

Beyond a lifting of the hairless eyebrows, Woudiver evinced neither surprise nor guilt. "A business affair. I occasionally deal with the under-folk."

"What sort of dealings?"

"This and that, one thing and another. Tonight I apologized for failing to meet certain commitments. Do you begrudge me my good reputation?"

"What commitments did you fail to meet?"

"Come now," chided Woudiver. "You must allow my few little secrets."

"I allow you nothing," said Reith. "I'm well aware that you plot mischief."

"Bah! What a canard! How should I plot anything trussed up by a chain? I assure you that I do not regard my present condition as dignified."

"If anything goes wrong," said Reith, "you'll be hoisted six feet off the ground by the same chain. You'll have no dignity whatever."

Woudiver made a gesture of waggish distaste and looked off across the room. "Excellent progress seems to have been made."

"No thanks to you."

"Ah! You minimize my aid! Who provided the hull, at great pains and small profit? Who arranged and organized, who supplied invaluable acumen?"

"The same man that took all our money and betrayed us into

the Glass Box," said Reith. He went to sit across the room. Traz and Anacho joined him. The three watched Woudiver, now sulking in the absence of his supper.

"We should kill him," Traz said flatly. "He plans evil for all of us."

"I don't doubt that," said Reith, "but why should he deal with the Pnume? The Dirdir would seem the parties most concerned. They know I'm an Earthman; they may or may not be aware of the spaceship."

"If they know they don't care," said Anacho. "They have no interest in other folk. The Pnume: another matter. They would know everything, and they are most curious regarding the Dirdir. The Dirdir in turn discover the Pnume tunnels and flood them with gas."

Woudiver called out: "You have forgotten my supper."

"I've forgotten nothing," said Reith.

"Well, then, bring forth my food. Tonight I wish a whiteroot salad, a stew of lentils, gargan-flesh and slue, a plate of good black cheese, and my usual wine."

Traz gave a bark of scornful laughter. Reith inquired, "Why should we coddle your gut when you plot against us? Order your meals from the Gzhindra."

Woudiver's face sagged; he beat his hands upon his knees. "So now they torture poor Aila Woudiver, who was only constant to his faith! What a miserable destiny to live and suffer on this terrible planet!"

Reith turned away in disgust. By birth half-Dirdirman, Woudiver vigorously affirmed the Doctrine of Bifold Genesis, which traced the origin of Dirdir and Dirdirman to twin cells in a Primeval Egg on the planet Sibol. From such a viewpoint Reith must seem an irresponsible iconoclast, to be thwarted at all costs.

On the other hand, Woudiver's crimes could not all be ascribed to doctrinal ardor. Recalling certain instances of lechery and self-indulgence, Reith's twinges of pity disappeared.

For five minutes longer Woudiver groaned and complained, and then became suddenly quiet. For a period he watched Reith and his companions. He spoke and Reith thought to detect a secret glee. "Your project approaches completion—thanks to Aila Woudiver, his craft, and his poor store of sequins, unfeelingly sequestered."

"I agree that the project approaches completion," said Reith.

"When do you propose to depart Tschai?"

"As soon as possible."

"Remarkable!" declared Woudiver with unctuous fervor. Reith thought that his eyes sparkled with amusement. "But then, you are a remarkable man." Woudiver's voice took on a sudden resonance, as if he could no longer restrain his inner mirth. "Still, on occasion it is better to be modest and ordinary! What do you think of that?"

"I don't know what you're talking about."

"True," said Woudiver. "That is correct."

"Since you feel disposed for conversation," said Reith, "why not tell me something about the Gzhindra."

"What is there to tell? They are sad creatures, doomed to trudge the surface, though they stand in fear of the open. Have you ever wondered why Pnume, Pnumekin, Phung and Gzhindra all wear hats with broad brims?"

"I suppose that it is their habit of dress."

"True. But the deeper reason is: the brims hide the sky."

"What impels these particular Gzhindra out under the sky which oppresses them?"

"Like all men," said Woudiver, somewhat pompously, "they hope, they yearn."

"In what precise regard?"

"In any absolute or ultimate sense," said Woudiver, "I am of course ignorant; all men are mysteries. Even you perplex me, Adam Reith! You harry me with capricious cruelty; you pour my money into an insane scheme; you ignore every protest, every plea of moderation! Why? I ask myself, why? Why? If it were not all so preposterous, I could indeed believe you a man of another world."

"You still haven't told me what the Gzhindra want," said Reith.

With vast dignity Woudiver rose to his feet; the chain from the iron collar swung and jangled. "You had best take up this matter with the Gzhindra themselves."

He went to his table and after a final cryptic glance toward Reith took up his tatting.

2

REITH TWITCHED AND trembled in a nightmare. He dreamt that he lay on his usual couch in Woudiver's old office. The room was pervaded by a curious yellow-green glow. Woudiver stood across the room chatting with a pair of motionless men in black capes and broad-brimmed black hats. Reith strained to move, but his muscles were limp. The yellow-green light waxed and waned; Woudiver was now frosted with an uncanny silver-blue incandescence. The typical nightmare of helplessness and futility, thought Reith. He made desperate efforts to awake but only started a clammy sweat.

Woudiver and the Gzhindra gazed down at him. Woudiver surprisingly wore his iron collar, but the chain had been broken or melted a foot from his neck. He seemed complacent and unconcerned: the Woudiver of old. The Gzhindra showed no expression other than intentness. Their features were long, narrow and very regular; their skin, pallid ivory, shone with the luster of silk. One carried a folded cloth; the other stood with hands behind his back.

Woudiver suddenly loomed enormous. He called out: "Adam Reith, Adam Reith: where is your home?"

Reith struggled against his impotence. A weird and desolate dream, one that he would long remember. "The planet Earth," he croaked. "The planet Earth."

Woudiver's face expanded and contracted. "Are other Earthmen on Tschai?"

"Yes."

The Gzhindra jerked forward; Woudiver called in a horn-like voice: "Where? Where are the Earthmen?"

"All men are Earthmen."

Woudiver stood back, mouth drooping in saturnine disgust. "You were born on the planet Earth."

"Yes."

Woudiver floated back in triumph. He gestured largely to the Gzhindra. "A rarity, a nonesuch!"

"We will take him." The Gzhindra unfolded the cloth, which Reith, to his helpless horror, saw to be a sack. Without ceremony the Gzhindra pulled it up over his legs, tucked him within until only his head protruded. Then, with astonishing ease, one of the

Gzhindra threw the sack over his back, while the other tossed a pouch to Woudiver.

The dream began to fade; the yellow-green light became spotty and blurred. The door flew suddenly open, to reveal Traz. Woudiver jumped back in horror; Traz raised his catapult and fired into Woudiver's face. An astonishing gush of blood spewed forth—green blood, and wherever droplets fell they glistened yellow . . . The dream went dim; Reith slept.

Reith awoke in a state of extreme discomfort. His legs were cramped; a vile arsenical reek pervaded his head. He sensed pressure and motion; groping, he felt coarse cloth. Dismal knowledge came upon him; the dream was real; he indeed rode in a sack. Ah, the resourceful Woudiver! Reith became weak with emotion. Woudiver had negotiated with the Gzhindra; he had arranged that Reith be drugged, probably through a seepage of narcotic gas. The Gzhindra were now carrying him off to unknown places, for unknown purposes.

For a period Reith sagged in the sack numb and sick. Woudiver, even while chained by the neck, had worked his mischief! Reith collected the final fragments of his dream. He had seen Woudiver with his face split apart, pumping green blood. Woudiver had paid for his trick.

Reith found it hard to think. The sack swung and he felt a rhythmic thud; apparently the sack was being carried on a pole. By sheer luck he wore his clothes; the night previously he had flung himself down on his cot fully dressed. Was it possible that he still carried his knife? His pouch was gone; the pocket of his jacket seemed to be empty, and he dared not grope lest he signal the fact of his consciousness to the Gzhindra.

He pressed his face close to the sack hoping to see through the coarse weave, unsuccessfully. The time was yet night; he thought that they traveled uneven terrain.

An indeterminate time went by, with Reith as helpless as a baby in the womb. How many strange events the nights of old Tschai had known! And now another, with himself a participant. He felt ashamed and demeaned; he quivered with rage. If he could get his hands on his captors, what a vengeance he would take!

The Gzhindra halted, and for a moment stood perfectly quiet. Then the sack was lowered to the ground. Reith listened but heard no voices, no whispers, no footsteps. It seemed as if he were alone. He reached to his pocket, hoping to find a knife, a tool, an edge. He found nothing. He tested the fabric with his fingernails: the wave was coarse and harsh, and would not rip.

An intimation told him that the Gzhindra had returned. He lay quiet. The Gzhindra stood nearby, and he thought that he heard whispering.

The sack moved; it was lifted and carried. Reith began to sweat. Something was about to happen.

The sack swung. He dangled from a rope. He felt the sensation of descent: down, down, down, how far he could not estimate. He halted with a jerk, to swing slowly back and forth. From high above came the reverberation of a gong: a low melancholy sound.

Reith kicked and pushed. He became frantic, victim to a claustrophobic spasm. He panted and sweated and could hardly catch his breath; this was how it felt to go crazy. Sobbing and hissing, he took command of himself. He searched his jacket, to no avail: no metal, no cutting edge. He clenched his mind, forced himself to think. The gong was a signal; someone or something had been summoned. He groped around the sack, hoping to find a break. No success. He needed metal, sharpness, a blade, an edge! From head to toe he took stock. His belt! With vast difficulty he pulled it loose, and used the sharp pin on the buckle to score the fabric. He achieved a tear; thrusting and straining he ripped the material and finally thrust forth his head and shoulders. Never in his life had he known such exultation! If he died within the moment, at least he had defeated the sack!

Conceivably he might score other victories. He looked along a rude, rough cavern dimly illuminated by a few blue-white buttons of light. The floor almost brushed the bottom of the bag; Reith recalled the descent and final jerk with a qualm. He heaved himself out of the sack, to stand trembling with cramp and fatigue. Listening to dead underground silence, he thought to hear a far sound. Something, someone, was astir.

Above him the cavern rose in a chimney, the rope merging with the darkness. Somewhere up there must be an opening into the outer world—but how far? In the bag he had swung with a cycle of ten or twelve seconds, which by rough calculation gave a figure of considerably more than a hundred feet.

Reith looked down the cavern and listened. Someone would

be coming in answer to the gong. He looked up the rope. At the top was the outer world. He took hold of the rope, started to climb. Up he went, into the dark, heaving and clinging: up, up, up. The sack and the cavern became part of a lost world; he was enveloped in darkness.

His hands burned; his shoulders grew warm and weak; then he reached the top of the rope. Groping, fumbling, he discovered that it passed through a slot in a metal plate, which rested upon a pair of heavy metal beams. The plate seemed a kind of trapdoor, which clearly could not be opened while his weight hung on the rope . . . His strength was failing. He wrapped the rope around his legs and reached out with an arm. To one side he felt a metal shelf; it was the web of the beam supporting the trapdoor, a foot or more wide. He rested a moment—time was growing short— then lurched out with his leg, and tried to heave himself across. For a sickening instant he felt himself falling. He strained desperately; with his heart thumping he dragged himself across to the web of the beam. Here, sick and miserable, he lay panting.

A minute passed, hardly long enough for the rope to become still. Below four bobbing lights approached. Reith balanced himself and heaved up at the metal plate. It was solid and heavy; he might as well have been shoving at the mountainside. Once again! He thrust with all his might, without the slightest effect. The lights were below, carried by four dark shapes. Reith pressed back against the vertical section of the beam.

The four below moved slowly in eerie silence, like creatures underwater. They went to examine the sack and found it empty. Reith could hear whispers and mutters. They looked all around, the lights blinking and flickering. By some kind of mutual impulse all stared up. Reith pressed himself flat against the metal and hid the pallid blotch of his face. The glow of the lights played past him, upon the trapdoor, which he saw to be locked by four twist-latches controlled from above. The lights, veering away, searched the sides of the shaft. The folk below stood in puzzled consultation. After a final inspection of the cavern, a last flicker of light up the shaft, they returned the way they had come, flashing their lights from side to side.

Reith huddled high in the dark, wondering whether he might not still be dreaming. But the sad desolate circumstances were real enough. He was trapped. He could not raise the door above him; it might not be opened again for weeks. Unthinkable to crouch bat-like, waiting. For better or worse, Reith made up his mind. He looked down the passage; the lights, bobbing will-o'-the-wisps, were already far and dim. He slid down the rope and set off in pursuit, running with long gliding steps. He had a single notion, a desperate hope rather than a plan: to isolate one of the dark figures and somehow force him to lead the way to the surface. Above burned the first of the dim blue buttons, casting a glow dimmer than moonlight, but sufficient to show a way winding between rock buttresses advancing alternately from either side.

Reith presently caught up with the four, who moved slowly, investigating the passage to either side in a hesitant, perplexed fashion. Reith began to feel an insane exhilaration, as if he were already dead and invulnerable. He thought to pick up a pebble and toss it at the dark figures . . . Hysteria! The notion instantly sobered him. If he wanted to survive he must take a grip on himself.

The four moved with uneasy deliberation, whispering and muttering among themselves. Dodging from one pocket of shadow to another Reith approached as closely as he dared, to be ready in case one should detach himself. Except for a fleeting glimpse in the dungeons at Pera, he had never seen a Pnume. These, from what Reith could observe of their posture and gait, seemed human.

The passage opened into a cavern with almost purposeful roughness—or perhaps the rudeness concealed a delicacy beyond Reith's understanding, as in the case of a shoulder of quartz thrusting forth to display a coruscation of pyrite crystals.

The area seemed to be a junction, a node, a place of importance, with three other passages leading away. An area at the center had been floored with smooth stone slabs; light somewhat stronger than that in the cavern issued from luminous grains in the overhead rock.

A fifth individual stood to the side; like the others he wore a black cloak and wide-brimmed black hat. Reith, flat as a cockroach, slid forward into a pocket of dense shadow close by the chamber. The fifth individual was also a Pnumekin; Reith could see his long visage, dismal, white and bleak. For an interval he took no notice of the first four and they appeared not to see him, a curious ritual of mutual disregard which aroused Reith's interest.

Gradually the five seemed to wander together, none looking directly at the others.

There came a hushed murmur of voices. Reith strained to listen. They spoke the universal tongue of Tschai; so much he could understand from the intonations. The four reported the circumstances attendant upon finding the empty sack; the fifth, an official or monitor, made the smallest possible indication of dismay. It seemed that restraint, unobtrusiveness, delicacy of allusion were key aspects of sub-Tschai existence.

They wandered across the chamber and into the cavern close by Reith, who pressed himself against the wall. The group halted not ten feet distant, and Reith could now hear the conversation.

One spoke in a careful, even voice: ". . . Delivery. This is not known; nothing was found."

Another said: "The passage was empty. If defalcation occurred before the bag was lowered, here would be an explanation."

"Imprecision," said the monitor. "The bag would not then have been lowered."

"Imprecision exists in either case. The passage was clear and empty."

"He must still be there," said the tunnel monitor; "he cannot be anywhere else."

"Unless a secret adit enters the passage, of which he knows."

The monitor stood straight, arms at his sides. "The presence of such an adit is not known to me. The explanation is remotely conceivable. You must make a new and absolutely thorough search; I will inquire as to the possibility of such a secret adit."

The passage-tenders returned slowly along the cavern, lights flickering up and down, back and forth. The monitor stood looking after them. Reith tensed himself: a critical moment. Turning in one direction the monitor must certainly see Reith, not six feet away. If he turned in the other direction Reith was temporarily secure . . . Reith considered an attack upon the man. But the four were still close at hand; a cry, a sound, a scuffle would attract their attention. Reith contained himself.

The monitor turned away from Reith. Walking softly he crossed the chamber and entered one of the side passages. Reith followed, running on the balls of his feet. He peered down the passage. Each wall was a ledge of pyroxilite. Remarkable crystals thrust forth from either side, some a foot in diameter, faceted like brilliants: russet-brown, black-brown, greenish-black. They had been artfully cleaned and polished, to show to best advantage: enormous effort had been spent in this corridor. The crystals offered convenient objects behind which to take concealment; Reith set off at a soundless lope after the gliding Pnumekin, hoping to take him unawares and put him in fear of his life: a primitive and desperate plan, but Reith could think of nothing better . . . The Pnumekin halted, and Reith jumped nervously behind a shoulder of glossy olive crystals. The Pnumekin, after a glance up and down the passage, reached to the wall, pushed at a small crystal, touched another. A segment of the wall fell aside. The Pnumekin stepped through; the portal closed. The passage was empty. Reith was now angry with himself. Why had he paused? When the Pnumekin had halted Reith should have been upon him.

He looked up and down the corridor. No one in sight. He went on at a fast trot and after a hundred yards came abruptly upon the rim of a great shaft. Far below gleamed dim yellow lights and a motion of bulky objects which Reith could not identify.

Reith returned to the door through which the Pnumekin had disappeared. He paused, his mind racing with angry schemes. For a desperate wretch like himself any course of action was risky, but the sure way to disaster was inaction. Reith reached out and worked at the rock as he had seen the Pnumekin do. The door fell aside. Reith drew back, ready for anything. He looked into a chamber thirty feet in diameter: a conference room, or so Reith deduced from the round central table, the benches, the shelves and cabinets.

He stepped through the opening and the door closed behind him. He looked around the chamber. Light-grains powdered the ceiling; the walls had been meticulously chipped and ground to enhance the crystalline structure of the rock. To the right an arched corridor, plastered in white, led away; to the left were shelves, cabinets, a closet.

From the corridor came a dull staccato knocking, a sound which carried a message of urgency. Reith, already as taut as a burglar, looked around in a panic for a place to hide. He ran to the closet, slid the door ajar, pushed aside the black cloaks hanging from hooks, and squeezed within. The cloaks and the black hats at the back gave off a musty odor. Reith's stomach gave a jerk. He huddled back and slid the door shut. Putting his eye to a crack, he looked out into the room.

Time stood still. Reith's stomach began to jerk with tension. The Pnumekin monitor returned to the chamber, to stand as if in deep thought. The queer wide-brimmed hat shadowed his austere features, which, Reith noted, were almost classically regular. Reith thought of the other man-composites of Tschai, all more or less mutated toward their host-race: the Dirdirmen—sinister absurdities; the stupid and brutish Chaschmen; the venal over-civilized Wankhmen. The essential humanity of all these, except perhaps in the case of the Dirdirman Immaculates, remained intact. The Pnumekin, on the other hand, had undergone no perceptible physical evolvement, but their psyches had altered; they seemed as remote as specters.

The creature across the room—Reith could not think of him as a man—stood quiet without a twitch to his features, just inconveniently too distant for a lurch and a lunge out of the closet.

Reith began to feel cramped. He shifted his position, producing a small sound. In a cold sweat he pressed his eye to the crack. The Pnumekin stood absorbed in reverie. Reith willed him to approach, urged him closer, closer, closer . . . A thought came to disturb him: suppose the creature refused to heed a threat against his life? Perhaps it lacked the ability to feel fear . . . The portal swung ajar; another Pnumekin entered: one of the passage-tenders. The two looked aside, ignoring each other. The newcomer spoke in a soft voice, as if musing aloud: "The delivery cannot be found. The passage and shaft have been scrutinized."

The tunnel monitor made no response. Silence, of an eerie dream-like quality, ensued.

The passage-tender spoke again. "He could not have passed us. Delivery was not made, or else he escaped by an adit unknown to us. These are the alternative possibilities."

The monitor spoke. "The information is noted. Transit control should be instituted at Ziad Level, Zud-Dan-Ziad, at Ferstan Node Six, at Lul-lil Node and at Foreverness Station."

"Such will be the situation."

A Pnume came into the chamber, using an aperture beyond Reith's range of vision. The Pnumekin paid no heed, not so much as glancing aside. Reith studied the oddly jointed creature: the first Pnume he had seen, except for a darkling glimpse in the dungeons of Pera. It stood about the height of a man and within its voluminous black cloak seemed slight, even frail. A black hat shaded its eye-sockets; its visage, the cast and color of a horse's skull, was expressionless; under the lower edge a complicated set of rasping and chewing parts surrounded a near-invisible mouth. The articulation of the creature's legs worked in reverse to that of the human: it moved forward with the motion of a man walking backwards. The narrow feet were bare and mottled, dark red and black; three arched toes tapped the ground as a nervous man might tap his fingers.

The Pnumekin tunnel monitor spoke softly into the air. "An abnormal situation, when an item of delivery is no more than an empty sack. The passage and the shaft have been scrutinized; the item either was not delivered, or it made evasion by using a secret adit of Quality Seven or higher."

Silence. From the Pnume, in a husky muffled murmur, came words. "Verification of delivery cannot be made. The possibility of a classified adit exists, above Quality Ten, and beyond the scope of my secrets.* We may properly solicit information from the Section Warden.†'

The tunnel monitor spoke in a voice of tentative inquiry. "The delivery, then, is an item of interest?"

The Pnume's toes drummed the floor with the delicacy of a pianist's fingers. "It is for Foreverness: a creature from contemporary Man-planet. Decision was made to take it."

Reith, cramped in the locker, wondered why the decision had been delayed so long. He eased his position, gritting his teeth against the possibility of a sound. When once again he put his eye to the crack the Pnume had departed. The monitor and the passage-tender stood quietly, taking no notice of each other.

Time passed, how long Reith could not judge. His muscles throbbed and ached, and now he feared to shift his position. He took a long slow breath and composed himself to patience.

At odd intervals the Pnumekin spoke in murmurs, looking aside all the while as if they addressed the air. Reith distinguished a phrase or two: ". . . The condition of Man-planet; there

---

*Secrets: the rough translation of a phrase signifying the body of lore proper and suitable to a particular status. In the context of Pnume society the word secrets conveys more accurate overtones.

†Again a rude rendering of an untranslatable idea: the title in Tschai terms connotes superlative erudition in combination with high authority and status.

is no knowing . . ." ". . . Barbarians, surface dwellers, mad as Gzhindra . . ." ". . . Valuable item, invisible . . ."

The Pnume reappeared, followed by another: a creature tall and gaunt, stepping with the soft tread of a fox. It carried a rectangular case, which it placed with delicate precision upon a bench three feet in front of Reith; then it seemed to lose itself in reverie. A moment passed. The passage-tender of lowest status spoke first. "When a delivery is signaled by the gong, the bag is usually heavy. An empty bag is cause for perplexity. Delivery evidently was not made, or the item gained access to a secret adit, over Ten in Quality."

The Warden turned aside and, spreading wide its black cloak, touched the locks of the leather case. The two Pnumekin and the first Pnume interested themselves in the crystals of the wall.

Opening the case, the Warden brought forth a portfolio bound in limp blue leather. The Warden spread it apart with reverent care, turned pages, studied a tangle of colored lines. The Warden closed the portfolio, replaced it in the case. After a moment of musing, he spoke in a voice so breathy and soft that Reith had difficulty understanding him. "An ancient adit of Quality Fourteen exists. It courses nine hundred yards northward, descends, and enters the Jha Nu."

The Pnumekin were silent. The first Pnume spoke. "If the item came into the Jha Nu, he might traverse the balcony, descend by Oma-Five into the Upper Great Lateral. He could then turn aside into Blue Rise, or even Zhu Overlook, and so reach the *ghaun*."*

The Warden spoke. "All this only if the item has knowledge of the secrets. If we assume his use of a Quality Fourteen adit, then we can assume the rest. The manner by which our secrets have been disseminated—if this is the case—is not clear."

"Perplexing," murmured the passage-tender.

The monitor said, "If a *ghian*† knows Quality Fourteen secrets, how can these be safe from the Dirdir?"

The toes of both Pnume arched and tapped the stone floor.

"The circumstances are not yet clear," remarked the Warden. "A study of the adit will provide exact information."

Ghaun: a wild region exposed to wind and weather. In the special usage of the Pnume: the surface of Tschai, with emphasized connotations of exposure, oppressive emptiness, desolation.
†*Ghian:* an inhabitant of the *ghaun:* a surface-dweller.

The low-status passage-tenders were first to leave the room. The monitor, apparently lost in reflection, sidled after them, leaving the two Pnume standing still and rigid as a pair of insects. The first Pnume went off, padding on soft, forward-kicking strides. The Warden remained. Reith wondered if he should not burst forth and attempt to overpower the Warden. He restrained himself. If the Pnume shared the fantastic strength of the Phung, Reith would be at a terrible disadvantage. Another consideration: would the Pnume become pliant with pressure? Reith could not know. He suspected not.

The Warden took up the leather case and turned a deliberate stare to all quarters of the chamber. It appeared to listen. Moving with uncharacteristic abruptness, it carried the case to an expanse of blank wall. Reith watched in fascination. The Warden slid forward its foot, delicately touched three knobs of rock with its toes. A section of wall fell back, revealing a cavity into which the Warden tucked the case. The rock slid back; the wall was solid. The Warden went off after the others.

3

THE ROOM WAS empty. Reith stumbled forth from the closet. He hobbled across the room. The wall showed no crack, no seam. The workmanship was of microscopic accuracy.

Reith bent low, touched the three protuberances. The rock moved back and aside. Reith brought forth the case. After the briefest of hesitations, he opened the case, removed the portfolio. From the closet he brought a carton of small dark bottles, approximately the same weight as the portfolio which he closed into the case, and replaced all into the cavity. He touched the knobs; the cavity closed; the wall was solid rock.

Reith stood in the center of the room, holding the portfolio, obviously a valuable article. If he were able to evade detection and capture, if he were able to decipher the Pnume orthography—all of which seemed intrinsically unlikely—he might conceivably discover a route to the surface.

From the closet he brought a cloak, which he draped about himself, and a hat, somewhat too small, but which by dint of twisting and stretching he managed to pull low over his head.

The Pnumekin habit of furtive unobtrusiveness would serve him well; no one would attempt greater furtiveness, less obtrusiveness, than himself. Now he must leave the immediate area, and find some secluded spot where he might examine the portfolio at his leisure. He tucked the portfolio into his jacket and set off along the white plastered corridor, putting one foot softly in front of the other as he had seen the Pnumekin do.

The corridor stretched long and empty ahead, at last opening upon a balcony which overlooked a long room, from which came a hum and shuffle of activity.

The floor of the chamber was twenty feet below. On the walls were charts and ideograms; in the center Pnumekin children took instruction. Reith had come upon a Pnumekin school.

Standing back in the shadows Reith was able to look down without fear of detection. He saw three groups of children, both male and female, twenty to each group. Like their elders they wore black cloaks and hats with flattened crowns. The small white faces were peaked and pinched, and almost laughably earnest. None spoke; staring into empty air they marched softly and solemnly through a drill or exercise. They were attended by three Pnumekin women of indefinite age, cloaked like the males and distinguishable only by lesser stature and somewhat less harshness of feature.

The children padded on and on through the exercise, the silence broken only by the shuffle of their feet. Nothing could be learned here, thought Reith. He looked in both directions, then set off to the left. An arched tunnel gave upon another balcony, which overlooked a chamber even larger than the first: a refectory. Tables and benches were ranked down the middle, but the chamber was vacant except for two Pnumekin, who sat widely separated, crouched low over bowls of gruel. Reith became aware of his own hunger.

He heard a sound. Along the balcony came a pair of Pnumekin, one behind the other. Reith's heart began to thump so loudly he feared they would surely hear the sound as they approached. He pulled down his head, hunched his shoulders, moved forward in what he hoped to be the typical Pnumekin gait. The two passed by, eyes averted, thoughts on matters far removed.

With somewhat more assurance Reith continued along the passage, which almost immediately expanded to become a roughly circular node, the junction for three corridors. A staircase cut from the natural gray rock curved down to the level below.

The corridors were desolate and dim; Reith thought them unpromising. He hesitated, feeling tired and futile. The charts, he decided, were of no great help; he needed the assistance, willing or otherwise, of a Pnumekin. He was also very hungry. Gingerly he went to the staircase and, after ten seconds of indecision, descended, begrudging every step which took him farther from the surface. He came out into a small anteroom beside the refectory. A portal nearby gave upon what appeared to be a kitchen. Reith looked in cautiously. A number of Pnumekin worked at counters, presumably preparing food for the children in the exercise room.

Reith backed regretfully away, and went off down a side passage. This was dim and quiet, with only a few light-grains in the high ceiling. After a hundred feet the passage jogged to the side and came to an abrupt end at the brink of a drop-off. From below the sound of running water: more than likely a disposal-place for waste and garbage, Reith reflected. He halted, wondering where to go and what to do, then returned to the anteroom. Here he discovered a small storage chamber in which were stacked bags, sacks and cartons. Food, thought Reith. He hesitated; the chamber must frequently be used by the cooks. From the exercise room came the children, walking in single file, eyes fixed drearily on the floor. Reith backed into the storage room: the children would discern his strangeness far more readily than adults. He crouched at the back of the room, behind a pile of stacked cartons: by no means the most secure of hiding places, but not altogether precarious. Even if someone entered the chamber he stood a good chance of evading attention. Reith relaxed somewhat. He brought forth the portfolio and folded back the limp blue leather cover. The pages were a beautiful soft vellum; the cartography was printed with most meticulous care in black, red, brown, green and pale blue. But the patterns and lines conveyed no information; the legend was set forth in undecipherable characters. Regretfully Reith folded the portfolio and tucked it into his jacket.

From a counter in front of the kitchen the children took bowls and carried them into the refectory.

Reith watched through a cranny between the cartons, more than ever aware of hunger and thirst. He investigated the contents of a sack, to find dried pilgrim-pod, a leathery wafer highly nutritious but not particularly appetizing. The cartons beside him contained tubes of a greasy black paste, rancid and sharp to the taste: apparently a condiment. Reith turned his attention to the serving counter. The last of the children had carried their bowls into the refectory. The serving area was vacant, but on the counter remained half a dozen bowls and flasks. Reith acted without conscious calculation. He emerged from the storage room, hunched his shoulders, went to the counter, took a bowl and a flask and retreated hurriedly to his hiding place. The bowl contained pilgrim-pod gruel cooked with raisin-like nubbins, slivers of pale meat, two stalks of a celery-like vegetable. The flask held a pint of faintly effervescent beer, with a pleasantly astringent bite. To the flask was clipped a packet of six round wafers, which Reith tasted but found unpalatable. He ate the gruel and drank the beer and congratulated himself on his decisiveness.

To the serving area came six older children: slender young people, detached and broodingly self-sufficient. Peering between the cartons, Reith decided that all were female. Five passed by the counter taking bowls and flasks. The last to come by, finding nothing to eat, stood in puzzlement. Reith watched with the guilty awareness that he had stolen and devoured her supper. The first five went into the refectory, leaving the one girl waiting uncertainly by the counter.

Five minutes passed; she spoke no word, standing with her eyes fixed on the floor. At last unseen hands set another bowl and flask down on the counter. The Pnumekin girl took the food and went slowly into the refectory.

Reith became uneasy. He decided to return up the stairs, to select one of the passages and hope to meet some lone knowledgeable Pnumekin who could be overpowered and put in fear for his life. He rose to his feet, but now the children began to leave the refectory, and Reith stood back. One by one, on noiseless feet, they filed into the exercise room. Once more Reith looked forth and once more retreated as now the five older girls issued from the refectory. They were alike as mannequins from the factory: slender and straight, with skins as pale and thin as paper, arched coal-black eyebrows, and regular, if somewhat peaked, features. They wore the usual black cloaks and black hats, which accentuated the quaint and eerie non-earthliness of the earthly bodies. They might have been five versions of the same person, although

Reith, even as the idea crossed his mind, knew that each made sure distinctions, too subtle for his knowing, between herself and the others; each felt her personal existence to be the central movement of the cosmos.

The serving area was empty. Reith stepped forth and on long quick strides crossed to the stairs. Only just in time: from the kitchen came one of the cooks, to go to the storage room. Had Reith delayed another moment he would have been discovered. Heart beating fast, he started up the stairs . . . He stopped short and stood holding his breath. From above came a soft sound: the pad-pad-pad of footsteps. Reith froze in his tracks. The sounds became louder. Down the stairs came the mottled red and black feet of a Pnume, then the flutter of black cloth. Reith hurriedly retreated, to stand indecisively at the foot of the stairs. Where to go? He looked about frantically. In the storage room the cook ladled pilgrim-pod from a sack. The children occupied the exercise-chamber. Reith had a single choice. He hunched his shoulders and stalked softly into the refectory. At a middle table sat a Pnumekin girl, she whose supper he had commandeered. Reith took what he considered the most inconspicuous seat and sat sweating. His disguise was makeshift; a single direct glance would reveal his identity.

Silent minutes passed. The Pnumekin girl lingered over the packet of wafers which she seemed especially to enjoy. At last she rose to her feet and started to leave the chamber. Reith lowered his head: too sharply, too abruptly—a discordant movement. The girl turned a startled glance in his direction and even now habit was strong; she looked past him without directly focusing her eyes. But she saw, she knew. For an instant she remained frozen, her face loose and incredulous; then she uttered a soft cry of terror, and started to run from the room. Reith was instantly upon her, to stifle her with his hand and thrust her against the wall.

"Be quiet!" Reith muttered. "Don't make any noise! Do you understand?"

She stared at him in a kind of horrified daze. Reith gave her a shake. "Don't make a sound! Do you understand? Nod your head!"

She managed to jerk her head. Reith took away his hand. "Listen!" he whispered. "Listen carefully! I am a man of the surface. I was kidnapped and brought down here. I escaped, and now I want to return to the surface. Do you hear me?" She made no response. "Do you understand? *Answer!*" He gave the thin shoulders another shake.

"Yes."

"Do you know how to reach the surface?"

She shifted her gaze, to stare at the floor. Reith darted a glance toward the serving area; if one of the cooks should happen to look into the refectory, all was lost. And the Pnume who had descended the stairs, what of him? And the balcony! Reith had forgotten the balcony! With a sick thrill of fear he searched the high shadows. No one stood watching. But they could remain here no longer, not another minute. He grasped the girl by the arm. "Come along. Not a sound, remember! Or I'll have to hurt you!"

He pulled her along the wall to the entrance. The serving area was empty. From the kitchen came a grinding sound and a clatter of metal. Of the Pnume there was no sign.

"Up the stairs," whispered Reith.

She made a sound of protest; Reith clapped his hand over her mouth and dragged her to the staircase. "Up! Do as I say and you won't be harmed!"

She spoke in a soft even voice: "Go away."

"I want to go away," Reith declared in a passionate mutter. "I don't know where to go!"

"I can't help you."

"You've got to help me. Up the stairs. Quick now!"

Suddenly she turned and ran up the stairs, so light on her feet that she seemed to float. Reith was taken by surprise. He sprang after her, but she outdistanced him and sped down one of the corridors. In desperation she fled; in equal desperation Reith pursued, and after fifty feet caught her. He thrust her against the wall, where she stood panting. Reith looked up and down the corridor: no one was in sight, to his vast relief. "Do you want to die?" he hissed in her ear.

"No!"

"Then do exactly what I tell you!" growled Reith. He hoped that the threat convinced her; and indeed her face sagged; her eyes became wide and dark. She tried to speak, and finally asked: "What do you want me to do?"

"First, lead the way to a quiet place, where no one comes."

With sagging shoulders she turned away, and proceeded along the corridor. Reith asked suspiciously, "Where are you taking me?"

"To the punishment place."

A moment later she turned into a side corridor which almost at once ended in a round chamber. The girl went to a pair of black flint cabochons; looking over her shoulder like a fairy-tale witch, she pushed the black bulbs. A portal opened upon black space; the girl stepped through with Reith close behind. She touched a switch; from a light-panel came a wan illumination.

They stood on a ledge at the edge of a brink. A crazy insect-leg derrick tilted over profound darkness; from the end hung a rope.

Reith looked at the girl; she looked silently back at him with a kind of half-frightened, half-sullen indifference. Holding to the derrick, Reith looked gingerly over the brink. A cold draft blew up into his face, and he turned away. The girl stood motionless. Reith suspected that the sudden convulsion of events had put her into a state of shock. The tight hat constricted his head; he pulled it off. The girl shrank back against the wall. "Why do you take off the hat?"

"It hurts my head," said Reith.

The girl flicked her glance past him and away into the darkness. She asked in a soft muffled voice, "What do you want me to do?"

"Take me to the surface, as fast as you can."

The girl made no answer. Reith wondered if she had heard him. He tried to look into her face; she turned away. Reith twitched off her hat. A strange eerie face looked at him, the bloodless mouth quivering in panic. She was older than her underdeveloped figure suggested, though Reith could not accurately have estimated her age. Her features were wan and dreary, so regular as to be nondescript; her hair, a short black mat, clung to her scalp like a cap of felt. Reith thought that she seemed anemic and neurasthenic, at once human and non-human, female and sexless.

"Why do you do that?" she asked in a hushed murmur.

"For no particular reason. Curiosity, perhaps."

"It is intimate," she muttered, and put her hands up to her thin cheeks. Reith shrugged, uninterested in her modesty. "I want you to take me to the surface."

"I can't."

"Why not?"

She made no answer.

"Aren't you afraid of me?" Reith asked gently.

"Not as much as the pit."

"The pit is yonder, and convenient."

She gave him a startled glance. "Would you throw me into the pit?"

Reith spoke in what he hoped to be a menacing voice. "I am a fugitive; I intend to reach the surface."

"I don't dare help you." Her voice was soft and matter-of-fact. "The *zuzhma kastchai** would punish me." She looked at the derrick. "The dark is terrible; we are afraid of the dark. Sometimes the rope is cut and the person is never heard again."

Reith stood baffled. The girl, reading a dire meaning into his silence, said in a meek voice: "Even if I wished to help you, how could I? I know only the way to the Blue Rise pop-out, where I would not be allowed, unless," she added as an afterthought, "I declared myself a Gzhindra. You of course would be taken."

Reith's scheme began to topple around his head. "Then take me to some other exit."

"I know of none. Those are secrets not taught at my level."

"Come over here, under the light," said Reith. "Look at this."

He brought forth the portfolio, opened it and set it before her. "Show me where we are now."

The girl looked. She made a choking sound and began to tremble. "What is this?"

"Something I took from a Pnume."

"These are the Master Charts! My life is done. I will be thrown into the pit!"

"Please don't complicate such a simple matter," said Reith. "Look at the charts, find a route to the surface, take me there. Then do as you like. No one will know the difference."

The girl stared with a wild, unreasoning gaze. Reith gave her thin shoulder a shake. "What's wrong with you?"

Her voice came in a toneless mutter. "I have seen secrets."

Reith was in no mood to commiserate with troubles so abstract and unreal. "Very well; you've seen the charts. The damage is done. Now look again and find a way to the surface!"

A strange expression came over the thin face. Reith wondered if she had gone mad for a fact. Of all the Pnumekin walking the corridors, what wry providence had directed him to an emotion-

---

*zuzhma kastchai: the contraction of a phrase: *the ancient and secret world-folk derived from dark rock and mother-soil.*

ally unstable girl? . . . She was looking at him, for the first time directly and searchingly. "You are a *ghian*."

"I live on the surface, certainly."

"What is it like? Is it terrible?"

"The surface of Tschai? It has its deficiencies."

"I now must be a Gzhindra."

"It's better than living down here in the dark."

The girl said in her dull voice, "I must go to the *ghaun*."

"The sooner the better," said Reith. "Look at this map again. Show me where we are."

"I can't look!" moaned the girl. "I dare not look!"

"Come now!" snapped Reith. "It's only paper."

"Only paper! It crawls with secrets, Class Twenty secrets. My mind is too small!"

Reith suspected incipient hysteria, although her voice had remained a soft monotone. "To become a Gzhindra you must reach the surface. To reach the surface we must find an exit, the more secret the better. Here we have secret charts. We are in luck."

She became quiet and even glanced from the corner of her eyes toward the portfolio. "How did you get this?"

"I took it from a Pnume." He pushed the portfolio toward her. "Can you read the symbols?"

"I am trained to read." Gingerly she leaned over the portfolio, to jerk instantly back in fear and revulsion.

Reith forced himself to patience. "You have never seen a map before?"

"I have a level of Four; I know Class Four secrets; I have seen Class Four maps. This is Class Twenty."

"But you can read this map."

"Yes." The word came with sour distaste. "But I dare not. Only a *ghian* would think to examine such a powerful document . . ." Her voice trailed away to a murmur. "Let alone steal it . . ."

"What will the Pnume do when they find it is gone?"

The girl looked off over the gulf. "Dark, dark, dark. I will fall forever through the dark."

Reith began to grow restive. The girl seemed able to concentrate only on those ideas rising from her own mind. He directed her attention to the map. "What do the colors signify?"

"The levels and stages."

"And these symbols?"

"Doors, portals, secret ways. Touch-plates. Communication stations. Rises, pop-outs, observation posts."

"Show me where we are now."

Reluctantly she focused her eyes. "Not this sheet. Turn back . . . Back . . . Back . . . Here.'" She pointed, her finger a cautious two inches from the paper. "There. The black mark is the pit. The pink line is the ledge."

"Show me the nearest route to the surface."

"That would be—let me look."

Reith managed a distant and reflective smile: once diverted from her woes, which were real enough, Reith admitted, the girl became instantly intense, and even forgot the exposure of her face.

"Blue-Rise pop-out is here. To get there one would go by this lateral, then up this pale orange ramp. But it is a crowded area, with administrative wickets. You would be taken and I likewise, now that I have seen the secrets."

The question of responsibility and guilt flickered through Reith's mind, but he put it aside. Cataclysm had come to his life; like the plague it had infected her as well. Perhaps similar ideas circulated in her mind.

She darted a quick sidelong glance again. "How did you come in from the *ghaun?*"

"The Gzhindra let me down in a sack. I cut my way out before the Pnumekin came. I hope they decide that the Gzhindra lowered an empty sack."

"With one of the Great Charts missing? No person of the Shelters would touch it. The *zuzhma kastchai* will never rest until both you and I are dead."

"I become ever more anxious to escape," said Reith.

"I also," remarked the girl with ingenuous simplicity. "I do not wish to fall."

Reith watched her a moment or two, wondering that she appeared to bear him no rancor; it was as if he had come to her as an elemental calamity—a storm, a lightning-bolt, a flood—against which resentment, argument, entreaty would have been equally useless. Already, he thought, a subtle change had come over her attitude; she bent to inspect the chart somewhat less gingerly than before. She pointed to a pale brown Y. "There's the Palisades exit, where trading is done with the *ghian*. I have never been so far."

"Could we go up at this point?"

"Never. The *zuzhma kastchai* guard against the Dirdir. There is continual vigilance."

Reith pointed to the other pale brown Y's. "These are other openings to the surface?"

"Yes. But if they believe you to be at large, they will block off here and here and here"—she pointed—"and all these openings are barred, and these in Exa section as well."

"Then we must go somewhere else: to other sectors."

The girl's face twitched. "I know nothing of such places."

"Look at the map."

She did his bidding, running her finger close above the mesh of colored lines, but not yet daring to touch the paper itself. "I see here a secret way, Quality Eighteen. It runs from the passage out yonder to Parallel Twelve, and it shortens the way by a half. Then we might go along any of these adits to the freight docks."

Reith rose to his feet. He pulled the hat over his face. "Do I look like a Pnumekin?"

She gave him a brief unsympathetic inspection. "Your face is strange. Your skin is dark from the *ghaun* weather. Take some dust and wipe it on your face."

Reith did as he was bid; the girl watched with an expressionless gaze; Reith wondered what went on in her mind. She had declared herself an outcast, a Gzhindra, without overmuch agony of the spirit. Or did she contrive a subtle betrayal? "Betrayal" was perhaps unfair, Reith reflected. She had pledged him no faith, she owed him no loyalty—indeed, something considerably the reverse. So how could he control her after they set forth through the passages? Reith pondered and studied her, while she became increasingly agitated. "Why do you look at me like that?"

Reith held out the blue portfolio to her. "Carry this under your cloak, where it won't be seen."

The girl swayed back aghast. "No."

"You must."

"I don't dare. The *zuzhma kastchai*—"

"Conceal the charts under your cloak," said Reith in a measured voice. "I'm a desperate man, and I'll stop at nothing to return to the surface."

With limp fingers she took the portfolio. Turning her back,

and glancing warily over her shoulder at Reith, she tucked the portfolio out of sight under her cloak. "Come then," she croaked. "If we are taken, it is how life must go. Never in my dreaming did I expect to be a Gzhindra."

She opened the portal and looked out into the round chamber. "The way is clear. Remember, walk softly, do not lean forward. We must pass through Fer Junction, and there will be persons at their affairs. The *zuzhma kastchai* wander everywhere; if we meet one of these, halt, step into the shadows or face the wall; this is the respectful way. Do not move quickly; do not jerk your arms."

She stepped out into the round room and set off along the passage. Reith followed five or six paces behind, trying to simulate the Pnumekin gait. He had forced the girl to carry the charts; even so, he was at her mercy. She could run screaming to the first Pnumekin they came upon, and hope for mercy from the Pnume . . . The situation was unpredictable.

They walked half a mile, up a ramp, down another and into a main adit. At twenty-foot intervals the narrow doorways opened into the rock; beside each was a fluted pedestal with a flat polished upper surface, the function of which Reith could not calculate. The passage widened and they entered Fer Junction, a large hexagonal hall with a dozen polished marble pillars supporting the ceiling. In dim little booths around the periphery sat Pnumekin writing in ledgers, or occasionally holding vague and seemingly indecisive colloquies with other Pnumekin who had come to seek them out.

The girl wandered to the side and halted. Reith stopped as well.

She glanced at him, then looked thoughtfully toward a Pnumekin in the center of the room: a tall haggard man with an unusually alert posture. Reith stepped into the shadow of a pillar and watched the girl. Her face was blank as a plate but Reith knew her to be reviewing the circumstances which had overwhelmed her pale existence, and his life depended on the balance of her fears: the bottomless gulf against the windy brown skies of the surface.

Slowly she moved toward Reith and joined him in the shadow of the pillar. For the moment at least she had made her choice.

"The tall man yonder: he is a Listening Monitor.* Notice how he observes all? Nothing escapes him."

For a period Reith stood watching the Listening Monitor, becoming each minute more disinclined to cross the chamber. He muttered to the girl, "Do you know another route to the freight docks?"

She pondered the matter. Having committed herself to flight, her personality had become somewhat more focused, as if danger had drawn her up out of the dreaming inversion of her former existence.

"I think," she said dubiously, "that another route passes by way of the work halls; but it is a long way and other Listening Monitors are on hand."

"Hmmf." Reith turned to watch the Listening Monitor of Fer Junction.

"Notice," he said presently, "he turns to look this way and that. When his back is toward us, I'll move to the next pillar, and you come after me."

A moment later the Monitor swung around. Reith stepped out into the chamber, sauntered to the nearest of the marble pillars. The girl came slowly after him, still somewhat indecisively, or so it seemed to Reith.

Reith could not now peer around the pillar without the risk of attracting the Monitor's attention. "Tell me when he looks away," he muttered to the girl.

"Now."

Reith gained the next pillar and, using a file of slow-moving Pnumekin as a screen, continued on to the next. Now a single open area remained. The Monitor swung about abruptly, and Reith ducked back behind the pillar: a deadly game of peek-a-boo. From a passage to the side a Pnume entered the chamber, coming softly on forward-padding legs.

The girl hissed under her breath, "The Silent Critic . . . take care." she drifted away, head downcast, as if in an abstraction. The Pnume halted, not fifty feet from Reith, who turned his back. Only a few strides remained to the north of the passage. Reith's shoulder blades twitched. He could bear to stand by the pillar no longer. Feeling every eye in the chamber pressing upon him he

---

*A somewhat unwieldy translation of the contraction *gol'eszitra*, from a phrase meaning "supervisory intellect with ears alert for raucous disturbance."

crossed the open area. With each step he expected a cry of outrage, an alarm. The silence became oppressive; only by great effort could he control the urge to look over his shoulder. He reached the mouth of the passage and turned a cautious glance over his shoulder—to stare full into the eye sockets of the Pnume. With pounding heart Reith turned slowly and proceeded. The girl had gone ahead. He called to her in a soft voice, "Run ahead; find the Class Eighteen passage."

She turned back a startled glance. "The Silent Critic is close at hand. I may not run; if he saw he would think it boisterous conduct."

"Never mind the decorum," said Reith. "Find the opening as fast as possible."

She quickened her step, with Reith coming behind. After fifty yards he risked a glance to the rear. No one followed.

The corridor branched; the girl stopped short. "I think we go to the left, but I am not sure."

"Look at the chart."

With vast distaste, she turned her back and brought the portfolio from under her cloak. She could not bring herself to handle it and gave it to Reith as if it were hot. He turned the pages till she said, "Stop." While she studied the colored lines, Reith kept his gaze to the rear. Far back, where the passage met Fer Junction, a dark shape appeared in the opening. Reith, every nerve jerking, willed the girl to haste.

"To the left, then at Mark Two-one-two, a blue tile. Style Twenty-four—I must consult the legend. Here it is: four press points. Three-one-four-two."

"Hurry," Reith said, through gritted teeth.

She turned a startled look back down the passage. *"Zuzhma kastchai!"*

Reith also looked back, trying to simulate the Pnumekin gait. The Pnume padded slowly forward, but with no particular sense of purpose, or so it seemed to Reith. He moved off along the passage and overtook the girl. As she walked she counted the number marks at the base of the wall: "Seventy-five . . . eighty . . . eighty-five . . ." Reith looked back. There were now two black shapes in the corridor; from somewhere a second Pnume had appeared. "One hundred ninety-five . . . two hundred . . . two hundred and five . . ."

The blue tile, filmed with an antique red-purple luster, was only a foot from the floor. The girl found press-points and touched them; the outline of a door appeared; the door slid open.

The girl began to shake. "It is Quality Eighteen. I should not enter."

"The Silent Critic is following us," said Reith.

She gasped and stepped into the passage. It was narrow and dim and haunted by a faintly rancid odor Reith had come to associate with the Pnume.

The door slid shut. The girl pushed up a shutter and put her eye to the lens of a peephole. "The Silent Critic is coming. It suspects boisterous conduct, and wants to issue a punishment . . . No! There are two! He has summoned a Warden!" She stood rigid, eye pressed to the peephole. Reith waited on tenterhooks. "What are they doing?"

"They look along the corridor. They wonder why we are not in view."

"Let's get moving," said Reith. "We can't stand here waiting."

"The Warden will know this passage . . . If they come in . . ."

"Never mind that." Reith set out along the passage and the girl came behind him. A queer sight they made, thought Reith, loping through the dark in the flapping black cloaks and low-crowned hats. The girl quickly became tired and further diminished her speed by looking over her shoulder. She gave a croak of resignation and halted. "They have entered the passage."

Reith looked behind. The door stood ajar. In the gap the two Pnume were silhouetted. For an instant they stood rigid, like queer black dolls, then they jerked into motion. "They see us," said the girl, and stood with her head hanging. "It will be the pit . . . Well, then, let us go to meet them in all meekness."

"Stand against the wall," said Reith. "Don't move. They must come to us. There are only two."

"You will be helpless."

Reith made no comment. He picked up a fist-size rock which had fallen from the ceiling and stood waiting.

"You can do nothing," moaned the girl. "Use meekness, placid conduct . . ."

The Pnume came quickly by forward-kicking steps, the white undershot jaws twitching. Ten feet away they halted, to contemplate the two who stood against the wall. For a half-minute none of the group moved or made a sound. The Silent Critic slowly raised its thin arm, to point with two bony fingers. "Go back."

Reith made no move. The girl stood with eyes glazed and mouth sagging.

The Pnume spoke again, in a husky fluting voice. "Go back."

The girl started to stumble off along the passage; Reith made no motion.

The Pnume watched him nonplussed. They exchanged a sibilant whisper, then the Silent Critic spoke again. "Go."

The Warden said in an almost inaudible murmur, "You are the item which escaped delivery."

The Silent Critic, padding forward, reached forth its arm. Reith hurled the rock with all his strength; it struck full in the creature's bone-white face. A crunch, and the creature tottered back to the wall, to stand jerking and raising one leg up and down in a most eccentric manner. The Warden, making a throaty gasping sound, bounded forward.

Reith jumped back, snatched off his cloak, and in an insane flourish threw it over the Pnume's head. For a moment the creature seemed not to notice and came forward, arms outspread; then it began to dance and stamp. Reith moved cautiously in and away, looking for an instant of advantage, and the two in their soundless gyrations performed a peculiar and grotesque ballet. While the Silent Critic watched indifferently Reith seized the Warden's arm; it felt like an iron pipe. The other arm swung about; two harsh finger-ends tore across Reith's face. Reith felt nothing. He heaved, swung the Warden into the wall. It rebounded and moved quickly upon Reith. Reith slapped tentatively at the long pale face; it felt cool and hard. The strength of the creature was inhuman; he must evade its grip, which put him in something of a quandary. If he struck the creature with his fists he would only break his hands.

Step by step the Warden padded forward, legs bending forward. Reith threw himself to the ground, kicked out at the creature's feet, to topple it off balance; it fell. Reith jumped up to evade the expected attack of the Silent Critic, but it remained leaning gravely against the wall, viewing the battle with the detachment of a bystander. Reith was puzzled and distracted by its attitude; as a result the Warden seized his ankle with the toes of one foot and with an amazing extension reached the other foot toward Reith's neck. Reith kicked the creature in the crotch; it was like kicking the crotch of a tree; Reith sprained his foot. The toes gripped his neck; Reith seized the leg, twisted, applied leverage. The Pnume was forced around on its face. Reith scrambled down upon its back. Seizing the head, he gave it a sudden terrible jerk backward. A bone or stiff membrane gave elastically, then snapped. The Warden thrashed here and there in wild palpitations. By chance it gained its feet and with its head dangling backward bounded across the tunnel. It struck the Silent Critic, who slumped to the ground. Dead? Reith's eyes bulged. Dead.

Reith leaned against the wall, gasping for breath. Wherever the Pnume had touched him was a bruise. Blood flowed down his face; his elbow was wrenched; his foot was sprained . . . but two Pnume lay dead. A little distance away the girl crouched in a shock-induced trance. Reith stumbled forward, touched her shoulder. "I'm alive. You're alive."

"Your face bleeds!"

Reith wiped his face with the hem of his cloak. He went to look down at the corpses. Drawing back his lips, he searched the bodies, but found nothing to interest him.

"I suppose we'd better keep on going," said Reith.

The girl turned and set off down the tunnel. Reith followed. The Pnume corpses remained to lie in the dimness.

The girl's steps began to lag. "Are you tired?" asked Reith.

His solicitude puzzled her; she looked at him warily. "No."

"Well, I am. Let's rest for a while." He lowered himself to the floor, groaning and complaining. After a moment's hesitation she settled herself primly across the passage. Reith studied her with perplexity. She had put the struggle with the Pnume completely out of her mind, or so it seemed. Her shadowed face was composed. Astonishing, thought Reith. Her life had come apart; her future must seem a succession of terrifying question marks; yet here she sat, her face blank as that of a marionette, with no apparent distress.

She spoke softly: "Why do you look at me like that?"

"I was thinking," he said, "that, considering the circumstances, you appear remarkably unconcerned."

She made no immediate reply. There was a heavy silence in the dim passage. Then she said, "I float upon the current of life; how should I question where it carries me? It would be impudent to think of preferences; existence, after all, is a privilege given a very few."

Reith leaned back against the wall. "A very few? How so?"

The girl became uneasy; her white fingers twisted. "How it goes on the *ghaun* I don't know; perhaps you do things differently. In the Shelters* the mother-women spawn twelve times and no more than half—sometimes less—survive . . ." She continued in a voice of didactic reflection: "I have heard that all the women of the *ghaun* are mother-women. Is this true? I can't believe it. If each spawned twelve times, and even if six went to the pit, the *ghaun* would boil with living flesh. It seems unreasonable." She added, as a possibly disconnected afterthought, "I am glad that I will never be a mother-woman."

Again Reith was puzzled. "How can you be sure? You're young yet."

The girl's face twitched with what might have been embarrassment. "Can't you see? Do I look to be a mother-woman?"

"I don't know what your mother-women look like."

"They bulge at the chest and hips. Aren't *ghian* mothers the same? Some say the Pnume decide who will be mother-women and take them to the crêche. There they lie in the dark and spawn."

"Alone?"

"They and the other mothers."

"What of the fathers?"

"No need for fathers. In the Shelters all is secure; protection is not needed."

Reith began to entertain an old suspicion. "On the surface," he said, "affairs go somewhat differently."

She leaned forward, and her face displayed as much animation as Reith had yet noticed. "I have always wondered about life on the *ghaun*. Who chooses the mother-women? Where do they spawn?"

Reith evaded the question. "It's a complicated situation. In due course I suppose you'll learn something about it, if you live long enough. Meanwhile, I am Adam Reith. What is your name?"

" 'Name'?* I am a female."

"Yes, but what is your personal name?"

The girl considered. "On the invoices persons are listed by

*Shelters: an inexact rendering of a word combining concepts of ageless order, quiet and security, the complexity of a maze.
*"Identification," "name," and "type" in the language of Tschai are the same word.

group, area and zone. My group is Zith, of Athan Area, in the Pagaz Zone; my ranking is 210."

"Zith Athan Pagaz, 210. Zap 210. It's not much of a name. Still, it suits you."

At Reith's jocularity the girl looked blank. "Tell me how the Gzhindra live."

"I saw them standing out on the wastelands. They pumped narcotic gas into the room where I slept. I woke up in a sack. They lowered me into a shaft. That's all I know of the Gzhindra. There must be better ways to live."

Zap 210, as Reith now thought of her, evinced disapproval. "They are persons, after all, and not wild things."

Reith had no comment to make. Her innocence was so vast that any information whatever could only cause her shock and confusion. "You'll find many kinds of people on the surface."

"It is very strange," the girl said in a vague soft voice. "Suddenly all is changed." She sat looking off into the darkness. "The others will wonder where I have gone. Someone will do my work."

"What was your work?"

"I instructed children in decorum."

"What of your spare time?"

"I grew crystals in the new East Fourth Range."

"Do you talk with your friends?"

"Sometimes, in the dormitory."

"Do you have friends among the men?"

Under the shadow of the hat the black eyebrows rose in displeasure. "It's boisterous to talk to men."

"Sitting here with me is boisterous?"

She said nothing. The idea probably had not yet occurred to her, thought Reith; now she considered herself a fallen woman. "On the surface," he said, "life goes differently, and sometimes becomes very boisterous indeed. Assuming that we survive to reach the surface."

He brought out the blue portfolio. As if by reflex Zap 210 drew herself back. Reith paid no heed. Squinting through the dim light he studied the tangle of colored lines. He put his finger down, somewhat tentatively. "Here, it seems to me, is where we are now." No response from Zap 210. Reith, aching, nervous and exhausted, started to reprimand her for disinterest, then caught his tongue. She was not here of her own volition, he reminded himself; she deserved neither reprimands nor resentment; by his actions he had made himself responsible for her. Reith gave a grunt of annoyance. He drew a deep breath and said in his most polite voice, "If I recall correctly, this passage leads over here"— he pointed—"and comes out into this pink avenue. Am I right?"

Zap 210 looked down askance. "Yes. This is a most secret way. Notice, it connects Athan with Zaltra; otherwise one must go far around, by way of Fei'erj Node." Grudgingly she came closer and brought her finger to within inches of the vellum. "This gray mark is where we want to go: to the freight-dock, at the end of the supply arterial. By Fei'erj it would be impossible, since the route leads through the dormitories and the metal-spinning areas."

Reith looked wistfully at the little red circles which marked the pop-outs. "They seem so close, so easy."

"They will certainly be guarded."

"What is this long black line?"

"That is the freight canal, and is the best route away from Pagaz Zone."

"And this bright green spot?"

She peered and drew a quick breath. "It is the way to Foreverness: a Class Twenty secret!" She sat back and huddled her chin into her knees. Reith returned to the charts. He felt her gaze and looked up to find her studying him intently. She licked her colorless mouth. "Why are you such an important item?"

"I don't know why I'm an 'item' at all." Though this was not precisely true.

"They want you for Foreverness. Are you of some strange race?"

"In a way," said Reith. He heaved himself painfully to his feet. "Are you ready? We might as well be going."

She rose without comment and they set off along the dim passage. They walked a mile and came to a white wall with a black iron door at the center. Zap 210 put her eye to the peep-lens. "A dray is passing . . . persons are near." She looked back at Reith. "Hold your head down," she said in a critical voice. "Pull the hat lower. Walk quietly, with your feet pointed straight." She turned back to the peephole. Her hand went to the door-catch. She pressed, and the door opened. "Quick, before we are seen."

Blinking and furtive, they entered a wide arched passage. The pegmatite walls were studded with enormous tourmalines which, excited to fluorescence by some means unknown, glowed pink and blue.

Zap 210 set off along the passage; Reith followed at a discreet distance. Fifty yards ahead a low dray loaded with sacks rolled on heavy black wheels. From somewhere behind them came the sound of hammers tapping at metal and a scraping noise, the source of which Reith never learned.

For ten minutes they plodded along the corridor. On four occasions Pnumekin passed, shadowed faces averted, thoughts exploring areas beyond Reith's imagination.

The polished pegmatite altered abruptly to black hornblende, polished back from veins of white quartz which seemed to grow like veins over the black matrix, the end-product of unknown centuries of toil. Far ahead, the passage dwindled to a minute black half-oval, which by insensible degrees grew larger. Beyond was black vacancy.

The aperture expanded and surrounded them; they came out on a ledge overlooking a void as black and empty as space. Fifty yards to the right a barge, moored against the dock, seemed to float in midair; Reith perceived the black void to be the surface of a subterranean lake.

A half dozen Pnumekin worked listlessly upon the dock, loading the barge with bales.

Zap 210 sidled into a pocket of shadow. Reith joined her, standing somewhat too close for her liking; she moved a few fastidious inches away. "What now?" asked Reith.

"Follow me aboard the barge. Say no word to anyone."

"No one objects? They won't put us off?"

The girl gave him a blank look. "Persons ride the barges. This is how they see the far tunnels."

"Ah," said Reith, "wanderlust among the Pnumekin; they go to look at a tunnel."

The girl gave him another blank look.

Reith asked, "Have you ever traveled on a barge before?"

"No."

"How do you know where this barge goes?"

"It goes north, to the Areas; it can go nowhere else." She peered through the gloom. "Follow me, and walk with decorum."

She set off along the dock, eyes downcast, moving as if in a reverie. Reith waited a moment, then went after her.

She paused beside the barge, looked vacantly across the black void; then, as if absentmindedly, she stepped across to the barge. She walked to the outboard side and merged with the shadow of the bales.

Reith imitated her demeanor. The Pnumekin on the dock, immersed in their private thoughts, paid him no heed. Reith stepped aboard the barge and then could not control the acceleration of his pace as he slipped into the shade of the cargo.

Zap 210, tense as wire, peered at the dock-workers. Gradually she relaxed. "They are disconsolate; otherwise they would have noticed. Do the *ghian* always lurch and lope when they move about?"

"I wouldn't be surprised," said Reith. "But no harm done. Next time—" He stopped short. At the far end of the dock stood a dark shape. It stirred, came slowly toward the barge, and entered the zone of illumination. "Pnume," whispered Reith. Zap 210 stood soundless.

The creature padded forward, oblivious to the dock-workers, who never so much as glanced aside. It stepped softly along the dock, and halted near the barge.

"It saw us," whispered the girl.

Reith stood heavy-hearted, bruises aching, legs and arms nerveless and dull. He could not survive another fight. In a husky whisper he asked, "Can you swim?"

A horrified gasp and a glance across the black void. "No!"

Reith searched for a weapon: a club, a hook, a rope; he found nothing.

The Pnume passed beyond the range of vision. A moment later they felt the barge tremble under its weight.

"Take off your cloak," said Reith. He slipped out of his own and, wrapping up the portfolio, shoved both into a crevice of the cargo. Zap 210 stood motionless.

"Take off your cloak!"

She began to whimper. Reith clapped his hand over her mouth. "Quiet!" He pulled the neck laces and, touching her fragile chin, found it trembling. He jerked off her cloak, put it with his own. She stood half-crouching in a knee-length shift. Reith, for all the urgency of the moment, resisted an insane desire to laugh at the thin adolescent figure under the black hat. "Listen," he said hoarsely. "I can tell you only once. I am going over the side. You must follow immediately. Put your hands on my shoulders. Hold your head from the water. Above all, do not splash or flounder. You will be safe."

Not waiting for her acknowledgment, he lowered himself over the side of the barge. The frigid water rose up his body like a ring of icy fire. Zap 210 hesitated only for an instant, then went over the side, probably only because she feared the Pnume more than the wet void. She gasped when her legs hit the water. "Quiet!" hissed Reith. Her hands went to his shoulders; she lowered herself into the water, and in a panic threw her arms around his neck. "Easy!" whispered Reith. "Keep your face down." He drifted in under the gunwale, and gripped a bracket. Unless someone or something peered over the side of the barge, they were virtually invisible.

A half-minute passed. Reith's legs began to grow numb. Zap 210 clung to his back, chin at his ear; he could hear her teeth chattering. Her thin body pressed against him, trapping warm pockets of water which pulsed away when one or the other moved. Once, as a boy, Reith had rescued a drowning cat; like Zap 210 it had clung to him with desperate urgency, arousing in Reith a peculiarly intense pang of protectiveness. The bodies, both frightened and wet, projected the same elemental craving for life . . . Silence, darkness, cold. The two in the water listened . . . Along the deck of the barge came a quiet sound: the click of horny toes. It stopped, cautiously started, then stopped once more, directly overhead. Looking up, Reith saw toes gripping the edge of the gunwale. He took one of Zap 210's hands, guided it to the bracket, then the other. Once free, he turned to face outward from the barge.

Unctuous ripples moved away from him; lenses of quince-colored light formed and vanished.

The toes over Reith's head clicked on the gunwale. They shifted their position. Reith, lips drawn away from his teeth in a ghastly grimace, lunged up with his right arm. He caught a thin hard ankle, pulled. The Pnume croaked in dismal consternation. It teetered forward and for a moment leaned at an incredible angle, almost horizontal, supported only by the grip of its toes. Then it fell into the water.

Zap 210 clutched at Reith. "Don't let it touch you; it will pull you apart."

"Can it swim?"

"No," she said through chattering teeth. "It is heavy; it will sink."

Reith said, "Climb up on my back, take hold of the gunwale, pull yourself aboard the barge."

Gingerly she swung behind him. Her feet pushed against his back; she stood on his shoulder, then clambered aboard the barge. Reith laboriously heaved himself up after her to lie on the deck, totally spent.

Presently he gained his feet, to peer toward the dock. The Pnumekin worked as before.

Reith moved back into the shadows. Zap 210 had not moved. The shift clung to her underdeveloped body. She was not ungraceful, reflected Reith.

She noticed his attention and huddled back against the cargo.

"Take off your undergown and put on your cloak," Reith suggested. "You'll be warmer."

She stared at him miserably. Reith pulled off his own sodden garments. In horror almost as intense as she had shown toward the Pnume, she jerked herself around. Reith found the energy for a sour grin. With her back turned she draped the cloak over her shoulders and by some means unknown divested herself of her undergarments.

The barge vibrated, lurched. Reith looked past the cargo to see the dock receding. It became an oasis of light in the heavy blackness. Far ahead showed a wan blue glimmer toward which the barge silently moved.

They were underway. Behind lay Pagaz Zone and the way to Foreverness. Ahead was darkness and the Northern Areas.

4

THE BARGE CARRIED a crew of two, who kept to the apron at the bow of the barge. Here was a small pantry, a cook-bench, an island of dim yellow illumination. There seemed to be at least two other passengers aboard, perhaps as many as three or four, who were even less obtrusive than the crew, and manifested themselves only at the pantry and the cook-bench. The food seemed to be free to the use of all. Zap 210 would not allow Reith to go forward for food. When the pantry and cook-bench were not in use

Zap 210 procured food for both: cakes of pilgrim-pod meal, candied plum-shaped objects which might have been fruit or possibly leech-like insects, bars of meat-paste, sweet and salty wafers of a delicate crisp white substance which Zap 210 considered a delicacy, but which left an unpleasant aftertaste in Reith's mouth.

Time passed: how long Reith had no way of knowing. The lake became a river which in turn became an underground canal fifty or sixty feet wide. The barge moved without a sound, propelled, so Reith guessed, by electric fields cycling along the keel. Ahead gleamed a dim blue light serving as a fix for the barge's steering sensor; when one blue light passed overhead, another always shone far ahead. At long intervals the barge passed lonesome little piers and docks, with passages leading away into unknown fastnesses.

Reith ate and slept; how many times he lost count. His cosmos was the barge, the dark, the unseen water, the presence of Zap 210. With nothing but time and boredom, Reith set himself to the task of exploring her personality. Zap 210, on her part, treated Reith with suspicion, as if begrudging even the intimacy of conversation: a skittishness and prim reserve peculiar in a person who, to the best of his knowledge, had not even a distorted understanding of ordinary sexual processes. Primordial instinct at work, Reith surmised. But how in good conscience could he turn her loose on the surface in such a condition of innocence? On the other hand the prospect of explaining human biology to Zap 210 was not a comfortable one.

Zap 210 herself never seemed to become bored with the passage of time; she slept or sat looking off into the darkness as if she watched passing vistas of great fascination. Vexed with her self-sufficiency, Reith would occasionally join her, taking no notice of her slight shift of fastidious withdrawal. Conversation with Zap 210 was never exhilarating. She had unalterable preconceptions regarding the surface: she feared the sky, the wind, the space of the horizons, the pale brown sunlight. Her anticipations were melancholy: she foresaw death under the club of a yelling barbarian. Reith tried to modify her views but encountered distrust.

"Do you think that we are ignorant of the surface?" she asked in calm scorn. "The *zuzhma kastchai* know more than anyone; they know everything. Knowledge is their existence. They are the brain-life of Tschai; Tschai is body and bones to the *zuzhma kastchai.*"

"And the Pnumekin: how do they fit into the picture?"

"The 'persons'? Long ago the *zuzhma kastchai* gave refuge to certain men from the surface, with some females and some mother-women. The 'persons' proved their diligence by polishing stones and perfecting crystals. The *zuzhma kastchai* provided peace, and so it has been, for all the ages."

"And where did men come from originally, do you know this?"

Zap 210 was uninterested. "From the *ghian*, where else?"

"Do they teach you of the sun and the stars and the other worlds of space?"

"They teach what we most want to learn, which is decorum and good conduct." She heaved a small sigh. "That is all behind me and gone; how the others would marvel at me now!"

So far as Reith could comprehend, Zap 210's principal emotion appeared to be for her own indecorous conduct.

The barge moved on. Blue glimmer appeared ahead, waxed to become a glare and pass overhead, with a new blue glimmer far in the distance. Reith became stale and restless. Darkness was almost complete, relieved only by a vague glow from the bow apron forward. The feminine voice of Zap 210, herself only a blur, began to work upon his imagination; certain of her mannerisms took on the semblance of erotic provocations. Only by conscious rational effort could he maintain his impersonality. How, he would ask himself, could she provoke or tease when she was totally unaware of the male-female relationship? Any urgings from her subconscious must seem a peculiar perversion, the most exaggerated form of "boisterous conduct." He remembered the vitality of her body when she had clung to him in the water; he thought of the look of her soaked body; he began to wonder if his instincts might not be more accurate than his reason. Zap 210, if she felt anything other than glumness and foreboding, gave no evidence, except a somewhat greater willingness to talk. For hours she spoke in a low monotone, of everything she knew. She had lived a remarkably drab life, thought Reith, without experience of gaiety, excitement, frivolity. He wondered as to the content of her imaginings, but of this she said nothing. She recognized differences in the personalities of her fellows: subtle variations of decorum and discretion which to her assumed the same significance as the more vehement personality traits of the surface. She was aware of biological differences between male and female, but apparently had never wondered as to their justification. All very strange, mused Reith. The Shelters would seem to be an incubator for a whole congeries of neuroses. Reith dared venture no inquiries; whenever the conversation skirted such matters, she became instantly taciturn. Had the Pnume bred sexdrive out of the Pnumekin? Did they administer depressants, drugs, hormones, to eliminate a troublesome tendency to over-reproduce? Reith asked a few cautious questions, to which Zap 210 gave such irrelevant and unapposite replies that Reith was sure she didn't know what he was talking about. From time to time, Zap 210 admitted, certain persons found the Shelters too staid; they were sent up to the surface, into the glare, the blowing winds, the empty nights with all the universe exposed, and never allowed to return below. "I wonder that I am not more fearful," she said. "Is it possible that I have always had Gzhindra tendencies? I have heard that so much space creates a distraction; I do not wish to be so affected."

"We're not on the surface yet," said Reith, to which Zap 210 gave a faint shrug, as if the matter were of no great importance.

Regarding the reproductive mechanisms of the Pnume she had no sure knowledge; she was uncertain whether or not the Pnume regarded the matter as secret, though she suspected as much. As to the relative number of Pnume and Pnumekin she was also uncertain. "There are probably more *zuzhma kastchai*. But many are never seen; they keep to the Deep Places, where the precious things are kept."

"What precious things?"

Again Zap 210 was vague. "The history of Tschai goes back beyond thought; just so far back go the records. The *zuzhma kastchai* are meticulous; they know everything that has ever happened. They consider Tschai to be a great conservatory, where every item, every tree, every rock is a cherished curio. Now there are off-world folk on the *ghian*: three different sorts, who have come to leave their artifacts."

"Three?"

"The Dirdir, the Chasch, the Wankh."

"What of men?"

" 'Men'?" Her voice took on a dubious tone. "I don't know. Perhaps men too are off-world. If so, four peoples sojourn in Tschai. But this has happened before; many times have strange folk come down to Old Tschai. The *zuzhma kastchai* neither welcome nor repel; they observe, they watch. They expand their collections; they fill the museums of Foreverness; they compile their archives."

Reith began to see the Pnume in a new light. It seemed that they regarded the surface of Tschai as a vast theater, on which wonderful millennium-long dramas were played out: the Old Chasch-Blue Chasch wars; the Dirdir invasion, followed by the Wankh counter-invasion; the various campaigns, battles, routs, and exterminations; the building of cities, the subsidence of ruins, the coming and going of peoples—all of which explained the acquiescence of the Pnume to the presence of alien races: from the Pnume point of view, they embellished the history of Tschai. As for Zap 210 herself, Reith asked if she had the same regard for Tschai. The girl made one of her small apathetic gestures: no, it meant nothing; she cared little one way or the other. Reith had a sudden insight into the processes of her psyche. Life for Zap 210 was a somewhat insipid experience to be tolerated. Fear was reserved for the unfamiliar; joy was beyond conjecture. He saw his own personality as it must appear to her: abrupt, brutal, crafty, harsh and unpredictable, in whom the worst excesses of boisterous conduct must always be feared . . . A sad creature, thought Reith, inoffensive and colorless. Still, remembering the feel of her clinging to his neck, he wondered. Still waters ran deep. In the dark, with nothing to occupy his mind, imaginings came to stimulate him and arouse his fervor, whereupon Zap 210, somehow sensing his turmoil, moved uneasily off into the shadows, leaving Reith sourly amused by the situation. What could be going on in her mind?

Reith invented a new game. He tried to amuse her. He invented grotesque incidents, extravagant situations, but Zap 210 was the fairy-tale princess who could not laugh. Her single pleasure, insofar as Reith could detect, was the sweet-salt wafer which served as a relish to the otherwise bland food; unfortunately, the supply of these delicacies was quickly exhausted, a day or two after they had boarded the barge. Zap 210 was taken aback by the deficiency. "There is always *diko* in our diet—always! Someone has made a foolish mistake!"

Reith had never seen her quite so emphatic. She became morose, then listless, and refused to eat anything whatever. Then she became nervous and irritable, and Reith wondered if perhaps the *diko* contained a habit-forming drug to arouse so pronounced a craving.

For a period which might have been three or four days she spoke almost not at all, and kept as far from Reith as was practicable, as if she held Reith responsible for her deprivation, which was actually the case, reflected Reith. Had he not blundered rudely into her cool gray existence, she would be conducting her ordinary routine, nibbling *diko* whenever she was of a mind. Her sulkiness waned; she became almost talkative; she seemed to want reassurance, or attention, or—could it be?—affection. So it appeared to Reith, who found the situation as absurd as any he had known.

On and on through the dark moved the barge, from blue light to blue light to blue light. They passed along a chain of underground lakes, through still caverns draped with stalactites, then for a long period—perhaps three days—along a precisely straight bore, with the blue lights spaced ten miles apart. The bore gave into another set of caverns, where they once again saw a few lonesome docks: islands of dim yellow lights. Then once again the barge rode a straight canal. The voyage was approaching its end—the feeling was in the air. The crew moved with a somewhat less deliberate gait, and the passengers on the starboard side went to stand on the forward apron. Zap 210, returning from the pantry with food, announced in a dolorous mutter: "We have almost come to Bazhan-Gahai."

"And where is this?"

"At the far side of the Area. We have come a long way." She added in a soft voice, "It has been a peaceful time."

Reith thought that she spoke with regret. "Is this place near the surface?"

"It is a trade center for goods from the Stang Islands and Hedaijha."

Reith was surprised. "We are far to the north."

"Yes. But the *zuzhma kastchai* may be waiting for us."

Reith looked anxiously ahead, at the far blue guide-light. "Why should they be?"

"I don't know. Perhaps they won't."

Blue lights, one after the other: Reith saw them pass with growing tension. He became tired, and slept; when he awoke, Zap 210 pointed ahead. "Bazhan-Gahai."

Reith rose to his feet. Ahead the gloom had lightened; the water showed a far luminous reflection. With dramatic majesty the tunnel widened; the barge moved forward, ponderous as fate. The cloaked shapes at the bow stood in silhouette against a great golden space. Reith felt a lifting of the spirit, a mysterious exaltation. The voyage which had started in cold and misery was at its end. The sides of the tunnel—fluted buttresses of raw rock—began to be visible, illuminated on one side, in black shadow on the other. The golden light was a blur; beyond, across calm water, white crags rose to a great height. Zap 210 came slowly forward, to stare into the light with a rapt expression. Reith had almost forgotten what she looked like. The thin face, the pallor, the fragile bones of jaw and forehead, the straight nose and pale mouth were as he recalled; additionally he saw an expression to which he could put no name: sadness, melancholy, haunted foreboding. She felt his gaze and looked at him. Reith wondered what she saw.

The passage opened and widened. A lake lay ahead, long and twisting. The barge proceeded along vistas of uncanny beauty. Small islands broke the black surface; great gnarled columns of white and gray rose to the vaulted ceiling far above. Half a mile ahead, under a beetling overhang, a dock became visible. From an unseen opening a shaft of golden light slanted into the cavern.

Reith could hardly speak for emotion. "Sunlight!" he finally croaked.

The barge eased forward, toward the dock. Reith searched the cavern walls, trying to trace out a route to the gap. Zap 210 said in a soft voice, "You will attract attention."

Reith moved back against the bales, and again studied the side of the cavern. He pointed. "A trail leads up to the gap."

"Of course."

Reith traced the trail along the wall. It seemed to terminate at the dock, now only a quarter of a mile distant. Reith noticed several shapes in black cloaks: Pnume or Pnumekin, he could not be sure. They stood waiting in what he considered sinister attitudes; he became highly uneasy.

Going to the stern of the barge, Reith looked right and left. He returned to Zap 210. "In a minute or so we'll pass close to that island. That's where we better leave the barge. I don't care to land at that dock."

Zap 210 gave a fatalistic shrug. They went to the stern of the barge. The island, a twisted knob of limestone, came abeam. Reith said, "Lower yourself into the water. Don't kick or flounder; I'll keep you afloat."

She gave him one unreadable side-glance and did as he bid. Holding the blue leather portfolio high in one hand he slid into the water beside her. The barge moved away, toward whoever or whatever waited on the dock. "Put your hands on my shoulders," said Reith. "Hold your face just above the water."

The ground rose under their feet; they clambered up on the island. The barge had almost reached the dock. The black shapes came forward. By their gait Reith knew them for Pnume.

From the island they waded to the shore, keeping to areas of shadow, where they were invisible to those on the dock, or so Reith hoped. A hundred feet above ran the trail to the gap. Reith made a careful reconnaissance, and they started to climb, scrambling over detritus, clinging to knobs of agate, crawling over humps and buttresses. A mournful hooting sound drifted across the water. Zap 210 became rigid.

"What does that mean?" Reith asked in a hushed voice.

"It must be a summons, or a call . . . like nothing I have heard in Pagaz."

They continued up the slope, sodden cloaks clinging to their bodies, and at last heaved themselves up on the trail. Reith looked ahead and back; no living creature could be seen. The gap into the outer world was only fifty yards distant. Once again the hooting sounded, conveying a mournful urgency.

Panting, stumbling, they ran up the trail. The gap opened before them; they saw the golden-gray sky of Tschai, where a tumbled group of black clouds floated. He took a last look down the trail. With the light of outdoors in his face, with tears blurring his vision, he could distinguish only shadows and dim rockshapes. The underground was again a world remote and unknown. He took Zap 210's hand, pulled her out into the open. Slowly she stepped forward and looked across the surface. They stood halfway up the slope of a rocky hill overlooking a wide valley. In the distance spread a calm gray surface: the sea.

Reith took a final look over his shoulder at the gap, and started down the hill. Zap 210, with a dubious glance toward the sun, followed. Reith halted. He removed the hated black hat and sailed it off over the rocks. Then he took Zap 210's hat and did the same despite her startled protest.

5

FOR REITH THE walk down the wide valley in the brown-gold light of afternoon was euphoric. He felt light-headed; his torpor had vanished; he felt strong and agile and full of hope; he even felt a new and tolerant affection for Zap 210. An odd wry creature, he thought, watching her surreptitiously, and pale as a ghost. She clearly felt uneasy in this sudden wilderness of space. Her gaze moved from the sky, along the sweep of hills to either side, out to the horizon of what Reith had decided must be the First Sea.

They reached the floor of the valley. A sluggish stream wandered between banks of dark red reeds. Nearby grew pilgrim plant, the pods of which formed the indispensable staple food of Tschai. Zap 210 looked at the gray-green pods skeptically, failing to recognize the shriveled dry yellow tablets imported into the Shelters. She ate with fatalistic disinterest.

Reith saw her looking back the way they had come, somewhat wistfully, he thought. "Do you miss the Shelters?" he asked.

Zap 210 considered her reply. "I am afraid. We can be seen from all directions. Perhaps the *zuzhma kastchai* watch us from the gap. They may send night-hounds after us."

Reith looked up toward the gap: a shadow, almost invisible from where they sat. He could detect no evidence of scrutiny; they seemed alone in the open valley. But he could not be sure. Eyes could be watching from the gap; the black cloaks made them conspicuous. He looked toward Zap 210. Almost certainly she would refuse to remove the garment . . . Reith rose to his feet. "It's growing late; perhaps we can find a village along the shore."

Two miles downstream the river spread wide to become a swamp. Along the opposite shore grew a dense forest of enormous dyans, the trunks on the periphery slanting somewhat outward. Reith had seen such a forest before; it was, so he suspected, a sacred grove of the Khors, a truculent folk living along the south shore of the First Sea.

The presence of the sacred grove, if such it was, gave Reith pause. An encounter with the Khors might immediately validate Zap 210's fears regarding the *ghaun,* and the unpleasant habits of those who lived there.

At the moment there were no Khors in sight. Proceeding

along the verge of the swamp they came out on a knoll overlooking a hundred yards of mud flat, with the sluggish First Sea beyond. Far to right and left were crumbling gray headlands, almost lost in the afternoon murk. Somewhere to the southeast, perhaps not too far, must lie the Carabas, where men sought sequins and where the Dirdir came to hunt.

Reith looked up and down the coast, trying to locate himself by sheer instinct. Zap 210 stared glumly off to sea, wondering what the future held. A mile or so along the shore to the southeast Reith noticed the crazy stilts of a pier extending across the mud flats, out into the sea; at the end half a dozen boats were moored. A swelling of ground beyond the swamp concealed the village which must lie at the head of the pier.

The Khors, while not automatically hostile, lived by a complicated etiquette, transgressions of which were not tolerated. A stranger's ignorance received no sympathy; the rules were explicit. A visit with the Khors thus became a chancy occasion.

"I don't dare risk the Khors," said Reith. He turned to look back over the desolate hills. "Sivishe is a long way south. We'll have to make for Cape Braise. If we get there we can take passage by ship down the west coast, although at the moment I don't know what we'll use for money."

Zap 210 looked at him in slack-mouthed surprise. "You want me to come with you?"

So here was the explanation for her melancholy inspection of the landscape, thought Reith. He asked, "Did you have other plans?"

She pursed her lips sullenly. "I thought that you would want to go your way alone."

"And leave you by yourself? You might not fare too well."

She looked at him with sardonic speculation, wondering at the reason for his concern.

"There's a good deal of 'boisterous conduct' up here on the surface," said Reith. "I don't think you'd like it."

"Oh."

"We'll have to go warily. These cloaks—we'd better take them off."

Zap 210 looked at him aghast. "And go without clothing?"

"No, just without the cloaks. They attract attention and hostility. We don't want to be taken for Gzhindra."

"But that is what I must be!"

"At Sivishe you may decide otherwise. If we arrive, of course. We don't help ourselves going as Gzhindra." He pulled off his cloak. With her face angrily turned away she removed her cloak and stood in her gray undergown.

Reith rolled the cloaks into a bundle. "It may be cold at night; I'll take them with us."

He picked up the blue portfolio, which now represented excess baggage. He wavered a moment and at last slid the portfolio between the inner and outer layers of his jacket.

They set off to the northwest along the shore. Behind them the Khor grove became a dark blur; the far headland grew bulky and dark. Carina 4269 moved down the sky and the sunlight took on a late afternoon richness. To the north, however, a bank of purple-black clouds threatened one of the sudden Tschai thunderstorms. The clouds moved inexorably south, muffling, half-concealing spasms of electric light. The sea below shone with the sallow luster of graphite. Ahead, close underneath the headland, appeared another grove of dyan trees. A sacred grove? Reith searched the landscape but saw no Khor town.

The grove loomed above them, the exterior boles leaning outward, the fronds hanging down in a great parasol. The headland conceivably concealed a village, but at the moment they were the only animate creatures under the half-black, half-golden-brown sky.

Reith imparted none of his misgivings to Zap 210, who was sufficiently occupied with her own. Exposure to the sunlight had flushed her face. In the rather flimsy and clinging gray undergown, with the black hair beginning to curl down on her forehead and her ears, she seemed a somewhat different person than the pallid wretch Reith had met in the Pagaz refectory . . . Was his imagination at fault? Or had her body become fuller and rounder? She noticed his gaze and gave him a glare of shame and defiance. "Why do you stare at me?"

"No particular reason. Except that you look rather different now than when I first saw you. Different and better."

"I don't know what you mean," she snapped. "You're talking foolishness."

"I suppose so . . . One of these days—not just now—I'll explain how life is on the surface. Customs and habits are more complicated—more intimate, even more 'boisterous'—than in the Shelters."

"Hmmf," sniffed Zap 210. "Why are you heading toward the forest? Isn't it another secret place?"

"I don't know." Reith pointed to the clouds. "See the black trails hanging below? That's rain. Under the trees we might stay dry. Then, night is coming soon, and the night-hounds. We have no weapons. If we climb a tree we'll be safe."

Zap 210 made no further comment; they approached the grove.

The dyans reared high overhead. At the first lines of boles they stopped to listen, but heard only a breath of wind from the oncoming storm.

Step by step they entered the grove. The sunlight shining past the clouds projected a hundred shafts and beams of dark golden light; Reith and Zap 210 walked in and out of shadow. The nearest branches were a hundred feet above; the trees could not be climbed; the grove offered little more security from night-hounds than did the open downs . . . Zap 210 stopped short and seemed to listen. Reith could hear nothing. "What do you hear?"

"Nothing." But she still listened, and peered in all directions. Reith became highly uneasy, wondering what Zap 210 sensed that he did not.

They proceeded, wary as cats, keeping to the shadows. A clearing free of boles opened before them, shrouded by a continuous roof of foliage. They looked forth into a circular area containing four huts, a low central platform. The surrounding boles had been carved to the semblance of men and women, a pair at each tree. The men were represented with long nutcracker chins, narrow foreheads, bulging cheeks and eyes; the females displayed long noses and lips parted in wide grins. Neither resembled the typical Khor man or woman, who, as Reith recollected, almost exactly resembled one another in stature, physiognomy and dress. The poses, conventionalized and rigid, depicted the act of copulation. Reith looked askance at Zap 210, who seemed blankly puzzled. Reith decided that she interpreted the not-too-explicit attitudes as representations of sheer sportiveness, or simple "boisterous conduct."

The clouds submerged the sun. Gloom came to the glade; drops of rain touched their faces. Reith scrutinized the huts. They were built in the usual Khor style, of dull brown brick with conical black iron roofs. There were four, facing each other at quadrants around the clearing. They appeared to be empty. Reith wondered what the huts contained. "Wait here," he whispered to Zap 210, and ran crouching to the nearest hut. He listened: no sound. He tried the door, which swung back easily. The interior exhaled a heavy odor, almost a stink, of poorly cured leather, resin, musk. On a rack hung several dozen masks of sculptured wood, identical to the male faces of the carved trees. Two benches occupied the center of the room; no weapons, no garments, no articles of value were to be seen. Reith returned to Zap 210 to find her inspecting the carved treetrunks, eyebrows lifted in distaste.

A purple dazzle struck the sky, followed immediately by a clap of thunder; down came rain in a torrent. Reith led the girl at a run to the hut. They entered and stood with rain drumming upon the iron roof. "The Khors are an unpredictable people," said Reith, "but I can't imagine them visiting their grove on a night like this."

"Why would they come at any time?" demanded Zap 210 peevishly. "There is nothing here but those grotesque dancers. Do the Khor look like that?"

Reith understood that she referred to the figures carved upon the treetrunks. "Not at all," he said. "They are a yellow-skinned folk, very neat and precise. The men and women are exactly alike in appearance, and disposition as well." He tried to recall what Anacho had told him: "A strange secret folk with secret ways, different by day and by night, or at least this is the report. Each individual owns two souls which come and go with dawn and sunset; the body comprises two different persons." Later, Anacho had warned: "The Khor are sensitive as spice-snakes! Do not speak to them; pay them no heed except from necessity, in which case you must use the fewest possible words. They consider garrulity a crime against nature ... Never acknowledge the presence of a woman, do not look toward their children: they will suspect you of laying a curse. Above all ignore the sacred grove! Their weapon is the iron dart which they throw with accuracy. They are a dangerous people."

Reith paraphrased the remarks to the best of his recollection; Zap 210 went to sit on one of the benches.

"Lie down," said Reith. "Try to sleep."

"In the noise of the storm, and this vile smell to all sides? Are all the houses of the *ghaun* so?"

"Not all of them," muttered Reith. He went to look out the door. The alternation of lightning glare and dying twilight upon the tree-statues presented the illusion of a frantic erotic jerking. Zap 210 might soon begin to ask questions to which Reith did not care to respond . . . Upon the roof came a sudden clatter of hail; abruptly the storm passed over, and nothing could be heard but wind sighing in the dyan trees.

Reith returned into the room. He spoke in a voice which rang false even to his own ears: "Now you can rest; at least the sound is gone."

She made a soft sound which Reith could not interpret, and went herself to stand in the doorway. She looked back at Reith. "Someone is coming."

Reith hurried to the doorway and looked forth. Across the clearing stood a figure in Khor garments: male or female Reith could not determine. It went into the hut directly opposite their own. Reith said to Zap 210: "We'd better leave while we have a chance."

She held him back. "No, no! There's another one."

The second Khor, entering the clearing, looked up at the sky. The first came from the hut with a flaring cresset on a pole, and the second ran quickly to the hut in which Reith and Zap 210 were concealed. The first took no notice. As the Khor entered Reith struck hard, ignoring all precepts of gallantry; in this case male and female were all the same. The Khor fell and lay limp. Reith jumped forward; the Khor was male. Reith stripped off his cape, tied his hands and feet with sandal thongs and gagged him with the sleeve of his black coat. With Zap 210's help he dragged the man behind the rack of masks. Here Reith made a quick search of the limp body, finding a pair of iron darts, a dagger and a soft leather pouch containing sequins, which Reith somewhat guiltily appropriated.

Zap 210 stood by the door gazing out in fascination. The first to come had been a woman. Wearing a woman-mask and a white frock, she stood by the cresset which she had thrust into a socket near the central platform. If she were perplexed by the disappearance of the man who had entered the hut she gave no sign.

Reith looked forth. "Now: while there's only one woman—"

"No! More come."

Three persons slipped separately into the clearing, going to the other three huts. One, in a woman-mask and white gown, emerged with another cresset which she placed in a socket and stood quietly like the first. The other two now came forth, wearing man-masks and white gowns like those of the women. They went to the central platform and stood near the women, who made no movement.

Reith began to understand something of the purpose of the sacred grove. Zap 210 stared forth in fascination.

Reith became highly uneasy. If events proceeded as he suspected, she would be shocked and horrified.

Three more persons appeared. One came to the hut where Reith and Zap 210 waited; Reith tried to deal with him as he had the other; but this time the blow was glancing and the man fell with a startled grunt. Reith was instantly upon him and shut off his breath until he fainted. Using sandal thongs and cape as before he tied and gagged the Khor and again robbed the man of his pouch. "I regret becoming a thief," said Reith, "but my need is far greater than yours."

Zap 210, standing by the door, gave a startled gasp. Reith went to look. The women—now there were three—had disrobed to stand nude. They began to sing, a wordless chant, sweet, soft, insistent. The three in the man-masks began a slow gyration around the platform.

Zap 210 muttered under her breath: "What are they doing? Why do they reveal their bodies? Never have I seen such a thing!"

"It is only religion," said Reith nervously. "Don't watch. Go lie down. You must be very tired."

She gave him a lambent look of wonder and distrust. "You don't answer my question. I am very embarrassed. I have never seen a naked person. Are all the folk of the *ghaun* so—so boisterous? It is shocking. And the singing: most disturbing. What are they planning to do?"

Reith tried to stand in front of her. "Hadn't you better sleep? The rites will only bore you."

"They don't bore me! I am astounded that people can be so bold! And look! The men!"

Reith took a deep breath and came to a desperate decision. "Come back here." He gave her a female mask. "Put that on."

She jerked back aghast. "What for?"

Reith took a man-mask and fitted it over his face. "We're leaving."

"But—" She turned a fascinated look toward the platform.

Reith pulled her back around, fitted one of the Khor hats on her head, arranged the other on his own.

"They'll certainly see us," said Zap 210. "They'll chase us and kill us."

"Perhaps so," said Reith. "Nevertheless we'd better go." He looked around the clearing. "You go first. Walk behind the hut. I'll come after you."

Zap 210 departed the hut. The women at the platform chanted with the most compelling urgency; the men stood nude.

Reith joined Zap 210 behind the hut. Had they been noticed? The chanting continued, rising and falling. "Walk out into the grove. Don't look back."

"Ridiculous," muttered Zap 210. "Why shouldn't I look back?" She marched toward the forest, with Reith twenty feet behind her. From the hut came a wild scream of fury. The chanting stopped short. There was stunned silence.

"Run," said Reith. Through the sacred grove they fled, throwing away the hats and masks. From behind came calls of passionate fury, but deterred perhaps by their nudity, the Khor offered no pursuit.*

Reith and Zap 210 came to the edge of the grove. They paused to catch their breath. Halfway up the sky the blue moon shone through a few ragged clouds; elsewhere the sky was clear.

Zap 210 looked up. "What are those little lights?"

"Those are stars," said Reith. "Far suns. Most control a family of planets. From a world called Earth, men came: your ancestors, mine, even the ancestors of the Khor. Earth is the world of men."

"How do you know all this?" demanded Zap 210.

"Sometime I'll tell you. Not tonight."

They set off across the downs, walking through the starry night, and something about the circumstances put Reith in a strange frame of mind. It was as if he were young and roaming a starlit meadow of Earth with a slim girl with whom he had become infatuated. So strong became the dream, or the hallucination, or whatever the nature of his mood, that he groped out for

---

*Later Reith learned more of the sacred groves, and the Khor inter-social relationships. In the towns and villages, men and women wore identical clothes; sexual activity was regarded as unnatural conduct. Only in the sacred groves, with nudity and the ritual masks to emphasize sexual disparity, did procreation occur. Men and women, in assuming the masks, assumed new personalities; children were regarded not as the issue of specific parents, but as the yield of archetypal Man and Woman.

Zap 210's hand, where she trudged beside him. She turned him a wan uncomplaining glance, but made no protest: here was another incomprehensible aspect of the astounding *ghaun*.

So they went on for a period. Reith gradually recovered his senses. He walked the surface of Tschai; his companion— He left the thought incomplete, for a variety of reasons. As if she had sensed the alteration of his mood Zap 210 angrily snatched away her hand; perhaps for a space of time she had been dreaming as well.

They marched on in silence. At last, with the blue moon hanging directly above, they reached the sandstone promontory, and found a protected niche at the base. Wrapping themselves in their cloaks, they huddled upon a drift of sand . . . Reith could not sleep. He lay looking up at the sky and listening to the sound of the girl's breathing. Like himself, she lay awake. Why had he felt so urgently compelled to flee the Khor grove at the risk of pursuit and death? To protect the girl's innocence? Ridiculous. He looked to find her face, a pale blotch in the moonlight, turned in his direction.

"I can't sleep," she said in a soft voice. "I am too tired. The surface frightens me."

"Sometimes it frightens me," said Reith. "Still, would you rather be back in the Shelters?"

As always she made a tangential response. "I can't understand what I see; I can't understand myself . . . Never have I heard such singing."

"They sang songs which never change," said Reith. "Songs perhaps from old Earth."

"They showed themselves without clothes! Is this how the surface people act?"

"Not all of them," said Reith.

"But why do they act that way?"

Sooner or later, thought Reith, she must learn the processes of human biology. Not tonight, not tonight! "Nakedness doesn't mean much," he mumbled. "Everyone has a body much like everyone else's."

"But why should they wish to show themselves? In the Shelters we remain covered, and try to avoid 'boisterous conduct.' "

"Just what is this 'boisterous conduct'?"

"Vulgar intimacy. People touch other people and play with them. It's all quite ridiculous."

Reith chose his words with care. "This is probably normal human conduct—like becoming hungry, or something of the sort. You've never been 'boisterous'?"

"Of course not!"

"You've never even thought about it?"

"One can't help thinking."

"Hasn't there ever been a young man with whom you've especially wanted to be friendly?"

"Never!" Zap 210 was scandalized.

"Well, you're on the surface and things may be different. . . . Now you'd better go to sleep. Tomorrow there may be a townful of Khors chasing us."

Reith finally slept. He awoke once to find the blue moon gone, the sky dark except for constellations. From far across the downs came the sad hooting of a night-hound. When he settled back into his cloak Zap 210 said in a drowsy whisper: "The sky frightens me."

Reith moved close beside her; involuntarily, or so it seemed, he reached out and stroked her head, where the hair was now soft and thick. She sighed and relaxed, arousing in Reith an embarrassed protectiveness.

The night passed. A russet glow appeared in the east, waxing to become a lilac and honey-colored dawn. While Zap 210 sat huddled in her cloak, Reith investigated the pouches he had taken from the Khors. He was pleased to find sequins to the value of ninety-five: more than he had expected. He discarded the darts, needle-sharp iron bolts eight inches long with a leather tail; the dagger he tucked into his belt.

They set out up the slopes of the promontory, and presently gained the ridge. Carina 4269, rising at their backs, shone along the shore, revealing another sweep of low beach and mud flats, with far off another promontory like the one on which they stood. The Khor town occupied a hillside slope a mile to the left. Almost at their feet a pier zigzagged across the mud flats and out into the sea: a precarious construction of poles, rope and planks, vibrating to the current which swirled around the base of the promontory. Half a dozen boats were moored to the spindly piles: double-ended craft, high at bow and stern like swaybacked dories fitted with masts. Reith looked toward the town. A few plumes of smoke rose from the black iron roofs; otherwise no activity was perceptible. Reith turned back to his inspection of the boats.

"It's easier to sail than to walk," Reith told Zap 210. "And there seems to be a fair wind up the coast."

Zap 210 spoke in consternation: "Out across so much emptiness?"

"The emptier the better," said Reith. "The sea gives me no worry; it's the folk who sail there . . . The same is just as true of the land, of course." He set off down the slope; Zap 210 scrambled after him. They reached the end of the pier and started along the rickety walkway. From somewhere nearby came a shriek of anger. They saw a half-grown boy racing toward the village.

Reith broke into a run. "Come along, hurry! We won't have much time."

Zap 210 came panting behind him. The two reached the end of the pier. "We won't be able to escape! They'll follow us in the boats."

"No," said Reith. "I think not." He looked from boat to boat, and chose that which seemed the most staunch. In front of the village excited black shapes had gathered; a dozen started at a run for the pier, followed by as many more.

"Jump down into the boat," said Reith. "Hoist the sail!"

"It is too late," cried Zap 210. "We will never escape."

"It's not too late. Hoist the sail!"

"I don't know how."

"Pull the rope that goes up over the mast."

Zap 210 clambered down into the boat and tried to follow Reith's instruction. Reith meanwhile ran along the pier cutting loose the other boats. Riding the current, pushed by the offshore breeze, they drifted away from the dock.

Reith returned to where Zap 210 fumbled desperately with the halyard. She strained with all her might and succeeded in fouling the long yard under the forestay. Reith took a last look toward the screaming villagers, then jumped down into the boat and cast off.

No time to sort out halyards or clear the yard; Reith took up the sweeps, fitted them between the thole pins and put way on the boat. Along the trembling pier surged the screaming Khors. Halting, they whirled their darts; up and out flew a volley of iron, to strike into the water an uncomfortable ten or twenty feet short of the boat. With renewed energy Reith worked the sweeps, then went to hoist the sail. The yard swung free, creaked aloft; the gray sail billowed; the boat heeled and churned through the water. The Khors stood silent on the pier, watching after their departing boats.

Reith sailed directly out to sea. Zap 210 sat huddled in the center of the boat. Finally she made a dispirited protest. "Is it wise to go so far from the land?"

"Very wise. Otherwise the Khors might follow along the shore and kill us when we put into land."

"I have never known such openness. It is exposed—frightfully so."

"On the other hand, our condition is better than it was yesterday at this time. Are you hungry?"

"Yes."

"See what's in that caddy yonder. We may be in luck."

Zap 210 climbed forward to the locker in the bow, where among scraps of rope and gear, spare sails, a lantern, she found a jug of water and a sack of dry pilgrim-pod cakes.

With the shore at last a blur, Reith swung the boat into the northwest, trimming the ungainly sail to the wind.

All day the fair wind blew. Reith held a course ten miles offshore, well beyond the scope of Khor vision. Headlands appeared in the murk of distance, loomed off the beam, slowly dwindled and disappeared.

As the afternoon waned the wind increased, sending whitecaps chasing over the dark sea. The rigging creaked, the sails bulged, the boat threw up a bow-wave, the wake gurgled, and Reith rejoiced at every mile so swiftly put astern.

Carina 4269 sank behind the mainland hills; the wind died and the boat lost way. Darkness came; Zap 210 crouched fearfully on the center seat, oppressed by the expanse of the sky. Reith lost patience with her fears. He lowered the yard halfway down the mast, lashed the rudder, made himself as comfortable as possible and slept.

A cool early morning breeze awoke him. Stumbling about in the pre-dawn gloom he managed to hoist the yard; then went aft to the tiller, where he steered half-dozing until the sun arose.

About noon a finger of land thrust forth into the sea; Reith landed the boat on a dismal gray beach and went out foraging. He found a brackish stream, a thicket of dark red dragon-berries, a supply of the ubiquitous pilgrim-pod. In the stream he noticed a number of crustacean-like creatures, but could not bring himself to catch them.

During the middle afternoon they once again put out to sea, Reith using the sweeps to pull the boat away from the beach. They rounded the headland to find a changed landscape shoreward. The gray beaches and mud flats had become a narrow fringe of shingle; beyond were barren red cliffs, and Reith, wary of the lee shore, put well out to sea.

An hour before sunset a long low vessel appeared over the northeast horizon, faring on a course parallel to their own. With the sun low in the northwest Reith hoped to evade the attention of those aboard the ship, which held a sinister resemblance to the pirate galleys of the Draschade. Hoping to draw away, he altered course to the south. The ship likewise altered course, coincidentally or not Reith could not be sure. He swung the boat directly toward the shore, now about ten miles distant; the ship again seemed to alter course. With a sinking heart Reith saw that they must surely be overtaken. Zap 210 watched with sagging shoulders; Reith wondered what he should do if the galley in fact overtook them. She had no knowledge of what to expect: now was hardly the time to explain to her. Reith decided that he would kill her in the event that capture became certain. Then he changed his mind: they would plunge over the side of the boat and drown together . . . Equally impractical; while there was life there was hope.

The sun settled upon the horizon; the wind, as on the previous evening, lessened. Sunset brought a dead calm with the boats rolling helplessly on the waves.

Reith shipped the sweeps. As twilight settled over the ocean he pulled away from the becalmed pirate ship toward shore. He rowed on through the night. The pink moon rose and then the blue moon, to project tremulous trails across the water.

Ahead, one of the trails ended at a mass of dead black: the shore. Reith stopped his rowing. Far to the west he saw a flickering light; to sea all was dark. He threw out the anchor and lowered the sail. The two made a meal on berries and pilgrim-pod, then lay down to sleep on the sails in the bottom of the boat.

With morning came a breeze from the east. The boat lay at anchor a hundred yards offshore, in water barely three feet deep. The pirate galley, if such it was, could no longer be seen. Reith pulled up the anchor and hoisted the sail; the boat moved jauntily off through the water.

Made cautious by the events of the previous afternoon, Reith sailed only a quarter of a mile offshore, until the wind died, half-way through the afternoon. In the north a bank of clouds gave portent of a storm; taking up the sweeps, Reith worked the boat into a lagoon at the mouth of a sluggish river. To the side of the lagoon floated a raft of dried reeds, upon which two boys sat fishing. After an initial stir they watched the approach of the boat in attitudes of indifference.

Reith paused in his rowing to consider the situation. The unconcern of the boys seemed unnatural. On Tschai unusual events almost always presaged danger. Reith cautiously rowed the boat to within conversational distance. A hundred feet distant on the bank sat three men, also fishing. They seemed to be Grays: a people short and stocky, with strongly-featured faces, sparse brownish hair and grayish skin. At least, thought Reith, they were not Khors, and not automatically hostile.

Reith let the boat drift forward. He called out: "Is there a town nearby?"

One of the boys pointed across the reeds to a grove of purple ouinga trees. "Yonder."

"What town is it?"

"Zsafathra."

"Is there an inn or a tavern where we can find accommodation?"

"Speak to the men ashore."

Reith urged the boat toward the bank. One of the men called out in irritation: "Easy with the tumult! You'll drive off every gobbulch in the lagoon."

"Sorry," said Reith. "Can we find accommodation in your town?"

The men regarded him with impersonal curiosity. "What do you here, along this coast?"

"We are travelers, from the south of Kislovan, now returning home."

"You have traveled a remarkable distance in so small a craft," remarked one of the men in a mildly skeptical voice.

"One which strongly resembles the craft of the Khors," noted another.

"For a fact," Reith agreed, "it does look like a Khor boat. But all this aside, what of lodging?"

"Anything is available to folk with sequins."

"We can pay reasonable charges."

The oldest of the men on the bank rose to his feet. "If nothing else," he stated, "we are reasonable people." He signaled Reith to approach. As the boat nosed into the reeds he jumped aboard. "So, then: you claim to be Khors?"

"Quite the reverse. We claim not to be Khors."

"What of the boat, then?"

Reith made an ambiguous gesture. "It is not as good as some, but better than others; it has brought us this far."

A wintry grin crossed the man's face. "Proceed through the channel yonder. Bear to the right."

For half an hour Reith rowed this way and that through a maze of channels with the ouinga trees always behind islands of black reeds. Reich presently understood that the Zsafathran either was having a joke or sought to confuse him. He said, "I am tired; you row the rest of the way."

"No, no," declared the old man. "We are now there, just left through yonder channel, and toward the ouingas."

"Odd," said Reith. "We have gone back and forth past that channel a dozen times."

"One channel looks much like another. And here we are."

The boat floated into a placid pond, surrounded by reed-thatched cottages on stilts under the ouinga trees. At the far end of the pond stood a larger, more elaborate structure. The poles were purple ouinga wood; the thatch was woven in a complicated pattern of black, brown and gray.

"Our community free-house," explained the Zsafathran. "We are not so isolated as you might think. Thangs come by with their troupes and carts, or Bihasu peddlers, or wandering dignitaries like yourselves. All these we entertain at our free-house."

"Thangs? We must be close upon Cape Braise!"

"Is three hundred miles close? The Thangs are as pervasive as sand-flies; they appear everywhere, more often than not when they are not wanted. Not too far is the great Thang town of Urmank . . . You and your woman both are of a race strange to me. If the concept were not inherently ludicrous—but no, to postulate nonsense is to lose my dignity; I will hazard nothing."

"We are from a remote place," said Reith. "You have never heard of it."

The old man made a sign of indifference. "Whatever you like; provided that you observe the ceremonies, and pay your score."

"Two questions," said Reith. "What are the 'ceremonies,' and how much must we expect to pay as a daily charge?"

"The ceremonies are simple," said the Zsafathran. "An exchange of pleasantries, so to speak. The charges will be perhaps four or five sequins a day. Go ashore at the dock, if you will; then we must take your boat away, to discourage speculation should a Thang or a Bihasu pass by."

Reith decided to make no objection. He worked the boat to the dock, a construction of withe and reeds lashed to piles of ouinga-wood. The Zsafathran jumped from the boat, and gallantly helped Zap 210 to the dock, inspecting her closely as he did so.

Reith jumped ashore with a mooring line, which the Zsafathran took and passed on to a lad with a set of muttered instructions. He led Reith and Zap 210 through the white pavilion and into the great free-house. "So here you are, take your ease. The cubicle yonder is at your service. Food and wine will be served in due course."

"We want to bathe," said Reith, "and we would appreciate a change of clothes if any such are available."

"The bathhouse is yonder. Fresh garments after the Zsafathran style can be furnished at a price."

"And the price?"

"Ordinary suits of gray furze for withe-cutting or tillage are ten sequins each. Since your present garments are little better than rags, I recommend the expense."

"Under-linen is included in this price?"

"Upon a surcharge of two sequins apiece under-linen is furnished, and should you wish new sandals, each must pay five sequins additionally."

"Very well," said Reith. "Bring everything. We'll go first class while the sequins last."

6

WEARING THE SIMPLE gray smock and trousers of the Zsafathrans, Zap 210 looked somewhat less peculiar and conspicuous. Her black hair had begun to curl; exposure to wind and sun had darkened her skin; only her perfectly regular features and her brooding absorption with secret ideas now set her apart. Reith doubted, however, if a stranger would notice in her conduct anything more unusual than shyness.

But Cauch, the old Zsafathran, noticed. Taking Reith aside, he muttered in a confidential voice, "Your woman: perhaps she is ill? If you require herbs, sweat-baths or homeopathy, these are available, at no great cost."

"Everything at Zsafathra is a bargain," said Reith. "Before we leave we might owe more sequins than we carry. In this case, what would be your attitude?"

"Sorrowful resignation, nothing more. We know ourselves for a destiny-blasted race, doomed to a succession of disappointments. But I trust this is not to be the case?"

"Not unless we enjoy your hospitality longer than I presently plan."

"No doubt you will carefully gauge your resources. But again, what of the woman's condition?" He subjected Zap 210 to a critical scrutiny. "I have had some experience in these matters; I deem her peaked and listless, and somewhat morose. Beyond this, I am puzzled."

"She is an unfathomable person," Reith agreed.

"The description, if I may say so, applies to you both," said Cauch. He turned his owlish gaze upon Reith. "Well, the woman's morbidity is your affair, of course . . . A collation has been served on the pavilion, which you are invited to join."

"At a small charge, presumably?"

"How can it be otherwise? In this exacting world only the air we breathe is free. Are you the sort to go hungry because you begrudge the outlay of a few bice? I think not. Come." And Cauch, urging them out upon the pavilion, seated them in withe chairs before a wicker table, then went off to instruct the girls who served from the buffet.

Cool tea, spice-cakes, stalks of a crisp red water-vegetable were set before them as a first course. The food was palatable, the chairs were comfortable; after the vicissitudes of the previous weeks the situation seemed unreal, and Reith was unable to subdue a nervous mannerism of looking warily this way and that. Gradually he relaxed. The pavilion seemed an idyll of peace. Gauzy fronds of the purple ouinga trailed low, exhaling an aromatic scent. Carina 4269 sprinkled dancing spots of dark gold light across the water. From somewhere beyond the free-house came the music of water-gongs. Zap 210 gazed across the pond in a reverie, nibbling at the food as if it lacked flavor. Becoming aware of Reith's attention she straightened primly in the chair.

"Shall I serve more of this tea?" asked Reith.

"If you like."

Reith poured from the bubble-glass jug. "You don't seem particularly hungry," he observed.

"I suppose not. I wonder if they have any *diko*."

"I'm sure that they have no *diko*," said Reith.

Zap 210 gave her fingers a petulant twitch.

Reith asked, "Do you like this place?"

"It is better than the vastness of the sea."

For a period Reith sipped his tea in silence. The table was cleared; new dishes were set before them: croquettes in sweet jelly; toasted sticks of white pith; nubbins of gray sea-flesh. As before Zap 210 showed no great appetite. Reith said politely, "You've seen something of the surface now. Is it different from your expectations?"

Zap 210 reflected. "I never thought to see so many mother-women," she murmured, as if talking to herself.

"'Mother-women'? Do you mean women with children?"

She flushed. "I mean the women with prominent breasts and hips. There are so many! Some of them seem very young: no more than girls."

"It's quite normal," said Reith. "As girls grow out of childhood, they develop breasts and hips."

"I am not a child," Zap 210 declared in an unusually haughty voice. "And I . . ." Her voice dwindled away.

Reith poured another mug of tea and settled back into his chair. "It's time," he said, "that I explained certain matters to you. I suppose I should have done so before. All women are 'mother-women.'"

Zap 210 stared at him incredulously. "This isn't the case at all!"

"Yes, it is," said Reith. "The Pnume fed you drugs to keep you immature: the *diko,* or so I imagine. You aren't drugged now and you're becoming normal—more or less. Haven't you noticed changes in yourself?"

Zap 210 sank back in her chair, dumbfounded by his knowledge of her embarrassing secret. "Such things are not to be talked about."

"So long as you know what's happening."

Zap 210 sat looking out over the water. In a diffident voice she asked, "You have noticed changes in me?"

"Well, yes. First of all, you no longer look like the ghost of a sick boy."

Zap 210 whispered, "I don't want to be a fat animal, wallowing in the dark. Must I be a mother?"

"All mothers are women," Reith explained, "but not all women are mothers. Not all mothers become fat animals."

"Strange, strange! Why are some women mothers and not others? Is it evil destiny?"

"Men are involved in the process," said Reith. "Look yonder, on the deck of that cottage: two children, a woman, a man. The woman is a mother. She is young and looks healthy. The man is the father. Without fathers, there are no children."

Before Reith could proceed with his explanation, old Cauch returned to the table and seated himself.

"All is satisfactory?"

"Very much so," said Reith. "We will regret leaving your village."

Cauch nodded complacently. "In a few poor ways we are a fortunate folk, neither rigorous like the Khors, nor obsessively flexible like the Thangs to the west. What of yourselves? I admit to curiosity regarding your provenance and your destination, for I regard you as unusual folk."

Reith ruminated a moment or two, then said: "I don't mind satisfying your curiosity if you are willing to pay my not-unreasonable fee. In fact I can offer you various grades of enlightenment. For a hundred sequins I guarantee amazement and awe."

Cauch drew back, hands raised in protest. "Tell me nothing upon which you place a value! But any oddments of small talk you can spare at no charge will find in me an attentive listener."

Reith laughed. "Triviality is a luxury I can't afford. Tomorrow we depart Zsafathra. Our few sequins must take us to Sivishe—in what fashion I don't know."

"As to this I can't advise you," said Cauch, "not even for a fee. My experience extends only so far as Urmank. Here you must go carefully. The Thangs will take all your sequins without a qualm. Useless to feel anger or injury! This is the Thang temperament. Rather than work they prefer to connive; Zsafathrans are very much on their guard when they visit Urmank, as you will see should you choose to go in our company to the Urmank bazaar."

"Hmm." Reith rubbed his chin. "What of our boat, in this case?"

Cauch shrugged, somewhat too casually or so it seemed to Reith. "What is a boat? A floating shell of wood."

"We had planned to sell this valuable boat at Urmank," said Reith. "Still, to save myself the effort of navigation, I will let it go here for less than its full value."

With a quiet laugh Cauch shook his head. "I have no need for so clumsy and awkward a craft. The rigging is frayed, the sails are by no means the best; there is only a poor assortment of gear and rope in the forward caddy."

After an hour and a half of proposals and counter-proposals Reith disposed of the boat for forty-two sequins, together with all costs of accommodation at Zsafathra, and transportation to Urmank on the morrow. As they bargained they consumed quantities of the pepper tea, a mild intoxicant. Reith's mood became loose and easy. The present seemed none too bad. The future? It would be met on its own terms. At the moment the failing afternoon light seeped through the enormous ouinga trees, pervading the air with dusty violet, and the pond mirrored the sky.

Cauch went off about his affairs; Reith leaned back in his chair. He considered Zap 210, who also had drunk a considerable quantity of the pepper tea. Some alteration of his mood caused him to see her not as a Pnumekin and a freak but as a personable young woman sitting quietly in the dusk. Her attention was fixed on something across the pavilion; what she saw astonished her and she turned to Reith in wonder. Reith noticed how large and dark were her eyes. She spoke in a shocked whisper. "Did you see . . . *that*?"

"What?"

"A young man and a young woman—they stood close and put their faces together!"

"Really!"

"Yes!"

"I can't believe it. Just what did they do?"

"Well—I can't quite describe it."

"Was it like this?" Reith put his hands on her shoulders, looked deep into the startled eyes.

"No . . . not quite. They were closer."

"Like this?"

Reith put his arms around her. He remembered the cold water of the Pagaz lake, the desperate animal vitality of her body as she had clung to him. "Was it like this?"

She pushed back at his shoulders. "Yes . . . Let me go; someone might think us boisterous."

"Did they do this?" Reith kissed her. She looked at him in astonishment and alarm, and put her hand to her mouth. "No . . . Why did you do that?"

"Did you mind?"

"Well, no. I don't think so. But please don't do it again; it makes me feel very strangely."

"That," said Reith, "is the effects of the *diko* wearing off." He drew back and sat with his head spinning. She looked at him uncertainly. "I can't understand why you did that."

Reith took a deep breath. "It's natural for men and women to be attracted to each other. This is called the reproductive instinct, and sometimes it results in children."

Zap 210 became alarmed. "Will I now be a mother-woman?"

"No," said Reith. "We'd have to become far friendlier."

"You're sure?"

Reith thought that she leaned toward him. "I'm sure." He kissed her again, and this time, after a first nervous motion, she made no resistance . . . then she gasped. "Don't move. They won't notice us if we sit like this; they'll be ashamed to look."

Reith froze, his face close to hers. "Who won't notice us?" he muttered.

"Look—now."

Reith glanced over his shoulder. Across the pavilion stood two dark shapes wearing black cloaks and wide-brimmed black hats.

"Gzhindra," she whispered.

Cauch came into the pavilion, and went to talk with the Gzhindra. After a moment he led them out into the road.

Dusk became night. Across the pavilion the serving girls hung up lamps with yellow and green shades, and brought new trays and tureens to the buffet table. Reith and Zap 210 sat somberly back in the shadows.

Cauch, returning to the pavilion, joined them. "Tomorrow at dawn we will depart for Urmank, and no doubt arrive by noon. You know the reputation of the Thangs?"

"To some extent."

"The reputation is deserved," said Cauch. "They cheat in preference to keeping faith; their favorite money is stolen money. So be on your guard."

Reith asked casually, "Who were the two men in black with whom you spoke half an hour ago?"

Cauch nodded as if he had been awaiting the question. "Those were Gzhindra, or Ground-men as we call them, who sometimes act as agents for the Pnume. Their business tonight was different. They have taken a commission from the Khors to locate a man and a woman who desecrated a sacred place and stole a boat near the town of Fauzh. The description, by a peculiar coincidence, matched your own, though certain discrepancies enabled me to state with accuracy that no such persons had been seen at Zsafathra. Still, they may discuss the matter with people who do not know you as well as I; to avoid any possible confusion of identities, I suggest that you alter your appearance as dramatically as possible."

"That is easier said than done," said Reith.

"Not altogether." Cauch put his fingers into his mouth, producing a shrill whistle. Without surprise or haste one of the serving girls approached: a pleasant creature, broad in hips, shoulders, cheekbones and mouth, with nondescript brown hair worn in a wildly coquettish array of ringlets. "Well, then, you desire something?"

"Bring a pair of turbans," said Cauch. "The orange and white, with black bangles."

The girl procured the articles. Going to Zap 210, she wound the orange and white cloth around the black cap of hair, tied it so that the tasseled ends hung behind the left ear, then affixed black bangles to swing somewhat in front of the right ear. Reith marveled at the transformation. Zap 210 now seemed daring and mischievous, a gay young girl costumed as a pirate.

Reith was next fitted with the turban; Zap 210 seemed to find the transformation amusing; she opened her mouth and laughed: the first occasion Reith had heard her do so.

Cauch appraised them both. "A remarkable difference. You have become a pair of Hedaijhans. Tomorrow I will provide you with shawls. Your very mothers would not know you."

"What do you charge for this service?" demanded Reith. "A reasonable sum, I hope?"

"A total of eight sequins, to include the articles themselves, fitting, and training in the postures of the Hedaijhans. Essentially, you must walk with a swagger, swinging your arms—so." Cauch demonstrated a mincing lurching gait. "With your hands—so. Now, lady, you first. Remember, your knees must be bent. Swing, swagger . . ."

Zap 210 followed the instructions with great earnestness, looking toward Reith to see if he laughed.

The practice went on into the night, while the pink moon sailed behind the ouinga trees, and the blue moon rose in the east. Finally Cauch pronounced himself satisfied. "You would deceive almost anyone. So then, to the couch. Tomorrow we journey to Urmank."

The sleeping cubicle was dim, cracks in the rattan wall admitting slits of green and yellow light from the pavilion lamps, as many more from the pink and blue moons shining from different directions to make a multicolored mesh on the floor.

Zap 210 went to the wall and peered through the cracks out toward the avenue which ran under the ouingas. She looked for several minutes. Reith came to join her. "What do you see?"

"Nothing. They would not let themselves be seen so easily." She turned away and with an inscrutable glance toward Reith went to sit on one of the wicker couches. Presently she said, "You are a very strange man."

Reith had no reply to make.

"There is so much you don't tell me. Sometimes I feel as if I know nothing whatever."

"What do you want to know?"

"How people of the surface act, how they feel . . . why they do the things they do . . ."

Reith went to where she sat and stood looking down at her. "Do you want to learn all these things tonight?"

She sat looking down at her hands. "No. I'm afraid . . . Not now."

Reith reached out and touched her head. He was suddenly wildly tempted to sit down beside her and tell her the tale of his remarkable past . . . He wanted to feel her eyes on him; to see her pale face attentive and marveling . . . In fact, thought Reith, he had begun to find this strange girl with her secret thoughts stimulating.

He turned away. As he crossed to his own couch he felt her eyes on his back.

7

THE MORNING SUNLIGHT entered the cubicle, strained by the withes of the wall. Going out upon the pavilion, Reith and Zap 210 found Cauch making a breakfast of pilgrim-pod cakes and a hot broth redolent of the shore. He inspected Reith and Zap 210 narrowly, paying particular attention to the turbans and their gait. "Not too bad. But you tend to forget. More swagger, lady, more shrug to your shoulders. Remember when you leave the pavilion you are Hedaijhans, in case suspicions have been aroused, in case someone waits and watches."

After breakfast, the three went out upon the avenue which led northward under the ouinga trees, Reith and Zap 210 as thoroughly Hedaijhan as turban, shawl and mincing gait could make them, to a pair of carts drawn by a type of animal Reith had not previously seen: a gray-skinned beast which pranced elegantly and precisely on eight long legs.

Cauch climbed aboard the first cart; Reith and Zap 210 joined him. The carts departed Zsafathra.

The road led out upon a damp land of reeds, water-plants, isolated black stumps trailing lime-green tendrils. Cauch gave a great deal of his attention to the sky, as did the Zsafathrans in the cart behind. Reith finally asked: "What are you watching for?"

"Occasionally," said Cauch, "we are molested by a tribe of predatory birds from the hills yonder. In fact, there you see one of their sentinels." He pointed to a black speck flapping across the southern sky; it appeared the size of a large buzzard. Cauch went on in a voice of resignation. "Presently they will fly out to attack us."

"You show no great alarm," said Reith.

"We have learned how to deal with them." Cauch turned and gestured to the cart behind, then accelerated the pace of his own cart, to open up a gap of a hundred yards between the two. Out of the southern skies came a flock of fifty or sixty flapping bird-creatures. As they drew near Reith saw that each carried two chunks of stone half the size of his head. He looked uneasily toward Cauch. "What do they do with the rocks?"

"They drop them, with remarkable accuracy. Assume that you stood in the road, and that thirty creatures flew above you at their customary height of five hundred feet. Thirty stones would strike you and crush you to the ground."

"Evidently you have learned how to frighten them off."

"No, nothing of the sort."

"You disturb their accuracy?"

"To the contrary. We are essentially a passive people and we try to deal with our enemies so that they disconcert or defeat themselves. Have you wondered why the Khors do not attack us?"

"The thought has occurred to me."

"When the Khors attack—and they have not done so for six hundred years—we evade them and by one means or another penetrate their sacred groves. Here we perform acts of defilement, of the most simple, natural and ordinary sort. They no longer can use the grove for procreation and must either migrate or perish. Our weapons, I agree, are indelicate, but typify our philosophy of warfare."

"And these birds?" Reith dubiously watched the approach of the flock. "Surely the same weapons are ineffectual?"

"I would presume so," Cauch agreed, "though for a fact we have never tested them. In this case we do nothing whatever."

The birds soared overhead; Cauch urged the dray-beast into a sinuous lope. One by one the birds dropped their stones, which fell to strike the road behind the cart.

"The birds, you must understand, can only compute the position of a stationary target; in this case their accuracy is their undoing."

The stones were all dropped; with croaks of frustration the birds flew back to the mountains. "They will more than likely return with another load of stones," said Cauch. "Do you notice how this road is elevated some four feet above the surrounding marsh? The toil has been accomplished by the birds over many centuries. They are dangerous only if you stand to watch."

The carts moved through a forest of wax-brown trees, seething with hordes of small white fuzz-balls, half-spider, half-monkey, which bounded from branch to branch, venting raucous little screams and hurling twigs at the travelers. The road then led twenty miles across a plain littered with boulders of honey-colored tuff, toward a pair of tall volcanic necks, each growing into an ancient weathered castle, in ages past the headquarters of hermetic cults but now, according to Cauch, the abode of ghouls. "By day they are never seen, but by night they come down to prowl the outskirts of Urmank. Sometimes the Thangs catch them in traps for use at the carnival."

The road passed between the peaks and Urmank came into view: a disorderly straggle of high, narrow houses of black timber, brown tile and stone. A quay bordered the waterfront, where half a dozen ships floated placidly at moorages. Behind the quay was the marketplace and bazaar, to which a flutter of orange and green banners gave a festive air. A long wall of crumbling brick bounded the bazaar; a clutter of mud huts beyond seemed to indicate a caste of pariahs.

"Behold Urmank!" said Cauch. "The town of the Thangs. They are not fastidious as to who comes and who goes, provided only that they take away fewer sequins than they brought."

"In my case they will be disappointed," said Reith. "I hope to gain sequins, by one means or another."

Cauch gave him a marveling side-glance. "You intend to take sequins from the Thangs? If you control such a miraculous power please share it with me. The Thangs have cheated us so regularly that now they regard the process as their birthright. Oh, I tell you, in Urmank you must be wary!"

"If you are cheated, why do you deal with them?"

"It seems an absurdity," Cauch admitted. "After all, we could bring a ship and sail it to Hedaijha, the Green Erges, Coad—but we are a wry people; it amuses us to come to Urmank where the Thang provide entertainments. Look yonder; see the area wrapped around with brown and orange canvas? There is the site of the stilting. Beyond are the games of chance, where the visitor invariably loses more than he gains. Urmank is a challenge to Zsafathra; always we hope to outwit the Thangs."

"Our joint efforts may yield a profit," said Reith. "At least I can bring a fresh outlook to bear."

Cauch gave an indifferent shrug. "Zsafathrans have tried to outdo the Thangs from beyond the brink of memory. They deal with us by formula. First we are enticed by the prospect of quick gain; then after we have put down our sequins the prospects recede . . . Well, first we will refresh ourselves. The Inn of the Lucky Mariner has proved satisfactory in the past. As my associate you are safe from thuggery, kidnap and slave-taking. However, you must guard your own money; the Thangs can be coerced only so far and no further."

The common room at the Inn of the Lucky Mariner was furnished in a style Reith had not seen previously on Tschai. Angular chairs of wooden posts and poles lined the walls, which were whitewashed brick. In alcoves glass pots displayed the movement of iridescent sea-worms. The chief functionary wore a brown caftan buttoned down the front, a black skullcap, black slippers and black finger-guards. His face was bland, his manners suave; he proffered for Reith's inspection a pair of adjoining cubicles furnished with couch, nightstand and lamp, which, with fresh body linen and foot ointment, rented for the inclusive sum of three sequins. Reith thought the figure reasonable and said as much to Cauch.

"Yes," said Cauch. "Three sequins is no great amount, but I recommend that you make no use of the foot ointment. As a new amenity, it arouses suspicion. It may stain the woodwork, whereupon you will be levied an extra charge. Or it may contain a pulsing vescient, the balm for which sells at five sequins the dram."

Cauch spoke in full earshot of the functionary, who laughed quietly and without offense. "Old Zsafathran, you are overskeptical for once. Recently we were required to accept a large stock of tonics and ointments in lieu of payment, and we have merely put these substances at the disposal of our guests. Do you require a diuretic or a vermifuge? We supply these at only a nominal charge."

"At the moment, nothing," said Cauch.

"What of your Hedaijhan friends? Everyone is the better for an occasional purge, which we offer at ten bice. No? Well then, for your evening meal let me recommend The Choicest Offerings of Land and Sea a few steps to the right along the quay."

"I have dined there on a previous occasion," said Cauch. "The substances set before me would have quelled the appetite of a High-castle ghoul. We will buy bread and fruit in the market."

"In that case, be so good as to patronize the booth of my nephew, opposite the depilatorium!"

"We will inspect his produce." Cauch led the way out upon the quay. "The Lucky Mariner's comparatively scrupulous; still, as you see, one must be alert. On my last visit, a troupe of musicians played in the common room. I stopped for a moment to listen and on my reckoning discovered a charge of four sequins. As far as the offer of purgative at little or no charge"—here Cauch coughed—"this is all very well. On a previous visit to Urmank a similar offer was put to my grandfather, who accepted and thereafter discovered a lock on the door to the convenience, and consequent usage charge. The medication, in the long run, cost him dearly. It is wise in one's dealings with the Thangs to examine every aspect of a situation."

The three strolled along the quay, Reith examining the ships with interest. These were all fat-bellied little cogs, with high poops and foredecks, propelled by sails when the wind was fair and an electric jet-pump otherwise. In front of each a board announced the name of the ship, the port of destination and the date of sailing.

Cauch touched Reith's arm. "It might be imprudent to evince too great an interest in the ships."

"Why?"

"At Urmank it is always the part of wisdom to dissemble."

Reith looked back up the quay. "No one appears to be heeding us. If they are, they will take it for granted that I dissemble and actually plan a journey overland."

Cauch sighed. "At Urmank life has many surprises for the unwary."

Reith halted by a board. "The ship *Nhiahar*. Destination: Ching, the Murky Isles, the South Schanizade Coast, Kazain. A moment." Reith climbed a gangplank and approached a thin and somber man in a leather apron.

"Where is the captain, if you please?"

"I am he."

"In connection with a voyage to Kazain: what fare would you demand for two persons?"

"For the Class A cabin I require four sequins per person per diem, which includes nutrition. The passage to Kazain is generally thirty-two days; hence the total fee for two persons is, let us say, two hundred and sixty sequins."

Reith expressed surprise at the magnitude of the amount, but the captain maintained an indifferent attitude.

Reith returned to the dock. "I need something over two hundred and fifty sequins."

"Not an impossible sum," said Cauch. "A diligent laborer can earn four or even five sequins a day. Porters are always in demand along the docks."

"What of the gambling booths?"

"The district is yonder, beside the bazaar. Needless to say, you are unlikely to overcome the Thang gamesters on their own premises."

They walked into a plaza paved with squares of salmon-pink stone. "A thousand years ago the tyrant Przelius built a great rotunda here. Only a floor remains. There: food-stalls. There: garments and sandals. There: ointments and extracts . . ." As Cauch spoke he pointed toward various quarters of the plaza, where the booths offered a great variety of goods: foodstuffs, cloth, leather; an earth-colored melange of spices; tinware and copper; black iron slabs, pads, rods and bars; glassware and lamps; paper charms and fetishes. Beyond the floor of the rotunda and the more or less orderly array of booths were the entertainments: orange tents with rugs in front where girls danced to nose-flutes and snap-blocks. Some wore garments of gauze; others danced bare to the waist; a few no more than a year or two from childhood wore only sandals. Zap 210 watched these and their postures with amazement. Then, with a shrug and a numb expression, she turned away.

Muffled chanting attracted Reith's attention. A canvas wall enclosed a small stadium, from which now came a sudden chorus of hoots and groans. "The stilt contests," Cauch explained. "It appears that one of the champions has been downed, and many wagers have gone by the boards."

As they passed the stadium Reith caught a view of four men on ten-foot stilts stalking warily around each other. One kicked forth with his stilt; another struck a blow with a pillow-headed club; a third caught unaware careened away, preserving his balance by a miracle, while the others hopped after him like grotesque carrion-birds.

"The stilt-fighters are mostly Black Mountain mica-cutters," said Cauch. "The outsider who wagers on the bouts might as well drop his money into a hole." Cauch gave his head a rueful jerk. "Still, we always hope. My brother's name-father won forty-two sequins at the eel-race some years ago. I must admit that for two days previously he burnt incense and implored divine intervention."

"Let's watch an eel-race," said Reith. "If divine intervention earns a profit of forty-two sequins, our own intelligence should produce at least as much and hopefully more."

"This way then, past the brat-house."

Reith was about to inquire what a brat-house might be, when a grinning urchin ran close and kicked Reith on the shins then, dodging back, made an ugly face and ran into the brat-house. Reith looked after the child in wrathful puzzlement. "What's the reason for that?"

"Come," said Cauch. "I'll show you."

He led the way into the brat-house. On a stage thirty feet distant stood the child, who upon their entrance emitted a hideous taunting squeal. Behind the counter stood a suave middle-aged Thang with a silky brown mustache. "Nasty tyke, don't you think? Here, give him a good pelting. These mud-balls come ten bice apiece. The dung-packets are six to the sequin and these prickle-burrs are five to the sequin."

"Yah, yah, yah!" screamed the urchin. "Why worry? He couldn't heave a rock this far!"

"Go ahead, sir, give it to him," suggested the operator. "Which will it be? The mud-balls? The dung-packets make a hideous reek; the brat despises them. And the thorn-balls! He'll rue the day he attacked you."

"You get up there," said Reith. "Let me throw at you."

"Prices double, sir."

Reith departed the brat-house with the taunts of both urchin and operator accompanying him to the reach of earshot.

"Wise restraint," said Cauch. "No sequins to be earned in such a place."

"One can't live by bread alone . . . but no matter. Show me the eel-races."

"Only a few steps further."

They walked toward the sagging old wall which separated the bazaar from Urmank Old Town. At the very edge of the open area, almost in the shadow of the wall, they came to a U-shaped counter surrounded by two-score men and women, many wearing outland garments. A few feet beyond the open end of the U a wooden reservoir stood on a concrete platform. The reservoir, six feet in diameter and two feet high, was equipped with a hinged cover and emptied into a covered flume which ran between the arms of the U, to empty into a glass basin at the far bend. The attention of the players was riveted upon the glass basin; as Reith watched a green eel darted forth from the chute and into the basin, followed after a moment or two by eels of various other colors.

"Green wins again!" cried out the eel-master in a voice of anguish. "Lucky lucky green! Hands behind the screen, please, until I pay the winners! I am sorely hit! Twenty sequins for this Jadarak gentleman, who risked a mere two sequins. Ten sequins for this green-hatted lady of the Azote Coast, who chanced a sequin on the color of her hat! . . . What? No more? Is this all? I have not been struck so sorely as first I feared." The operator cleared the boards of sequins laid down upon the other colors. "A new race will now occur; arrange your bets. Sequins must be placed squarely upon the chosen color, if you please, to avoid misunderstanding. I set no limit; bet as high as you please, up to a limit of a thousand sequins, since my total wealth and reserve is only ten thousand. Five times already I have been bankrupted; always I have climbed back from poverty to serve the gambling folk of Urmank; is this not true dedication?'" As he spoke, he gathered the eels into a basket and carried them to the upper end of the chute. He hauled on a rope which, passing over a frame, lifted the lid of the reservoir. Reith edged close and peered down into the pool of water contained within. The eel-master made no objection. "Look your fill, my man; the only mysteries here are the eels themselves. If I could read their secrets I would be a rich man today!" Within the reservoir Reith saw a baffle which defined a spiral channel originating at a center well and twisting out to the chute, with a gate to the center well which the eel-master now snapped shut. In the center well he placed the eels and closed down the lid. "You have witnessed," he called out. "The eels move at random, as free as though they traveled the depths of their native streams. They whirl, they race, they seek a ray of light; when I raise the gate all will dash forth. Which will win the race to the basin? Ah, who knows? The last winner was Green;

will Green win again? Place your bets, all bets down! Aha! A grandee here wagers generously upon Gray and Mauve, ten sequins on each! What's this? A purple sequin upon Purple! Behold all! A noblewoman of the Bashai backlands wagers a hundred-value on Purple! Will she win a thousand? Only the eels know."

"I know too," Cauch muttered to Reith. "She will not win. Purple eel will loiter along the way. I predict a win for White or Pale Blue."

"Why do you say that?"

"No one has bet on Pale Blue. Only three sequins are down on White."

"True, but how do the eels know?"

"Herein, as the eel-master avers, lies the mystery."

Reith asked Zap 210: "Can you understand how the operator controls the eels to his profit?"

"I don't understand anything."

"We'll have to give this matter some thought," said Reith. "Let's watch another race. In the interests of research I'll put a sequin down upon Pale Blue."

"Are all bets made?" called out the eel-master. "Please be meticulous! Sequins overlapping two colors are reckoned to fall on the losing color. No more bets? Very well then, please keep hands behind the screen. No more bets, please! The race is about to begin!"

Stepping to the reservoir, he pulled a lever which presumably lifted the gate in front of the spiral baffle. "The race is in progress! Eels vie for light; they cavort and wheel in their joy! Down the chute they come! Which is to win?"

The gamblers craned their necks to watch; into the basin streaked the White eel. "Ah," groaned the operator. "How can I profit with such uncooperative eels? Twenty sequins to this already wealthy Gray; you are a mariner, sir? And ten to this noble young slave-taker from Cape Braise. I pay, I pay; where is my profit?" He came past, flipping Reith's sequin into his tray. "So then, everyone alert for the next race."

Reith turned to Cauch with a shake of his head. "Perplexing, perplexing indeed. We had better go on."

They wandered the bazaar until Carina 4269 went down the sky. They watched a wheel of fortune; they studied a game where the participants bought a bag of irregular colored tablets and sought to fit them together into a checkerboard; a half-dozen other games, more or less ordinary. Sunset arrived; the three went to a small restaurant near the Inn of the Lucky Mariner, where they dined upon fish in red sauce, pilgrim-pod bread, a salad of sea-greens and a great black flask of wine. "In only one phase of existence," said Cauch, "can the Thang be trusted: their cuisine, to which they are loyal. The reason for this particularity escapes me."

"It goes to demonstrate," said Reith, "that you can't judge a man by the table he sets."

Cauch asked shrewdly, "How then can a man judge his fellows? For example, what is the basis of your calculation?"

"Only one thing I know for certain," said Reith. "First thoughts are always wrong."

Cauch, sitting back, inspected Reith under quizzical eyebrows. "True, quite possibly true. For instance, you probably are not the cool desperado you appear on first meeting."

"I have been judged even more harshly," said Reith. "One of my friends declares that I seem like a man from another world."

"Odd that you should say that," remarked Cauch. "A strange rumor has recently reached Zsafathra, to the effect that all men originated on a far planet, much as the Redeemers of Yao aver, and not from a union of the sacred xyxyl bird and the sea-demon Rhadamth. Furthermore, it was told that certain folk from this far planet now wander Old Tschai, performing the most remarkable deeds: defying the Dirdir, defeating the Chasch, persuading the Wankh. A new feeling is abroad across Tschai: the sense that change is on its way. What do you think of all this?"

"I suppose the rumor is not inherently absurd," said Reith.

Zap 210 said in a subdued voice: "A planet of men: it would be more strange and wild than Tschai!"

"That of course is problematical," remarked Cauch in a voice of didactic analysis, "and no doubt irrelevant to our present case. The secrets of personality are mystifying. For instance, consider the three of us. One honest Zsafathran and two brooding vagabonds driven like leaves before the winds of fate. What prompts such desperate journeys? What is to be gained? I myself in all my lifetime have not gone so far as Cape Braise; yet I feel none the worse, a trifle dull perhaps. I look at you and ponder. The girl is frightened; the man is harsh; goals beyond her understanding propel him; he takes her where she fears to go. Still, would she go back if she could?" Cauch looked into Zap 210's face; she turned away.

Reith managed a painful grin. "Without money we won't go anywhere."

"Bah," said Cauch bluffly, "if money is all you lack, I have the remedy. Once a week, each Ivensday, combat trials are arranged. In point of fact, Otwile the champion sits yonder." He nodded toward a totally bald man almost seven feet tall, massive in the shoulders and thighs, narrow at the hips. He sat alone sipping wine, staring morosely out upon the quay. "Otwile is a great fighter," said Cauch. "He once grappled a Green Chasch buck and held his own; at least he escaped with his life."

"What are the prizes?" Reith inquired.

"The man who remains five minutes within the circle wins a hundred sequins; he is paid a further twenty sequins for each broken bone. Otwile sometimes provides a hundred-worth within the minute."

"And what if the challenger throws Otwile away?"

Cauch pursed his lips. "No prize is posted; the feat is considered impossible. Why do you ask? Do you plan to make the trial?"

"Not I," said Reith. "I need three hundred sequins. Assume that I remained five minutes in the ring to gain a hundred sequins . . . I would then need ten broken bones to earn a further two hundred."

Cauch seemed disappointed. "You have an alternative scheme?"

"My mind reverts to the eel-race. How can the operator control eleven eels from a distance of ten feet while they swim down a covered chute? It seems extraordinary."

"It does indeed," declared Cauch. "For years folk of Zsafathra have put down their sequins on the presumption that such control is impossible."

"Might the eels alter color to suit the circumstances? Impractical, unthinkable. Does the operator stimulate the eels telepathically? I consider this unlikely."

"I have no better theories," said Cauch.

Reith reviewed the eel-master's procedure. "He raises the lid of the reservoir; the interior is open and visible; the water is no more than a foot deep. The eels are placed into the center well and the lid is closed down: this before betting is curtailed. Yet the eel-master appears to control the motion of the eels."

Cauch gave a sardonic chuckle. "Do you still think you can profit from the eel-races?"

"I would like to examine the premises a second time." Reith rose to his feet.

"Now? The races are over for the day."

"Still, let us examine the ground; it is only five minutes' walk."

"As you wish."

The area surrounding the eel-race layout was deserted and lit dimly by the glow of distant bazaar lamps. After the animation of the daytime hours, the table, reservoir and chute seemed peculiarly silent.

Reith indicated the wall which limited the compound. "What lies to the other side?"

"The Old Town and, beyond, the mausoleums, where the Thangs take their dead—not a place to visit by night."

Reith examined the chute and reservoir, the lid to which was locked down for the night. He turned to Cauch. "What time do the races begin?"

"At noon, precisely."

"Tomorrow morning I'd like to look around some more."

"Indeed," mused Cauch. He looked at Reith sidewise. "You have a theory?"

"A suspicion. If—" He looked around as Zap 210 grasped his arm. She pointed. "Over there."

Across the compound walked two figures in black cloaks and wide black hats.

"Gzhindra," said Zap 210.

Cauch said nervously, "Let us return to the inn. It is not wise to walk the dark places of Urmank."

At the inn Cauch retired to his chamber. Reith took Zap 210 to her cubicle. She was reluctant to enter. "What's the matter?" asked Reith.

"I am afraid."

"Of what?"

"The Gzhindra are following us."

"That's not necessarily true. Those might have been any two Gzhindra."

"But perhaps they weren't."

"In any event they can't get at you in the room."

The girl was still dubious.

"I'm right next door," said Reith. "If anyone bothers you—scream."

"What if someone kills you first?"

"I can't think that far ahead," said Reith. "If I'm dead in the morning, don't pay the score."

She wanted further reassurance. Reith patted the soft black curls. "Good night."

He closed the door and waited until the bolt shot home. Then he went into his own cubicle and, despite Cauch's reassurances, made a careful examination of floor, walls and ceiling. At last, feeling secure, he turned the light down to a glimmer and lay himself upon the couch.

8

THE NIGHT PASSED without alarm or disturbance. In the morning Reith and Zap 210 breakfasted alone at the café on the quay. The sky was cloudless; the smoky sunlight left crisp black shadows behind the tall houses and glinted on the water of the harbor. Zap 210 seemed less pessimistic than usual, and watched the porters, the hawkers, the seamen and outlanders with interest. "What do you think of the *ghian* now?" asked Reith.

Zap 210 at once became grave. "The folk act differently from what I expected. They don't run back and forth; they don't seem maddened by the sun-glare. Of course"—she hesitated—"one sees a great deal of boisterous conduct, but no one seems to mind. I marvel at the garments of the girls; they are so bold, as if they want to provoke attention. And again, no one objects."

"Quite the reverse," said Reith.

"I could never act like that," Zap 210 said primly. "That girl coming toward us: see how she walks! Why does she act that way?"

"That's how she's put together. Also, she wants men to notice her. These are the instincts that the *diko* suppressed in you."

Zap 210 protested with unusual fervor: "I eat no *diko* now; I feel no such instincts!"

Reith looked smiling off across the quay. The girl to whom Zap 210 had drawn attention slowed her step, hitched at the orange sash around her waist, smiled at Reith, stared curiously at Zap 210, and sauntered on.

Zap 210 looked sidelong at Reith. She started to speak, then held her tongue. A moment later she blurted: "I don't understand anything of the *ghian*. I don't understand you. Just now you smiled at that odious girl. You never—" Here she stopped short, then continued in a low voice: "I suppose you blame 'instinct' for your conduct."

Reith became impatient. "The time has come," he said, "to explain the facts of life. Instincts are part of our biological baggage and cannot be avoided. Men and women are different." He went on to explain the processes of reproduction. Zap 210 sat rigid, looking across the water. "So," said Reith, "it's not unnatural that people indulge in this kind of conduct."

Zap 210 said nothing. Her hands, so Reith noticed, were clenched and her knuckles shone white.

She said in a low voice, "The Khors in the sacred grove—is *that* what they were doing?"

"So I suppose."

"And you took me away so I wouldn't see."

"Well, yes. I thought you might be confused."

Zap 210 was silent a moment. "We might have been killed."

Reith shrugged. "I suppose there was a chance."

"And those girls dancing without clothes—they wanted to do *that*?"

"If someone gave them money."

"And everyone on the surface feels this way?"

"Most of them, I should say."

"Do you?"

"Certainly. Sometimes, anyway. Not all the time."

"Then why—" she stuttered. "Then why—" She could not finish. Reith reached out to pat her hand; she snatched it away. "Don't touch me!"

"Sorry . . . But don't be angry."

"You brought me to this horrible place; you deprived me of life; you pretended to be kind—but all the time you've been planning—*that*!"

"No, no!" cried Reith. "Nothing of the sort! You're quite wrong!"

Zap 210 looked at him with eyebrows coolly raised. "You find me repulsive then?"

Reith threw his hands up in the air. "Of course I don't find you repulsive! In fact—"

"In fact, what?"

Cauch, arriving at the table, provided, for Reith, a welcome interruption. "You spent a comfortable night?"

"Yes," said Reith.

Zap 210 rose to her feet and walked away. Cauch drew a long face. "How have I offended her?"

"She's angry with me," said Reith. "Why—I don't know."

"Isn't this always the case? But soon, for reasons equally unknown, she will again become benign. Meanwhile, I am interested in hearing your ideas in regard to the eel-races."

Reith looked dubiously after Zap 210, who had returned to the Inn of the Lucky Mariner. "Is it safe to leave her alone?"

"Have no fear," said Cauch. "At the inn you and she are known to be under my sponsorship."

"Well, then, to the eel-races."

"You understand that they are not yet in operation? The races do not start till noon."

"So much the better."

Zap 210 had never been so angry. She half-walked half-ran to the inn, through the dim common room to the cubicle where she had spent the night. She entered, furiously shot the bolt and went to sit on the couch. For ten minutes she let her thoughts rage without control. Then she began to cry, silently, tears of frustration and disillusionment welling down her cheeks. She thought of the Shelters: the quiet corridors with the black-robed figures drifting past. In the Shelters no one would provoke her to anger or excitement or any of the other strange emotions which from time to time colored her brain. They would give her *diko* once more . . . She frowned, trying to recall the flavor of the crisp little wafers. On sudden impulse she rose to her feet, examined herself in the mirror which hung on the side wall. The previous evening she had looked at herself with no great interest; the face which looked back seemed just a face: eyes, nose, mouth, chin. Now she studied herself earnestly. She touched the black hair curling down her forehead, combed it with her fingers, studied the effect. The face which looked back was that of a stranger. She thought of the lithe girl who had regarded Reith with such insolence. She had worn a garment of blue cloth which clung to the figure, different from the shapeless gray smock which Zap 210 now wore. She pulled it off, stood in her white undergown. She turned, studied herself from all angles. A stranger now for certain. What if Reith could see her now: what would he think? . . . The idea of Reith made her furiously angry. He considered her a child, or something even more ignoble: she had no word for the concept. She felt herself with her hands and, staring in the mirror, marveled at the changes which had come over her . . . Her original scheme of returning to the Shelters dwindled. The *zuzhma kastchai* would give her to the darkness. If by chance she were allowed to keep her life, they would feed her *diko* again. Her lips twitched. No more *diko*.

Well, then, what of Adam Reith, who considered her so repulsive that—her mind refused to complete the train of thought. What was to become of her? She studied herself in the mirror and felt very sorry for the dark-haired girl with thin cheeks and sad eyes who looked back at her. If she ran away from Adam Reith how could she survive? . . . She slipped into her gray smock, but decided against tying the orange cloth around her head. Instead she tied it around her waist as a sash, as she had noticed other girls of Urmank doing. She examined herself in the mirror again and rather liked the effect. What would Adam Reith think?

She opened the door, looked up and down the corridor and ventured forth. The common-room was empty but for a squat old woman who scrubbed the stone floor with a brush and looked up with a sneer. Zap 210 hastened her pace and went out into the street. Here she hesitated. She had never been alone before, and the sensation was frightening, if thrilling. Crossing to the quay, she watched porters unloading a cog. Neither her vocabulary nor her stock of ideas contained the equivalent of "quaint" or "picturesque"; nevertheless, she was charmed by the bluff-brown craft moving gently to the heave of the water. She drew a deep breath. Freak or not, repulsive or not, she had never felt so alive before. The *ghaun* was a wild cruel place—here the *zuzhma kastchai* had not dissembled—but after living in the golden-brown sunlight, how could anyone choose to return to the Shelters?

She walked along the quay to the café, where somewhat diffidently she looked for Reith. What she would say to him she had not yet formulated; perhaps she would sweep to her seat with only a haughty glance to let him know what she thought of his opinions . . . Reith was nowhere to be seen. A sudden terrible fear came over her. Had he taken the opportunity to escape, to be rid of her? Impulses urged upon her; she wanted to cry out: "Adam Reith! Adam Reith!" She could not believe that the reassuring form, so taut and economical of motion, was nowhere to be seen . . . She turned to leave and stepped full into the advancing body of a tall massive man, wearing pantaloons of dove brown leather, a loose white shirt and a vest of maroon brocade. A small brimless cap clung to the side of his bald head; he gave a soft grunt as she walked into him and held her away with two hands on her shoulders. "Where do you go in such haste?"

"Nowhere," stammered Zap 210. "I was looking for someone."

"You have found me, which is not the worst of luck. Come along; I have not yet had my morning wine. Then we will discuss our affairs."

Zap 210 stood paralyzed by indecision. She tentatively tried to shrink away from the man's grasp, which only tightened. Zap 210 winced. "Come," said the man. She stumbled with him to a nearby booth.

The man signaled; a jug of white wine and a platter of fried fishcakes was set before them. "Eat," the man told her. "Drink. I stint no one, either in bounty or hard knocks." He poured her a liberal goblet of wine. "Now, before we proceed, what are your fees? Certain of your number, knowing me for Otwile, have attempted nothing less than larceny—to their dissatisfaction, I may say. So then: your price?"

"Price for what?" whispered Zap 210.

Otwile's blue eyes widened in surprise. "You are an odd one. What is your race? You are too pale for a Thang, too slender for a Gray."

Zap 210 lowered her eyes. She tasted the wine, then searched desperately over her shoulder for Reith.

"Ah, but you are shy!" declared Otwile. "And delicate of manner as well!"

He began to eat. Zap 210 tried to slip away. "Sit!" snapped Otwile. She hastily returned to her seat. "Drink!" She sipped at the wine, which was stronger than any she had yet tasted.

"That is better," said Otwile. "Now we understand each other."

"No," said Zap 210 in her soft voice. "We don't! I don't want to be here! What do you want of me?"

Otwile again stared at her in disbelief. "You don't know?"

"Of course not. Unless—you don't mean *that*?"

Otwile grinned, "I mean precisely that, and more."

"But—I don't know anything about such things! I don't want to learn."

Otwile put down his fishcakes. He said incredulously, "A virgin, wearing a sash. Is that how you represent yourself?"

"I don't know what such a thing is . . . I must go, to find Adam Reith."

"You have found me, which is somewhat better. Drink wine, to relax yourself. Today is to be that particular day you will remember to the end of your time." Otwile poured full the goblets. "Indeed, I will join you, to relax myself. Truth to tell, I myself have become somewhat excited!"

Reith and Cauch walked through the bazaar, where the fish and produce vendors called attention to their merchandise by means of peculiar ululations.

"Are they singing?" asked Reith.

"No," said Cauch, the cries were no more than devices to attract attention. "The Thang have no great feeling for music. The selling-screams of the fish-wives are inventive and emotional, true; listen and you will hear how they try to outdo each other!"

Reith conceded that certain of the advertisements were remarkably intricate. "In due course the social anthropologists will record and codify these calls. But for the moment I am more interested in the eel-races."

"To be sure," said Cauch. 'Though, as you will notice, they are not yet in operation."

They crossed the compound and stood appraising the vacant tables, the reservoir and the chute. Looking across the wall, Reith noticed the fronds of a gnarled old psilla. "I want to look on the other side of the wall," he said.

"Just so," said Cauch, "and I have the fullest sympathy with your curiosity. But are we not at the moment directing our energies to the eel-races?"

"We are," said Reith. "I see a portal through the wall, opposite that vendor of amulets. Do you care to accompany me?"

"Certainly," said Cauch. "I am always alert to learn."

They walked along beside the old wall, which in the remote past had been faced with brown and white tiles, most of which had fallen away, revealing patches of dark brown brick. Passing through the portal, they entered Urmank Old Town: a district of huts built of broken tile, brick, fragments of stone, and odd lengths of timber. Some were abandoned ruins, others were in the process of construction: a continuing cycle of decay and regeneration, in which every shard, every stick, every fragment of stone had been used a hundred times over twice as many generations. Low-caste Thangs and a squat, big-headed variety of Gray peered forth from the doorways as Reith and Cauch went past; stench thickened the air.

Beyond the huts lay an area of rubble, puddles of slime, a few clumps of angry red bristle-bush. Reith located the psilla of which he had taken note: it stood close beside the wall, overhanging a shed built of well-laid bricks. The door was solid timber bound with iron, secured with a heavy iron lock. The shed backed firmly up against the wall.

Reith looked around the landscape, which was vacant except for a group of naked children paddling in a rivulet of yellow slime. He approached the shed. The lock, the hasp, the hinges were sound and solid. There was no window to the shed, nor any opening other than the door. Reith backed away. "We've seen all we need to see."

"Indeed?" Cauch dubiously inspected the shed, the wall, the psilla tree. "I see nothing significant. Are you still referring to the eel-races?"

"Of course." They went back through the dismal huddle of huts. Reith said: "Very likely we could make all our arrangements alone; still, the help of two trustworthy men might prove convenient."

Cauch eyed him with awe and incredulity. "You seriously hope to take money from the eel-race?"

"If the eel-master pays all winning bets, I do."

"No fear of that," said Cauch. "He will pay, assuming that there are winnings. And on this supposition, how do you propose to share?"

"Half for me, half for you and your two men."

Cauch pursed his lips. "I perceive something of an inequity. From a mutual project, one man should not derive three times the share of the others."

"I believe that he should," said Reith, "when otherwise the other three gain nothing whatever."

"The point is well-taken," Cauch admitted. "The affair shall go as you recommend."

They returned to the café. Reith looked for Zap 210, who was nowhere to be seen. "I must find my companion," he told Cauch. "No doubt she waits at the inn."

Cauch made an affable gesture; Reith went to the inn, but found Zap 210 nowhere. Making inquiries of the clerk he learned that she had come and gone, leaving no intimation as to her destination.

Reith went to the doorway and looked up and down the quay. To the right porters in faded red kirtles and leather shoulderpads unloaded a cog; to the left was the bustle of the bazaar.

He never should have left her alone, he told himself, especially in her mood of the morning. He had taken her stability for granted, never troubling to divine the state of her mind. Reith cursed himself for callousness and egocentricity. The girl had been undergoing the most intense and dramatic emotional strains: all the fundamental processes of life at once. Reith strode back to the café. Cauch eyed him with calm benevolence. "You appear concerned."

"The girl who accompanies me—I can't find her."

"Pah," said Cauch. "They are all alike. She has gone to the bazaar, to buy a trinket."

"No. She has no money. She is utterly inexperienced; she would go nowhere—except . . ." Reith turned to look toward the hills, the way which lay between the ghoul-castles. Would she seriously consider going down into the Shelters? . . . A new idea came to turn his bones to ice. The Gzhindra. Reith summoned the Thang servant-boy. "I breakfasted this morning with a young woman. Do you recall her?"

"Yes, indeed; she wore an orange turban, like a Hedaijhan, at least on that occasion."

"You saw her another time?"

"I did. She sat yonder, wearing the sash of solicitation and consorting with Otwile the champion. They drank wine for a period, then went off."

"She went of her own free will?" asked Reith in wonder.

The servant gave a shrug of indifference, covertly insolent "She wore the sash, she uttered no outcry, she leaned on his arm, perhaps to steady herself, for I believe her to have been somewhat drunk."

"Where did they go?"

Again the shrug. "Otwile's chambers are not too far distant; perhaps this was their resort."

"Show me the way."

"No no." The servant shook his head. "I am at my duties. Also I would not care to vex Otwile."

Reith jumped at him; the servant stumbled back in a panic. "Quick!" hissed Reith.

"This way then, but hurry; I am not supposed to leave the café."

They ran through the dank back alleys of Urmank, in and out of the brown light of Carina 4269, which occasionally slanted down past the crooked gables of the tall houses. The servant halted, pointed along a walkway leading into a garden of green and purple foliage. "At the back of the shrubbery are Otwile's rooms." He scuttled back the way he had come. Reith ran along the walkway, through the garden. At the back stood a cottage of carved timber and panels of translucent fiber. As Reith approached he heard a sudden wordless cry of outrage from within. "Unclean!" Then there was the sound of a blow, and a whimper. Reith's knees shook, he tottered forward, thrust open the door. On the floor crouched Zap 210, glassy-eyed and nude; above her stood Otwile. Zap 210 stared at Reith; he saw a red welt on her cheek.

Otwile spoke in a voice of hushed outrage. "Who are you to intrude in my house?"

Reith ignored him. He picked up Zap 210's undergown, a torn tangle of cloth. He turned to look at Otwile. Cauch spoke from the doorway. "Come, Adam Reith; fetch the girl. Do not trouble yourself."

Reith paid no heed. He moved slowly toward Otwile, who waited, smiling coldly, hands on hips. Reith approached to within three feet. Otwile, six inches taller, smiled down at him.

Zap 210 said in a husky croak: "It wasn't his fault. I wore an orange sash . . . I didn't know . . ."

Reith turned slowly away. He found Zap 210's gray gown,

pulled it over her slender body. He saw what had outraged Otwile; he could hardly control a great cry to express sorrow and pity and terrible grim amusement. He put his arm around Zap 210 and started to lead her from the room.

Otwile was dissatisfied. He had been awaiting a touch, a motion, even a word, to serve as a trigger for his muscles. Was he to be denied even the gratification of beating the man who had invaded his chambers? The bubble of his rage burst. He bounced forward and swung his leg in a kick.

Reith was pleased to find Otwile active. Twisting, he caught Otwile's ankle, pulled, dragged the champion hopping out into the garden, and sent him careening into a thicket of scarlet bamboo. Otwile sprang forth like a leopard. He halted, stood with arms out, grimacing hideously, clenching and unclenching his hands. Reith punched him in the face. Otwile seemed not to notice. He reached for Reith, who backed away, hacking at the heavy wrists. Otwile came forward, crowding Reith against the side-wall. Reith feinted, punched with his left hand and rapped his knuckles into Otwile's face. Otwile gave a small flat-footed jump forward, and another, then he gave a hideous rasping scream, and swung his great arm in an open-handed slap. Reith ducked below, hit Otwile full in the belly, and as Otwile jerked up his knee, seized the crooked leg, heaved up, and sent Otwile down flat on his back with a thud like a falling tree. For a moment Otwile lay dazed, then he slowly struggled to a sitting position. With a single backward glance Reith led Zap 210 from the garden. Cauch bowed politely toward Otwile and followed.

Reith took Zap 210 to the inn. She sat on the couch in her cubicle, clutching the gray gown about herself, limp and miserable. Reith sat down beside her. "What happened?"

Tears dripped down her cheeks; she held her hands to her face. Reith stroked her head. Presently she wiped her eyes. "I don't know what I did wrong—unless it was the sash. He made me drink wine until I became dizzy. He took me through the streets . . . I felt very strange. I could hardly walk. In the house I wouldn't take off my clothes and he became angry. Then he saw me and he became even angrier. He said I was unclean . . . I don't know what to do with myself. I'm sick, I'm dying."

Reith said, "No, you're not sick or dying. Your body has

started to function normally. There's nothing whatever wrong with you."

"I'm not unclean?"

"Of course not." Reith rose to his feet. "I'll send in a maid to take care of you. Then just lie quietly and sleep until I return—I hope with enough money to put us aboard a ship."

Zap 210 nodded listlessly; Reith departed the cubicle.

At the café Reith found Cauch and two young Zsafathrans who had come to Urmank aboard the second cart. "This is Schazar; this is Widisch," said Cauch. "Both are reckoned competent; I have no doubt but that they will fulfill any reasonable requirements."

"In that case," said Reith, "let's be off about our business. We haven't too much time to spare, or so I should judge."

The four sauntered off down the quay. Reith explained his theories: "—which now we must put to the test. Mind you, I may be wrong, in which case the project will fail."

"No," said Cauch. "You have employed an extraordinary mental process to adduce what I now see to be limpid truth."

"The process is called logic," said Reith. "It is not always dependable. But we shall see."

They passed the eel-race table, where a few folk had already settled at the benches, ready for the day's gambling. Reith hurried his steps: under the portal, through the dismal byways of Urmank Old Town, toward the shed under the psilla tree. They halted fifty yards away and took cover in a ruined hut at the edge of the wastelands.

Ten minutes passed. Reith began to fidget. "I can't believe that we've come too late."

The young man Schazar pointed across the wastes, to the far end of the wall. "Two men."

The men strolled closer. One affected the flowing white robes and square white hat of an Erze Island Sage: "The eel-master," muttered Cauch. The other, a young man, wore a pink skullcap and a light pink cape. The two walked casually and confidently along the trail and parted company near the shed. The eel-master continued toward the portal. Widisch said: "Easier merely to waylay the old charlatan and divest him of his pouch; the effect, after all, is the same."

"Unfortunately," said Cauch, "he carries no sequins on his

person, and makes the fact well known. His funds are brought to the eel-races daily by four armed slaves under the supervision of his chief wife.''

The young man in pink strolled to the shed. He fitted a key in the lock, turned it three times, opened the ponderous door and entered the shed. He turned with surprise to find that Reith and Schazar had also pushed into the shed beside him. He attempted to bluster. ''What is the meaning of this?''

''I will speak one time only,'' said Reith. ''We want your unstinting cooperation; otherwise we will hang you by the toes to yonder psilla. Is that clear?''

''I understand perfectly,'' said the young man with a quaver.

''Describe the routine.''

The young man hesitated. Reith nodded to Schazar, who brought forth a coil of hard cord. The young man said quickly, ''The routine is quite simple. I undress and step into the tank.'' He indicated a cylindrical pool four feet in diameter at the back of the shed. ''A tube communicates with the reservoir; the level in the tank and that in the reservoir are the same. I swim through the tube to the reservoir and come up into a space in the peripheral frame. As soon as the lid is lowered, I open a partition. I reach into the reservoir and move the specified eel to the edge of the chute.''

''And how is the color specified?''

''By the eel-master's finger-taps on the top of the lid.''

Reith turned to Cauch. ''Schazar and I are now in control. I suggest that you now take your places at the table.'' He spoke to the young man in pink: ''Is there sufficient space for two under the reservoir?''

''Yes,'' said the young man grudgingly. ''Just barely. But tell me: if I cooperate with you, how will I protect myself from the eel-master?''

''Be frank with him,'' said Reith. ''State that you value your life more than his sequins.''

''He will say that as far as he is concerned, affairs are reversed.''

''Too bad,'' said Reith. ''The hazard of your trade. How soon should we be in position?''

''Within a minute or so.''

Reith removed his outer garments. ''If by some ineptness we

are detected . . . surely the consequences are as plain to you as to me."

The apprentice merely grunted. He doffed his pink robe. "Follow me." He stepped into the tank. "The way is dark but straight."

Reith joined him in the tank. The young man drew a deep breath and submerged; Reith did the same. At the bottom, finding a horizontal tube about three feet in diameter, he pulled himself through, staying close behind the apprentice.

They surfaced in a space about four feet long, a foot and a half high, a foot wide. Light entered through artfully arranged crevices, which also allowed a view over the gaming tables; Reith thus could see that both Cauch and Widisch had found places along the counter.

From near at hand came the eel-master's voice. "Welcome all to another day of exciting races. Who will win? Who will lose? No one knows. It may be me, it may be you. But we all will enjoy the fun of the races. For those who are new to our little game, you will notice that the board before you is marked with eleven colors. You may bet any amount on any of the colors. If your color wins, you are paid ten times the amount of your bet. Note these eels and their colors: white, gray, tawny, light blue, brown, dark red, vermilion, blue, green, violet, black. Are there any questions?"

"Yes," called Cauch. "Is there any limit on the betting?"

"The case now being delivered contains ten thousand sequins. This is my limit; I pay no more. Please place your bets."

With a practiced eye the eel-master appraised the table. He lifted the lid, set the eels into the center of the reservoir. "No more betting, please." On the lid sounded *tap-tap tap-tap*.

"Two-two," whispered the apprentice. "That's green." He pushed aside a panel and reaching into the reservoir, seized the green eel and set it into the mouth of the chute. Then he drew back and closed the panel.

"Green wins!" called the eel-master. "So then—I pay! Twenty sequins to this sturdy seafarer . . . Make your bets, please."

Tap tap-tap-tap sounded on the lid. "Vermilion," whispered the apprentice. He performed as before.

"Vermilion wins!" called the eel-master.

Reith kept his eye to the crack. On each occasion Cauch and

Widisch had risked a pair of sequins. On the third betting round each placed thirty sequins on white.

"Bets are now made," came the eel-master's voice. The lid came down. *Tap tap* came the sounds.

"Brown," whispered the apprentice.

"White," said Reith. "The white eel wins."

The apprentice groaned in muted distress. He put the white eel into the chute.

"Another contest between these baffling little creatures," came the complacent voice of the eel-master. "On this occasion the winning color is—brown . . . Brown? White. Yes, white it is! Ha! In my old age I become color-blind. Tribulation for a poor old man! . . . A pair of handsome winners here! Three hundred sequins for you, three hundred sequins for you . . . Take your winnings, gentlemen. What? You are betting the entire sum, both of you?"

"Yes, luck appears to be with us today."

"Both on dark red?"

"Yes; notice the flight of yonder blood-birds! This is a portent."

The eel-master smiled off into the sky. "Who can divine the ways of nature? I pray that you are incorrect. Well, then, all bets are made? Then in with the eels, down with the lid, and let the most determined eel issue forth the winner." His hand rested a moment on the lid; his fingernail struck the surface a single time. "They twist, they search, the light beckons; we should soon have a winner . . . Here comes—is it blue?" He gave an involuntary groan. "Dark red." He peered into the faces of the Zsafathrans. "Your presages, astonishingly, were correct."

"Yes," said Cauch. "Did I not tell you as much? Pay over our winnings."

Slowly the eel-master counted out three thousand-worth of sequins to each. "Astonishing." He glanced thoughtfully toward the reservoir. "Do you observe any further portents?"

"Nothing significant. But I will bet nonetheless. A hundred sequins on black."

"I bet the same," declared Widisch.

The eel-master hesitated. He rubbed his chin, looked around the counter. "Extraordinary." He put the eels into the reservoir. "Are all bets laid?" His hand rested on the lid; as if by nervous mannerism he brought his fingernails down in two sharp raps.

"Very well; I open the gate." He pulled the lever and strode up to the end of the chute. "And here comes what color? Black!"

"Excellent!" declared Cauch. "We reap a return after years of squandering money upon perverse eels! Pay over our gains, if you please!"

"Certainly," croaked the eel-master. "But I can work no more. I suffer from an aching of the joints; the eel-racing is at an end."

Reith and the apprentice immediately returned to the shed. The apprentice donned his pink cape and hat and took to his heels.

Reith and Schazar returned through the Old Town to the portal, where they encountered the eel-master, who strode past in a great flapping of his white gown. The normally benign face was mottled red; he carried a stout stave, which he swung in short ominous jerks.

Cauch and Widisch awaited them on the quay. Cauch handed Reith a pleasantly plump pouch. "Your share of the winnings: four thousand sequins. The day has been edifying."

"We have done well," said Reith. "Our association has been mutually helpful, which is a rare thing for Tschai!"

"For our part we return instantly to Zsafathra," said Cauch. "What of you?"

"Urgent business calls me onward. Like yourselves, my companion and I depart as soon as possible."

"In that case, farewell." The three Zsafathrans went their way. Reith turned into the bazaar, where he made a variety of purchases. Back at the hotel he went to Zap 210's cubicle and rapped on the door, his heart pounding with anticipation.

"Who is it?" came a soft voice.

"It is I, Adam Reith."

"A moment." The door opened. Zap 210 stood facing him, face flushed and drowsy. She wore the gray smock which she had only just pulled over her head.

Reith took his bundles to the couch. "This—and this—and this—and this—for you."

"For me? What are they?"

"Look and see."

With a diffident side-glance toward Reith, she opened the bundles, then for a period stood looking down at the articles they contained.

Reith asked uneasily, "Do you like them?"

She turned to him a hurt gaze. "Is this how you want me to be—like the others?"

Reith stood nonplussed. It was not the reaction he had expected. He said carefully, "We will be traveling. It is best that we go as inconspicuously as possible. Remember the Gzhindra? We must dress like the folk we travel among."

"I see."

"Which do you like best?"

Zap 210 lifted the dark green gown, laid it down, took up the blood-orange smock and dull white pantaloons, then the rather jaunty light brown suit with the black vest and short black cape. "I don't know whether I like any of them."

"Try one on."

"Now?"

"Certainly!"

Zap 210 held up first one of the garments, then another. She looked at Reith; he grinned. "Very well, I'll go."

In his own cubicle he changed into the fresh garments he had bought for himself: gray breeches, a dark-blue jacket. The gray furze smock he decided to discard. As he threw it aside he felt the outline of the portfolio, which after a moment's hesitation he transferred to the inner lining of his new jacket. Such a set of documents, if for no other reason, had value as a curio. He went to the common room. Presently Zap 210 appeared. She wore the dark green gown. "Why do you stare at me?" she asked.

Reith could not tell her the truth, that he was recalling the first time he had seen her: a neurasthenic waif shrouded in a black cloak, pallid and bone-thin. She retained something of her dreaming wistful look, but her pallor had become a smooth sun-shadowed ivory; her black hair curled in ringlets over her forehead and ears.

"I was thinking," said Reith, "that the gown suits you very well."

She made a faint grimace: a twitch of the lips approaching a smile.

They walked out upon the quay, to the cog *Nhiahar*. They found the taciturn master in the saloon, working over his accounts. "You desire passage to Kazain? There is only the grand cabin to be had at seven hundred sequins, or I can give you two berths in the dormitory, at two hundred."

9

A DEAD CALM held the Second Sea. The *Nhiahar* slid out of the inlet, propelled by its field engine; by degrees Urmank faded into the murk of distance.

The *Nhiahar* moved in silence except for the gurgle of water under the bow. The only other passengers were a pair of waxen-faced old women swathed in gray gauze who appeared briefly on deck, then crept to their dark little cabin.

Reith was well-satisfied with the grand cabin. It ranged the entire width of the ship, with three great windows overlooking the sea astern. In alcoves to port and starboard were well-cushioned beds as soft as any Reith had felt on Tschai, if a trifle musty. In the center stood a massive table of carved black wood, with a pair of equally massive chairs at either end. Zap 210 made a sulky appraisal of the room. Today she wore the dull white trousers with the orange blouse; she seemed keyed up and tense, and moved with nervous abruptness in jerks and halts and fidgeting twitches of the fingers.

Reith watched her covertly, trying to calculate the exact nature of her mood. She refused to look toward him or meet his gaze. At last he asked: "Do you like the ship?"

She gave a sullen shrug. "I have never seen anything like it before." She went to the door, where she turned him a sour twitch of a smile—a derisive grimace—and went out on deck.

Reith looked up at the overhead, shrugged, and after a final glance around the room, followed her.

She had climbed the companionway to the quarterdeck, where she stood leaning on the taffrail, looking back the way they had come. Reith seated himself on a bench nearby and pretended to bask in the wan brown sunlight while he puzzled over her behavior. She was female and inherently irrational—but her conduct seemed to exceed this elemental fact. Certain of her attitudes had been formed in the Shelters, but these seemed to be waning; upon reaching the surface she had abandoned the old life and discarded its points of view, as an insect molts a skin. In the process, Reith ruminated, she had discarded her old personality— but had not yet discovered a new one . . . The thought gave Reith a qualm. Part of the girl's charm or fascination, or whatever it was, lay in her innocence, her transparency . . . transparency?

Reith made a skeptical sound. Not altogether. He went to join her. "What are you pondering so deeply?"

She gave him a cool side-glance. "I was thinking of myself and the wide *ghaun*. I remember my time in the dark. I know now that below the world I was not yet born. All those years, while I moved quietly below, the folk of the surface lived in color and change and air."

"So this is why you've been acting so strangely!"

"No!" she cried in sudden passion. "It is not! The reason is you and your secrecy! You tell me nothing. I don't know where we are going, or what you are going to do with me."

Reith frowned down at the black boil of the wake. "I'm not sure of these things myself."

"But you must know something!"

"Yes . . . When I get to Sivishe I want to return to my home, which is far and remote."

"And what of me?"

And what of Zap 210? wondered Reith. A question he had avoided asking himself. "I'm not sure you'd want to come with me," he replied, somewhat lamely.

Tears glinted in her eyes. "Where else can I go? Should I become a drudge? Or a Gzhindra? Or wear an orange sash at Ur-mank? Or should I die?" She swung away and marched forward to the bow, past a group of the spade-faced seamen, who watched her from the side of their pale eyes.

Reith returned to the bench . . . The afternoon passed. Black clouds to the north generated a cool wind. The sails were shaken out, and the cog drove forward. Zap 210 presently came aft with a strange expression on her face. She gave Reith a look of sad accusation and went down to the cabin.

Reith followed and found her lying on one of the couches. "Don't you feel well?"

"No."

"Come outside. You'll be worse in here."

She staggered out upon the deck.

"Keep your eyes on the horizon," said Reith. "When the ship moves, keep your head level. Do that for a while and you'll feel better."

Zap 210 stood by the rail. The clouds loomed overhead and the wind died; the *Nhiahar* lay wallowing with slatting sails . . . From the sky came a purple dazzle, slanting and slashing at the sea—once, twice, three times, all in the flicker of an eye-blink. Zap 210 gave a small scream and jerked back in terror. Reith caught her and held her as the thunder rumbled down. She moved uneasily; Reith kissed her forehead, her face, her mouth.

The sun settled into a tattered panoply of gold and black and brown; with the dusk came rain. Reith and Zap 210 retreated to their cabin, where the steward served supper: mincemeat, sea-fruit, biscuits. They ate, looking out through the great windows at the sea and rain and lightning, and afterwards, with lightning sparking the dark, they became lovers.

At midnight the clouds departed; stars burnt down from the sky. "Look up there!" said Reith. "Among the stars are other worlds of men. One of them is called Earth." He paused. Zap 210 lay listening, but Reith for some obscure reason could say no more, and presently she fell asleep.

The *Nhiahar*, driven by fair winds, plunged down the Second Sea, crashing through great white billows of foam. Cape Braise reared up ahead; the ship put into the ancient stone city of Stheine to take on water, then fared forth into the Schanizade.

Twenty miles down the coast a tongue of land hooked out to the west. Along the foreshore a forest of dark blue trees shrouded a city of flat domes, cambered cusps, sweeping colonnades. Reith thought to recognize the architecture, and put a question to the captain: "Is that a Chasch city?"

"It is Songh, most southerly of the Blue Chasch places. I have taken cargoes into Songh, but it is risky business. You must know the games of the Chasch: antics of a dying race. I have seen ruins on the Kotan steppes: a hundred places where Old Chasch or Blue Chasch once lived, and who goes there now? Only the Phung."

The city receded into the distance and disappeared from view as the ship passed south beyond the peninsula. Not long after a cry from one of the crew brought everyone out on deck. In the sky a pair of airships fought. One was a gleaming contrivance of blue and white metal, shaped to a set of splendid curves. A balustrade contained the deck, on which lay a dozen creatures in glistening casques. The other craft was austere and bleak: a vessel sinister, ugly, gray, built with only its function in mind. It was slightly smaller than the Blue Chasch ship and somewhat more agile; in the dorsal bubble crouched the Dirdir crew, intent at the work of destroying the Chasch ship. The vessels circled and swung, now high, now low, careening around each other like venomous insects. From time to time, as circumstances offered, the ships exchanged volleys of sandblast fire, without noticeable effect. Far up into the gray-brown sky spun the sparkling shapes, to spiral giddily down, one after the other, veering only yards above the ocean's surface.

The whole company of the *Nhiahar* came on deck to watch the battle, even the two old women who had not previously shown themselves. As they scanned the sky the hood fell back from the head of one of them to reveal a keen pale countenance. Zap 210, standing beside Reith, uttered a soft gasp, and quickly turned away her gaze.

The Blue Chasch ship slid suddenly down; the bow guns struck under the counter of the Dirdir ship, knocking it up, tumbling it over and down into the sea, where it struck with a soundless splash. The Blue Chasch vessel swung in a single grand circle, then cruised back toward Songh.

The old women had disappeared below. Zap 210 spoke in a tremulous whisper: "Did you notice?"

"Yes. I noticed."

"They are Gzhindra."

"Are you sure?"

"Yes, I am sure."

"I suppose Gzhindra make voyages like other folk," said Reith, somewhat hollowly. "So far at least they've done nothing to bother us."

"But they are here, aboard the ship! They do nothing without purpose!"

Reith made another skeptical sound. "Perhaps so—but what can we do about it?"

"We can kill them!"

Zap 210, for all the strictures of her upbringing, was still a creature of Tschai, thought Reith. He said: "We'll keep close watch on them. Now that we know who they are, and they don't know that we know, the advantage is ours."

It was Zap 210's turn to make a skeptical sound. Reith nevertheless refused to waylay the old women in the dark and strangle them.

The voyage proceeded, southwest toward the Saschan Islands. Days passed without event more noteworthy than the turn of the heavens. Each morning Carina 4269 broke through the horizon into a dull bronze and old rose dawn. By noon a high haze had formed, to filter the sunlight and lay a sheen like antique silk on the water. The afternoons were long; sunsets were sad glories; allegorical wars between dark heroes and the lords of light. After nightfall the moons appeared: sometimes pink Az, sometimes blue Braz, and sometimes the *Nhiahar* rode under the stars.

For Reith the days and nights would have been as pleasant as any he had known on Tschai except for the worry which nagged him: what was happening at Sivishe? Would he find the spaceboat intact or destroyed? What of crafty Aila Woudiver; what of the Dirdir in their horrid city across the water? And what of the two old women, who might be Gzhindra? They never appeared except in the deep of night, to walk the foredeck. One dark evening Reith watched them, the hair prickling at the nape of his neck. Either they were Gzhindra or they were not, but lacking information Reith felt obliged to assume the worst—and the implications were cause for the most dismal foreboding.

One pale umber morning the Saschan Islands loomed out of the sea: three ancient volcanic necks surrounded by shelves of detritus where grew groves of psilla, kianthus, candlenut, lethipod. On each island a town climbed the central crag, beehive huts stacked one on the other like the cells of a wasp-nest. Black openings stared out to sea; wisps of smoke rose into the air.

The *Nhiahar* entered the inner bay and, swerving to avoid a ferry, approached the south island. On the dock waited bow-legged Saschanese longshoremen in black breech-clouts and black roll-toed ankle-boots. They took the hawsers; the *Nhiahar* was warped alongside. As soon as the gangplank settled into place the longshoremen swarmed aboard. Hatches were opened; bales of leather, sacks of pilgrim-pod meal, crated tools were taken to the dock.

Reith and Zap 210 went ashore. The captain called dourly after them: "I make departure at noon exactly, aboard or not."

The two walked along the esplanade, the crag and its unnatural encrustation of huts rearing above them. Zap 210 glanced over her shoulder. "They are following us."

"The Gzhindra?"

"Yes."

Reith grunted in disgust. "It's definite then. They have orders not to let us out of their sight."

"And we are as good as dead." Zap 210 spoke in a colorless voice. "At Kazain they will report to the Pnume and then nothing can help us; we'll be taken down into the dark."

Reith could think of nothing to say. They came to a small harbor protected from the sea by a pair of jetties, which narrowed to become a ferry slip. Reith and Zap 210 paused to watch the ferry arrive from the outer islands: a wide scow with control cabins at either end, carrying two hundred Saschanese of all ages and qualities. It nosed into the slip; the passengers debarked. As many more paid toll to a fat man sitting before a booth and surged aboard; immediately the ferry departed. Reith watched it cross the water, then led Zap 210 to a waiting area set with benches and tables beside the ferry slip. Reith ordered sweet wine and biscuits from a serving boy, then went to confer with the fat fare-collector. Zap 210 looked nervously here and there. In the shadow of a flight of steps she thought to glimpse two shapes robed in gray. *They wonder what we're doing,* Zap 210 told herself.

Reith returned. "The next ferry leaves in something over an hour—a few minutes before noon. I've already paid our fares."

Zap 210 gave him a puzzled inspection. "But we must be aboard the *Nhiahar* at noon!"

"True. Are the Gzhindra nearby?"

"They've just taken seats at the far table."

Reith managed a grim chuckle. "We're giving them something to think about."

"What should they think about? That we might take the ferry?"

"Something of the sort."

"But why should they think that? It seems so strange!"

"Not altogether. There might be a ship at one of the other islands to take us somewhere beyond their knowledge."

"Is there such a ship?"

"None that I know of."

"But if we take the ferry the Gzhindra will follow, and the *Nhiahar* will leave without all of us!"

"I expect so. The captain would have no qualms whatever."

The minutes passed. Zap 210 began to fidget. "Noon is very close." She studied Reith, wondering what went on in his mind.

No other man of Tschai—at least none she had yet seen—resembled him, he was of a different sort.

"Here comes the ferry," said Reith. "Let's go down to the slip. We want to be the first in line."

Zap 210 rose to her feet. Never would she understand Reith! She followed him down to the waiting sea. Others came to join them, to push and squirm and mutter. Reith asked: "What of the Gzhindra?"

Zap 210 glanced over her shoulder. "They're standing at the back of the crowd."

The ferry entered the slip; the barriers opened and the passengers surged ashore.

Reith spoke in Zap 210's ear. "Walk close by the collector's hut. As we pass, duck inside."

"Oh."

The gate opened. Reith and Zap 210 half-walked, half-ran down the way. At the collector's hut, Reith lowered his head and slipped within; Zap 210 followed. The embarking passengers pushing past, handed their fares to the collector and marched down to the ferry. Near the end of the line came the Gzhindra, trying to peer through the surge ahead of them. They moved with the crowd, down the ramp, aboard the ferry.

The barrier closed; the ferry moved out. Reith and Zap 210 emerged from the hut. "It's almost noon," said Reith. "Time to return aboard the *Nhiahar.*"

10

SOUTHEAST TOWARD KISLOVAN gusty winds drove the *Nhiahar.* The sea was almost black. The swells which rolled up and under the ship spilled rushes of white foam ahead.

One blustery morning Zap 210 joined Reith where he stood at the bow. For a moment they stood looking ahead across the heaving water to where Carina 4269 dropped prisms and fractured shards of golden light.

Zap 210 asked, "What lies ahead?"

Reith shook his head. "I don't know. I wish I did."

"But you worry. Are you afraid?"

"I'm afraid of a man named Aila Woudiver. I don't know whether he's alive or dead."

"Who is Aila Woudiver, that you fear him so?"

"A man of Sivishe, a man to fear . . . I think he must be dead. I was kidnapped out of a dream. In the dream I saw Aila Woudiver's head split open."

"So why do you worry?"

Sooner or later, thought Reith, he must make all clear. Perhaps now was the time. "Remember the night I told you of other worlds among the stars?"

"I remember."

"One of these worlds is Earth. At Sivishe I built a spaceship, with Aila Woudiver's help. I want to go to Earth."

Zap 210 stared ahead across the water. "Why do you want to go to Earth?"

"I was born there. It is my home."

"Oh." She spoke in a colorless voice. After a reflective silence of fifteen seconds, she turned him a sidelong glance.

Reith said ruefully, "You wonder if I am insane."

"I've wondered many times. Many, many times."

Though Reith himself had put the suggestion, he was nonetheless taken aback. "Indeed?"

She smiled her sad grimace of a smile. "Consider what you have done. In the Shelters. At the Khor grove. When you changed eels at Urmank."

"Acts of desperation, acts of a frantic Earthman."

Zap 210 brooded across the windy ocean. "If you are an Earthman, what do you do here on Tschai?"

"On the Kotan steppes my spaceship was wrecked. At Sivishe I've built another."

"Hmmf . . . Is Earth such a paradise?"

"The people of Earth know nothing of Tschai. It's important that they do know."

"Why?"

"A dozen reasons. Most important, the Dirdir raided Earth once; they might decide to return."

She gave him her swift side-glance. "You have friends on Earth?"

"Of course."

"You lived there in a house?"

"In a manner of speaking."

"With a woman? And your children?"

"No woman, no children. I've been a spaceman all my life."

"And when you return—what then?"

"I'm not thinking past Sivishe right now."

"You will take me with you?"

Reith put his arm around her. "Yes. I will take you with me."

She heaved a sigh of relief. Presently she pointed ahead. "Beyond where the sun glints—an island."

The island, a great crag of barren black basalt, was the first of a myriad, to scarify the surface of the sea. The area was home to a host of sea-foragers, of a sort beyond Reith's previous experience. Four oscillating wings supported a cluster of dangling pink tentacles and a central tube ending in a bulbous eye. The creatures drifted high and low, dipping suddenly to seize some small wriggling sea-thing. A few drifted toward the *Nhiahar;* the crewmen lurched back in dread and took shelter in the forecastle.

The captain, who had come up on the foredeck, sneered in disgust. "They consider these the guts and eyes of drowned seamen. We sail the Channel of Death; these rocks are the Charnel Teeth."

"How do you navigate by night?"

"I don't know," said the captain, "for I have never tried. It is risky enough by day. Around each of those rocks lies a hundred hulks and heaped white bones. Do you notice, far ahead, the loom? There is Kislovan! Tomorrow will find us docked at Kazain."

As evening approached long strands of clouds raced across the sky and the wind began to moan. The captain took the *Nhiahar* into the lee of one of the larger black rocks, nosing close, close, close, until the sprit almost scraped the wet black stone. Here the anchor was dropped and the *Nhiahar* rode in relative safety as the wind became a screaming gale. Great swells drove through the black crags; foam crashed high up and fell slowly back. The sea boiled and surged; the *Nhiahar* wallowed, jerking at the anchor line, then floating suddenly loose and free.

With the coming of darkness the wind died. For a long period the sea rose and fell in fretful recollection, but dawn found the Charnel Teeth standing like archaic monuments on a sea of brown glass. Beyond lay the bulk of the continent.

Proceeding through the Charnel Teeth under power, the *Nhiahar* at noon nosed into a long narrow bay and by late afternoon drew alongside the pier at Kazain.

On the dock two Dirdirmen paused to watch the *Nhiahar.*

Their caste was high, perhaps Immaculate; they were young and vain; they wore their false effulgences aslant and glittering. Reith's heart rose in his throat for fear that they had been sent to take him into custody. For such a contingency he had no plans; he sweated until the two sauntered off toward the Dirdir settlement at the head of the bay.

There were no formalities at the dock; Reith and Zap 210 carried their belongings ashore and without interference made their way to the motor-wagon depot. An eight-wheeled vehicle stood on the verge of departure across the neck of Kislovan; Reith commissioned the most luxurious accommodation available: a cubicle of two hammocks on the third tier with access to the rear deck.

An hour later the motor-wagon trundled forth from Kazain. For a space the road climbed into the coastal uplands, affording a view over the Channel of Death and the Charnel Teeth. Five miles north the road swung inland. For the rest of the day the motor-wagon lumbered beside bean-vine fields, forests of white ghost-apple, an occasional little village.

In the early evening the motor-wagon halted at an isolated inn, where the forty-three passengers took supper. About half seemed to be Grays; the rest were people Reith could not identify. A pair might have been steppe-men of Kotan; several conceivably were Saschanese. Two yellow-skinned women in gowns of black scales almost certainly were Marsh-folk from the north shore of the Second Sea. The various groups took the least possible notice of each other, eating and returning at once to board the power-wagon. The indifference Reith knew to be feigned; each had gauged the exact quality of all the others with a precision beyond any Reith could muster.

Early in the morning the power-wagon once more set forth and met the dawn climbing over the edge of the central plateau. Carina 4269 rose to illuminate a vast savanna, clumped with alumes, gallow-trees, bundle-fungus, patches of thorn-grass.

So passed the day, and four more: a journey which Reith hardly noticed for his mounting tension. In the Shelters, on the great subterranean canal, along the shores of the Second Sea, at Urmank, even aboard the *Nhiahar*, he had been calm with the patience of despair. The stakes were once again high. He hoped, he dreaded, he strained for the power-wagon to go faster, he shrank from the thought of what he might find in the warehouse on the Sivishe salt flats. Zap 210, reacting to Reith's tension, or perhaps beset with premonitions of her own, retired into herself, and took small interest in the passing landscape.

Over the central plateau, down through a badlands of eroded granite, out upon a landscape farmed by clans of sullen Grays, went the power-wagon. Signs of the Dirdir presence appeared: a grey butte bristling with purple and scarlet towers, overlooking a rift valley, walled by sheer cliffs, which served the Dirdir as a hunting range. On the sixth day a range of mountains rose ahead: the back of the palisades overlooking Hei and Sivishe. The journey was almost at an end. All night the motor-wagon lumbered along a dusty road by the light of the pink and blue moons.

The moons set; the eastern sky took on the color of dried blood. Dawn came as a skyburst of dark scarlet, orange-brown, sepia. Ahead appeared the Ajzan Gulf and the clutter of Sivishe. Two hours later the motor-wagon lumbered into Sivishe Depot beside the bridge.

11

REITH AND ZAP 210 crossed the bridge amid the usual crowd of Grays trudging to and from their work in the Hei factories.

Sivishe was achingly familiar: the background for so much passion and grief that Reith found his heart pounding. If, by fantastic luck, he returned to Earth, could he ever forget those events which had befallen him at Sivishe? "Come," he muttered. "Over here, aboard the transit dray."

The dray creaked and groaned; the dingy districts of Sivishe fell behind; they reached the southernmost stop, where the wagon turned east, toward the Ajzan shore. Ahead lay the salt flats, with a road winding out of Aila Woudiver's construction depot.

All seemed as before: mounds of gravel, sand, slag; stacks of brick and rubble. To the side stood Woudiver's eccentric little office, beyond the warehouse. There was no activity; no moving figures, no drays. The great doors to the warehouse were closed; the walls leaned more noticeably than ever. Reith accelerated his pace; he strode down the road, with Zap 210 walking, then running, then walking.

Reith reached the yard. He looked all around. Desolation. Not a sound, not a step. Silence. The warehouse seemed on the verge of collapse, as if it had been damaged by an explosion. Reith went to the side entrance, looked within. The premises were vacant. The spaceship was gone. The roof had been torn away and hung in shreds. The workshop and supply racks were a shambles.

Reith turned away. He stood looking over the salt flats. What now?

He had no ideas. His mind was empty. He backed slowly away from the warehouse. Over the main entrance someone had scrawled ONMALE. This was the name of the chief-emblem worn by Traz when Reith had first encountered him on the Kotan steppes. The word prodded at Reith's numbed consciousness. Where were Traz and Anacho?

He went to the office and looked within. Here, while he lay sleeping, gas had stupefied him; Gzhindra had tucked him into a sack and carried him away. Someone else now lay on the couch—an old man asleep. Reith knocked on the wall. The old man awoke, opening first one rheumy eye, then the other. Pulling his gray cloak about his shoulders, he heaved himself erect. "Who is there?" he cried out.

Reith discarded the caution he normally would have used. "Where are the men who worked here?"

The door slid ajar; the old man came forth, to look Reith up and down. 'Some went here, some went there. One went . . . yonder." He jerked a crooked thumb toward the Glass Box.

"Who was that?"

Again the cautious scrutiny. "Who would you be that doesn't know the news of Sivishe?"

"I'm a traveler," said Reith, trying to hold his voice calm. "What's happened here?"

"You look like a man named Adam Reith," said the caretaker. "At least that's how the description went. But Adam Reith could give me the name of a Lokhar and the name of a Thang that only he would know."

"Zarfo Detwiler is a Lokhar; I once knew Issam the Thang."

The caretaker looked furtively around the landscape. His gaze rested suspiciously on Zap 210. "And who is this?"

"A friend. She knows me for Adam Reith; she can be trusted."

"I have instructions to trust no one, only Adam Reith."

"I am Adam Reith. Tell me what you have to tell me."

"Come here. I will ask a final question." He drew Reith aside and wheezed in his ear: "At Coad Adam Reith met a Yao nobleman."

"His name was Dordolio. Now what is your message?"

"I have no message."

Reith's impatience almost burst through his restraint. "Then why do you ask such questions?"

"Because Adam Reith has a friend who wants to see him. I am to take Adam Reith to his friend, at my own discretion."

"Who is this friend?"

The old man waved his finger. "Tut! I answer no questions. I obey instructions, no more, and thus I earn my fee."

"Well, then, what are your instructions?"

"I am to conduct Adam Reith to a certain place. Then I am done."

"Very well. Let's go."

"Whenever you are ready."

"Now."

"Come then." The old man started down the road, with Reith and Zap 210 following. The old man halted. "Not her. Just you."

"She must come as well."

"Then we cannot go, and I know nothing."

Reith argued, stormed and coaxed, to no avail. "How far is this place?" he demanded at last.

"Not far."

"A mile? Two miles?"

"Not far. We can be back shortly. Why cavil? The woman will not run away. If she does, find another. So was my style when I was a buck."

Reith searched the landscape: the road, the scattering of huts at the edge of the salt flats, the salt flats themselves. No living creature could be seen: a negative reassurance at best. Reith looked at Zap 210. She looked back with an uncertain smile. A detached part of Reith's brain noted that here, for the first time, Zap 210 had smiled—a tremulous, uncomprehending smile, but nonetheless a true smile. Reith said in a somber voice: "Get in the cabin; bolt the door. Don't open it for anyone. I'll be back as soon as I can."

Zap 210 went into the cabin. The door closed; the bolt shot home. Reith said to the old man: "Hurry then. Take me to my friend."

"This way."

The old man hobbled silently along the road, and presently turned aside along a path which led across the salt flats toward the straggle of huts at the edge of Sivishe. Reith began to feel nervous and insecure. He called out: "Where are we going?"

The old man made a vague gesture ahead.

Reith demanded, "Who is the man we are to see?"

"A friend of Adam Reith's."

"Is it . . . Aila Woudiver?"

"I am allowed to name no names. I can tell you nothing."

"Hurry."

The old man hobbled on, toward a hut somewhat apart from the others, an ancient structure of moldering gray bricks. The old man went up to the door, pounded, then stood back.

From within came a stir. Behind the single window was the flicker of movement. The door opened. Ankhe at afram Anacho looked forth. Reith exhaled a great gusty breath. The old man shrilled: "Is this the man?"

Anacho said, "Yes. This is Adam Reith."

"Give me my money then; I am anxious to have done with this line of work."

Anacho went within and returned with a pouch rattling with sequins. "Here is your money. In a month come back. There will be another waiting for you if you have held your tongue meanwhile."

The old man took the pouch and departed.

Reith asked: "Where is Traz? Where is the ship?"

Anacho shook his long pale head. "I don't know."

"What!"

"This is what happened. You were taken by the Gzhindra. Aila Woudiver was wounded but he did not die. Three days after the event the Dirdirmen came for Aila Woudiver, and dragged him off to the Glass Box. He complained, he implored, he screamed, but they took him away. I heard later that he provided a spectacular hunt, running in a frenzy like a bull marmont, braying at the top of his lungs . . . The Dirdirmen saw the ship when they came to take Aila Woudiver; we feared that they would return. The ship was ready to fly, so we decided to move the ship from Sivishe. I said that I would stay, to wait for you. In the middle of the night Traz and the technicians took the ship up, and flew it to a place that Traz said you would know."

"Where?" Reith demanded.

"I don't know. If I was taken, I wanted no knowledge, so that I could not be forced into betrayal. Traz wrote 'Onmale' on the shed. He said that you would know where to come."

"Let's go back to the warehouse. I left a friend there."

Anacho asked: "Do you know what he means by 'Onmale'?"

"I think so. I can't be sure."

They returned along the trail. Reith asked, "Is the sky-car still available for our use?"

"I carry the call-token. I see no reason why there should be difficulty."

"The situation isn't as bad as it might be then . . . I've had an interesting set of experiences." He told Anacho something of his adventures. "I escaped the Shelters. But along the shore of the Second Sea Gzhindra began to follow. Perhaps they were hired by the Khors; perhaps the Pnume sent them after us. We saw Gzhindra in Urmank; probably these same Gzhindra boarded the *Nhiahar*. They are still on the Saschanese Islands, for all I know. Since then we apparently haven't been followed, and I'd like to leave Sivishe before they pick us up again."

"I'm ready to leave now," said Anacho. "At any instant we may lose our luck."

They turned down the road leading to Woudiver's old warehouse. Reith stopped short. It was as he had feared, in the deepest darkest layer of his subconscious. The door to the office stood ajar. Reith broke into a run, with Anacho coming after.

Zap 210 was nowhere in the office, nor in the ruined warehouse. She was nowhere to be seen.

Directly before the office the ground was damp; the prints of narrow, bare feet were plain. "Gzhindra," said Anacho. "Or Pnumekin. No one else."

Reith gazed across the salt flats, calm in the amber light of afternoon. Impossible to search, impossible to run across salt marsh and flat, looking and calling. What could he do? Unthinkable to do nothing . . . What of Traz, the spaceship, the return to Earth which now was feasible? The idea sank from his mind like a waterlogged timber, with only the umbral shape, the afterimage, remaining. Reith sat down upon an old crate. Anacho watched a moment, his long white face drawn and melancholy, like that of a sick clown. Finally, in a somewhat hollow voice, he said, "Best that we be on our way."

Reith rubbed his forehead. "I can't go just yet. I've got to think."

"What is there to think about? If the Gzhindra have taken her, she is gone."

"I realize that."

"In such a case, you can do nothing."

Reith looked toward the palisades. "She will be taken back underground. They will swing her out over a dark gulf and after a time drop her."

Anacho hunched his shoulders in a shrug. "You cannot alter this regrettable fact so put it out of your mind. Traz awaits us with the spaceship."

"But I can do something," said Reith. "I can go after her."

"Into the underground places? Insanity! You will never return!"

"I returned before."

"By a freak of fate."

Reith rose to his feet.

Anacho went on desperately: "You will never return. What of Traz? He will wait for you forever. I can't tell him you have sacrificed everything—because I do not know where he is."

"I don't intend to sacrifice everything," said Reith. "I intend to return."

"Indeed!" declared Anacho with a sneer of vast scorn. "This time the Pnume will make sure. You will swing out over the gulf beside the girl."

"No," said Reith. "They will not swing me. They want me for Foreverness."

Anacho threw up his arms in bafflement. "I will never understand you, the most obstinate of men! Go underground! Ignore your faithful friends! Do your worst! When do you go below? Now?"

"Tomorrow," said Reith.

"Tomorrow? Why delay? Why deprive the Pnume of your society a single instant?"

"Because this afternoon I have preparations to make. Come along: let's go into town."

12

AT DAWN REITH went to stand at the edge of the salt flats. Here, months before, he and his friends had detected Aila Woudiver's signals to the Gzhindra. Reith also held a mirror; as Carina 4269 lifted into the sky, he swept the reflection back and forth across the salt flats.

An hour passed. Reith methodically flashed the mirror, apparently to no avail. Then from nowhere, or so it seemed, came a pair of dark figures. They stood half a mile away, looking toward Reith. He flashed the mirror. Step by step they approached, as if fascinated. Reith went to meet them. Gradually the three came together, and at last stood fifty feet apart.

A minute passed. The three appraised each other. The faces of the Gzhindra were shaded under low-crowned black hats; both were pale and somewhat vulpine, with long thin noses and bright black eyes. Presently they came closer. In a quiet voice one spoke: "You are Adam Reith."

"I am Adam Reith."

"Why did you signal us?"

"Yesterday you came to take my companion."

The Gzhindra made no remark.

"This is true, is it not?" Reith demanded.

"It is true."

"Why did you do this?"

"We hold such a commission."

"What did you do with her?"

"We delivered her to such a place as we were bid."

"Where is this place?"

"Yonder."

"You have a commission to take me?"

"Yes."

"Very well," said Reith. "You go first. I will follow."

The Gzhindra consulted in whispers. One said: "This is not feasible. We do not care to walk with others coming at our backs."

"For once you can tolerate the sensation," said Reith. "After all, you will thereby be fulfilling your commission."

"True, if all goes well. But what if you elect to burn us with a weapon?"

"I would have done so before," said Reith. "At the moment I only want to find my companion and bring her back to the surface."

The Gzhindra surveyed him with impersonal curiosity. "Why will you not walk first?"

"I don't know where to go."

"We will direct you."

Reith spoke so harshly that his voice cracked. "Go first. This is easier than carrying me in a sack."

The Gzhindra whispered to each other, moving the corners of their thin mouths without taking their eyes off Reith. Then they turned and walked slowly off across the salt flats.

Reith came after, remaining about fifty feet to the rear. They followed the faintest of trails, which at times disappeared utterly. A mile, two miles, they walked. The warehouse and the office diminished to small rectangular marks; Sivishe was a blurred gray crumble at the northern horizon.

The Gzhindra halted and turned to Reith, who thought to detect a fugitive flicker of glee. "Come closer," said one of the Gzhindra. "You must stand here with us."

Reith gingerly came forward. He brought out the energy gun which he had only just purchased, and displayed it. "This is precautionary. I do not wish to be killed, or drugged. I want to go alive down into the Shelters."

"No fear there, no fear there!" "Have no doubts on that score!" said the Gzhindra, speaking together. "Put away your gun; it is without significance."

Reith held the gun in his hand as he approached the Gzhindra.

"Closer, closer!" they urged. "Stand within the outline of the black soil."

Reith stepped on the patch of soil designated, which at once settled into the ground. The Gzhindra stood quietly, so close now that Reith could see the minute creases in the skin of their faces. If they felt alarm for his weapon they showed none.

The camouflaged elevator descended fifteen feet; the Gzhindra stepped off into a concrete-walled passage. Looking over their shoulders they beckoned. "Hurry." They set off at a swinging trot, cloaks flapping from side to side. Reith came behind. The passage slanted downward; running was without sensible effort. The passage became level, then suddenly ended at a brink;

beyond stretched a waterway. The Gzhindra motioned Reith down into a boat and themselves took seats. The boat slid along the surface, guided automatically along the center of the channel.

For half an hour they traveled, Reith looking dourly ahead, the Gzhindra sitting stiff and silent as carved black images.

The channel entered a larger waterway; the boat drifted up to a dock. Reith stepped ashore; the Gzhindra came behind, and Reith ignored the near-transparent glee with as much dignity as he could muster. They signaled him to wait; presently from the shadows a Pnumekin appeared. The Gzhindra muttered a few words into the air, which the Pnumekin seemed to ignore, then they stepped back into their boat and slid away, with pale backward glances. Reith stood alone on the dock with the Pnumekin, who now said: "Come, Adam Reith. We have been awaiting you."

Reith said, "The young woman who was brought down yesterday: where is she?"

"Come."

"Where?"

"The *zuzhma kastchai* wait for you."

A sensation like a draft of cold air prickled the skin of Reith's back. Into his mind crept furtive little misgivings, which he tried to put aside. He had taken all precautions available to him; their effectiveness was yet to be tested.

The Pnumekin beckoned. "Come."

Reith followed, resentful and shamed. They went down a zigzag corridor walled with panes of polished black flint, accompanied by reflections and moving shadows. Reith began to feel dazed. The corridor widened into a hall of black mirrors; Reith now moved in a state of bewilderment. He followed the Pnumekin to a central column, where they slid back a portal. "You must go onward alone, to Foreverness."

Reith looked through the portal, into a small cell lined with a substance like silver fleece. "What is this?"

"You must enter."

"Where is the young woman who was brought here yesterday?"

"Enter through the portal."

Reith spoke in anger and apprehension: "I want to talk to the Pnume. It is important that I do so."

"Step into the cell. When the portal opens, follow, follow the trace, to Foreverness."

In a state of sick fury Reith glared at the Pnumekin. The pale face looked back with fish-like detachment. Demands, threats, rose up in Reith's throat only to dwindle and die. Delay, any loss of time, might result in terrible consequences, the thought of which caused his stomach to jerk and quiver. He stalked into the cell.

The portal closed. Down slid the cell, dropping at a rapid but controlled rate. A minute passed. The cell halted. A portal flew open. Reith stepped forth into black glossy darkness. From his feet a trail of luminous yellow dots wound off into the gloom. Reith looked in all directions. He listened. Nothing, no sound, no pressure of any living presence. Burdened with a sense of destiny, he set off along the trace.

The line of luminous spots swung this way and that. Reith followed them with exactitude, fearing what might lie to either side. On one occasion he thought to hear a far hushed roar, as of air rising from some great depth.

The dark lightened, almost imperceptibly, to a glow from some unseen source. Without warning he came to a brink; he stood at the edge of a darkling landscape, a place of objects faintly outlined in gold and silver luminosity. At his feet a flight of stone steps led down; Reith descended, step after step.

He reached the bottom and halted in an uncontrollable pang of terror; in front of him stood a Pnume.

Reith pulled together the elements of his will. He said in as firm a voice as he could muster: "I am Adam Reith. I have come here for the young woman, my companion, whom you took away yesterday. Bring her here immediately."

From the shape came the husky Pnume whisper: "You are Adam Reith?"

"Yes. Where is the woman?"

"You came here from Earth?"

"What of the woman? Tell me!"

"Why did you come to Old Tschai?"

A roar of desperation rose in Reith's throat. "Answer my question!"

The dark shape slid quietly away. Reith stood a moment, undecided whether to stand or follow.

The gold and silver luminosities seemed to become brighter;

or perhaps Reith had begun to cast order upon the seemingly un-related shapes. He began to see outlines and tracts, pagoda-like frameworks, a range of columns. Beyond appeared silhouettes with gold and silver fringes, as yet unstructured by his mind.

The Pnume stalked slowly away. Reith's frustration reached an intensity where he felt almost faint; then he experienced a rage which sent him bounding after the Pnume. He seized the harsh shoulder-element and jerked; to his utter astonishment the Pnume dropped as if falling over backward, the arms swinging down to serve as forelegs. It stood ventral surface upmost, head swiveling strangely down and over, so that the Pnume took on the aspect of a night-hound. While Reith gaped in awe and em-barrassment the Pnume flipped itself upright, to regard Reith with chilling disfavour.

Reith found his voice. "I must talk to responsible folk among you and quickly. What I have to say is urgent—to you and to me!"

"This is Foreverness," came the husky voice. "Such words have no meaning."

"You will think differently, when you hear me."

"Come to your place in Foreverness. You are awaited." Once more the creature set off. Tears brimmed in Reith's eyes; vast out-rage rose up behind his teeth. If anything had happened to Zap 210, they would pay, how they would pay! regardless of conse-quence.

For a space they walked and presently passed through a col-umned portal into a new underground realm: a place which Reith associated with some elegant memorial garden of old Earth.

Away and along the gold- and silver-fringed prospect stood brooding shapes. Reith had no opportunity for speculation. Cer-tain shapes moved forward; he saw them to be Pnume, and ad-vanced to meet them. There were at least twenty; by their extreme diffidence and unobtrusiveness Reith understood them to be of the highest status. Facing the twenty shadows in this shadow-haunted corner of Foreverness he could not help but wonder as to the state of his mind. Was he wholly sane? In such surroundings orderly mental processes were inapplicable. By sheer brutal energy he must impose his personal will-to-order upon the devious environment of the Pnume.

He looked around the shadowed group. "I am Adam Reith," he said. "I am an Earthman. What do you want of me?"

"Your presence in Foreverness."

"I'm here," said Reith, "but I intend to go. I came of my own volition; are you aware of this?"

"You would have come in any event."

"Wrong. I would not have come. You kidnapped my friend, a young woman. I came to fetch her away and take her back to the surface."

The Pnume, as if by signal, all took a simultaneous slow step forward: a sinister movement, the stuff of nightmare. "How did you expect to effect so much? This is Foreverness."

Reith thought for a moment. "You Pnume have lived long on Tschai."

"Long, long: we are the soul of Tschai. We are the world itself."

"Other races live on Tschai; they are people more powerful than yourselves."

"They come and go: colored shadows to entertain us. We expel them as we choose."

"You do not fear the Dirdir?"

"They cannot reach us. They know none of our precious secrets."

"What if they did?"

The dark shapes approached another slow pace.

Reith called out in a harsh voice: "What if the Dirdir know all your secrets: all your tunnels and passages and pop-outs?"

"A grotesque situation which can never be real."

"But it can be real. I can make it real." Reith brought forth a folder bound in blue leather. "Examine this."

The Pnume gingerly accepted the portfolio. "It is the lost master-set!"

"Wrong again," said Reith. "It is a copy."

The Pnume set up a low whimpering sound, and Reith once again thought of the night-hounds; he had often heard just such soft calls out on the Kotan steppes.

The sad half-whispered wails subsided. The Pnume stood in a rigid semicircle. Reith could feel their emotion; it was almost palpable, a crazy, irresponsible ferocity he heretofore had associated only with the Phung.

"Be calm," said Reith. "The danger is not imminent. The

charts are hostage to my safety; you are secure unless I do not return to the surface. In this case the charts will be given over to the Blue Chasch and the Dirdir."

"Intolerable. The charts must be secured. There is no alternative."

"That is what I hoped you would say." Reith looked around the half-circle. "You agree to my conditions?"

"We have not heard them."

"I want the woman whom you brought down yesterday. If she is dead, I plan to exact a terrible penalty from you. You will long remember me; you will long curse the name Adam Reith."

The Pnume stood in silence.

"Where is she?" demanded Reith in a rasping voice.

"She is in Foreverness, to be crystallized."

"Is she alive? Or is she dead?"

"She is not yet dead."

"Where is she?"

"Across the Field of Monuments, awaiting preparation."

"You say that she is not yet dead—but is she alive and well?"

"She lives."

"Then you are fortunate."

The Pnume surveyed him with incomprehension, and certain of the group gave near-human shrugs.

Reith said: "Bring her here, or let us go to her, whichever is faster."

"Come."

They set out across the Field of Monuments: statues or simulacra representing folk of a hundred various races. Reith could not avoid pausing to stare in fascination. "Who or what are all these creatures?"

"Episodes in the life of Tschai, which is to say, our own lives. There: the Shivvan who came to Tschai seven million years ago. This is an early crystal, one of the oldest: the memento of a far time. Beyond: the Gjee, who founded eight empires and were expunged by the Fesa, who in turn fled the light of the red star Hsi. Yonder: others who have dropped by along their way to oblivion."

Along the avenues the group moved. The monuments were black, fringed with luminous gold and silver: creatures quadruped, triped, biped; with heads, cerebral bags, nerve-nets; with eyes, optical bands, flexible sensors, prisms. Here towered a massive bulk with a heavy cranium; it brandished a seven-foot sword. The creature Reith saw to be a Green Chasch bull. Nearby a Blue Chasch chastened a group of crouching Old Chasch, while three Chaschmen glowered from the side. Beyond were Dirdir and Dirdirmen, attended by two men and two women of a race Reith failed to recognize. To the side a single Wankh, alone and austere, surveyed a gang of toiling men. Beyond these groups, except for a single empty pedestal, the avenue led away, down a black slope to a slow black river, the surface marked by drifting silver swirls. Beside the river stood a cage of silver bars; huddled in the cage was Zap 210. She watched the group approach with an impassive face. She saw Reith; her face crumpled into opposed emotions; grief and joy, relief and dismay. She had been stripped of her surface clothes; she wore only a white shift.

Reith took pains to control his voice; still he spoke thickly. "What have you done to her?"

"She has been treated with Liquid One. It invigorates and tones, and opens the passages for Liquid Two."

"Bring her forth."

Zap 210 emerged from the cage. Reith took her hand, stroked her head. "You are safe. We're going back to the surface." He stood for a few minutes quietly waiting while she wept in relief and nervous exhaustion on his shoulder.

The Pnume came close. One said: "The return of all charts is demanded."

Reith managed a thick laugh. "Not yet. I have other demands to make of you—but elsewhere. Let us leave this place. Foreverness oppresses me."

In a hall of polished gray marble Reith faced the Pnume Elders. "I am a man; I am disturbed to see men of my own kind living the unnatural lives of Pnumekin. You must breed no more human children, and the children now underground must be transferred to the surface and there maintained until they are able to fend for themselves."

"But this means the end of the Pnumekin!"

"So it does, and why not? Your race is seven million years old or more. Only in the last twenty or thirty thousand years have you had Pnumekin to serve you. Their loss will be no great hardship."

"If we agree—what of the charts?"

"I will destroy all but a very few copies. None will be delivered to your enemies."

"This is unsatisfactory! We would then live in constant dread!"

"I can't worry as to this. I must retain control over you, to guarantee that my demands have been met. In due course I may return all the charts to you—sometime in the future."

The Pnume muttered disconsolately together a few moments. One said in a flat whisper: "Your demands will be met."

"In this case, conduct us back to the Sivishe salt flats."

At sunset the salt flats were quiet. Carina 4269 hung in a smoky haze behind the palisades, glinting upon the Dirdir towers. Reith and Zap 210 approached the old warehouse. From the office came Anacho's spare form. He stepped forward to meet them. "The sky-car is here. There is nothing to keep us."

"Let's hurry then. I can't believe that we're free."

The sky-car lifted from behind the warehouse and swept north. Anacho asked: "Where do we go?"

"To the Kotan steppes, south of where you and I first met."

All night they flew, over the barren center of Kislovan, then over the First Sea and the Kotan marshlands.

At dawn they drifted over the edge of the Steppes while Reith studied the landscape below. They crossed a forest; Reith pointed to a clearing. "There: where I came down to Tschai. The Emblem camp lay to the east. There, by that grove of feather-bush: there we buried Onmale. Drop down there."

The sky-car landed. Reith alighted and walked slowly toward the woods. He saw the glint of metal. Traz came forth. He stood quietly as Reith approached. "I knew that you would come."

Traz had changed. He had become a man: something more than a man. On his shoulder he wore a medallion of metal, stone and wood. Reith said: "You dug up the emblem."

"Yes. It called to me. Wherever I walked upon the steppe I heard voices, all the voices of all the Onmale chieftains, calling to be taken up from the dark. I brought forth the emblem; the voices are now silent."

"And the ship?"

"It is ready. Four of the technicians are here. One stayed at Sivishe, two lost heart and set off across the steppes for Hedaijha."

"The sooner we depart the better. When we're actually out in space I'll believe that we've escaped."

"We are ready."

Anacho, Traz and Zap 210 entered the spaceship. Reith took a last look around the sky. He bent, touched the soil of Tschai, crumbled a handful of mold between his fingers. Then he too entered the unlovely hulk. The port was closed and sealed. The generators hummed. The ship lifted toward the sky. The face of Tschai receded; the planet exhibited rotundity, became a gray-brown ball, and presently was gone.

Jack Vance was born in 1920 and educated at the University of California, first as a mining engineer, then majoring in physics and finally in journalism. He has since had a varied career: his first story was written while he was serving in the U.S. Merchant Marine during the Second World War. During the late 1940s and early 1950s he contributed a variety of short stories to the science fiction and fantasy magazines of the time. His first published book was *The Dying Earth* (1950). Since then he has produced several series—for example, the *Planet of Adventure, Durdane* and *Demon Princes* series—as well as various individual novels.

Jack Vance has won the two most coveted trophies of the science fiction world, the Hugo Award and the Nebula Award. He has also won the Edgar Award of the Mystery Writers of America for his novel *The Man in the Cage* (1960). In addition, he has written scripts for television science fiction series.

Jack Vance's non-literary interests include blue water sailing and early jazz. He lives in Oakland, California.